SEVEN BREATHS OF THE DRAGON
The Secret History of the Gurkha-Dragon War

By Robert St Michael

OUR UNIVERSE IS STRANGER THAN WE can IMAGINE

Persistence of Content™ LLC

Seven Breaths of the Dragon
The Secret History of the Gurkha-Dragon War

ISBN: 978-1-947043-10-7
Library of Congress Control Number: 2018950108

Cover design by Bianchi Art.

Back cover illustration "Action by Lieutenant CJW Grant, VC, at Thobal, Manipur, 1 April 1891" by Edgar Alfred Holloway.

Persistence of Content, LLC
P.O. Box 769111
Roswell, Georgia 30076

For Krista.

SEVEN BREATHS OF THE DRAGON
The Secret History of the Gurkha-Dragon War

"The Primordial Seven, the First SEVEN BREATHS OF THE DRAGON of Wisdom, produce in their turn from their Holy Circumgyrating Breaths the Fiery Whirlwind."

From *The Book of Dzyan, Stanza V.1.*
The Secret Doctrine (1888)
By H. P. Blavatsky

OUR UNIVERSE IS STRANGER THAN WE can IMAGINE

Part I. The Letter

"I have no doubt that in reality the future will be vastly more surprising than anything I can imagine. Now my own suspicion is that the Universe is not only queerer than we suppose, but queerer than we can suppose."

From *Possible Worlds and Other Papers* (1927)
By J. B. S. Haldane

Dramatis personæ

In order of appearance (*denotes a fictional character)

1947 London

Mary Innes-Howie (née Winchester)	Anti-Slavery Society activist, 81
Sir Henry Tizard	Scientist-engineer, inventor of radar, 62
Sir Stewart Menzies	Chief of Britain's Secret Service, 57
Alice*	Librarian, Heath Library, 41
James	British secret agent, 37
Siriman*	Nepali Gurkha soldier, 23
Donald*	American physicist, 29

1891 Manipur

Siriman Sunwar*	Havildar (sergeant), 44th Gurkha Rifles, 20
Bahadur Thapa*	Naik (corporal), 44th Gurkha Rifles, 22
Ethel Saint Clair Grimwood	Wife of British political agent, 24
Karna (dream sequence)*	Disembodied voice, 22
Colonel Skene (dream sequence)	Expedition commander, 42nd GR, 47
Batsa Gurung*	Naik (corporal), 42nd Gurkha Rifles, 23
Zoluti	Angelic blonde woman in white, 25

Chapter 1. The Premonition

Morning, Thursday, 8 May 1947...

Mary

Misty showers passed and a cloudless sky burned bluer than Ceylonese sapphires. Soft breezes buffed young leaves greener than polished Jaipuri emeralds. Nature unveiled a new year's spring, another beginning for a majestic world alive with God's annual promise of better days ahead. Mary closed her eyes and savored the fragrant flavor of violets and lilacs on cool air.

A pleasant day for gardening, courtesy of the gentle morning rain.

Willow warblers chattered, thrilling Mary as if tiny cherubs trilled a heavenly chorus. They returned each spring, reoccupying the budding oak in their garden haven, communicating as birds do, in the languages of song and motion, fluttering, perching, and scanning the surroundings.

Mary called, "Back from your winter holiday?"

Her Scottish lilt sparked no surprise—the birds sang even happier—so Mary returned to her gardening and smiled.

Ignore them in return! The brazen creatures proclaim dominion over my garden. Fine—I prefer it that way. So peaceful!

"Such a romantic!" Eyes moistened as Mary chuckled. "Old on the outside, but younger inside than anyone imagines!"

Other than the birds, no one heard—no one visible, at least. Since Harry passed, Mary often spoke aloud when alone, as if he might be close by, listening.

A white strand escaped her kerchief and dangled over a blue eye. She stuck out her lower lip and blew a blast. Her hair had once been golden-blond, but her angelic eyes remained steel blue. She sat on a patch of blue fescue, reached for her trowel, and glimpsed a cap duck out of sight, behind the brick wall.

Spying. On me? Why?

Mary shouted at the wall, "Nosey neighbors! Am I that interesting?" She shook her head. "Which is worse, I wonder? Spied on by neighbors or ignored by birds?"

Mary wore Harry's baggy gardening trousers. Busybodies found her attire unladylike but Mary dressed as she wished when digging in *her* dirt in *her* garden.

She thrust the trowel into moist soil and struck something hard. Ears perked at the sound—a clink. Mary sighed, not expecting hard objects buried in her garden. A frown darkened her sunny face as if clouds of dread cloaked the sun.

"Oh, blast! I swear I tilled every inch of this garden."

Then she realized.

The birds stopped singing!

Mary turned and looked to the branches. Tiny eyes peered back from little feathered heads and restless stick-feet paced, as if the birds took a sudden interest in her digging.

"Now what? Birds snooping! Drat you, nosey birds. I am not bothering you—nothing ominous happened." Mary turned away, tucking her chin. "*Now* they want my attention—to lord it over me—but I refuse to give them the satisfaction. I hit a rock. So what? It means nothing."

Mary shifted attention to the matter at hand—metal clinking on stone. An ordinary sound—innocent, clean, and insignificant—not an ominous portent. It meant digging, prying, and lifting. She used the trowel edge to scrape topsoil and find the surface of the hard object.

"That answers the question!" She spoke as if announcing news to someone near expecting a different answer. "It is a rock."

The flat stone was a foot across—an uncommon size and shape for her region. She removed black dirt from the edge and traced a trench around the outline.

Not thick—two inches. I can dislodge it.

Mary enjoyed fending for herself, so she began the rewarding task, sticking the trowel nose under a corner and prying. The stone rose, and a gloved hand slid under and lifted.

Not large but heavy.

Mary toppled the stone onto the grass, preparing herself for those tiny creatures one finds hiding in a flower garden.

The depression is clean and dry!

No worms, ants, or pill bugs scurried from sudden sunlight disturbing a happy home. Instead, lying in the shallow depression was a flat rectangular object.

"An envelope? Here?"

The envelope-shaped object was letter-sized, six by ten inches. Mary removed a glove and fingernails peeled the envelope from the flattened soil. The paper was slick, coated end-to-end in a faded-yellow waxy substance. Mary's heart skipped a beat.

I have seen its kind.

"Can it be?" she gasped. "Another after—how long?" She worked the math, and eyes widened. "Has it been fifty-six years?"

Mary examined both sides.

Someone applied wax to repel the elements.

The hard, cloudy coating obscured the addressee. Her thumb pressed, trying to remove wax where a name should be.

Mary rubbed harder and one-by-one, letters appeared—first a capital followed by three lowercase letters.

Mary

She smiled. "That settles it! A letter in the post! You know what that means…"

Mary clutched the envelope to her chest. With the other hand, she reached into her blouse, drew forth a fine golden chain with a dangling golden cross, touched the cross to her lips, and let it fall. She next reached deeper inside her blouse and brought out a silvery chain necklace bearing a pewter-gray metal ring. A raised pattern encircled the ring face—the engraved likeness of a serpentine winged dragon devouring its tail. Mary clutched the ring, closed her eyes, and took a deep breath. She exhaled, smiled, and raised her eyes to inspect the sky.

Clouds rolled in as if with quiet, authoritative purpose and a drifting haze dimmed the sun. Mary doffed her kerchief and, as if on cue, the cool wind quickened, and white hair flew into greater disarray. The birds chattered with alarm and rose, taking flight.

"Now you have done it—you have further upset the birds! Get up, old bones!"

She struggled to stand, brushed dirty trousers, and cracked a wry smile. "Such is the price of premonitions. Company is coming—three old friends. Your house needs cleaning and so do you. No time to waste. Oh—one more thing."

She raised her voice, Scottish accent full force, and directed an unabashed pronouncement at the wall.

"You better stop talking to yourself. Someone will report you as batty, and cackle with glee as they take you away!"

Chapter 2. The Knights of the Realm

Later that morning...

Mary

Mary moved with efficiency. She made the house presentable, then bathed, and dressed for company, donning her proper-looking pattern dress—the light-green one with the white dots—chosen with careful consideration. Over it, she wore her favorite kitchen apron as she stood at the sink, washing the cutlery and dishware, gazing out the window at her walled English garden. The haze had passed and, once again, the rays of the smiling sun splashed across the rectangular patch beyond the oak canopy.

Dishes clinked underwater, and the kettle hissed, working toward a boil. A nondescript melody on the BBC Light Programme scratched and crackled from the wooden Lissen radio glowing on the parlor buffet.

A chipped china plate, the last dish, took its place atop a stack of sibling chipped china plates. The cupboard door squeaked and Mary faced a dozen coats of pastel yellow paint, trying in vain to hide cracks in old wood. Mary sighed. The dated kitchen screamed last century.

An update would be nice—but imagine the cost.

Mary lived in Hampstead, on Nassington Road, across the tracks north of Gospel Oak. For over fifty years, she lived in the same clinker-brick cottage, hugging the brick lane, crowded behind guardian oaks. Gospel Oak was a peaceful borough nestled between Hampstead Heath and Dartmouth Park, perched on the higher ground north of London. The prim and proper neighborhood of fine Victorian homes had a proud history stretching back a thousand years. Days in Hampstead were quiet and, at night, even the puffing, clanking, and rumbling of steam engines at Gospel Oak station was familiar and comforting. Years earlier, during the war and the blacked-out nights of the Blitz, residents hid crouching and praying in fear below ground. Mary comforted refugee friends and relatives in her cellar. She crouched and prayed alongside, but she had no fear—she had lived through far worse. When the Blitz ended months later, scattered bombs had damaged many homes, but Mary's home stood, conspicuous and untouched.

After the war, the borough rebuilt and tall mansions rose, crowding the little cottage. Snooty neighbors whispered that the small old house had become out-of-place in fashionable Hampstead Heath. Harry insisted they keep the home they loved, and after he passed, Mary respected his wishes and ignored the complaints.

"Neighbors spying again, Mister Who." Mary addressed the white porcelain owl figurine on the kitchen countertop. "They want me gone, taken away. Thanks for not taking their side. I am thankful I reached my eighty-first summer but, when the time comes, they will carry me away kicking and screaming. I am fit and ready for adventure."

The figurine stared back in silence.

"Yes, adventure!" Mary said. "Imagine—signaled by a clink. The birds knew straight away as always. How do I know?"

Mary felt for spectacles in her apron pocket and touched something slick. She whipped out the envelope and shook it at the owl.

"I found *this*! After fifty-six years, another buried letter." She stowed the envelope back in the apron. "I must not forget where I put it. I will examine it once I finish my chores." Donning her glasses, she turned to inspect the calendar. Fine script in her handwriting filled the day's square.

White Lotus Day

Mary tapped the calendar and winked at the figurine. "Why today? There is the answer. Today is May 8th, Nineteen Hundred and Forty-seven."

The porcelain owl did not move.

"White Lotus Day! The fifty-sixth anniversary of *her* passing. Fifty-six years should be enough time for my friends to complete their mission and return. I expect them soon. I foresaw—today will be the day." An unmistakable slam startled her. "Aha! A car door—discerned despite the radio."

Mary placed the copper kettle on a back burner, removed her apron, and dried her hands. As she walked into the parlor and switched off the radio, the wooden floor creaked. Mary winced.

The lamps, chairs, and rugs in my parlor—everything dates from the turn-of-the-century.

"Dratted rug. Awful doilies." She kicked the oval throw rug and straightened the crocheted cloths draped over the arms of the parlor chairs. "Too old! They must go!" She caught herself. "Why fuss? They will find my old furniture familiar. The incandescent lamp light will be the marvel."

At the front window, Mary tugged the curtains and peeked. A short stone walkway jutted amidst the sparse grass, tethering her porch to the brick street. Tall oaks swayed and sunlight played in the shade. A black Humber sedan sat at the curb where a uniformed man held the rear passenger door as two civilians exited.

Good. Three men. The expected number.

From Mary's vantage, the driver wore the garb of a junior military officer—ballooning tan trousers with olive drab uniform jacket and peeked visor cap. She could not discern his age. The two other men—old, or late middle-aged, at least, and well-dressed in suits and ties—approached the walkway with hats in hand.

Mary scampered down the hall, shoes clattering, stopping to primp by the hall mirror. Sweaty hands patted hair and straightened her dress before taking a final look.

You will do for now.

The bell rang. She took a deep breath, grasped the knob, and opened the door to face the visitors. Mary's jaw dropped. They were strangers, not the friends she expected.

Who are they?

The men were similar in dress, face, and figure—they were English gentlemen of medium height, with gray mustaches and thinning gray hair. One had the air of a professor, wearing eyeglasses and a well-worn, gray tweed vested suit. The other was more refined and handsome—slender, warm smile, sporting a less-worn, dark blue suit with faint gold pinstripes.

The man with spectacles cleared his throat and spoke. "Miss Winchester?"

Mary tightened her jaw and frowned. "I prefer Missus Innes-Howie."

The bespectacled man squirmed and blushed. "So sorry, my mistake. Yes, Missus Innes-Howie is whom we seek." Then he straightened and beamed. "Good morning! My name is Tizard. Henry Tizard." He touched the sleeve of the man at his side. "This is my associate, Mister Menzies."

"How may I help you, gentlemen?"

"We are—civil servants, one could say—from His Majesty's government. Do you recall receiving letters from the Defense Research Policy Committee?"

Mary shook her head. "Letters?"

Tizard nodded. "Yes, I corresponded several times."

Mary's eyes narrowed. "My neighbors put you up to this."

"Neighbors?"

"Have you come to take me away?"

"Take you—?" Open-mouthed, Tizard shook his head, and then chuckled. "No, no! I was hoping to ask a few questions. When you did not respond to my letters, Sir Stewart—err, Mister Menzies, I mean—suggested we take a drive on the chance you were home. I hope we are not interrupting your holiday."

"Holiday?" Mary's eyebrows raised. "You mean White Lotus Day?"

Tizard cocked his head. "Sorry? White—? I mean VE Day—Victory in Europe. Two years ago today it was, amazing as that sounds."

Mary stood blinking and an awkward silence followed.

Where are my friends? The premonition failed me. How? Why?

"Is another time more convenient?" Tizard said. "We could send the car later. The lieutenant could take you to us."

Take me away!

Mary shook her head and opened the door wider. "Please come in, gentlemen. You are just in time for elevenses." She stepped aside, and as the men passed, Mary nodded toward the car. "What of your driver? He is welcome." The officer's face appeared young compared to the civilians.

"Well…," Menzies said, speaking his first word. He glanced at the uniformed man and shook his head. "The lieutenant should stay behind—in case the vehicle requires moving."

Mary closed the door. "I own no motorcar. Nowhere to park, you see." She collected and hung hats, then ushered the men into the parlor. "Gentlemen, make yourselves comfortable while I fetch tea and biscuits."

"Please," Tizard said, "no need to trouble yourself."

"No trouble. The kettle is hot." She returned in minutes, carrying a tray laden with cups and saucers, a teapot, sugar cubes, and a plate of biscuits. Seconds later, the three partook of the refreshments.

"Very hospitable of you, Missus Innes-Howie," Menzies said. His warm voice had a neutral, educated accent. Mary smiled back.

Tizard, chewing, nodded agreement. "You said something earlier," he mumbled between sips, "when I mentioned today being a holiday. What did you call it—white something?"

"White Lotus Day." Mary took another sip and lowered her cup. "Today is the fifty-sixth anniversary of the death of Madame Blavatsky. Theosophists celebrate the date, calling it White Lotus Day."

Menzies straightened. "Well, were you acquainted with the old Russian sorceress?"

Who are these men? Menzies knows things, many secrets.

Mary frowned. "She was no sorceress, and she was Ukrainian, not Russian. I did not know her well. She and my mother were friends—before my birth."

Menzies leaned closer. He was not smiling. "Well, did she summon spirits or do parlor magic?"

Mary reddened. "There is no such thing as magic! If you came to question me about Helena Petrovna Blavatsky, I have nothing further to say. I am no theosophist. I am a God-fearing Christian woman, and I do not believe in mediums."

"You have no belief in the supernatural?"

"No! None."

Menzies studied Mary through pale blue eyes. "What of dragons? Men from other worlds? Or..." He fumbled with a folded paper slid from a coat pocket, held the crumpled sheet at length, and squinted. "Tall, shape-shifting lizard men?"

Mary's eyes widened. She stiffened, turned pale, and then looked toward the window and relaxed, lifting her teacup. She sipped and smiled. "The sky is blue again. I should get back to my gardening—hate to waste such a fine day."

Tizard signaled and Menzies shut his mouth. Tizard cleared his throat. "I say! We have gotten off on the wrong foot here. I apologize for Sir Stewart—I mean Mister Menzies—he has a keen interest in matters related to Russia, but he sometimes shows better judgment of things than people."

"That is the second time you have called him Sir." Mary looked at Menzies. "I presume I am in the company of Sir Stewart Menzies."

Tizard looked at Menzies who nodded. Mary continued.

"I do not know what you do, Sir Stewart, but I sense secrets are your business. Secrets surround you like a swarm of gnats. You found a file, dated 1891, hidden at Secret Service headquarters. Correct?"

Menzies shifted and cracked a smirk.

"Frank Rhodes was such an awful person," she said. "I told him what he wanted to hear. Brackenbury had him assigned to Bombay, and he never bothered me again. Here we are, fifty-six years later. Why fifty-six? Why not forty, or fifty, or fifty-seven?"

"Well...," Menzies said. "Why does it matter how many years? What is in a number?"

"Everything, God hides in numbers—try dividing by zero. You mentioned dragons. Did you know 1940—the year of Dunkirk and the Blitz—was a year of the dragon?"

"Do you believe in Chinese astrology?"

"I do not, nor do I believe in coincidences. May I ask you a question, Sir Stewart?"

Menzies winked at Tizard. "Please."

"Why did Hitler lose the war?"

Menzies shifted in his seat. "Not sure what you mean."

"It is a simple question."

Menzies and Tizard exchanged glances.

"Well...," Menzies said, "the conventional answer is Hitler invaded Russia and then the Americans entered the war."

"Ah, but why invade Russia? By 1940, Germany had conquered Europe. Russia was no threat. England could not have prevented a German blitzkrieg across North Africa, seizing Suez, and allying with the Aryans of Persia. Japan could have pushed through Manipur, conquered India, and darkness would have fallen."

Menzies crossed his arms. "Yes, yes! Instead, Hitler bombed Britain, ignored history, and invaded Russia. No one knows why he did, but it was the beginning of the end. What is your point?"

"I will give you a clue," Mary said. "Do you know of a town called Dnipropetrovsk?"

"In the Ukraine?"

"Yes. Its original name was Ekaterinoslav and is the birthplace of Madame Blavatsky. Look for your answer there."

"Well...," Menzies said, "so you believe Hitler invaded Russia because of Madame Blavatsky, seeking..." He stopped, leaned forward, and pressed fingers to forehead.

He realizes. Now he believes.

"I have another question," she said. "Before the war why were Nazi SS officers searching the mountains of Tibet?"

Tizard raised a hand. "Excuse me! We are off track, far afield from the purpose of my visit. Allow me to explain. I am working on a research project. I hope to receive funds to hire a team, but in the beginning, I am one to do things, rather than watch others, and I must see for myself."

"So, you must be Sir Henry Tizard—the inventor of radar."

Tizard blushed. "In truth, my team of engineers did the work."

"Tut, tut! False modesty is not becoming, Sir Henry. I lavish credit where due. It is not every day knights of the realm honor me with a visit."

"The honor is ours. I have been negligent, failing to mention my admiration of your efforts against slavery in Northeast India."

Mary pursed her lips and tilted her head. "Kind of you. Please tell me of your current research project."

"Thank you, I shall. Have you heard the names Eileen Arnold or Albert Lancaster?"

Mary shrugged and shook her head. Tizard continued.

"In 1942, months apart, these two English citizens claimed to have had—shall we say, unusual encounters?"

"Ah, and so now you want to ask of flying saucers."

"Saucers?" Tizard said. "Not disks? Interesting." He turned his tea saucer upside down, studying it. "Hum—had not realized drawings resemble saucers. I fancy the term and shall remember it! Now, as I began my research, Sir Stewart discovered a file, from 1891, as you said. It contained reports of events aligned with my interests. He shared the reports, and after that, I wrote, hoping we could meet. You have convinced me we came to the right place."

"Perhaps."

"Now," Tizard said, "I must ask—is the report factual? Did you claim to have flown in a disk—a flying saucer?"

Mary looked at her empty cup and at the window. "I never lie, but sometimes—best to stay silent. I must think on this. Another day is better. Today being VE Day, no doubt you have celebrations to attend."

"I see," Tizard said, exchanging glances with Menzies. "We are moving too fast. When would be a better time? The lieutenant can come by and collect you—bring you to us."

"Next week?" Mary said.

"Wonderful, the lieutenant will come a week from today, at—shall we say ten o'clock?"

Mary nodded.

Tizard stood, followed by Menzies. "We will show ourselves out. Thank you for the tea and biscuits. We look forward to seeing you next Thursday." The men walked toward the door.

"Do not forget your hats!" After the door closed, and Mary heard the car drive away, she slumped in her seat. She sniffed and swiped a tear. "Today is not proceeding as planned."

Chapter 3. The Heartaches and the Taxi Cab

Continued...

Mary

Mary resolved to stop brooding.

Pointless to mope.

She roused and shuffled to the buffet and switched on the radio. Her frown faded as the dulcet voice of Billy Williams filled the room, singing Sammy Kaye's "The Old Lamp-Lighter."

She hummed along, collected the cups and saucers, and returned the tray to the kitchen. Minutes later, with the set washed and stowed in the yellow cupboard, and the kettle refilled for afternoon tea, dread descended as if a vulture alighted atop her slouching shoulders. Mary wiped a tear with an apron corner and faced her friend, the porcelain owl.

"My premonition failed, Mister Who." She shook her head. "No other way to say it. I swear, when I foresaw three men arriving, I saw my friends. Their faces were clear, easy to recognize. They were unchanged—unaged, as if they left yesterday. I know that cannot be, but—mistaking them for strangers? I am slipping, losing my skill—too old and confused. My heart is aching."

As if on cue, Harry James' rendition of "Heartaches" shattered her gloomy introspection.

I love this song. There are no coincidences! It must be a sign!

Mary tried to whistle along where Elmo Tanner would have in the Ted Weems version. "Too slow!" Both recordings were receiving airplay, making comparison easy. "Ted Weems's is cheerier, Mister Who. Why did Harry James bother if he could not improve it?"

As the song ended, a box on the counter caught Mary's eye. She pawed through a stack of recent correspondence—old condolence notes deserving replies, unpaid bills, and unopened letters from the Defense Research Policy

Committee. She opened Tizard's messages and found each stronger and more insistent than the prior.

"I should have read these earlier. Sir Henry is persistent. I can understand his impatience and decision to pop by my house. Still…" She tossed the note aside and glanced at the clock.

Eleven fifty-six. Fifty-six, fifty-six!

"Why fifty-six years?" She wrinkled her brow and cupped her chin. "Why today?"

The owl showed interest but, as usual, offered no comment.

"Nothing to contribute, Mister Who?" Mary set her jaw, stood, and walked to the front door. She donned a light coat and called down the hall, "I am off to the library. The stroll will do me good."

Mary trekked a half mile under a high sun and deep blue sky, arriving at Heath Library in ten minutes. Once inside, she located her friend Alice the librarian at lunch and interrupted to explain her interest in learning the meaning—historical or metaphysical—of a certain number.

"What number," Alice mumbled, chewing, "in particular?"

Mary's eyes darted each way before leaning closer to whisper, "Fifty-six."

Alice, still munching, raised a finger, asking for the time to think. She stood and disappeared into the rows of shelves, returning minutes later with two books—Aristotle's *Metaphysics* and *Excavations at Stonehenge* by William Hawley.

"These may help," Alice said. "Read what Aristotle says about cosmic spheres, and in Hawley, you may find the Aubrey Holes interesting."

"Right," Mary said. "You are ever a wonder. I have a final favor to ask. Have you something scientific—not too scientific; mind you—discussing the passage of time during…" She glanced side to side and moved close to Alice's ear. "Travel—through outer space."

Alice raised an eyebrow. "By coincidence, something new arrived just today. In fact, I examined it right before lunch." She presented a small volume.

ONE TWO THREE… INFINITY
Facts and Speculations in Science
George Gamow

"Pay particular attention to chapter five," Alice placed a bookmark at the proper spot. "Relativity of Space and Time."

Mary accepted the books with thanks. "Alice," she said, winking, "no coincidences." After those parting words and a quick wave, Mary hurried home with her stack of reading material. After a quick bite, she settled at the kitchen table. With spectacles donned, she immersed herself—flipping pages, scanning for keywords, and pausing here and there to read a salient passage.

"Alice is an angel, Mister Who," Mary announced, eyes glued to the page. "Aristotle describes fifty-six layers in the cosmos—the Earth, surrounded by fifty-five spheres of ether. That must mean something."

Mary turned next to Hawley, per Alice's instruction, and read of Stonehenge. One hundred miles west, alone on Salisbury Plain, Stonehenge stood for thousands of years. No one knew who quarried and moved the massive stones. No one knew its purpose, but there were always theories, myths, and claims. A circle of chalk-filled depressions ringed the trilithons—the Aubrey Holes.

Mary cocked her head. "Fifty-six stark-white Aubrey Holes, Mister Who. Another clue!"

One theory claimed Druids advanced stones from hole to hole, year by year, marking out a fifty-six-year cycle. She shuddered, imagining hooded ghosts in the freezing fog, counting the passage of the years.

Could one such fifty-six-year cycle have passed?

Mary opened the final book at Alice's marker. "Now, for Mister Gamow!"

The author had a humorous style and a common way with words, but the concepts left her scratching her head. Four-dimensional space-time, light-carrying ether, and Michelson's experiment to detect the ether wind, Fitz-Gerald contractions—the math was beyond her. At the point of giving up, key passages caught her eye.

...the expansion of time becomes noticeable only at velocities approaching the speed of light...

The slowing down of the speed of time in moving systems has an interesting implication in respect to interstellar travel...

In fact, if you move, for example, at 99.99999999 per cent of the speed of light, your wristwatch, your heart, your lungs, your digestion, and your mental processes will be slowed down by a factor of 70,000...

Mary looked at the clock.

It is almost four! I frittered away the afternoon.

Still mulling her reading, she put on the kettle. A moment later, a familiar tinny bang came from outside, at the front of the house.

A car door! Government men again! This time to take me away!

She contemplated hiding in the cellar, but when two more car doors slammed, she shrugged.

I suppose I should at least check.

At the front window, she peeked through parted curtains. Three men climbed out of a taxicab—one of those new box-shaped, black Oxford taxis appearing around London.

Why must automobiles always be black and box-shaped? What is wrong with color and curves?

Three well-dressed men in dark business suits exited the cab, closed umbrellas in hand. Turned backs and Foxhound hats hid faces and hair.

Mary smiled. Post-war rationing frustrated many, as the government exported English clothing to rebuild the British textile industry. Londoners often wore American garb, but Mary found it amusing.

"Ha! How fashionable. As if Americans would visit me!" The tallest visitor spoke to the driver while paying the fare. "He is asking the cabbie to wait until they are certain I am home."

Then, the realization struck. She dropped the curtains. Although she could not see faces, they were the right number, size, and shape—she knew...

They are not from the government! They are the visitors my premonition foretold—my three, long-lost friends!

Mary hurried to the kitchen to primp. After wiping her hands a final unnecessary time, she set the apron aside. In the hallway, she took a quick look in the mirror on the wall, straightened her dress, and sighed.

Nothing like I imagine.

A young woman with golden hair faced the mirror and a white-haired lady smiled back—attractive considering age, but an eighty-one-year-old woman.

What do they expect? How will they react? What should they expect?

She leaned closer to the reflection and threw in a self-assured harrumph. "What rights have they to expect anything?"

Mary dreaded that momentary shock—the first glimpse of friends not seen in years. Everyone ages, but that irrational jolt—a friend looking older than recollected—was as if she should age while others remained frozen like old photographs buried in a bottom drawer.

You are fine!

"No worse than they will appear. You will look younger than they do. It is silly to worry, because, Old Girl..."

The bell rang and Mary started for the door. A second later the teakettle in the kitchen whistled. Startled by competing sounds, she danced in harried indecision.

Visitors first—the kettle can wait!

Mary reached for the doorknob and stopped. Seconds of indecision passed, and then she returned to the window.

"One final peek before answering." Trembling fingers touched the curtain. "I was saying, Old Girl, time moves on and no one can keep from aging. It happens..."

Mary dropped the curtain, pressed back to wall, and panted. Heart raced, blood pounded, and a hand leapt to her chest to still a beating drum. The kettle screamed. The top of her head burned as if lightning bolts started a wildfire. That moment Mary learned old age did not happen to everyone.

"Fifty-six years, and they have not aged a day!"

Chapter 4. The Visitors from the Past

A few heartbeats later...

Mary

Mary trembled, wide-eyed and panting, back to the wall. The doorbell rang a second time.

What is that bell?

Friends at the door.

Harry? What do I do?

Pull yourself together and answer the door.

I am unprepared for this. They are—fifty-six years—not aged.

You knew this was possible. Admit it.

Why? How could I?

You suspected. Remember—Gamow. Why did you ask Alice for a book on space and time?

Right!

Good girl! Relax. Have fun. See what happens.

Mary gulped and forced a whisper. "A week older perhaps, but no more!" She shut her eyes, concentrated until breathing slowed, and then she gulped again, managing an unforced smile. The doorbell rang a third time.

Open the door! You can face them.

She reached for the knob...

Wait! What is that screaming?

"Oh, drat! Blasted kettle is intolerable!"

Dress shoes clattered across hard wood as Mary scurried back to the kitchen to tend the kettle. "Thanks for nothing, Mister Who! You are no help at all!" With the shriek silenced, Mary clip-clopped the return route, stopping for final nervous preening before the hall mirror. As she reached for the knob, the bell rang a fourth time. The door crept open. On the porch, three young-looking men stood at polite attention. One by one, they lifted hats and smiled. The difference in appearance between the three was distinct.

The tallest was shy of six feet and looked late thirties in age.

As dapper as ever!

Handsome, brown hair groomed long on the sides, and moustache poised above a wry smile.

The shortest was just over five feet tall, but of sturdy build, and in his early twenties. He had Asian features, no facial hair, and a swarthy complexion. His straight dark hair was medium length and combed. A wide grin brightened his face.

Looks as if he cannot wait to share a joke!

The third visitor was slender and between the others in height and age—standing five-foot-eight or nine and in his mid-to-late twenties. His sandy hair...

Is too long—as usual! At least he combed it for once!

The man's face was clean-shaven. He wore wire-rimmed glasses, and he was not smiling.

He could crack a grin at any moment if he permitted it.

Mary coughed into her fist to keep from laughing.

He reminds me of a young American college student in one of those silly comedies at the cinema.

"Yes," Mary said in her meekest tone.

"Mary?" The tallest man leaned forward, head cocked.

"I am Missus Innes-Howie, if you please. How may I help you?"

My voice must sound old, thin, and weak to their ears.

Mary bit her lip, struggling to keep a straight face. The men stood in silence, casting sideways glances with puzzled-looking expressions.

Got them! Speechless!

The Asian squirmed, as if unable to stand it any longer, and blurted in a high-pitched lilt, "Memsahib, do you not recognize us?"

The looks on their faces are too much to bear!

Mary broke character with a huge smile and a loud laugh. "Yes, I recognize you! I played a cruel joke. Shame on me. I expected you since this morning. Now, please come in before anyone sees you."

The tallest visitor wrinkled his brow, turned, and scanned in every direction. "Is there a problem?" he said with a Scottish accent.

"I will explain." She stepped back and held the door wide. "Come in first—please. You are in time for afternoon tea." She leveled a stern glare at the Asian. "Siriman, will you ever call me Mary?" He grinned but kept quiet.

The tallest waved to the cab driver, and the black cab pulled forward from the brick walk and drove away. Mary held the door as the men entered, and after final quick glance up and down the street, shut the door and raised her arms. Tears ran as she hugged each, from tallest to shortest. She studied each face, making certain her friends were as young as they appeared.

They show no sign of shock at my age. They show less surprise at my age than I do at theirs as if they made sense of all this!

Mary sobbed and started another round, embracing the tallest. He returned her hug and the other two gathered and patted her shoulders.

Harry, I am sorry I never introduced you.

Sobs became croaks. "I missed—each of you—more than words can express." She cleared her throat. "I love you all beyond measure, and now you came back safe and sound."

The visitors, unable to hide emotions any longer, swiped tears with knuckles. Mary tried to laugh, but coughed and choked back more tears. At last, she pushed away and held her hands to her face. "I did not expect I would sob this way. I promised myself this morning I would not, but here I am, a blubbering baby."

The tall man presented a handkerchief. She buried her face, and the men gave space.

"We wanted to—make contact—before coming," the tallest said. "You do not have a—what do you call it?"

"Telephones, you mean?"

"Yes, that is it."

"No, no telephone," she said, finishing wiping her eyes. "My nosey neighbor has one. He may allow me to use it as long as he can eavesdrop. Why, this morning…" Eyes narrowed, she studied the tall man. "James, where is your cane?"

The man Mary called James jerked and scanned his surroundings wide-eyed, as if caught in that instant of terror when one first realizes a precious possession is missing. He steadied himself, chuckled, and smiled red-faced. "They fixed my leg!"

I wonder what else they can fix.

"I no longer need a cane."

"Wonderful!" Mary hugged the man tighter and then frowned.

That cane is no ordinary cane!

"Worry not!" James said, as if guessing her concern. "I tucked it away in a safe place."

With joyful hugs and the wiping of tears finished, Mary straightened and cleared her throat. "How long have you been back?"

"A week—right?" The blond man nodded and Siriman shrugged. "Yes," James repeated, "it has been six or seven days."

"A week!" Mary could not disguise her surprise and hurt.

"Oh, um...," James blushed and stammered, "we hurried over—as soon as we—well, we had errands."

"Errands?"

"We needed somewhere to stay, and proper clothing, so we—blend into the crowd..."

"Lost, like three fish out of water," Siriman said.

"Look what cabs have become!" The blond man's voice had a bland accent with a slight twang typical of a mid-western American. He pushed up his glasses and frowned, waving his hands, as if struggling for the right word, at last managing, "Self-propelled!"

"Automobiles."

"Right," James said. "Look at how everything has changed. Imagine our shock."

"You fooled me." Mary shook her head. "Earlier, acting as if you had things sorted out."

"Us? No, no. It confused us for days. We landed up north, in the country—we cannot land inside London as we once could."

"No?"

"The fog no longer provides enough cover."

"Oh?"

"We must be cautious of—technical advances—the military can detect..."

"Radar," Mary said. "How did you learn I was alive? At my age, you must have worried."

"That was my first errand," James said.

"Easy for a secret agent, I imagine."

"It would surprise you to learn what I went through, but look, Mary—we came as soon as we could manage it. Coming to see you was essential."

Mary blushed. "Why? Where are you going next?"

"They said you would tell us."

"Me? How?" She paused, frowned, and bit her lip.

The letter!

"Ah, perhaps I have a way. Enough tears and hurt feelings!" She spoke with a tone of finality and discipline. "Where are my manners? Let me hang those up for you."

Mary covered the hallway pegs with hats and umbrellas and latched onto the arms of the two tallest. "Come this way, please. To the parlor! We have much to discuss. You cannot imagine how I have prayed for this day to arrive. We must have tea."

"Fabulous," James said. "You cannot imagine how long it has been since I had a good cup of tea."

Mary stopped, turned, and leaned close to study James's face with a frozen smile and narrowed eyes. "True. I cannot imagine how long it has been. Pray, tell us."

James glanced at his associates, but they averted eyes.

"Is this a sensitive topic?"

"Not to us."

"Right, then! No sense beating around the bush. The year is 1947." She paused, waiting for a reply, but received only polite smiles. "You are all aware of that, I hope."

James squirmed, frowning, but the other two heads nodded in unison.

"Good! Pressing on—you left in 1891 so I calculate that, for me, it has been fifty-six years. How long has it been for you? A day, a week, or a month?"

James turned to his spectacled comrade. "Donald? You are the scientist. That sounds like a technical question. It should be a dolly for you. Perhaps you should take it."

"I used this." Donald, the blond man, held up a pocket watch. "If one is observant, uses discipline, and keeps exact logs…"

"You still have James's timepiece!" Mary said. "I would have expected you to have returned it by now."

"I remind him each day!" James eyed the timepiece. "It is not a gift—it was a loan."

"You trust him with it?"

"If I must tell the truth…" James paused for dramatic effect. "No!"

Donald and Siriman smirked.

"So then, Donald," Mary said. "How long has it been?"

"According to my calculations—three years."

Mary's hands covered her cheeks. "That long? I was far from the mark. I guessed a week, but at first, I swore you had not aged a day. It does not seem possible."

"They warned us this would happen," Donald said, "but could not explain the phenomena."

"They should talk to Mister Gamow!"

"Who?"

"Or better, they should see Einstein."

"Who is that?"

"Oh, he is the most amazing scientist. You must try to meet him. He is in America—at Princeton University. You would have much to discuss. You would be the living proof of his theories—if he believed you. He is so famous he would be harder to meet and convince than the other scientist—the one back in 1891."

"You mean Tesla."

"Yes, poor Mister Tesla. He passed away four years ago, alone and penniless—he never received his due. Everyone thought he was insane."

"Insane?" Donald said. "Impossible. His theories—electrical energy, the ether—they were right, brilliant, and critical to the..."

"The death ray? The world regards it as a fantasy—or a joke."

"Dragons do not find it humorous..."

"Sorry to interrupt," James said, "but at the door, you said you expected us and sounded worried—as if afraid someone might see us."

"Yes, and I promised to explain, so I shall!" Mary winked and, with Siriman following, towed James and Donald into the parlor. "But first, I shall tend the kettle." She motioned to the couch and chairs. "Gentlemen, please take a seat. I apologize for these old chairs but I hope they will do." Mary hurried to the kitchen and reappeared in seconds carrying her apron. "The pot will whistle in no time." She dug into the pocket, retrieved the unopened wax-coated envelope, and raised it into view. "I found this today—under a rock."

James leapt to his feet, arms raised, beaming. "Another hidden letter? After all this time? Do you think she wrote it?"

"Who else?" Mary said. "By strange chance, today is the fifty-sixth anniversary of her passing."

"There are no coincidences!" Eyes turned, and the Asian shrugged. "So the memsahib always says."

"Is the letter addressed to anyone?" Donald said.

"It says Mary and I assume that means me. After I found it, I had a premonition. I sensed someone would come today, and I saw you three—the soldier, the scientist, and the secret agent—standing at my door, looking as young as ever."

"Incredible," James shook his head. "Another letter hidden under a rock—like the one Colonel Burnaby found."

"And Solon Bailey!" Donald raised a finger. "He also found his letter under a rock."

"Me, too!" Siriman said. "Well—under bricks, not a rock." He looked at Mary. "And addressed to someone else."

"Have you read it yet, Mary?" James said.

"I have yet to open it. My morning took an even stranger turn. My premonition failed me—instead of you, three other men arrived."

"What men?"

"If you can believe it, a soldier, a scientist, and a secret agent—men from the government. I thought I had lost my mind."

"Who were they?"

"Tizard, for one. Sir Henry Tizard—a scientist of sorts. He invented radar—it detects flying craft—the reason you landed out in the country."

"What did he want?" James said.

"He asked questions—about flying saucers."

"What did you tell him?"

"Little or nothing. I changed the topic."

"Who else came?"

"Menzies—Sir Stewart Menzies. He is a secretive man—quiet, scary, with smoldering eyes that burned holes in my soul. I think he is in the secret service. He uncovered a report from 1891—asked how I knew Madame Blavatsky, and of dragons and lizard men. They know things. They are coming back for me in a week—to bring me in for interrogation. I am worried."

"You have good cause," James said. "Given this information, we have scant time."

"No time? You only just arrived! I thought we would visit for a while at least."

"It is not safe here. Someone is likely watching—you know I would be. Our cab will return in an hour. Collect your things and come with us."

"Where are we going?"

"Yes," James said, "where? They said you would tell us."

"How would I know? Oh!"

Mary turned the envelope over and back.

The letter!

She tore at one end with shaking hands and fumbled, grasping at empty air and the envelope fell with a plop onto the wooden floor.

"Memsahib!" Siriman stood, reached into his coat, and produced a wicked-looking curved knife. He stooped and picked up the letter. "May I open it for you?"

"Ever the soldier and a gentleman!" Mary eyed the blade. "Are you ever without that thing?"

"Oh no, memsahib. You know a Gurkha is never without his kukri knife."

"You once before did me this exact favor."

The Gurkha worked the point of the blade into the wax, under the flap. The knife sliced the end and Siriman handed the letter back. Mary shook the envelope and a crisp, folded piece of paper dropped into her lap. She unfolded the sheet—ordinary letter-size, off-white, medium-grade stock. Dense ink script in steady thin lines covered both sides. She held the page at arms' length and squinted. "Oh, my, I shall need my spectacles. They are on the kitchen table." A shriek came from the kitchen. "And that would be the teapot! Tea and biscuits first, then the letter."

As she hurried toward the kitchen, Siriman scrambled to follow. "Memsahib! Please allow me to help!"

Mary threw an arm over Siriman's shoulders and gave him a hug so warm and genuine that any observer would believe no gesture could seem more natural.

Chapter 5. The Dragon Slayer

Fifty-six years earlier; midnight, Wednesday, 25 March 1891...

Siriman

The moon glared at Manipur like the judgmental eye of a merciless god. Torches flickered atop high brick walls and turbaned sentries paced, casting long shadows in the bright darkness. Crickets chirped and tree frogs croaked—their song echoed, punctuating the still night air. Jungle vegetation smoldered on the far side of the misty river and a smoky odor wafted past the bustees (shanty villages).

Across the ditch and two hundred yards west, wiry men in khaki uniforms—Nepali Gurkha riflemen—stood guard behind a mud wall. Flashes in the moonlight marked the bright steel of bayonets. A tenuous calm hovered above the British Residency (embassy) like a circling flock of scavenger birds waiting to swoop.

Twenty-year-old Gurkha soldier Siriman Sunwar sharpened his kukri knife and slid the blade back into the yak-hide sheath on his belt.

Midnight. Two hours gone and the sahibs are still inside the citadel.

Sounds of sudden activity at the opposing fort disrupted the calm—rustling leather and cloth, clanking steel and hushed voices barking orders in a strange tongue. Siriman leapt onto an empty ammunition crate and stood tiptoe, stretching his five-foot-two frame. As he peered over the mud wall, the torches atop the high brick ramparts extinguished and the dark figures of the sentries vanished.

Something is wrong!

Then, with flashes and mighty booms, twin field guns erupted. Shells shrieked and burst among the treetops sending branches crashing earthward. More shrieks followed and more incendiary shells fell and detonated above the confines. Comrades scurried as musket bullets whistled. Siriman covered his ears and winced. Sharp screams from the falling shells hurt like stabbing needles, but to Siriman, the sounds signified something more painful—there could be one explanation for the assault…

The truce ended! The parlay failed!

Siriman dropped behind the mud wall and crouched. Nine hundred feet away, down a tree-lined gravel lane stood a sprawling white stucco building—the home of the British ambassador—and its thatch roof burned in several places.

A shell exploded above one wing!

With a crack and a mighty crash, the roof of the wing collapsed.

The memsahib!

Siriman prepared to abandon his post and rush to help, and then stopped. In the bright moonlight, he saw fellow soldiers near the structure shouting and scurrying. The fearless Gurkhas formed a bucket brigade and transferred water from the nearby lake to fight the blaze. Siriman turned back to the wall as outside, a familiar high-pitched Nepali voice wailed.

"Open the gate!"

Siriman remounted the wooden crate and peered over the wall for confirmation. "Scout returning!" Heads of nearby comrades raised at his call. "Open the barricade!" Siriman ignored the incoming fire and pulled the man through the opening. "Thapa! Are you hit?"

Thapa caught his breath. "No—dragon slayer—not hit!"

"Stop calling me dragon slayer! Where were you hiding?"

The Gurkha pointed north. "In the brush, outside the Western Gate. I ran hard the whole way, but the Manipuris did not shoot at me."

"What happened? Why did you come back?"

"No time! Must speak to the sahibs!"

This is my chance! I can see to the memsahib's safety.

"Right!" Siriman gripped Thapa's arm. "I will go with you."

Naik (corporal) Thapa grinned and nodded. "Yes, dragon slayer. I mean, yes, Havildar (sergeant)!"

The two Gurkhas sprinted the long path to the house. Boots pounded, crunching gravel, as bullets hissed. Once reaching the verandah, Gurkha sentries led the men inside and into the durbar hall (formal meeting chamber) to speak with Captains Butcher and Boileau.

"I hid in the brush, sahib," Thapa said. "Manipuris could not see me, but knew someone was hiding. After the guns fired, someone yelled…"

The Gurkha paused, mouth open, and stared at the door. Siriman followed his gaze.

The memsahib!

Captain Boileau motioned. "Come in, Missus—this concerns you, too."

A slim, dark-haired woman entered the room. It was Missus Ethel Grimwood, the young wife of the ambassador, Political Agent Frank Grimwood. Siriman smiled and breathed a sigh of relief.

Safe!

The captain turned back and bade Thapa continue his report.

"The voice spoke in Manipuri…" Thapa stopped again and looked at Missus Grimwood.

"Please go on," Ethel said. "I know my husband is in danger. Tell us what you heard."

"A man on the wall said…," Thapa paused, swallowed, and blurted, "'the sahibs will not return!'"

"You are certain?" Captain Boileau said.

"Yes, sahib!"

"You understand the Manipuri tongue?"

"Yes, sahib! At least—I understood that much."

Butcher and Boileau whispered. Siriman studied the face of Missus Grimwood for reaction.

She shows no surprise. She expected this news.

Siriman and Thapa remained stoic as the officers conferred in hushed whispers.

The news is dire. They worry.

Captain Butcher turned and nodded to the Gurkhas. "That will be all."

Siriman and Thapa saluted and turned to leave. As he passed, Siriman caught Missus Grimwood's eye and the young woman returned his smile.

She recognized me!

Once outside, Siriman and Thapa joined a gathering of Gurkhas awaiting orders. The soldiers mingled near the shattered windows of the durbar hall and chattered in Gorkhali (a mix of Nepali, Hindi, and English). Through the bullet-riddled glass, a passionate debate was underway and Missus Grimwood's voice resounded.

"Do something!" she said. "We must evacuate! You had your chance!"

Siriman exchanged glances with his comrade.

"What is happening?" Thapa said.

Siriman held a finger to his lips and cocked an ear. "The memsahib is angry at the captains. I am not sure what—indecisiveness—means, but it must be bad. She wants to escape and take others. She will not listen to the sahib captains."

"What of the other sahibs—inside Kangla?"

Siriman shrugged. Five senior British leaders, including Missus Grimwood's husband, had entered the Manipuri gate to parlay and were still inside the fort.

Likely held captive!

"She wants to go west," Siriman said. "To Cachar. She says reinforcements will come that way. The captains do not know the road. She says she does, even in the dark."

The front door burst open and the young woman stormed off the verandah. She pointed and barked orders, directing servants and household staff.

"The memsahib has taken charge," Siriman said. "She is organizing an evacuation—including the wounded."

European women were rare in Northeast India, and to the Gurkhas, the young memsahib was the most beautiful European woman they had beheld. Siriman admired her vocal leadership in the face of her husband's plight, and from observing attentive stares, he knew the British officers concurred.

"See the sahibs—how they look at her," Thapa said.

Siriman nodded. "Everyone is alert when she is close. I will hate to see her leave."

"Yes," Thapa said, "someone must carry the wounded from danger, but what about us?"

"What of us?"

"We should go, too. Defeat is inevitable."

"Only the sahib captains can order a retreat," Siriman said.

By a quarter to one o'clock, the evacuation was well underway. The Residency's majordomo assembled embassy non-combatants near the garden behind the house—household staff, bunnias (merchants), coolies (laborers), and camp followers jostled and shouted. Doctor Calvert, the company's medical officer and surgeon, directed the kahars (carriers) to bear the wounded on doolies (stretchers) up from the cellar's makeshift infirmary.

Siriman recognized a young British officer among the wounded. They were from the same regiment and had fought together in the earlier action. Siriman edged closer.

I must offer encouragement.

The young man opened his eyes and smiled at Siriman. The Gurkha squeezed the officer's hand, and the man winced in pain, coughed, and then managed a whisper.

"Dragon—slayer…"

"Stand back!" Doctor Calvert said, pushing past Siriman.

Missus Grimwood rushed to the officer's side. Siriman retreated and watched as the officer succumbed to his wounds. Sobs wracked the woman's slender frame. The kahars carried the body back into the cellar.

Hiding his body. No time for burial.

A small company of Gurkha sepoys (native soldiers) marched around the corner and joined the memsahib's party.

"Did the sahib captains reconsider?" Thapa said. "Are we joining the retreat?"

"Those men are escorts," Siriman said, "chosen to guard the memsahib and help carry the doolies—too few kahars."

"They are lucky."

"They are not the best," Siriman said. "The sahibs need us at the wall."

The remaining four hundred Gurkhas gathered under fire near the verandah at the front of the house to hear the captains' orders. A shell exploded in the canopy of a tall oak behind the house, causing wild panic among the evacuees. With shouts and shoves, the retreating party struggled past hedges and moved west, crossing the walls, ditches, and streams surrounding the Residency grounds. Once the party had disappeared into the brush, Captain Butcher addressed the troops.

"There will be no general retreat. We will not abandon the officers inside the fort. While hope for a negotiated release remains, we will defend these grounds."

Butcher divided the Gurkhas into four companies. Each would take a turn guarding the Residency's perimeter mud wall for one hour, then rotate, relieved on the hour by the next company. The watch would continue, even under bombardment, until they could discover the fate of the captives. The subadar (native officer) motioned to Siriman.

"Sunwar, you are company leader of the first watch."

"What of ammunition?" Siriman said. "We have little and soon none. We cannot return fire."

"Exchange Martinis for Sniders."

Gurkhas from the 43rd Regiment had newer model Martini-Henry rifles, but were out of ammunition. Soldiers from the 42nd and 44th regiments had older model Snider-Enfield rifles, and a few remaining rounds. Gurkhas traded new rifles for old as the subadar doled precious rounds to each.

"Affix bayonets!" Siriman said to his company. "Assume positions behind the wall!"

At a quarter past one o'clock, as the bombardment continued, Siriman led his company forth. The other three companies remained stationed at the house watching the western flank and waiting their turn at the wall.

One hundred and six Gurkhas scurried under fire to the outer perimeter, spreading out across the north, east, and south sides of the mud wall. The soldiers crouched as bullets whistled in the moonlight. A bright moon and clear sky defeated the cloak of darkness, but musket-wielding Manipuris were poor shots at that distance, and the five-foot-tall Nepali warriors made difficult targets. The six-foot-high barrier afforded adequate protection when the Gurkhas stood close.

Siriman went to the eastern wall where, on either side of the gate, stone masonry ancillary buildings straddled a road fronting the southwestern wall of the Manipuri fort. He waited near the treasury, the left stone building housing the telegraph station—silent since the Manipuris cut the wires, perhaps miles away, to end communication with the outside world. Siriman sharpened his bayonet and fingered the point. Bullets flew and shells exploded overhead, and still he waited.

When will the ground assault come?

"Dragon slayer!" Siriman spun to face Thapa, returned from his rounds. "Sentries are in place, but with ammunition depleted, if the Manipuris attack the wall, as they did yesterday, there will be nothing to fight with except bayonets and kukri knives."

Siriman drew his kukri and studied the moon's reflection. "Then they will taste our steel."

"True, but, we cannot hold the wall for long."

"Kafar hone bhanda morne ramro (Better to die than to be a coward)."

"I am no coward," Thapa said, "but mottos will not save us."

"Motto? It is our way of life and…"

"Death!" Thapa said. "I do not fear death, but I and others wonder at our predicament. Two days ago Manipur welcomed us, now we fight for our lives."

"We could have beaten the Manipuris, even with their greater numbers, but…" Siriman paused and shook his head. The sahibs' ways were always mysterious, but the mission seemed wrong from the start. Something had to explain their situation.

Nothing makes sense.

"Subadar Chund wondered, too!" Thapa said. "I overheard him at Sengmai, talking to Sahib Brackenbury. He asked why we brought no mountain guns, only older rifles, and with only forty rounds to a man. We should have had at least five times as much ammunition. It is as if someone sent us here wanting a defeat."

"It is not our place to question." Siriman sheathed his knife. "Focus on something useful. Make your rounds again. Tell each man—stay alert, recite the motto."

Thapa nodded and left, shaking his head. Siriman repeated the motto until he grew tired of waiting and risked a quick look. He crept along the wall, stepped onto an empty ammunition crate, and stretched until his eyes just cleared the top of the wall. Through raised field glasses, he studied the royal banner of Manipur unfurled high above the battlements. A herald shone in the bright moonlight—a golden dragon on a green field, coiled, and devouring its tail.

"Dragons again!" A shot rang, Siriman ducked, and jumped off the box. He turned and sat, back against the wall, and shook his head. "Why does everything have to involve dragons?"

At a quarter past two o'clock—more than an hour since the memsahib's evacuation—shells and bullets continued raining as Siriman glanced back toward the Residency.

Where is our relief? The second watch should have come. Why have they not doused the fires at the house?

He rose and, as he stood next to the treasury, cannon fired, and a shell screamed, louder than the earlier rounds.

Falling right on us!

Siriman fell flat and threw arms over head. A furious explosion burst the treasury into a cloud of dust and shards, stinging arms and torso, and then blackness came.

Chapter 6. The Waxy Envelope

Continued...

Siriman

From a distance, came a voice. "Havildar…"

Siriman did not answer as he drifted on in a warm darkness.

Leave me in peace. I do not want to speak until the pain stops.

"The company depends on you. You are havildar now."

I am not a havildar—I am a naik.

"No, you received a promotion—remember?"

No. When? How?

"Yesterday. Before the bombardment. Look, I will show you…"

Siriman stood in the durbar hall of the Residency. British and Gurkha officers stood close. It was still daylight—the low sun poured through the broken glass.

"Naik Sunwar," Colonel Skene said, "you are receiving a brevet promotion."

Siriman stood at attention, wearing the endearing, never-ending grin of the Gurkhas. The colonel studied the soldier's face and frowned. "Do you know what I mean by a brevet promotion?"

"No, sahib!" Siriman stood ramrod straight, eyes fixed ahead.

"Right." Skene rubbed his chin. "Well, the point is, I am promoting you to havildar rank. Lieutenant Simpson recommended you. Good show today at the dry ditch and later at the river bank—helping rescue Lieutenant Brackenbury, and all that."

Siriman gave a crisp salute and grinned wider. The colonel offered his hand and Siriman returned the firm shake. He strode from the room in brisk fashion, exited through the front door, and hopped down the verandah steps to meet a crowd of comrades offering warm congratulations.

I remember now—Colonel Skene promoted me. What did he mean— brevet promotion?

"It is a promotion given during the heat of battle," the voice said. "If you escape and live, the promotion could become permanent—assuming someone is alive to vouch for you. Sometimes no record exists to verify a brevet promotion, but that should be the least of your concerns. With higher rank comes new responsibility."

The colonel—he is...

"Yes, the colonel remains captive inside the fort with the other sahibs."

Then—how...?

"The scene I showed you happened yesterday evening."

Who are you?

"You know."

Karna?

No answer came.

Karna—if you are there—I am sorry! Can you forgive me?

"Avenge me, Siriman."

Avenge—it was I who...

"No. You did the needful."

From whom do I seek vengeance—the Manipuris?

"No!" the voice said. "You know..."

Dragons? How can I?

"The time will come, Siriman, and remember..."

What?

"Avoid the dragon's eyes."

Karna!

No answer came.

Wait! Please, do not go!

Siriman sobbed, caring nothing for promotions—brevet or otherwise. The bitter memory of a loss consumed him. An evil moment had befallen despite every effort to prevent it.

I pray to—to whichever god looks after soldiers such as me—please forgive me, help me forgive myself, help this bitter memory fade...

"Havildar?"

"Karna! Please come back!"

"Havildar?"

Siriman opened his eyes and found himself sprawled facedown. A low hum and a painful hiss filled his ears, and large, jagged rocks stood on either side of his throbbing head.

I was lucky—either rock could have crushed my skull!

The Gurkha shook his head and struggled to a kneeling position. He gulped, trying to clear his ears. The hiss and hum grew fainter, but in their place was—nothing. No cracking of muskets or booming of field guns from the walls of Kangla—only silence.

"I have gone deaf!" Siriman said, certain he had suffered hearing loss from the concussive force of the explosion, but then, "Hold! There are crickets chirping—and the other jungle night sounds."

"Havildar?"

"Not deaf? Who?" Siriman blinked and his vision cleared, revealing the toes of boots. He looked up, past trousers and a khaki shirt, to the wide eyes and open mouth of Naik Batsa Gurung.

"Havildar," Gurung whispered, "are you injured? The explosion..."

Siriman spat a mouthful of dust. "Thik chha (all is right). Not injured...," he coughed, "I need time—to recover."

"Recover then, but hurry! Something is happening!" Gurung scurried back to his place at the wall.

Siriman turned and sat. As he patted his shirt, brushing away stone dust and fragments, something rustled, and he discovered a stiff, flat, rectangular shape hiding inside his uniform.

What is that?

Siriman unbuttoned his shirt, reached inside, and touched something cool and slippery. He drew out a wax-coated object shaped like a letter-sized envelope.

How did this get into my shirt?

He turned the object over, studying the slippery surface in the moonlight, and then...

I remember!

The day before, during the heat of battle, as he climbed over a wall to enter Kangla Fort, Siriman found the unusual item hidden under bricks. He had slipped it inside his shirt for safekeeping and later examination, intending to deliver it to the sahibs, but soon forgot.

Inside must be a letter or document.

Siriman could not read or write and had little experience with letters, documents, or envelopes. He had sent and received a few letters from back home in Nepal. He had always found a babu (scribe) and paid the chap a rupee to listen and write as he dictated, then another rupee to stamp and send the letter. Likewise, rupees would entice the babu to read aloud the few letters he received. This envelope was larger than those his letters came in, and someone had sealed it with a thin coat of paraffin, or other waxy substance.

Something someone told me long ago. Was it a dream? Why can I not remember? I must try.

In the bright darkness, Siriman made out symbols under the wax—a few characters of the English alphabet. Most Gurkhas, and even many British soldiers and officers, had little formal education. Siriman received little schooling in Nepal, other than religious instruction. Then, at age fifteen, he lied about his age and enlisted. In the five years since, he received only military training. He was bright, motivated to learn, and taught himself the characters of the English alphabet. He learned to sound out words, in particular those on signs posted around British camps.

Perhaps I can read this.

He rubbed his thumb over the wax and unveiled the first two characters. He spotted a "Z" and an "o" and then sounded the letters.

"Zo," he whispered, with a quiver of pride in his voice.

It cannot mean the Zo people. They cannot write.

The Zo people were a wild tribe of headhunting natives of the Lushai Hills of Mizoram, a mountainous jungle country southwest of Manipur.

Gurung called, "Havildar! Are you coming?"

No time to decipher now. Later perhaps.

Siriman stuffed the envelope inside his shirt, refastened the buttons, and stood. He snatched his cap, beat it against his shirt and trousers, knocking away dust and masonry fragments, and then snugged it atop his head. His rifle served as a crutch as he hobbled toward the wall.

"What is happening?" he asked the sepoy. "What do you see?"

"See for yourself."

Siriman leapt onto a crate and took another cautious peek over the wall with his field glasses. The bright moonlight showed a clear expanse leading toward the moat and high brick walls of Kangla. The gold and green dragon banner still hung from the battlements. Nothing moved. It was quiet save for the sounds from the jungle on the far side of the river.

"All is clear," Siriman said. "I see nothing and I hear nothing."

"Yes! It is quiet—too quiet."

"Right! Something has happened inside the fort. This quiet will not last long."

The quiet did not last long, but rather than guns firing, unexpected faint sounds drifted over the walls of Kangla. The sounds grew louder.

"What is that?" Gurung said.

"Drums!"

The slow tempo of the beating drums increased. Voices followed—cheering, singing, and chanting—then more drums.

"It sounds like a celebration," Siriman said.

A Gurkha below tugged at Siriman's trouser leg. "Dragon slayer..."

"Good," Siriman said, "you are back, Thapa. I need you."

"What is happening?"

"Can you tell what they are chanting?"

Thapa cocked an ear. "Happy words—of victory, or revenge. A prophecy—but that makes no sense."

"Our relief is late!" Siriman jumped off the box. "The Residency is still burning. I fear the worst. Hurry to the house and find the sahibs—the captains, the subadar, anyone. Tell them what is happening. Find out if we have new orders."

Thapa sprinted away down the long gravel drive. Siriman cupped his hands to his mouth and shouted to the nearest soldiers.

"Stand by for new orders! Pass it forward!"

The Gurkhas relayed the message north and south along the wall. Agonizing minutes crept by and the sounds of celebration continued. Siriman grew impatient.

"Gurung," Siriman said, "I cannot wait for Thapa any longer. I am going to the house. Take command until I return."

Siriman ran up the gravel path and, near the house, discovered Thapa kneeling beside a downed soldier. Thapa looked up as Siriman approached. "Gone! All gone!"

"Who?"

"Everyone. The others at the Residency! There is no one left! We are alone!"

Chapter 7. The Golden-haired Angel

An instant later...

Siriman

Siriman stared wide-eyed at Thapa. "What are you saying?"

"The sahibs, the soldiers—everyone at the Residency—gone! They retreated and left us at the wall."

"How do you know?"

Thapa pointed. "*He* told me."

Nearby lay a motionless Gurkha. A dark red stain soaked the front of the man's uniform and a frozen grimace distorted his face.

"Who is—who was he?"

"Naik Rom Tamang," Thapa said. "I found him here—wounded, dying. He spoke his last words, moments ago."

"What did he say?"

"He coughed so much blood—so hard to understand—but he said the subadar sent him to tell us to retreat. A Manipuri bullet caught him as he ran—a lucky shot."

"Unlucky for poor Tamang." Siriman shook his head. "What else did he say?"

"He said twenty, maybe thirty, minutes after we took the first watch the sahibs changed their minds and ordered the retreat."

"To follow the memsahib?"

"Right," Thapa said. "Everyone fled at once, caught up in the retreat."

"No one came to help him?"

"He said it was chaos, a mad rush to leave, and likely no one saw him fall."

"If it was chaos," Siriman said, "it was silent chaos. No bugler blew retreat. Were we so focused on the wall?"

Thapa shrugged.

"Did the captains leave any specific orders?"

"All Tamang said was—disengage, retreat, head west to Cachar and to…" Thapa squirmed.

"To do what?"

"To manage as best we can. Those were his final words."

"Manage as best we can?" Siriman turned away in disgust. He clenched his fists and bit a knuckle.

Doomed from the start—now stranded! They have a half-hour head start. The Manipuris will overwhelm us—that much is certain.

Siriman fumed—leaderless, abandoned, low on provisions, ammunition depleted, outnumbered at least fifty-to-one, a hundred miles of dangerous, unfamiliar terrain stretched ahead. He put his hand to his forehead. His temples still throbbed from the explosion.

Surrender is not a choice. The Manipuris will show no mercy.

Siriman had to decide and soon. He spoke aloud as he paced. "The sahibs said to manage as best as we can. So we will. We cannot stay here and defend this place. Our best chance is to retreat and try to catch them. We must leave at once before this lull ends."

Siriman turned to Thapa. "Go to the south wall. Spread the word— withdraw and assemble by the house—at the verandah. We are leaving this deathtrap now!"

Thapa shouted agreement and sprinted away. Siriman hurried up the drive shouting for Gurung. The word spread along the perimeter and soon one hundred and six Gurkhas, with jaws set and rifles slung over shoulders, trotted in silence toward the house. Siriman cocked his head and listened. Coarse khaki rubbed, leather creaked, and boots crunched gravel—sounds drowned by jungle noises and the drumming and singing from the fort.

Then, a loud sound hit Siriman's ears—it was more of a sensation—a pulsing, pounding, reverberating, deep rumble. Siriman covered his ears to no avail—it was as if a steam locomotive had parked inside his head.

What is happening? Have I gone deaf again from the explosion?

Comrades stopped. Confused faces. Hands flew up to cover ears. A few dropped to their knees.

They hear it, too!

Then a red light broke like a sudden dawn—a blinding, downward beam illuminated the Residency grounds. Siriman shielded his eyes and tried to locate the source, but had to turn his head, unable to withstand the brilliance. Then something large and bright dropped from the sky and disappeared. The sprawling white house appeared stark and desolate, still smoldering, blocking the eerie light like a dark moon eclipsing a blood-red sun.

Siriman and the leading members of his party halted fifty feet from the house. The remaining Gurkhas arrived in dribbles and gathered. All eyes focused on the verandah. Inside, through the broken windows and wide-open front door, they could see flames flickering.

Shapes moved in the firelight. The wavering illumination cast long, writhing shades—like eerie silhouettes of tall humanoids. Shadows like gangling arms reached outward from the open door, spilled across the verandah and stretched onto the ground. Dark fingers writhed as if grasping at Siriman's boots. His jaw dropped, his eyes widened, and he took a step back.

"Maar patsaa (what to do)?" he whispered.

Then, with a great whoosh, as if a giant had inhaled and sucked the air from the house, the flames extinguished and the shadows vanished.

"Are we trapped in a nightmare?" Thapa said.

"Asuras (demons)," Gurung said. "Or Rakshasas (shapeshifters)."

"We are dead," another said. "It is Yama (god of death). We are at the gates of Naraka (hell)."

Beyond the open door lay a still interior. Flames glimmered in the thatch above, but the verandah roof remained intact and blocked the bright moon. A red light pulsed behind the house, keeping time with the deep throbs. Then another shadow darkened the door.

"Something moves inside," Siriman said. He drew his kukri blade and took a step forward.

Kafar hone bhanda morne ramro.

"Havildar, wait," Thapa said. "What is it?"

"I will find out. Go around the outside if you wish."

"We cannot go around," Thapa said. "There is something behind the house—we saw the red light, we hear the sounds. Do you think—is it a dragon?"

"Ha! Ridiculous! A machine is my guess." He pointed his knife at the door. "We must go forward. Something is inside and if it stands in my way, I will kill it. I go through the house."

He took two strides toward the verandah steps.

At that instant, the dark shadow at the door became a white form. The Gurkhas stiffened. The shape was human—feminine—a hooded woman in a white dress appeared on the verandah like a ghost in the mist. She wore a white pilgrim's dress with her face half-covered by a hood. With a quick motion, she tossed the hood back, and the Gurkhas gasped.

"A—a—an angel…," a soldier stammered.

Angel?

The word struck a chord. Siriman stared, dumb founded, and his mind raced as if time had frozen.

An angel? Why does that strike me odd? There was—something, like a dream. Why can I not remember?

The woman glowed like a moonlit apparition with flowing, golden blond hair, and sparkling, steel blue eyes. She seemed young, with the radiance of a woman in her twenties. Not tall, but she looked taller than any Gurkha. To Siriman's eye, she was European, and yet—there was something different…

Something in her eyes—an eastern look…

"Hullo," she said. "Please lower your weapons and listen to what I have to say."

With those words, the spell of the frozen moment ended. Her soft voice was clear and direct, with a quiet authority, as if she could tell someone to jump off a cliff and expect immediate compliance. He considered the other European woman—the memsahib, Missus Grimwood—and compared the two. The memsahib was dark haired, slender, and sultry—he had thought her beautiful beyond compare, but the angelic young woman before him captured top honor in his heart.

"I know this looks a wee bit frightening…"

Is she a Scot?

"Believe me—you are among friends. The others with me—they are not ready to show themselves. The right time will come. Meanwhile, I will speak for them. We are here to help you—if you let us. We have little time."

Siriman mustered the courage to speak. "What are you?"

She paused, cocked her head, as if considering an idea, facing a consequential decision, and then she nodded and smiled. A lock of blond hair fell across her face and she raised a hand to brush it away.

"My name is Zoluti." She stuck out her lower lip and blew a blast to knock a final strand away from her eye. "I am—a messenger of sorts. My message to you is this—you are in great danger—but you know that. If you stay and resist, they will overwhelm and kill you to the last man. If you retreat to the brush, you might escape, but more likely, your enemy will hunt down and kill each one before you can make ten miles. You could stay here and try to surrender—beg for mercy, but expect none. You know I am right."

Siriman glanced at the wide eyes of his comrades.

She terrifies even the bravest.

"Memsahib," he said, "we understand the danger. What do you want from us?"

"Come with us now," Zoluti said. "Leave this place. Live to fight another day."

"What of the sahibs? Those still inside the fort—if we leave them, what will be their fate?"

"They are in God's hands," she said. "No one can change their fate."

The sahibs—can there be no hope?

"You must move on," she continued. "Your officers have abandoned you as they abandoned the men inside the fort. Now you must leave."

"We want to leave," Siriman said, "but, forgive me, you are in our way."

"See here!" she said, crossing her arms. "You cannot make it on your own. Come with us."

"With—with whom?"

The woman took a quick glance over her shoulder, as if in answer to a call, then returned and smiled. "We have no time. If you follow me and come with us, I promise we can take you to safety, but you must decide—now. We are leaving. God bless you all."

With those words, she stepped inside the door and vanished.

Siriman stood speechless, kukri still in hand. All Gurkha eyes turned toward him. Seconds crawled.

"Havildar?" Gurung said.

Siriman did not answer.

"Lead us," Thapa said. He grasped Siriman's arm and locked eyes. "We trust you, Havildar—with our lives."

Many voices murmured agreement.

"Tell us what to do," Gurung said. "If you say stay and fight, we stay and we fight. Say retreat into the brush and we follow. If you say trust these—these beings, whoever or whatever they are—I, at least, will follow you."

"As will I," Thapa said, "even to our doom, if so fated."

Siriman glanced behind at the looming walls of Kangla Fort. The drums and chants of the celebration had ceased. He sheathed his kukri and faced his men.

"Orders are to manage as best we can. I will manage by trusting the memsahib. If you trust me with your lives, then follow me now."

Siriman strode forward and leapt up the verandah steps. Without waiting to see who followed, he entered the house. Inside, no open flames but smoke rose from smoldering woodwork. He coughed and his eyes watered as he passed the durbar hall and entered the kitchen. The backdoor stood open. He paused, took a deep breath of the fresh night air, and then stepped outside to face—the machine.

Red lights pulsed and a low hum rumbled from a massive, disk-shaped machine, at least a hundred feet in diameter.

Like giant saucers, turned face-to-face.

Three telescoping struts angled downward from the hull and met the ground. A long ramp descended from the underside. The golden-haired woman waited at the foot of the ramp.

"Good," she said, smiling. "I am glad you came. I know it must be difficult to place your trust in someone, or something, so strange."

Siriman looked up the ramp toward a looming hole overhead.

"Yes," she said.

Siriman cocked his head and frowned.

"You were wondering if I meant for you to climb the gangway to the hold. The answer is, yes—please do."

Siriman paused, looking to see if anyone followed. He smiled, thrilled by the sight of a crowd of Gurkhas lining behind him. More streamed from the back door. He waved his arm and motioned the men to climb.

The first Gurkhas ventured with caution, then more crowded behind pushing and it became a rush. Siriman tallied as they streamed past.

"I make it one hundred and five," he said, pointing at the last man.

"So counting you, that makes one hundred and six."

Zoluti climbed the gangway with Siriman at her side.

"Memsahib," the Gurkha said, "are you—an angel?"

Zoluti threw back her head and laughed. Siriman smiled, taken aback, but her laugh was endearing, charming, and disarming. As they took the final steps into the hold, she threw her arm over Siriman's shoulders. She gave the Gurkha a hug so warm and genuine that any observer would have believed no gesture could have seemed more natural.

Chapter 8. The Flying Saucer

Seconds later...

Siriman

The Gurkhas gathered in the hold. Siriman followed the golden-haired woman, edging through the milling crowd. A second gangway lowered and Zoluti led the soldiers to a higher deck of the saucer-shaped craft where a sprawling alleyway circled the outer rim. Every eye blinked in bright white light emanating from the overhead. There was six and a half feet of headroom—comfortable for the woman, and the shorter Gurkhas.

The taller sahibs would be uncomfortable.

The gangway raised behind, sealing shut, and Siriman searched in vain for lines where the hatch closed. His attention turned to his men—navigating the crowd, encouraging individuals, and conversing with groups—listening to questions and grumbles, offering assurances they would be safer once far from Manipur.

"When do we meet these strange new sahibs?" one said.

Siriman shrugged and looked to Zoluti.

"In time." She motioned the group to sit.

The men spread around the compartment, finding ample space on the stark deck. Siriman rubbed his hand over the surface—non-metallic, warm, and firm, and tiny dimples gave it a rough texture. He rapped knuckles on the deck and frowned, puzzled by the hollow thud. He knocked on the inner hull with similar results. There were no visible seams—as if someone had poured the deck, bulkhead, and overhead in a single, flowing sheet.

This material is not wood or metal. I have not seen its kind.

He studied the white glow from the overhead but could not find the source. The light dimmed and soon the only illumination came from moonlight streaming through circular windows in the angled hull. The crystalline portholes, spaced at intervals of a dozen feet, offered outside views. Zoluti took a place standing next to an aperture facing the rear of the house. Siriman scooted closer, looked out, and observed flames raging once more.

"Memsahib," he said, looking up, "we saw this—this machine…"

She answered without turning. "It is a vessel—a craft."

"This—craft—came from the sky?"

"It did."

"Will we now fly away?"

"Oh, yes—in a wee bit you will see."

Siriman closed his eyes and waited, bracing for the invisible tugs of acceleration and inertia, but nothing happened. He opened his eyes and jerked, surprised by the scene in the porthole. The house and the entire Residency grounds—the trees, lakes, gardens, tents, outbuildings, and perimeter mud wall—had dwindled to miniscule size. In the moonlight, he made out the line of the dirt road, the villages and bustees, the bazaar, and the high brick walls of Kangla. The craft rose higher, with no physical sense of motion, passing over the fields, forests, and rivers of the Imphal valley.

We must be high. What prevents us falling to our deaths?

Siriman placed ear to deck—the same powerful throb sensed earlier.

How can engines make the craft float, as if grasping thin air?

"Memsahib," he said, "what magic holds us aloft?"

She stared ahead. "There is no such thing as magic."

"I have heard of balloons—they can fly. Are we in a balloon?"

"Not at all."

The view out the porthole shifted. Without physical sense of movement, Kangla and the Residency became dots and disappeared in the distance.

We travel southwest! Not west to Cachar, not north to Kohima. Where is she taking us?

Thick jungles in the valley gave way to a wooded hill country. "Memsahib," he said, "are those the Lushai Hills?"

"Yes."

"Memsahib, are you taking us to Mizoram?"

"No!" She turned her face that time. "Please call me Zoluti."

"Mem—I mean, Zoluti—Memsahib, do you know Mizoram?"

"I do. The hills are beautiful in the moonlight, are they not?"

Siriman glanced at the landscape and the young woman. "Your name—Zoluti—is it a name from the Zo tribes?"

"It was my home once..." She gave a wistful sigh. "A long time ago. When I was a child."

"It must have been frightening and dangerous. The Zo people are cruel and—and..."

"Primitive?"

"Yes," he said. "Their warriors sweep down from the hills and attack the tea gardens. They capture slaves—take white heads."

"How do you know of Mizos?"

"From stories. The British send Gurkhas to fight the Zos. That land is no place for European girls—unless... The subadar once told a campfire story of a young girl captured by a Zo tribe and..."

Siriman trailed off and studied the young woman's face. She turned away from the porthole and he could see her sparkling eyes and moonlit smile.

Could it be she?

"There is goodness there. They treated me as a princess. Someday they will learn God's mercy and give up violence and slavery. I expect it to happen in my lifetime."

The little girl—a grown woman?

Zoluti shrugged and looked at Siriman. "What is your name, Soldier? You are the leader—correct?"

"Oh, yes, memsahib," he said, "but I became havildar—yesterday, it was. I am Siriman Sunwar, 44th Gurkha Rifles, but the men are a mix from the 42nd, 43rd, and 44th regiments. We are from Nepal, and soldier in the service of Queen Empress Victoria."

"Impressive!" She grinned and offered a hand. "Pleased to make your acquaintance, Siriman Sunwar. Please call me Zoluti."

The overhead lights blinked and then lit to a bright white. "Goodness," Zoluti said, looking up, "our light is back."

Siriman remembered.

Zo...

He unbuttoned his shirt, reached inside, and retrieved the envelope. He rubbed the waxy coating, trying to uncover more characters. As shapes appeared, he moved his lips and mouthed the letters, spelling "Zoluti." Siriman grinned with pride and, beaming, presented the envelope.

"Memsahib," he said, "For you!"

She frowned as she reached, took the envelope, and studied the front. "Where did you get this?"

"I found it yesterday. It was an accident..."

Zoluti struggled, trying to tear the waxy end.

"Please," Siriman said, unsheathing his kukri blade, "allow me to help."

She offered the envelope. He inserted the point beneath the sealed flap, sliced open the end, and returned it.

"That is a wicked blade you have there," she said. "Thank you. You are a kind gentleman."

She removed and unfolded a single sheet of paper. Her eyes grew wide as she read.

Siriman waited, looking around, and noticed comrades watching. Several stood and moved closer. "Um...," he ventured. "Zoluti Memsahib?"

"Huh," she mumbled, not taking her eyes from the page.

"Is the letter interesting?"

"Huh? Yes—immeasurably."

"Immeasurably..." He repeated the new word, chewing it, savoring the flavor, and guessing at the meaning.

I think she likes it. It must be for her.

A thought gnawed at his mind.

There is something else. Something from years ago.

It came to him in a flash.

I remember!

He raised both hands and his mouth dropped open. He trembled as he tried to articulate his realization.

"Is the letter...?"

"Yes?"

"Is it from—the Smoking Woman?"

"What...?" Zoluti yanked the page from her face and burning eyes glared as if Siriman had blundered his way into a private moment. "How do you know *her*?"

Siriman shrank, as if retreating from hot sparks shot from blue eyes. "I remembered. It—was a dream from long ago—five years. She told me I would find a letter, and when I did, I should give it to the angel." His chin drooped and his shoulders slumped.

Zoluti's eyes softened. "Oh, Siriman Sunwar...!" She laughed and tossed her long golden hair. "I underestimated you, but will not repeat that mistake. She chose her messenger wisely."

Chapter 9. The Service of the Queen Empress

Continued...

Siriman

Zoluti left the porthole and touched a shaded circle shoulder-high on the bulkhead. She stood aside as another ramp lowered from the overhead, and took slow steps up the incline, eyes glued to the letter.

"Memsahib, wait! Where are you going?"

Zoluti paused, turned to Siriman, and raised the paper toward the higher deck. "To discuss this letter of yours—with our friends."

"Where are we being taken?

"I cannot say yet."

"When will we learn?"

"Soon, I hope."

I am being forward, but the situation is forcing my hand.

"This craft..." His face reddened. Zoluti waited as he sputtered, struggling to find the right words, before at last blurting, "Does it have a blind alley?"

"Sorry?"

"A latrine."

"Oh, my Lord!" Hands covered a red face.

"And a mess hall? Maybe pans of water for washing first, and cloth towels. We have seen many hours of action, and... ah... the men need to... um... we need food, drink, and... freshening. If you understand me."

"You poor dears! Where are my manners? Let me show you the head, the galley, and the other facilities."

Zoluti stepped down, touched the circle, and the ramp returned to the overhead. Three steps away, she touched another circle, a hatch slid open, and she motioned. Siriman followed into a smaller compartment.

"This is a head," she said. "You and your men can freshen here. I will show you how to use it."

Zoluti unleashed a rapid explanation of the room's operation. She pointed at mechanisms, describing each's purpose, but Siriman struggled to understand. She touched a glowing circle, and a hatch opened.

"Here," she said, "you can place your dirty clothing. Now, closing the hatch like so." She tapped another circle, and the cover snapped shut. "Then, touch this circle—like so." She pointed at another spot in the bulkhead. "Soon, over here, another hatch will open and the uniform will return, clean and dry, and..."

"What strange magic..."

Zoluti wagged a finger, shaking her head. "There is no such thing as magic. There is a simple principle..."

Zoluti tried to explain the technical aspects, but it was more than Siriman could comprehend. He grasped something about sound waves.

Whatever those are.

Zoluti next pointed to a tall tube of clear material like glass, but warmer and softer to the touch.

"If you were to remove your clothing and step in..." She unleashed a stream of incomprehensible words, followed by, "it would clean your body, and—oh, no!"

Zoluti gasped—eyes wide and face beat red. Siriman stood on one leg, leaning against the bulkhead, struggling to remove his trousers.

"Not yet!" she said, shaking her head. "Let me show you how everything works first. Then you can organize your men and see everyone accommodated."

Zoluti turned away while a red-faced Siriman yanked up his trousers. When he finished, she motioned and led him into the corridor.

"A similar compartment is opposite us on the deck. I will show it to you, and you can divide everyone in two groups. Perhaps things will move faster that way."

Siriman nodded.

"Next," she said, "I will show where you get provisions."

Zoluti spent the next half hour instructing the soldiers in other amazing features the craft offered for cleanliness, sustenance, and overall personal comfort. Soon the Gurkhas were attending to their personal needs, and Siriman noticed Zoluti had disappeared.

Up the ramp, I suppose, taking the letter to see... Whom?

Siriman was soon clean, dry, and ready to attend to hunger and thirst. Solid provisions came in colored packages—the colors denoted different flavors and consistency. The Gurkhas learned which foods they preferred and which colors went with less palatable flavors. They sifted through the bins, arguing and bargaining over the preferred colors. Siriman settled on green packages containing crunchy, fruity-flavored bars. He gobbled those and topped his meal off with a dark liquid sucked through a nipple at the end of short yellow cylinder. The drink had a tangy taste, reminiscent of a mixture of vegetable juices.

Gurkhas soon rested, sleeping or conversing, but overall, in a far better mood. Siriman laid back, thirst quenched and his stomach full, blinking at the bright light. He tried to stay alert, but eyelids grew heavy and he settled into a mellow haze, drifting in and out of consciousness. He lost track of time, and then woke and sat up, thankful for the rest.

Now I must decide our next steps. I must get answers.

He was thinking, working through a list of questions that needed answering, when someone sighed. He found Zoluti, returned from her visit to the upper deck, standing over, arms folded.

"I hoped to go home," she said, "but instead, because of your waxy letter, we are going to Peru."

"Peh-roo, memsahib? Where in India is Peh-roo?"

"Peru is…" Zoluti covered her mouth and cleared her throat. "Not in India—in South America."

"Oh," Siriman said, frowning. "Is that far?"

"The far side of the world. It will not take long—this craft travels fast."

"Yes, I am sure, memsahib."

She unfolded her arms. "I said before, you do not have to call me memsahib. Call me Zoluti."

Siriman climbed to his feet. "Thank you, Zoluti Memsahib."

"Zoluti."

"Zoluti." He bowed. "Kind memsahib."

She threw her hands up and laughed. "I surrender!"

"If you have time—I have questions."

"I can guess your questions." She counted using the fingers of one hand. "Whom am I? Who are those you have not seen? Why did we rescue you? What is this strange craft and how does it fly? Where are we going next? Have I missed any?"

"Oh, yes, memsahib!" he said. "I mean, no, Zoluti. I mean correct! You must have read my mind."

She smiled. "Oh, to be sure. Gather around and I will explain what I can."

Soldiers within earshot gathered and others followed. Soon a crowd of Gurkhas surrounded her, bright eyed and eager for news.

"Who I am does not matter," she began, "but I came from England—yesterday, it was. Before I came to find you, I was in London. It is a long story best saved for later. I am here to act as translator. I understand the language of the others—your saviors—the operators of this craft. Who they are, they are not ready to say, but I can say with certainty they are your friends."

We are making progress!

"Do they have a name?" Siriman asked.

"I call them the scientists. It is the best translation I can give."

"Scientists?"

"Yes—experts in the scientific fields." Blank stares came in answer. "Science—you know about science?" Shrugs and twisted smiles. "Oh, come now, you must know of physics, astronomy, chemistry, geology, biology, botany, zoology…"

"Zoo!" a Gurkha shouted.

A chattering hubbub erupted.

"I heard Madras has a zoo!" another cried.

"We are going to Madras!"

"Madras is far away!"

"No!" Zoluti said, tearing at her hair. "Not a zoo! Not Madras! Never mind about science for now." She paused, waiting for quiet. The chatter continued until Siriman clapped and motioned for silence. "Now," she said, "about this vessel. Why can it fly? That is beyond my knowledge. In fact, I am not convinced the scientists understand either. The craft does not use steam power—an ether force is at work. As for why they saved you…"

Zoluti paused, searching all eyes, as if ensuring she had everyone's attention. "They rescued you because they need your help."

Chatter rose. Siriman raised his hand. "Our help? What can we do? We know nothing of science. We are soldiers."

Gurkhas nodded, and many mumbled agreement.

"That is the point," Zoluti said. "You *are* soldiers. In fact, they told me the Gurkhas are the finest soldiers in the world."

More chatter, mixed with smiles and nodding heads.

"True, memsahib," Siriman said, "Gurkhas are the best, but we swore ourselves to the service of Queen Victoria."

"And—if the Queen were in danger…?"

"Is she…?"

"If she was…?"

The chatter died and there was a long silence, broken by Siriman. "We swore to fight and die for the Queen. If she was in danger, and our officers sent us to fight, we would fight."

"And—if your officers were not around to give orders…?"

"Memsahib, why are you asking these questions? Are you saying these scientists want us to fight for the Queen? She has armies all over the world. Our place is with our regiments. We should go back right away."

"And—if that was not possible…?"

Siriman rubbed his chin.

Why is she asking strange questions? What agreement is she seeking from me?

He crossed his arms and his face reddened.

Without officers, I must use my initiative. I trusted this woman to lead us to safety. Did I make a mistake?

He curled a lip and his nostrils flared.

I must not lead them from the frying pan into the fire. I will answer her questions with my own.

"Memsahib…," he said.

"Zoluti!"

"Huh?"

"Call me Zoluti!"

"Oh, yes, memsahib—Zoluti—I am confused. I fail to understand."

"Not true—you understand what I am saying."

"I mean, I cannot understand why you ask such questions or how I should answer. You are trying to trap me into saying something I should not say. We do not know these scientists who rescued us. What do they want of us?"

"I told you," she said, face tightening, "they need your help. You are soldiers, they are not, and soldiers fight, so they want you to help them by fighting and teaching them how to fight."

"To fight?" he said. "For the scientists?"

"Yes…"

"You vouch for them but who vouches for you? All we have seen are shadows—like the shades of demons."

"Shadows can deceive…"

"Why do they hide? Why should we trust them?"

Siriman rubbed the back of his neck and as he threw up his hands, a familiar voice nudged inside his head.

Ask her. Whom will you fight?

I fear what she will say.

Do you expect to hide forever? Not possible.

I think I will be sick.

Ask her!

When he returned his attention, Zoluti was speaking.

"They are peaceful, but now is a time for fighting and someone must teach them. They hope you will fight at their side until they can learn to fight alone. I can imagine this sounds strange, but the matter is crucial, and…"

Siriman raised his hand. "Memsahib…"

Zoluti stopped and bit her lip, waiting.

"Who—or what—do we fight?"

They locked eyes and slow seconds ticked.

Not the sparks again!

You know what she will say, and she knows you do.

Why must it be like this?

Because it must. Be ready.

Zoluti's answer came in a terse whisper.

"Dragons!"

Part II. The Jeweled Land

"Once that a student abandons the old trodden highway of routine, and enters upon the solitary path of independent thought—Godward—he is a Theosophist, an original thinker, a seeker after the eternal truth, with 'an inspiration of his own' to solve the universal problems."

The Theosophist, Vol. I, No. 1, October 1879
By Helena Blavatsky

Dramatis personæ

In order of appearance (*denotes a fictional character)

1857 Manipur

Old Maiba*	Vaishnavist priest, Sanamahist shaman, 77
Helena Blavatsky	Ukrainian clairvoyant, traveler, adventurer, 26
Jatly	Manipuri Thang-ta dancer, 12
Young Maiba*	Old Maiba's chela (disciple), 15
Lungthoubu	Tongol Captain, king's protector, 41
Major William McCulloch	British political agent to Manipur, 41
Chandra Kirti Singh	Maharaja of Manipur, 26
Watcher*	Shapeshifting reptilian, ??
Kangmeiza	Cavalry officer, Jatly's father, 49

Chapter 10. The Old Maiba

Thirty-four years earlier; midday, Saturday, 10 May 1857...

Helena

A bent man clutching a staff hobbled out of the shade, straightened, and gazed over the courtyard. The midday sun cast short shadows and beads of sweat sparkled as if tiny fires ignited between strands of white hair. A bony finger extended and the thin sleeve of his white robe dropped to his elbow.

"Behold Kangla!" the old man cried in Hindi, pointing, turning like a weather vane in a shifting breeze. "The center of the world!"

Women in colorful sarongs slowed, lowering baskets. Turbaned passersby paused, squinting in the glint of the temple dome.

The priest continued, "We stand amidst the works of Maharaja Chandra Kirti Singh—greatness foretold by ancient prophecy. On this high ground, the raja builds his royal house—a spark, reawakening forgotten sacred places."

After a minute, one by one, men drifted, and soon women returned to their business, hurrying home with goods from the bazaar. Not a holy day—too hot and humid to spend listening to rants in a language few spoke.

A short distance away, a woman in a hooded black dress climbed a flight of steps opposite the priest and observed from the cooler shade of the verandah. The hooded black attire was a stark contrast to the colorful garb in the courtyard. Helena tossed her hood, exposing unkempt brown hair, intense, azure-colored eyes, and the fresh face of a European woman in her twenties.

"Ni Pukha, Ni Pyera!" she muttered in Russian while lighting a cigarette—wishing the priest good luck as one might tell an actor to break a leg. "He should get out of the sun," she added in English, "before he suffers heat stroke."

The sermon droned as the priest switched from Hindi, which Helena understood, to Meithei, of which she knew little.

Prattle on, old man! Nothing impresses this crowd.

After a final drag, she tossed her hand-rolled cigarette onto the patio, and stooped, digging in a carpetbag at her feet, rummaging for another smoke. She gave up and shut the bag.

I should wait. The old man might finish soon.

Helena rubbed out the butt with the hard toe of her black shoe and studied the crushed tobacco on the red brick. Her eyes lifted past the red brick temple columns and followed the sweep of the old man's wrinkled hand. She observed masons laying red bricks in the busy courtyard. Beyond, more brick construction was underway on the rising walls of the fort and the nearby palace.

Bricks, bricks, bricks. Where ever one looks—red bricks.

The well-burnt, oven-fired, red clay bricks were everywhere in Kangla. Manipur was a free country on the rise, and the Manipuris managed the construction on their own, with no British involvement. Helena chuckled.

Brits are scarce here. I like that. The world's secret center!

Manipur—the Jeweled Land—a green country hidden in a valley, a plateau in the foothills of the Himalayas. Britain found little use for Manipur, other than as a buffer between India and the warlike Burmese, but that would soon change.

The old fellow is still ranting. Maybe I will have that smoke!

Helena stooped and rummaged again, finding a crooked cylinder that time, rolled and waiting. She lit the stick and took a deep drag.

I hope he finishes soon—I need to leave in a few days.

Helena arrived at Manipur's capital two weeks earlier, after booking passage with a Haw caravan out of India, departing from Cachar, Assam. She accomplished her goal—putting British-held territory many days behind her.

Just in time—no doubt!

Manipur was to be a two-day pause along the trade route to Burma—but sensing hidden mysteries and wisdom, curiosity got the better of her. She stayed two weeks to explore, study, and learn of ancient Manipur.

Another caravan will be along soon.

How ancient is Manipur? Thousands of years—no one knows. The *Mahabharata* speaks of Manipur, and scholars believe the book is over five thousand years old. Yet, the more Helena tried to learn the history of the ancient land, the harder the challenge became. The citizens hid behind walls of fear and silence, ignoring questions of the ancient times. Then a child—a young girl who befriended Helena in the bazaar—had the courage to send her to the gold-domed temple inside Kangla Fort.

I hope the priest has answers. This humidity is oppressive.

Helena smoked, staring past the monotonous priest, and sweat stung her eyes. She wiped streaks from her cheeks with a black sleeve. When her eyes cleared, she beheld her friend—a twelve-year-old Manipuri girl— milling at the foot of the steps, beaming and waving, trying to get Helena's attention. The girl wore a colorful sarong and, typical of Manipuri girls, had long dark hair with straight bangs cut above her eyebrows.

She wants to join me up here. Now is not the time.

Helena glared, waved a stern dismissal, and the girl's face fell. She turned and wandered a short distance, kicking at pebbles, then turned back and smiled once more as if hoping Helena would change her mind. Helena frowned, shook her head, and from a distance, saw the glisten of young tears. Moisture again stung Helena's eyes.

Wonderful—sweat mixed with tears.

Helena's heart softened. She wiped her eyes and raised a hand to summon the girl, but the child had vanished—melded into the passing crowd.

"Jatly!" Helena called, adding in Hindi, "Vaapas aao (come back)!"

She tossed her smoke and dug into her bag again, fetching a well-worn pair of French opera glasses. She scanned the stream of saris and turbans and caught sight of the girl.

There—by the dragons!

Helena's dragons were massive, masonry beasts, four times the height of a man—twin statues, reminiscent of mythical Chinese foo-lions, except with multi-point antlers; head and torso like a dragon and thick legs and paws like a lion. The monsters stood guard in a nearby courtyard, northwest of the Durbar Hall, heads back and jaws open wide, as if waiting to drink cool rain pouring from heaven.

Now who is that?

Through the glasses, a man wearing a uniform and a dark turban approached and spoke to her friend. He had a thick gray moustache with dark piercing eyes under bushy gray eyebrows. Suspicion and an instinctive, protective dislike for the man filled Helena's heart. The child pointed toward the temple and the man looked in Helena's direction.

"Enjoying the sights of Kangla, madam?"

Helena realized the priest stood by her side.

Sermon over at last.

Helena took a quick final glance through the glasses, but the uniformed man and her young friend had disappeared. She lowered the glasses and turned to the priest, trying not to look startled.

"You speak English," she said, smiling. "I did not expect that in Manipur."

The priest smiled back. "Hindu School in Calcutta. I was the oldest student when the doors opened, but I was one of the first to graduate."

"Ah," she said. "Congratulations."

"You are the English sorceress someone told me to expect."

"My name is Blavatsky and I—I am not English—I am Ukrainian! Why do you call me a sorceress? I am a mere traveler!"

"Madame Blavatsky," the priest murmured, nodding. "My information may be incorrect. A traveler? A young European woman, traveling alone? It is a dangerous world."

"I have traveled alone for eight years," she said. "I have been around the world."

"And the road led you to Manipur."

"For a time. I am seeking…"

"You came to the Temple of Shri Govindajee for knowledge."

"Govindajee?" Helena raised her eyebrows. "This is a Vaishnavist temple?"

"The people of Manipur have worshiped Lord Krishna for centuries."

"Centuries? That is not long. I heard of another—an ancient, local religion—predating the days of Krishna. Older than the *Mahabharata*. Older than Vedic times."

"Ah," the priest said, "you seek a maiba—a priest of Sanamahi—the old faith." He pointed northwest. "See the tall temple—beyond the walls of the inner fort?"

Helena squinted and made out a distant tower. "The tall, square building with balconies and an iron roof?"

"Yes," he said. "The private temple of the maharaja. There one still finds idols of old local gods and goddesses—hundreds. There you may find what you seek. My temple is not ancient—only ten years old."

Helena studied the old man's face.

He is lying.

She shook her head. "No! Someone told me to find ancient wisdom here. This temple! She was specific."

"The young girl told you, I suppose."

"You know Jatly?"

"Yes." He nodded. "I know her. She is—different—special."

"Jatly sent me here because this site is much older, rebuilt after an earthquake destroyed the old temple. She said you are the man to teach me—you have books…"

"Books?"

He has conflicts, is trying to decide if he can trust me, and will shift the discussion.

"Did you come out of India?"

"Yes," Helena said. "Two weeks ago."

"South from Kohima?"

"No, east from Cachar—with a Haw caravan."

"Ah," he said, smiling, "so then your first sight of Manipur came as you crossed the mountain pass at the Peak of Leimatak?"

"Yes!" She could not restrain her exhilaration. "The sight of the green valley took my breath away—the hills, dense forests, blue lakes, rivers, and green fields…"

"The Jeweled Land!" He beamed with pride. "You beheld the jewels of the gods." He paused and then shifted topics again. "The girl…"

"Jatly."

"Yes—how did you meet her?"

"At Khwairamband—the women's bazaar," she said. "Girls were dancing with swords and spears—a strange, hypnotizing dance."

"It is an ancient art—called Thang-ta."

"The girls showed impressive skill—leaping, spinning, and whirling— blades crashing and sparks flying. We met later by chance. She speaks a little Hindi, and we became fast friends."

My turn to change topics.

"You said Jatly is different, special—how do you know her?"

The priest stared back, biting his lower lip, as if trying to decide if he should answer. "Come inside," he said at last.

He turned and hobbled toward the temple door, staff clacking on the bricks. Helena gathered her bag and followed.

"You are correct," he said. "This temple stands over the ruins of an older structure—a new temple built with well-burnt bricks."

"So I see," Helena said. "Manipur loves its red brick."

"A skill learned hundreds of years ago from Chinese prisoners of war." The priest led her to an ambulatory passage. "Come, we will follow the Pradakshina Path."

They followed the traditional clockwise route, keeping the inner sanctum hall to their right, and soon stumbled upon a gaping hole in the floor. Helena inched forward to look, but saw no bottom. She leaned farther.

How deep is it? Where does it lead? I wish I could drop a burning torch and watch it fall.

"Take care! There may be no bottom."

Helena remained frozen at the edge, peering into the depths. She detected a stale breeze rising from the deep, and a sound—as if steel claws scratched stone.

My imagination?

The sound stopped, the breeze vanished, and Helena inched away from the edge, heart pounding in her ears.

I cannot breathe!

The priest's eyes widened and he broke into a smile. "You sensed it!"

"What—did I sense?" she said, gasping.

"The dragon."

Chapter 11. The Dragon-god of Manipur

Seconds later...

Helena

Helena backed further away and took a deep breath. "Did you say—dragon?"

"Yes," the priest said.

"In the hole, I mean. A live dragon? With scales, claws, wings, and..."

"According to tradition."

"Have you seen it?"

He shook his head. "No one in my lifetime has seen it, only sensed it."

"You?"

"No." He scratched his head. "Not yet. I hope someday to prove worthy."

"You said someone sensed it. Who?"

"To this point, you—and the girl."

"Jatly?"

"Yes, but please—keep that secret."

"Why?"

"She could be in danger if others learned. I found your reaction intriguing—you must describe your feelings."

Helena recounted her experience, but struggled for adequate words.

"You are no mere traveler," he said, eyes narrowing. "Will you stay in Manipur long? Others may be upset that a European woman sensed..."

"Then say nothing," Helena said, staring at the opening and inching closer. "What is this—hole?"

"It is a cave—a surung. Its name is Khuman. Ahead are two more—named Luang and Mangang."

"Caves?" she said. "A temple floor with cave openings—with no railings? Is that not dangerous?"

The priest shrugged. "Visitors learn to take care." He added, smiling. "Most visitors."

"Where do the—surungs—lead?"

"To bigger caves? To the vast, underground kingdom of the Dragons— no one knows. No one dares explore and find out."

"Why?"

"Surungs are holy places. Legends say Pakhangba, the god-king of Manipur, ascended from one of these caves."

"A man? Ascended from a cave?"

"Pakhangba is a dragon—the dragon-god of Manipur."

"A dragon?" she said. "The king of Manipur was a dragon?"

"Man by day, dragon by night."

Helena shook her head.

The priest offered a hand. "Follow me—with care. I will explain."

He led her past the surung, skirting two similar holes, and they reached the inner sanctum where an open door led to an antechamber. In the center, behind a stack of books, a robed figure sat hunched at a table, reading by torchlight. As Helena and the priest entered, a teenage boy looked up wide-eyed and leapt to his feet.

The priest waved off the boy. "My young chela." The youth scrambled and backed into a corner, far from the table. "Someday—not too soon, I hope—he will take my place and become the new, much younger maiba. For now, I allow him to listen and, I hope, learn."

"Maiba?" Helena said. "So—you *are* a maiba—a shaman, a priest of the ancient religion."

"Yes," he said. "I counsel devotees of Lord Krishna, and I help the maharaja keep the Sanamahi ways alive in the shadows."

"Alive? What do you mean?"

"God has a million names. Each region of India has local gods and goddesses—remnants of older religions. Over thousands of years, the ancient religions melded into Hinduism. Manipur was different—an isolated valley, a land of jungles and fertile plains, hidden in the foothills. The old Sanamahi ways survived."

"Until when?"

"Hindu missionaries brought the Sanskrit ways to Kangleipak four centuries ago. Then, one hundred and fifty years ago, King Gharib Nawaz saw Krishna in a vision and, after converting, imposed the Hindu faith. He renamed the country Manipur, the ancient Hindu name from the *Mahabharata*, and became maharaja.

"We call that time the Puya Meithaba—the Time of Great Burning. The maharaja ordered scriptures destroyed and the old gods banished."

"Books burned!" Helena's hands covered her face. "A terrible loss!"

"A few survived." The maiba pointed toward the stacks. "Here—hidden in a temple rededicated to Krishna."

"Once a temple to Pakhangba?"

"Yes—hiding in plain sight, you could say. This book, for example." He lifted a thick volume. "The *Panthoibi Khongul* holds the origin of Pakhangba. May I tell you?"

Helena nodded, so he began the tale.

The Origin of Pakhangba

From emptiness came Atiya, who is God. He created the gods and goddesses, the earth, sun, moon, stars, and planets. He married the earth goddess, and she bore him two sons—Kuptreng, the oldest and most powerful, and Shentreng, younger but wiser, and the most like his father. Atiya knew he would leave the earth to one of his sons, but wondered—which traits were most worthy of his successor. Would age decide the birthright or would wisdom and loyalty prove more worthy? He tested his sons.

Atiya took the disguise of a dead cow and floated down a river. The trick fooled Kuptreng, who saw a bloated corpse, but not Shentreng, who saw the truth and called his father's name. Atiya rewarded Shentreng with the title Pakhangba, which means, the one who knows his father. Kuptreng grew jealous.

Atiya tried another test. He announced he would hand his throne to whichever son could first circle the four corners of the earth. Kuptreng sped away, faster than the wind, but Pakhangba stood his ground. He circumambulated his father's throne, making a circle at each corner. When finished, he bowed and asked for the throne. Atiya saw wisdom in the deed. A wise and loyal son sees his father as his entire world.

Atiya gave the throne to Pakhangba and charged him to sustain and protect life on earth.

Kuptreng returned to find Pakhangba on the throne. He burned with anger and swore to kill his brother. Atiya intervened. A crack opened and swallowed the throne. Pakhangba fled deep underground and hid in Patala, the dragon kingdom. While Pakhangba hid, Kuptreng seized the title Sanamahi, the sustainer of life. Pakhangba sought help from Ananta, the dragon king, but Ananta pledged support to Sanamahi. Vasuki, Ananta's younger brother, stole a magic gem from Ananta's crown and presented it to Pakhangba. The jewel transformed Pakhangba into a dragon, too powerful to kill. Pakhangba remained underground, watching, waiting for his time to regain rightful dominion of earth. He appears to those worthy, and his spirit guides the kings of Manipur.

"These stories offer three lessons," the maiba said. "First, we learn to crown the wisest; second, travel seeking wisdom leads to truth; and third, no higher religion than truth exists."

"I have heard these tales before," Helena said, "except the gods had different names—Brahma, the creator, instead of Atiya, and Vishnu, the sustainer, instead of Sanamahi. Ganesha outsmarted his brother Karthikeya by circling Shiva, his father. Where does that leave Pakhangba? In the role of Shiva, the destroyer?"

"You see!" the maiba said. "They stole our gods; corrupted our stories!"

"Are you certain the opposite did not happen?"

"In the *Mahabharata*, Arjuna came to Manipur, Manipur did not seek Arjuna."

"Arjuna came and took a wife…"

"Who gave him a son, Babhruvahana," he said, "and he became king of Manipur."

"And he later killed Arjuna…"

"True, but Babhruvahana used the magic gem—the Mani—to bring Arjuna back to life."

"The Mani?"

"The jewel," he said, "the magic gem of King Ananta, the Sheshanaga, king of the dragons, the jewel that turned Pakhangba into a dragon."

"That jewel is the Mani?"

"Yes—the namesake of Manipur, the jeweled land—naval of the world. Beneath Manipur lies the kingdom of the dragons."

"What happened to the gem?"

"That is another tale."

The maiba lifted a heavy volume from the table. He flipped pages, stopping at a painted image of a serpent-like dragon, coiled with tail in mouth.

"There," he said, "is Pakhangba."

"I have seen this symbol before," Helena said. "Dragons appear in many cultures, by many names—called the Jörmungandr by the Vikings, Quetzalcoatl in South America, the Klu in Tibet, the Lung in China, and Naga in India. The symbol of a coiled dragon eating its own tail is a powerful image, shown in the Egyptian Book of the Dead. The ancient Greeks named it Ouroboros. In India the symbol is kundalini energy, or dragon power, a coiled and dormant potential force."

"Pakhangba surrounds the four corners of the world," the maiba said. "He is the symbol of Manipur—since before the Aryans, before the days of the *Mahabharata*."

"Five thousand years?"

"Older," he said.

"Older than the time of the *Ramayana?*"

"Yes, older."

"Nine thousand years?" she said.

"Older. Before the Devas and the Asuras fought, and the death of Vritra released the flood of water from the great ice. Thirty thousand years, or older."

"How do you know this?"

He shrugged and laughed. "It is my job to know."

"Why show Pakhangba so much respect? Why not his older brother Sanamahi, the sustainer, as the symbol of Manipur? The religion's name is Sanamahi."

"Sanamahi protects the earth, but in Manipur, dragons house the external soul of the king. The kings of Manipur keep the spirit of Pakhangba alive."

Helena frowned. "External soul?"

"One of the six souls of the elements."
"Six? Six souls?"
The maiba began another tale.

Elemental Souls, the External Soul, and Pakhangba

The Hakchang, the body, is a cage. It holds the immortal Thawai. When the heart stops, at the final breath, the Thawai flies away like a bird freed from its cage. The Thawai finds a new Hakchang and is reborn in an endless cycle.

Six souls make the Thawai—one for each of the five elements, earth, wind, fire, water, plus the ether, the elemental fabric of space. The sixth soul—the mi—is the immortal self, the shadow, the reflection in the mirror, the essential essence of existence.

While alive, the Hakchang can transmigrate any of the five elemental souls to an external object. The object can be valuable—an idol or relic, a piece of jewelry, or a sword—or even a living creature. Transmigrating an elemental soul can protect the mi in difficult times. During childbirth, for example, a mother can project her soul of fire to an idol, to reduce the pain of childbirth. After birth, the mother reclaims the fire.

The elemental soul imbues the external object with magnified power. The possessor benefits by wielding the power. Summon fire, bend space, or inhabit the consciousness of a creature—earth soul to beast, water soul to sea-creature, or wind soul to bird. The possessor becomes the creature—directs its actions, sees with its eyes, hears with its ears, or tastes what it eats.

Pakhangba projected his elemental souls to the Mani and gave the jewel to the first king. In later days, the line of kings failed. Then, two thousand years ago, a warlord rediscovered the surungs. Pakhangba appeared from the cave and presented the magic gem. The Mani transformed the warlord into Pakhangba, the first god-king, ruling the empire by day as a man, roaming at night as a dragon.

"How is it done?"

The maiba raised his eyebrows and cocked his head.

"How," she said, "is an elemental soul projected—to become an external soul?"

"With help from a maiba."

Helena chuckled. "Convenient! Suppose no maiba is available?"

"Difficult," he said, "but faith is the key—believing without question."

"A projected elemental soul imbues an object with magnified powers?"

"With proper effort, it can," he said.

"How long does the power last?"

"Until the original owner takes back the soul."

"What if the owner dies first?"

"The soul stays embedded in the object forever. There are few treasures more prized than an object of power holding an external soul."

"Can it work in opposite fashion? That is—could a dragon project its own elemental soul and walk as a human."

After a long pause, the maiba nodded. "It is possible."

"Is there more to tell about Pakhangba?"

The maiba nodded and continued his tales.

Pakhangba and Polo

Pakhangba created a game called Sagol (pony) Kangjei (ball-stick). Players ride ponies across a wide field while swinging mallets. They strike a ball, and sometimes each other. The original field is inside Kangla. Manipur's passion is Sagol Kangjei. Men trade wives for good ponies. The British adopted Sagol Kangjei and renamed the game polo.

Pakhangba and the Lallup

Pakhangba created a system of mandatory service by the able-bodied men of Manipur. Ten days out of every forty, the men serve in the militia or support roads and bridges. Pakhangba created an annual foot race called the Lamchel. The winner's reward is a lifetime exemption from the Lallup.

Pakhangba and Thang-ta

Pakhangba ruled one hundred and twenty years, and now sleeps in deep water, the primary element of the dragon. His descendants ruled in a direct line until three hundred years ago. When the line failed, as warlords fought for control, China saw weakness and invaded, led by a giant demon named Moydana. Still, the warlords stayed divided.

The warlord Mungyamba prayed to Pakhangba. The god-king appeared in a dream and taught a new way to fight. Then he led the warlord to a secret chamber holding weapons forged by Atiya at the dawn of time. Mungyamba took the weapons—the Tang (sword) and the Ta (spear)—and, legends say, the Mani, the magic gem of Manipur.

Mungyamba met the demon in battle in the Kabaw Valley. The warlord danced and dodged, leapt and spun—as shown in the dream—and slew the demon, saving Manipur and India. The demon lies buried beneath a great boulder. To this day, no festival is complete without Thang-ta. Boys and girls give exhibitions of the martial art created by the dragon god Pakhangba.

"This giant…," Helena said, "the demon…"

"Moydana."

"Yes, what manner of being was he? A Rakshasa (tall, shape-shifting demon)?"

"Who can say?"

A latter day David and Goliath myth?

"And Pakhangba the god-king—ruling for one hundred and twenty years—how is that possible? Do you believe these myths?"

"Myths?" the maiba said. "Perhaps you find the tales amusing?"

"I do not!" Helena said. "Science, history, myth, and religion—all are pieces leading to the same truth. The dragons—the two large statues outside in the courtyard…"

"The Kangla-sha."

"What dragon breed are they? They do not resemble the picture you showed me."

"Swear to keep a secret and I will tell you of the Kangla-sha."

Chapter 12. The Kangla-sha Prophecy

Continued...

Helena

Helena searched the maiba's eyes for signs of deceit, or mockery, but discerned sincerity and concern.

After trusting me to this point, what gives him pause now?

"Are the statues so secret? They are in plain sight, larger than life."

"It is necessary," the maiba said.

"In that case, I swear. I will tell no one what I learn."

"I trust you," he said, nodding, and began another tale.

The Kangla-sha

Dragons existed millions of years before mankind. They are intelligent, serpentine beings with scales, wings, and claws, living in hidden civilizations. The *Ramayana* and *Mahabharata* both speak of the subterranean kingdoms of the dragons.

The Kangla-sha statues are fixtures of Kangla Fort and Manipuri culture. What does the name mean? *Kangla* means dry land. Kangla— where Pakhangba circled the throne; where Arjuna married a princess; and where, two thousand years ago, the god-king Pakhangba founded an empire. *Sha* means the body and spirit of a person or animal, living or dead. The Kangla-sha statues represent the strength and power of Kangla. The statues guard the coronation hall of the kings and herald future glory.

Mungyamba conceived of the Kangla-sha after defeating Moydana, the Chinese demon. He became king, blessed by the dragon-god. If he had the magic gem, he hid it, and the Mani became a distant memory.

Mungyamba brought captured Chinese artisans to Kangla. The prisoners of war taught the art of brick construction and built the Kangla-sha. Scholars say the half-dragon-half-lion creatures depict the war, in which the singh (lion) of India defeated the lung (dragon) of China.

Khagemba succeeded his father, and during his reign, Sanamahi mystics wrote the book of prophecy, *Ningthoural Singkak*. One of its prophecies mentions the Kangla-sha.

Seventy-five years later, King Gharib Nawaz became maharaja, imposed Krishna worship, restored the ancient name Manipur, and burned the scriptures. Old gods hid in the shadows. The Mani became a myth, lost in the smoke of burning books. Prophecy became a rumor, or a song sung by children at play.

Burma conquered Manipur and destroyed the Kangla-sha, but Manipur drove out the Burmese and rebuilt stronger statues. Now we live in the era of Maharaja Chandra Kirti Singh, the time described in the prophecy—the dawn of a new age.

"Is the prophecy the great secret I swore to protect?" Helena said. "Something of the Kangla-sha statues?"

"Yes."

"You are now unsure if you will tell me?"

He lifted another book from the table. "Here," he said, "is the *Ningthoural Singkak*."

"The book of prophecy—not burned?"

"This copy escaped, as you see."

The maiba opened to a place marked by a silk ribbon. The page appeared worn from frequent reading over many years. His finger moved down the page, stopping at a passage of flowing script, translating aloud.

He shall come in 1771.
He shall reconstruct the capital in 1779.
Know, ye, on this high ground,
He shall build a royal house.
The ruling king in this time shall be a spark.
He shall build many sacred places.
Four years, the next king shall rule.
Three years, the following king shall rule.
One year, the next king shall rule.
In his reign, five white heads shall fall at the feet of the Kangla-sha.

Helena smiled. "The prophecy is behind the times—1771 and 1779 have passed. This is 1857."

The maiba closed the book. "So it would seem, but the years cited use an ancient calendar. The British and Manipuri calendars differ by seventy-eight years. Hence, 1771 becomes 1849—the first year in the reign of Maharaja Chandra Kirti Singh, the current king of Manipur. Likewise, 1779 becomes 1857, this year, the eighth year of his reign."

"I take your word on that."

"None can dispute the maharaja has been a spark. He rebuilds temples, walls of the fort, and a new palace. He reopened the door to Sanamahi. People are leaving the shadows and whispering the name of Pakhangba."

"What of the rest?" she said. "Five white heads—sounds ominous. Human white heads?"

"The prophecy is silent on that."

"White human heads means European heads. Does the prophecy describe human sacrifice?"

"Never!"

"Execution?"

He scoffed. "Most unlikely!"

"What then?"

He shrugged. "Animal sacrifice, sheep—five white sheep. That is the likely interpretation."

"What happens after sacrificing five white sheep?"

"There is much speculation," the maiba said. "I believe someone will find the jewel—the Mani—and awaken its power. A new day will dawn—a golden age for Manipur. The Sanamahi faith restored—so the ancient scholars believed."

A high voice cracked from the corner. "Tell her the rest of the prophecy."

The maiba glared at the teenager. "Chela! Be silent!"

The youth trembled.

He was so quiet I forgot him!

"It took bravery to speak," Helena said. "You speak English, too. Impressive. Tell me the rest, young man."

The boy looked at his master.

The maiba shrugged. "Tell her."

The youth gulped, cleared his throat, and spoke.

Close the west gate and the east gate shall open.
White heads shall fall before the Kangla-sha,
Three kings with armies shall come by three roads, and
The kingdom shall fall.

"What does it mean?"

"Three roads—the meaning is clear. The north road leads to Kohima, in Nagaland, the west road to Cachar, in Assam, and the south road to Burma, and to Chittagong on the Bengal. The rest is less clear—the west gate never closes—always stays open, and the east gate never opens."

"Closing and opening of gates is significant," she said. "This is not a joyful prophecy. The executioner will not cleave the necks of sheep."

The maiba shook his head. "Do not make a hasty judgment…"

"Do you not see the truth?" she insisted. "The Kangla-sha statues do not celebrate the collision between India and China—they foretell the conquest of the dragon, Manipur, by the lion, Great Britain. The five white heads will not be the heads of sheep—oh no, they will be British white heads. After which three British armies will march and Manipur becomes yet another piece of the British Empire."

"That is one interpretation…"

"This must not happen!" Helena said. She paced, shaking her head, waving her arms. "You must not allow it."

"Why should I believe you?"

"Why tell me this prophecy? You wanted my confirmation of the meaning—that this golden age will be a nightmare—delivered with the British Empire's heavy boot on Manipur's throat. Manipur must stay free! You must not allow this evil to happen!"

"I am old," the priest said. "The maharaja's reign will last years. I will not live to see the prophecy fulfilled."

Helena pointed to the chela cowering in the corner. "He can stop it."

"Him? My chela? He is a…"

"A boy? He will soon be a man. This will be his destiny."

The priest averted his eyes. "This task is beyond him."

Helena took the boy's hands. "Do you understand?"

He nodded, as his face grew pale.

"You know the danger? You swear, when the time comes, you will take steps to prevent the fulfillment of this prophecy?"

The boy's voice cracked. "What can I do? I am but one."

"Where one leads, others will follow."

She released his hands and faced the priest. "I came from the Tibetan mountains and traveled India the past year. Everywhere is talk of rebellion. Ukrainians do not love the British Empire. I hope someday a strong Asia, perhaps led by Russia, can unite to resist England. Meanwhile, Manipur must avoid India's problems. The Jeweled Land must survive."

Helena fell still. Courtyard sounds filtered in—men shouting, playing children screaming, women chattering, and somewhere in the distance, an elephant trumpeted.

"You speak the truth," the priest said. "I told you the prophecy to hear your interpretation and I will do as you say. I will prepare my chela for the day when he must stop the prophecy."

"Forgive the interruption, Maiba." A Manipuri soldier watched from the door. His deep-set eyes glowered beneath bushy eyebrows, and his lips tightened below a thick, gray moustache. "The Maharaja requests your presence."

It is he—from the courtyard, by the Kangla-sha. The man who spoke to Jatly. How long has he been standing there?

"What is His Highness's pleasure?" the maiba said.

"State dinner—at the Durbar Hall…" He looked at Helena with burning eyes. "The European madam must come, too."

"The maharaja?" Helena said, blushing. "How does he know me?"

"Nothing happens in Manipur without the maharaja's knowledge."

Chapter 13. The Vision in the Durbar Hall

Later that evening...

Helena

Major William McCulloch, British political agent to Manipur, struck an imposing figure. His dress uniform—red tunic, gold buttons, black shoulder straps, studded collar with star emblems—glittered with a smattering of medals and regimental emblems.

The major's eyes darted sideways as he hoisted his goblet. Across the long dinner table sat a slender man wearing a formal white uniform, a black jacket, and a white turban.

The major addressed Helena in English. "His Highness told me you are a spiritualist. Or would you prefer I say, a clairvoyant?"

Helena studied the monarch's reaction. Chandra Kirti Singh, Maharaja of Manipur, cocked his head, listening as the maiba translated. Behind the maharaja hung a banner—a great standard with a green field and a golden dragon coiled in loops, devouring its tail.

The symbol of Pakhangba, the royal emblem of Manipur.

"Perhaps," the major continued, "you prefer the word sorceress?"

The maharaja smiled, listening while chewing ngri (fermented fish).

He finds the major's rude questions amusing.

Helena stared at the officer, refusing to acknowledge his comments, and felt piercing eyes peering from around the room.

I feel crude, coarse, and out of place. Awkward. Uncouth.

She wore the same black pilgrim's dress she had worn all day—no opportunity to change or freshen. It did not matter—her dresses all looked the same. She feared her curly hair appeared wild, unkempt.

I look horrible—unfit for a maharaja.

Helena guessed her age matched the king. She had a noble heritage, but in her own eyes, she was a misfit—plainer, shorter, dumpier, and older...

An older soul, at least.

She was uncomfortable, and worse…

I am dying for a cigarette. I wish this dinner would end.

The maharaja wiped his mouth and rose. The maiba translated.

"His Majesty apologizes for the size of the dinner party. The table seats more, but His Majesty's oldest son, is too young, and the princes, His Majesty's cousins, could not attend." The maiba paused, whispered to the maharaja, and then added, "Due to an ongoing, family squabble."

Ministers lowered cutlery and tittered. In a corner, the old maiba's chela fidgeted. Near the door, arms folded, eyes glowering, stood the gray mustachioed soldier who led Helena and the maiba to the durbar hall.

I dislike him. I suspect the feelings are mutual.

"His Majesty," the maiba continued, "hopes this intimate gathering will suit his honored guests." The maharaja raised his goblet to Helena and the major in salute. "He hopes everyone can speak with open candor and enjoy the company."

The maharaja sat and murmurs of thanks and good wishes went round the table. An awkward silence followed. Cutlery clinked and overhead, the punkah fan swished. The slow and steady rope creaked, drawn by a punkahwallah (fan servant) in a different room.

Major McCulloch kept his eyes on Helena as he lifted his fork and stabbed beans and mixed vegetables in his plate of yongchak. He swallowed and broke the silence.

"His Highness told me you are Russian."

Helena finished chewing and spat back. "I am Ukrainian!"

The clinking stopped. Diners froze mid-bite and eyes darted from Helena to the maharaja.

McCulloch smiled. "Is there a difference?"

Helena glared. "To a Ukrainian, yes!" Her fork stabbed the final bite of ngri. She waved the impaled chunk of fish at the major. "Is there a difference between an Englishman and a Scotsman? You remind me of my father, except my father is a colonel, not a mere major, and he is an educated nobleman, not a pompous, crude, and illiterate scot. Upon further reflection, you are nothing like him." She thrust the fork into her mouth.

"Your father is a colonel in the *Russian* army!"

She answered with mouth half-full. "And you a British redcoat!"

The major's tone was rife with suspicion, and Helena did not appreciate it. The British had misgivings about every European foreigner on the Indian subcontinent, suspecting they were spies there to foment rebellion. Russia alone had the power to challenge Britain's dominance, and Russia longed for warm seaports in India. The bloody Crimean war between England and Russia had ended the year before, and Russia still stung from the disadvantageous terms of the negotiated peace.

The maharaja stood and spoke as the maiba translated.

"Come, come," the maiba said. "His Majesty welcomes you as guests in Manipur. We do not play the so-called Great Game of intrigue between rival imperial powers. We play happier games, such as polo. Madame Blavatsky, it pleases His Majesty for you to watch him play polo against his cousin princes' team tomorrow evening. You are in luck—end of the playing season and Sunday evenings are the best matches. His Majesty is an excellent rider."

"I am honored," Helena murmured.

"Wonderful," the maiba said, "and you, too, Major. Unless you would prefer to ride in the match, it would please His Majesty if you watched from your usual place with Madame Blavatsky. He suggests you explain the rules of the game to our lady guest."

The major stiffened, grunted, and nodded. The maharaja smiled and whispered to the maiba.

He is testing us—as if he were a young boy, with two exotic insects in a jar, watching them fight, separating them before one kills the other.

"You please His Majesty," the priest translated. "He asks Madame Blavatsky to forgive him for talking about you earlier with the major. Your reputation precedes you—a daughter of nobility, a world traveler, and well-versed in religion, science, and the occult. His Majesty hopes he said nothing improper or inaccurate."

Helena remained silent and cast a cold stare at the major. She knew British political agents were a mix of ambassador, spy, and unofficial administrator, representing the empire while keeping a close watch on allied states such as Manipur. The Residency (embassy) sat outside Kangla's walls—a large white house, a stable and outbuildings, gardens, a lake, and spacious wooded grounds, surrounded by a ditch and mud wall. No doubt, the major attended many state dinners at the durbar hall, but still…

His probing—he spies, making sure I leave.

The maharaja spoke through the maiba. "Madame Blavatsky," he said, "you would honor His Majesty if you graced us with tales of your world travels—the road that led you to Manipur."

Helena told her tale. She left Odessa in 1849 and traveled the world for eight years—to Europe, the Middle East, Canada, the American West, Mexico, South America, Kashmir, Tibet, and India. She arrived by caravan in Manipur two weeks earlier, pausing on her way to Burma.

"I come from wealth and nobility," she said, "but, as you can see, I am now a pilgrim of modest means. I must earn my livelihood as I progress."

"How do you earn your livelihood?" the major asked.

"I tell fortunes. The Cachar road leads to the women's bazaar outside the gates of Kangla. The women allowed a table for fortunes and counseling. I do not speak Manipuri, but I met a young girl and..."

The maiba glowered.

He does not want me to mention Jatly.

"She knows Hindi, so I pay her to be my translator, and..."

"On which day," the major said, interrupting, "will you leave Manipur?"

"Oh, I am in no hurry. Next caravan—the day after tomorrow."

"Hem!" the major grunted. "I trust you found what you were looking for during your visit."

"I did." She nodded toward the old maiba. "Thanks to the priest. I spent the afternoon at the temple and learned a great deal."

The maharaja spoke to the maiba who nodded and turned to Helena. "His Majesty asks if you regard yourself as a prophet."

"No," she said, "prophets are holy. I could not pass for holy."

"But, all the same," McCulloch pressed, "you tell fortunes."

"I predict events that have not yet happened."

"These events—sometime come true?" the maiba said.

"They always come true."

"Can you see your own future?" the major asked.

She sighed. "No. I am blind to my fate."

The table erupted. During the hubbub, the maiba and maharaja huddled and argued, as if the maharaja was overruling the maiba's objections.

"Please indulge us," the maiba said. "His Majesty requests you show us your talents."

"The maharaja wants to know the future of Manipur?"

"Guests first. His Majesty asks, please tell the major his future."

McCulloch let out a guffaw and fidgeted. Then he wiped his mouth with his napkin, tossed it onto the table, and faced Helena. "Right!" His cheeks reddened. "If it pleases His Highness—madam, do me the honor."

The room quieted, eyes turned to Helena. She squared her shoulders and sat straight, eyes closed, hands folded in her lap. There was a faint knock, like the sound of a knuckle striking wood. Another knock followed, then others, each louder. At first, Helena tried to concentrate and ignore the sounds. The knocking grew louder, more frequent—and then came a rattling. She opened her eyes and observed the heads of the maharaja and his frantic dinner guests turning in each direction. Helena, too, searched in vain for the sounds' origin.

"Are we having an earthquake?" the major said.

"No," the maiba replied. "The ground is stable."

Knocks grew louder—from the ceiling, from the walls, and sometimes from beneath the long dining table. Rattling became sharper, like china dishes clanking in a cabinet, though no cabinet was visible.

Helena stood, looked at the ceiling, and shouted. "Stop!"

As if by her command, the knocking and rattling ceased. The others froze in their seats, eyes wide and blood draining from faces. Helena sank into her chair, closed her eyes, and pressed fingers to forehead. She reopened her eyes to nervous glances. She faced the major with a glassy stare and spoke as if miles away.

"In a few days," she said, "you receive a letter from Assam—a dispatch from district headquarters. It is a coded message. You decode it."

"Ha!" the major scoffed. "You describe my typical day!"

The maharaja raised a hand for silence, head cocked, as the maiba translated. Helena ignored the major's interruption, and the spell continued.

"You read the message, learning that days before—on this day—growing unrest erupted into open rebellion. War and strife—blood washes over India. Multitudes on both sides die—women and children, innocents slaughtered in hatred and anger. The battle rages for months, with heroism by patriots, both Muslim and Hindu of all castes, but at the end, India loses. Lines of gallows with bodies hanging, twisting at the ends of ropes. Others blindfolded, strapped to cannons, and blown apart. The lion of Britain prevails, crushing the rebellion. Ninety more years pass before India is free."

The spell broke. Helena lifted her goblet and drank. Chattering erupted around the table.

"I say," the major scoffed, "how unpleasant! I hope she saved something promising for His Majesty."

The maharaja raised his hand, ignoring the major and stopping the maiba from further translation. He faced Helena and spoke in Hindi.

"Manipur kya bhavishyavaanee (what prediction for Manipur)?"

Helena set her goblet down and wiped her mouth.

"Manipur—its people," the maiba added. "Did you see anything?"

"I saw—something." She switched to Hindi for the maharaja. "Tongol kaun hai (who is Tongol)?"

The maharaja's face twisted, as if confused, and said, "Tongol?"

"Tongol is a tribe," the maiba said. "Not a man. Nagas of the northern hills. His Majesty himself is part Naga."

"Daravaaje se aadamee (the man by the door)," the maharaja said, pointing. "Lungthoubu mera dost (Lungthoubu, my friend)—unhonne kaha ki ek Tongol hai (he is a Tongol)."

Helena looked toward the door. The man with the bushy gray mustache stood attentive, arms unfolded, glowering. Their eyes met and locked. Helena broke the stare, looked away, and continued in English.

"I see a man of strength. Others will call him the Tongol. A fire burns in his heart, and he will join the rebellion, leading others to defeat and death. He will escape and rise, but in time, death shadows the patriotic, and the gallows beckon." She waited for the maiba to translate and then looked into the maharaja's eyes. "Do not trust your cousins. They are ambitious and foolish. Manipur must avoid the rebellion. Stay neutral. Better—side with Britain."

"Good advice!" McCulloch said, smiling.

"What of the maharaja?" the maiba said.

"I see a cape of blue and white, and a star—the light of heaven will be his guide." Her chin dropped and eyes closed. "I can say no more."

Every eye in the silent room studied the maharaja. He smiled and clapped hands, signaling to the servants to clear the table. He spoke in Manipuri as the maiba translated.

"The day is long," the maiba said. "His Majesty thanks his guests, but wishes to retire." The maharaja nodded to the major. "He hopes we see the major and Madame Blavatsky at the polo grounds tomorrow." The maiba looked at Helena. "His majesty offers Madame Blavatsky the hospitality of his home tonight."

Helena bowed her head.

Chapter 14. The Watcher

Minutes later...

Helena

The durbar hall emptied, and the parties went separate ways. Major McCulloch galloped toward the Western Gate as Helena mingled with the maharaja's entourage. She accepted the offer of a spare pony, secured her travel bag, and mounted. As she rode away, the old maiba stood in torchlight near the Kangla-sha, talking to the glowering man the maharaja named Lungthoubu.

I do not trust that man. Now I wonder if I should trust the maiba. I am glad I am leaving Manipur soon.

The pony riders left the inner citadel via the Northern Gate and turned west. The maharaja lived in a walled compound a short distance away, between the inner and outer walls. Helena trotted beside the maharaja who pointed at the approaching arched gate.

"When the new palace is complete," he said in Hindi, "I will move there. Someday this estate will be the home of my oldest son, the Yuvraj (crown prince)."

As they rode through the entrance, Helena nodded toward a looming tower. "Is that the temple of the maharaja?"

"It is the Temple of Vrindavan Chandra."

"Another Krishna temple? The maiba said it houses idols of the gods of old Manipur."

"That, too."

"But I thought..."

"Manipur worships Lord Krishna," he said, "but a museum is in the temple. Would you care to see?"

"Yes!"

No need to ask twice. A chance to study the old religion.

The maharaja dismounted and servants led the ponies to the stables. Helena joined, and they entered the arched doorway. Her black shoes clattered on the bricks and echoed in the tall, torch-lit chamber. The maharaja beckoned and approached the inner sanctum. Helena peered through the door at an altar and tall statue. She took a step to enter, and he grabbed her arm.

"This chamber is for Lord Krishna. There is nothing to see in there." He pointed at a brick stairway wrapping around the inside walls, circling the sanctum. "What you seek is up those stairs."

The maharaja signaled for servants to bring torches. Firelight cast long shadows as they climbed four flights to the upper shrine. They reached a dark chamber with arched doors opening onto high balconies overlooking the compound. A rectangular inner column housed another stairway leading to the roof. The torch moved toward the central chamber and Helena's eyes widened.

The light showed altars and shelves adorned with a myriad of statues—large ones, chiseled from plain rock, and smaller, intricate pieces carved from precious stones. Hundreds of idols of exotic gods and goddesses, all unrecognizable to Helena.

"An idol per deity," the maharaja said. "Each deity has a name—over three-hundred gods and goddesses in Sanamahi…"

"Three hundred and sixty-five." She smiled. "To be exact."

He returned the smile. "One for each day of the year."

Helena stepped toward an altar and a green reflection caught her eye. The maharaja motioned to the servant to bring the torch closer. Helena caught her breath—she beheld an intricate, jade-green figurine. It was a dragon—winged, coiled, and devouring its tail. Tiny emerald eyes glittered. One claw grasped a round red gem as if protecting a precious egg.

"Pakhangba?"

The maharaja shrugged. "Perhaps."

"You do not know?"

He smiled, but said nothing.

"It is so beautiful," she said. "So tiny for such a mighty god. The jewel—is it…?"

"Is it what?"

"The Mani?"

"Here?" His eyes twinkled as he cracked a smile. "The mighty Mani, magic gem of ancient legend? Perhaps! Who can say?"

"May I touch... the figurine?"

The maharaja nodded.

Helena reached. The tip of her finger grazed the edge of one wing. A bright flash. An exploding vision—a vivid panorama.

A mighty continent, triangular-shaped and green, set in the center of a warm ocean. Thick jungles and high mountains. A steamy tropical mist trailed dark-bottomed, white-topped clouds. Tall, silvery spires rose high, stabbing the blue sky, and sparkling in the bright sun. Sleek air ships beyond count paraded past the towers. Winged, four-legged, reptilian creatures perambulated the wide causeways.

Dragons!

She did not know how she knew, but without question, the winged creatures were dragons. Each had a tall, dark-skinned humanoid at its side. Verbal communication was unnecessary. A voice spoke inside her head.

Behold Lemuria at its peak—millions of years ago!

The view shifted to outer space. A huge rock—an asteroid—raced through the cold reaches of the ether, bearing down on the tiny blue planet. Destruction was imminent, unstoppable.

Death. Extinction. Time is short, mere decades away. There is one answer.

Like wispy seeds exploding from a feathery pod, great ships by the thousands sailed from the tiny world and plummeted into darkest space.

They are leaving, by the millions—a great diaspora. Those remaining hide—safe underground, cut off from passing time.

"Madame Blavatsky?"

Helena yanked her hand from the figurine and shook her head, blinking.

"Are you all right?"

"I—I thought—I saw something." She caught her breath. "I am fine now." She fanned her face with one hand.

"You sensed..." He paused and looked at the servants holding torches. "The maiba told me you—perhaps we should retire to my home now. We have all had a long day. Come."

The maharaja held Helena's arm as they descended the stairway. They exited the temple and walked a short distance to the nearby palace. Before turning in, he asked Helena to join him in the candle-lit parlor for a nightcap. The two sat close, sipping cups of Yu (rice liquor), conversing in Hindi, and sharing confidences.

The maharaja did not ask, so Helena avoided discussing her vision in the tower. Instead, she told more of her history. She spoke of her childhood and her grandfather's influence, awakening of her esoteric interests. She spoke of her disastrous marriage as a teenager to a man in his forties.

"I had to run away," she said. "Three months was all I could take."

The maharaja told of fleeing Manipur as a child after a power dispute with his father's cousins. He returned in triumph as a young man and recaptured the throne. He owed the British for protecting him in during those years in exile in Assam, but McCulloch sided against him when he returned. That he could not forget.

"After eight years, I still distrust the British. My cousins resent me deposing their father, my uncle, so I keep them under a watchful eye."

"Wise of you."

"I am trying to rebuild my country, but I walk a tightrope."

"Time to choose," she said. "Know your enemies from your friends—sort out those whom you can and cannot trust."

"Yes, but to be certain of the difference, I must watch everyone—enemies and friends."

"At dinner—the man by the door. You said he was of the Tongol tribe…"

"Lungthoubu," he said. "He is a loyal friend, a protector of my family, and I owe him my throne. When exiled, he led us to Assam. When I returned to claim my throne, he rode at my side, rallied support, and turned the tide. I would trust him with my life. Why do you ask of him?"

"Has he been spying on me?"

The maharaja scratched his chin as if measuring his next words. "A maharaja must know everything going on in his realm."

"I see. So what did you learn?"

"That you are no threat to Manipur."

"In my visions this evening…," Helena said, "I believe he is the one—the Tongol. I saw him siding with your cousins against the British in the rebellion. It will go ill for Manipur."

"That was not an act? You foresaw a rebellion. Are you certain?"

"Yes."

"Then great danger comes, but with it, opportunity. You gave me an idea this evening—I thought of a way to solve the problem of my cousins. The man you are worried about will help me. I should say no more."

They toasted each other's health and said goodnight. A servant led Helena to a guest chamber and closed the door. Helena lit candles and took a seat at a writing table next to her bed. She opened her carpetbag and rummaged for tobacco.

First things first.

She lifted a pouch to her nose, closed eyes, and sniffed.

Running low. I hope I can find more in Burma.

She sifted and pinched, dolling the remaining clump of dry leaf and rolling a line of cigarettes. She studied the meager remains in the pouch and shook her head.

I hope I do not have to fall back on chewing paan.

Paan, a smokeless chaw, blended beta root with tobacco leaf. The ancient addictive chaw was a far more popular pastime in Asia than smoking, and so it could be the best she could do for a while.

Helena pulled writing paper, a pen, a Pounce pot, and a bottle of ink from the travel bag. She arranged the materials on the table and slid a burning candle closer. She took the pen and a clean piece of paper and jotted the first lines of a letter to her sister Vera in Pskov. Helena scratched a few words then scribbled over and started once more. After several false starts, she gave up, wadded the paper, and tossed it at an empty chair near the closed door.

Sometimes—I wish—it would be nice to have company.

Helena stared at the flickering candle. The smoke rose from her cigarette and drifted toward the window. She thought of the dinner and her unsettling performance. She had seen more than she told. Peripheral events danced, spinning like eddies in the stream of the yet-to-happen. She closed her eyes and focused, trying to recall and follow the swirls, but the images eluded her grasp.

Helena opened her eyes and drew back. Sheets of paper lay scattered, each covered with scribbled sketches of dragons, looping and devouring their tails. Surrounding each dragon were swastikas—the Sanskrit symbol of good fortune.

A sound, like chair legs dragged across a stone floor, screeched near the door. She glanced and glimpsed a tall figure. She turned, eyes open wide, hopeful yet dreading, but no...

An illusion!

Shadows from the flickering candle danced over the empty chair.

The chair has moved.

Helena set the smoldering cigarette on the edge of the table and reached for another sheet of paper. She picked up the pen, dipped it in ink, and prepared to write. A deep voice spoke in a strange accent.

"Good performance this evening."

She dropped the pen and faced a smiling man in a turban and sherwani (long tunic). He had a black beard and eyes deep-set like darkened lairs. Though sitting, the slender man's frame stretched tall—implying a height over eight feet—and with a turban and elongated head, closer to nine feet. A yellow light flashed in his reptilian eyes and the beard could not hide the scales on his swarthy skin.

"What are *you* doing there?" Her voice trembled, betraying surprise and relief.

"Watching, as usual." His thin lips smiled. "Watching is what Watchers do, after all—we watch."

"I suspected it was you making that racket tonight. Was it necessary?"

"I thought it was a nice touch."

"Amateur theatrics of the worst kind."

He covered his heart, feigning hurt feelings. "You should thank me. I have good news—your vision this evening was correct. Exact."

"What part?" she said. "Do you mean the rebellion?"

"Today was the day." His smile took a devilish twist. "As you predicted. Well done!"

"That is not good news!" Tears flowed, and she shook her head. "Where did it start? Was it Lucknow?"

"Closer to the Punjab—Meerut—but it will spread from there."

"What was the final spark?"

"You should know."

"Not the rifle cartridge!"

"The same!" He laughed and clapped. "You should be proud. You warned about those greasy cartridges for weeks."

The East India Company had introduced the 1853 pattern Enfield muzzle-loading muskets. To load the rifles, the Indian sepoys had to bite open the greasy cartridges. Someone started a rumor that the grease came from animal fat and the rumor spread everywhere.

"The Muslims believed the grease came from pigs and the Hindus thought it came from cows—as you told them."

"I was speculating…"

"In convincing fashion."

"I did not intend…"

"The British," he said, "were oblivious or too proud to contradict the rumors. It was a matter of time before a revolt erupted. You see why I told you to leave India?"

"Damn you!" Helena hung her head and sobbed. Tears smeared the ink on a sketch. "You told me to say it! Damn you to Hell!"

His laugh rumbled like distant thunder.

"This is not a laughing matter!" she screamed. "Innocents will die by the thousands. Nothing good will come of it. The blood will be on my hands."

The tall man threw back his head and laughed louder. Helena clenched fists as her face reddened. She glanced at the travel bag at her feet.

If I could reach my loaded muff-pistol, I could get off a shot before he moved.

"No, you could not!" he said. "Shame on you for such thoughts."

Helena's heart sank.

"You are looking at this all wrong." A long, bony finger wagged as he pursed lips. "Something good hides in every bad event. If the cartridge had not sparked the revolution, it would have been something else, and if it were not you, it would be someone else. It was time, it was inevitable, and we are players in the game, doing what we must do. The wheel turns, the sun will come up tomorrow, and everything happens for a reason."

"You and your trite witticisms sicken me!" She sobbed again. "If I cannot blow out your brains, I should put the bullet through mine. The British will suspect me. I will never return to India, will I? They will hound me. I will look over my shoulder for the rest of my life."

"Posh and nonsense! You will return to India someday. When you do, let them spy on you—what does it matter? Meanwhile the British have full hands and enough blame to spread. At least this revolt will mark the end of the East India Company. It will force Victoria to do something. This helps India. Today, a hundred countries, not one. Someday, little by little, year by year, India will become one country. In time, it will be. Meanwhile, put as much distance between you and India as possible. Move on to Burma as planned and continue your studies. There are amazing temples there, I hear.

Maybe Java should be next, and afterward, perhaps you should return to South America—yes, go to Peru. Then go home. You have been away too long. Meanwhile, I believe you have work to do this evening."

Helena looked at the pen and paper. "You mean to write letters?"

She turned, and the chair was empty. The tall man—vanished without a trace.

As if it had been a dream.

She lifted her smoldering cigarette and took a deep draw.

How long can I stay this course?

Her miniature French pistol held a single shot, but one shot would be all she would need.

I should end things here and now.

She wept anew. When her tears dried, she picked up the pen and wrote. As the pen scratched, Helena looked into emptiness, not at the paper, jotting without knowing what she jotted. She wrote as if an automaton, dipping the pen, again and again, until the page was full. She picked up the Pounce pot and dusted the page with fine powder. After the inked dried, she folded and inserted the paper into an envelope.

Candle tipped, dripping wax, sealing the letter. The pen scratched the name—Zoluti—in bold print across the front of the envelope. The name meant nothing—a nonsensical word.

Next Helena pulled a block of paraffin from her bag. She held it above the candle until it softened and rubbed the dripping wax over each side of the envelope. She rubbed, reheated, dripped, and rubbed, until she had coated the entire envelope in the sealing wax.

Still in a trance, she lifted the envelope, stood, and walked out the door. She drifted down a hallway and stepped out into a moonlit garden. The night sounds of the jungle croaked and chirped. She made a ghostly figure in her black dress as she approached a ruined garden wall.

The outer wall showed signs of impact, perhaps struck during the last war with Burma. Piles of Kangla red bricks lay scattered at the foot of the broken wall. Through the breach, the moonlight exposed a wide dry ditch, once a moat. Helena strolled to the breach, turned, and followed the ragged line of the wall. Her fingertips caressed the bricks—up and up—her fingers rose until she reached unbroken structure. Hands grasped, pushed, and pulled until a cap atop a brick baluster wiggled free. She placed the envelope on top of the baluster and maneuvered the heavy cap into its original position.

Turning from the wall, still lost in a dream, she stared straight ahead and strolled back to her quarters. When Helena reached her room, she plopped into her chair at the table, reached for her still smoldering cigarette, and finished her smoke.

The candle burned out and still she sat, staring straight ahead, as hours passed.

When the first hint of day intruded on the darkness, she still sat, frozen, staring. In the distance, a rooster crowed, and Helena, at last, stirred.

Where am I?

Her writing materials lay strewn across the table. She returned her things to her bag. She went to the window, stretched, smiled a rare smile, and said, "Looks to be a nice day for polo!"

Chapter 15. The Rings, the Pond, and the Polo Match

Sunday, 11 May 1857...

Helena

Helena hefted a silver-gray object in her palm.

The ring is heavier than it looks!

She raised a jeweler's eyepiece and scrutinized the band. The bezel featured an engraved relief of a winged dragon looped, devouring its tail.

"Ask her," she said in Hindi, "of what material are the rings made."

Jatly chattered at the Manipuri woman in the red sari behind the bamboo table and translated as the old woman spoke.

"She says—rings made from finest Siamese pewter. She says—ring smith from Nagaland. Workmanship exceptional. Quality good."

"Um, yeah." Helena stared closer at the ring. "Ask her if she knows what the design signifies."

The girl cocked her head and rubbed her chin.

"The dragon! On the ring—what does it mean?"

"Oh!" Jatly nodded.

The old woman listened. With narrowed, shifting eyes, she looked each way, and then answered, "Nongda Lairen Pakhangba."

"The old woman says..."

Helena cut the girl off with a raised hand. "I understood that much. The dragon king sent by the gods—and we all know his name."

Helena handed the old woman the ring, muttering, "No fear of Krishna here. These people grow bolder by the day." She turned to Jatly. "Try to negotiate a fair price for that ring. Try to buy the smaller one, too. Fight for a lower price for the pair."

Helena soon strolled out of the shade and into the hot sun, holding a lit cigarette with one hand as two pewter rings clinked in the other palm. The Women's Bazaar fell behind as they crossed the dusty road toward the Western Gate of Kangla. Her young friend Jatly trudged behind, struggling to keep up, lugging Helena's heavy travel bag.

"So...," Jatly said, huffing, "you bought—two rings?" She pulled beside Helena and grinned, cocking her head, trying to make eye contact.

"I did—with your help. Thank you."

"Very nice rings!"

"Yes—very."

"Good price, too!"

"True," Helena said. "Can you guess why I bought the pair?"

"Um—hum...," Jatly said, puffing, "one is—larger than the other." She looked at Helena's face with a smile and eager bright eyes. "Perhaps one is for you—and one is a gift for someone."

"Perhaps..."

"For me?"

"Outstanding guess! I intend to give you one of these rings and keep the other for myself. Can you guess why?"

Jatly stopped, dropped the heavy bag, and slouched. Helena paused and took a drag from her cigarette.

She knows.

"You are leaving tomorrow!" Jatly took a deep breath and choked back a sob. "My ring is a going away gift!" She broke into tears.

Helena put the rings in a pocket and tossed her cigarette. She threw her arms around Jatly, squeezing the girl to her breast.

"Have you spoken to the old maiba today?"

"No."

"No?" Helena grasped the girl by the shoulders and studied her face.

Jatly averted her eyes. "Young maiba."

"Who?" Helena frowned and then grinned. "Oh, I understand now—the chela. I forgot about the boy. Ha! Yes, he was at the durbar hall last night. You two are close?"

"He is my friend."

"Um...," Helena said, "do you two speak often?"

The girl shrugged and blushed.

"Let me serve as an example—attraction to older men is dangerous."

"What do you mean?"

Helena changed topics. "The Monsoons start soon. The caravan for Burma is here now and leaves tomorrow. I plan to be on it."

"Did you book passage? You did not ask my help!"

"You helped," Helena said. "The veiled woman in the black hijab..."

"I brought her to you!"

"Yes, yes. She is a Kashmiri Sufi Muslim—a fellow mystic. She offered me a ride—on an elephant! We should have much to discuss."

Jatly's shoulders drooped, chin trembling, as Helena took her hands.

"Oh, dear Jatly," Helena said. "Please do not make this hard. You have been such a good friend during my time here—recruiting my customers, acting as my translator, and your father let me sleep under his roof. I will cherish our time together, and I cannot repay you, but I must leave."

"I hoped you would stay longer." Tears trickled down Jatly's face. "I want to go, too. I want to see the world."

A mist gathered in Helena's eyes. "Come. Let us find a place to talk. Somewhere shady."

Helena lifted her bag and Jatly led the way through the outer gate of the fort. They passed shops and stables, soon entering the inner gate. The Kangla-sha stood straight ahead and, past a bustee, the polo field and durbar hall lay on their right. To their left was a large pond ringed by a rocky shore, stacked stones, and shady trees. The calm waters reflected low clouds and deepest blue. The two took seats in the cooler shade on soft grass.

"This is the Nungjeng Pukhri." Jatly nodded toward the pond. "It is a sacred place. Lord Pakhangba sleeps here, they say."

"Pakhangba the man or Pakhangba the god?"

"Pakhangba the dragon." Jatly pointed. "He sleeps out there. Deep in the cold water—the spirit element of dragons. He will stay there until his time of awakening."

"When will that be?"

"No one knows."

"There must be a backdoor. He comes up from the cave sometimes."

Helena laughed, but Jatly turned away and tossed a pebble at the pond.

She will be hard to cheer.

Helena bit her lip, folded her hands, and cleared her throat. "Jatly, how familiar are you with Pakhangba and the Sanamahi faith?"

Jatly shrugged, still looking away. Helena squirmed.

I hate to, but I must press her.

"Why," Helena said, "do you associate with the old maiba?"

"I do not associate with him." Jatly tossed a larger pebble. It landed with a plop a few feet from shore.

"He knows of you, and wants to keep you a secret, all to himself. He said you sensed the dragon."

"Yes, so he says." She wiped her eyes on her sleeve. "I am not sure."

"What were you doing in the temple?"

"I sneaked inside—to visit with my friend."

"The chela? That boy again?"

"Yes."

"How did you two meet?"

"He watched me dance Thang-ta. He watched me a lot. Then he spoke." She shrugged. "I spoke back. He wanted to be friends, so—we are friends." She tossed another stone, a larger one, farther out into the pond where it made a bigger splash.

Helena chuckled, and said, "He is cute, I suppose."

"He works at the temple," Jatly said, blushing. "He sits for hours, all alone at a table, copying books. I missed him and felt sorry for him. I wanted to keep him company. It was so hot—so cooler in the shade—so I went into the temple. That is all I remember."

"There must be more."

"The old maiba found me. I was looking down—into a surung. He said I almost fell. Maybe true—I remember little. He asked questions."

"Questions like what?"

"What did I see? Did I hear anything, or sense anything? Questions like that. All I remembered was I had a dream of the dragon. In my dream, I heard a scratching, like climbing. I smelled its breath, felt its heartbeat, and I imagined that it spoke, but I understood nothing."

"A dream? Are you certain?"

Jatly shrugged. "Maybe it was real." She picked up a large rock and threw it as far as she could. It hit with a great splash and ripples raced toward the shore.

"Should you be doing that?" Helena said. "What if you hit Pakhangba?"

"Do not jest—but you are right. I should not."

"Anything else about the old maiba?"

"Not much. He wants me to keep coming to the temple—to learn."

"Like a chela?"

"Yes. Somewhat."

"What would you learn?"

"Rituals, dances, memorize sacred texts—things like that."

"In Manipur, are girls allowed to become maibas?"

"No!" Jatly said, aghast. "How could they?"

"No?" Helena frowned.

"Girls become maibis, silly, not maibas!"

"Oh, I see." Helena could not help laughing. "Big difference—men and women. Anything else?"

"Maibis are more necessary than maibas. Maibas are shamans, but maibis are oracles, possessed by a god or a goddess."

"Hm. I see. Are there maibis?"

"No, at least, none in the open. Old maiba says, the maharaja will bring back the old religion. Not Krishna only. Old gods and maibis—in daylight."

"Interesting," Helena said. "How does a girl become a maibi?"

"The old maiba said, best if the girl starts young, by age seven, but I am not yet a woman. Then there will be a ritual, called Lai Nupi Thiba. It means the girl marries a god. The ritual will take place during a festival called Lai Haraoba—there has not been one for a hundred years."

"Did he say?" Helena bit her lip. "Which god would you marry?"

"Pakhangba. The dragon."

Helena's face darkened.

The old man hid the truth. He wants the dragon to reawaken on earth, inside the mind of this poor girl.

"How do you feel about marrying a dragon?"

Jatly threw her arms around Helena's neck and sobbed. "I refuse to be a maibi." Tears streaked her face. "The dream was evil. I do not want a god inside my head. I want a husband—not a god."

Jatly tore herself away and picked up a large rock.

"Jatly!" Helena said. "No!"

"Leave me alone, dragon!" Jatly flung the rock far out into the pond. "I want to be myself!"

As the stone struck the still water, the smooth mirror of the blue sky vanished, replaced by green ripples. Helena peered at the dark expanding circles and beheld a flash followed by a vision.

It was night. The full moon was brighter than any moon Helen had seen. A man knelt beside the pond. He lifted a chain necklace, draped it around his neck, and slipped a medallion into his tunic.

Who is he? Somehow, I sense—he is a prince.

Men approached—a young man carrying an older man—and the prince called, as if he recognized them.

"General!"

The word elicited no reaction from the newcomers.

He is invisible to them—like a ghost.

The young carrier set the old man by the bank. The old man wore a green uniform and a violet turban, and his hair and bushy mustache were gray.

General? He looks like the Tongol, but many years older!

The general knelt, splashed water then plunged his head in and came up sputtering.

"Please help me." The general extended his arms toward the water. "Lord Pakhangba, please tell me what I should do."

A dark voice answered from far away. *"You know what to do."*

"What do I do? Tell me!"

"It is time. Fulfill the prophecy."

"General!" the prince said. "No!"

The general looked, but stared through the invisible prince.

He noticed his voice that time, but still cannot see him.

Helena called to the prince, "Who are you?"

The prince spun and stared through Helena.

He perceived me, too, but he cannot see me!

"Helena?"

Jatly's voice jarred Helena awake, eyes blinking in sudden daylight.

Back to reality!

"What happened?" Jatly said.

"A vision came, but it passed. I must ask something. This morning when you talked to the boy, the chela—did he say anything of what happened at the dinner?"

"He said something, but not much."

"A vision came then, too—I spoke of the future, but not everything I saw. I kept secret events such as your future. I saw you as a grown woman. You were not a maibi, possessed by a dragon. You were a mother, with a beautiful little girl, and you spoke to the girl in English."

"Me—married?" Jatly clasped her hands under her chin. "A mother? Speaking English?"

"All that and more. Do you know a man—strong, middle-aged? He wears a turban and uniform, has deep-set eyes and a bushy gray mustache. I saw you two talking yesterday by the Kangla-sha."

"He knows my father," Jatly said. "He is a captain. I call him the Tongol. He is a bad man."

"Why? What did he do?"

"The Tongol and his men destroyed entire villages—they killed everyone, including the animals. My father said the Tongol gave the order."

"Why did he do that?"

"The village refused to obey the Lallup—the call to the maharaja's service. My father rode in the attack—the Tongol forced him. The Tongol laughed and called the attack a nautch."

"Nautch?"

"A sacred dance," Jatly said. "Like the Ras Lila nautch."

"If the Tongol raised a war company, would your father join?"

Jatly cocked her head and frowned. "A few years ago, but not now. Father is older and has been sick—too sick for fighting."

"Too sick to serve the maharaja?"

"The Tongol would not call upon men unless it was for the service of the maharaja. Yes, if the need were great, the Tongol would expect my father to join him. My father would not refuse."

Jatly's chin quivered. "You are frightening me." She grabbed Helena's arm with a trembling hand. "What have you foreseen?"

"I fear I planted a seed in the mind of the maharaja. Rebellion broke out yesterday in India. I think the maharaja will use the Tongol to trick his cousins into joining the rebellion. Then he will betray them to the British. Your father must not follow the Tongol. He could die—killed in battle or executed. If he is lucky, the Sirkar (government) will put him in prison. If your father is old and sick, a man like the Tongol would regard him as expendable."

Jatly grew shrill. "What do I do?"

"You and your father must leave Manipur."

"Where do we go?"

"Go west. Go to Assam. Look for work in the tea gardens. You will meet your future husband there."

"How can we leave? This is all so sudden."

"First, you must convince your father—make him understand. Buy time while he sells things you will not need. Go to the old maiba. Tell him you want to learn to be a maibi but first you want him to teach you English. Learn as much as you can—simple phrases at first—it will be a start. You will learn the rest in Assam.

"When do we go?

"Soon—within two weeks. No longer. The monsoons are coming. Go sooner if possible."

"How will I know?"

"Watch the old maiba. One day he will speak to the Tongol. Then the old maiba will ask you to leave home and move in with him. He will say you can concentrate on your studies better. When that day comes, time to leave. Slip out of Manipur in secret. Run as fast as you can. Do not look back."

Jatly grasped Helena's hand. "Take me with you!"

"Your father would die, fighting for a lost cause. He needs you now. He will help you meet your English husband."

Helena patted Jatly's hand. The girl sat still, staring with glazed eyes. *Stunned!*

"There is one more thing. Do you know of the five elemental souls— earth, wind, fire, water, and ether—and the sixth soul, the mi?"

"Yes," Jatly said. "Everyone knows this."

"If you could have one of my elemental souls, as a gift, which would you want?"

"I—do not know. That is a funny question." She leaned back with one eye closed, scratching her head, and then brightened. "Wind! I love the wind. Whenever it touches my face, I wish I could be a bird, take wing, and fly!"

Helena pulled the rings from her dress pocket, clutched the smaller ring, and raised her fist. "This ring will cement a bond between us. I project my elemental soul of the wind to this ring as my external soul." She handed the ring to Jatly. "Use it in time of need. Think of me when you do."

Jatly cradled the ring in her palms, accepting it wide-eyed. Her lips parted. "I want to give you one of my souls." She broke into a brighter smile. "Which would you prefer?"

"You choose."

"Water," Jatly said. "I choose water—the dragon's element. Without the water soul, the dragon has no power over me."

Helena presented the ring, and the girl performed the ceremony. Helena slipped on the ring and they hugged. They spent the next two hours confiding, discussing the mysteries of boys and the duties of a mother. At last, it was time to leave.

Jatly waved. "I will see you off tomorrow." She ran toward the Western Gate and home.

Late afternoon turned to early evening. Helena finished her cigarette and strolled to the polo grounds, looking for Major McCulloch. She found him under one of the shamiana tents erected on the north side. Members of the royal family sat under a colorful shamiana at the west side.

No doubt to avoid the glare of the setting sun.

Helena shaded her eyes as McCulloch pointed out members of the royal party. There was the queen with her sisters and cousins, and the young son Sura Chandra and his ayah nursemaid. A woman in the entourage waved. Helena smiled and returned the gesture.

The uniformed riders trotted onto the polo field, preparing to begin the match. Helena and major were cordial, and each showed the other no animosity. The major was a serious aficionado. He explained that the ball was three-and-one-half inches in diameter and made of bamboo root.

"You British always make up your own names," Helena said. "Why do you call Sagol Kangjei polo?"

McCulloch shrugged. "Have not the foggiest."

"Polo derives from the Tibetan word pulu," she said, "meaning a willow wood knot—what the Tibetans use for a ball."

The field was two hundred yards long and one hundred yards wide. There were seven riders on each side and each rider carried a four-foot long mallet. The mallet head was hardwood, set at an obtuse angle. A player hitting the ball sometimes met an opponent in a test of strength called a mukna.

In the right hands, the mallet makes a fearsome weapon.

There were no goal posts—the ball had to cross goal lines to score. The game lasted eight periods called chukkas, each seven minutes long. Players on the teams wore colors to signify their pana, or class in society, and the teams only played within their pana.

The maharaja wore the white uniform and turban of the Ahallup pana. He rode his polo pony hard and played well, but his team lost. The other team impressed Helena by not acting intimidated or having played any less hard because they were competing against the maharaja.

After the match, Helena thanked the major and retired. She lugged her carpetbag and trudged back to the maharaja's walled estate where she would spend her final night in Manipur.

On to Burma. Tomorrow I will ride an elephant.

Chapter 16. The Wind and the Wings

Early in the morning of the next day, Monday, 12 May 1857...

Jatly

Jatly leaned over the southeastern wall under a clear sky. Twenty feet below the battlement, the crowded caravan assembled near the river and prepared to cross the ford. On the other side, the dirt road ran due east, and then angled south toward Burma and vanished, swallowed by the jungle.

"Helena!" Jatly shouted, jumping and waving.

The figure below showed no sign of recognition. Jatly's voice fell flat, drowned by the din.

Turbaned boys tugged mules and coaxed into line sturdy pack ponies laden with goods. Water buffaloes strained, hauling bullock carts full of heavy crates and barrels. Porters prodded and pushed the beasts as they guided the huge wooden wheels in and out of muddy puddles in the rugged road.

Pangal Muslim muleteers with pistols in their belts and talwars at their sides, brandished whips as they rode sturdy horses up and down the line. They were the caravan's drivers and its guardians from bandits, ever a threat. Here and there in the surge and flow ambled elephants—magnificent beasts, draped in colorful carpets, saddled with tented howdahs. Dark-skinned, loin-clothed, mahout handlers mounted on the elephants' shoulders, grasping at the ears with their ankusa hooks. There, Jatly spied Helena, under one elephant's howdah, seated next to a woman wearing a hijab and veil.

"Goodbye, Helena!" Jatly called. "I hope you learn more in the Buddhist temples of Burma!"

It is hopeless. She cannot hear me.

Jatly sighed and stepped aside, jostled by the crowd. A younger, more aggressive child—a boisterous boy—shoved forward to take her place. He strained on tiptoe, peering over the wall. The commotion below and the yelling and pushing crowd above had conspired to stymy Jatly's farewell. She resolved to regain her spot and try once more.

If I cannot say a proper goodbye, at least I will watch her as long I can.

Jatly pushed forward through the gathered onlookers and engaged the boy in a shoving match, securing her place at the parapet once more. She leaned over the wall, straining for a clearer view of the caravan, and something cool struck her cheek.

A raindrop!

Jatly frowned and studied the sky. Moments before, the heavens had been clear and blue. Without warning, gray rain clouds drifted in from the south. She shook a clenched fist at the dark billows.

"This will not do!" she shouted. "Helena must have a good sendoff. Rain will spoil everything!"

She slapped her hands on the bricks in anger. There was a dull, metallic clink.

My new ring!

Helena's gift from the day before, the dragon-embossed pewter ring, had struck the bricks. As Jatly studied the gray band, the boy pushed and shoved his way back into her place. This time Jatly yielded and stepped back, peering at the clouds while fingering the raised dragon image.

"External soul of the wind! Hum—I wonder."

She twisted the ring off her finger, gripped the band, and closed her eyes. Then, with as much intensity as she could muster, she wished…

I wish for the wind to stir and chase the rain clouds away.

She opened her eyes and, to her astonishment, it happened. A soft wind blew, then gathered strength from the north, and pushed the dark-bottomed clouds south, away from the caravan.

Jatly belly laughed. She danced and spun and the brisk wind blew her wild hair. The breeze calmed, the sun peeked, and the caravan was across the river, out of sight. Onlookers turned away, returning to other business. Soon Jatly found herself alone atop the wall.

"Incredible!" she shouted. She spread her arms wide and spun around on the empty battlements.

Was it a coincidence? Did the wind appear because I wished for it?

She looked at the ring in her open palm. "With your help, I meant to say."

Should I chance another try? Would I be tempting fate?

With the reckless abandon of youth, the thrill of the experience had its way.

What other magic tricks can I try?

She gripped the ring and glanced around for something, anything—a bird caught her eye. The bird had flown from the nearby bamboo thickets and landed atop the battlement a few feet away. In a spot where, minutes earlier, onlookers had been standing, the bird turned its head to one side and studied the bricks. It pecked its black beak into cracks, gobbling insects from the red bricks.

How pretty! My favorite.

The little bird was a streak-throated Fulvetta. Its gray-brown feathers flashed violet in the sunlight. It hopped on stick-thin feet, stopped to puff its feathers, and arched its tail upward. The tiny head turned and one eye fastened on Jatly. The girl returned the gaze, locking eye-to-eye.

How would life be as a bird?

Jatly gripped the ring tighter. She pictured herself inside the head of a bird—the sights, sounds, and emotions—the hot rush and pitter-patter of a tiny heart. She blinked and, instead of a bird, before her stood a thin girl in a blue and red sari, long black hair blown to disarray.

Can that be how I look? I am hideous! I will never find a husband!

Jatly studied her appearance in closer detail, too enthralled to wonder how it was possible, and noticed a pungent flavor in her beak.

Insects! Terrible!

Then, with a sudden jerk, she was back in her body, seeing through her own eyes. The bird leapt from the wall and flew toward the jungle and the safety of the bamboo thickets.

There was a clink. She had dropped the ring onto the bricks. She clasped her hands to the sides of her head, and wild-eyed, with heart pounding, she yanked disheveled hair.

"What happened?"

The ring! Could it be...?

Could the same magic that commanded the wind give her the ability to cast her external soul into the bird?

That is the only explanation!

Jatly retrieved the ring and resolved to wait for another bird to land and, if one did, try to repeat what had happened. She waited several minutes, but no bird came. Then she realized...

The first bird ate all the insects!

She scampered, looking around the battlements for more tiny crawlers, located and scooped a few beetles, and raced back to the earlier spot. She placed the insects onto the bricks, took several steps back, and waited, leaning against a nearby baluster, still gripping the ring. A few minutes later another Fulvetta appeared.

A twin of the first? Maybe the same one, back for dessert?

Fulvettas, by nature, keep to the forest undergrowth and bamboo thickets, staying away from people and places such as the top of the wall of Kangla Fort. Once was unusual, but to appear twice...

It cannot be a coincidence! It must be a sign—an omen!

"Our fate is to be together!"

She resolved to repeat the feat—staring at the bird, gripping the ring. The bird pecked at insects and into cracks, gulped, raised its head, and regarded the girl. With head cocked, feathers puffed, and tail raised, it returned the stare.

Jatly followed the same steps as before, staring back, imagining herself as the bird, trying to feel the pitter of its tiny heart. This time, she did not stop to agonize over her disheveled appearance, and instead, considered Helena and the caravan.

Is it possible to catch them? I must try.

Then Jatly, the little gray-brown bird, turned, leapt from the wall, and sped toward the forest. She discovered there was no need to think of flapping her wings. She picked a place, and there she went—wings flapping on their own.

Flying seems much easier than I expected.

She made it to the nearest tree and looked back at Kangla, noting the distance flown and eying the river. The caravan was out of sight, down the jungle road toward Burma.

Can I make it across the river? It looks far away.

Without fear, she leapt and sped to the nearest tree on the other side.

Yes—easy!

She vaulted and sped down the road, flitting side to side, pausing on a tree limb, and speeding off, following the route of the caravan. Jatly lit on a bough, lifted a cautious eye, and scanned the sky.

Predators could be hunting. Do not be a falcon's meal!

She threw caution to the wind and sped away. Soon horses and ponies came into sight.

The end of the caravan!

Further ahead were the elephants.

Helena's mount should be in the middle of the pack.

Jatly flitted side-to-side, high as the lowest branches, examining rumbling beasts and riders. At last, she caught sight of Helena under the canopy of a howdah. She sped ahead, circled, and brought her stick feet down for a landing on the elephant's head in front of the mahout boy.

Helena wore her usual black dress but atop her head was a pith sun helmet. She sat under the howdah tent, engaging in animated conversation with the veiled woman, flinging her hands, as if to hammer home a philosophical point.

"Helena! Helena!" Jatly screeched. "Look here! It is me, Jatly!"

She screamed at the top of her lungs, but only shrill chirps and cackles emerged from her beak.

The mahout boy shouted and waved his ankusa hook. He swung, trying to knock Jatly off the elephant's head, but she hopped and fluttered over the stick. He swung faster and came closer but Jatly avoided his blow.

Jatly attempted a second time to attract Helena's attention, but all she accomplished was louder chirping. That time Helena noticed—she turned, nudged the woman at her side, and pointed at the funny little bird. The women smiled at the bird's antics, and then Helena leaned forward, peering. Her face changed—head cocked, eyes widened, and then she cracked a sly smile.

"Well done, Jatly!" Her voice carried authority. "Now, best you go home!"

The mahout boy swung his stick a final time. Jatly leapt from the elephant's head and flitted to safety on a nearby tree branch. She panted and rested a moment.

Now what can I try?

There was a jerk and a skinny girl in a sari stood looking at open hands holding a ring. She stood once more atop the walls of Kangla Fort. Another jerk—a woman shook her shoulders. Jatly frowned—sad her adventure had ended.

"Young girl," the woman said, "are you ill? You kept staring at your hands—as if in a trance. Is anything wrong?"

Jatly broke into a huge smile. She skipped away, spun, shook her fists in the air, and laughed.

"No!" she shouted. "Everything is perfect! Wonderful!"

Jatly took the ring from her fist, slipped it onto her finger, and skipped away humming. She broke into a merry song and sang as she made her way down the brick stairway. She continued to sing as she skipped and hopped across the courtyard until she neared the Kangla-sha statues.

Drums! Music!

Musicians played and young girls danced. A friend called to her. Jatly ran and joined the circle, linking hands. She danced with her friends, circling the musicians, until she broke free and bent over, hands on knees, laughing and trying to catch her breath. With hands on hips, she stood straight, facing the tall dragons.

"Oh, so mighty and menacing are we today?"

The wide-open mouths of the dragon statues gaped skyward, and she imagined they were laughing, too—laughing at her.

"Go ahead!" she said. "Laugh at me—see if I care."

She turned away and gazed west toward the sacred pond with its dark unknown depths, then at the polo grounds, emptied because of the coming monsoons. The music continued. The drumbeats pounded.

I will miss this place.

She reached into her sari, pulled out a silvery thin chain necklace, and undid the clasp. The chain slipped through the dragon-embossed ring. She refastened the clasp, replaced the chain over her head, and lifted the dangling ring.

"From now on," she said to the ring, "I save you for emergencies." She dropped the necklace into her sari, out of sight, and patted her chest. "I will hide you as my most precious secret."

Jatly turned toward the temple. In the distance, an old man in a white robe stood on the verandah clutching a staff, looking her direction.

Staring at me! How long has he been watching?

She ran to the temple and climbed the steps.

"What mischief are you making this morning?" the priest asked.

"Oh, seeing my friend's caravan leave."

"I hope the madame has a safe and comfortable journey."

Jatly nodded, bit her lip, looked down, and kicked at a pebble. She looked up and grinned. "I have decided something."

The maiba cocked his head and smiled back. "Yes?"

"I have decided. I will learn to be a maibi—if—if…"

"If what?"

"First—I want to learn English. I want you to teach me as you taught the young maiba."

"Who?"

"You taught English to the boy."

"Oh, him! My chela! Is it like that now? I am the old maiba and he is the young maiba?" The priest threw back his head and laughed. Jatly skipped down the stairs. "English!" he called through cupped hands. "Whatever will you do with English?"

Jatly skipped away backward, waving and smiling.

"When will you start?"

"See you tomorrow!" She ran hard for home.

Chapter 17. The Tongol

Two weeks later, Monday morning 26 May 1857...

Jatly

Jatly studied the brown pages, struggling to read the spidery writing, sounding each word inside her head. She found classical Meitei script challenging despite two weeks of instruction.

So many unknown words.

She sensed a gaze, glanced up, and caught the dreamy-eyed chela, head cocked, lips parted, ogling her from across the table. The lad's eyes darted aside, and he blushed.

"Why?" She used the English word.

He returned to his copying. "Why what?"

"Why me you look?"

He averted his eyes. "Your English is terrible."

"You English talk—me English learn."

The boy sighed and rolled his eyes. "I cannot teach you English," he said in Meiteilon. "It is too hard for you. You are too stupid to understand. English verbs are not always last."

"Not stupid!" She threw her hands up and switched back to the Manipuri tongue. "I—will understand—soon!" She fumed in silence, wondering what a verb was, and trying to think of a way to avenge her honor.

The old maiba said—something useful!

Jatly gave the youth a sideways glance and cracked a wry smile. "You want to be a girl! Why?"

"What? I want no such thing. Why do you say that?"

"You keep trying to commune with Pakhangba." The sight of the boy's bugged-out eyes thrilled her. "I saw you standing by the surung. The old maiba says gods prefer maibis, and goddesses prefer maibas. If a maiba communes with a god, he has to pretend to be a girl. He has to dress as a girl and act as a girl."

"You liar!"

"I am not a liar! That is the truth!"

"Stop!" The old maiba stood at the doorway. "You!" He jabbed his staff at the chela. "See to your copying, and you!" He beckoned to Jatly. "Come with me."

The old maiba left the library. As Jatly closed her book and stood, preparing to follow, the chela screwed up his eyes and sneered. She made an ugly face and stuck out her tongue as she closed the library door. The old maiba waited outside in the sanctum.

"I was explaining to the boy...," she said.

The old maiba cut her short. "No time for childish fights! You need to do something. Go straight home and say goodbye to your father. Gather your things. You will stay here now."

"Why?" A chill raced down her spine and moisture filled her wide eyes.

It is time! As Helena said would happen!

"You will concentrate better on your studies that way. I must keep my eye on you here. You must learn discipline."

"But—my father..."

"Your father will be fine without you as a burden. Now be off with you. Be swift. Return as fast as you can."

Jatly looked down, forced a dejected frown, and shuffled away.

"Now!"

She broke into a run down the perambulatory passage, skirted the surungs without a glance, and ran out of the temple. She cleared the verandah steps and sprinted toward the Western Gate. A mile past the women's bazaar and another mile up a hill, she reached a rundown bustee. A friendly pack of dogs chased after, scattering a flock of clucking hens. She jumped over a muddy puddle and burst through the rickety wooden door of the mud hut.

"Father! We must go—now!"

Their packs were waiting, ready for a quick departure. Once Jatly was certain no one was watching, she led her father out of the hut and into the brush behind the bustee. After an hour of uphill hiking, Jatly and her father reached a flat spot high on a rocky crag and set down backpacks and walking sticks. The hilt of a dao knife (single-edged blade) extended from the larger pack.

"Rest here." She pointed at a large flat rock. "The bushes shield us from sight."

Her father panted as he sat. "Are you—certain...?" He coughed. "About leaving Manipur this way?"

Jatly nodded and patted his shoulder. She took his knife, cut a flowery shoot from a Karot Akhabi bush at the edge of the crag, and offered red cherry-shaped fruit from a yellow gourd.

"Here, this will help your cough."

"If the captain catches us running away, he will butcher me and feed me to the pariah dogs. I hate to think what he will do to you."

"You warned me before," she said. "They will not catch us."

"They will catch us on the road in the broad daylight."

Jatly said nothing. She looked around to get her bearings, crawled back to the spot she had cleared, and leaned over the rocky crag. Far below, she saw the thatch roof of the mud hut that had been their home.

No sign yet of the Tongol.

She crawled back to her father. "I remember now," she said. "I know where we are. Farther up the hill is a cave—well, an overhang. We can take shelter there and hide until nightfall. We will travel at night."

A half hour later, they reached the spot. She pointed and her father crawled deep beneath the overhanging rocks. "The cave seems smaller than I remember," she said.

He chuckled. "You have grown!"

"A tight fit, but it will do. Settle in—try to sleep."

He grasped her hand. "Where are you going?"

"To have a look." She peeled his hand, scooted from under the rock, and then turned. "Which way is Assam?"

He pointed west toward a mountain. "That is the Peak of Leimatak. We can avoid the road as long as we keep the peak in sight. We will need the road to cross over the mountain into Assam."

Jatly reconnoitered their surroundings, found the area safe, but too high, and out of the line of sight of their hut. She sat and folded her arms.

Hours until sundown. What to do now?

A chirp came, and she found a Fulvetta sitting on a branch of a nearby bush. She cracked a wry smile. "You came back!"

Minutes later, Jatly flew high. She dove, swooping low over the hillside, and caught sight of the bustee. A bearded man in a soiled shirt wandered the dirt lane near the hut. Four horse riders rounded a bend. One rider held the reins of a fifth, riderless horse.

Horses! Real horses! Not ponies.

Ponies were common in Manipur, for both polo and cavalry, but heavy horses were rare, saved for the best warriors. The bearded man waited as the riders approached. Jatly flitted to a branch on a nearby Monkey Jack tree, studied the men, and recognized the lead rider.

The Tongol!

Riders drew beside the bearded man and halted before the hut. The Tongol shouted, "Kangmeiza! Come out! We must talk."

No sign of movement. A rider dismounted, strode to the hut, and pounded on the wooden door. No answer. He pushed the door open and entered. After a minute, he reappeared.

"No one is here!" the rider said. "Empty! They took everything!"

"You!" The Tongol pointed at the bearded man. "Where is the man who lives here?"

"Kangmeiza?" the bearded man said. "See for yourself. Gone!"

"Where?"

"What does it matter? It is my hut now. He sold it, I bought it!"

"When did he leave?"

The bearded man shrugged, saying, "Today—maybe yesterday—I do not know. Gone! Moved away! Try another village."

"What of the girl?" the Tongol said.

"What girl?"

"Kangmeiza's daughter. A young girl, twelve years old."

The bearded man spread his palms and shrugged. "How would I know? She is his daughter—why would he leave her here?"

The Tongol leaned, reached into his saddlebag, and pulled out a dark bottle. A dirty rag extended from the open neck. A struck flint set fire to the rag.

"What are you doing?" the bearded man shouted, grabbing the Tongol's arm. "Stop! This is my house!"

A boot kicked the bearded man square in the jaw. He flew backward, arms flung wide. Chickens scattered as he slid headfirst into a muddy puddle. The Tongol ambled his horse closer to the hut and tossed the burning bottle onto the thatch roof. Flames rose from the dry straw.

Jatly had seen all she needed. She leapt and sped away. From higher up, she circled and watched the flickering fire consume the mud hut.

Our house! Our poor little home!

Jatly would never again live in the shanty, but the emotional attachment remained. She had grown up there, her mother had died there, and Helena had slept there. The bearded man was a stranger, but she felt comfort knowing someone her father knew would make a home there. The bird's little heart pattered.

Must have revenge!

The spell ended. Jatly sat and blinked, finding herself atop the hill. She fumed, red-faced, looked at the clear sky, and shook her head.

Where are the monsoons?

She clenched her ring and closed her eyes. The breeze stirred and became a wind. Dark clouds rushed from the north. Lightning flashed, thunder boomed, and the sky opened. She spun, arms spread wide, laughing in the rain.

"Take that! Have a little monsoon, Tongol!" She clapped hands. "That should give them a good soaking and chase them back to Kangla!"

A lightning flash came closer. As the rumble shook, she ran for the little cave and crawled inside next to her father.

"There you are," he said. "I was preparing to search for you."

"Not to worry! The storm will not last long. Once clear, at dark, we start for Assam. Take a safe rest."

Part III. The Sun Never Sets on the British Empire

"The British Empire: This vast empire on which the sun never sets and whose bounds nature has not yet ascertained..."

From *The Journal of George Macartney* (1773)
By The First Earl Macartney

Dramatis personæ

In order of appearance (*denotes a fictional character)

1890 Manipur and Assam

Frank Saint Clair Grimwood	British political agent to Manipur, 36
Albert Edward Heath (dream)	Former political agent (died 4 April 1889), 40
Bearer	Major-domo at British Residency, 50
Tongol General's daughter	Frank's mistress, 19
Sura Chandra Singh	Maharaja, Chandra Kirti's oldest son 34
Ethel Saint Clair Grimwood	Frank's wife, 23
Lieutenant Walter Simpson	43rd Gurkha Rifles, piano player, 30
Captain Alan Boisragon	Royal Irish Guards, Ethel's step-brother, 30
Lieutenant Berkeley	Residency staff officer, Bengal infantry, 30
Watcher*	Shapeshifting reptilian, ??
William Henry Cossins	Assistant to Chief Commissioner of Assam, 27

1891 London

William T. Stead	Journalist, editor, author, publisher, 41
Jay Dee	Lame vagrant, former soldier, 34
Baboula	Gujarati, personal valet to HPB, 26
Annie Besant	Writer, orator, activist, theosophist, 43
Helena Petrovna Blavatsky	Writer, spiritualist, theosophist, 59
Mister Doughty (top hat)*	Hansom cab driver, 40
Cecil John Rhodes	Industrialist, Cape Town prime minister, 37
Reginald Baliol Brett	Viscount Esher, fixer, Queen's advisor, 38
Mister Doughty (bowler hat)*	Private detective, cab driver's brother, 45
Captain James Dunbar Guthrie	Former artillery officer, secret agent, 34

Chapter 18. The Shots in the Dark

Thirty-three years later, 2:00 a.m., Saturday, 20 September 1890...

Frank

At the musket crack, Frank Saint Clair Grimwood ran. He chanced an over-the-shoulder glance and saw a pack of men in hot pursuit.

Manipuris!

Frank reached a bridge where the pack coalesced into a jumble of arms, legs, and fists. He burst out, untouched and beyond belief, was first over the moat and through the great Western Gate of Kangla. With each pounding step, his lead increased, and he laughed, amazed by his ability to outpace the younger, more athletic competitors.

What am I doing here? What is this race? A footrace with much younger Manipuri men—and I am winning!

Frank enjoyed a good game of polo, riding ponies and playing with competitive zeal. He gave as he took, but knew his limits—a middle-aged English gentleman, no athlete, and in no shape to run so hard. Yet, on he ran, not the least bit winded, without the foggiest idea why. Then he remembered.

Now I place it—the Lamchel.

The Lamchel footrace was one of the great Manipuri traditions—created by the god-king Pakhangba two thousand years earlier. The first man to touch one of the Kangla-sha dragon statues wins a lifetime reprieve from the Lallup, the mandatory service to the maharaja of Manipur.

So what? I am English, not Manipuri. The Lallup means nothing!

The wide-open entrance to the inner citadel reared. He sped forward, burst through the gate, and pressed on toward the polo grounds. A shape entered his peripheral vision and Frank did a double take—the newcomer wore a riding habit.

A woman runner!

"Hullo!" Frank said. "What are you doing here? Ladies are not eligible!"

The hazy face sharpened.

Ethel!

His young wife ran at his side, matching his pace.

"I did not—fancy you a runner!" he shouted between rapid breaths. "In fact—I cannot recall—ever seeing you run!"

Ethel smiled, and he grinned in return.

So young, so pretty!

Seeing her at his side melted Frank's heart. He reached and their hands clasped.

So warm, so reassuring!

"Come, Frank!" Ethel said. "We are nearing the finish!"

Love her sweet, authoritative voice!

Ethel pressed forward—eyes straight ahead, jaw set with a thin smile—pushing harder and faster toward the goal. Their matched strides became leaps—blurred and unnatural, as if gravity had no hold—springing further in front of the pack with each step.

"There!" Frank said, nodding ahead.

The goal approached—the mighty twin dragon statues loomed, heads raised high, jaws open wide, as if laughing at the gods.

Two loud cracks.

"What was that?"

Three cracks followed. The heads of the statues jerked, dropping with each crack, until the stone eyes stared at Frank and Ethel. The jaws opened wider.

"Laughing at me!" Frank said. "They knew all along I would win."

Ethel will know what to do next. She always knows!

Frank turned to ask, but his wife vanished. He glanced behind and the other runners disappeared. Alone and feeling winded, Frank slowed and stopped. A man appeared—an Englishman—standing next to the statues,

"Come on, Frank!" he said, waving. "Hurry!"

"Heath?"

"Finish the race and join me."

"Join you?" Frank looked around, scratching his head, but did not move. "This cannot be happening. Heath—you are dead!"

Frank woke in the dark with a start and sat up, twisting his head side to side, stretching his stiff neck.

What a nightmare! I have not had a good night's sleep in weeks—waking at all hours at the slightest sound.

Loud cracks sounded, and that time it was no dream.

Gunfire! Now what?

Frank stood, reached for a rumpled cloth, pulled on a long silken robe, and tied the sash. With the robe his sole cover, he slipped out of the bedroom, and met the bearer (major-domo) coming down the hall.

The bearer is up—coming to wake me. When does he sleep?

Frank raised forefinger to lips, pointed to his ear, and nodded, letting the bearer know he heard the sounds. The bearer nodded, led the way, and held the front door as Frank stepped onto the verandah.

Must appreciate the situation.

The rain had stopped, and the moon cast a dim light through breaks in the clouds, shimmering on the calm surface of the little lake. Muggy, clingy night air signaled more rain ahead.

A breeze would be nice.

More cracks echoed in the moonlight.

"Shots in the dark." Frank addressed the moon and the night air. "From where?"

"Kangla, sahib," the bearer said, pointing northeast toward the outer wall of the fort. As more cracks echoed, his finger moved south until it aligned with the palace, hidden behind the inner and outer walls.

Sounds traveled unimpeded in the dark quiet—darkness tempered by the light of the moon in its first quarter, and quiet defined by chirping crickets and croaking tree frogs.

"Blast those bloody brat princes!" Frank shouted, clenching fists. "Constant arguing does not satisfy them. Now they have to kill one another."

Tension between the royal brothers reached a boiling point in recent days. Frank shook a fist at the sky.

"If their father could see them now!"

Two Gurkha sepoys ran up the gravel drive from the gate and the leader slowed, seeing Frank.

"Sahib!" the Nepali said. "Gunshots at Kangla!"

"Rouse the guard!" Frank ordered. "Secure the main gate!"

"Yes, sahib!"

"Wait!" Frank shouted, stopping the man before he could run away. "Wake the stable hands. I want a saddled horse and a rider here—by the verandah—straight away."

The short soldier in khaki saluted, shouted orders to his cohort, and scurried toward the stables.

No further shots, but sounds of human activity drifted from Kangla— voices, angry shouts, and a few screams. Frank looked down, realizing he wore a sheer silk robe, barefoot, sticky, and sweating. The house was stirring.

A robe is not proper attire for the British Political Agent to Manipur, at least, not when entertaining guests.

Frank stepped inside and met his khidmutgar (valet) awaiting his order.

"Tea," Frank said, adding, "Please." He would love to have instead said, "Sorry for the commotion. I am so glad you are awake. Will you please put on the tea? So generous of you!"

Simple instructions work best on the natives.

The servant bowed, turned, and proceeded to the kitchen as Frank padded down the hall to his sleeping chamber. He closed the door, fumbled in the dark, and struck a match to light an oil lamp. As the key twisted as far as it would turn, warm yellow light flooded the room. A wide wooden fan hung motionless above the bed, and a limp rope dangled from the fan to a hole in the wall.

Damned punkahwallah—dozing again. I must speak to the bearer later.

The bed was a mess of feather pillows and silk covers. The tangled pile stirred, and a shapely young woman surfaced, blinking and frowning at the sudden brightness. Her long, dark hair was in wild disarray. She gripped the thin sheet, pulled it under her chin, and rose from her pillow, squinting in the yellow light, wearing nothing but sheets.

An attractive mess, but—time to go.

"What is happening?" The woman spoke in Meiteilon, the language of the Meiteis of Manipur.

Frank sighed and replied in the same tongue, "Shots fired at Kangla. Out of bed! Dress yourself!"

"Now?"

"Now! There will be visitors—high-ranking—soon. I would prefer they not find you here in this state. You of all people should understand."

Imprudent of me—allowing her to spend the night—again.

The young woman was not Frank's wife, nor was she a run-of-the-mill, casual bedmate from the bustees. She was the daughter of the venerable Tongol General—national hero and legendary commander of the native militia of Manipur.

Without questioning Frank's tone or command, she tossed aside the sheet and leapt out of the bed, retrieving dress and underclothing from a crumpled pile on the floor.

Frank fished his used underclothes, shirt, and trousers from a nearby chair, tossed his robe aside, and dressed.

No time to wash. I can splash my face after she leaves.

While looking for his shoes, he sneaked a longing glance at tawny skin on a smooth backside.

Once dressed, Frank steered the woman down the hall, visible to several members of the household staff, pulled her out the front door and down the verandah steps. Without a kiss, or a pat, or a word of goodbye, Frank hoisted her onto the back of the waiting horse, behind the Gurkha rider. He shouted instructions to the sepoy and watched the horse gallop up the drive. Gurkha sentries opened the gate and the rider and passenger disappeared toward Kangla.

Blast! Someone will recognize the horse—and the girl.

There were few horses in Manipur and Frank's was recognizable—as was its passenger. Between Frank's impropriety, the household servants, and the nosey locals, Frank's dalliances with the Tongol's daughter had graduated from rumor to common knowledge.

What excuse this time? Too much Yu to drink?

Frank shook his head and shrugged.

Forget that poor excuse. Ethel is certain to learn the truth—from someone.

Frank's wife Ethel was away in Assam, waiting out the monsoons—at least, that was what they told everyone. The monsoon season was ending and the cooler, drier Indian winter would start any day, and whispers spread. "Where is Ethel? Will she return? Has she left Frank? Is it for good this time?"

Ethel's recent letters spoke of wonderful times at the hill station of Shillong—the Scotland of the East. Her stepbrother arrived—a gallant officer, related not by blood, but via her father's second marriage. Then there was the dashing Lieutenant Walter Simpson—Frank and Ethel's mutual friend—who also turned up in Shillong, joining the fun.

By sheer coincidence.

Ethel was attractive and engaging—exceeding expectations for a European woman trapped on the Indian subcontinent.

Here I stand while there she is...

"Amongst the scenery—cool breezes through tall trees, rushing streams, and splashing waterfalls—swooning as Simpson pounds the piano keys, belting out drinking songs; mingling with the haughty subset of humanity trying to pass for English high society."

While I stand here sweating in the humid Manipuri night.

More cracks echoed through the semi-darkness.

"Do you see?" Frank shouted at the quarter moon. "I must make nice to a fat, ugly, worthless maharaja and his bleeding, bloody, spoiled brat prince brothers. Not one of them fit to fill their father's boots. Let them kill each other. Meanwhile, what is Ethel up to—dancing, flirting, and making the other women jealous? No wonder she does not return."

What was it she said she overheard? I remember the look on her face when she told me.

"She said, 'Manipur is a strange place—mysterious and unlucky—where political agents meet unfortunate ends.'"

She changed after that.

Ethel complained of dreams, premonitions, and uneasy feelings.

She asked me to seek a new assignment—a different role or another district—but I refused.

Frank stroked his mustache, remembering taking photographs of Ethel playing tennis. A flowering garden stood near the court.

Missus Johnstone's prize rhododendrons.

Beside the garden sat the tiny graveyard where Frank planted the remains of his unfortunate immediate predecessor.

Heath, Agent Trotter, and Lieutenant Beaver—side by side.

Frank shouted at the graveyard, "Heath, you poor bastard! You pushed me out just as Ethel and I settled in—seniority, you called it. Dysentery—a painful way to go, Queen and Country aside. Too bad. Now—I will thank you to stay the hell out of my dreams!"

No wonder Ethel stays in Shillong...

"She sleeps without a care in the world," Frank muttered. "I wonder if she sleeps alone."

Frank stepped through the door.

Tea first. Sort out the rest later.

Chapter 19. The Supernatural

An hour later…

Frank

Frank winced as pudgy fingers smudged the glass.

"Your work shows improvement," the short man said, "and as always, your wife looks lovely."

The photograph showed Frank's wife Ethel, racket mid-swing, playing tennis on the Residency's court. To Frank's eye, Ethel looked like a ghost—pale and thin, dressed in white—a lightweight, long skirt, a loose-fitting blouse, and a wide-brimmed straw hat. The picture was one of many framed photographs on display in the British Residency. Frank hated seeing his prized works of art handled—but a cavalier attitude toward a picture of Ethel rankled him in particular.

The fat, pockmarked face leered at Frank from beneath a snow-white turban. An overwhelming urge surged…

I want to punch his smirking face.

The face Frank wanted to strike belonged to Sura Chandra Singh—son of the late, legendary Chandra Kirti Singh, maharaja of Manipur. Legends are always difficult to replace, and Sura Chandra could not fill the shoes. Crowned following his father's death, Sura Chandra was far from the most intelligent or best-qualified son, but he was the eldest, so no one debated the matter. Of the eight sons of the former maharaja, Frank respected Sura Chandra the least, because…

He is a bad king.

Frank smiled, ignoring the mention of Ethel, and staying pleasant, shrugged and said, "I enjoy photography."

"It must be an expensive pastime," Sura Chandra said.

"It can be—with delicate equipment and hard-to-get chemicals."

"How was everything transported to Manipur?"

"With great difficulty." Frank kept a nervous eye on the picture. "And at great expense."

Sura Chandra perused the entire wall, studying each photograph, keeping a relaxed grip on the frame. When the maharaja reached the end of the line, he cracked a wry smile and said, "I understand others exist." He sounded like a conspirator revealing he was in on a secret.

Frank frowned. "Others?"

"Other, more interesting photographs—ones not on display."

Frank reddened.

He knows! Who told?

Months earlier, Ethel held a garden party for the Manipuri princesses and the teenage girls played in the Residency's lake. The party got out of hand with the girls jumping in and out of a rowboat, splashing and laughing, and soon their scanty dresses were soaking wet. Frank captured every wild moment on film. Frank fancied himself an artist, and it was his most adventurous and artistic photographic session. He felt no guilt for taking pictures he regarded as art, but he feared putting the images on display. Though he treasured the pictures as his finest work, he suspected they would appeal to the prurient interests of many.

Ethel! She must have told someone. Tikendra Jeet! She is too thick with that one.

Tikendra Jeet, the maharaja's half-brother, better known as the Senapati, or commander of the Manipuri military, in Frank's opinion, worked too hard at making friends with Ethel.

She is around that rascal too much!

"I am glad you feel better," Frank said, voice trembling, close to losing his temper. "But you did not come to my home in the middle of the night, chased by gunfire, to discuss the fine art of photography."

The maharaja only smiled, and Frank studied the faces of the entourage on the other side of the durbar hall.

No sign of concern at my comment. Nor sympathy.

"No," Sura Chandra said, "you are right. We must discuss more salient matters." The maharaja offered the frame to Frank, but then stopped. He raised the photograph, turned the frame around so Frank could see, and pointed to a spot on the picture. "What is this misty shape?"

"Mist? Where?"

"Here," the maharaja said, pointing, "in the lower corner."

Frank took the frame, pulled out his kerchief, and wiped away the fingerprints. He peered at the spot where Sura Chandra had pointed—beyond the tennis court and the garden, at the little cemetery nearby. There, Frank noticed for the first time a misty shape—a faint image like a man, standing and observing from the graveyard.

"Heath," Frank murmured, remembering his dream.

Sura Chandra took the picture back from Frank and held it close to his nose.

"Try to not touch the glass," Frank said. "Please."

"Ah, yes! The shape resembles Mister Heath—your predecessor. An unfortunate passing. Dysentery, as I recall. Painful and so tragic."

Sura Chandra offered Frank the frame. Frank accepted and, with fumbling, hung it in its original place.

"Considering your remark," Sura Chandra said, "I must now ask…"

A chill coursed Frank's spine. "Yes?"

Here it comes—he will ask about sleeping with the Tongol's daughter.

"Mister Grimwood…," Sura Chandra began, and then stopped to study Frank's eyes. "Do you believe in the supernatural?"

Frank jerked, wide-eyed, shocked by the question, but then breathed a sigh of relief.

I must sort out this squabble.

Frank cleared his throat. "I do not." He looked around the room at the monarch's entourage. "Perhaps we should continue our discussion in private."

Sura Chandra motioned and his supporting cast of brothers and advisors moved to leave. An officer leaned close, whispered, and Sura Chandra cleared his throat.

"About my men's weapons…"

I should have expected this.

"I gave the order," Frank said.

Hundreds of Manipuri sepoys had followed the maharaja through his gates. Frank's Gurkhas collected every dao knife, rifle, and pistol for safekeeping. Frank looked out the window and saw a mob milling in the dim light.

"The Gurkhas will return the weapons when you leave."

"But my guards worry for my safety, and…"

"You are in a safe place," Frank interjected. He tried to sound calming, reassuring. "Your men act jumpy, not knowing whom to trust. They may shoot each other."

Sura Chandra nodded, motioned his counselors to leave, and took a seat as Frank closed the door. Frank poured and offered tea, but Sura Chandra waved off the cup.

"My caste forbids eating or drinking in the house…"

"Of an Englishman?" Frank said, laughing. "Now? Here? In private, behind closed doors. After all that has happened tonight?"

Sura Chandra frowned, but Frank continued to hold out the cup. The maharaja sighed in resignation, accepted the tea, and after another moment of hesitation, took a sip.

"How safe are we?" Sura Chandra asked, setting down the cup.

"The bullets flew high over your head. If your brothers wanted you dead, they would have shot someone long before any of you made it past my gate."

Sura Chandra slumped and maintained a pained expression for a long minute. As if resurfacing from a deep pool, he straightened. "Where were we?" he said. "You were preparing to explain why you believe in ghosts."

Frank let out a guffaw. "Not at all! I am sorry I said that! Heath popped into my dream last night and was on my mind. Defects in the development process caused the mist. It is all a coincidence."

"In my experience," Sura Chandra replied, "coincidences do not exist. May I share a story? Or, I should say, a story within a story?"

Frank yawned and looked at his pocket watch, but Sura Chandra charged ahead.

"Ten years ago, Chief Commissioner Bayley awarded my father a great honor—Knight Commander of the Star of India. Perhaps you knew this."

Frank nodded. "I heard."

"I was at the ceremony. My father wore a blue and white cape. The commissioner pinned a gold star medallion on his uniform. No son was ever more proud of his father."

"I can imagine."

"The medallion read, 'Heaven's light our guide.'"

Frank rubbed his eyes. "Hm."

"Later that night, at the celebration, Young Maiba—do you know Young Maiba?"

Frank jerked. "Huh?" He rubbed an eye. "Oh, you mean the priest—the chap in the white robe at the temple with the golden dome."

"The same."

"Why call him a young maiba? He is not young. He looks middle-aged. Is there an older maiba somewhere?"

"The old maiba died," Sura Chandra said. "Young Maiba was chela to Old Maiba so long the name stuck."

"Ah!" Frank suppressed a laugh. "I see." He glanced at his watch. "Continue."

"Young Maiba drank too much Yu that night. Many did. He accosted me at the celebration and told me a story. He accused my father of treason."

"Treason!"

"Well, not treason, perhaps. He said Britain had knighted my father for betraying India and staying loyal to the East India Company during the Great Rebellion."

"That was harsh," Frank said. "Several states did the same—Mysore, Hyderabad, the Sikhs of the Punjab, and others. Manipur was not alone."

"Young Maiba said my father tricked his cousins into joining the rebellion. The Tongol convinced them if they led the way my father would join, but he betrayed them to the British—all killed or imprisoned. The Tongol, as part of the conspiracy, escaped and survived. He hid for a few years, changed his name, and reappeared stronger than ever. Soon he was back at my father's side."

"I did not know this," Frank said. "Quite an accusation. How does Young Maiba know this?"

"As the rebellion was breaking out, a European woman—a fortune-teller—visited Manipur. My father invited her to dinner at the durbar hall. Young Maiba observed the dinner—as he was chela to the old maiba. He said the fortune-teller made a prophecy. She predicted the rebellion, my father's knighthood, the trouble with the cousin princes, the Tongol—everything. It all came true as she predicted."

"Interesting." Frank scratched his head. "But what is the point?"

"There are three points," Sura Chandra said. "First, I learned my father sided with Britain in the Rebellion because of a warning, and also because he knew it was best for Manipur, his country."

"And?"

"Second, whose absence would you call conspicuous?"

"Ah," Frank said. He squirmed and suppressed a cough. "The Tongol General."

Now it comes. Here is where he tells me he knows of my affair with the old man's daughter.

"Correct—the old Tongol. He, who risked his life for his maharaja, my father, all those years ago, is missing when I, his current maharaja, have the greatest need. The Tongol has passed judgment upon my performance. The Tongol has chosen, as did my father, to betray one part of the family and support the other. Most likely, as before, he did what he did because he felt it was best for Manipur."

Frank breathed a sigh of relief. "Perhaps." He glanced at his watch. "Describe the attack again—slower this time."

"I was asleep," Sura Chandra began. "Someone climbed the palace walls and fired shots through my windows. Unlike you, I believe the shots were to kill, not frighten."

"Did you raise the guard?"

"No," the maharaja said. "I do not trust the guard. Not anymore."

"Do you believe the Tongol General ordered the attack?"

"My brothers Zillah and Angao Sena led the charge—there were witnesses to that—and soldiers fired the shots. That means the guard is against me. My brother—Tikendra Jeet, the Senapati—commands the palace guard. Only Tikendra Jeet could have ordered the attack."

Brother against brother—a house divided against itself...

"And—the Tongol?" Frank asked, reluctant to speak the name.

"It appears the general has chosen sides—with Tikendra Jeet."

"Why would Tikendra Jeet want you dead?"

"He would become Yuvraj—one step closer to the crown."

"What of your brother Kula Chandra, the current Yuvraj?"

"He will deny any involvement," Sura Chandra said. "He is in Bishnupur—by coincidence—at the Vishnu temple, far from any struggle."

"By coincidence? I thought you..."

"Correct—I do not believe in coincidences." Sura Chandra grabbed Frank's arm. "The half-brothers conspire—they want me dead!" His voice quivered. "You must understand! It is not my fault—the girl—Maipakbi."

Sura Chandra described the bitter rivalry between Pucca Senna and Tikendra Jeet. The brothers vied for the affections of Maipakbi, a beautiful young woman, a seductive dancer, and the daughter of a rich goldsmith. Tikendra Jeet encouraged younger brother Zillah to impugn Pucca Senna during council meetings. Sura Chandra banned Zillah from further durbar council meeting, over the strong objections of Tikendra Jeet.

"Maipakbi is a flirt," Sura Chandra said. "Never trust women! They are behind many civil wars and the fall of kingdoms."

I cannot believe my ears!

"Forgive my saying so," Frank interjected, "but as the maharaja, you should not take sides in these squabbles between your brothers. You have seven brothers total, and observers say you always side with your full-blood-brothers—never with your half-brothers. Is it necessary to side with Pucca Senna? He is a trouble-maker."

"Perhaps I make mistakes," Sura Chandra said. "I am not the man my father was—I recognize that—but for that, do I deserve to die?"

"Zillah and Angao are your brothers," Frank insisted. "They only wanted to frighten you. Allow me to negotiate. I will arrange a meeting— we can find a peaceful resolution."

"What peace can there be now?" Sura Chandra turned away. "They have made their intension clear."

"You must decide on a course of action."

"I *have* decided." The maharaja faced Frank. "I will leave Manipur."

"Leave? Why run away?"

"Run? I am no coward!" Sura Chandra cried. "It is for the best."

Frank grabbed Sura Chandra by the shoulders. "You cannot leave now. You endanger the Ghuddi (throne) if you do so. The country will be in turmoil—ripe for civil war."

"Despite that, I will leave." The maharaja stood, looked up, and pressed hands together. "Many Manipuris strayed from Lord Krishna. My father allowed it—he permitted the old religion to return. This corruption should have ended long ago. Now I must leave while I can."

"Where will you go?" Frank asked. "What will you do?"

"I will take a pilgrimage to sacred Matura and Vrindavan, become a fakir, and worship Lord Krishna. Any that wish may follow, and I will pray the gods lift the shadow."

"Do you intend to abdicate?"

"What does this word mean—abdicate?"

He does not know.

Frank spoke slower. "Do you intend to proclaim, in writing, you are no longer maharaja, and henceforth surrender all claim to the throne of Manipur?"

"I have not heard of this practice." Sura Chandra sat with a plop and his face went blank. "Why would I do that?"

"You cannot just walk away," Frank explained, trying to stay calm. "You cannot leave, become a fakir, and expect to keep the throne. Without an official transition of power, there would be riots, civil war."

"I cannot—abdicate."

"In that case," Frank said, "if you want to keep your throne, you must fight for it. Or, better, negotiate."

"Fight? A civil war?" Sura Chandra shook his head. "Against my brothers? With what? Tikendra Jeet commands the army. The Tongol General is on his side. Will Britain send troops to fight a war against Manipur to restore my throne?"

"Not my place to say, but doubtful."

"Yet Britain claims to be an ally to Manipur."

Frank rubbed his eyes and looked at his pocket watch.

I have had enough.

"Think on this," Frank said. "I will send in your counselors. Meanwhile, I will telegraph my headquarters for further instructions."

Frank opened the door and left the durbar hall.

Wait!

He remembered something, halted, and reentered the room.

"What is the third?" Frank asked.

"Third?"

"You said there were three points to your story…"

"Ah," Sura Chandra said. "The final point, which I learned myself, and I would caution you to learn now, is this—do not discount the supernatural. Many powers beyond our understanding exist in this world. When they speak, you must listen. Ignore these supernatural messages at your peril."

Chapter 20. The Hill Station of Shillong

Four days later, Tuesday afternoon, 24 September 1890...

Ethel

Lieutenant Walter Henry Simpson pounded the keys, tossed back his head, and sang at the top of his lungs. Captain Alan Maxwell Boisragon and fellow off-duty British officers crowded the piano and joined in, belting out the chorus.

```
             "Macdermott's War Song" (1877)
                    By G.W. Hunt

                       Chorus

   We do not want to fight, but by jingo, if we do…
   We have got the ships; we have got the men, and got
                     the money too!
     We have fought the Bear before—and while we are
                      Britons true,
        The Russians shall not have Constantinople…
```

Ethel Saint Clair Grimwood stood unseen, a few steps behind the rowdy group, gripping a piece of paper. Her wandering eyes scanned the social hall. She avoided the stares of the officers, because if she made eye contact, the officer would avert his gaze. Women mingled or chatted, joining the men in a drink or watching officers play billiards. As she met female faces, each woman nodded and returned a half-hearted smile.

It is no fantasy—I annoy the hell out of these women.

Ethel had grown accustomed to the reaction and the attention during her time in India, in particular when visiting Shillong. In fact, she thrived on it. She had no misconceptions—she was not beautiful in the classical sense, but was certain she was, in a dark, sultry way, at least attractive. She maintained a pleasant, outgoing personality, but one bordering on flirtatious. In India, where young, attractive European women were rare, she stood out, and she took advantage while she could.

The song faded as Walter Simpson tinkled the high keys with a flourish. Amidst the applause, Ethel cleared her throat. Walter cocked his ear, turned, and laughed.

He has enjoyed a pint too many.

"Attention, gentlemen!" he said, louder than necessary. "On your best behavior! Look, Alan, your sister, the lovely Missus Grimwood, joined us for song and drink."

"You officers are so…" Ethel winced, blushing, struggling for the right word, then blurted, "Rowdy!"

"And you, my dear," Walter said, "are always welcome amongst the rowdy." Walter stood and hoisted his mug. "Chaps! A toast to Missus Grimwood!"

The officers at the piano and by the billiard tables raised their mugs. Ethel tried not noticing the narrowing eyes of the women.

"Hear! Hear! Missus Grimwood!"

"No mug!" Walter said, feigning outrage. "Allow me to procure a draught."

Ethel bit her lip and shook her head.

"Not thirsty?" Walter shrugged. "Then join us in another round of Macdermott's."

"No thank you, gentlemen." Ethel shook her head. "Must you always sing war-mongering songs? Are you so eager to see war?"

"It is our profession," Walter said. "We fight whenever the Queen asks, but we cannot fight a war without a good fighting song, and we must keep our voices in practice." He lifted his mug once more. "Gentlemen, another toast—to the Queen's good health!"

A thicket of mugs hoisted and clanked. Ale sloshed as inebriated officers laughed and shouted in honor of Victoria. The entire hall, including the ladies, returned the cheer.

"God save the Queen!"

Simpson shouted to his mates, "Since she does not like war songs, boys, give her a round of McCloskey!"

"Throw Him Down, McCloskey" (1890)
By S.W. Kelley

Chorus

Throw him down, McCloskey, was to be the battle cry!
Throw him down, McCloskey; you can lick him if you
try;
And future generations, with wonder and delight,
Will read on history's pages of the great McCloskey
fight!

"Excuse me," Ethel said, but the singing continued. "I hate to interrupt…" The piano clanged, and the voices rang. She shouted, "Walter!"

With a final bang of the keys, Walter Simpson stopped, turned, slapped palms on knees. He cocked a smile as if to say Ethel had the floor.

"Thank you," Ethel said. "I hate that song, too! I find it disgusting." She pinched the paper until her fingers trembled. "Before you go any further, I brought news of Frank."

Walter and Alan Boisragon exchanged glances.

"Frank?" Walter said. "What news?"

"May I have a word with you two somewhere private?"

Walter nodded toward the French doors. "The patio?"

Alan led and held the door. Ethel sensed a roomful of stares following every move as she stepped outside onto the stone pavers.

Shillong loves a scandal. Everyone is dying to learn what I will say.

The bright afternoon sun shone on the lawn below but the air was cooler and pleasant on the shaded patio. Chirping birds flitted limb to limb in the nearby tall pine trees. From somewhere higher in the hills came distant sounds of water crashing onto rocks.

Walter and Alan took spots leaning against the stone balustrade, arms folded, waiting for Ethel to speak. She stood before them, staring at the paper.

"Is it a letter?" Walter said.

"No—a telegram, from Frank. Chief Commissioner Quinton received it today and gave me a transcript."

"Kind of Quinton," Alan said. "What does Frank say?"

Ethel cleared her throat and read from the transcript.

```
Maharaja has formally abdicated in favor of Yuvraj and
goes to Vrindavan as fakir. This is his wish.

I told him I could guarantee his personal safety at
Residency, but refused to allow him to collect armed
men in Residency grounds. Also told him if once
abdicated, he could not return to Manipur or Cachar;
but he persists in his resolution.

Senapati agrees to supply Maharaja with all necessaries
of journey. This seems to be best solution.

Yuvraj has held aloof from both sides, and could
therefore be acknowledged Maharaja if you approve.

Maharaja leaves to-night. Am sending escort—41 rifles.
Also insisting on Pucca Senna going, too. He is primary
cause of all the trouble.
```

Ethel folded the sheet. "This will be in the newspaper soon. Then letters will follow—from Frank, and—from the Senapati."

"Senapati?" Walter said. "Tikendra Jeet?" He snorted. "Frank blames Pucca Senna, but it sounds more like Tikendra Jeet mischief. You are friends, I understand, but should steer clear of that one."

"You are worried," Alan said to Ethel.

"I am. I detest Manipur—ever since Heath died, and Frank had to return, I felt a dread. A few nights ago I had another dream…" She stopped.

"Tell us!"

"It was frightening. I was running alongside Frank, toward those dragon statues in front of the palace. Then Frank disappeared, and I was walking toward that temple—the one with the gold dome. That priest was there—the one they call Young Maiba—intent on hurting someone."

"Young Maiba?" Walter said, chuckling. "He is harmless!"

"You both think it sounds silly!"

"I do not," Alan said. "What will you do?"

Ethel bit her lip and stared at the forest. A cooler breeze blew her hair into a subtle disarray. She crossed her arms and shivered.

Walter unbuttoned his jacket. "Are you chilled?"

"No." Ethel raised her hand. "I am fine, but torn. I should be with Frank, but I have lingered here in Shillong, finding silly excuses not to return."

"Silly excuses!" Walter held a hand over his heart. "All this time, I thought you enjoyed our company."

Ethel managed a weak smile. "I do. You two must learn first—I am returning to Manipur. Frank needs me and my place is with him. I can help. Prince Tikendra Jeet and I are friends and..."

Walter cocked his head. "And?"

"And—I am certain I can help."

"When do you leave?" Alan asked.

"As soon as I can manage. It will be a difficult, two-week journey. It will take Moonia and me time to prepare."

"Moonia?" Walter's voice dripped with scorn. "That old witch still following you?"

Ethel gasped. "Walter! How rude! She is a loyal servant."

"She seldom leaves your side—always muttering that Vedic Hindu mumbo jumbo." Walter snapped his fingers. "She must be the source of those bad dreams!"

"Oh, stop!"

"Now, Ethel," Alan said. "If Manipur frightens you, do not go. Stay here until matters subside. Frank can manage on his own."

Walter cracked an impish smile. "Perhaps I can help."

Ethel raised eyebrows, then frowned and shook her head.

Ever joking, making light. When is he ever serious?

Walter smiled. "You think I am joking, but I am serious for once. I should say nothing, but I drank too much and ask your discretion."

"What is it?" Alan said.

"I met with General Collett this morning," Walter said. "I am going to Manipur."

Ethel threw up her hands. "You knew! The entire time—yet you said nothing. You let me go on, talking of nightmares and..."

"Discretion, my dear," Walter said. "Frank sent Berkeley and most of his Gurkhas with Sura Chandra. I leave for Golaghat tomorrow. I will gather a hundred fresh rifles, send half down to replace Berkley's troop, then follow later with the other half to shore up Frank's defense."

Ethel clapped hands to face and beamed.

"I will also inspect the Manipuri weapon stores," Walter added. "I will need to be inconspicuous."

"Wonderful!" Ethel said. "The Manipuris store arms and ammunition in the arsenal—I can draw a map."

"I can find my way around Kangla, but need the Senapati to allow me inside the arsenal."

"Here is an idea," she said. "The Senapati is always showing off, firing his mountain guns, and blowing up trees and such. The guns are in the arsenal. He must open it, and…"

"Brilliant!" Walter said. "Sounds like fun."

"One moment," Alan said. "This does not seem prudent. You should not entice Ethel to involve herself in your spy mission. As her brother, I protest…"

"Stepbrother." Walter gave Ethel a sly wink. "You have not a single drop of blood in common." Ethel blushed.

Alan glared. "Regardless, it sounds dangerous and I do not think…"

"Nonsense!" Walter laughed. "No need for drama. Manipur is not dangerous. Tell Ethel about danger."

Alan shook his head and Ethel furrowed her brow.

Walter raised an eyebrow. "Has Alan not told you of Abu Klea?"

"You mean…," she said, "the Nile Expedition?"

"Yes, yes! The bloody Nile Expedition! Tell her, Alan!"

Boisragon shook his head. "I am not yet drunk."

"I am, so I will." Walter addressed Ethel. "You know Alan was in the Sudan with the Nile Expedition in '85. There they were, at Abu Klea, one thousand of the Queen's finest, with the sun beating down without mercy…"

"Who is being dramatic now?" Alan's voice quivered. "Why tell her this?"

Ethel raised a hand. "It is all right, Alan. I want to hear."

"Right," Walter said. "Surrounded by thousands of Dervishes and Fuzzy-Wuzzies, outnumbered—what, Alan? Ten-to-one? Twenty-to-one?"

Alan shrugged. "I do not recall exact numbers. Beyond count. Greater than ten-to-one."

"Whatever the count," Walter continued, "outnumbered by a multitude. Alan and his comrades formed a square. Navy chaps had a Gardner, but the bloody thing jammed. Dervishes mowed the poor blokes down, and the devils breached the line! Fuzzy-Wuzzies broke a British Square! Picture it—hooded sheiks on horseback, leaping over the line, planting black colors, waving wicked scimitars—complete chaos. Right, Alan?"

"Alan," Ethel said, eyes wide, "you mentioned little of Africa or the Nile Expedition. You are fortunate to have survived. Many must not have."

"A lot of the enemy killed—hundreds," Alan replied. "Seventy-five on our side."

"And heroism," Ethel said. "Many earned the Victoria Cross?"

Alan wrinkled his brow. "One—now you mention it."

"That man must have done something incredible!"

"It was—queer." Alan scratched his head. "An artillery officer—an acquaintance, Guthrie was his name—fumbled with his screw gun and a Dervish stuck a spear in his leg. A gunner named Smith jumped in, grabbed the handspike, and swung it like a mad man, knocking Dervishes willy-nilly, like Samson with the ass's jawbone against the Philistines. I caught a glimpse while otherwise occupied. It was quite a sight. Smith earned his VC that day."

"So—this Smith fellow, saved Guthrie's life. How grateful Guthrie must have been!"

"Oh, Guthrie died a few days later. I doubt he ever knew what happened."

"Guthrie died?" Ethel cocked her head, confused. "A VC awarded for saving Guthrie's life, but Guthrie died anyway?"

"Right," Alan said. "Smith is a good chap, nothing against him, but it seemed strange his was the sole VC given. I saw many heroic acts."

"At least the mission was a success," Ethel said.

Alan snorted. "It was an abject failure! We were too late—Khartoum fell, Gordon died. The Mahdi won—killing or enslaving every starving man, woman, and child. We sailed back down the Nile, tails between our legs. Politicians only know how to dither."

An uncomfortable silence ensued. Walter cleared his throat. "Ah hem, yes. This conversation took a turn I did not expect. The point is I am certain nothing at all like Abu Klea is in store for us in Manipur."

Ethel noticed a row of noses pressed against windows of the officer's social hall. Walter and Alan followed her gaze, and the faces disappeared.

Prying eyes—always spying, looking for scandal.

"Gentlemen," Ethel said, "let us go back. It appears Walter and I will join Frank in Manipur."

Alan frowned as Simpson signaled thumbs-up, beaming.

"And," Ethel continued, smiling, "I will have that drink now!"

Chapter 21. The Temple of Kancha Kanti

Nine days later, Thursday evening, 2 October 1890...

Sura Chandra

The ruins appeared without warning. The toppled stone structure stood on the north side of the road, catching the final rays of a blood-soaked sun. Farther west, thatch-roofed mud huts loomed and yellow pariah dogs roamed, marking the outskirts of a rundown bustee. Lieutenant Berkeley drew his horse to a halt, raised a hand, and pointed at the ruins.

"There is our landmark!" the officer said. "We are in time. The sun will be down soon. This is where we make camp."

Berkeley dismounted and led his horse off the dirt road. Twenty pony riders followed onto a rocky field. Next came forty hikers wearing black turbans and bearing supplies. Forty Gurkha riflemen, dressed in khaki uniforms and round caps, marched at the rear.

Berkeley crossed the field and stopped at a grassy clearing atop a cliff overlooking a broad, curving river valley. He handed the reins to a Gurkha and turned to survey the area.

"Here," Berkeley said. "This is the place."

The men in turbans and the Gurkha soldiers spread out, dropped packs, and unrolled tents. A sturdy brown pony walked up near side to Berkeley and a swarthy-faced man wearing a white turban slid off and handed his reins to a servant.

Berkeley greeted the plump man. "Welcome to Cachar!"

Sura Chandra Singh, the former maharaja of Manipur, nodded and returned the smile.

Berkeley pointed west. "The road improves from this point. With an early start tomorrow, we can cover the remaining seven miles to Silchar. We should arrive at the district headquarters by late morning."

"Excellent, Lieutenant!" Sura Chandra said. "Silchar—I look forward to meeting Chief Commissioner Quinton at last."

"I am certain he looks forward to seeing you, too!"

Sura Chandra looked around, hands on hips. "What place is this where we camp?"

Berkeley pointed south. "That is the Barak River. We are on the outskirts of the tea gardens of Lakhipur. Sometimes troops muster here, in this field, before proceeding uphill." He pointed the way they had come—the road to Manipur. "Tonight, we will have the site to ourselves."

Sura Chandra nodded while rubbing his hands and squinting at the red sun in the pink-and-dark-blue sky.

"Winter is coming." Berkeley said.

"Lord Indra willing," Sura Chandra replied, nodding, "we will have no rain, and Lord Agni willing, our bright fires will burn all night."

"The jungle is behind us," Berkeley said. "We can enjoy the campfire without worry of tigers or gibbons."

Berkeley excused himself and left to inspect the assembly of the camp. Sura Chandra looked back at the road to Manipur. The narrow dirt path wound up the hill, through the brush, and disappeared into a tropical evergreen forest.

It has been a hard nine days.

Eight days earlier Sura Chandra departed the British Residency in Manipur. He claimed to be embarking on his new career as a fakir, making a pilgrimage to sacred Vrindavan on the Ganges. The new, so-called fakir took along three brothers—Pucca, Samu, and Gopal. He also brought trusted aides and a host of loyal servants.

Not the trappings of a poor ascetic surviving on alms.

Frank Grimwood assigned Lieutenant Berkeley and forty Gurkhas for his protection. Grimwood claimed headhunters from the Lushai Hills were making trouble along the border.

The escort's true purpose was to make sure I do not return.

The party slogged west on the rough road from Kangla, covering over one hundred miles. They trekked past fields, through jungles, over mile-high hills, and across rivers and raging streams. On rainy nights, they huddled, sweating in tents. On clear nights, insects swarmed, biting in the moonlight; invisible tigers growled in the dark forest; and singing hoolocks hid in the trees, laughing at their campfires.

On the eighth day—Sura Chandra's yesterday—the party reached the border of Assam. They crossed the Jihiri River and camped near a Thana (lookout post) where Gurkhas kept watch for raiding headhunters from the Lushai hills. A chattering swarm of naked Kuki and Naga tribesmen surrounded them, seeking work as coolies.

They scattered when Berkeley fired shots in the air.

During the nine-day journey, Sura Chandra had ample time for reflecting upon his life, his short career as a maharaja, and his supposed new avocation as a fakir. He replayed the events—his fall from power—in his mind. Sura Chandra concluded his half-brother Tikendra Jeet masterminded the coup that stole his throne, and Frank Grimwood, the British political agent to Manipur, had forced his abdication.

My brothers betrayed me, but Grimwood legitimatized their theft of my throne. When I meet with Quinton, I will name the primary villains— Tikendra Jeet and Grimwood—and I will demand Britain lend aid to Manipur, its true friend and ally. Quinton must punish the villains and support my right to the throne.

Berkeley cupped hands to mouth. "Dinner!"

Sura Chandra turned to the setting sun. As he strolled to the camp, the nearby stone ruin caught his eye. During the meal, his interest piqued, Sura Chandra's eyes stole to the dark silhouette of the toppled structure. The meal wore past the last glimmer and, as darkness enveloped the camp, the ruin faded into black under the stars. After dinner, Sura Chandra and his brothers sat close to the campfire and Berkeley lit his pipe.

Sura Chandra pointed. "The ruin over there. What is it?"

Berkeley glanced, puffed his pipe, and shrugged. "After so many trips, I pay scant attention—other than as a landmark. The locals call it Kancha Kanti Mandir (temple). Why do you ask?"

"No reason." Sura Chandra shrugged back. "It caught my eye. I became curious."

"Not much to see," Berkeley said. He took a long, thoughtful draw on his pipe. "Now considering, I should have picked a different spot. Somewhere not as close. It is a morbid place."

"Why do you say morbid?" Sura Chandra asked.

"Legends say it was a temple to Kali—the evil, blood-thirsty Hindu goddess of death and destruction."

"Kali is not evil!" Sura Chandra said, raising his voice. "That is a British misconception—a Christian lie. Kali is Devi, Goddess, and Mother of the Universe."

"Blimey, Man!" Berkeley said. "Human sacrifices took place there! The murderous Thuggee cult worshiped Kali. Children of Kali, they called themselves. Until the East India Company wiped them out. Before my time, but I wager it was a Thuggee temple destroyed in battle."

"Bah!" Sura Chandra spat. "The West knows nothing!" He turned and motioned to a servant who delivered an unlit torch. Sura Chandra thrust the long brand into the fire, stood, and held the flame aloft. "I will look at this temple of Kali, Goddess of Time, Destroyer of Evil."

"I would steer clear, Mate!" Berkeley said. "But if you must go, I will send sepoys along for safety sake."

"I go alone!" Sura Chandra asserted. "I need no ayahs (nursemaids)."

"At least," Berkeley insisted, "take my Enfield for good luck." He handed Sura Chandra his handgun.

Sura Chandra accepted the weapon, hefted the revolver in each palm, and then stuffed the barrel into his sash, beneath an ample stomach. The servant offered a dao knife, but Sura Chandra waved it away, and strode from the campsite.

Berkeley called after, "If we hear a shot, someone will come running. I promise!" He chuckled as he struck a match and relit his pipe. "Scream if you see a ghost!"

Sura Chandra walked north toward the temple, ignoring echoing laugher from his three brothers. The campfire light dwindled. He took care crossing the rocky field until he reached the road, surrounded by darkness.

Sura Chandra raised the torch and illuminated the stone ruin. Four barren walls and a collapsed roof, open to the stars, comprised the temple.

Nothing ornate.

Sura Chandra halted before the door, knees shaking and palms sweating. A desperate dialogue played in his head.

Why are you doing this?

To prove I am no coward.

To whom?

Berkeley, to my three brothers, and above all—myself.

How does entering this temple prove this?

It is a start, at least.

Sura Chandra's clammy hand dug under his gut and gripped the handle of the pistol. He raised the torch, trembling, and with a pounding heart, stepped through the open door.

Flickers illuminated a stone idol, toppled to one side—a tall figure, female but inhuman—chipped in places but otherwise intact. Sura Chandra had expected Kali to have eight arms, but counted four. One hand held a scimitar, one a mace, and the other two cradled a human male's severed head. The goddess's insulting tongue stabbed forth from a grimacing mouth.

So far so good.

He expected to find angry eyes beneath wild hair. Instead, a warrior's helmet crowned a serene face.

"It is not Kali," rumbled a deep voice from a dark corner.

Sura Chandra spun. "Who is there? Step forward. Show yourself!"

"But I am sitting!"

Sura Chandra thrust the torch, revealing a man in lotus position, back against the corner. A tall turban topped a long bearded face. Cold eyes glowed yellow in the firelight.

"Stand!" Sura Chandra commanded, voice quivering. He waved the pistol. "Stand, I say!"

The man stood up—higher and higher. A towering, rail-thin figure— nine feet tall, at least—dressed in a long, jet-black sherwani, loomed over the former maharaja. Sura Chandra looked up, wide-eyed and gasping.

The bearded face spoke from on high. "She is Kancha Kanti—a more temperate goddess, blending Durga and Kali, but followers deemed her worthy of human sacrifices."

Sura Chandra stood speechless and shaking.

"Kindly remove your hand from your weapon," the giant said.

Sura Chandra eased his grip and returned the pistol to his sash. His cold fingers trembled and then his hand dropped to his side.

"Thank you," the tall man said.

Sura Chandra managed a shrill warble of a whisper. "Who are you? What are you?"

The tall man ignored the questions. "Is this the way a fakir dresses these days, Maharaja?"

"What do you mean? How do you know who I am?"

"I saw that little farce between you and your brothers—your abdication ceremony. Nine days ago, was it not?"

"How…?" Sura Chandra gasped.

"Handing over the keys, the sword of the state—to Tikendra Jeet."

Sura Chandra stuttered. "I—I…"

"You promised not to return." The tall man chuckled. "Your brothers—half-brothers I should say—are in the palace now, drunk on Yu, laughing. Laughing at you."

"You cannot know…"

"And Grimwood," the giant said, "you think you hate him, but at least he tried to get Tikendra Jeet to let you keep your throne."

Sura Chandra clenched his eyelids, but when reopened, the giant remained. "Who are you?" Sura Chandra struggled to keep his voice calm. "How can you know these things?"

"I like to watch."

"Are you—a Rakshasa?"

The giant chuckled in a deep baritone. "Consider me a teacher, a counselor. I can help with consequential decisions. Life is full of decisions, every minute. Most are inconsequential, mattering not which path one takes, but other choices can change the course of history. Tomorrow you will face such a choice. You can continue on your announced path, go to Vrindavan, and learn to live as a fakir—as a beggar—without the comforts of a maharaja…"

The giant paused.

"Or?" Sura Chandra said.

"Instead, you can do something else."

"What?"

"You will know when the time comes. I will be interested to see the choice you make. One last thing—I suggest looking under that stone." The giant extended a long arm and bony finger. "There—past the idol."

Sura Chandra turned and followed the gesture. In the torchlight, he perceived a stone block.

Could have cracked from the base when the idol toppled.

He turned back. "What is it?" The giant had vanished.

Sura Chandra hurried to the door, torch in hand. Nothing but darkness. He returned and knelt, setting aside the torch. With all his might, he strained, lifted, and turned the block on its side. There on the dusty stone floor lay an object—flat, shiny, and rectangular.

It appears to be an envelope.

Trembling fingers reached and touched the waxy coating.

A few minutes later, Sura Chandra was back at the campfire, flaming torch in hand.

"Hullo!" Berkeley called. "Back so soon? You make a ghostly figure in the darkness."

Sura Chandra stepped into the circle and drew close to the fire. He handed the torch to the servant, and the pistol, butt-first, to the lieutenant. He reclaimed his seat but remained silent.

"Satisfied?" Berkeley puffed his pipe. "Anything mysterious to report?"

Sura Chandra reached inside his tunic, found the object, and pinched the waxy coating.

It is real—not a dream.

"No," he muttered, shaking his head. "Nothing of interest."

Chapter 22. The Decision at Silchar

The next day, Friday morning, 3 October 1890...

Sura Chandra

At first daylight, following a brisk breakfast of tan (flatbread, rice, and lentils) and changaang (sweetened black tea) Sura Chandra sat alone and read the letter. The wax-coated envelope lay at his feet, sliced open. Thin, spidery Sanskrit script covered the top half of the sheet. The curious and poetic phrases filled Sura Chandra's heart with cold fear mixed with nervous pride. The mysterious author left no signature, but Sura Chandra knew without question that the author intended the message for him.

Is this message serious?
Remember what you said to Grimwood.
Yes, I told him one ignores supernatural messages at one's peril.
Therefore, you must...

"A letter?" a cheery voice said. It was Sura Chandra's brother, Samu, looking over his shoulder. "From whom?"

Sura Chandra jerked and refolded the letter. He picked the slick envelope up from the ground, slid the sheet back into its sheath, and restored the package to its hiding place in his tunic.

"I prefer not to discuss it!" He glanced around and stood. "I see we are breaking camp. We are departing."

The party struck camp, packed, and lined up, awaiting Berkeley's order. Berkeley mounted and waved the column forward. Pony riders and marchers followed, and the party abandoned the rocky field for the hardened dirt and dust of the Silchar-Manipur road.

As they headed west, Sura Chandra stole rear glances until the stone ruin of Kancha Kanti Mandir was no longer in sight. The party marched without incident along the north side of the Barak River, past the bustees and tea gardens of Lakhipur. After a few miles, the river swept south in a wide lazy curve, but the road continued west. The travelers rendezvoused with the river on its northward route at the ferry crossing to Badrighat. Once across, the road veered north and the outskirts of Silchar came into sight.

Human activity increased, first in a trickle, then a torrent. Palanquins, gharry cabs, and bullock carts clogged the road. Chickens, dogs, and cattle wandered the roadside, along with women in saris carrying baskets and children playing kho-kho (tag).

What is that horrible wailing? Are those bagpipes?

A company of Scotts in kilts marched ahead—the King's Own Borderers, returned from punitive action in the Lushai Hills. Elephants followed, lumbering, bearing mountain guns, flanked by lines of marching Gurkhas.

Berkeley led his party past a polo field. Sura Chandra stood in the stirrups, taking noticeable interest in the dapper English riders on trotting ponies. Berkeley pulled his reins, drew back beside the former maharaja, and pointed at the grassy field.

"British soldiers founded the first polo club outside Manipur here," Berkeley said, "a few years before the rebellion."

"Hum," Sura Chandra grunted, with a hint of surprise mixed with feigned disinterest. When Berkeley rode ahead, Sura Chandra peered closer at the riders with a jealous eye.

Should I feel complimented that Britain appropriated Manipur's national pastime?

Berkeley led on and the party reached the rocky riverfront where docked steamships awaited bales of tea stacked for shipment. At the nearby markets, bustling with traders and the din of open commerce, Berkeley dismissed his Gurkhas, sending them marching to the nearby camp of the Bengal Infantry.

"Are you abandoning us now?" Sura Chandra asked.

"Not at all!" Berkeley said, laughing. "Come, follow me."

Berkeley led on, and soon the remaining party reached the Cachar District Headquarters. Berkeley dismounted and hitched his horse.

"Excuse me," he told Sura Chandra. "I will return in a moment with the chief commissioner."

The pony riders remained mounted. Berkeley jogged up the steps, sauntered past the kilted Scottish guards standing at attention at either side of the door, and disappeared inside the building. Ten minutes passed, then fifteen. The morning was passing and the hot sun was high overhead. Sura Chandra remained calm but his brothers grew restless.

"Impolite!" Pucca said. Gopal and Samu nodded agreement. "They should not keep you waiting on the doorstep!"

"I trust Berkeley will return soon," Sura Chandra said. After another minute, he wiped his brow.

"Where is Quinton," Samu said. "This is most rude."

After another minute, the door to district headquarters burst open and Berkeley reappeared, trotting down the short flight of stairs. A slender, bookish man in a brown suit with vest and tie followed. The bookish man bore a thin mustache and wore his short brown hair parted on the left.

Sura Chandra dismounted and waited as the men approached.

"Excellency...," Berkeley began, and then stopped and fidgeted. His eyelids fluttered as he looked at the bookish man at his side.

"Ah!" Sura Chandra smiled and folded hands. "Chief Commissioner Quinton, I presume. We meet at last!"

"Um—hum...," stammered Berkeley, "the truth is—well, meet Mister Cossins, the chief commissioner's assistant. The commissioner is..."

"William Henry Cossins!" The slender man stepped forward and bowed. "At your service, Maharaja Singh!"

"Assistant?" Sura Chandra said, frowning. "Where is..."

"I wish to apologize," Cossins said. "There appears to be a miscommunication. Chief Commissioner Quinton is not here at present. He is away on holiday with his family at the hill station in Shillong."

Sura Chandra's face clouded as his heart sank.

The letter spoke the truth.

Sura Chandra huffed and his nostrils flared. "But—Mister Grimwood assured me..." His face turned darker. "I am certain he informed Mister Quinton I was coming. He made himself clear. I expected to meet the chief commissioner when I arrived. The lieutenant can vouch for me. Correct, Lieutenant?" Sura Chandra looked to Berkeley for support but the lieutenant stared at his boots.

"I see," Cossins said. "That was—ten days ago, I believe. If you would care to come inside and make yourself comfortable, I will wire the chief commissioner and let him know of your arrival."

Sura Chandra motioned and drew Berkeley aside. Out of earshot, the former maharaja expressed his displeasure. Berkeley spread his hands and shrugged. After two full minutes, the men faced Cossins.

"Mister Cossins," Berkeley said, "Maharaja Singh will join you inside while you try to contact the chief commissioner. Meanwhile, I will take the rest of the party and secure suitable quarters."

Cossins led Sura Chandra inside and sent a telegram to Quinton. Cossins offered tea and biscuits but Sura Chandra refused with a half-smile and polite wave of hand. Quinton's reply came an hour later. A dour-faced Cossins paraphrased the message as a native babu translated to Bengali.

"The chief commissioner sends his regrets for missing Maharaja Singh's arrival. He had a long-scheduled holiday with his wife and daughter. So sad, but he cannot return to Silchar. He reminds the maharaja of the danger in returning to Manipur. He wishes the maharaja well on his religious pilgrimage. Mister Cossins is at his service during his stay."

Sura Chandra's face turned ashen gray.

"I am sorry, Excellency," Cossins said. "As the commissioner said, I will do whatever I can to make your stay in Silchar comfortable."

"How would one travel to Shillong?"

"It is a five-day journey. Three days march west to Sylhet and a day north to Companyganj. From there, take the river steamer north to Tharia, and then a new railway line connects to the hill station."

"I see," Sura Chandra said. "I propose to travel to Shillong to see the chief commissioner. Please send a message and confirm he will meet with me in five days."

Cossins frowned, but nodded and left to compose the message. A half an hour later he returned, looking glum. "In three days," he said, "Mister Quinton and his family will leave Shillong and travel to Golaghat and Kohima. They will not be back in Shillong for several weeks."

Sura Chandra sat in silence for a full minute.

Cossins fidgeted. "As the chief commissioner mentioned, I am at your service. How else can I help you?"

"Does the chief commissioner have a superior?"

"That would be the Viceroy—Lord Lansdowne."

"Where would I find him?"

"In Calcutta."

"Tell me Mister Cossins," Sura Chandra said, "how would one travel from Sylhet to Calcutta?"

"Also difficult to do. One would first take a river steamer south to Goalundo—a tortuous, winding water route. There one would find the nearest rail station. The rail line connects first to Kushtia and then to Calcutta."

Sura Chandra considered his predicament and weighed his options.

Quinton wants nothing to do with me...

It was clear Quinton was avoiding Sura Chandra. He had washed his hands. He had no intension of meeting the former maharaja.

I can continue the pilgrimage—slink off like a dog with my tail between my legs...

His party could continue west to Sylhet, replenish provisions, and continue twelve hundred miles west to Vrindavan as planned. Doing so would forever end any chance to lay claim to the throne of Manipur.

On the other hand...

Sura Chandra could cast caution to the wind, turn south to Calcutta, and appeal his case to the Viceroy of India, commander of the British Raj. He recalled the tall stranger in the temple and the boney finger pointing at the stone hiding the letter. Sura Chandra reached inside his tunic and fumbled for the wax-coated envelope.

It is still there.

He decided.

This is my moment. Here I show the world I am no coward. I was once a maharaja. I will reclaim my birthright and become a maharaja once more.

"Mister Cossins, you have been most helpful. May I trouble you for another favor?"

"Anything! I am at your service!"

"Kindly compose and send two more telegrams. First, please inform your superior Mister Quinton of my regrets at our not being able to meet. Convey my best wishes to him and his family for a pleasant holiday. Second, please inform Viceroy Lansdowne that as Britain broke its promise to defend the crown of Manipur and forced my hand in the matter, I am rescinding my abdication. I am proceeding south with my party and will arrive by train in Calcutta. I expect to meet with Lord Lansdowne and discuss Britain's plan to restore my rightful place on the throne of Manipur."

Sura Chandra's words were as pebbles slipping down a mountainside, bouncing, striking other stones, and starting a landslide. His decision, intentional or otherwise, altered the course of history.

Chapter 23. The Dragon Sketch

Four months later, Sunday afternoon, 1 February 1891...

W.T. Stead

As the monsoon season of 1890 turned to autumn in India, a world away in England mild weather dominated during October and November. Then high pressure descended from Scandinavia and winds from the east brought two months of snow and bitter cold. The sun disappeared behind impenetrable clouds. The Angel of Death tread with iron boots as the Russian flu struck. At the end of January, the sun broke through, lifting spirits and foretelling a milder February.

On a sunny Sunday afternoon, the first day of February, a hansom cab delivered a passenger to number 19 Avenue Road, Saint John's Wood. A well-dressed, middle-aged man stepped down from the cab and paid the driver. The dapper man had a trim beard, a top hat, a thick coat, and held a notebook and papers under his arm. As the horse-drawn two-wheel cab pulled away, the dapper man sidestepped a dingy patch of ice and approached a wrought-iron gate between two red brick columns. Behind the short brick wall and a phalanx of bare trees stood a homey, two-story brick manor.

A few yards away, a disheveled man dressed in a long, ratty coat and a wool scarf rounded the sidewalk corner. The wretched-looking chap was above average height, had long, matted hair and a bushy beard flecked with gray and icicles. His gait had a surprising rapidity considering his use of a cane to compensate for a dreadful limp. His left leg dragged to catch up with his right and the man winced with each painful step.

"I say, Governor!" the lame man called to the well-dressed man. He breathed steam in the cold air as he huffed and puffed from the exertion. "May I have a word?"

The dapper man turned and smiled. He had arrived early for his appointment and curiosity got the better of him, so he stopped and waited.

Ridiculous accent. The poor chap is a Scottie. Whom does he think he is fooling?

"Thank you for waiting, Governor," the disheveled man said. "A gentleman—I can see that. Beautiful day. Good to feel the sun's rays."

"What can I do for you?"

"Governor, I was wondering if you could spare something to help a wounded former soldier."

"Soldier, huh!" The dapper man studied the disheveled man head to toe. "In which of Her Majesty's little wars did you last take part?"

"The Nile Expedition, Governor. In '85. Took a spear point in the leg at Abu Klea."

"Fuzzy-Wuzzy was it?"

"No, Dervish, but those fuzzy little beggars were as bad. They broke the British square, you know."

"Yes, I know," the dapper man said. "It may surprise you to learn Gordon was a good friend of mine."

"Blimey!" The disheveled man straightened. "Chinese Gordon—your friend? I would love to shake the hand of a friend of the general's." He thrust a hand forward, and then stopped, peering at the dapper man's face. "I say, Governor! You look familiar. Have we met?"

"Perhaps you remember seeing my picture in the newspaper. My name is Stead—William T. Stead. Once editor of the *Pall Mall Gazette*."

"Ha! You are the one!" the lame man shouted. "TOO LATE!" he added, making broad sweeps of his palm as if painting two massive words across the sky. "Never a bigger or more proper headline."

"You saw the paper in the Sudan?"

"Well—it was later, I mean—after I returned from Egypt. A friend kept a copy." The disheveled man extended his hand. "Dee is my name—Jay Dee. Served with 1 Battery, Southern Division; Royal Artillery."

"Well met, Mister Dee!" William Stead gave the outstretched hand a quick shake. "Here, my good man." He fumbled in his pocket, drew out, and handed a shilling to the former soldier.

"A bob! Bless you, Governor!"

Stead eyed the man, stroking his beard. "So, you read then, Mister Dee?"

"Read?" Dee cocked his head. "Oh—the newspaper. You mean, *can* I read? Oh, Governor, yes I can read, but I seldom read, not being able to afford proper reading material, if you take my meaning."

"Here." Stead handed Dee another shilling, and a printed journal titled *Review of Reviews*. "Perhaps you would appreciate a signed copy of my new monthly and…"

The door to the manor burst open, and a short, swarthy young man wearing a white sherwani and turban, brandishing a long-handled buggy whip, ran out screaming.

Dee shoved the coins and the journal into a coat pocket. "God bless you, Governor!" He cast nervous glances at the approaching whip. "I best be on my way."

Dee turned to limp away, leaning on his cane and dragging his lame left leg. The wrought-iron gate swung open with a screech, and the turbaned man jumped forward.

"Away with you, begging devil!" the Indian cried, striking the former soldier across the back. "How dare you accost the madame's visitor?"

"Ow! Bloody…!" Dee raised an arm to block the blows. "Are you blind? Can you not see I am trying to leave?"

A woman shouted from the open door. "Stop, Baboula! Mister Dee is leaving as fast as he can manage."

The lame man limped off, mustering greater urgency than during his arrival. He muttered under his breath and shot evil looks over his shoulder at the short man holding the threatening whip handle.

"Most sorry, Sahib Stead," the turbaned young man's high voice hissed through gritted teeth, still watching Dee's departure through narrow eyes. "I swear I will make of him a sacrifice to Kali and flay him alive."

Dee took a final glance over his shoulder, limped around the corner, and vanished. Baboula stuck the buggy whip under his arm, turned to Stead, pressed two palms together, and bowed, saying, "Namaste!"

"Namaste," Stead answered with a quick nod.

Baboula held the gate as Stead shuffled along the icy path.

"Welcome, William!" The woman held out a hand. "So nice to see you. I see you met our local spy, Mister Dee."

The woman had short curly hair, brown with a hint of gray. She was attractive if not a classic beauty, dressed for warmth and comfort in a long dark dress and a light-colored shawl. Her voice carried an air of elegance with no hint of pretension.

"Dear, Annie," Stead said, clasping her hand in both of his. "Thank you for inviting me. Did you say spy? I took the man for a vagrant—a rare species, seldom found in Saint John's Wood."

"Please, come inside out of the cold," Annie said. "So good to see the sun, but the winter air remains brisk. You, too, Baboula. Horrid and foolish of you to run outside without a coat."

Stead and the Indian entered, chased by a final frigid gust before Annie could close the door.

"HPB believes Dee is a spy." Annie took Steed's coat and hat. "She is certain he has been following her, in disguise, since her last trip to India. Was he asking of us?"

Stead chuckled. "He was asking for a handout! We were discussing how a Dervish spear wounded his leg. I gave him two shillings and a copy of *Review of Reviews*."

Annie shook a finger. "You are too generous! See how he works his magic—I suppose you told him your name. He has an uncanny way of appearing from nowhere and interrogating any new visitor."

Stead frowned. "I have a friend in the cabinet, and deal with Melville at the Yard. I can make inquiries and have him arrested."

"HPB insists we leave him alone. She says he is harmless, and someone worse would take his place. Better, the devil you know, they say." She changed topics. "I am so appreciative you could come here to meet us. As I mentioned in my note, she has seldom left the house since moving here. With the Russian flu going around, I fear it would be the death of her."

"How is she doing?" Steed whispered.

"Not well—I fear for her. I am thankful she agreed to move here during the summer. This winter has been brutal."

"She is fortunate to have you to persuade and care for her."

"I am the fortunate one," Annie said. "I owe you a debt of gratitude for choosing me to review her *Secret Doctrine*. She and I would not have met otherwise."

"I imagine no one is better qualified than Annie Besant."

Annie blushed. "Come, William, she is expecting you. Perhaps Baboula could fetch tea for his mistress and her guest." Besant led Stead to a darkened parlor. "Mind the books and papers as you enter."

The crowded room overflowed with bookshelves, chairs, and desks. Books and papers covered every surface, even the hardwood floor. Stead stepped over a stack and faced, alone in a lamplit corner, a gray-haired woman seated in a plush leather chair. Lazy smoke rose from an ashtray next to the lamp. The woman wore a black dress over her large frame. A black shawl draped her head, and a blanket covered her lap and legs. A walnut card table stood before her where she was laying out cards. She seemed to take no notice of her visitors as they approached. Stead looked down and studied the cards.

"Playing fortune, madame?"

"Patience! They call the game Patience." She continued laying cards without glancing at Stead. "It is the one thing that relaxes me. It will not tell the future, but they say bad luck follows if one lays cards on a table without a tablecloth." She rapped the dark wood tabletop.

Annie gasped. "I will have Baboula fetch a tablecloth straight away!"

"Nonsense," the smoking woman said, chuckling, "the game is my passion. The demon of bad luck always follows a passionate player." She played her final card, sighed in disgust, and pushed the cards into a pile. Then she raised her voice. "Flapdoodle! Thirteen games in a row lost. Does it foretell bad luck? If so, I face a lifetime of bad fortune." She looked up at Stead and held out her hand. "How are you, Stead? We meet in the flesh once more. How long has it been?"

Stead took her hand. "Two or three years. I am well, thank you, madame, and please, call me William."

"I shall call you William if you call me Helena. My friends call me H-P-B, you know. I encouraged them to do that, but I refuse to call you W-T-S."

Stead laughed. "That is a relief! You honor me. Helena it shall be."

"Good! Please, William, you and Annie, take a seat."

Stead sat in a facing chair. "I hope you accepted my apology gift—the book I sent you."

"*The Truth about Russia*—a presumptuous title," Helena said. "Truth can be a slippery eel, but no religion is higher than truth. Are you a religious man, William?"

"A prescient question, Helena. It touches on my reason for wanting to meet with you. I hope you will keep my visit confidential. I am as yet unwilling to discuss this topic at large."

"You have now piqued my interest," she said. "How may I help?"

Stead reached for his notebook. He thumbed until he found the page he sought. He stopped with four fingers holding the place.

"I mentioned at our first meeting, my interest in the occult goes back ten years, but other preoccupations kept me from further study until a few nights ago."

"Something happened?"

"Yes," Stead said, "I had a strange experience I wish to relate."

"Please do."

"I had been sitting alone in my parlor with a notebook and pencil, thinking of ideas for articles and books. The clock on the wall read eight o'clock. I must have drifted off for next I knew the clock read nine o'clock. When I looked at my notebook, an unusual pencil drawing had appeared on the page as if by magic. No one else was home, so only I could have made it."

"May I see it?"

Stead lifted his notebook, thumb behind the cover, and four fingers gripping the bottom edge.

"I am no artist," he said. "I am not capable of such work."

A detailed pencil drawing filled the paper—a winged dragon, with clawed feet and a long, looping tail held by sharp teeth.

"Ouroboros," Helena said with a disinterested tone. She presented an ornate signet ring—a crown topping a looping dragon encompassing a cluster of symbols including two interwoven triangles and a swastika. "You knew this dragon symbol was part of the emblem of the Theosophical Society, so you thought of me, but Ouroboros is one part of the signet. You will find the Seal of King Solomon, the Sanskrit word Sat, or Truth, and other symbols."

"Your signet is part of why I am here," he said. "There was something else."

Stead grasped the book by its top edge. "Beneath the drawing I discovered writing..." He removed his fingers from the bottom edge, uncovering three scrawled phrases.

TELL HPB
MANIPUR BLEEDS
SEEK MW

"'Tell HPB' has an obvious meaning," Stead said. "That is the foremost reason I am here—hoping you will shed light on the two remaining phrases."

Helena sat forward and peered at the page. Seconds passed. At last, she settled back and frowned. Stead shot a glance at Annie, who sat in silence nearby, legs crossed, hands folded on her hap. A dark curtain of concern crossed her face.

"Manipur," Helena whispered. "The Jeweled Land. Many years since I thought of Manipur."

"What is Manipur?"

"It is a country in northeast India. It lies along the road between Assam and Burma. I visited there once, long ago. I was fleeing India, on my way to Burma to escape the Great Mutiny."

Helena paused and stared at a ring on her other hand. Stead regarded the ring from a distance. It appeared to be plain pewter, engraved with a relief of a looping dragon. A wistful smile crossed her face, and she said, "So long ago."

Stead glanced at Annie who shrugged and shook her head.

"Is there a connection?" Stead asked.

"Between what?"

"The dragon and Manipur?"

"Oh, yes! The looping dragon is the royal symbol of Manipur—an ancient god, predating Vedic times."

"Forgive me," Stead pressed, "but Manipur seems to have impressed you. Is the symbol of Manipur the reason for your interest in the dragon—on your emblem, and on your—rings?"

"Perhaps. Who can say? So many experiences factor into one's being."

"The phrase MANIPUR BLEEDS—any thoughts?"

"No. I am sorry."

"Do the initials MW mean anything to you? Anyone you know?"

Helena picked up the smoldering cigarette, took a deep drag, turned her head to exhale, and set the cigarette back in the ashtray. She squared on Stead and her stare bored holes.

"I fear I am not much help. The two letters could mean anything. This experience of yours is a known phenomenon. It has a name—automatic writing. This ability to receive messages as drawings or written words is a gift. I encourage you to develop it further. Perhaps more messages will come and, in time, offer clarity."

Stead's face drooped, unable to mask his disappointment.

"All right, Helena," he said. "I will try to develop this gift, as you call it. Perhaps more messages will come, but please realize, Manipur meant nothing. The sender intended this message for you. Why I am an intermediary, I cannot fathom. You must decide how to use the message."

"Point taken, William." Helena's face remained emotionless. "Everything has a reason. You are an intermediary and in time, you will learn the reason. It always works that way."

Stead squirmed. The woman's daunting presence left him struggling for words.

She knows more than she will admit. How can I break down the wall?

A knock came and Baboula entered to serve tea. Time wore on and the conversation shifted to lighter subjects. When Stead next glanced at the clock, he realized an hour had passed.

"I see I have exhausted my time."

"So soon?"

"I did not intend to take too much advantage of your hospitality. I told my driver to return in one hour. Thank you so much for agreeing to meet. It was an honor to visit in person. Please consider the message meaning further and drop me a note if something comes to you, or if I can do anything to help. Meanwhile, I will do as you suggest and wait to receive more automatic writing messages."

They said their goodbyes and Annie accompanied Stead to the door. He donned his hat and coat, stepped back out into the crisp winter air, and walked to meet his ride. The driver sat tall in the seat behind the cab, smart as a whip in his long black coat and top hat. His ruddy face broke into a bright smile at the sight of Stead.

"Where to, Mister Stead?"

"Home, please, Mister Doughty. And—Mister Doughty?"

"Yes, Mister Stead?"

"Are you and your brother available for hire this coming Saturday morning?"

"For you?" The driver drew himself tall and squared his shoulders. "Yes, sir, Mister Stead!"

"Outstanding! Please be in front of my house at eight o'clock sharp."

"As you wish, Mister Stead."

"Oh and—Mister Doughty?"

"Yes, Mister Stead?"

"Kindly remind your brother to bring his service revolver."

Chapter 24. The Little Secret Society

Four days later, Thursday afternoon, 5 February 1891...

W.T. Stead

On Thursday, the promising sun of February hid behind the gray bluster of winter and a white wind howled. That afternoon, William Stead sank into a plush, red leather chair before a brick hearth, basking in a crackling glow, oblivious to the cold and snow.

Stead lit a cigar, puffed, and aromatic smoke billowed. He sat, warm and cozy, in the quiet comfort of the library of London's exclusive East India Club at 16 Saint James's Square. Ornate oil paintings of renowned former members hung between bookcases. The faces, all heroes of the British Empire, stared in stern disapproval.

I wonder—should I smoke in the library?

"Ah, hum!"

Stead turned to find the waiter, tall, black-suited with a starched white collar, standing close behind, tray in hand. The waiter sniffed. "Mister Stead, is it?"

Stead nodded.

"Forgive the reminder—the board prefers members not smoke in the library."

"Right!" Stead said. He looked for an ashtray, but saw none handy, so he tossed the cigar into the fireplace atop burning logs. The draft pulled the tobacco smoke up the flu but the aroma lingered.

The waiter winced and then extended his tray. "Brandy, Mister Stead?"

Alone again, Stead held the snifter aloft and studied the room through a golden lens.

I say, is that a new map?

One wall featured a large world map hung between glowering portraits, and Stead rose and approached. Mapmakers, in customary fashion, shaded British possessions rosy-red, showcasing a vast presence stretching around the world—an empire upon which the sun could never set. As the empire expanded, maps required updating, and proper application of red.

I appreciate an up-to-date map!

Stead pointed at London—the center of the known universe—and the rose-colored islands of Great Britain and Ireland. He traced a path south to Gibraltar, the Mediterranean isles of Malta and Cyprus, and then east to Suez. His finger moved south across Africa to Nigeria in the west and Kenya in the east, and vast stretches of unnamed grasslands in the south until reaching the Cape Colony.

He pointed east across island possessions in the Indian Ocean to Ceylon. The rose-colored subcontinent of India stretched north to the Himalayas, west to the border of Afghanistan, and east into Burma.

Where did HPB say Manipur was? Oh, yes, there, in the northeast corner—it must be that white spot between Assam and Burma.

"Manipur?" A man spoke. "Where in the world is Manipur? What makes *it* so critical?"

"In good time," a second answered. "Oh, look, here is William. He is busy studying the map, looking for Manipur, no doubt. We are late to the party—he found brandy and cigars!"

Stead jumped as if caught in mischief, and turned from the map, shaken, red-faced, and trembling.

Manipur?

He faced two middle-aged English gentlemen. Cecil Rhodes and Reginald Brett entered the library and the three friends exchanged greetings.

"We can call for more brandy," Stead said, "but no cigars, sad to say. The waiter chastised me for lighting one and I had to toss it."

"No!" Rhodes said, laughing. "This is a cozy place, but next meeting is at Chatham House. I ordered a round conference table. We can seat ourselves like Knights of the Round Table and smoke all we want!"

Rhodes' laughter became chokes, and he sank sputtering into a chair, hand on heart.

I hope he lives that long! The rumors of his bad heart must be true.

Brandy arrived, signaling the start of the meeting—the first of the venture Rhodes dubbed "our little secret society."

"Now, gentlemen," Rhodes said, raising his snifter, "let us plot the conquest and civilization of the world!"

Like a three-legged stool, the three men represented sturdy pillars of publicity, secrecy, and wealth.

Stead's prominence in revolutionizing the fast-growing news industry and his reputation as a tireless campaigner against injustice in Britain made his unfiltered printed words popular, authoritative, and influential.

Reginald Brett worked his magic in secret inside the government. The son of Lord Esher had become the most connected man in the British Empire, mingling with the wealthy and powerful. He had a flair for political intrigue and the ear of the Queen.

Cecil Rhodes brought limitless wealth to the venture. Stead's friend Rhodes was a private man—quiet, a confirmed bachelor, and one of the wealthiest men in the British Empire. English-born, his business and political interests had led him to South Africa and control over most of the world's diamond and gold production.

The simple plan was to unite the world under the English language. Superiority obliged the Anglo-Saxon race to offer peace, freedom, and equality through education, liberal enlightenment, and the stability of firm but sensible British rule.

A difficult and expensive proposition? Not for Cecil Rhodes, Prime Minister of Cape Colony. By age thirty-seven Rhodes had accumulated wealth and power beyond the dreams of most men. His expansive agenda in South Africa was pushing native Africans off their lands to make room for white civilization and the industry and agriculture that typified British imperial progress.

Rhodes impressed Stead with his grand ideas and recruited him into the fold. With help from Stead and Brett, Rhodes could create a secret society and put his fortune to good purpose achieving his vision and extending British civilization throughout the world.

The three men agreed on a structure and plan to expand the secret society. The triumvirate of Stead, Brett, and Rhodes formed the "Junta of the Three," the core of the society. Rhodes would be the general, financier, and spiritual leader of the movement. Brett would use his connections to infiltrate and influence high-level government policy. The three would recruit prominent members in key places of the church, government, and high society into the "Circle of Initiates." Stead's influence in journalistic circles would create the "Association of Helpers" to propagate a positive, receptive image. The society would fund colleges, create scholarships, train worthy scholars in the skills needed, create a pipeline of talent sharing the vision, and advance English domination.

Rhodes, Brett, and Stead had a plan and were ready to begin.

"Reginald…!" Rhodes coughed and caught his breath. "Shall we move to the next topic? You said you wanted to discuss Manipur."

"Ah, yes!" Brett clapped. "Manipur, the Jeweled Land!"

A shiver froze Stead's spine. He stopped taking notes, set his book aside, and gave Brett his rapt attention.

"A convenient opportunity," Brett continued. "I propose an experiment—a small exercise before tackling bigger things." He scanned and found the map. "Ah, outstanding!"

Brett approached, gripping a wooden pointer, and jabbed at the small white spot Stead had earlier located. "Here!" he said, pointing. "Manipur is right here."

"That little white spot?" Rhodes said. "Surrounded by red! Why is Manipur not red like India and Burma?"

"Right!" Brett said. "Why is it not red? Long kept as a buffer between India and Burma, but now Burma is red. Manipur is smaller than Wales, but big things have small beginnings. We should bring Manipur into the empire and color the little spot on the map red as a test of our society's muscles."

"Hum," Rhodes said, scratching his chin. "You called it the Jeweled Land. What jewels? Are we going after diamonds, rubies, or emeralds?"

"Ha!" Brett said, chuckling. "I knew jewels would grab your attention. Sorry, no gems—an Indian legend is all—thousands of years old."

"Tell me," Rhodes said, leaning forward. "What legend?"

"Oh, stuff and nonsense!" Brett said. "Myths of dragons and magic gems. The locals are all Hindus—even they no longer believe it. Precious stones are not relevant to our exercise."

Brett recounted a brief history of Manipur from the Great Mutiny of 1857 to the death of Maharaja Chandra Kirti Singh in 1886. He described the power struggle between his eight sons and the coup that sent the oldest son Sura Chandra Singh into exile.

"Singh took pilgrimage as a fakir but turned up in Calcutta on the Viceroy's doorstep. He claims the political agent pushed him to abdicate. He accuses England of shirking its duty as an ally and demands the Crown take steps to reclaim his throne."

"What did Lansdowne say?" Stead said.

"Lansdowne thinks Singh is a fool and should stay in exile. He proposes recognizing a half-brother, the current regent, as maharaja. To placate Singh—and assert British authority—the viceroy further proposes to exile a half-brother prince, mastermind of the trouble."

Stead squirmed. "The relevance this information escapes me. How is this an opportunity? It sounds like imperial balderdash, political intrigue in the hinterlands."

"There is more," Brett said. "Ten days ago in Calcutta, Singh, the former maharaja, met with Nicholas, the future tsar of Russia, during a stop on his eastern journey."

"Bah!" Stead said. "Russia seeks warm ports and Manipur is land-locked. Nicholas will have no interest."

"Other than…" Brett started.

"To embarrass Victoria!" Rhodes finished.

"Right!" Brett said. "Would we rather see Russia secure a toehold in India?"

Rhodes crossed arms and cupped his chin. "We will deal with Nicholas in two months—in Japan—far from British territory."

"What does that mean?" Stead said. "Deal with Nicholas how?"

"Save that for next meeting," Rhodes said. "Back to Manipur. I understand what Reginald is saying. If Lansdowne's plan works, he exiles a troublemaker and Manipur has a new king. He placates the former maharaja and his half-brother lives in exile on a tidy pension. Life goes on, Manipur remains independent, but chastened."

"Right—so far," Brett said.

"If the plan fails," Rhodes continued, "war breaks out. England wins and annexes Manipur, coloring the little white spot on the map red. Is that the sum of it?"

"A precise rendering!" Brett said. "Well done, Cecil!"

"I am still not clear," Stead said. "Are you proposing to start a war? If so, I am a pacifist. I cannot support such a plan."

"We would not *start* the war," Brett said. "We let conditions dictate the inevitable."

"How?" Stead asked.

"Simple—bureaucracy—uncontrollable complexity, but I excel at manipulating the uncontrollable. The chief commissioner proposes to visit Manipur, recognize the new maharaja, and convince this troublemaking prince to accept exile. If the prince accepts the deal, he lives in wealthy comfort in Assam."

"What is wrong with that plan?"

"Too simple, Stead!" Brett said. "Simple plans never survive a bureaucracy. Many levels must assert authority. A civil servant will suggest the commissioner take policemen. Another civil servant will insist it be at least fifty policemen, then double it to one hundred. Not to be outdone, another authority will say policemen alone are insufficient, and will demand adding fifty soldiers. Soon they will forgo the policemen, double the force to two hundred soldiers, and then double again to four hundred. The commissioner will lead an intimidating column of troops into Manipur. The visit will not appear peaceful. Manipur will feel threatened and become desperate."

"A good plan, Reginald," Rhodes said, "but it leaves too much to chance. A force of such size may have its way. Once at full strength, instruct officers to expect no resistance, so limit the amount of ammunition each soldier may take, for speed in completing the mission—less weight to carry. Oh, and no field guns—too heavy."

"Good points, Cecil," Brett said. "It requires one more touch— Lansdowne must tell the chief commissioner his career depends on success. Under no circumstance is he to return to Assam without the rebellious prince."

"That should do it," Rhodes said.

Stead shook his head. "You are proposing to trap the commissioner into causing Manipur to start a war. You limit our soldiers' ability to defend themselves assuring an embarrassing defeat. Brutal retribution and conquest are certain to follow. You sacrifice soldiers to make Manipur's blood stain the map red?"

"Who? Us?" Brett protested. "My dear Stead! A shocking suggestion! We have little to do with it. Bureaucracies work that way. Manipur will start the war or it will not. If Manipur submits, so be it. If Manipur takes a stand and war breaks out, Parliament will have no choice but to insist England defends her honor."

"Look at the bigger picture," Rhodes said. "It will end in a few weeks, resulting in a better Manipur. This is our goal, is it not? We are humanitarians. We committed ourselves to bettering our fellow man. Soon English schools will open and children will receive proper English educations. Best thing for them!"

Brett clapped. "Thank you, Mister Rhodes! Settled! I will speak to my contacts in the foreign office and begin the process. One more thing…"

"Yes?" Rhodes drawled.

"I shall need—financing—for persuasion and such…"

Rhodes inspected his fingernails. "Right!"

Brett raised his brandy snifter. "To a successful experiment!"

"Hear, hear!" Rhodes answered, raising his glass.

Stead followed with his glass, but made no comment.

Rhodes stood and joined Brett at the map, pointing and asking questions. Stead picked up his notebook and flipped the pages.

What have I done? This is not what I imagined.

He stopped flipping when he reached the dragon sketch.

The royal symbol of Manipur—Manipur bleeds. Have I solved the mystery? Was the message for me alone, or for HBP, too? MW—who or what is it? Who or what must we seek?

Stead turned the page in his notebook to another pencil sketch made the night before in a second try at automatic writing. A large ocean-going vessel stood on end, sinking, with lifeboats afloat, and nearby stood an iceberg. A cold moon glared upon circles in the water, heads of the drowning. He shivered as if stinging cold numbed his arms and legs as he struggled to stay afloat.

Stead rose and looked out a window. Snow fell, the wind gusted, and the afternoon sky was dark and gray. Pedestrians on the street struggled, hands on hats, headfirst against the gust, marching through the snow. It would soon be time to leave and a horse-drawn cab and driver, the loyal, irrepressible Mister Doughty, would wait for him at the door. Unlike the poor blokes slogging through the snow, Stead would only spend a moment in the cold. Stead shook his head, shuddered, and turned away from the window.

What am I becoming? What is happening to the world? I want to be a good man. Am I doing the right thing?

Chapter 25. The Spy in the Fog

Two days later, Saturday morning, 7 February 1891...

W.T. Stead

On Friday evening, the snow ceased and a pea soup fog dropped over London like a dirty blanket. On the morning of the following day, a hansom cab emerged from the dingy mist, clip clopping along Avenue Road in Saint John's Wood. The tall driver sat in the usual place behind the cab. The ruddy-faced man wore a long black coat and top hat and had ice cycles clinging to his handlebar mustache. A second, shorter man stood in an unusual place—squeezed beside the driver, atop the spring, gripping a rooftop support. The shorter man wore a black coat and bowler hat, lower face hidden by a black wool scarf. When the cab stopped, the shorter man leapt to the street.

The driver tapped the horse's flank with his long whip. "Step up, there, my good fellow!" The horse walked forward, making a wide turn at the corner, and slipped into the fog.

Inside the cab, a passenger knocked, and the driver lifted the trapdoor. "Yes, sir!"

"Around the block, Mister Doughty," the passenger said.

"Yes, Mister Stead!" The door slammed shut.

The cab ambled through the mist, wheels rattling over cobblestones and bricks, and after three right turns, Stead knocked again. The cab stopped beside an iron gate framed by red brick columns. Stead squinted through the obscuring mist, discerning an engraved brass sign bearing the number 19. The figure of the man in the bowler cap emerged from the fog and stood by the gate as Stead watched and waited.

The man in the bowler faced the street and fidgeted—shivering and rubbing gloved hands. He twice leaned to study the number as if expecting a rescue from the cold and ensuring he had the correct house. A moment later, something came—a dark, lumbering shape emerged from the fog.

Here comes our spy!

A raggedy, bearded man loomed in the murk, walking with a cane, dragging his left leg. As the bedraggled man closed in on the man in the black bowler, Stead knocked again, and the hansom trotted forward. The cab stopped before the dark shape and the door opened.

"Get in, please, Mister Guthrie," Stead said.

"Sorry, Governor?" The lame man peered into the cab but stood firm. "The name is Dee."

Stead showed his face and barked from the open cab door, "You heard me, Lieutenant!"

"Mister Stead is it?" The man leaned further inward, squinting. "Jay Dee, Mister Stead. We met the other day."

The man in the bowler stuck a revolver into Dee's back. "Come along nice and easy." The barrel jabbed deeper. "Do as Mister Stead says."

"That will not be necessary, Mister Doughty," Stead said. "Not yet, at least. Please stow the pistol for now and secure yourself in the back. Ask your brother to wait a moment."

Bowler Hat Doughty slipped the revolver into a coat pocket and climbed behind the cab, assuming his prior position next to his brother, Top Hat Doughty.

Stead spoke in a softer voice, "Now, please get in, Mister Guthrie." Dee shrugged and reached for the door, waving off Stead's offered hand. "Hand me your cane at least," Stead said.

Dee yanked the cane away from Stead's open hand and winced, struggling with his left leg before turning and dropping into the empty seat. Dee gave the head of his cane a quick twist.

A hidden sword in that thing?

Stead rapped and the trap door opened. "Around the block a few times please, Mister Doughty." The horse stepped forward, hoofs echoing.

Dee spoke first. "You are making a mistake, Governor…"

Stead raised a hand, cutting off Dee. "Drop the fake accent. You are no good at it."

Dee shut his mouth and folded his arms. The cab trotted along in the fog. Both passengers sat silent for a full a minute, and then Stead spoke.

"I thought it would surprise you I discovered your name, but it occurred to me—you wanted me to know who you are. Am I right?"

Dee stared ahead, jaw clenched.

"When we met," Stead continued, "you acted as if you did not know whom I was, but you recognized me the moment I exited the cab. You did not want to preserve your anonymity."

Dee spoke. "What makes you say that?"

"Oh, you provided several clues. You could have picked any of the little wars England fought in recent years, yet you said the Nile Expedition and Abu Klea knowing I knew every detail."

"I told the truth."

"Yes, you did, and when I guessed a Fuzzy-Wuzzy spear wounded your leg, you could have agreed—everyone has heard of the Fuzzy-Wuzzies. Instead, you insisted it was a Dervish spear, knowing it made your story more credible."

"Story?"

"You named your unit, narrowing the field, but you omitted your rank. Every soldier announces his rank along with his unit. You hoped it would make me suspicious—that you hid your rank—raising questions was your goal. Could a vagrant be a former officer?"

"Fourteen hundreds of us there that day. I am down on my luck."

"The most outrageous ploy was your name—Mister Jay Dee! Which officer at Abu Klea received a Dervish spear wound in the left leg? Why, none other than Lieutenant James Dunbar Guthrie—or, should I say, J. D. Guthrie, or Jay Dee."

Dee's face turned dark red.

"Rather than conceal," Stead said, "you strove to divulge your identity. There is one problem with my theory—any guesses?"

Dee kept silent, but his red face tightened.

"J. D. Guthrie is dead. Yes, poor Guthrie died—three days after gunner Alfred Smith saved his life, earning the sole Victoria Cross awarded that day."

"Smith is a good chap," Dee said.

"Yes, for certain, but how can a dead man spy on Annie Besant's home in Saint John's Wood? There is a real mystery for you."

Dee's fists tightened, fingernails biting into palms.

"Not so mysterious if the dead man was a Scottish artillery officer—a breed favorable to Her Majesty's Secret Service—recruited during the expedition, I wager, by Brackenbury himself. I further wager you are a Freemason, making the picture perfect. One last mystery—perhaps the most critical. What motivated you to *want me* to discover your identity?"

The clip-clop of the horse's hoofs and the rattle of the wheels changed as brick became cobblestones. Dee turned his head and studied Stead's eyes. He opened his mouth, as if to speak, then he bit a lip and looked away.

"I have friends," Stead continued. "You do not want me to have this conversation with General Brackenbury at Military Intelligence or Inspector Melville at Scotland Yard."

Dee squirmed, looked down, and then gazed at Stead.

"I am now Captain Guthrie." He spoke with a light Scottish tap on his R's. "For future reference, I could have snapped the neck of your Mister Bowler Hat back there, and he would not have known. Fair warning—think twice before you have a lackey jab a revolver in my back."

"Ah!" Stead said, clapping. "Progress! Perhaps we should leave the tale of your resurrection for another time, *Captain* Guthrie. I still wonder why you sought this conversation. You had to realize it would compromise your station as a spy."

Guthrie's eyes shifted. His arms unfolded, he placed hands on knees, and sighed. Tension released, his frame settled.

"It is hard to explain, Mister Stead. Something changed—the world is not right. I do not know how else to describe the feeling. I watched Madame Blavatsky for years. People in high places believe she is a Russian agent. She is not. I have reported as much, but the opinion persists. I do my job as long as they give orders—and pay me. Something will happen—soon—something extraordinary and queer. I needed to tell someone and, as luck had it, it was you. It may cost me my career, but, if so, I will find another way to solve the mystery."

Stead tried to picture the miserable chap washed, groomed, and dressed in a crisp, clean uniform. "It may surprise you, Captain," he said, "but I understand what you are saying."

Guthrie cocked his head, studying Stead's face.

"I, too, believe something queer is afoot. Here..." Stead lifted his notebook, thumbed to a page, and presented his pencil drawing of the looping dragon. "Have you ever seen anything like this?"

"More than once," Guthrie said, "in dreams—strange, unsettling dreams."

"We have even more in common then!" Stead snapped the book shut. "Perhaps we can help each other, Captain. I need an investigator—someone to solve a mystery—and I suspect you may be the man for the job. I will pay one hundred pounds for your trouble."

"A tidy sum," Guthrie said, shaking his head, "but I do not need your money. In fact, a few days ago I stopped in on Saint Marylebone. I said a prayer for you and dropped your two bob into the poor box. I kept the signed journal—an interesting read."

"Thank you. I may need your prayers, and more. Let us leave payment aside for the moment. There is a mystery connected to Madame Blavatsky to which I wish to find an answer. I need to discover the meaning two letters or initials. The initials are MW."

Guthrie's eyes opened wide as he blushed and grinned. "Why, Mister Stead, this proves something strange is happening. I need not investigate—I can answer that mystery for you now and you can have your Mister Doughty drop me off at the next corner. 'MW' stands for Mary Winchester."

Part IV. The Mad Dogs and Englishmen in the Noonday Sun

"Only mad dogs and Englishmen go out in the noonday sun."

Indian Proverb

Dramatis personæ

In order of appearance (*denotes a fictional character)

1891 Manipur

Karna Sunwar*	Sepoy (private), 43rd GR, Siriman's cousin, 22
Lieutenant Walter Simpson	Bengal infantry, 43rd Gurkha Rifles, 31
Leishna (name fictionalized)	Tongol General's daughter, Frank's mistress, 19
Frank Saint Clair Grimwood	British political agent to Manipur, 37
Ethel Saint Clair Grimwood	Frank's wife, 24
Prince Tikendra Jeet Singh	Yuvraj (crown prince), former Senapati, 35
Moonia	Ethel's Assamese ayah (personal maid), 60
Bearer	Major-domo at British Residency, 50
Rassik Lal Kundu	Head chuprassy (messenger), 40
Tongol General	Senior military leader, king's protector, 74
Prince Angao Singh	Senapati (royal military commander), 25
Head chuprassy's Wife	Naga, Rassik Lal Kundu's wife, 35
Groom*	Stable hand, animal herder, 16
William Melville	Superintendent of telegraphs, Assam, 37

Chapter 26. The Dragon's Murmur

Two weeks later, Saturday afternoon, 21 February 1891...

Karna

As cold and fog lingered in London, winter brought drier air to the northeast corner of the Indian subcontinent. There were fewer hot and humid days, but as luck would have it, Karna Sunwar drew sentry duty on one of the hottest days. The Gurkha stood guard in the merciless sun. His rimless cap kept his skull from frying and his brains from boiling but could not keep his brow's sweat and the sun's glare from stinging his eyes. He stood at the gate of the British residency in Manipur for three hours, watching and waiting.

The life of a Gurkha soldier—hours, days, weeks, and months of monotonous duty, drilling and practicing, sometimes under miserable conditions, always ready for action when duty called...

When?

The service was rich with a camaraderie. There were fun and rewarding times, but the good times of soldiering were far from Karna's mind. His thoughts centered on when.

When will this shift end, when can I eat, and when will I see women?

Karna always thought of women, but he did what sentries do—he paid attention to everything. As the hot day wore on, his stamina weakened. From a few hundred yards north, at the women's bazaar, melodic voices floated on the still air. He wished he was there—it was so tantalizing, so close. He tried to imagine...

Many women at the women's bazaar—Manipuri women!

Despite limited ability to mingle, Karna regarded Manipuri women attractive—very attractive.

You always are thinking of girls!

His younger cousin Siriman said so and was right. Karna thought of women and one in particular. Karna had left a pretty girl behind in Nepal, the girl of his dreams, the girl he hoped to marry someday, and her name was…

What is her name? Strange—I do not remember. Five years since leaving Khiji and I forgot her name. If I stayed—but the priest was right—I had no choice.

Distant activity interrupted Karna's thoughts—something required his undivided attention. He arched his hand as if in mock salute to the sun and shielded his watery eyes. Something was approaching from the north, past an expanse of Kangla's walls, near its main gate, on the road passing the bazaar. A uniformed man on horseback followed by a company of men shouldering rifles. The small column turned south and headed toward the Residency. The company's pace quickened. Dust rose from the dry road and a trailing cloud formed in the shimmering heat. Karna raised his field glasses. Through the dust, he recognized the man on horseback as a British officer. He counted fifty Gurkha sepoys marching behind, two by two. After a few more paces, the officer's face became clear. It was his commanding officer, Sahib Lieutenant Simpson of the 43rd Gurkha Rifles. It was the second half of the contingent sent to secure the Residency. Karna had marched south from Kohima weeks earlier with forty-nine fellow Gurkhas, bringing supplies and replacing the forty rifles sent to Silchar as escort to the deposed maharaja.

They are here at last! The second company has marched the final twelve miles from camp at Sengmai.

Karna turned and shouted in Gorkhali to the nearby guards. "Make ready to open the gate! Prepare the guard of honor!"

The company turned onto the final stretch and reached the entrance to the Residency. The British officer raised his hand, and the company halted. Sentries opened the gate, shouldered their rifles, and stood at attention. Karna saluted. Simpson waved forward, and the march resumed. The company passed the gate and proceeded toward the Residency. The gate closed.

Karna tracked the company's march down the nine hundred feet of the carriage lane, sheltered beneath overhanging trees, and arrival at the verandah of the white thatch-roofed house. Karna should have turned his attention back to the perimeter, but he peered through his field glasses. Sahib Simpson dismounted in front of the veranda. A sepoy took the reins and led the horse toward the stables. Simpson dismissed the fifty Gurkhas.

The soldiers stacked Martini-Henry rifles, doffed backpacks, and spread out into the cool grass under the trees.

The shade looks so cool and inviting.

As Simpson approached the house, the front door opened, and two figures emerged. Karna recognized the figures of Sahib and Memsahib Grimwood. Simpson stepped onto the verandah and Sahib Grimwood shook the Lieutenant's hand. Memsahib Grimwood gave Simpson a warm hug and Karna frowned.

Too warm, too long!

Karna's stare lingered, devouring every line of the memsahib's face. They separated, and he lowered the glasses as the three disappeared. His cousin's words echoed.

You always are thinking of girls! You are a Gurkha—you will never know the secret pleasures of the sahibs.

Karna sighed and turned attention to his duty. Another hour passed, and no one relieved him.

When will this duty end? Who is managing assignments?

The sun beat on Karna like a blacksmith at the forge. His pounding pulse became a rhythmic whisper. Karna stiffened, recognizing a voice.

It is back!

The whisper was not a sound or memory, but a faint murmur in his head—a satin voice in a strange tongue. The voice had a name—Siriman, who had never heard it, named it—the dragon's murmur. It began five years earlier, in happier times, after Siriman and Karna suffered a catastrophe. Siriman described the event, but Karna had no recollection. Karna took Siriman at his word—his cousin never lied. The voice returned after Karna arrived in Manipur though he could not remember the exact day. Karna resisted, and the murmur passed—he hoped for good.

What is it saying? What does it want from me? Is it enticing me? What is it promising? I will go mad if it does not stop.

The murmur became a muffled grumble. It spoke rhythmic nonsense—sometimes soothing, sometimes gnawing. Karna shook his head.

I must assert control.

"Stop!"

That helped. The murmur vanished, but left a headache. Siriman had taught Karna to assert his authority to stop the voice. Karna stared at his feet and rubbed his forehead, not caring if other sentries observed. When the ache faded, Karna refocused attention on his surroundings.

The road had little traffic. An occasional pony rider, a bullock cart, or a group of locals walking near the bustees clustered around the southern wall of Kangla. To stay focused and pass the time, Karna played a game. He trained his eyes on each traveler and tried to imagine what they were doing, where they were going, and what they were thinking. He hoped one, any one, for any reason, would stop, approach, and give him something to do. The scene played out in his mind—what he would say to turn them away.

What is your business? You have no appointment! Sahib cannot see you today! Move! Go on your way!

A solitary bullock cart lumbered down the road. Behind the driver sat a slim figure. Karna watched and played his game. He willed the cart to stop and—it stopped. A lithe young woman jumped off, trilling thanks to the driver. As the cart trundled on, the woman sashayed toward the gate.

Karna observed through narrowed eyes. The woman was attractive—a young Manipuri woman, fair-faced, slender, with long unkempt hair. She wore a loose-fitting white dress with a black bodice and thin red ties around the bare neck and shoulders.

Shameless and enticing!

Karna guessed she was nineteen or twenty. She renewed his conviction that all Manipuri women were beautiful.

You are always thinking of girls! Do your duty!

The woman reached the gate. Karna addressed her in broken English. "What business?"

She jabbered back in a melodious voice. Karna shook his head. She spoke the Manipuri tongue and he could not fathom a word. He replied in Hindi, Gorkhali, and broken English, but the girl shook her head, blurting at last in English, "See Sahib Frank!"

A sentry approached and whispered in Karna's ear. "She is the sahib's mistress. When the memsahib returned, the sahib left strict orders. Do not admit this one. You must send her away."

Karna nodded and turned back to the young woman, barking, "You have no appointment! The sahib cannot see you! Go away!"

The woman's face clouded, and she unleashed Manipuri invectives.

She grasped the gist of my order.

The woman pouted and shook the bars.

She is pleading for me to open the barricade.

Her voice droned—a sweet, intoxicating sound like comforting music. Karna listened without expression while admiring the lines of her face. She reminded him of the girl he left behind in Nepal...

Yet all pretty girls remind me of—what is her name? Oh, yes, now I remember. Her name is Akuti.

The young woman facing Karna became Akuti.

How? What is Akuti doing here?

Akuti's voice became rhythmic, humming, and pulsing. The pulse softened and slowed to a low rumble, like a velvet hand patting a bass drum. Karna blinked in the bright sunlight and grew woozy.

The dragon's murmur has returned.

The droning rhythm slowed. Akuti vanished. Blackness. Karna touched his eyes. The lids were open.

I have gone blind.

The heat became a warm blanket. Karna nestled in a soft cocoon where he could listen to the murmur in comfort and imagine its meaning.

There are pleasures beyond my imagination waiting for me. I must learn to understand and appreciate my destiny.

No, I must fight. I must regain consciousness.

Give in—let the murmur take me. It is only fair. I have been on duty far longer than expected. I will let the dragon speak.

A voice shouted in his ear. "Sunwar! What are you doing?"

Karna jerked awake. A sentry shook his shoulders. He looked around, aware of his surroundings.

Akuti—I mean, the young woman vanished. That is a relief!

"I must have heat stroke," Karna rubbed his eyes. "I have been on duty too long. How long have I stood here?"

"Why admit her? I told you, the sahib left strict orders—if she comes, turn her away!"

"What do you mean? I let in no one!"

The sentry pointed. Karna spun and his jaw dropped. He saw the young Manipuri woman, half way down the carriage lane, nearing the house.

Karna cried in anguish, "Oh, no! How did that happen?"

"You did it!" the sentry shouted. "I saw you! You opened the gate. You let her in despite orders. This is not good. Sahib will be angry! What is wrong with you?"

"I do not know!" Karna held hands to head. "No time! Take my rifle!"

Karna bolted, chasing after the young woman.

Chapter 27. The Golden Flower in the Lake

An hour earlier, as Simpson's company approached Kangla...

Frank

Frank Grimwood's afternoon began with excitement and intrigue. First, a cable arrived—the second telegram in two days. The message was from his superior, Chief Commissioner Quinton. Later that afternoon, Frank and Ethel sat in the parlor at the Residency, hiding from the sun's heat, and resting under the gentle, steady swish of the punkah fan. At Ethel's request, Frank read the cryptic message aloud—for the third time.

```
I propose to visit Manipur soon. Have roads and rest
houses put in order. Further directions and dates to
follow.
```

"Short on specifics," Ethel said, "no matter how many times you read it."

"He leaves too much to the imagination."

"We must make plans!" Ethel said. "This calls for a feast."

Frank and Ethel began dinner event planning. Fish, fowl, or an odd goat here or there, made up the list of available meats—bland fair for a major feast. The number of officers in Quinton's company and length of the visit were mysteries—they needed something more—befitting a chief commissioner's party. Pork and beef were inconceivable. They settled at last on mutton. After further debate, they agreed on five as a suitable quantity of the wooly creatures.

"White sheep only," Ethel insisted. "I will have no one wondering if they are eating the black sheep of the flock."

Frank composed a message, summoned a chuprassy (clerk), and sent the fellow off to telegraph Cachar to requisition five white sheep. As they were preparing to discuss the entertainment aspect of the plan, the bearer entered. Frank straightened and grew attentive. He always listened to the bearer.

"Memsahib," the man said, bowing first to Ethel, and then adding, "Sahib," as he bowed to Frank. "You have company. An officer arrives soon, followed by fifty sepoys."

"Is it Simpson?"

"Yes, sahib."

"What?" Ethel exclaimed. "Walter—coming here? Now?" She ran to the parlor window and parted the curtains. "No one! How do you...?" When she turned, the bearer had vanished.

Frank chuckled. "You wonder how, but he always knows—everything. It is a mystery how the man does it, but he knows everything going on at the Residency before anyone."

"But—no one is there," Ethel insisted.

"If the bearer says Simpson will be here soon, he will be. The bearer has either omniscient foresight or a sixth sense for things like that."

"Did *you* know Walter was coming today?"

Frank did not answer. Simpson had wired from twelve miles away, at the telegraph station at Sengmai. His message informed Frank of his imminent arrival, but Frank had neglected to inform Ethel.

"He sent a cable yesterday," Frank said at last, biting his lip.

Ethel's eyes narrowed. "You said nothing."

"I am sorry, dear—slipped my mind."

That was a lie. So why did I not tell her? Two reasons—the first being, I wanted to test the powers of the bearer, and he passed with flying colors.

"Slipped your mind?" Ethel said. "As if a telegram arrives every day."

"Well, that makes two in two days." Frank pointed toward the door, trying to change topics. "Come. Let us wait on the verandah. Good he came—I can use help with the roads. Maybe he knows why Quinton is coming."

Frank stepped toward the door but Ethel stopped, saying, "Wait! I am not in proper dress for company! I must change into something more suitable." She took a step and then stopped. "What of you?"

Frank mumbled, "Oh, I am fine. Simpson is no bigwig or..."

Ethel did not wait for Frank to finish. She scurried as if in a panic down the hall toward her dressing chamber. "Moonia!" she shouted, "I need to change!"

"Walter will appreciate you being underdressed," Frank mumbled once Ethel was out of earshot.

She shows enthusiasm, no question about that! That is the second reason—I wanted to see her reaction when she learned of Walter's imminent arrival.

Frank stepped alone onto the verandah. As predicted, at the end of the long tree-lined drive, Walter Simpson was there—on horseback, riding through the gate followed by a marching company of Gurkha riflemen.

He reopened the door and shouted, "Walter *is* here!"

"One minute!" Ethel's faint voice came from down the hall.

"Take your time," Frank muttered, closing the door.

Why am I so dour?

Frank hated himself acting so suspicious.

Am I jealous? Is Ethel smitten?

Smitten or not, Frank thought Walter was a good bloke. Walter had done a stint at the Residency and he and Frank became friends. They had grand times with Ethel away, drinking and carousing—aside from polo there was not much else to do in Manipur.

Ethel had met Walter in Shillong later, during her long absence from Manipur. After Ethel's return, Frank and Ethel rode to Kohima to meet Quinton and there, reunited with Walter. After a drink or two, Ethel swooned whenever Walter played the piano and sang.

Too bad—no piano in Manipur. The man can play up a storm.

Frank could see what attracted Ethel to Walter. He was British and good company—a rare combination in Manipur.

Admit it—he is a good chap. You like him, too. Do not act jealous. You have your own dirty laundry to sort out.

Ethel had not mentioned Frank's indiscretions, but Frank was certain, between whispers and secret letters, she knew everything.

Act confident and supportive. Let matters play out.

Frank opened the door and called down the hall, "Hurry, dear! Walter is at our doorstep!"

Frank tucked in his shirt and straightened his hair—for Ethel's sake.

Simpson will not care.

Ethel emerged from her room wearing a lighter-weight, looser-fitting dress.

The neckline could be a little higher.

"You look—cooler." Frank looked Ethel over, arms folded, trying to decide if the dress was too revealing. "In fact, ravishing."

"Do not lie!" Ethel blushed.

"In all earnest—Walter will be appreciative."

"That is not…"

"Never mind," Frank turned to see Walter handing his reins to a sepoy. "Here he is now. Let us go greet him."

Frank and Ethel stepped down from the veranda as Walter approached. Frank had to admit—the mustachioed young Lieutenant Walter Simpson was a handsome and dashing fellow in his cap and uniform.

After hours on the road, on horseback, in the hot sun.

Ethel's face lit. "Walter! Welcome! This is a pleasant surprise."

Frank and Walter shook hands. Ethel stepped forward and threw her arms around the officer. Walter stiffened, looked at Frank, then relaxed and returned the embrace. At that instant, twin flashes from the vicinity of the gate caught Frank's attention.

What was that? Reflection from field glasses—a sepoy is spying on us—or, more likely, on Ethel.

"Did Frank not tell you I was coming?" Walter glanced at Frank, wide-eyed. "I wired from Sengmai yesterday."

Ethel pulled away after what seemed to Frank an eternity. "No." She cast a sidelong glance at Frank. "He says he forgot. With all the excitement over the chief commissioner's wire, I can understand."

"A wire?" Walter's face twisted in surprise. "News from Shillong?"

Frank told Walter of Quinton's telegraph.

"That is news," Walter said, scratching his head, "but short on details."

"Let us get you inside and out of the heat," Frank said. "The khidmutgar is serving tea."

The three sat in the parlor and partook of tea and biscuits. They discussed happenings in Manipur since Walter's last visit to Kohima and then turned to the events of that day.

"What is your guess?" Walter asked Frank. "Why is Quinton coming to Manipur?"

"It must have something to do with Sura Chandra's abdication," Frank said. "I hope he will end this state of limbo and award Kula Chandra formal recognition as the new maharaja. He has proven himself an improvement. The people support him. Sura Chandra was a disaster."

Simpson nursed his tea. "Frank," he said at last, "I may need your help. My assignment is to take an inventory of the weapon stores at the Residency."

"Not a problem," Frank said. "I have a considerable stack of ammunition boxes locked in the treasury. You can see them whenever you wish."

"What manner of shell?"

"Metal-cased Boxer cartridges—for Snider-Enfield rifles."

"Sniders? Interesting. How many rounds—any guess?"

"Thousands," Frank said, "maybe ten thousand rounds or more. We can go count them anytime you wish."

"Right—in a moment. I have another problem. I will need your help—and Ethel's, too."

Frank and Ethel exchanged glances. Ethel shrugged.

"Such as?" Frank said.

"I need to get inside Manipur's arsenal and take inventory."

"Oh," Frank said. "That could be a problem."

"Yes," Walter said. "Manipur is protective of its weapon store. My entire time in Manipur I never got close."

"What do you propose?"

"I was thinking…" Walter looked at Ethel and smiled. "Ethel may have powers of persuasion over the Senapati."

"Do you mean Prince Tikendra Jeet?" Frank said.

"None other."

Ethel spoke. "He is no longer Senapati."

"Why not?"

"When Sura Chandra abdicated, everyone moved up a notch—Kula Chandra to maharaja, Tikendra Jeet to Yuvraj, and Prince Angao Sena to Senapati."

Walter snorted. "Angao! Is he the Senapati? Can he talk? He used to stuff his mouth with wads of betel nut."

"He still does," Ethel said. "Chomps all the time."

Walter laughed and said, "He will rot his mouth off one day. I think we all know, call him Yuvraj or not, Tikendra Jeet will not surrender control of the military to Angao. He worked something out with the Tongol General and they pretend Angao is Senapati. I need permission to enter the arsenal and it will have to come from Tikendra Jeet."

"Supposing you are right," Frank said, "how can Ethel help?"

Walter shrugged. "She is close friends with Tikendra Jeet."

Frank looked at Ethel.

"I suppose I should mention," Walter added, "I discussed my assignment with Ethel back in Shillong, after she told me and Alan she was going back to Manipur. She offered to help."

"So," Frank said. He looked at Ethel and stiffened.

"Well," Ethel said, "I suggest..."

Outside, a voice called, "Frank!" A Manipuri woman was is distress somewhere close. "Frank! Help me!"

They heard another voice. "Stop!" It was the high-pitched voice of a Gurkha. "Get out! Now! You must leave—now!"

Frank, Ethel, and Walter Simpson ran for the verandah. From the railing, they looked across the grassy slope leading to the nearby lake and beheld a singular scene. Two figures splashed in the lake. The wild ducks scattered, quacking and flapping. A young Manipuri woman struggled to avoid the grasp of a Gurkha sepoy. She was soaked, and her white dress clung to her slender figure, leaving little to the imagination. The soldier stood at her side, water up to his belt. He grabbed for the woman's arm but she pulled away. The Gurkha lunged, encircled her waist from behind, and lifted the struggling woman. She kicked, and the man lost his balance. Both toppled backward, submerged with an explosive splash, and resurfaced seconds later, coughing, and sputtering. The woman's long black hair hung straight, dripping, and the soldier lost his cap—it floated upside down and the ripples pushed it out of arm's reach.

Frank and Walter stood, wide-eyed, but smiling. Ethel froze, open-mouthed and grimacing. None could look away from the spectacle. Frank at last glanced at Ethel and found her standing with arms folded. She met Frank's eyes with an icy stare.

"Who is that woman?" Ethel said. "It seems she knows you."

"I...!" Frank turned back toward the lake, finding it hard to take his eyes off the young woman. "She is—a friend—somewhat..."

"I see," Ethel said. "What is her name?"

"Leishna," Frank answered, still staring. "Her name is Leishna."

"Does that mean flower?"

"Yes...," Frank replied. "A golden flower, to be correct."

"So, Frank," Ethel said, arms still folded, "why do we have a scanty-clad young woman named Leishna splashing in our lake?"

"I cannot say—with confidence."

"From where did she come?"

"Kangla—one supposes."

"How do you know her?"

"She is the Tongol General's daughter."

Ethel turned to the railing, fuming. "So *she* is the one."

She knows.

"I can explain," Frank said.

"Oh, I am sure you can!" Ethel watched as the struggle continued. "Walter, is that man one of yours?"

Simpson tore himself away. "Why, yes, I believe he is."

"How long must we endure this—this…?" She struggled to describe the scene.

"Walter," Frank said, "will you help me?"

Frank and Walter left the veranda and walked toward the lake. Once out of earshot, Walter murmured, "Nice of Ethel—not making a scene."

"Because you are here," Frank said. "I will catch it later."

"Sorry, old boy."

A sudden thought struck Frank. "I say, Walter, I need a favor. This— friend of mine—could you take her off my hands?"

"Me?"

"She is a hopeless devotee of British authority figures. You are a young, single fellow."

"So, you want me to…" Walter did not finish.

"If you do not mind. She is a handful, and I offer fair warning—she loves to drink Yu."

"What of the old man—her father?"

"I should mention something," Frank said. "I think she is a spy."

"Are you sure?"

"Why else would the General allow his daughter to sleep with an Englishman?"

"I see," Walter said. "Perfect. Well, Frank, old man…" Walter cracked a wry grin and offered his hand. "My duty as a friend! I will give it my best shot."

The Gurkha and Leishna continued struggling. The soldier hoisted the woman onto his shoulder, carried her kicking and screaming out of the lake, and tossed her, soaking wet, onto the grass.

"Stop, Leishna!" Frank shouted.

The wet soldier looked up, saw Lieutenant Simpson, and snapped to attention. A hand went to his head and felt, then his eyes sprung wide—his cap still floated in the lake. Leishna sat up but remained on the wet grass.

Frank switched to Manipuri. "You cannot be here," he said, addressing the girl. "You must leave." Frank placed a hand on Walter's shoulder. "This man is Lieutenant Simpson. He is..." Frank and Simpson exchanged glances. "A British army officer and a fine gentleman. He will take you home now."

Walter Simpson smiled at Leishna and nodded. The girl blushed and looked away. Then Walter placed hands on hips and walked a circle around the drenched Gurkha, inspecting the soldier head to toe.

"You—sepoy!" Walter barked in Gorkhali. "Sunwar—is it?"

"Yes, sahib!"

"You look ridiculous!"

"Yes, sahib!"

"What is behind this? How did she pass the gate?"

"Sahib," Sunwar answered, "it was my fault. It will not happen again."

"Right!" Walter shouted. "Go to the stable. Tell the hands to ready my horse and have it brought around to the verandah. Then go dry yourself."

"Yes, sahib!" the Gurkha shouted. He saluted and jumped back into the lake to retrieve his hat, then climbed out and stomped. His soaked boots sloshed.

"Put yourself down for a week of extra duty!"

The soldier nodded and trotted away. Frank offered the young Manipuri woman a hand and helped her to her feet.

Walter studied the sopping wet damsel. "Does she speak English?"

"Not much," Frank replied. He scratched his head. "At least, I do not think so, but sometimes I wonder. She may know more than she admits."

"I see," Simpson said. "Anything else?"

"Oh! One more thing—since she is a spy, I hope you do not talk in your sleep."

Chapter 28. The Prince's Invitation

Nine days later, Monday afternoon, 2 March 1891...

Ethel

Women sense when a man's interest extends beyond casual conversation. Ethel Grimwood became adept at divining the intension of attention. She reveled in and encouraged attention. Ethel was, in a word, a flirt. It was wrong for married women to flirt, but Ethel could not help herself. Flirting made Ethel feel special, desired, and excited. Had Frank's attention faded—or had she changed? Either way, she was young and vibrant while Frank was fifteen years older with a roving eye.

He has no business complaining of anything I do! How many attentive gentlemen friends do I have strung on my line?

Ethel ticked off a count of her followers.

Walter.

Lieutenant Simpson would top the list, but he displeased Ethel by picking up Frank's cast off—that alluring-but-contemptible daughter of the venerable Tongol General. Ethel extracted the full story from Frank, and she would forgive him in time. She was not sure of Walter—not after Frank said the girl was a spy, passing secrets to her father.

Alan.

If Ethel could be honest with herself, her line of flirting targets included her stepbrother Captain Boisragon whom she had encountered and then left behind at Shillong. No blood connected them so nothing wrong in the attraction, yet somehow it seemed unfitting. Tongues wagged in Shillong, as always, but it was nothing serious.

Lieutenant Williams.

That morning Ethel had written a letter to Charles Williams of the 43rd Gurkha Rifles. Charles was an officer Ethel had not seen in months yet she wrote, spilling details she had no business spilling, of Quinton's coming expedition to Manipur.

Expedition! A new word. It rolls off the tongue.

As soon as Ethel learned Colonel Skene would lead Quinton's large contingent of soldiers, she stopped calling it a visit and called it an expedition. It sounded so much more intriguing and consequential. Quinton had not told them the true purpose of his expedition but suspicions abounded and Ethel loved the guessing game.

Lionel.

Lieutenant Lionel Brackenbury, nephew of the head of the British Secret Service, left Manipur months before when his assignment ended. The man reminded Ethel of Walter, except younger and more sensitive, taller and more handsome, and he played the banjo instead of the piano. Ethel sensed Lionel's interest and made a mental note to write a letter soon, to keep the interest warm.

Lieutenant Grant.

Frank and Ethel encountered Charles Grant at his remote outpost in Tamu during their recent foray across the border into Burma. Ethel's appearance shocked and embarrassed poor Charles who never imagined finding an Englishwoman at his hut! Ethel smiled remembering how Charles scrambled to get dressed. Frank, Ethel, and Charles laughed so hard when they tried to bake a cake—with disastrous results! Charles was a splendid fellow—bright, charming, and handsome. He could not take his eyes off of her and she had not stopped thinking of him.

Prince Tikendra Jeet. Are you serious, Ethel?

Crown Prince Tikendra Jeet Singh of Manipur was an intriguing fellow—military mastermind, engineer, civic organizer, and legendary tiger hunter. He was intelligent, cultured, suave, not too terrible to look at—more handsome than not, at least when he shut his mouth, hiding his teeth. The prince was a first-class rogue. He had nine wives yet he had his eye on Ethel, seeking every opportunity to spend time and make conversation. Ethel had the prince hooked, and she sought to leverage the situation.

What to do with him?

Walter expected Ethel to use feminine wiles to get permission to inspect the Manipuri weapon stores. Against better judgment, but with the thrill of adventure, Ethel did something she had never done—she asked to meet with Prince Tikendra Jeet.

I am playing a dangerous game!

The prince was too intelligent to fool—he would sense something was afoot. As rumors of Quinton's expedition flew, suspicions would grow. As one known for his violent temper, Tikendra Jeet was not one to trifle. A concession would have a price.

I hope the price will not be too steep.

The mountain gun erupted with a mighty boom, destroying Ethel's train of thought. She covered her ears as the shell landed, exploding inches from the target flag on the rifle range. Prince Tikendra Jeet turned away from the gun with a wide grin. He looked smart and dignified in his uniform and turban, but Ethel winced at the sight of his broken teeth.

His eyes are his best feature. If his teeth were not so...

"Direct hit!" the prince called, raising both arms, beaming with pride.

Alone among the princes of Manipur, Tikendra Jeet mixed Hindi and English into his conversations. Ethel's Manipuri language skills deteriorated during long months in Shillong and she appreciated the prince's attempts at English, a product of the English school established by Colonel Johnstone. Wise future leaders of Manipur invested in learning English.

"Well done!" Ethel shouted, louder than necessary, ears ringing from the explosion. The prince smiled and Ethel smiled back, clapping.

Ethel's attentive escort, a young Gurkha, stood fifty feet away, Martini-Henry rifle slung over his shoulder. He showed no reaction to the explosion, but Ethel's exclamation alerted him, and he coiled, ready for action.

The Gurkhas are so impressive!

Ethel found the little chaps fabulous soldiers—focused and dedicated. She recognized the Gurkha as the same one she saw tangling with the Tongol General's daughter, dragging the dreadful girl wet and kicking from the lake. Walter sent him with her as an extra duty—punishment for letting the girl past the gate.

My protection should not be a punishment, but I feel safer in his presence.

Prince Tikendra Jeet approached, offered Ethel his hand, and led the way to a table shaded by a tall oak. Servants stood ready, proffering fresh fruit and flasks of Yu, cups filled and waiting.

"Join me in a toast?" The prince picked up his cup, still smiling...

Thank God, not his wide grin!

Ethel returned the smile and lifted her cup. "To what shall we toast?"

"To the friendship and alliance between Manipur and Great Britain," the prince said. "It shall last a thousand years!"

His voice and eyes project sincerity.

Ethel laughed. "Happy to drink to that!" They clinked cups and Ethel sipped as the prince gulped.

Tikendra Jeet locked eyes. "May I ask a question?"

"Yes—you—may ask."

Did I sound uncertain?

"Thank you. I am wondering to what I owe the pleasure of your company—or do you prefer I guess?"

"Oh? Have you a guess?"

"I do," he said. "My guess is this—it has something to do with the impending visit to Manipur by Chief Commissioner Quinton. You wish to confide in me, disclosing the reason for his visit. Am I close?"

"No, I am not privy to the reason for Quinton's visit."

"Ah, too bad—then I am intrigued. To what *do* I owe this pleasure?"

"I needed to ask a favor." Ethel studied the prince's eyes.

He pursed his lips and cocked his head. "Ask your favor."

"As you know," Ethel said, "England and Manipur, as partners and allies, have shared in the defense of the eastern frontier of India."

"Yes, true for many years."

"And Manipur received much weaponry from England."

"True also—gifts from Queen Victoria herself."

"Walter—Lieutenant Simpson, I mean—is the ranking military officer in the district. He must take a physical inventory of Manipur's weapon stockpile and report to the Raj."

"Ah," Tikendra Jeet said. "So Simpson wants into our arsenal."

"In simple terms—yes."

"Perhaps the Sirkar expects an invasion?" The prince smiled. "From Burma? Or China perhaps?"

"Invasions do not seem imminent, but I assume the report is a formality—for preparedness and such."

"Why not ask me himself? Why send you?"

"He said last year you declined when he asked."

"Ah!" The prince nodded. "That, too, is true."

"So, Lieutenant Simpson assumed you would decline once more."

"You understand I am no longer Senapati. My brother Angao Sena now has responsibility for the military."

"Walter knows this, but he assumes Angao will support your policy. He is hoping you will speak to your brother ahead of time and suggest an exception to the policy. It need not appear Walter went over your brother's head."

Tikendra Jeet handed his empty cup to the servant for a refill. He closed his eyes, gulped the second helping, and then exhaled, wiping his mouth on his sleeve.

"Simpson asked a favor of you, to ask a favor of me, to ask a favor of my brother."

Ethel laughed. "A correct assessment!"

"And does Simpson's mission relate to Melville's ongoing inspection of the telegraph lines?"

Nothing escapes this man!

"Somewhat," Ethel said. "The telegraph connects Manipur with the empire. Mister Melville maintains all wires from Assam to Burma."

Ethel set her half-empty cup down and waved off a refill.

Must stay calm. Must not allow my voice to quiver.

"Ah yes," the prince said. "The telegraph wires—source of a recent mysterious message saying someone will soon catch a big tiger in Manipur."

"What? I—I—do not...," Ethel stammered. "Is a maneater prowling?"

"No, but perhaps Quinton wishes to hunt—something. Koireng (tiger hunter) is another of my names. Should I worry about Quinton?"

"I know nothing." Ethel clasped her hands. "With Quinton visiting soon, British officials like Lieutenant Simpson and Mister Melville have many measures to take. No reason you should worry."

Tikendra Jeet studied Ethel's eyes. "I love to look into a beautiful woman's eyes. Do you know why?"

Ethel shook her head, blushed, and looked away.

"I search for truth," the prince said. "Eyes always show truth or falsehood."

A chill traversed Ethel's spine. She grabbed her cup, took a gulp, and then returned the man's gaze. For several silent seconds the two locked eyes.

Tikendra Jeet smiled. "I believe you."

Ethel breathed a sigh of relief.

"I will consider the lieutenant's petition," the prince said. He paused and handed his cup for a refill. "As I consider, and before I give an answer, I ask a favor from you."

Here it comes!

"Yes?" Ethel murmured.

"I will consider Lieutenant Simpson's petition on condition you have dinner with me this evening."

Ethel paused and glanced at her nearby Gurkha escort. When she looked back, the prince grinned bright-eyed, waiting as if with great anticipation.

"Where?" Ethel asked.

Tikendra Jeet raised an eyebrow.

"Dinner…," she added. "Where will we be dining?"

"Why, at my home! The Yuvraj's compound. Inside Kangla, between the inner and outer walls."

What can it hurt to have dinner? I will have my protection—my Gurkha escort.

"Yes, I will dine with you," Ethel said. "As long as you allow me to send a message informing Frank why I delayed my return."

"Done at once!" He clapped his hands with glee. "Let us retire to Kangla!"

The prince motioned to the servants to pack up the cannon, munitions, and sundries of the picnic. He ordered the ponies brought forth and he and Ethel mounted, beginning the short ride back to Kangla.

Ethel glanced over her shoulder to see if her Gurkha was staying close. Her escort trotted behind her pony, rifle in hand. Ethel caught his eye, and she smiled but the soldier's expression did not change. Ethel turned and faced the approaching red brick walls of Kangla.

Chapter 29. The Yuvraj's Proposition

A short time later...

Ethel

Ethel rode next to the prince as the entourage followed—servants riding, walking, and leading pack ponies laden with field guns and supplies. Close behind Ethel's clip-clopping pony trotted her indefatigable escort. Ethel marveled at the wiry Gurkha.

He shows no sign of tiring!

The Kohima road led southeast to the Northern Gate in the outer wall of Kangla. A wide dry ditch, once a deep moat, fronted the ancient citadel. The northwest corner, the brick wall to their right, stood in disrepair, damaged decades earlier in a war with Burma.

The party passed beneath a brick arch and entered the outer confines of Kangla. Ahead lay a wet ditch—an interior moat defending the high brick walls of the inner citadel. To their left, the river swung in a lazy curve. A one-thousand-foot-long mud wall broken by two masonry arches stretched along their right. They turned at the first arch and entered the Yuvraj's compound—a spacious enclosure filled with mud-walled, thatch-roofed buildings. The largest was the palace of the Yuvraj, surrounded by guesthouses, supply holds, stables, and quarters for soldiers and servants. The most impressive structure was a fifty-foot-tall brick temple. All four sides featured tall columns framing arched doorways with high balconies overhead. The rooftop was open, encircling an upper tower topped by a corrugated iron roof with gilded eaves.

Ethel and the prince entered the palace and servant women led Ethel to a boudoir where she could freshen before dinner.

The dinner was a traditional Manipuri feast of chicken, fish, and mixed vegetables. Above the table, the lazy punkah fan swished as servants filled goblets, set the table, and brought forth dinner courses, removing empty dishes. Ethel gobbled her food as if she was starving, but went easy on the wine.

Nervous energy. I must keep my wits. I almost have him where I want him.

Ethel's Gurkha escort received a plate and drink and sat at the far end of the dining room. His Martini-Henry rifle stood leaning in a corner within easy reach. The soldier's manner comforted Ethel—always present, observant, aware of his mission, yet almost invisible. The prince had yet to acknowledge or question the man's presence, though the Gurkha was the only other person seated at their dinner.

Odd that Tikendra Jeet's wives stay hidden!

Conversation progressed in good humor and as Tikendra Jeet finished his last bite, he revisited Lieutenant Simpson's petition to inspect Manipur's arsenal.

"His assignment confuses me," the prince said. "With the Burmese now subjugated, absorbed into the British Empire, I question, why show such interest in the pitiful weapon stores of Manipur?"

Ethel cocked her head and shrugged while chewing her final mouthful.

"That aside," he continued, "to honor my late father, who was always a good friend to Britain, and to thank you for your company, I will grant the petition..."

Ethel dropped her fork, clasped her hands, and swallowed.

"On two conditions," he finished.

Ethel could not suppress her surprise. "More conditions?"

"Yes," he said. "First, during the inspection, you will go with Lieutenant Simpson."

"Oh, that will be no problem." Ethel broke into a self-satisfied smile. "I would love to see the inside of the arsenal. What is the other condition?"

"You agree to join me now in an after-dinner stroll around the grounds. We shall converse as our dinners settle."

"All right." Ethel forced another little smile and dropped her napkin on the table. "That sounds nice."

The prince rose and she followed. As the servants approached the table, her escort stood and slung his rifle strap over his shoulder. Ethel followed the prince to the courtyard, a few steps ahead of her Gurkha. They walked toward the nearby brick tower and reached a tall arched doorway.

"This is the temple of Vrindavan Chandra. It has been in my family for decades—at least since the time of my grandfather. Let us enter."

They entered a cavernous chamber lit by torches. Their footsteps echoed as they approached the inner sanctum. Ethel craned her neck, looking past the prince. The chamber featured alters and statues.

"Which gods do you worship here?"

"Lord Krishna," he said, "but come, I will show you something."

"In there?" She nodded toward the sanctum.

He cocked his head toward a brick staircase, and motioned, pointing toward the ceiling. "Up those steps."

Ethel and her escort followed as the prince climbed the brick staircase. They scaled four long flights around the tall sanctum and reached an upper alcove. Each side of the chamber featured a high balcony extending above a temple entrance. Along the walls of the inner tower stood tables, shelves, and an altar exhibiting statues and idols, large and small. Ethel and the prince approached the altar as the Gurkha escort watched from the top stair.

"Represented here," the prince said, "are hundreds of deities of Manipur—the ancient gods and goddesses from before the Krishna awakening. The family of the maharaja worships here in private. It is a tradition to keep the memory of the old gods alive."

Ethel approached a table to examine the many figurines and statues. She reached to touch one, but stopped and turned. "Is it permitted?"

Tikendra Jeet nodded. Ethel selected and lifted an intricate figurine—a green-eyed jade dragon with wings, scales, and claws. Its long body looped multiple times, and many-toothed jaws devoured its tail. A claw grasped a sparkling red gem as if it was an egg. Ethel held her breath as she gripped the statue. The stone was smooth and cool—a pleasant sensation tingled her palm. She glanced and observed the prince studying her interest in the idol.

"You admire it!"

"I do—very much so! I have seen nothing like it."

"Do you know what it signifies?"

"No. What?"

"Of all the idols," he said, "you selected Pakhangba, the dragon-god—ancient symbol of Manipur."

"It is beautiful."

"I would like you to have it—as a gift."

"Oh, I could not!" she said. "It must be far too precious. It belongs here in the temple though I admit I am taken by its beauty."

"As I am with yours." The prince locked eyes.

Ethel caught her breath. "Please, do not say that." She moved to restore the statue to the altar.

The prince caught her hand. "I do not apologize for speaking the truth. I insist you keep the statue—as my gift. A thing of beauty given to honor a beauty."

Ethel gripped the figurine and drew it close to her breast. The tingling sensation grew stronger.

"You must take it," he insisted. "I expect to find it on display in the durbar hall, the next time I am a guest at the Residency."

"If you insist," Ethel murmured. "Thank you."

"Excellent! Now come! There is something else I must show you before the fall of darkness."

The prince entered the base of the central tower where another staircase led upward. Ethel waited for her Gurkha escort and held out the jade dragon. "Please keep this safe for me until we are back at the Residency."

The Gurkha took the statue and looked at it while Ethel walked up the stairs. She glanced back to see the soldier stuff the object into a shirt pocket, shoulder his Martini, and follow.

They climbed three short flights. The door opened onto the rooftop where brick coping and balusters interspaced with iron rails formed the parapet of a spacious four-sided balcony fifty feet high.

"Oh, my!" Ethel went to the western parapet and beheld the blood-red sun setting behind the tall hills. "One can see everything from here!"

She looked down at the compound and the thatch roof of the Yuvraj's palace and raised her eyes to the northwest corner. The brick wall facing the dry ditch lay broken in ruin. The damaged wall and its scattered bricks drew her eyes. She focused on a pier cap atop a brick baluster. As the evening breeze blew through her hair, a thought flashed through her mind.

Something queer—something vital—hides there.

She turned to find the prince standing close. Her Gurkha escort observed from the doorway by the top stair. She edged away, turned back, and pointed.

"Why is the wall in such disrepair? It has been so my entire time in Manipur."

Tikendra Jeet drew closer, looking where Ethel pointed. "Now you mention it, it has been like that my entire life. Burmese guns caused the damage decades ago. Something always prevents the work from starting—heavy rain, or other more essential construction projects. With Burma no longer a threat, it has not received priority. Come—let me show you something."

The prince led Ethel around the central tower to the eastern side. Ethel's line of sight cleared the walls of the inner citadel and she looked out upon the vast expanse of Kangla. She saw the royal ceremonial hall and the maharaja's palace; the setting sun glinting on the golden-roofed temple of Shri Govindajee; a nearby grove of trees; the durbar hall; great dragon statues; polo grounds; and the arsenal. High brick walls surrounded the squat brick structure.

"Magnificent—is it not?" His hand swept an arc past the scene. "What do you think?"

"Of Kangla?" Ethel said. "It is impressive—and beautiful."

"We are a small country," he said. "Once mighty, we could be mighty again. All of this could be yours."

"What do you mean?" Ethel bit her lower lip.

"I could give it to you." The prince searched her eyes as if seeking the bottom of a deep well.

"How…?" Ethel found his stare uncomfortable and turned away.

"If you were my queen."

"But—but…," Ethel stammered. "You are not the maharaja. Britain will soon recognize your brother the regent as the maharaja."

"So is that the reason for Quinton's visit? Formal recognition of my brother Kula Chandra as the maharaja?"

"I do not know," Ethel said. "Quinton has not said. Perhaps he intends to recognize your brother. Would it not make sense?"

"Unnecessary," he said. "My brother is the maharaja in the eyes of Manipur. Britain cannot dictate who rules, yet rumors persist the Viceroy wants Sura Chandra returned to the throne. Rumors say Quinton will use force to reinstate my brother. Manipur does not want Sura Chandra back."

"I know nothing of that. It does not change the truth—you are not the maharaja."

"Your husband has taught us how to rectify that situation. The word is 'abdicate.'"

"But, you are a married man—with nine wives! How can you make such a suggestion? You cannot be serious."

"I am serious," he said. "If you accept my proposal, I will divorce my other wives if that is what it takes to please you. You would be all I need."

"You forget—I am a married woman."

"Married—yes—to a perverted, philandering English civil servant. I myself wrote you of his scandalous indiscretions. You deserve better. He could die of dysentery, like Heath, or get a new assignment. As his wife, you will follow him to another remote corner of the British Empire. You will not have this chance again—a chance to be influential, to be royalty—I offer you the chance to be a queen."

Ethel's heart pounded. She fought off a surge of fantasies, fear, longing, and a warm arousal.

This is where my game has led me—to the edge! I cannot accept, but if I reject him now, I risk his refusal to let Walter inspect the arsenal.

"Tell me your thoughts." He gripped her hand and drew her close. "Will you accept?"

She gasped. "I cannot." She turned. "Please stop. It is not possible."

"My proposition impressed you," he said. "I can tell. I can see it in your eyes. You express no outrage and make weak objections. You cannot hide it—my offer intrigues you."

This is not about me. The timing is no accident. He fears Quinton's coming—that is clear—and suspects he is in danger. He seeks protection, imagining he can save himself by concocting a political marriage.

"I—I am tired," she said. "I want to go home."

Ethel tried to pull away from his grasp. She glanced to one side—her Gurkha escort had taken his rifle from his shoulder and held it ready.

"I ask *you* a favor now," Tikendra Jeet said. "I ask for your answer before you go."

Ethel looked away. Thoughts raced.

Do not fall for his trap and break the spell of good feelings, but do not give false hope. Play for more time to think.

"You upset me," she said. "This is too sudden and unexpected. I cannot make a quick decision on a matter of such gravity. I need time to consider your proposition. The chief commissioner is coming and I will be busy helping Frank. Please allow me time—until after Quinton's visit. Then I will give you my answer."

Tikendra Jeet released Ethel's hand. "Look once more into my eyes."

Tears welled. Ethel raised wet eyes to meet his stare. She kept control and counted ten seconds—an eternity. The prince nodded and broke his gaze.

"I will await your answer," he said, "after the chief commissioner's visit. Thank you for granting me the pleasure of your company. I look forward to our next visit, and I hope you have similar feelings."

"Thank you for a lovely dinner," Ethel replied.

Tikendra Jeet turned away and moved toward the stairs without looking back, passing the Gurkha without a glance. The prince had taken no notice of the escort the entire day and evening. The Gurkha looked at Ethel and their eyes met. In that gaze, Ethel saw his understanding and read his emotions—concern, anger, and an urge to defend her honor and punish the prince. Ethel smiled and shook her head.

"Time to go home."

Chapter 30. The Goat and the Fire god

Continued...

Ethel

The red sun disappeared behind the western hills and darkness crept over the walls of Kangla. Ethel and her Gurkha escort departed for the Residency. Ethel swayed in silence on the back of her pony, exhausted, emotions spent. The Gurkha led the way on foot, reins in hand. They crossed the bridge over the moat and entered the inner citadel. At the Kangla-sha, they turned west and followed the main thoroughfare toward the Western Gate. As Ethel sat on the pony, she realized they were yet half a mile from home. Her escort, who had spent much of the day trotting after her, walked before her. Guilt got the better of Ethel and she took pity.

"You poor thing," she said. "Are you not exhausted? Ride in my place!"

The Gurkha did not look back. "Oh, no, memsahib must ride."

It was the first time Ethel had heard his high-pitched Nepali lilt.

What an endearing voice.

"Gurkhas walk," he said, adding, "Sunwar not tired."

"Sunwar? Is that your name?"

"Oh, yes, memsahib," he said. "Sepoy Sunwar, 43rd Gurkha Rifles, Bengal Infantry, memsahib."

"Well, Sepoy Sunwar, I appreciated having you nearby today. You made me feel safe. I understand it was—a punishment."

He turned and grinned. "Not punishment, memsahib! All pleasure for Sunwar!"

"I am sorry you had to witness that scene in the temple tower."

"Memsahib, forgive Sunwar," he said, "not for Gurkha to say, but prince is clever—very dangerous man. Memsahib should not be alone with him. Sunwar happy to watch and keep memsahib safe—anytime."

"Thank you, Sepoy Sunwar. I appreciate your concern. Your advice is sound and welcome."

Ethel remained lost in her thoughts the rest of the trip. The two soon reached the Residency gate, and Sunwar led the pony the final distance up the carriage lane to the verandah. There they parted, she toward the house and he toward the cluster of tents in the bivouac area.

Ethel's servant Moonia greeted her at the door. The old woman held a bony finger to her lips, signaling for quiet, and led Ethel to the parlor door. Ethel looked inside to find Frank asleep in a chair. A spilled cup lay nearby on the floor, surrounded by empty Yu flasks. Ethel sighed and shook her head. She dialed the lamp down to a glimmer and followed Moonia to the dressing chamber. Ethel doffed her riding habit and dressed in the bedclothes Moonia had laid out. As the ayah brushed Ethel's hair, Ethel had a mischievous thought.

"Moonia," Ethel said, "the British dignitaries are coming soon. Frank and I wish to throw a feast in their honor, but we have a problem. We grow tired of fish, chicken, duck, and geese. We know beef and pork are out of the question. Frank requisitioned five sheep from Silchar, but they only sent four. Yesterday we learned none of the sheep survived the long journey. Now we have nothing to serve our guests. The bearer recommends goats. Goats fatten slower than sheep so we must act with urgency while still time. I hope to select worthy subjects tomorrow. What are your thoughts?"

Ethel knew she was making mischief. She smiled at Moonia's hateful expression at the mention of the bearer. The old woman detested the bearer, and they were forever at each other's throats. Ethel received guilty pleasure egging on the woman.

Moonia's face darkened and she exploded in anger. "No goats! Evil will come!"

"Why do you say that?"

"Do not trust bearer! Agni will be angry!"

"Agni?" Ethel said. "The Hindu god of fire? Why?"

"Goats sacred. Willing stead of Agni. Offend Agni and there will be death, fire, and evil."

Ethel shook her head and laughed. "But, Moonia, no one forbids eating goats."

Moonia wagged her head. "Not forbidden, but permitted only with proper rituals—tapasya and vrata. Without tapas, Agni will bring death, fire, and evil. British sahibs—all ignorant of tapas. Did bearer not mention this? Memsahib must not trust bearer!"

Ethel laughed. "Goodnight, Moonia. We can discuss this tomorrow."

The woman grumbled as she crawled off, curling up in her usual spot, wrapped in blankets on the floor outside Ethel's bedchamber and was asleep in seconds. Ethel, meanwhile, tossed and turned. Her mind raced as she replayed the events of the day and contemplated the implications. Instead of counting sheep, she assembled a list of tasks for the next day.

Ask Frank if he has heard anything more from Quinton.

Write a letter to Lionel Brackenbury.

Draw a map of Kangla for Walter.

Tell Walter to contact Prince Tikendra Jeet and schedule inspection of the arsenal.

Select and buy a goat.

Find a spot in the durbar hall to display the dragon figurine...

"The idol!" She bolted upright in panic. "The Gurkha still has it!"

No worry! Gurkhas are not thieves. He forgot about it, as did I. He will keep it safe for me. Tomorrow I will speak to Walter.

Ethel settled back, mind still racing, and soon drifted into a sleep filled with frustrating dreams. She wandered in desperation, lost on the streets of Calcutta. She was seeking the docks in time to board a steamship bound for England. Then she was back at the Residency grounds with cold stars glinting overhead. She wandered in the darkness and found herself among the line of tents in the bivouac area. She approached one tent and peeked. A Gurkha lay sleeping, flat on his back, arm draped over his face. His lips moved, whispering in a strange language. His fingers held an object and his thumb caressed the smooth surface.

It is my dragon! He intends to keep it!

She woke, early in the morning, nursing a headache. She rose and threw on the clothes Moonia had earlier laid out. After a light breakfast alone, she went to her study, fidgeted at her writing desk, and commenced work on her list of tasks. Moonia, ever underfoot, followed and took the guest chair by the window where she sat and darned in silence.

Per the mental note she made the prior day, Ethel composed a warm letter to her friend Lieutenant Lionel Brackenbury. She finished, sealed and addressed the envelope, set down the pen, and buried face in hands.

Is the letter too friendly—too intimate, too personal? Why am I getting myself deeper into another flirtatious relationship? What will I say if he appears?

Ethel debated. Should she send the letter as it was, come what may, or burn it and start a new letter?

Just burn the letter and forget writing to Lionel?

She picked up the sealed envelope and moved it close to the nearby candle—then stopped and plopped the envelope on the desk. As if to emphasize a point, she opened her ivory vanity box, removed a vial, lifted the stopper, and placed a drop of vetiver perfume on each corner.

I will send the letter, written as is, and I will do so today!

Ethel next selected a large sheet of parchment, found a straight edge, arranged her pen and a bottle of ink, and began her next task. At that instant, a rumpled mess appeared at her door. Frank stood yawning, bags under his eyes, scratching a disheveled head of hair.

Ethel glanced at Frank and frowned. "You look as if you lost a fight with a tiger." She turned her eyes back to her paper.

Moonia glanced up from her darning, scowled, and muttered a stream of Hindi curses under her breath.

"Hello to you, too, Moonia!" Frank said, bright and chipper. "Good morning, Ethel. Sorry I missed you last night. Were you back late?"

Ethel's eyes stayed focused on her drawing. "Not too late."

"How was your afternoon and evening?"

"Wonderful," Ethel said. "The prince is clever as ever at blowing things up with his field guns."

"Ah…," Frank said. "Um—he invited you to dinner, huh?"

"Yes. He did."

"Ah—hum!" Frank waited for Ethel to elaborate. "How was it?" he asked at last.

"Fine," she said, still not looking. "Afterward he showed me Kangla from the rooftop of his temple."

"Oh!" Frank's eyebrows raised. "Interesting. How did things end?"

"In what sense?"

"You know—Walter's mission. You went to ask…"

"Ah yes!" Ethel looked up and smiled. "The good news is…" She paused, watching Frank's pitiful expression of anticipation. "At dinner's end…"

"Yes?"

"He agreed to let Walter inspect the arsenal."

"Brilliant news!" Frank exclaimed. "Mission accomplished! Jolly good show!"

"Yes," Ethel murmured, "I suppose it was." She turned back to her drawing, putting pen to paper. "Jolly good."

Frank inched closer, attempting to look over Ethel's shoulder. "What is that you are making?"

Ethel drew a long straight line. "I am drawing a map of Kangla. Walter may need it."

"Why would Walter need a map?"

"It is hard to explain—a feeling. Yesterday I noticed details for the first time. I want to get it all down while I have it fresh in my mind."

Frank first nodded, but then cocked and shook his head. He took a step, stopped, and stood fidgeting in the doorway.

He is struggling, trying to find the right way to broach a sensitive topic.

Ethel's coolness at last ran its course. She warmed and broached a topic of her own. "There is something else I should mention from yesterday."

Frank straightened and raised his eyebrows. "Yes?"

Ethel addressed her servant. "Moonia, please leave us alone for a moment."

The woman gathered her work, stood, and left grumbling. Frank waited until she was out of sight and then took the empty chair by the window.

"Tikendra Jeet has heard rumors," Ethel announced. "He believes Quinton is out to get him and will return Sura Chandra to the throne. The man knows things. I think the woman you tossed at Walter—the general's daughter—is spying and Walter is not good at keeping secrets."

She returned to her drawing.

How will Frank react to that?

Frank took his time before responding. He sighed and shook his head. "Yes, I know," he said. "The Tongol General cornered me yesterday while you were with the prince. He probed and prodded, asking pointed questions. Ever since word got out of the size of Quinton's expedition, rumors have sprouted like weeds. Keeping the details secret in his first message has made matters worse. I wired Quinton yesterday, asking for more details, pushing for a reason for the visit, but so far no response."

"What should we do?" Ethel asked, still bent over her drawing.

"I have been thinking," he said. "Thinking of the concerns you raised after Heath died and we moved back—how you wanted to leave; how you begged me to ask for a different assignment."

Ethel put her pen down and gave Frank her full attention. "And…?" she said.

"I decided you are right. We should leave."

Ethel's heart skipped a beat. "When?"

"After Quinton's visit. I cannot leave until after, so I will tell him before he leaves Manipur."

Ethel's eyes welled with tears. "Oh, Frank!"

"You should leave as soon as possible," he said. "It is no longer safe here, if it ever was. If Quinton arrives leading an army and brings the former maharaja with him, all hell could break loose. I made inquiries by wire yesterday—into steamship schedules and such. I have reserved passage for you on a steamer out of Calcutta at the end of the month. You must leave soon—within a week, at least, I would say—a long trip back to Calcutta and the sooner you start the better."

Ethel quivered as a thrill surged up her spine. She had wished they could move away from Manipur, be together somewhere safe, to start over, and to reconnect as husband and wife. They had moved to India right after their marriage. If they could live somewhere else, somewhere—she hated to say it or think it—more civilized, they could find happiness together.

"It would be grand," she said, "to return to England, at least for a while, but—how can I leave, without you?"

"I will follow as soon as possible."

Ethel stared off and smiled.

"I take it you agree?" he said.

"Yes!" Ethel exclaimed. "Oh, yes, dearest Frank, yes!"

He grinned and looked as if a weight had lifted. "That settles it then— but we will keep it our secret as long as possible. I have told no one except you. Let us wait a day or two before you pack. The longer we can keep your departure a secret the better. Now, I must make myself presentable and eat something."

Frank stood and left Ethel to her drawing. As he walked toward his dressing room, Ethel noted he showed no signs of his earlier grogginess. He had a slight spring in his step and whistled as if the conversation had lifted a load. Ethel's mind raced and her body surged with adrenalin.

London! Tikendra Jeet will be furious when he learns! Walter must inspect the arsenal before the prince discovers the secret.

Ethel's head swam, feeling as if the walls were closing around her.

So much to do—so little time!

She wanted to be everywhere, doing everything at once.

Must finish one thing before starting another! Finish the map!

She focused, scratching another series of lines. She drew the river and the polo grounds; the inner and outer walls and moats; the durbar hall and the palace. She marked the prince's walled compound with "The Yuvraj" and drew a square denoting the tall temple. At the northwest corner of the outer perimeter of Kangla, she wrote "Dry Ditch" and "Wall Broken."

Ethel lowered her pen. "That is the weakest point," she whispered. "I would attack there if it came to war, and I were an enemy."

Frank returned an hour later, dressed and hair combed, as Ethel finished the final strokes and set down her pen. Frank addressed Ethel from the door.

"Dearest," he said, "a small commotion is brewing. The bearer is calling for you—seems he has located a goat."

"One goat?"

Frank nodded.

"Well—let us have a look then."

Ethel joined Frank, and they rushed to the verandah. The bearer stood out front with a large tethered goat, ready to present for inspection.

"Fine goat!" He puffed with pride. "Bearer found best goat in all Manipur. Good price if sahib buy today. Memsahib likes goat?"

Ethel smiled and whispered to Frank, "It had to be the best goat in all Manipur if it was the one goat he could find."

"And priced to sell," Frank whispered back.

Ethel and Frank walked down the stairs to examine the goat. Ethel looked up, startled to find Walter Simpson had strolled over from bivouac.

"It appears we have a committee of four to make this decision," Ethel said, laughing.

Walter joined the examination, and after discussion, the three agreed the bearer had found a fine goat –a large withered buck. Once fattened, it would make an excellent feast for important company.

"Oh, but wait...," Ethel said to the bearer. "What do you know of— tapasya?" Ethel smiled at Frank and Walter with a twinkle in her eye. "Moonia insists Agni, the Hindu god of fire, has an issue with goats."

The bearer threw up his hands, shouting, "Old woman is a witch! Memsahib must not listen to Moonia! Bearer can find memsahib a younger, better servant anytime!"

Frank, Ethel, and Walter burst out laughing. Upon further discussion, the goat committee voted and agreed to table any concerns over fire gods and Vedic magic.

The bearer led the animal to its new home behind the house. Workers had erected a pen in the garden outside the kitchen, far from the graveyard and the tennis courts. The groom from the stable took the rope and led the goat into the pen.

"Why was the pen built here?" Walter asked.

"Far from pink flowers," the bearer said. He explained that twenty years earlier Missus Johnstone, wife of the former political agent, had cultivated a unique breed of rhododendron. The bushes still bloomed in the garden next to the graveyard. The bearer insisted the goat pen had to be far from the enticing but toxic pink flowers.

"No flowers!" Ethel told the groom, "but make sure the goat eats all else it wants and more. Give him the best the garden has to offer. There is not much time for fattening."

As they returned to the verandah, Ethel broke the news to Walter—how Tikendra Jeet had agreed to allow inspection of the arsenal.

"Outstanding!" Walter said.

"One condition," she added. "I have to attend."

"Is that so?" Frank said.

As with Frank, Ethel said nothing of her stressful rooftop scene with Tikendra Jeet and his marriage proposition. As Frank requested, she also said nothing of the plan for her escape to London.

"Superb!" Walter laughed and clapped. "Well done! We must go today if possible." He looked at Frank. "Can you send a chuprassy to make the arrangements?"

Frank nodded, but squirmed and frowned. "Any reason I cannot tag along with you two?"

Ethel shrugged. "He did not say who else could. I assume it would be up to Walter who he wants to have in his inspection party."

"I have no objection," Walter said. "The more the merrier!"

"Oh, and Walter," Ethel interjected, "before I forget, the sepoy you sent with me yesterday for my protection…"

"Sunwar," Walter said.

"Yes," she continued. "His performance was exemplary and professional. I appreciated his presence."

"Good!"

"Is he back in camp? He has something of mine. I asked him to carry it for me last night. I forgot to ask for it back."

"You missed him," Walter said. "I sent him off early this morning. He will complete his extra duty at the cantonment at Langthabal. He will be back next week. Should I send someone after him?"

"Oh, no. It is not critical." Ethel bit her lower lip. "I am sure it can wait."

She scratched her palm. She had held the figurine for only a moment but craved its cool tingle.

I may never see it again!

Frank summoned Rassik Lal Kundu, the head chuprassy—a pompous fellow in a red uniform. Frank dictated a short letter to Prince Angao Sena, the Senapati, proposing inspection of the arsenal that afternoon. Before the chuprassy could run off, Ethel handed over the letter she had written to Lieutenant Brackenbury, asking the clerk to include it in the next post to Kohima.

Soon after, Walter departed to see about his troops and Frank headed to his telegraph office in the treasury—the stone building next to the main gate. Ethel returned to the Residency and found an ashen-faced Moonia waiting inside near a window.

She watched!

"Evil will come from goat!" she spat. "Moonia loves memsahib. Memsahib must not trust bearer, must not trust chuprassy!"

Chapter 31. The Arsenal, the Spy, and the Fight

That afternoon, Tuesday, 3 March 1891...

Ethel

Frank received an answer from Prince Angao Sena within two hours. Tikendra Jeet had kept his promise—he told his brother Angao to meet the inspection party and allow Simpson into the arsenal.

Ethel made final touches to her drawing. After lunch, she inspected the goat, ensuring it had plenty to eat and ate what it had. Then she joined Frank and Walter before the verandah where the horses waited and the three rode to Kangla. They soon entered the inner citadel and arrived at the arsenal. The cube-shaped fifteen-foot-tall brick building sat next to the palace, well defended inside twenty-foot-high brick walls—a fortress inside a citadel within a fort.

A line of Manipuri sepoys guarded the iron door. The princes Tikendra Jeet and Angao Sena stood waiting at their side, along with, to no one's surprise, the Tongol General. The venerable officer glowered, but appeared otherwise fit and looked regal in his green uniform and orchid-colored turban. Prince Angao Sena, as usual, chomped a wad of betel nut stuffed into his plump cheek, making his face appear peculiar and lopsided.

Simpson dismounted, met Angao, and the pair disappeared into the arsenal. Before Frank helped Ethel down, the Tongol General pulled him aside, and the two drifted away out of earshot. Ethel observed the old soldier shaking his head and punctuating his comments with wild gestures.

Probing Frank again about Quinton's expedition.

Tikendra Jeet offered Ethel his hand, and she slipped off her horse. As she stepped toward the door, the prince tugged her arm, spinning her.

"I thought we were going inside," she said, frowning.

"Not yet!"

Tikendra Jeet motioned and led her around a corner. Once out of sight of Frank and the general, he stopped, took her hands, and studied her eyes. Ethel stole nervous glances over her shoulder to see if anyone had followed.

Alone!

The prince spoke in a harsh whisper. "I learned you are leaving for London. Why?"

"What!" Ethel's eyes widened and her face reddened. "How can you...?"

"Do not imagine you can keep secrets," he hissed. "I find out everything that happens within the borders of this kingdom. Why did you say nothing yesterday?"

"I learned today!" Her voice quivered. "Frank arranged my departure without my knowledge."

"So—then you will not go?"

Ethel looked away, unable to bear the prince's stern gaze. "I am going to London. It is Frank's wish, and I will respect his authority in this matter."

"But you do not wish to go."

Ethel said nothing. Tikendra Jeet's face grew redder and pulsing veins rose on his temple.

"So your answer to my generous offer is that you will run away? Will you not wait until after Quinton's visit as you promised? Will nothing change your mind?"

Ethel tried to pull away, but he held fast. "Release me, or I will call for help! Calm your famous anger. I cannot discuss this now. We must rejoin the others."

He pulled her closer. "I see the truth in your eyes. Quinton will bring back my brother. There will be war. You are escaping while you can."

"Please let me go!"

Tikendra Jeet released his grip, turned, and stormed away, cursing. Ethel wiped tears, and still trembling, followed. She turned the corner to find Frank walking her way.

"There you are!" Frank called. His voice was bright, but with a hint of relief. "Where is Tikendra Jeet headed to in such a rush? I finished with the general. He was in fine form today. I noticed you were missing and was coming to look..."

Frank stopped and stared. Ethel could not hide her reddening cheeks or the sparkle in her moistening eyes.

"What is wrong?"

"Nothing—something caught in my eye."

Frank helped Ethel mount and did not press for details. Instead of going inside the arsenal, Frank mounted and waited for Walter to finish his inspection. During the ride back, Frank asked Walter what he had learned.

"They have a huge store of weaponry," Walter said. "I counted four seven-pounder mountain guns, and limitless rounds of ammunition—I could not tally all the crates. There are few modern rifles, but I saw muskets, perhaps two thousand—Enfield 53 pattern—and a few matchlocks, at least two thousand Brown Besses, and a wealth of ammunition."

"What does it all mean?" Ethel asked.

"It means our Manipuri friends can quite defend themselves," Walter replied. "They can arm a force of several thousand with artillery to back them. I will have to wire this information to Golaghat as soon as possible."

After a minute, Frank asked Ethel, "What happened back there, between you and Tikendra Jeet?"

Walter leaned forward in the stirrups. "Something happened?"

"He knows." Ethel burst into tears. "He said he heard I am going to London."

"What?" Walter looked at Frank. "What does she mean, going to London?"

Ethel told Walter of Frank's plan for her departure and then told him and Frank of her conversation with Tikendra Jeet outside the arsenal. Once more, she omitted any mention of the marriage proposal made the night before atop the tower.

Frank shook his head. "How can it be possible? I told you this morning—and only you. I am positive no one else knew."

"Someone else did," Ethel said. "Someone told him."

"A spy inside the Residency! We must discover who."

"I am still confused," Walter said. "What business is it of Tikendra Jeet if Ethel goes to London? Why was he so upset?"

Ethel thought long and hard before answering. "I mentioned to Frank earlier, Tikendra Jeet thinks Quinton is coming for him—to land a big tiger. He thinks I am escaping because there will be war. Perhaps he is right."

The three riders ambled through the gate and stopped when Ethel pointed. "Look ahead! What is happening?"

They observed, at the end of the carriage path, a crowd gathered near the verandah. Household servants, grounds staff, and Gurkha soldiers clustered in a circle surrounding a smaller group. Two women shouted and spat at each other as they struggled, held apart, each gripped by two sepoys.

Frank broke into a gallop and pulled up near the crowd. He had dismounted and reached the commotion by the time Walter and Ethel arrived.

"What is all this?" Frank shouted.

Ethel looked at the struggling women and her eyes opened wide, shocked by the sight of a familiar face.

Moonia!

One of the two women was Ethel's ayah. Cuts and bruises disfigured Moonia's face and blood trickled from a gash on her forehead. Ethel did not recognize the other, but she appeared to be a Manipuri or Naga village woman. Her injuries were scratches and scrapes instead of cuts and bruises. Moonia received the worst of the battle. On the ground lay two sticks—one was thick, almost qualifying as a log, the heavy end splattered with blood and strands of gray hair.

"That one—evil dog," the old ayah shouted, "She attacked Moonia!" and then she released a stream of Hindi curses.

"It is true, sahib!" one Gurkha said.

"She is an evil witch!" the second woman answered. "She called my husband a spy!"

The sturdy woman lunged forward, pulling and twisting. She was strong. The wiry Gurkhas planted their feet and gripped her wrists but had their hands full.

Through an avalanche of swearing and accusations on both sides, a story emerged. The second woman was the wife of Rassik Lal Kundu, the head chuprassy. Moonia had argued with his wife and accused the clerk of being a spy for Tikendra Jeet. Rassik's wife had flown into a rage and attacked Moonia. The fight had opened with words, escalated to kicks and bites, then punches, and at last sticks. The chuprassy's wife had scored with the heavier club.

Frank drew Ethel and Walter aside for a private conference.

"Is it possible?" Ethel whispered. "The chuprassy our spy?"

Frank considered the possibility. "He *was* in and out of the treasury as I was using the telegraph yesterday. Damned chuprassies are useless—always strutting around in their red uniforms, too pompous to be of much use."

Walter raised a finger. "Ah! I have a thought. Is old Moonia the spy?"

"How?" Ethel said.

"How else could she have known there was a spy? She may have feared the prince would confront you at the arsenal on leaving for London. She could use the accusation to cover her tracks."

Ethel bit her lower lip and shook her head. "I cannot believe faithful Moonia is a spy. She has been with me for years—ever since we first arrived in Silchar. When Frank and I discussed me leaving, we were alone."

"Moonia *was* there," Frank said, "until you asked her to leave."

"True," Ethel said. "I suppose anything is possible. The house is large with many nooks and crannies. When Frank is away, if I hear noises at night, I send Moonia off to explore—I am too afraid. She has been everywhere—the basement, attic, and crawlspaces. Maybe she discovered places for eavesdropping."

"You both raise good points," Frank said. "Who else could it be?"

"What of the bearer?" Ethel said. "Eyes in the back of his head. He always knows everything before anybody. If anyone were to know the hidden nooks and crannies of the house, it would be he."

"Perhaps you should end this," Walter suggested. "We have three suspects. Keep eyes on them and watch for clues."

Frank nodded and turned back to the impromptu trial. After another ten minutes of interrogation, he extracted no further information from either party. He ruled the chuprassy's wife had used excess violence. He gave her a warning and ordered her to pay a fine of one rupee. Then Frank directed the two Gurkhas to escort the woman home.

"She must pay more!" Moonia screamed. "Moonia will have revenge."

Frank cautioned Moonia against false accusations but before pronouncing judgment, the old woman twisted free and ran away cursing. She flew up the stairs onto the verandah and disappeared into the house.

Chapter 32. The Jade Figurine

One week later, Tuesday, 10 March 1891...

Ethel

Ethel threw her hands up in disgust. Straw fluttered to the rug alongside the half-packed wooden crate.

"This is impossible!" she cried, shaking her head. "Two days remaining! If I miss the deadline I shall..." She clutched two fists full of dark hair. "I shall tear out my hair. I refuse to leave without my belongings."

Ethel was packing and the slow progress was infuriating. The servants seemed oblivious to her predicament. To Ethel's eye, they were dragging their feet.

At least, more so than usual!

Moonia had sulked off alone, refusing to help the instant she saw the bearer, her archenemy, hovering near Ethel. Once word of Ethel's impending departure got out, a parade of Manipuris lined up each day. They pestered her and stole her time, forcing her to answer again and again why she was leaving, and showering her with pleas to stay. Tikendra Jeet and the Tongol General each came more than once, always probing, digging for clues on the purpose of Quinton's visit. She answered that in all honesty she was as clueless as they were.

Ethel turned from the crate in disgust and walked out onto the verandah. As she fought back tears of frustration, she looked at her hands.

I am doing it again!

She realized she had been scratching her palm. There was an itch, or a tingling feeling in her palm that would not stop. To be precise –absence of a tingle. A tingle she craved. She knew the reason.

The figurine! Where is it? It has been a week. I must not leave without it!

She strode off the verandah into the sun and marched beneath the shady trees toward the bivouac area. She passed the thatch-roofed barracks, canvas tents, and mud huts, sidestepping stacks of Martini-Henry rifles. Her eyes darted, side-to-side, examining the smiling faces of the diminutive Gurkhas. She searched each for that one particular face.

A sepoy stood, pointed her way, and his high-pitched voice called, "Sahib!"

The face of Walter Simpson popped above the heads of a circle of Gurkhas kneeling around the pieces of a dissembled rifle. "Ho! Ethel!" Walter called, hurrying to meet her. "What brings you out here?"

"Where is Sunwar?" She turned each way, searching. "Has he returned from Langthabal?"

Walter frowned. "Sunwar?" He snapped his fingers. "Oh—right! I remember—he has something of yours. Yes—he returned this morning."

He led Ethel to a group soldiers who snapped to attention. Walter addressed one of the Gurkhas, "Sunwar! Do you have a belonging of the memsahib's?"

Karna's smile vanished and his face darkened. He scuffed the ground with the toe of his boot.

"Do you have it?" Walter pressed.

Karna looked sheepish as he unbuttoned a shirt pocket and dug out a jade-green dragon figurine. His hand moved toward Ethel. "Memsahib, forgive Sunwar." He dropped his eyes, "Idol is—is…"

"Yes?" Ethel studied the young man's eyes. Karna remained silent as Ethel and Walter exchanged glances.

"What is the problem?" Walter said.

"Memsahib—must not hold too long. Dragon is—is no good for memsahib." Karna held out the figurine.

"I see…" Ethel smiled and snatched the idol from Karna's hand. "Thank you for keeping it safe." She turned and walked away as Walter followed.

"What was all that?" After a few steps, when Ethel would not answer, Walter changed the topic. "How is the packing going?"

"Terrible," Ethel replied. "I am so frustrated I could scream. It is a long trip to Calcutta. I must leave in two days or I will miss my steamer. It appears I will have to leave my belongings behind and trust Frank to bring them when he follows. The servants are slow and pitiful. All day I deal with a line of suitors begging me to stay."

"You can lump me into that group of beggars," Walter said with a chuckle. "Would it help if I got down on one knee?"

Ethel blushed. "Walter, do not make light. I am serious."

"Would it help if I sent men to do the packing for you?"

Ethel laughed. "It might! But if you send Sunwar, he needs to keep his hands off my figurine."

"What is that thing? Where did you say you got it?"

"A gift from Tikendra Jeet." She bit her lip.

Do not say too much.

"May I see it?"

Ethel held up the idol, keeping it in hand. She blinked as the dragon sparkled bright red and green.

Walter leaned forward to inspect. "A regal present—it should be in a museum. It seems too precious to be a gift."

She stuck out her lower lip. "To the likes of me, you mean?"

"Oh stop," he said. "It is beautiful. What will you do with it?"

Ethel said nothing as she slipped the ornament into a dress pocket.

"Look, Ethel," Walter said, "I suppose I have no right to say anything of your leaving. My assignment here is temporary, and I received orders this morning to return to Golaghat. I did my job and took inventory of the arsenal—thanks to you. I sent my report straight away. The roads and rest houses are ready as Quinton ordered. One hundred Gurkhas garrisoned and on alert. Nothing left for me to do."

"That is not true!" Ethel shouted. She glanced around at faces turning her way and lowered her voice. "Walter, you must be here during Quinton's visit. Frank needs you. You speak fluent Manipuri. You know everyone and where they keep everything."

"Yes, yes, I know all that. That is why I wired back and petitioned to stay longer—at least through Quinton's visit. Frank put in a good word, too. I hope to hear soon."

They chatted further until they reached the verandah where they parted. Walter offered to check on the goat and Ethel hurried back into the house. Unable to face the packing quagmire, Ethel walked past the crate and into the durbar hall. She looked down at her fist gripping the cool figurine. The smooth surface once more tingled in her palm, and she realized how desperate she had been to hold it again.

Why? At the temple, I only held it a moment.

She set the idol on a curio shelf beneath a set of Frank's photographs and stepped back to admire the presentation. She rearranged knickknacks, setting the idol in front. Then she moved it back and forward. She set it to one side then the other. After placing the figurine in front again, she snatched it off the shelf.

What am I doing? What difference does it make how it looks on the shelf? I will leave soon and will not leave it.

With an effort, Ethel returned the figurine to the shelf and stepped back. She reached for it once more, intending to move it somewhere else, and yanked her hand back.

Stop it! You are becoming obsessed. Let it sit there for now. You can always grab it before you leave.

She leaned to examine the dragon in the good light—her first chance to study. It was so intricate—so beautiful. The green scales sparkled in the daylight and she imagined the tiny eyes followed her movements. The delicate wings were assertive—erect and potent—but appeared too small to support flight. One clawed foot held the red jewel. The end of the looping tail thrust between the beast's sharp teeth.

How does it taste?

"What are you doing?"

Ethel stiffened, startled by Frank's voice and embarrassed.

How long was he at the door?

"A knickknack," she said. "One I must make certain to take with me. What are you doing?"

"I have news! Quinton responded to my appeal for information. He wired to say he is *not* bringing Sura Chandra back to Manipur. The Raj will not interfere in Manipur's choice of a maharaja. Her majesty will recognize Kula Chandra. Do you realize what this means?" Frank grinned, wide-eyed, expecting Ethel's answer.

"There is no reason for Manipur to fear Quinton's expedition," Ethel said. "There should be no chance of war."

"Correct!"

"Wonderful news!"

"You must help me spread the word," Frank said. "To Walter, to the Residency staff, to Tikendra Jeet, and the Tongol General."

"Yes! The women at the bazaar, any strangers we meet—we tell everyone and the sooner the better."

"Right! We can diffuse this tension. Everyone is so worried and depressed."

"Yes!"

"Oh, and…," Frank added, "Walter can stay longer, at least through Quinton's visit—headquarters approved that, too. Could the news be more fabulous?"

"Brilliant…" Ethel's voice trailed off as another thought occurred. "Do you know what else this means?"

Frank leveled a puzzled look and shrugged.

"It means—no reason for me to leave." Ethel bit her lip. "At least not right away. My leaving made everyone jumpy. If I keep packing and go forward with the plan to leave now, who will believe us? Should we wire the steamer company and delay the date of my departure to after Quinton leaves?

Frank's jaw dropped. "By Jove, you are right, as usual! We can leave together after Quinton has departed."

"Good! I will stay and enjoy all the fun with you and Walter, yet…"

"Yet what?"

"Did Quinton mention Tikendra Jeet? What of his worry—that Quinton is coming to take him away?"

"No," Frank said. "He mentioned nothing of that sort." He paused, looking thoughtful. "I am certain all will go well. No worries."

Chapter 33. The Last Ride

Eleven days later, Saturday morning, 21 March 1891...

Ethel

Anxiety became anticipation, and excitement grew with each passing day. Word spread like English ivy that Sura Chandra would never return to power—Quinton was coming to recognize Kula Chandra as maharaja.

All Manipur prepared for the visit. Chefs planned celebratory feasts for hundreds. Women and young girls prepared entertainment—festivities highlighted by exhibitions of Thang-ta, music, and dancing, including Manipur's famous classical play, the Ras Leela Nautch.

Ethel's decision to stay in Manipur was joyous news. Prince Tikendra Jeet visited the Residency to inspect his gift on display in the durbar hall and to see for himself the truth in her eyes. Ethel passed the test.

As things looked up, Quinton's party left Kohima and marched south, following the road through the Naga Hills. Then, as the column crossed the border into Manipur, anxiety returned. Reports spread south that Quinton's escort was larger than expected. Estimates varied, but settled on more than a dozen British military officials and native officers, and over four hundred crack Gurkha riflemen. Quinton appeared prepared for a fight few expected and no one wanted.

"Why so many soldiers?" was a question whispered everywhere, from the bustees by the citadel walls to the booths of the women's bazaar. The marshal prowess of the Gurkhas was legendary. Four hundred battle-hardened warriors teamed with the one-hundred Gurkhas already at the Residency formed a fighting force five-hundred strong. Rumors of Sura Chandra sightings spread and the newfound hope vanished. Quinton's expedition once more became an ominous event, and with each mile marched, anxiety grew. The tromping of Gurkha boots echoed like footsteps of doom.

On the day before Quinton's arrival, Ethel sat in the durbar hall watching the morning sun sparkle on the tips of the wings of the dragon figurine. The idol nestled in her palm, emanating a pleasant tingle.

Who is there?

Ethel sensed a presence—the bearer, standing in the doorway. She stood to return the idol in its place on the shelf, and right away, missed the sensation. She reached to retrieve the figurine, but suppressed the urge and turned away.

The bearer bowed. "Memsahib, time to inspect goat."

"Oh, yes!" Ethel looked at the clock. "Today is the eve of his command performance as the star of the feast."

As they proceeded to the kitchen, Moonia glowered from a chamber doorway. "Moonia," Ethel said, "do you wish to inspect the goat with us?"

I should not torment her. It perturbs her so, seeing me with the bearer.

Moonia shook her head, scowled, and sulked away.

She is such a tough nut to crack.

Days earlier, Ethel tried to extract an explanation for Moonia's allegation that the head chuprassy was a spy. Her efforts had been in vain, and the mystery of the spy remained unsolved. As Ethel entered the goat pen in the garden, Moonia glared from a kitchen window. Ethel smiled but Moonia's face vanished.

"Evil witch!" the bearer muttered.

"You always say that!" Ethel said. "Why?"

The bearer shut his mouth and said nothing further.

I will never understand the animosity between those two.

The stable groom waited in the garden next to the goat, smiling, eager to show off his work. The beast appeared cared-for, fattened, and in fine health.

"See, memsahib!" the groom said, pointing to the little shelter he had erected in the pen. "Goats not like being wet!"

"So you kept him dry! That is so outstanding!" Ethel said. "What of his diet? I assume goats eat most anything."

"Oh, no!" the groom said. "Goats picky eaters! Goat had pick of finest in garden!"

The groom next opened the goat's mouth, showing off intact molars and incisors. He pulled the skin over the goat's shoulders several times. Each time the hide snapped back.

"See, memsahib!" the groom said, beaming with pride. "Well-watered goat!"

The inspection continued as the boy's hands probed every nook and cranny. He checked the beast's temperature, respiration, and pulse. He pawed through its wattles and fleece checking for any sign of parasites or disease.

"No problems, memsahib! Fine, very healthy goat! Groom prepared goat well. Ready for sahibs to eat. Sahibs will have happy feast tomorrow."

"You both did well!" Ethel agreed, complementing the groom and the bearer on the fine work. They had prepared the goat for his big day in a short amount of time.

As Ethel turned to return to the kitchen, flashes caught the corner of her eye. She looked toward the bivouac area.

Two reflections! Someone is spying with field glasses. Sunwar!

Ethel's only justification for her suspicion of Karna was that he was the one Gurkha she knew by face and name.

The flashes stopped!

Insecurity crept into Ethel's mind.

My dragon figurine! Where is it? The durbar hall!

Ethel abandoned the groom and bearer, scurried inside, and ran to the durbar hall. She arrived at the curio shelf, frazzled, panting, heart pounding, looked for her treasure, and—there the dragon sat—in the exact spot where she left it.

It is still there. What is wrong with me? I am so foolish.

Ethel reached out, intending to pick up the statue, but hesitated and drew back when men's voices came from the verandah. She recognized Frank's voice, but not the other Englishman. She reached, wanting to touch the dragon once more. Instead, she yanked her hand back, straightened her dress, and entered the foyer. Frank stood holding the door, about to admit a middle-aged, mustachioed man.

"Why, Mister Melville!" Ethel said. "What a pleasant surprise! Back so soon?"

I feel so foolish for not recognizing his voice.

William Melville, the superintendent of telegraphs for Assam, stepped inside and removed his hat.

"So soon?" Melville shot a glance at Frank and chuckled. "Why, Missus Grimwood, it has been a month."

Ethel blushed.

Has it been a month? Is it possible?

Melville passed through Manipur a month earlier before Walter Simpson's arrival, inspecting and testing telegraph wires from Nagaland to Burma before Quinton's arrival.

"So sorry! I did not realize…"

"I had planned to ride on to Sengmai," Melville said, "but considering Frank's news, I am glad I stopped."

"News?" Ethel raised her eyebrows.

"A wire came in," Frank said. "Quinton's expedition reached Sengmai this morning. The party is twelve miles from Kangla. They are camping by the telegraph station and will start the final leg at dawn tomorrow. The grounds will soon crawl with visitors."

"I heard surprising rumors of the party's size," Melville said. "Did Quinton's message confirm?"

"Yes," Frank said, "the rumors are true on that score at least. Over four hundred rifles." Frank turned to Ethel. "Dearest, I must ride to Sengmai. Quinton wants me at the camp for a private conference."

"Did he say why so many soldiers?"

Frank shook his head. "He questioned William on the condition of the road to Burma."

Melville nodded.

"What could that mean?" Ethel asked.

"Perhaps that is the next stop for the expedition," Melville suggested.

"Another rebellion?" Frank said. "There was one in Wuntho last month."

"Um, perhaps…," Melville said, removing his spectacles. After a moment, he shook his head, saying, "Seems unlikely. Things are quiet in Burma now—General Wolseley has things under control. Kawlin and Wuntho are far from Tamu."

"Then the sooner I leave for Sengmai the sooner we shall learn the answer. I hope to end this speculation on the former maharaja."

Frank left to change into riding clothes while stable hands saddled a fresh horse. Minutes later Frank galloped up the carriage drive on his way to Sengmai—a twelve-mile ride, six miles past the bridge over the Imphal River. Melville stayed behind and went to inspect Frank's telegraph station at the treasury. Ethel hurried to give Walter the news.

Activity at the Residency soon reached a fever pitch as last-minute preparations shifted to full chisel. Three hours later Melville appeared at the door with a cable from Frank. Ethel read and her eyes opened wide.

```
Grounds to quarter over four hundred more rifles and
expect eleven more for breakfast.
```

"Eleven British officers and officials! In addition, Frank, myself, Walter, and you, Mister Melville, that makes fifteen all together—here, in my house, for breakfast tomorrow! Where is the bearer? We have work to do!"

The bearer was better prepared than Ethel expected and matters were soon in hand. Yet, excitement and nervous energy overwhelmed her and she could not keep still. She checked on the goat, admired the figurine, inspected the house, and then she admired the figurine again. She checked on the preparations for breakfast a second time, checked on the goat again, and admired the figurine once more.

Outside, a voice called, and she exited onto the verandah. There at the foot of the stairs stood Walter Simpson, dressed for riding, holding the reins of two saddled horses.

"Let us take a ride," he said. "You need to work off that anxiety. We can ride north toward the river. Perhaps we will meet Frank returning and learn what fate has in store."

Following a quick change into her riding habit—and a final unnecessary inspection of the goat and the figurine—Ethel and Walter galloped off toward Kangla. As they rode up the Kohima Road and neared the firing range, Walter pointed to a neighboring hill.

"Ready for a break?" he said. "From that rise we have a clear view of the road down to the river. We should see Frank returning."

The horses followed a winding path up the hill. At the top, while Walter tethered the horses, Ethel admired the panoramic view of the Imphal River valley. The Kohima Road ran a mile north to the bridge and snaked off into the jungle, disappearing into the mist. A chain of telegraph poles ran alongside the road, like the spine of an armored serpent. The wires formed a lifeline—a fragile link to the world outside Manipur. Ethel turned to remark on the beauty of the view and jumped, startled to find the officer standing close. Walter had a blanket draped over one arm as his hand gripped a dark bottle by the neck. In his other hand, he held two delicate glasses by their stems.

"Picnic?" he said, grinning.

Walter spread the blanket over a soft place beneath the shade of a tall oak. The point provided a clear view of the road. Ethel took a seat and smiled in anticipation as Walter opened the bottle.

"Is that real red wine I see?" she said.

"Shillong's finest!"

"I am so tired of drinking Yu. How on earth did you get that?"

"Oh, I pilfered it and the glasses from the officer's hall. They have sat hidden in my saddlebag ever since, waiting for the right moment. Tomorrow this adventure comes to a happy end. Calls for a celebration. Agree?"

"Oh, hurry and pour!" Ethel said laughing.

Three rounds later, the bottle was empty. Ethel and Walter lay back on the blanket and Walter pointed at the sky.

"That cloud looks like a dragon," he said.

Ethel hiccupped. "Clouds always—look like dragons—in Manipur."

"Oh? I had not noticed."

A peaceful moment of silence followed before Walter spoke. "I was thinking of the last time you and I polished off a bottle of wine. Do you remember?"

"I do," she said. "In Shillong. A similar place as I recall. Except the rocky hills went up higher beyond the woods. We listened to the waterfall, crashing onto the rocks."

"Correct! That was the time and place. Remember when Alan left us alone?"

"Yes, he sneaked off for a dip."

"I was so intoxicated," he said, "I almost made inappropriate advances."

"Did you?" Ethel turned to one side, elbow bent, head propped in hand. She pursed her lips and whispered, "What stopped you?"

Walter turned. "I—I heard a sound." Flushed faces moved close, lips almost touching.

"What sound?"

"Sticks snapping, like footsteps in the brush. I thought it was Alan, returning from his dip."

"And was it Alan?"

"No," he said. "I looked, but no one was there. Maybe it was an animal."

"Then what happened?"

"I feared someone was watching, so I did nothing. It turned out, Alan did not return for another twenty minutes. A magical moment spoiled."

"And what is your excuse this time?" Her lips parted, waiting.

Walter paused, so Ethel leaned forward, eyes closed, until their lips met. Walter's arms circled her in a warm embrace. He freed a hand to fumble with the buttons on her blouse. Ethel reached to help when Walter stopped and sat up with a lurch.

"What is wrong?" she said.

"Shush! I think I heard something."

"Oh, bloody hell!" Ethel moaned. "Now what?" She laid back and threw an arm over her face.

Walter stood, with difficulty, and stumbled toward the horses. He pulled a set of field glasses from a saddlebag and approached the eastern edge of the hilltop. He stared for a minute and then ran to the western side and raised the glasses.

"What is it? What do you see?"

"Come see for yourself," Walter said.

Ethel sighed and sat up, buttoning her blouse. As she stood, she placed a hand on the rough tree bark, righting her uncertain balance. She ambled over to Walter and he handed her the glasses. Below, in the distance, tiny figures lined the Cachar Road—clumps of five, ten, or twenty. All were men, heading for Kangla, most carrying long dao knives, and a few shouldered muskets. Further on, more men came. She hurried to the other side. The Kohima Road was much the same. Manipur was alive and its able-bodied men were streaming to Kangla.

Ethel lowered the glasses. "What does it mean?"

"Manipur," Walter said, "is preparing for war."

Chapter 34. The Secrets and the Goat Omen

Continued...

Ethel

Lieutenant Simpson stowed the blanket and wine glasses into his saddlebag. He tossed the empty bottle into the brush, and when he turned, Ethel stood close. She wrapped her arms around his waist and laid her head on his shoulder. Walter returned the embrace—a gentle kiss caressed the top of her head, and he drew a long, deep sniff, as if memorizing her scent.

"Ethel," he whispered, "what happened by the tree—I am sorry..."

"Do not be!" Ethel spoke with firm tenderness. "I am not sorry—I wanted it—longed for it to happen."

"No—I mean—I am glad your thoughts mirror mine, but I mean I am sorry I could not finish what I started. That is twice. Not in the stars, I suppose."

"Who can say?"

"We must get back," he said. "Quinton arrives tomorrow. After he departs, you and Frank will steam off to London and I will ride north to Golaghat, or another miserable place. When will I ever see you? How will we get another chance?"

Ethel looked up, blinking back tears. "Promise to write whenever you can—I shall. You will not be in India forever. Come to England—find us—in London, or wherever. Frank adores you as I do. It will all be fine between the three of us. We will be together—I promise."

She raised her lips, and he kissed her—full and deep. When their lips parted, she opened moist eyes to see Walter smiling.

"At least," he said, "you are no longer angry with me."

"Hum?"

"I thought I upset you forever when I took up with the Tongol's daughter."

Ethel laughed and said, "It was not real anger towards you. It was jealousy—of her!"

"Why?"

"She is with you! She is so young, pretty, and carefree—living the dangerous life of a spy."

It was Walter's turn to laugh. "But you are young and pretty! What cares have you? A houseful of servants does everything for you."

"That is not fair…"

"And why a spy?" he said. "She is not so good at it. That we all know she is a spy proves the point."

"I am not so young—I will be twenty-five. Frank will expect children soon. I want many things I cannot have—lives I dream of but will never live. Why must we live but one life?" Ethel drew back and her face clouded. "I must confide in someone. Promise you will not spill a word to anyone—not to Frank, in particular. I think I should tell you, given the circumstances."

Ethel told every detail of her dinner with Tikendra Jeet and the prince's proposal delivered atop the temple tower.

"That—scoundrel!" Simpson fumed, shaking clenched fists. "I am horrified—I put you up to that. If I had known—I should go now, find him, and strangle him with my bare hands. I will yet, given half a chance!"

"You do no such thing," Ethel said. "I have another sinful confession. I place implicit trust in you with this secret. For a time, I desired the life he offered. I imagined myself his queen, helping rule this beautiful country, mingling as an equal with royalty."

"Why?"

"I would make something of this land. I say I want to leave, and I do, but I changed—I respect the people more. There is a simple honesty here. The Manipuris treat their women and girls with respect. Manipur could become a modern, cultured, and educated country. I would build schools and museums. I would make it the jewel of all India. Can you understand? I could influence people's lives, live a meaningful life, do great things, and be someone who mattered…"

"Ethel!" Walter clasped her shoulders square on and stared at her hard. "This can never be! How long do you think England will let Manipur stay free? The Empire continues to grow. I wager within five years, under a pretense, Manipur will become a princely state, and the monarchy will become figureheads, window dressing, with no power. I have seen the pattern repeat. You would not make the snooty ladies of Shillong jealous— they would laugh and sneer behind your back."

Ethel sighed and laid her cheek against Walter's breast. "It was a silly dream. Lucky for me, the dream faded. The guilt was strong, and I had to clear my conscience by telling someone."

"Come." Simpson took Ethel's hand. "We should get back to the Residency before Frank returns."

"Do not worry what Frank will think. I have long sensed Frank has been expecting this to happen. It would please him—an odd but convenient manner of penance."

"Perhaps you are right, but I have concern for all the traffic on the road. We should find out what is happening at Kangla so we can warn Frank. I hope we have not missed him."

They mounted, guided the horses down the meandering path, and galloped across the field to the Kohima road where they cantered amidst the growing swarm of armed sepoys. As they grew close to Kangla, they reined the horses back and snaked through the thick crowd clustered around the Western Gate.

Walter shouted to a turbaned man carrying a rifle. "You, there— Sepoy!"

"Sahib?"

"What is happening here?"

The man pointed to the tall battlement. A great banner fluttered in the breeze—a golden dragon on a green field, coiled, and devouring its tail.

"Pakhangba unfurled, sahib! The maharaja called the Lallup!"

Walter nodded and urged his horse forward.

"What did he mean?" Ethel asked.

"The Senapati has raised his irregulars. All those thousands of rifles I counted in the armory—there will be hands to use them. I hope Quinton knows what he is doing, for all our sakes."

They arrived at the Residency surprised to discover Frank had not yet returned. The bearer, as usual, was waiting for them on the verandah.

"Memsahib!" he shouted. "Come! The goat!"

Ethel and Walter hurried through the house and burst out the kitchen door. A crowd had gathered in a circle in the garden. Ethel pushed her way to the middle, and in the center, the stable groom knelt next to the goat. The poor creature lay on its side, a puddle of vomit near its mouth.

"Goat most sick—dying!" the young man cried. "Drink may help—spirits, Yu, something!"

The bearer shouted to a servant who ran into the house and returned with bottles of Yu, brandy, and beer. The groom forced the liquids down the goat's throat. It was a desperate measure to no avail. The beast expelled a gurgling froth. With a shudder and a groan, it exhaled and passed.

"No!" Ethel cried. "How can this be possible? I saw him a few hours ago—he was fine. He was in perfect health!"

The groom examined the foamy earth near the dead animal's mouth and looked up, holding a palm full of pink petals.

"Poisoned!"

"What are those?" Walter said.

"Flower petals!" Ethel gasped. "Missus Johnstone's rhododendrons—from the bushes in the garden on the other side of the house."

"Lovely flowers."

"But poisonous! Lethal to goats. We were careful to keep the goat far away. How could the goat eat the flowers?"

"Goats are agile creatures," Walter said. "They can vault high fences. It could have jumped out."

"And then jumped back?" Ethel scoffed. "Doubtful. Besides, it has had a tether the entire time."

"Then someone may have picked the flowers—threw them over the fence to the goat. Perhaps the person thought it would be a treat."

"Goats not like eat food tossed on ground," the groom said.

"Goats are social creatures." Ethel sniffled, tears welled, and her voice trembled. "They graze all day long. Someone picked the flowers, walked up to the goat, and fed them to him, branch after branch, knowing the flowers would kill. The poor beast trusted the person and gobbled poison."

"Poor chap," Walter muttered. "But—how ironic—we planned his slaughter for tomorrow." He chuckled. "At least the goat escaped the evil fate of becoming a feast for a crowd of hungry sahibs."

Ethel did not smile. She wiped tears, turned away, and stared at the house. An empty kitchen window overlooked the garden. The same window at which, hours earlier, she had last seen Moonia glowering at her, the groom, and the bearer.

What had she said? Goat is sacred, willing stead of Agni. There will be death, fire, and evil, if we offend Agni.

"Where is Moonia?" Ethel asked.

"Old witch gone," the bearer answered.

"What do you mean gone?"

The bearer shrugged. "Packed bag. Left house. Out gate. Gone! House happier without her."

Ethel scratched her palm. A horrid thought sprang into her mind. She bolted for the house and ran to the durbar hall. She pawed through the knickknacks on the shelf. Her heart sank further, and she collapsed, sobbing, onto the couch.

A few minutes later, Walter entered. "There you are. I had the goat hauled off for proper burial and…"

Ethel sat, arms folded, staring into space. Tear tracks lined her red cheeks.

"What now?" he murmured.

Ethel sobbed. "Gone! My little jade dragon figurine—the gift from Tikendra Jeet. It was so precious, and so beautiful. She stole it."

"Who?"

"Moonia!"

"How do you know?"

"Who else?" Ethel cried. "She killed my goat, stole my treasured possession, and deserted me. The bearer is right—she *is* an evil witch! How could I have missed it?"

Walter put a comforting hand on Ethel's shoulder. She looked up, wiping tears and sniffling.

"I must speak with Sunwar!" she said.

"Why? What has he done?"

"Perhaps nothing, but he knows something. I must see him right away."

Walter led the way to the bivouac area. The Gurkha looked up and stood. He fidgeted and his face reddened as Ethel and the lieutenant approached. Ethel strode straight up and looked the young soldier in the eye.

"Were you spying on me?"

"Spy?" Karna's voice became shrill. "Sunwar not a spy!"

"Were you watching me?" Ethel pressed. "Earlier today, with field glasses, when I was in the garden."

The Gurkha looked down and nodded. "Sunwar wants to protect Memsahib. Sunwar worried about bad prince."

Walter and Ethel exchanged wide-eyed glances.

"So then," she said, "did you watch the house this afternoon while Lieutenant Simpson and I were away?"

Sunwar nodded.

"What did you see?" Walter said. "Anything suspicious?"

"Saw old woman. She plucked flowers by graveyard, feed to goat. Saw old woman leave through gate, walked in big hurry."

Ethel grasped the man's shoulders. "Which way did she go?"

Sunwar pointed at Kangla, then south, toward the cluster of bustees outside the walls near the Burma Road. A dark cloud passed over the Gurkha's face, and he gritted his teeth. "Did old woman hurt memsahib?"

"No," Ethel said, "but she killed my goat and stole my little dragon—the one you kept safe for me."

Ethel looked toward the distant bustees, scratching her palm.

"Sunwar warned!" Karna said, pointing to Ethel's hands. "Idol not good! Warned memsahib not to hold idol too much. Sunwar knows!"

Ethel stopped scratching, red-faced. Her hands dropped to her side.

The Gurkha's frown vanished. "Sunwar will find old woman." His eyes lit up, and he clenched his fists. "Make her give statue back."

"You will not!" Walter shouted. "You are not to leave the grounds without a direct order." The lieutenant looked toward the gate. A man on horseback galloped down the carriage path. Walter dismissed the Gurkha. "That will be all, Sepoy. Return to duty." He pointed toward the drive. "Look, Ethel. Frank is back."

Frank cleared the tree-lined lane and arrived at the verandah. He handed his reins to a servant and hurried into the house.

"Why is he so late?" Ethel said. "It is almost seven."

Walter and Ethel rushed to the house. The bearer directed them to Frank's study. The door was open part way. Ethel knocked and peeked through the crack. Frank had hung his coat, rolled his sleeves, and sat at his desk writing a note. A redcoat chuprassy stood waiting as Frank finished scribbling. He handed the note to the messenger who sidestepped Ethel and Walter, scurrying away. Frank's face expressed welcome and weariness, as if they were customers arriving one minute before bank closing time.

"Well!" Ethel said. "At last!"

"Greetings to you, too," Frank said.

"You worried us! You were away such a long time."

Frank set his jaw and his face turned sullen. "Sorry, dear." He nodded at Simpson. "Good evening, Walter."

The lieutenant nodded back. "Can you share any news?"

"I can share a part," Frank said. "Sura Chandra, the former maharaja, is *not* with Quinton's expedition. I can vouch for that. He is not at the camp—I would have seen him."

"Good news!" Walter said and Ethel nodded.

Frank continued. "The Raj *will* recognize Kula Chandra. The regent will become the maharaja in the Queens's eyes. I saw the paperwork. It is all official. I sent word to the palace notifying Kula Chandra, and all of his brothers, to be here tomorrow at noon sharp for a durbar. A reception follows that I hope will please the regent. Oh, and, Walter—full dress uniform."

Simpson smiled and nodded.

"You brought wonderful news, Frank!" Ethel said. She stood with clasped hands, wide eyes, and a bright smile, expecting more good news.

"Now," Frank muttered, "if you do not mind—I hate to be a wet blanket, but I had a long, exhausting day. I hope you and Melville do not mind dining without me."

"What of you?" Ethel said. "Your dinner…"

"I will have the khidmutgar bring something to my room later." Frank placed elbows on the desk, looked down, and pressed his fingers to his forehead. "Now, if you will both excuse me."

Ethel's face reddened. She expected—something more—she did not know what she expected from her husband at that moment, but raw, irrational emotion surged. She knew something was wrong, and she wanted to help, to have Frank's confidence. Her day had taken a bad turn—her goat was dead, her precious figurine stolen, and Moonia had fled. Instead of a chance to share, she felt ignored, cut off cold, and dismissed. She succumbed to impulse, performing the most outrageous stunt she could imagine. She turned to Walter, threw one arm around his waist, placed the other hand behind his head, and drew him forward into a passionate kiss on the mouth. Walter pulled away, red-faced. Frank glanced up, but kept his fingers on his forehead. Ethel faced her husband, prepared for a severe reaction, but Frank paid scant attention.

"Well—Frank…," Walter said, sputtering. "I understand. Goodnight, then. Join us later if feeling better." He stopped at the door and held out his hand to Ethel. "Are you coming?"

Ethel shook her head, saying, "I need to talk to Frank."

Walter nodded and left as Ethel closed the door.

You have done it—you have crossed the Rubicon! Prepare yourself for what comes next.

She turned to face Frank and found him standing at the coat tree, digging into a jacket pocket. He pulled out a shiny disk attached to two long black tubes. He inserted the tube ends into his ears and, head cocked, held the shiny, flat mechanism against the wall, as if listening for something.

Ethel stared. "What…"

Frank raised a finger to his lips. He moved along the wall, pausing here and there to listen at open spots. Once he had completed a pass over the interior walls, he laid the device on the desk.

"What is that you have there?" Ethel whispered. "Is that a…?"

"Yes—a Stethoscope. I borrowed it from Doctor Calvert, the surgeon for Quinton's company."

"Are you listening for rats?"

"For spies—in the walls. One cannot be too careful."

"I think we resolved that mystery." Ethel told Frank about the goat, the missing figurine, and Moonia's disappearance.

Frank smiled for the first time. "Well—good! One less thing." His face darkened. "We have to discuss something."

"About the kiss…"

Frank held up a hand and shook his head. "Ethel, I mean this— whatever is between you and Walter is fine with me. I give my blessing. In fact, if something happens, I hope Walter can be there for you."

"What are you saying?"

"I want you to know, I love you, but now I must discuss something more critical. I must have your total commitment to secrecy. No one must know what I say. Not Walter, Melville—no one."

Ethel nodded as blood drained from her face.

"I have made an egregious error," he continued. "Pray, forgive me, but I should not have allowed you to stay. I should have insisted, made you return to London when the opportunity was in our hands. Too late now."

"You are scaring me." She took a deep breath. "What is it? Too late for what?"

"Quinton confided in me for the first time, and so far, in me alone. He told me the true, primary purpose of the expedition."

"Not Tikendra Jeet…"

Frank nodded. "He is coming to arrest Tikendra Jeet. He will charge the prince as the villain behind the coup, deliver the verdict, and take him away to exile under armed guard. The Raj wants to make an example—show Manipur and other states, the Empire will not tolerate political intrigue."

"Manipur is not part of the Empire!"

"I tried that argument," Frank said. "The Raj believes otherwise."

"Manipur will not stand for it! It will be a disaster."

"Let us pray it will not be."

"It makes no sense," Ethel said. "You must convince them. It would be madness."

"Trust me—I spent the entire day trying, but to no avail. Quinton has sympathy, but he cannot, or will not, alter the plan. He has the bit between his teeth. Someone has tied his hands. There is a conspiracy of incompetence that reaches high."

"This is—terrible news," Ethel said.

"I fear I have even worse news."

She shook her head. "What *could* be worse?"

"The reason Quinton told me, and no one else, is because he expects me, as the political agent, to make the arrest."

"No!"

"I will hold the durbar, under the pretense of recognizing the regent as the maharaja, and then arrest Tikendra Jeet. Quinton put the burden on me. I must level the charges, deliver the verdict, and take Tikendra Jeet into custody."

Ethel rushed to Frank's arms, sobbing against his chest. "What can we do?"

"No way to stop this," he said. "All we can do is our duty, help Quinton any way we can, and hope and pray his plan succeeds."

Ethel kissed Frank full on the mouth. He drew back at first, but responded and their embrace tightened. Ethel feared to let Frank go as if clinging could avert the disaster.

Frank lifted Ethel in his arms and carried her next door to the bedchamber where they made love with fiery passion not felt for years.

Part V. The Gurkhas

"Faith there's little small about him
Save the question of his size
From the mountains which beget him
To the laughter in his eyes
His sport, his love, his courage
Preserve the sterling ring
Of the simpleminded Hillman
With the manners of a king."

From *To a Gurkha* (1915)
By Lt-Col William Ross Stewart

Dramatis personæ

In order of appearance (*denotes a fictional character)

1891 Manipur

Lieutenant Lionel Brackenbury	44th Gurkha Rifles, banjo player, 23
James O'Brien	Signaler, Assam telegraphs, 35
Heema Chund	Subadar (major), 44th Gurkha Rifles, 50
Gunna Ram	Bugler, 44th Gurkha Rifles, 23
Siriman Sunwar*	Naik (corporal), 44th Gurkha Rifles, 20

1886 Nepal

Siriman Sunwar*	Khiji village boy, cowherd, 15
Karna Sunwar*	Khiji village boy, Siriman's cousin, 17
Manu Sunwar*	Siriman's father, 38
Jeet Sunwar*	Karna's father, Siriman's uncle, 40
Pandit Ramnath Bhatt*	Puja Hari, Shaivanist priest, 72
Smoking woman (dream sequence)	Writer living in Germany, 54
Gallawalla Ram Thapa*	Havildar (sergeant), Gurkha recruiter, 50

1891 Manipur

Lieutenant Edward J. Lugard	D.S.O. (1890), 42nd Gurkha Rifles, 26
Lieutenant J.B. Chatterton	42nd GR, Skene's staff officer, 29
Captain Thomas S. Boileau	Senior officer, 44th Gurkha Rifles, 40
James Wallace Quinton	Chief Commissioner, Assam, 57
Colonel Charles M. Skene	Expedition commander, 42nd GR, 47
Prince Angao Singh	Senapati (royal military commander), 25
Prince Tikendra Jeet Singh	Yuvraj (crown prince), former Senapati, 35
Frank Saint Clair Grimwood	British political agent to Manipur, 37
Karna Sunwar*	Sepoy (private), 43rd GR, Siriman's cousin, 22
Lieutenant Walter Simpson	Bengal infantry, 43rd Gurkha Rifles, 31
Tongol General	Senior military leader, king's protector, 74
Moonia	Ethel's former ayah (personal maid), 60

Chapter 35. The Scented Letter

Earlier that same Saturday evening, 21 March 1891...

Lionel

The lieutenant struck a match and a trembling hand lit the pipe.

Why smoke so soon? Why smoke so much?

You know why!

Lionel Brackenbury puffed the bowl of tamped tobacco to a bright glow and watched the billows rise.

The letter from Manipur is to blame.

Two weeks earlier, he received a letter from a friend. The note reached him in Golaghat, and that same day, at a moment of despondency, he reached for the pipe. The mere thought of the letter excited Lionel, making him want to examine it for the...

How many times today? A half-dozen at least!

His legs trembled and butterfly flutters filled his stomach, crackling with nervous energy like a teenage boy at his first dance. Rereading the letter would worsen his nervousness, but he could not help himself.

You thought smoking would calm your jittery nerves. You were wrong.

Lionel chomped the stem and puffed harder. To read, he needed more than moonlight. An oil lantern hung nearby, on a post before the Sengmai telegraph office, but the light was dim. A few feet further, a torch flickered. Torches circled the camp perimeter and campfires roared by the tents. Fire kept wild jungle creatures at bay.

No. Stay clear of open flames! Cannot risk burning the precious letter.

Lionel moved toward the lantern. The glow did little to help nighttime reading, but the moon and the lantern were the best he could do. Before turning in, he had to read his treasured letter one more time. He pulled the envelope from his breast pocket, raised it to his nose, and sniffed.

Is that her perfume I smell? What else could it be?

He had pondered the scent too many times to count. He pictured her delicate hand placing a few drops of her favorite fragrance onto the letter—to capture his attention, spark his imagination, and remind him of her.

As if, the letter was not enough.

Lionel unfolded two crisp sheets of stationery and read the delicate script. He imagined the slender fingers of her hand holding the quill, dipping it in the ink, and scratching out the tender words that touched his heart. The letter's words alone had not moved him—it was how she said them. He closed his eyes and sighed.

Ah, the lovely and delightful Missus Ethel Grimwood.

Her letter spoke of ordinary things she and Lionel had in common—shared experiences from his time in Manipur.

> *Polo is in full swing. You used to play the game so well! I took such delight in watching you!*

He almost heard her sweet laughter as she reminisced about her pets—two otters that followed her around like dogs, the tame deer, the cranes, and three pet monkeys…

> *Do you remember the time Jacko the monkey escaped his tether and led us on a merry chase about the garden? The little creature destroyed every flower in his wake.*

Ethel raised a bear from a cub and one day the full-grown bear escaped his pen.

> *He chased me down and I was lucky to escape with a few scratches. Frank had the poor beast taken far away and released into the wild. Do you remember how sad I was to see him go?*

She reminded him of the hunting expedition when they ducked, fearing for their lives, as Pucca Senna, one of the seven princes, fired with reckless abandon at anything that moved. There was the time Tikendra Jeet showed his skill firing his field gun, blowing up flags at the target range. They applauded while wincing in pain from the sound of the explosions. They bit their tongues that day to keep from laughing.

Do you remember the deformed lunatic fellow who jumped out, frightening me in the bazaar—until Tikendra Jeet had the man locked up during the hours of my visits? I have not seen him for a time and wonder what became of the poor fellow.

Such good times!

Then her letter turned serious. Ethel told of rumors that tempered her excitement over the impending visit by Quinton.

Frank and I worry Quinton may try to restore Sura Chandra, the former maharaja, to the throne.

I wonder if Frank knows more of the mission now. He must after today.

Ethel's husband Frank spent most of that day in the camp meeting with Quinton. Frank and Lionel had a brief reunion and exchange as Frank departed. Frank muttered a quick greeting, but his face seemed pale. Then Frank rode away at a gallop, racing the sun to get home before dark.

Frank seemed disturbed after his long meeting with Quinton.

Lionel glanced at the nearby command tent. Lantern light cast shadows of men moving. The man Ethel mentioned—James Wallace Quinton—was one shadow. The chief commissioner of Assam, the leader of the expedition, was still meeting with the senior officers.

Lionel did not know the purpose of the expedition, but he knew they were not in Manipur to reinstate a deposed monarch. No Manipuris in the column—only British officers, civil servants, and a great number of Gurkhas—the crack soldiers of the Indian army, none in the world more deadly. Over four hundred of the little Nepali killing machines made the march.

Lionel skipped ahead in Ethel's letter to the part he found most intriguing—the section where Ethel delved into delicate matters. Her candid words spoke of her displeasure with Lieutenant Walter Simpson.

Lieutenant Simpson upset me by taking a young native mistress. If you can believe it, she is the daughter of the Tongol General. Worse, it shocked and humiliated me to learn she had been intimate with Frank while I was away on holiday in Shillong.

Ethel shared private details as if speaking to a close confidant—someone to whom she was reaching out, as if—yearning to rekindle a close friendship. The exciting idea, while worrisome, was the reason he was in Sengmai. His next assignment was to have been Burma but after the letter arrived and he learned of Quinton's expedition he went to Captain Boileau and requested assignment to Manipur.

"Ah, hah! A fellow kapnosmologist."

Lionel turned to find James O'Brien, the telegraph signaler, stepping out of his office, lighting his own pipe.

"Sorry?" Lionel said. "Oh, hullo, O'Brien. What did you say?"

"Kapnosmology!" O'Brien drew against the flame and shook the match dead as he puffed.

"What is that?"

"Kapnos is Greek—means smoke. Kapnosmology—the study of smoking." O'Brien pointed to his pipe. "A pipe is more befitting a sahib than scrambling after hard ups in the dirt."

"A science for everything these days," Lionel said, "but I wager you invented that word."

"If not a word, it should be."

"Hum—busy day?"

"Very busy," O'Brien said. "Coded messages all day, back and forth. Quinton and Grimwood. All gibberish. So you army blokes will reach the Residency tomorrow morning."

"That is the plan."

"Lucky bastards!"

"In what way?"

"The memsahib there—the Missus Grimwood."

Lionel's eyes narrowed. "What of her?"

"A treat for the eyes, that one!" O'Brien cracked a devilish smile and blew a smoke ring at the moon. "Looks as if the moon will be full soon. More than full, by its look!"

"It may surprise you to learn," Lionel said, "Ethel—Missus Grimwood—is a good friend of mine."

"Ah, say no more." O'Brien chuckled as he puffed. "Lucky for you, and excellent company, I should add."

"What do you mean by that?"

"Word has it she makes the rounds, if you know what I mean." O'Brien winked. "It could be a happy and productive visit."

"See here!" Lionel took a step toward the signaler. "I take exception…"

A voice called out. "Perusing the letter again, Lieutenant?"

Lionel turned to see Subadar Heema Chund approaching. He refolded the letter, inserted it back in its envelope, and slipped it into his breast pocket. He shook a finger at O'Brien and said, "Watch your gob, signaler!" before turning to walk away.

O'Brien laughed behind his back and muttered something unintelligible, but Lionel ignored the man and continued toward the newcomer. The two met and strolled back toward the camp.

"A letter worth re-reading," the subadar said, "is a letter of great importance. From a family member or a lady friend, perhaps?"

Lionel knew he was blushing and was thankful for the darkness. The subadar was in his regiment, though subordinate to any of the British officers, and Lionel and the others respected the battle-tested veteran, treating him as an equal. Lionel held the man in great esteem and was at ease sharing intimate details in confidence. No comment or question from the subadar was inappropriate.

"A lady friend," Lionel admitted.

"Very nice," the subadar said.

"A married woman."

"Oh! Well, say no more. I understand, but a soldier must always consider his legacy and be thinking of settling down in marriage."

"What of you?" Lionel asked. "You have not settled."

"I have soldiered long, but give thought to it. In fact, I am thinking of retiring and moving back to Nepal after this expedition."

"What would you do with yourself?"

"Perhaps become a gallawalla (recruiter)," the subadar said. "Or, better, find a young bride, and start a family—raise sons to follow in my footsteps."

"Hum!" Lionel grunted. "I have similar thoughts. My brother died six years ago at the Bolan Pass. My father, a major general, died last summer— he was fifty-nine. He had a heart attack while traveling by rail. My entire family is military, and I love the service, but am I wrong to want a different future?"

The elder soldier walked in silence, chin down, and hands behind his back. "I have concerns about our mission," the subadar said at last. "I am wondering if you have any insights."

He changed topics. Did my comments lead him in that direction?

"Of what kind?" Lionel asked.

Lionel expected questions on the purpose of the mission, such as those raised by Ethel's letter, but instead the subadar rattled off technical military concerns.

"Why no screw guns?"

The Gurkhas always took one or two of the easy-to-assemble mountain guns on expeditions. They at least could spare one pack pony to carry one small cannon. The orders were, no cannon allowed.

"Why was each man issued only forty rounds?"

Gurkha riflemen always carried seventy to one hundred rounds of ammunition and the pack animals should carry an equal amount in reserve. Instead, the order stated no man was to carry over forty rounds, and none held in reserve.

"Why Sniders?"

The sahibs had issued the Gurkhas from the 42nd and 44th rifle regiments older, obsolete Snider-Enfield rifles, instead of the newer, standard-issue Martini-Henry models.

"You ask good questions but I have no answers," Lionel said.

"I am finished grousing," the subadar said. "Wherever the sahibs ask us to march is thik chha to us Gurkhas."

Their stroll brought the pair near the tents. The subadar pointed to a roaring fire, surrounded by seated Gurkhas, talking and laughing.

"I will visit the campfire," the subadar said. "Would you care to join?"

"Yes, I would love that."

"Wonderful! Oh, and Lieutenant...," the old soldier added.

"Yes?"

"The men were wondering—could you please bring along your banjo?"

Chapter 36. The Campfire Tale of a Princess and Dragons

Continued...

Lionel

Unlike other regiments in the Indian army, native soldiers and British officers in Gurkha regiments developed close relationships. The officers, the junior officers in particular, associated often with the troops. This association fostered a bond of trust, respect, and mutual admiration between the Gurkhas and their officers. Officers unable to gain trust did not last long in Gurkha regiments.

Lionel hurried to his tent and retrieved his banjo. American minstrel music had become popular in British music halls and Lionel had purchased an imported Sweeny five-string. By the time he enlisted and departed for India, he was adept at the Clawhammer style and quick to play catchy folk tunes. Shy by nature, with the instrument in his hands Lionel unleashed an alter ego, popular at camp and the officer halls. He exhibited a preference for comic tunes and developed a surprising singing voice.

The subadar led the way to the main campfire. Sparks popped and smoke rose toward the bright moonlight. The lively sounds of laughter and storytelling echoed in the dark. Gurkhas have keen senses of humor and smiling faces lit by flickering flames greeted the officers. The soldiers closest to the fire rose, but Lionel motioned to stay seated.

"Gentlemen," Lionel said, speaking in Gorkhali, "may we join you?"

Affirmative murmurs came from every direction. The soldiers took seats, all save one. Gunna Ram, bugler of the 44th Regiment, remained standing. He lifted a bundle from a nearby stack. With a bang, a snap, and the flourish of a stage magician, the bugler assembled a canvas campaign chair.

The bugler offered the chair with an open palm. "Please, sahib. Have a seat."

Lionel thanked him and sat. Gunna Ram next presented the flat stump on which he had been sitting to the subadar. "For you, Subadar, please sit and enjoy."

With the pot on his lap and the neck in his left hand, Lionel strummed a few chords and tuned the banjo.

"I did not mean to interrupt," he said, cocking his head.

"Oh, no problem, sahib," the bugler said. "So happy to have you join."

"What is the topic this evening?"

"We were telling stories of missions and battles seen over the years. Perhaps sahib has a story to share?"

The Gurkhas murmured agreement, encouraging the lieutenant.

"I am too inexperienced," Lionel demurred. "No tales worth telling. Subadar Chund has many stories after—how many years, Subadar?"

The older officer's chest puffed with pride and recited the count without a pause. "Thirty-two years!"

"You see!" Lionel pointed at the subadar. "Longer than I have been alive!" The Gurkhas clapped, laughed, and whooped a cheer. "And your medals," Lionel continued, over the laughter, "You earned those in which campaigns?"

The subadar looked down at his khaki shirt. He wore no medals, but pointed at empty places and grinned. The soldiers laughed as, one by one, he called out the invisible medals.

"This one is for the Naga Hills, this for Burma, and this one for the hill country of the Lushai."

"Tell us," Lionel said, "which mission was the most—interesting?"

The subadar enjoys being the center of attention.

"Hum…" The subadar scratched his head. "I took wounds in my first action, in the Khasiah Jantia Hills. That is something I will always remember. If I must choose one, the Lushai Expedition was the most worthy of a tale."

A chorus arose. "Tell us!" Gurkhas shouted. "Tell the tale, Subadar!"

The old soldier held up hands, protesting. "I am sure most know this story…"

The Gurkhas demanded a repeat. Lionel set his banjo down, struck a match, and relit his pipe, puffing through clenched teeth until at last the subadar shrugged. Lionel picked the banjo back up and gave the instrument a loud strum.

"Well, Subadar," he said, laughing, "we are all ears! I think I have heard this one. Tell the tale and I will play accompaniment—proper mood music."

Cheers rose and then silence fell and the young crowd gave rapt attention as if the curtain had risen upon a set stage. Lionel strummed an introduction and faded to silence. As the subadar prepared to begin, the campfire issued pops, hisses, and crackles as hoots, howls, and screeches came from the jungle.

"Twenty years ago," the subadar began, "before mothers bore a few of you—I was younger than now."

Laughter.

"I know—hard to imagine, but even then, I was a veteran of twelve years."

Lionel plucked a happy, basic forward roll.

"The British taste for tea grew," the subadar continued, "and planters cleared land in the north, planting tea gardens in the fertile Himalayan foothills of Assam."

Lionel shifted to a slower roll with an ominous drone.

"Zos and Kookies, the wild dangerous Lushai hill tribes, took notice, displeased that white settlers pushed the frontier. Naked headhunters struck back, armed with wood-blade swords, spears, and clubs. The warriors attacked settlements, beheaded many, and captured a few as slaves. The Indian army was slow to answer—a few skirmishes but no major retaliation—so the settlers fought back on their own, refusing to abandon their plantations."

Lionel picked up the pace.

"Then, one winter day, a war party from Lushai ventured deeper than ever into Assam. They attacked a tea garden, killing the parents of a British child, a girl five years old. Wild men killed many and carried the child into captivity, facing slavery or death."

Lionel struck a loud chord, paused for the fade, then shifted to a somber rendition of *Rule Britannia*.

"Back in Britain, the public learned of the attack and the little girl's capture. *This means war!* Was the cry. *Raise an army! Rescue the child!* The people demanded revenge. Summer came and then the monsoons. The months drifted."

Lionel picked up the pace, breaking into his best rendition of a Gurkha regimental favorite, the *Old Monmouthshire* march.

"After a year, the British launched the Lushai expedition to punish the tribes and rescue the girl—if she still lived. My column trekked up steep hills and hacked through dense jungles. For ten weeks, we skirmished with wild warriors, but sickness struck and more Gurkhas died from disease than wounds.

"We learned the girl lived—a captive in a village stockade. We surrounded the fort, and a battle raged. The surrender, not the battle, was the interesting part.

"The Zos agreed to each term but one—they would not give up the child. So we destroyed the Zo crops and grain stores—and then at last the Zos agreed to release the girl, but—on one condition…"

The subadar held up a finger, pausing for dramatic effect.

"Tell us!" shouted a Gurkha. "What condition?"

"The British must let the Zos cut off and keep the child's long locks of golden hair as a talisman of power!"

Lionel hit a strong chord and then pretended to ruffle imaginary locks of hair. The Gurkhas howled with laughter.

The subadar shrugged. "Why not give them the hair? It would grow back and was likely infested by vermin!"

More laughter.

"So we entered the camp and found the child. She was pretty—a six-year-old by then—but dirty, with long, wild golden hair, and half-naked. Now here is the funny part…" He paused again.

"What?" the crowd shouted.

"She was smoking a pipe, speaking in the Zo tongue, and ordering Zos around like a general!"

The men burst out laughing and clapping. Lionel finished with a wild flourish on the banjo.

A Gurkha called out, "What happened to the child?"

"We cut off her hair," the subadar replied. "We bathed her and sent her home to England. She steamed away, never heard of again. The little princess of the wild…"

"Until rescued!"

"Yes—until rescued by Gurkhas, best soldiers of the greatest empire on Earth!"

When the laughter and applause died down, Lionel spoke. "How," he asked, "could a little English orphan girl, five or six years old, enslaved by wild savages, unable to speak or understand the language, wield power over head-hunters?"

A Gurkha who seemed to know the tale called, "They say, she was not pure-English. She was a half-caste!"

Another answered, "They say, her mother was a Manipuri witch! The little girl was a witch, too! She bewitched the Zos and used magic to make the British rescue her!"

A third Gurkha, younger than the other two, jumped in, saying, "It was not the girl, or her magic. It was dragon power. All of this land sits over dragons."

The Gurkhas grew silent. Lionel removed his pipe and leaned forward, squinting in the firelight, studying the face of the young soldier. "Did you say dragons? What do you mean?"

Eyes turned to the young soldier. He scratched his head and squirmed. "Sahib," he continued, "all this country—from the Himalayas, Tibet, and Nepal; from Bhutan, known as Druk Yul, the Land of the Thunder Dragon; the foothills of Nagaland, or land of dragons; Manipur who once worshiped dragons; Burma and the Toe-nayar dragon; and the Lushai hills—all these lands sit above the underground kingdom of dragons. Dragons hide under the mountains, foothills, and in the waters. It has been long since they walked in the open. They watch us from hills and lakes. They bide their time."

Silence. Painful seconds ticked by, then murmurs began.

"An intriguing tale," Lionel said. "What is your name soldier?"

"Sunwar, sahib," the Gurkha answered. "Siriman Sunwar, naik, 44 GR, sahib."

"Sunwar, eh?" Lionel said. "Many Sunwars in the Indian army?"

"No, sahib, few Sunwars. Many Gurungs, Magars, and Thapas!"

The soldiers exploded in laughter. Gurung, Magar, and Thapa were the names of many of the Gurkhas present—tribal surnames more common among Gurkhas than Smith, Jones, and Williams in England.

"You may be the one Sunwar in the corps," Lionel speculated. "At least, you are the only one I have met."

"No, sahib, not the only. There is at least one other. My cousin is a sepoy, 43 GR, and here in Manipur."

"Perhaps you will soon have a happy reunion," Lionel said, smiling.

"Yes, sahib," Sunwar said. "Perhaps."

"Tell us, Sunwar," Lionel continued. "You claim to know much of dragons, but you cannot believe dragons exist."

"Dragons are real, sahib—even if not believed in by anyone."

"Have you seen a dragon?" Lionel asked, winking at the subadar. "Are there living, breathing dragons in Nepal?"

"Yes, sahib, I have seen," Sunwar said. "They are very dangerous."

"Did the dragon breathe fire?"

At that instant, with a crack and a pop, a red-hot log split and collapsed, flames rose and sparks flew, startling many including Lionel, but Sunwar did not flinch.

"No, sahib. Dragons shoot fire, but do not breathe fire."

"That must have been a singular event! Will you tell us your tale?"

"My tale, sahib?" Sunwar asked.

"The time you saw a dragon…"

Silence followed, save for the crackling of the dying fire. All eyes turned to Sunwar. The shy young Gurkha looked at the ground.

"I am sorry, sahib," he answered. "I have said too much. Please excuse Sunwar."

The Gurkha stood, saluted, and walked toward the tents. Whispers followed, but he walked on, oblivious. Lionel almost called after the young man, but stopped himself. He watched until the soldier disappeared into a tent. He scratched his head and drew on his pipe.

I must get to know the chap. There is something about him…

Lionel lightened the mood by strumming his banjo and running through a series of rolls.

"Who wants something more cheery?" he said. "Any requests, gentlemen?"

Chapter 37. The Defenders of Cows

Five years earlier, a spring day in 1886...

Siriman

The bullock cart rattled down a rocky path. Two villager boys bounced in their seats, hurrying home from the day's chores. The sun was setting and in two hours, the warm spring day would end. Nepal is all mountains and hills separated by a few warm valleys. Nepalis are always going uphill or downhill. The boys spent the day uphill working and ended the day tired and hungry, going downhill, but with a long journey still ahead.

"Siriman, mind the hole!" Karna Sunwar shouted. "Too late!"

With a horrible *crack* and a sickening lurch, a wooden wheel dropped into a hollow. The cart toppled, dumping a stack of dry timber, and sending the teenagers flying into the brush. The two oxen pulling the cart bellowed in confusion, straining at their harnesses, struggling to keep their footing.

Fifteen-year-old Siriman Sunwar scrambled on all fours and crawled out of the brush. He ignored the bloody scratches crisscrossing his naked chest and sprang to his feet, shouting, "Karna! Come help with the oxen!" He jumped to grab the harness and unfasten the straps lashing the yoke over the beasts' withers.

Close behind, Siriman's seventeen-year-old cousin exited the foliage and rushed to join the action. The two half-naked, loin-clothed, bloodied-and-scratched youths struggled to free the worried oxen. Once released, the beasts calmed and wandered a short distance. The boys turned their attention to the cart. Over the years, the teenagers had developed close attachments to their chore-mates. They trusted the castrated males named Saktisali and Baahubali would stay close.

The contents of the cart lay sprawled—a tangled stack of dry firewood, the fruits of their day's labor. The cart appeared serviceable—if the boys could set it right. First, they had to lift the tall wooden wheel out of the hole. The youths squabbled as they set to the task, arguing over who had been at fault. Karna insisted his younger cousin should have been a better driver and avoided the hole. Siriman countered his older cousin should have seen the hole and shouted a warning sooner.

"You were not paying attention!" Siriman shouted. "You were thinking of Akuti! It is always the girls with you!"

More like brothers than cousins, they spent days in much the same routine—working hard, side-by-side, but fighting and arguing. Siriman was two years younger than Karna but his equal in size, appearance, and everything—unless it came to girls. Siriman had shown interest but his cousin had a two-year head start. Akuti, a pretty girl in their village, was Siriman's age but, as do many girls, she had eyes for older boys, including Karna.

The youths lived nearby in quiet Khiji, ten miles northwest of Okhaldhunga, in the Sunuwar hill country of Eastern Nepal. They had spent that day, as most days, searching the higher hills for dead trees and limbs. They chopped and carted firewood for their families to sell, trade, or burn.

Further uphill and miles north, the majestic peaks of the mighty Himalayas, the Abode of Snow, rose in the distance, disappearing in the clouds. Prominent among the nearest peaks stood an imposing mountain the Nepalis named Sagarmatha. The Tibetans called the peak Chomo Lung Ma, or Goddess Mother of Mountains. Impressed by the massive peak, the highest in the world, and disinterested in discovering if it already had a name, the British dubbed it Mount Everest.

"No time to waste!" Karna said. "Debate later—work now."

A boulder became a fulcrum and using the longest of the logs as a lever, they strained with wiry strength that belied their size and age. They lifted the heavy wooden wheel and pushed the cart back onto the path. Then they gathered the yoke and ropes to reattach their hoofed friends.

"Where are the oxen?" Karna shouted, frantic, looking each way.

"There!" Siriman said, pointing. The end of a tail disappeared around a distant rocky corner. "They wandered."

"No doubt seeking water."

One hundred yards away, a wide gash in the rocks marked the entrance to a gorge. The stony bed of a dry rivulet curved between two short tree-topped cliffs. Earlier that day when the boys had gone uphill, a swift, steady rush had flowed through the exact place they stood.

"Here is a mystery," Siriman said. The rivulet had diminished to a tiny trickle winding down the rocky hill.

"What happened to the water? It was here earlier." Karna looked down at the damp rocky bed where the cart had toppled.

"Yes," Siriman said. "It became a mere trickle."

"We better get the oxen first," Karna suggested, "and worry over what happened to the water later."

Siriman grabbed the reins. After a struggle with the knots, he pulled his kukri knife from its leather sheath and sliced the ropes free of the cart. He held one rope, tossed the other to his cousin, and the boys ran after the wandering oxen.

With growling stomachs, the teenagers trudged uphill, following the trickle through the winding ravine. They soon spied the trailing ox Baahubali, plodding.

"Where is Saktisali?"

"He must be farther ahead," Siriman said. "Around that bend."

The boys looped the rope over the animal's head. The beast stood its ground, reluctant to turn from the path. After tugging and straining, they pulled Baahubali to one side. Karna fastened the rope to a sturdy bush jutting from the rocky cliff wall while Siriman continued after Saktisali.

After laboring a hundred yards further up the winding bed of rocks, a horrible sound tore at Siriman's heart—a bellowing scream of unimaginable agony and terror. He ran harder, worried but resolved to rescue his charge from any danger.

He rounded a turn and froze, stunned by the scene ahead. The ox Saktisali lay crumpled on the rocks of the dry streambed. Across its back lay a creature from a nightmare. A winged beast with a long tail and green-scaled hide gripped the back of the ox, clinging with sharp talons. The monster's body appeared larger than the ox's, but it loomed even larger with its outstretched wings and tail. The monster's head bent over the neck of the ox, powerful jaws snapped, the long snout lifted, and the head shook. Sharp teeth grasped flesh and hide as hot blood shot forth.

Siriman whispered under his breath. "Maar patsaa!"

He roused, letting out an angry scream. Raising his kukri blade high, he ran toward the monster, swearing aloud to the deities of Swarga Loka he would have his revenge.

The startled creature turned toward the screaming Gurkha. It leapt with surprising agility and ran away on all fours. Its wings folded back and its tail trailed as it scampered up the path of the rivulet and disappeared around a bend.

Siriman reached the side of the dying ox as dark blood spurted from a gaping hole in the animal's neck. As he knelt on the sticky rocks at Saktisali's side, he sensed his cousin's arrival. Siriman glanced behind and saw Karna, wide-eyed, stunned by the sight of the mutilated ox. Karna's face turned blood red. He drew his kukri, let out a war cry, and ran with reckless abandon after a villain he had been too late to see.

"Wait!" Siriman called. "You do not know the danger!"

Karna ran on and disappeared around the corner. Siriman wept and prayed as he knelt next to the dying animal. The ox shook with labored breath as its lifeblood drained.

The pain must be horrible!

The proper, sanctified way to end the misery would be to behead the creature with one swift stroke of his kukri. Siriman knew he lacked the strength and the day's work had dulled the blade. He took the next best available choice and with care, drew his knife across the throat of his hooved companion, ending the sacred beast's suffering.

Siriman dipped a forefinger into the sticky puddle and traced red streaks across his naked chest and forearms, then cheeks and forehead. He stood, looked down at the dead animal, closed his eyes, and whispered a final farewell to Saktisali. He turned away, broke into a run, and followed the uphill trail of his cousin.

Siriman leapt as he ran, avoiding the sharper rocks and the weathered ruts in the bed. The gully of the dry rivulet meandered upward. He rounded one bend and then another and then saw his cousin.

Karna stood frozen, eyes locked on something ahead. His arms hung limp at his sides, hands open, and his kukri knife lay on the rocks at his feet. Siriman drew close and grabbed his cousin's arm to announce his arrival, but Karna took no notice.

The gorge had reached a narrow end where sharp boulders piled high before a shallow puddle. Water trickled from the yawning mouth of a cave, crossed the rock face, and dropped ten feet into the puddle. Thick foliage hung, cloaking part of the cave mouth. The boys had reached the source of the dry rivulet. Something had blocked the flow.

Jutting between the vines, the head, shoulders, and fore-claws of the monster protruded from the entrance. Its cold eyes fixed on Karna and his cousin stared back.

"What are you doing?" Siriman shouted to Karna. "Stop! Do not look at it!"

Karna did not break his gaze. "We must stand here." He spoke in a monotone drawl. "We must not move."

"What are you saying? Stop looking at it, I said!"

"We must not leave. We must wait here."

Siriman turned to the monster. Without stopping to think, he measured the distance, reared, and heaved his kukri.

Kukri knives have many uses, but lack the balance for throwing. Siriman's kukri was typical—a curved blade thirteen inches long with a four-inch wooden handle—used in chores such as clearing brush. A skilled warrior with a similar blade can turn an upward diagonal swipe into a beheading blow. Siriman, in the heat of the moment, did not consider the knife's limitations. Since it was his one weapon, without thinking, he had aimed and thrown. By luck, or fate, or perhaps the knife chose its own path, but against all logic, the blade flew, turned a complete circle, and struck the monster's left shoulder. The knife impaled itself deep into the green-scaled flesh.

The beast screeched in agony and broke its gaze. Its eyes turned toward the wound and talons clawed at the handle. The kukri tore free, clattered down the face of the boulders, and splashed into the puddle. Red blood gushed, and the monster howled as it pulled back from the cave opening.

Siriman had no time to admire his knife throwing skills, contemplate the providence of his good luck, or wonder how grievous a wound he inflicted on the monster. He grabbed Karna by the shoulders and gave him a vigorous shake.

"Karna! Come! We must leave—now!"

Karna stared back. "We must stay. We must not leave."

Siriman grabbed Karna by the wrists, turned him around, and pulled, walking backwards, dragging him from the spot. The monster's head reappeared at the entrance, then its shoulders, arms, and claws. It worked at something and metal glinted.

The beast has a weapon!

The device appeared to be the barrel of a rifle. In that instant Siriman realized they were not dealing with a wild animal.

The monster has intelligence!

"Now we run!" Siriman said.

He leaned, lunged forward, and drove his shoulder into Karna's stomach. With his arms around his cousin's waist, Siriman hoisted the older lad and draped him over one shoulder like a heavy sack of rice. He ran fast, back the way they came—away from the cave.

Siriman trudged, wobbling under the load, and approached the first bend in the gully. A sound, an instinct, or a lucky guess warned him—he never knew which—but he sensed danger.

I must get out of the monster's line of sight! Now!

With a last burst of strength, he reached the first bend, turned left, and dove forward, heaving Karna over his head onto the ground. Siriman hit the gravel as a ravenous flame erupted. In a bright streak, heat scorched the cliff face behind and to his right. Darkened rocks glowed, and the charred remains of scrawny bushes smoldered.

Stay flat! Crawl farther away!

Siriman slithered and grabbed Karna under his armpits. His cousin lay prone and motionless. Siriman dragged Karna a few feet farther around the curve, turned, and buried his head under his arms as the flames erupted again. The beam played back and forth, up and down, hitting the rocky face full force, creating a maelstrom of fire within the bend of the gorge. The flames raged overhead, just missing the prostrate youths. Siriman shrank lower as the scorching heat seared his naked back. He cried, and he prayed.

Please, Lord Shiva, save us! Please let us survive.

As if in answer to his prayer, the flames ceased. Siriman waited, counting to thirty before taking his chance and standing. He bent, grabbed Karna by the arms, and dragged him farther forward. With a strength he should not have possessed, Siriman stood the older youth and hoisted him once more onto his shoulder. He ran, stumbling, back down the path of the dry rivulet. He passed Saktisali's carcass without stopping and trudged on, rounding each bend with urgency, until at last they reached Baahubali. Siriman gave thanks the patient ox was waiting, still tied to the bush. With his final burst of strength, Siriman tossed Karna over Baahubali's back, and sank exhausted to the ground.

Must rest! No, you must not! Get up and move!

Siriman forced himself to rise. He untied the ox and led the beast with Karna draped over his back, taking springy steps, freed from the heavy load of his cousin.

He led the plodding ox forward, and the survivors emerged from the gash between the cliffs. When they reached the bullock cart, Siriman checked Karna's condition. He pulled his cousin down and stood him against the flank of the ox. Karna wobbled, gazing as if lost in a dream.

"Wake up, Karna!" Siriman shook his cousin's shoulders.

Karna looked at Siriman with an evil glint. He spoke in a garbled voice as if an entity spoke through him from afar.

"I know you, Siriman Sunwar," Karna said, "who you are and where you live. I will follow and kill you. You cannot escape."

Siriman shook Karna again. "What are you saying? What is wrong? Wake!"

Karna lunged without warning. His hands grasped Siriman's neck, tightened his grip, and pressed his thumbs into the boy's throat. Siriman pressed his hands together as if in prayer. His arms shot straight between Karna's arms, forearms knocking away Karna's hands. Siriman gasped, red-faced, then lunged forward in anger.

He struck Karna in the face, knocking him backward. Karna tripped and fell to the ground. Siriman jumped forward, sat on Karna's chest, and slapped his face hard, again and again. Each smack turned Karna's head to one side.

"Karna, wake up!" Siriman shouted with each blow.

When Siriman lost count of the blows, a change came. Karna became less limp, less passive, his chest tensed, a sense of awareness returned.

"Siriman!" Karna groaned. "Why are you hitting me? Stop!"

Siriman grabbed Karna's shoulders. "Karna? Is it you?"

"Yes—I am Karna! Idiot! Who do you think I am? What are you doing?"

Siriman turned Karna, pinned his cheek to the ground, and gripped his wrists behind his back.

"Is it gone?" Siriman said.

"What are you saying?"

"The monster."

"What monster?" Karna squirmed. "Get off me!"

Siriman took a chance, stood, and backed away from his cousin. Karna rolled, both arms across his face, moaning. Siriman offered a hand but Karna shook his head no.

"Take it!" Siriman demanded.

Karna paused, frowning, then accepted the hand, and let Siriman pull him to his feet. Once standing, Karna twisted his head, patted his cheeks, and shook his arms. He looked around at the cart and the pile of spilled wood.

"I remember now," he said. "I fell off the cart. Was I unconscious this entire time?"

"You do not remember?" Siriman studied his cousin's eyes.

"I remember you ran the cart into a hole and I fell. The cart is out of the hole. How did you move it without my help?"

"You do not remember the monster?"

"What are you talking about?" Karna massaged his neck with one hand and looked each way. Baahubali the ox stood nearby. "Where is Saktisali?"

"Come, Karna." Siriman shook his head. "We must go home. I will tell you on the way."

"What of the cart?"

"Leave it. We will come for it tomorrow—with luck we will have help."

Siriman took the rope holding Baahubali and offered a hand. Karna stared at it and then took it. Siriman gave one last glance at the gorge.

All seems safe.

Siriman turned and led the way as the three companions began the long walk home.

Chapter 38. The Raging Rivulet

The afternoon of the next day...

Siriman

Siriman trudged uphill, gripping a tether, leading Baahubali the ox. He stopped and shielded his eyes, squinting in the glare of the high sun. Ahead lay the gorge opening—a rugged gash between rocky, tree-topped cliffs.

Siriman pointed. "There! The ravine."

He glanced over his shoulder making sure two swarthy men still followed. The closest was Manu Sunwar, Siriman's father, and the other was Jeet Sunwar, Siriman's uncle. Uncle Jeet led a second beast of burden, a draft bull named Nandi. Both men bore rifles slung over shoulders.

"Are you certain?" Jeet asked Siriman.

"This is the place, Jeet," Manu said. "There is the cart."

The empty bullock cart was a short distance ahead, still parked by the tumbled pile of dead timber.

"I see," Jeet said, "but the stream..."

A few feet away, foamy water raced, surging and splashing among the sharp rocks of the ford. The water tumbled over stair-stepping boulders on its way to the larger tributary.

"Is this the same rivulet?" Manu asked Siriman.

"Yes, sir."

"The one you said yesterday was dry?"

"Yes, sir—I swear it was dry yesterday. It flowed in the morning, but when we came back down, it was a trickle, almost bone dry."

The ox and bull drank from the stream, and then Siriman lashed the tethers to the cart. Manu and Jeet scanned the surrounding area.

Jeet pointed to scuffed ground near the cart. "There you fought Karna?"

Siriman nodded but withheld further comment. Karna had stayed behind at the village, quiet, resting, and keeping away from bright light. He complained of headaches and blacked out twice.

I hope the pummeling I gave Karna did not cause permanent damage.

Siriman also worried over the words Karna spoke while possessed by the monster—a chilling threat of revenge and murder.

Did the hypnotic stare burn a trace of the monster into Karna's mind?

"Shall we go upstream?" Manu asked.

"Better load first," Jeet said.

The men unslung their P53 rifles; bit the ends of paper cartridges; poured powder into the muzzles; seated the Minni balls with the ramrods; and then cocked and placed fresh caps over the nipples.

Manu nodded toward the ravine. "Lead us."

Siriman stared at his father's rifle, then at his empty kukri sheath. Manu smiled, drew his kukri, and presented it to Siriman. The youth cracked a wide grin and accepted the blade handle. With a weapon in hand, Siriman strode toward the gorge with renewed confidence.

The three shuffled over the rocks, careful to keep close to the cliff wall. They followed the course of the rivulet upstream through the ravine, scanning the high cliffs for signs of danger. They soon reached the site where Saktisali's carcass had lain.

"Here," Siriman said. "The monster killed Saktisali here."

They stopped at the edge of the rushing water to inspect the area. No visible sign of the attack remained, as if the inundating torrent had cleansed the bed of blood, gore, and carcass.

"Are you certain?" Manu asked.

Siriman nodded.

"Then the dragon ran around that bend ahead?" Jeet said.

Dragon?

Uncle Jeet had startled Siriman by using the word dragon. Something about the word bothered him. He had never used the word dragon in any of his descriptions of the attack. Instead, he had always called the creature a monster. Siriman knew what a dragon was, and he supposed the monster he had encountered fit the description—it had green-scaled skin, wings, claws, and a tail. He had seen pictures of the dragon statues at the temples and palaces of Kathmandu, but those looked more like lions or dogs, not at all like his monster.

Monster—dragon—why should either word matter?

"Yes, Uncle." Siriman gave the easiest answer. "Karna chased—the dragon—first. Then after I…" It was still too hard to talk of Saktisali.

"No sign of the carcass," Manu said.

"No, Father." Siriman hesitated. "I—I suppose the dragon—could have dragged the body into the cave after we fled. Or perhaps when the water flowed again, it washed the body downstream."

How fantastic my story must sound!

Siriman led the men onward, holding his breath as they neared the next bend. When he saw the scorched wall, he breathed easier. Black scarred the rocky surface, and the charred remains of scrawny bushes jutted from fissures. His father and uncle eyed the blackened canes and scalded branches on the cliff side.

"*That*," Jeet said, "is where the dragon breathed fire at you and Karna?"

Siriman was thankful for the surviving signs of scorching heat, but his uncle's question again gave him pause.

I can put up with the term dragon but "breathed its fire" goes too far!

"Uncle Jeet, sir," Siriman said, "If you recall, I said before, the monster did not breathe fire. It had a weapon. The monster stuck the weapon out the cave mouth and fired at us."

Uncle Jeet did not reply. The two older men surveyed the clifftops and surroundings, Enfield P53s loaded and at-the-ready.

"We are near the end," Siriman said. "The entrance is around the bend. Be certain of your target. It—the dragon—moves fast. You will not have time to reload."

They inched past the curve. A short way further ahead lay the pool where a white turmoil of mist and spray boiled and rushed to form the rivulet, raging between the tall cliffs.

"*That* is the spot where you wounded the dragon?" Manu said.

How to answer Father's question?

The entrance was no longer an open hole—a torrent of ice-cold water poured from the mouth. The gushing water fell ten feet, battering boulders on its path downstream, and crashing against the face of the rocky cliff where a foaming whirlpool formed, boiling around the bend.

Manu pointed at the waterfall. "You said the fall was not flowing yesterday, and the rivulet was dry?"

"Yes, Father." Siriman suppressed a sigh from having to repeat himself. "Almost bone dry—a trickle of water yesterday."

The men trained their rifles on the spout. The barrels rose and turned, scanning the entire cliff top. Siriman eyed the waterfall spouting from the cave and at the raging pool. Somewhere beneath the churning waters lay his lost kukri.

I wish I could recover the blade.

He shook his head, knowing the violent waters would batter him against the rocks and sweep his bloody, lifeless body downstream.

Siriman had nothing to add—he had said everything worth saying and had no other way to explain his experience. His father broke the silence.

"Legends and myths speak of dragons as intelligent—capable of thought and speech. Yet I cannot imagine such a creature civilized, creating weapons that shoot fire."

"There are eyewitness accounts of dragons in Nepal," Uncle Jeet added, "but described as wingless, legless creatures, like huge snakes creeping through the jungle, devouring creatures they find. Slow moving, often mistaken for massive logs—no intelligence in those beasts."

"This waterfall has flowed as long as I can remember," Manu added. "Traditions say an underground stream runs deep under the mountain. The waters come from the melting glaciers up higher. In the worst of mountain winters, I have not seen the waterfall freeze, nor has it stopped flowing in the driest of summers..."

Manu's voice trailed off and Siriman recognized his father's tone and implication. If Siriman's story was true, the dragon not only wielded a fiery weapon, but it lived in an impregnable fortress. No one could get past the raging waterfall blocking the entrance.

The monster somehow shut off the water!

The dragon must have blocked the flow to leave the lair, roam, and kill. If the dragon can come and go at will, what could stop it from finding and killing whomever it pleased? Karna, or something speaking through Karna, had threatened to find and kill Siriman.

The dragon wants to kill me.

Siriman studied his trembling hands.

Do not give in to fear!

There was physical evidence—a missing ox, two lost kukri knives, a scorched cliff wall, and a few burned bushes. The cart and the pile of dumped firewood stood where Siriman said it would be. These few pieces would never convince a skeptic of his veracity. Arguing against the story's truth, a missing carcass, the rivulet flowed strong as always, and Karna had no recollection of the events.

He vouched for it being dry when we walked home. That is something, at least.

Siriman had an impeccable reputation for honesty and dependability—the last boy expected to invent a fantasy.

Why would I? What would I gain?

The death of Saktisali was a grave loss, but not enough to concoct a wild story to avoid blame. His father and uncle said they believed his story, but Siriman suspected they hoped to find the missing ox alive and well, meandering homeward.

They exited the mouth of the ravine and found the bullock cart, still waiting by the pile of timber. Two oxen waited nearby, safe and still tethered to a tree. Siriman breathed a sigh of relief.

No sign of another attack!

Manu and Jeet helped Siriman reload the wood onto the cart, and Siriman yoked Baahubali and Nandi. They stored the loaded rifles in the back, uncocked, and Siriman handed the kukri back to Manu. As Siriman drove the cart home, everyone remained quiet, deep in thought, until his father broke the silence.

"Son," Manu said, "tomorrow we should go to the temple in Okhaldhunga. You should tell your story to the priest."

At least he is not sweeping my story aside.

"Yes, Father."

Siriman considered his father's decision a positive sign, but contemplated the purpose of the visit to see the priest.

What does a priest know of monsters?

Siriman was unsure the priest could offer wise insights.

Unless father wants the priest to force the truth out of me!

Most Sunwars were Buddhists, but Siriman's family was Hindu, as were most Nepalis. It was months since last making the trek to the temple.

What will the priest think of that?

Siriman remembered his piercing stare.

He makes me nervous!

"Do you believe me, Father?" Siriman asked.

Manu spoke without pausing. "Yes." He drove the cart in silence for a minute before speaking. "Others will not believe you. Yet we cannot stay silent and put others at risk. The priest may know what to do."

When they reached home, the three unloaded and divided the firewood. After tending the draft animals, Siriman went next door to check on his cousin. He found Karna awake, sitting in a dark corner of the cabin.

"How are you feeling?" Siriman asked.

"Tell no one," Karna confided, "but I have strange dreams. I hear a sound deep inside my head—a voice, but like a rumble, or slow drumming, using words of an unknown language."

"Dreams while sleeping?"

"No—waking dreams," Karna said. "The words seem to be asking questions, pushing me, to do something. I do not know what."

Karna tried to describe the sound of the voice. Siriman listened until Karna ran out of words, threw up his hands, and shrugged.

"Have you told your parents?" Siriman asked.

"No!" Karna was emphatic, shaking his head for emphasis. Siriman did not press—he understood the universal reluctance of teenagers to discuss intimate matters with elders.

"Do you hear it now?"

"No, not now. It comes and goes."

"When it comes next," Siriman said, "you must tell it to stop!"

"Tell what to stop?"

"The sound—the voice—the dragon's murmuring. You can be the master of your mind and your body if you try. You must demand the voice stop."

Karna closed his eyes, and a determined smile crossed his face. "I will! I will be master of my mind. Thank you, Siriman!"

"For what?"

"For saving my life yesterday."

"But—you said you did not remember..." Siriman frowned. "Are you remembering now?"

"No—I still do not remember..." Karna smiled. "But I believe you."

"But, I struck you...," Siriman protested. "Many times."

"Yes, you did...," Karna said, laughing. "And it hurt, but I know you saved me. You are my loyal friend and nothing else matters."

Chapter 39. The Devas and the Asuras

The morning of the following day...

Siriman

Siriman had a restless night. He woke before the sun and attacked his morning chores, working off nervous energy. When finished, he helped his uncle with Karna's chores. Karna seemed better, but Siriman insisted he rest. After a modest breakfast, the boys ventured into the dim early morning light.

"I am well!" Karna insisted. "I want to see the priest."

Enthusiasm for a long trip! That shows a marked improvement!

Karna hopped on the back of the bullock cart and sat behind Siriman and Manu, next to gifts for the priest's trouble. There was a caged egg-laying hen, two medium-sized bags of rice, and a basket of fruit and wild flowers. The cart pulled away, bouncing over ruts and rocks.

Uncle Jeet waved and called, "Someone in this family must work!"

The boy's mothers insisted on proper dress for the temple. Their sons must not arrive half-naked. Each boy wore a Daura-Suruwal outfit—a long tunic over loose-fitting trousers. The boys were uncomfortable, used to wearing little more than loincloths and sandals. They itched and scratched, dreading the heat to come as the sun rose further.

The cart rolled, and the sun climbed. Every half mile, Siriman turned to check on his cousin. Karna shaded his eyes with one hand, squinting at the bright blue sky.

"How is your headache?"

Karna shrugged. "No complaints."

Baahubali and Nandi trudged on, never tiring. They pulled the cart over hills, grinding out the hard miles on the rugged cart path from Khiji to Okhaldhunga. Twice the cart became stuck, and the cousins had to jump out and push. By mid-day, they drew near their destination, and Manu coaxed the oxen up the final hill to the picturesque town. At the bazaar, they halted near the Mahadev temple and tethered the ox and bull.

Karna laughed and said, "Look, Nandi!" He grabbed the bull by the horns and turned its head toward the nearby statue of a resting bull. "It is your namesake!"

After a quick snack of fruit, they lifted the gifts out of the cart. Manu carried the chicken cage, Siriman toted both heavy bags of rice, and Karna's face turned red, holding only the light basket of fruit and flowers.

Siriman smiled and said, "No one will notice."

Outside the temple, near the statue of Nandi, they sat the gifts and removed their sandals. A young boy of ten or eleven years with a bowl and water jug stood before stacks of shoes, hawking his services as a footwear guardian. Manu negotiated, and the boy agreed to a half-rupee payment for all three travelers, plus another half-rupee for his water bowl the travelers used, washing faces and hands. Leaving the sandals in the boy's care, they retrieved their gifts and approached the temple. Since it was not a holy day, the crowd was light. A few children played nearby and women, young and old, entered and exited the temple.

The priest wore a red silken robe draped over one shoulder. He stood by the entrance, smiling and spreading his slender arms, blessing and welcoming the arriving faithful. His straggling beard was long and white, and the few remaining strands of hair on his head were fine and colorless.

Siriman and Karna watched and waited as Manu motioned the priest aside and whispered in his ear. As the priest listened, his white eyebrows rose, and he glanced sideways at the boys and the gifts. The somber man nodded and motioned to a place to deposit his gifts. Manu set the hen cage down and Siriman placed one rice bag at its side.

"He said he eats eggs," Manu whispered to the boys.

An old woman sat before the temple holding a Vibooti bowl (sacred ash). She requested another half-rupee, and Manu slipped her the coin. She dipped a forefinger and marked the center of their foreheads. They carried the remaining gifts into the temple.

Manu and the boys entered the dark chamber, faced north, and lay prostrate before the lingam (column). They rose and offered a silent prayer, asking the Mahadev to find them worthy to set foot into His home. Three circumambulations followed, past stations of worship. Misty vapors of fragrant incense rose. They chanted praises in salute of the temple deities, and left gifts of rice, fruit, and flowers. When they returned to the entrance, they faced north, lay prostrate before the lingam a final time, and chanted the Holy Five Syllables of the supreme mantra.

"Na—mah! Shi—vaa—ya!"

They emerged, blinking in the bright light, and finding the priest waiting, retrieved their sandals and followed to a shady spot. The priest motioned to stone benches beneath a camphor tree and took one. Manu took another and Siriman and Karna shared the third.

The priest spoke first. "You know my name?"

The three nodded and answered in unison. "Pandit (scholar) Puja Hari (priest) Ramnath Bhatt."

After a prayer, the priest asked Manu the reason for the visit. Manu introduced himself, Siriman, and Karna, providing name, age, and relationship. Then he asked Siriman to tell his story, and the boy did so using few words and without emotion or embellishment. Ramnath listened, nodding at parts, frowning at times, but always with eyes fixed on Siriman. He studied the boy's face and Siriman met the priest's gaze.

When Siriman finished his tale, Ramnath probed the details. Siriman noticed the priest asked questions more than once but in different ways as if searching for inconsistencies. Siriman told the truth and never worried about being consistent. Soon the priest turned his attention to Karna.

Karna was at first reluctant to answer questions. He denied knowledge of the events. He turned away from the priest, unable to bear his gaze. Questioning continued and buried facts emerged. Karna confirmed Siriman's account of the rivulet being dry. At first, Karna could not remember dropping his kukri. Later, he remembered dropping it, but could not say where or why. After a pause, Ramnath launched a stream of strange words. Karna tensed. His eyes turned wild, his face darkened, and he clenched his jaw. Then he relaxed as if a dark cloud had passed.

The language the priest used seemed familiar.

"Please, Puja Hari," Manu asked, "what did you say to Karna?"

"The language is Sanskrit," Ramnath said. "The ancient tongue of the gods. I quoted the Rig Veda. I spoke the challenge Indra issued to Vritra the dragon who had caused a great drought. As Indra prepared to battle Vritra, he spoke these words."

I am Indra.
I rule the heavens and the storms obey my commands.

Do thou that which I command of thee or
I will release upon thee the full fury of my powers.

Ramnath turned to Karna. "Young man, I found your reaction interesting. Minds win or lose—not bodies. Your mind won this day, but new battles lie ahead. You must be strong and prepare for battle."

Where have I heard the dragon tale?

Siriman interrupted. "Please, Puja Hari. This—Vritra—you said it was a dragon?"

"A powerful dragon with sharp teeth, claws, scales, wings, and a tail—much like the monster you described."

"And he stopped the water?"

"Vritra was the Lord of the Asuras. As in your story, Vritra stopped the flow of the rivers. Vritra took wing and Indra flew after in his golden chariot. They battled in the sky. Indra impaled Vritra with his lightning and cast him onto the mountainside. The drought ended."

"Asuras…," Siriman asked, "are dragons?"

Does he think I should know this?

Ramnath's grin had teeth missing. "Asuras are demons of the underworld. Forces of darkness and chaos. The Devas are the gods of light and order, opposing the Asuras—two forces in a constant battle. Each side knows victory and defeat. Indra is the king of the Devas—god of sky, winds, and rain. Indra cast down the dragon, shattering the Asuras' fortress. The Asuras fled, banished to Patala, their hidden kingdom beneath the Himalayas."

"But—are they all dragons?"

"No, not all," Ramnath said. "There are demons called Rakshasas—tall, shape-shifters, part-human, and part-dragon. Dragons are water spirits. Legends say Patala holds a vast underground sea. In the time of Vritra, the Asuras hoarded water behind the mountains—locked in a vast sea of ice, a sheet miles thick, holding the water for thousands of years."

"No water?"

"The rivers dried, many lakes vanished, and the shores of the sea retreated. Dry land appeared and new continents rose. Ancient civilizations built mighty temples and great stone cities on the new land. Ships sailed the seas to the far corners, spreading language, culture, and learning."

"What happened to the old world?"

"When Indra destroyed Vritra, he released the frozen waters. A great flood followed. The oceans rose, and the continents sank. Great cities vanished, swallowed beneath the waves. It was an age of calamity. Mankind perished, all that is…"

"I remember!" Siriman said, beaming with pride.

"Do not interrupt!" his father scolded.

"No!" Ramnath held up a hand. "Tell us what you remember."

"Everyone perished except Manu and the Seven Rishis! Saved by—saved…"

Ramnath finished his thought. "By Lord Vishnu. In the form of his avatar Matsya."

"Yes!" Siriman said. "The great fish! He pulled their ship to the mountains."

Ramnath nodded. "The floods subsided, but then the oceans rose. Great cities gone, lost forever, but rivers flowed once more. The land grew fertile and repopulated. In time, new civilizations rose—Indra's gift to the worshipful survivors."

"Puja Hari," Siriman said, "the dragon that killed Saktisali—was it an Asura?"

Ramnath paused. He cocked his head, closed his eyes, and licked his lips, as if savoring his words before beginning. "To have faith," he said, at last, "means believing in that which no one can prove. The Asuras and Devas are matters of faith. If a matter of faith proves true, does that solidify the faith? Does solving a mystery reduce the need for faith? It took a Deva, a mighty god, to slay the dragon Vritra. Can your dragon be an Asura? Can a mortal boy slay an immortal demon?"

"I wounded it."

"You wounded it and it bled. The creature is flesh and blood—a mortal being and the mortal die. Are Asuras mortal? What of Lord Indra if Asuras are mortal? Is he mortal, too? These are questions I cannot answer—questions for the wise in Kathmandu."

"Kathmandu?" Siriman murmured, awed by the name.

Ramnath turned to Manu. "There is a sacred temple to Lord Shiva in Kathmandu. The Pashupatinath temple stands on the banks of the Bagmati River. Wise men—priests of great learning—should hear Siriman's tale and give thought to these questions."

"How?" Manu said. "It is so far away."

"I have long hoped to take a pilgrimage to Kathmandu," Ramnath said. "At my age the journey would be too hard for me alone. With a chela to travel with me—to support and protect me—I could make this journey."

"Two chelas!" Karna erupted, having sat silent for a long time.

Manu glared at Karna and then turned to the priest. "You ask my son, and my nephew—mere boys—to leave Khiji, and their families because of this?"

"The wise ones may help Karna."

"What of us?" Manu protested. "The danger remains. The dragon killed my ox. It threatened to kill Siriman. How can we protect our village?"

"Who knows of this so far?"

"No one, outside our immediate family."

"Why not?"

"We were hoping to get your advice. I hoped you could uncover the truth behind the story."

Siriman eyes opened wide and looked at his father in dismay.

Truth? Father still hoped my story would prove false!

"I believe the story," Ramnath said. "Tell no one else of the dragon. Tell the other families in your village a large predator killed your ox. Say your son and nephew found the body and went for help. When you returned, the carcass had vanished. These statements are all true. Warn everyone to be alert to danger. Tell them to take precautions, arm themselves when traveling, guard the livestock, and let no beast stray."

"Prudent steps," Manu said, "but what of Karna? The dragon spoke through him and swore to kill Siriman. How can we protect the boys?"

"The danger may be greater if they stay in Khiji. Karna needs help for his—dragon sickness. He may find help in Kathmandu. With distance from the threat, he could heal the wounds in his mind."

"This requires thought and discussion. I must confer with my wife, my brother, his wife, and the boys."

"Your son and your nephew are no longer boys," Ramnath said. "They are young men. Their size, strength, and maturity in the face of danger show this."

"I want to go!" Siriman exclaimed.

"And I!" added Karna. "I want to go to Kathmandu!"

Manu shook his head. "We can discuss this later at home. The journey would be dangerous."

"Yes," Ramnath said. "Footpaths go many miles through the hills. Rope bridges over rocky gorges and raging rivers. The journey is over one hundred miles. It would take many days."

"What of the other villagers?" Manu said. "What reason would we give for the boys going to Kathmandu?"

"The truth is always the best answer. Tell the villagers, the wise say opportunities do not linger. Say, the young men are Ramnath's chelas."

"When would they return?"

"Who can say?" Ramnath said. "They may never return."

"Never?"

"There is more in Kathmandu than temples. Many young men leave quiet farming villages to see the world and never return. When I was their age, my brother and I and two friends journeyed to Kathmandu. I returned alone—as a priest."

"The others?"

"My brother and our two friends became soldiers. They left Nepal to fight for the British in India. There are many possibilities to consider."

Soldiers? For the British?

Afterward, Siriman thought of little else.

Chapter 40. The Smoking Woman

Two days later...

Siriman

Parents may plead but teenagers on the verge of adulthood make their own choices. The choice Siriman and Karna made was to leave the nest, seek safety in adventure, and follow Ramnath to Kathmandu. Two days later the young men had backpacks and walking sticks ready and prepared to set off on foot.

The cousins added woolen caps and jackets to their Daura-Suruwal attire. The long hike would lead over taller hills with cooler climes and lonely nights. In place of his thin robe, the priest wore a long, pleated kurta tunic, trousers, and matching purple turban. His thin tethered beard shone white in the bright morning sun.

Siriman patted a comforting weight on his hip. A new kukri knife hung in its yak-hide sheath. The young men had received replacement blades as parting gifts. The village's Kaami blacksmith had fashioned and sharpened the knives to razor edges. Siriman had confidence his skill with the blade could master any opponent—wolf, tiger, bandit, or the most terrible foe imaginable.

Their mothers cried, but their fathers were stoic and understanding. Their sisters joined the crying chorus, but tears turned to laughter, hugs, kisses, and well-wishing waves of goodbye. Playful dogs barked and nipped at the young men's hands. Brothers and young neighbors swarmed, chattering in high voices, begging to join the travelers. Siriman smiled and returned the waves. He caught sight of Akuti, the girl he thought he could love, given a chance. She was crying and Siriman's heart leapt, but when he saw the look in Karna's eyes, he realized her tears were for someone else.

The trio left Khiji village and the old priest kept pace as they climbed the narrow footpath with the sun at their backs. At the hilltop, Siriman sought a final glimpse, but the village was out of site. His eyes opened, as if the first time, to the beauty of Nepal—rocky hills, green forests, and in the distance, white glint of the mighty snow-capped Himalayas. His heart ached.

Will I ever see anything as beautiful?

Siriman sniffed, wiped a tear, and suppressed guilty thoughts of leaving his family. His stomach growled, and he recalled parting words of Nepali wisdom from his father.

If you depend on others, you will soon go hungry.

Siriman smiled and shook his head.

Quiet, stomach! Many more hours of hiking ahead before eating.

Their backpacks held provisions for a few days, but not the entire journey. The travelers would ration until they reached the east-west caravan road where they would find villages.

They hiked four days in the cool hills and slept three nights in warmer ravines. On the fourth night, they camped near a cold stream under a milky-white river of stars, flowing across a brilliant dome of sparkling diamonds. At the campfire, Ramnath told the story of Samudra Manthan, the churning of the ocean of milk.

"So the Asuras are not always evil," Siriman said at the story's end. "Nor are the Devas always good."

Ramnath cracked a wry smile. "And why do you say that?"

"The Asuras conquered the Devas in a fair fight. They ruled heaven, but still cooperated in churning the ocean of milk. The treasures benefited each side, but Lord Vishnu awarded the greatest prize—the Amrita nectar—to the Devas alone. The gods cheated the Asuras, drove them underground, and they have tried ever since to regain their rightful power."

Ramnath smiled. "Very perceptive, young man. You recognized the balance of the universe—light and darkness, good and evil—all things seek balance. When the balance is disturbed, it must restore itself."

Siriman took first watch that night as Karna and Ramnath dozed. The fifteen-year-old sat cross-legged on his wool blanket and studied the sparks and flames as he stabbed and stirred the burning branches. Through the smoke, two yellow orbs appeared behind nearby trees, gleaming as if the firelight was reflecting from watchful eyes. He stood to investigate and, as if a sitting giant stood in answer, the yellow beacons rose, higher and higher, and vanished. He reached the spot and found the space empty, save three pieces of dry timber.

How did we miss these earlier when we policed the camp perimeter for firewood?

Siriman noted the unusual lightness of the wood as he returned and fed the campfire. Fragrant smoke hissed from the new fuel and a curtain formed above the dancing flames.

Is it a door?

The door cracked and light streamed from a hallway. Siriman found himself inside a house—dark, yet comfortable—strange, yet desirable. Siriman had seen nothing like it.

This is a European house! How do I know that? Because no house like it exists in Nepal!

He approached an open door and peered into a dim room. A stout European woman in a loose-fitting black dress sat at a writing desk. A white shawl draped her neck beneath a tight gray bun of hair. An oil lamp cast a warm, yellow glow upon stacks of papers and books.

The woman wrote and the simple act amazed Siriman. Her hand flew, dipping the pen, scratching the page, and dipping once more. Siriman caught sight of a flash on one finger—reflection from lamplight striking polished gold and jewels. An ornate ring adorned her hand. The woman stopped and squinted into space as if reading words in midair. Then she turned and continued writing.

A hand-rolled cigarette smoldered in a large ashtray. The wispy smoke drifted upward as if from a tiny campfire. Ashes and crooked remains of smokes beyond count filled the tray.

Siriman wanted to enter and see inside, and even speak to the woman, but he —yes, he who thought himself fearless—trembled with fear. The woman was enticing, yet intimidating. He dared not speak, let alone enter.

"You planning to stand there all night, or enter?" she barked. The woman continued writing without looking up, scratching hurried script across empty expanses.

"I—I should go," Siriman muttered.

"Flapdoodle!" the woman shouted and Siriman jumped. Head down, her writing continued. "You invaded my privacy, like the rest—no, you are not the first today! Why must I endure this long line of intruders?"

Siriman had no answer.

The woman softened. "You may as well enter." She sighed, as if resigned to her fate, and nodded at an empty chair. "Take a seat. Make yourself comfortable. I will reach a breaking point in a moment."

Siriman stepped into the room and padded toward the chair. The wooden floor creaked, but the woman took no notice. He sat and his wide eyes explored the room. Books were everywhere—more books than he could imagine existing in the world—on shelves, stacked on tables, and piled on the floor. Strange paintings lined the paneled walls.

The woman put down her pen, arranged a pile of papers into a neat stack, and pushed it to one side. Stained fingers lifted the cigarette from the tray and she inhaled. Her head tilted back and exhaled like an erupting volcano as she flicked ashes.

"So, what will it be? What will satisfy you? What can I say so you will leave me in peace?"

That language—my ears hear strange words but my mind understands!

"I do not know. I was on my way to Kathmandu. How did I get here? Who are you?"

"You think you know little." Her voice matched her stern eyes. "You know more than you think." She raised the cigarette for another drag. "Yes, I see now." She exhaled. "You are one of *them*."

"One of whom?" Siriman said, more confused, if possible.

"Never mind. It is not your fault. You are new to the Great Game— young, but significant. You will grow up fast—like it or not."

"I want to grow up!" he exclaimed. "But—why am I here?"

"Young man," she said, chuckling, "the world's libraries have shelves of books attempting to answer that exact question, but none—including my writing—ever present a satisfactory answer."

Siriman stared back, face blank, mouth open, ready to answer, but no reply issued.

"Oh, never mind." She sighed. "I am sorry, we are wasting time." She looked around the room and nodded. "This is the home of a friend—in Wurzburg, Germany."

Siriman shrugged.

"Europe," she said. "Have you heard of Europe?"

"Yes!" He did not want her to think he was dull-witted.

"Europe, Germany—no matter. I am—never mind—not relevant. You are here because your soul seeks guidance. I will give it to you so you can leave and let me return to my work." The woman inhaled and exhaled another drag. Siriman suppressed a cough with his fist. "Kathmandu, huh?" she asked, flicking more ashes.

"Yes, I am going to Kathmandu."

"Hum. No, that is not where you..."

"Yes—I am—I..."

"Do not interrupt! Before Kathmandu, you will reach a fork in the road and will have to choose. As a free agent, choose whichever course you wish, but you will choose not to go north to Kathmandu."

"Where else *is* there to go?"

"South! Turn away from the mountains and toward your future."

"When?"

"When it feels right."

The woman twisted the cigarette stub in the tray and exhaled the last of her smoke.

"Will south lead away from the dragon?"

She laughed and coughed. "Ah—now—we come to it!" She shook her head and chuckled. "The nub of the matter at last! You will avoid danger— for a while. You can grow up, prepare for battle, then face the challenge later, on your terms and with help, but you must face them."

"'*Them*'? Are there more dragons?"

"All that territory—the Himalayas, Tibet, Nepal, Bhutan, northeast India, and Burma—dragon country. Those lands sit above Agartha, secret underground kingdom of the dragons. They watch, wait, bide their time beneath mountains, foothills, and waters. Fate marked you. Delay reckoning while you can, but you must come to terms."

"What of the priest?" he said. "I promised I would go with him to Kathmandu."

"He will be fine! Let him go alone. His part is to lead you to where you need to be."

"My cousin...?"

"Hum..." She paused long seconds. "I have less confidence. I am tempted to say leave him behind but on second thought—do not go south alone. He must go, too—that is essential."

Another rolled cigarette reached the smoking woman's mouth. She fumbled striking a match and her hand shook as she puffed.

"One last thing...," she said, rustling through papers. She held up an envelope. "Do you see this?"

"Yes."

"Take a good long look!"

"I see it—but what is it?"

"Never mind—for now. Remember the shape. Someday you will find something similar. When you do, save it, and give it to the angel."

"Angel? Will I meet an angel?"

"Yes."

"How will I...?"

"When the time comes, you will know. Now, what else?"

"I—I do not..."

"None of you ever do! Now, please go—let me work!"

The woman set the smoldering cigarette in the tray, turned back to her papers, and reached for her pen. Siriman stood and walked to the door. He turned and fidgeted, trying to decide how best to phrase a final question.

"Yes?" The woman spoke without looking.

"Am I—is this real—or am I dreaming?"

"I am real! You may be in a dream, but dreaming does not mean something is not real. Now, shoo!"

Siriman reentered the dark hallway. The door closed behind him with a...

Bang!

Chapter 41. The Lok Geet Piper

Continued...

Siriman

Siriman woke, wide-eyed and cross-legged on his blanket. Cold stars glinted in the dark sky with the faintest hint of sunrise in the east. A chill settled over the camp. He shivered in the night air and drew the woolen blanket closer. Lazy smoke rose from the dying campfire, so he jabbed a branch into the red embers and rejuvenated the flame.

What a dream! I slept through my watch. Wild animals could have attacked us.

Karna and Ramnath remained asleep but tossed, restless under their blankets.

The priest will wake soon. I slept through all three watches. How could I do that?

Bright eyes shone behind foliage near the stream and Siriman peered back, wary of danger. He stood and reached for the cooking pot. As he moved toward the brush to investigate, the eyes blinked once and disappeared. He found the spot and searched for tracks, but found no clear sign.

Whatever it was, it has gone, leaving no trace.

As Siriman dipped fresh water from the stream, rustling sounds came from the camp's direction. He returned carrying the pot and found the priest awake, tossing dry branches into the rekindled fire.

Ramnath nodded in Karna's direction and whispered, "Your cousin struggles, locked in a battle."

Siriman set the pot next to the fire and bent over Karna. His cousin had an arm draped over his eyes and his lips moved. Siriman turned an ear but heard nothing.

"It is as if he is conversing."

"Do not wake him! Watch and wait."

Ramnath emptied part of the water into drinking cups, then added rice, lentils, and spices to the remaining water. He set the pot to cook over the fire and Siriman sighed at the thought of another bland breakfast.

Dal and bhat stew again. At least we still have dried fruit and a few lapsi nugget sweets.

Ramnath turned and smiled. "Rationing will end soon—I promise. Villagers along the east-west road welcome pilgrims, and will offer hot meals for blessings and counsel from a priest."

Siriman's stomach grumbled, and he licked has lips at the thought of a proper meal of curried chicken and sweet meats.

As Father said, if you depend on others, you will soon go hungry.

As the priest stirred the pot, back turned, Siriman thought of his dream and failure to stay awake during his watch.

How best to confess and explain the events?

Ramnath surprised Siriman by speaking first. "I had an unusual dream last night."

"Oh?" Siriman bit his lip, trying not to seem jolted. "What happened?"

The priest finished stirring, turned, and motioned Siriman close. "I saw a man playing a pipe. The music pleased me—a traditional Lok Geet (folk tune). Children followed the piper—skipping, laughing, and singing—and he led them away from their parents. I saw no clear destination, but sensed they were going toward danger. I saw you and your cousin, and shouted after you two, but you did not hear, or would not listen. You ran to join the children and follow the piper. Soon you all disappeared from sight. I felt alone, lost, and empty. Then I woke."

"A strange dream—and sad," Siriman said. "What can it mean? We do not want to leave you. We promised to go with you to Kathmandu."

"I fear the dream foretells a different fate. We will meet the piper in a form we will not recognize at first. He will try to lure the two of you away."

Siriman did not reply at once.

Should I tell him of my dream and admit sleeping during my watch?

Siriman decided the dream was too significant to stay secret.

"I planned to not say anything," he said, "but I now feel I must. I am sorry to say I fell asleep during my watch and also had a strange dream."

Siriman described his dream of the visit with the smoking woman and the events before and after—the yellow eyes in the darkness, the cut firewood. It surprised Siriman how many of the details he remembered. As he finished he waited, expecting the priest to chastise him for falling asleep. Ramnath sat silent as if deep in thought.

Siriman broke the silence. "Is the smoking woman real?"

Ramnath shrugged. "What is real? Your dream seemed more real than my dream."

"Why me?" Siriman continued. "What did she mean by saying I was one of them? What role do we play? Who expects anything of me and Karna?"

"So many good questions. A better question may be why does your soul need her? Much in our dreams seems hard to dismiss. Both may represent different visions of the same future."

"Is there a place called Jehr Mahn Hee?"

"Huh? Jehr? Oh! Ha—Germany!" Ramnath chuckled. "Yes, a country, somewhere in Europe."

"The smoking woman said the dragons live in Agartha. You mentioned a different place."

"I used the Hindu name—Patala. Agartha is the Buddhist name. Different names for the same place—a kingdom under the Himalayas, reachable from caves. Legends say the Asura cave in Pharping, near Kathmandu, leads there."

Karna stirred, moaning, sat bolt upright, and screamed, "No!"

Siriman rushed to his side. "Karna, are you all right? You were dreaming. Was it the dragon's murmur?"

"Perhaps," Karna said. He stood and wobbled, holding his head. "It has faded. I do not remember."

"You should not...," Siriman said, grabbing his cousin's arm.

The boy pulled away and rubbed his eyes. "I am fine—and awake now." He left, staggering down to the stream.

As Karna walked off, Ramnath motioned to Siriman who followed and then hurried back to the campfire.

"I fear for him," Ramnath said.

"Karna is all right. He is groggy but washing himself. When he cried out—saying, no—it was as if he struggled with the dragon. He fought back and challenged its power."

Ramnath sighed and shook his head. "The demon is still a heavy burden. I had hoped time away would clear his mind and free him from torture."

"It *has* helped," Siriman insisted. "I know given more time he will be fine. This was the first incident in days. Perhaps it was not the dragon, but a dream like ours. What of the strange wood I found and placed on the fire? It had a pleasing aroma. Could it affect us, causing our strange dreams?"

The priest knelt near the edge of the fire and sifted through dying embers. He found a charred piece, still intact. He hefted the wood, testing its weight, and then held it to his nose and sniffed.

"Sandalwood perhaps," Ramnath said. "The aroma is similar, but the weight—too light. Sandalwood is heavier. Perhaps you are right. Sandalwood incense can aid meditation. It clears the mind and lifts one's mood. Maybe it caused our vivid dreams and aided your cousin in his struggle."

"How could three cut timbers of Sandalwood appear out there?" Siriman pointed toward the spot in the brush where he found the wood. "Perhaps those eyes I saw?"

"So many mysteries! Your faith in your cousin is strong. Perhaps someone else has faith in him, too. I suspect Karna has a role to play, with you there to help."

After Karna returned, the travelers ate and broke camp early. Near mid-day, they reached a rope bridge stretched between two cliffs. Far below white foam splashed over jagged rocks as a raging rivulet ran through a deep gorge. Karna skipped across while Ramnath inched forward with Siriman close behind, supporting. Later they hiked up and over a tall hill and caught sight of a critical landmark—the great east-west road.

The old road was like a tributary—a remnant of the ancient Silk Road—meandering northwest toward Kathmandu. Once on the road, the journey became easier. For the first time, they encountered human activity. Traffic flowed in both directions, pilgrim hikers on foot and villagers in bullock carts laden with goods. Villages appeared around each turn. Ramnath proved correct. The villagers always welcomed the priest's wisdom and blessings, replenishing supplies and keeping bellies full. The three sometimes camped in stables, but always slept in safety.

On it went until the road led to the east corner of the Kathmandu Valley. One bright morning, eight miles from Kathmandu, the three travelers entered the ancient city of Bhaktapur.

Ramnath shouted over the din of the crowd. "There is a festival underway! There always are festivals in Bhaktapur. Come! Follow me. I remember this place well. I could lead the way blindfolded."

Ramnath found new energy, straightening and taking the lead. Relying less on his walking stick for support, he strode a weaving path through the crowded markets. They passed throngs of Nepalis of every age and social status and skirted a parade of dancers and musicians. Siriman and Karna gazed in wide-eyed, open-mouthed amazement at the temples, stone monuments, and golden statues of a myriad of gods and kings.

Two centuries earlier Bhaktapur was a trading center along the caravan route between India and Tibet. It grew rich and prosperous and became the capital of Nepal. After the royal family moved the capital to Kathmandu, Bhaktapur declined, but remaining a center of art and culture, holding a festival every two or three weeks. The city was always busy, either holding a festival or preparing for the next.

As the parade passed, a young man wearing a khaki uniform and a black Dhaka Topi hat caught sight of the three travelers and approached.

"You!" He pointed at Siriman and Karna. "Yes, you two! You are late!" He then pointed down the street. "You will miss it if you do not hurry. You must get to the Layaku! To the Durbar Square! You must go right away and hurry. The gallawalla starts soon! It is not good to be late. Go now. Run!"

Siriman and Karna exchanged wide-eyed looks and stared back open-mouthed at the uniformed youth.

"That way!" the young man yelled, pointing to his right. "The Durbar Square is that way! Go to the bell!"

"Bell?" Siriman shouted against the noise of the crowd. "What bell?"

"The Barking Dog Bell! Now go! Run!"

Siriman and Karna ran in the direction the young man pointed with no idea where they were running or why. Siriman grabbed Karna's sleeve and yanked, realizing they were leaving behind their master.

"Stop! Wait for the Puja Hari!"

The old priest hobbled to his chelas, energy spent, walking stick clacking on paving stones.

Siriman shouted over the din. "Sir, what is a barking dog bell? What is a gallawalla?"

"Go on, you two!" Ramnath shook his head and waved his stick. "Do as he said. I will catch up with you. I think I see now—the Lok Geet Piper awaits. Go!"

Chapter 42. The Gallawalla

Continued...

Siriman

Siriman and Karna did not argue—they turned and ran, dodging children, old women, and street merchants. When they reached a stair-stepped temple guarded by an imposing pair of stone lion statues, Karna grabbed the sleeve of a passerby.

"Barking dog bell?" he asked, smiling.

A bell rang somewhere near, deep tones reverberated, followed by the faint yelps and howls of a chorus of barking dogs.

The man smiled and pointed. "Past the lions."

Siriman thanked him, and the cousins sped on, keeping left of the statues. They skirted a tall temple and a crowded courtyard to reach an open, rectangular plaza. There they stopped, eyes wide, amidst a crowd of young men their age, milling in an expanse surrounded by statues, temples, and palaces. Elephant statues reared before a tall temple, guarding stone-block steps. To the right, atop a wall, square pillars rose to support an arch featuring carvings of two encircled six-pointed stars. Beneath the arch hung a massive bronze bell, still reverberating as stray dogs in the plaza yapped and bayed.

The barking dog bell?

A late-middle-aged Nepali man in a soldier's garb stood atop the wall and addressed the crowd of young men. "Tomorrow, I lead those selected on a journey. We travel many days west and south, cross the border to India, and go on to Nautanwa. From there we go further south to Gorakhpur where British officers will be waiting. They will test you and choose the brightest and fittest. Those chosen will become Gurkha soldiers in the service of Queen Empress Victoria. If selected, the British will feed, clothe, train, and pay you more than you deserve. Many Gurkhas send rupees home to their families."

"Paid!" Karna whispered to Siriman. "In rupees!"

"Send rupees to our families?"

"As a soldier in a Gurkha regiment," the soldier continued, "you will find glory and honor. You will learn to fight with many types of weapons. Learn to shoot the best rifles, wield a bayonet, and assemble and fire mountain guns. Learn to use a kukri in ways you cannot now imagine. You will train to become true Gurkhas—the finest soldiers in the world."

Karna and Siriman exchanged glances and inched closer.

"But first you will undergo tests. The testing will be hard and even the strongest may fail. Listen—if you cannot meet the challenge, stay home. Save yourself the long journey and save embarrassing me by your failure."

Karna opened his mouth, but Siriman said, "Shush! Listen!"

"They will test your strength and endurance. You must lie flat and sit up twenty-five times in less than one minute. Then you will continue until exhausted."

"We can do that," Karna whispered, and Siriman nodded.

"You must run three miles in less than twenty-four minutes, and can take no longer than ten minutes on the last mile and a half."

"We can do that, too," Karna murmured.

"Wear a seventy-five pound backpack, run up a one-half-mile-high hill, and return down the same three-fourths mile-long path in less than thirty-five minutes."

The cousins nodded in unison.

"They will test your mind…"

"Huh-oh!" Siriman chuckled and jabbed an elbow into Karna's side.

"Stop!" Karna hissed and jabbed back.

"You will work in teams on obstacle courses to prove you can think and cooperate with others. You must show alertness and respect for superiors at all times, obey each order, and never complain or show weakness. Any failure of these challenges and you face a long walk home alone, so go home now, without shame."

The soldier jumped from the wall. "Now I will inspect this sad mob up close. Line up in two rows at attention!"

The candidates scrambled to follow the order. Karna took a step toward the group but Siriman grabbed his arm and motioned to stay back and watch from a distance.

The soldier walked the lines and stopped to peer at one candidate. He asked the youth something. Siriman and Karna stood too far away to hear the question or answer.

"Go home!" The soldier pointed and the rejected young man slinked away.

The soldier continued his inspection. One young man smiled and whispered to a candidate at his side. A clenched fist from nowhere struck the whisperer's stomach, doubling over the lad. The soldier pointed and a second candidate left the ranks dejected. The process continued and, one by one, the ranks thinned.

Ramnath hobbled into the plaza and drew close to watch the process, leaning on his staff.

The Puja Hari appears weary.

The soldier stared at the recruits with hands on hips. He looked down, then shook his head, and walked away. For the first time, his face turned to Karna, Siriman, and Ramnath standing nearby. To Siriman's surprise, the man strode toward them with jaw set, eyes fixed on the two youths.

"Are you here for the recruitment?" he barked, studying the boys. "If so then you are late!"

Ramnath leveled a steady glare. "They are not late—they are with me."

"Who are you?"

"Ramnath Bhatt, a disciple of Shiva, a priest from Okhaldhunga in the east. These young boys are my chelas."

Young boys? I thought we were mature young men.

"Why are you here then?"

"We are on a pilgrimage," Ramnath said. "We travel to Kathmandu, and after many days, we at last are near our destination."

Puja Hari is not happy the soldier is looking at us.

The soldier looked hard at the priest while tugging his chin. "Okhaldhunga is far away. You must be spry and your chelas must be of hardy stock. We have seen few recruits from the east. We spend all our time with tribes such as Magar, Gurung, Tamang, Rai, and Limbu." He turned to Karna and Siriman. "So, you are from a hill tribe?"

"Yes, sir," Karna said, "the Sunuwar tribe."

"Sunuwar—huh?"

"Please, sir," Siriman said, "tell us who are you?"

"I am Ram Thapa. Retired regimental havildar with the 1st Goorkhas, and I am a gallawalla."

"Gallawalla!" the cousins exclaimed in unison. "What is a gallawalla?"

"I recruit Gurkha warriors—young men like you two." The gallawalla puffed out his chest and seemed to grow taller. "I select the best and lead them to India to face British officers staffing Gurkha regiments for the Indian army where they…"

Ramnath interrupted, shouting, "I know you gallawallas! What you are doing is illegal! The king has outlawed your kind." His face grew dark and his voice shook as he waved his hand toward the thinned lines of candidates. "How can you recruit in the middle of the city square? Nepal has closed the Indian border. Anyone caught leaving Nepal to join the British army goes to prison."

The gallawalla smiled. "That is old news, priest. True last year, but no longer. Nepal signed a new treaty with the British. The Nepali Durbar now recruits for the Raj and, under the treaty, must meet quotas for recruits."

Ramnath shook his head and his face twisted in disgust. "How can it be possible?"

The gallawalla laughed. "Times change, priest! Leaders come and go—money always talks. Money, rifles, and mountain guns can change many things."

"Sad that Nepal accepts guns and money to send its young boys to fight and die for the British?"

"It is an honor," the gallawalla said. "The British officers still cannot cross the border, but yes, gallawallas now recruit in the open. The Durbar rounded up this crop you see here." He pointed, frowning, at the two lines of young recruits.

"Wealth can be both a friend and an enemy," Ramnath muttered. "A wealth of recruits, yet you are unhappy?"

The gallawalla shook his head. "These—these…," the gallawalla spat. "The Durbar sends farm boys and mamma's city boys. They are dimwitted weaklings from the Kathmandu valley. The British want warrior stock from the hills. I hope the British will reject them all."

"Why wait?" Ramnath asked. "Why not reject them all now and send them home?"

"Politics! I cannot dismiss them and meet my quota. The British can dismiss the ones with no chance, but even those selected may not survive first action. I have no choice but to take what the Durbar sends me and filter out the worst of the worst. I am forced to take quantity over quality."

Ramnath grabbed Siriman's arm and hit Karna's leg with his walking stick. "Come—I am finished listening. We leave now!"

"Wait!" the gallawalla shouted. "These are the sort I need. What of it, young men? Compared to this lot, you will have great success."

"These two are not..."

Karna interrupted. "We can send rupees home to our families?"

"Yes, many do."

"How would we be certain it reached them?" Siriman asked.

"You will write your family. Gurkhas have fought for the British for seventy years. If money did not reach families, we would know."

"How many rupees is the pay?" Karna asked.

Siriman smiled, surprised by the joyful look on his cousin's face.

"Far more than you will make herding cattle up and down hills," the gallawalla said.

"Siriman, Karna!" Ramnath shouted. "Remember Kathmandu. We go now!"

The gallawalla folded his arms and cracked a smug smile. "Are you their master?"

"Yes! They are my chelas—my responsibility."

Siriman pulled Ramnath aside, whispering, "Puja Hari, what of the words of the smoking woman?"

Before the priest could answer, the gallawalla addressed Karna, "What is your age?"

"Seventeen, sir," Karna replied.

"Perfect!" The gallawalla smiled and turned to Siriman. "You?"

"Fifteen!" Siriman snapped back.

The gallawalla's smile vanished. He turned, clapped his hands, and walked back to the lines of candidates. The youths had milled, whispering, and eyeing the soldier conversing to the side with the three travelers. At the first clap, they leapt back in line and snapped to attention.

"Listen!" he shouted. "This is paramount!" He waited until all stood at attention, eyes forward. "A candidate's age must be at least seventeen. I assume you all are at least seventeen or you would not be here. The British will ask your age. If you answer less than seventeen, you go home. If you answer wrong, even if by mistake, no second chances. Practice your response. They will ask the month, day, and year of your birth. Be prepared to answer with either British or Nepali years. They will try to trip you up and catch you in a lie. Have I made myself clear?"

The gallawalla paused, studying the faces of the remaining candidates. Siriman's face burned.

"Another thing! After we reach Gorakhpur, from that point forward, you will call all European men sahib. Repeat the word—loud so I can hear you!"

"Sahib!" the company shouted.

The gallawalla continued. "Should you meet a European woman, you will call her memsahib. Say the word!"

"Memsahib!" the company shouted, louder that time.

Siriman surprised himself by joining in the shouting.

"Again!" the gallawalla shouted. The word rang out. "Show respect to the memsahibs, or face a beating. I will beat you myself, given the chance!"

The gallawalla walked back and strode up to Siriman. "How old did you say you were?"

"Seventeen, sir!" Siriman shouted. He stood ramrod straight, eyes forward, grinning as if he had never been happier.

Ta-da-ta-da! Ta-da-ta-da! Ta-da-ta-da-dee!

"What is that sound?" Siriman asked, rubbing his eyes.

The flap lifted and gray early morning daylight poured into the tent.

"Wake up, dragon slayer!" It was the smiling face of bugler Gunna Ram. "Time to pack and march to Manipur!"

Chapter 43. The Burning Bridge

4:00 a.m., an hour before sunrise, Sunday, 22 March 1891...

Lionel

As the first faint glimmer of day challenged the darkness, a rousing clarion call stirred the camp. The short reveille played by bugler Gunna Ram provoked Lionel Brackenbury from his restless doze.

The final twelve-mile march to Kangla lies ahead.

Lionel pulled on his field uniform and then folded and packed his red dress coat for the noon ceremony at the Residency. He held the envelope to his nose, closed his eyes, and sniffed a final time before slipping the scented letter into a breast pocket.

How will she behave toward me? Will she be expecting me, or act surprised to see me?

Lionel had managed little sleep, fretting over questions, hoping he would soon have answers.

I deserve answers!

Ethel's letter could not have been an inconsequential note to a friend. Lionel interpreted the message as a plea—a cry for help, a signal she desired the comfort of his presence. He had to discover if his interpretation was fantasy or fact and, if fact, what else the plea implied. He dreaded the possibility of rejection.

Will she act happy to learn I am a member of the expedition? Will she act distant, as if she had not sent the letter, and make me feel foolish?

Lionel put the thoughts aside and tended his packing. He tapped his pipe against his palm, emptying the ashes, and stuck the stem into a side pocket.

No more tobacco until this evening!

Gurkhas broke down the junior officers' tent as Lionel stood, hands on hips, watching his belongings carried to his horse. "Careful with that banjo case!" he shouted. Further inspecting the camp activity, he caught sight of James O'Brien standing in the doorway of the telegraph office. Lionel frowned and, had eyes met, he would have shot O'Brien a farewell evil glare.

I should settle things with that insulting cad.

The signaler was observing a crowd of Gurkhas—men from the 42nd Regiment gathering at the stable. Lionel set aside his quibble with O'Brien and strode to the building where he found Lieutenant Lugard supervising. Each soldier in the party stepped forward and deposited his kit in the stable, forming a stack next to heavier baggage. Lugard counted each kit, and a sepoy wrote the names in a ledger. Lionel watched until the lieutenant finished.

"Morning, Lugard," Lionel said. "What is all this?"

Lugard jumped, acting startled. "Orders from Skene." He frowned and cleared his throat. "We are leaving any heavy baggage we will not need from this point. I am to command a detachment of one hundred rifles. Eighty of those men will leave kits here but march with us to Manipur. Twenty will stay in Sengmai and guard the baggage. My company might make a quick return march to Kohima."

"When?"

"As soon as tomorrow afternoon. I have yet to receive further details."

Lionel scratched his chin. "Interesting. Primed for a fast get-away?"

Lugard shrugged. "Your guess is as good as mine."

It at least means we are not going on to Burma. The mystery deepens!

"Brackenbury!" a voice called. Lionel turned and found Lieutenant Chatterton, Colonel Skene's staff officer, approaching. "Captain Boileau is asking for you."

Lionel spun, looking everywhere. "Where is he?"

Chatterton pointed. "Back that way. There—with Skene and Quinton."

Lionel broke into a trot and hurried to join the senior officers. He saluted upon arrival.

"Ah, here is Brackenbury," Captain Boileau said. "Lieutenant, I was explaining to the chief commissioner you served a term in Manipur. You know the country, its language, customs, and the royal family knows you, too. Is that a fair accounting?"

"Yes, sir," Lionel said, and then he gave Quinton a thumbnail sketch of his time in Manipur.

Quinton listened and nodded. The gray-haired civil servant in a brown tweed suit studied Lionel with eyes set beneath bushy gray eyebrows.

"Jolly good," Quinton said.

Colonel Skene spoke. "Since crossing the border, spies shadow us—not a surprise, I suppose. Our own spies report a welcoming party is gathering six miles ahead at the river crossing. Uncertain what we face there."

"Right," Quinton said. He nodded at Lionel. "I would like you, Lieutenant, next to me at the front. You do the talking. I do not trust the native translators. Are you up to the task?"

"Yes, sir!" Lionel saluted and ran to retrieve his horse, excited to join the party of senior officers, and excited by an idea.

This is my chance!

Two members of the expedition, Lieutenants Gurdon and Woods, had risen from regimental ranks to become assistant commissioners under Quinton. If Lionel could do his assignment well, he could show the chief commissioner his worth. A career in civil service seemed a safer path than soldiering if he hoped to marry, start a family, and live a long and happy life.

The expedition broke camp and began its loaded tab-march. Eleven British officers and dignitaries led the way on horseback with four hundred Gurkhas trekking behind, four-a-breast. The damp road headed south from Sengmai, following the line of telegraph poles leading to Kangla, and entered a dank jungle. They turned east and came upon Sengmai stream. The low water trickled over gravel and around flat rocks, offering easy ford. Once across, the jungle deepened, and the column skirted forested hills to their left. The path straightened toward the southeast and after another mile, the jungle fell away, replaced by a fertile plain dotted by farmers' mud huts.

Lionel surveyed the column and recognized a face, marching three rows behind—Siriman Sunwar—the Gurkha who spoke of dragons the prior night. Lionel pulled the reins and waited for Sunwar to come alongside.

"Good morning, Naik Sunwar," Lionel said. "Did you get much sleep?"

"Yes, sahib," Siriman replied, smiling. "A good sleep."

"No nightmares?"

"Oh, no, sahib. Never."

Lionel smiled. "I heard you have a new nickname—because of your story last night—dragon slayer."

"Yes, sahib," Siriman answered, chuckling, "but dragon slayer is a bad nickname."

"Why is that?"

"I did not slay the dragon, sahib."

"No?"

"No, sahib. I wounded the monster."

Lionel threw back his head and guffawed. "Naik Sunwar," he said shaking his head, "you and I must talk further. I must hear more of this story of yours before finishing this mission."

"Yes, sahib!" Siriman broke into a wide grin. "With pleasure."

Lionel looked toward the front of the column and noticed Quinton craning his neck as if looking for someone. He urged his horse forward and rejoined the senior leaders at the front.

"Oh, there you are, Brackenbury." Quinton pointed ahead. "What do you know of this next river crossing?"

"It is the Imphal River," Lionel said. "It flows much stronger than the stream back at Sengmai."

"How will we cross?" Colonel Skene asked.

"The road leads straight to a wooden bridge," Lionel said. "The construction is crude—a deck of wooden planks over pilings—but sturdy. It should be serviceable and meet our needs."

"Capital!" Quinton replied.

"We should make good time then," Skene said, "since the river will not slow us."

The gray sky burned to deep blue, threatening a hot day ahead, and the rising sun baked the dirt road into a dusty trail. The column trooped forward and a gritty cloud rose from the tramping hoofs and boots. As the mist cleared, a band of thick vegetation appeared—a snaking swathe of forest marking the path of the approaching river valley. The expedition had reached the halfway point, covering six miles without incident.

As the forest grew nearer, Subadar Heema Chund pointed above the tall trees and shouted. "Smoke!"

A thick black column rose above the forest roof. Colonel Skene raised a hand and called the column to a halt.

"Would I state the obvious," Quinton said, smiling, "if I said, fire and smoke go hand-in-hand?"

"What is burning?" Skene asked.

"Sir," Lionel said, "the smoke appears near the bridge."

Quinton frowned. "Our welcoming party?"

"Colonel," Captain Boileau said, "I suggest Brackenbury and I ride ahead to appreciate the situation."

Skene nodded. "All right, Captain, but move with caution. We will follow at double-time. If it looks like a trap, fire warning shots. We will take proper action."

Lionel and Boileau urged their horses to a gallop and covered the final quarter mile. They entered the river valley forest and rounded a bend. As they reached the northern riverbank, the horses reared and squealed in fear. A raging inferno engulfed the long bridge. A blast of heat from ruby flames singed their faces, and noxious fumes from coal-black smoke choked their lungs. The entire wooden structure was ablaze—the pilings, headers, beams, and planks. Visible through the shimmering heat, a mob crowded the facing southern bank. Two thousand turbaned irregulars waited, scowling, muskets at the ready. Front and center, four turbaned men sat mounted on sturdy ponies, staring across the flaming gulf.

"Manipuris!" Lionel had to shout over the roar of the flames and the rumble of fast water twenty feet below crashing past rocks.

"Armed Manipuris!" Boileau added. "I make it two regiments at least."

"Our welcoming party, I presume."

The officers coughed and backed their mounts away from the fire.

"Do you recognize anyone?" Boileau asked.

"Yes." Lionel pointed. "See the man in the center—the one with a mouth full of betel-nut?"

"I see."

"He is Prince Angao Sena, a minor player. To his right—that is Tikendra Jeet, his older brother."

"The Senapati?"

"Right," Lionel said. "Commander of the military. On his left, in the green uniform and purple turban—that is the old Tongol General. He is the highest-ranking officer in the army."

"On the pony behind—who is that?"

"I do not recognize him."

"We should ask their intentions," Boileau said.

"This is no diplomatic welcoming party," Lionel said. "Manipur does not have a large standing army. These men are irregulars—a militia assembled to prevent our crossing."

"Find out," Boileau said. "Ask them why they burned the bridge."

Lionel cupped his hands to his flush cheeks. "Is that the Senapati I see?" He called in Meiteilon, the language of the royal family of Manipur.

"Who is asking?" Prince Angao Sena replied, chomping all the harder.

"I was asking Prince Tikendra Jeet."

"Can that be Brackenbury I see?" Tikendra Jeet shouted.

"The same!"

"Well, well, Lieutenant," the prince said, "welcome back to Manipur. If you wish to speak to the Senapati, speak to my brother Angao Sena—he is Senapati now."

"I was not aware of that change."

"You will find many changes in Manipur since your last visit. I am now the Yuvraj."

"Congratulations on your promotion! What is happening here?"

"The bridge caught fire."

"So we see." Lionel flashed a grim smile. "Is this how Manipur welcomes Her Majesty's emissaries? With a sneak attack?"

"Sneak attack?" Tikendra Jeet said. "Ha! We did no such thing. I have a question for you. Is my older brother Sura Chandra with your company? There are rumors."

At that moment, the rest of the British column arrived. Mounted officers and dignitaries galloped up, followed by the sprinting column of Gurkhas. Soldiers fanned out along the northern bank and formed two rows—front row kneeling and second row standing. The Gurkhas raised, cocked, and aimed their rifles, ready to fire. On the opposing bank, the Manipuris trained their muskets in return.

Lionel glanced down and found Siriman kneeling close to his horse. Quinton and Skene drew their mounts close to Lionel and Boileau. Lionel summarized the conversation to that point. Quinton frowned, nodded, and offered a response for Lionel to convey.

Lionel translated, shouting back at Tikendra Jeet, "We can assure you, your brother, the former maharaja is not with us. We are not sure where he is. Calcutta perhaps."

"I know you are a man of honor, Lieutenant Brackenbury," Tikendra Jeet said. "I trust you."

"Is that your only comment?" Lionel shouted. "Would you have ordered your men to open fire had your brother been with us? Is Manipur eager for war over such a trivial matter?"

"Not at all," Tikendra Jeet said. "This is a misunderstanding. It serves both sides best by lowering weapons."

Lionel translated.

"Is he insane?" Quinton asked. "If he fired on us, no matter how many he killed, it would be the end of Manipur. He must realize that."

"He may be crazy," Lionel said, "but he is no fool."

"I suggest we trust them," Skene said, "for the time being at least. We could show good faith by lowering our weapons first."

Quinton nodded, and Skene gave the order. The captains shouted, and the Gurkhas lowered the barrels of four hundred Snider-Enfield rifles. Across the gulf, muskets lowered in reply.

"I still would like to hear his explanation for the bridge," Quinton said.

Lionel turned back to Tikendra Jeet. "What of the bridge? Is a fire-breathing dragon loose in Manipur?"

The Manipuri officers and sepoys burst into laughter.

"What is so funny?" Quinton asked.

Lionel made no reply, waiting for the prince to respond.

My cohorts would not appreciate my weak try at humor.

"No dragon," Tikendra Jeet said. "Agni, god of fire, could be angry. Assure Quinton this fire is an unfortunate accident."

"Accident? What sort?"

"Knowing Quinton was coming, I had this bridge repaired and waterproofed with pitch. During final inspection before sunrise, a careless sepoy tripped and dropped his torch. You can see the pitch is flammable."

Lionel relayed the prince's story. Skene snorted and burned red. "Balderdash! If the fire had ignited that early, we would have seen the smoke from a greater distance. They lit the bridge on fire right before our arrival, and with intent of blocking our path."

"I agree," Quinton added. "It is fortunate we do not have the former maharaja. We might have walked into a volley from those muskets."

"Sahib Colonel!" Subadar Chund hid his mouth with a cupped hand. Skene leaned low and turned his ear. "I recognize the man on the pony next to the general. He is a half-cast Gurkha. His name is Niranjan. He is a deserter from the 34th Madras infantry."

"Turncoat, huh," Skene said. "The Manipuris must use him as an advisor. Keep an eye on him, but keep it a secret you recognized him."

Quinton spoke to Lionel. "Tell the new Yuvraj we intend to cross the river—by whatever means we can manage. Ask if he is here to block our path or to welcome us."

Lionel relayed the message.

"You wound me!" Tikendra Jeet held a hand over heart in mock pain. "We are here to escort the chief commissioner and his party to Kangla. Given the fire, if too hard to cross, we understand if he turns back."

Lionel translated.

"How generous of him!" Quinton scoffed. "How *do* we cross?"

The British and Gurkha officers convened a council. Skene assigned Lionel and Subadar Chund to inspect the riverbank and rapids. After the pair examined the scene and devised a scheme, they returned to the circle.

"We must avoid the flames," Lionel said, "but we believe the area just below the bridge offers the safest point of crossing."

"It looks dangerous," Quinton said.

"The rocks will be slippery and the current is swift, but the bridge site was once a ford, and the water here is at its lowest depth. The horses and riders should cross without a problem, but the men on foot must use caution. If anyone slips, the river will carry him away."

"Can we reduce the risk?" Skene asked.

"Rope, sahib," the subadar said.

"The subadar believes," Lionel said, "and I agree, if we could stretch a rope across near the water line, the men could hold on as they cross."

"Have we any rope?" Quinton asked.

A quick inventory of the soldiers' packs produced several lengths of strong cord. Gurkhas tied the rope into a continuous coiled line.

Enough to stretch between the banks.

"Someone will have to cross first." Lionel turned toward Siriman. "It requires someone who can do a proper job—someone not afraid of fire."

"Sahib!" Siriman Sunwar leapt to his feet.

"Right!" Lionel said. "Sunwar and I will do it." He looked at the Gurkha and smiled. "A job for someone not even afraid of dragons' fire."

The lieutenant and the Gurkha followed a narrow path and descended the twenty-foot-high bank. Once reaching the riverbed, they doubled back toward the burning bridge. The subadar tossed down the coil of rope. Lionel secured one end to a scrubby-looking pine growing between the rocks. The Gurkha dropped his pack and rifle, tied the other end of the rope around his waist, and ventured into the current. Lionel fed the slack as Siriman inched his way along the slippery rocks, avoiding the burning pilings. As Siriman reached the halfway point, he slipped and toppled headfirst into the rushing current.

The white foam washed over the Gurkha and carried him a short distance until a boulder blocked his path.

"Are you all right?" Lionel shouted, holding fast to the line.

Siriman signaled with a wave, and Lionel pulled the rope, hand over hand, dragging the solder back to shore. Siriman crawled out and stood dripping by the tree.

"Can you do this?" Lionel asked.

"Yes, sahib," Siriman said. "This time, Sunwar will not fall."

Lionel glanced up and noted soldiers on both sides of the tall banks watching. Lionel's heart raced as the Gurkha made a second try. The soldier inched forward, hip deep in the rushing water, struggling to keep his balance on the rocks. Siriman wobbled, but regained his footing. At last, the far shore grew closer, the water became shallower, and Siriman reached the other side. The soldier strode onto the rocky bank and stomped his boots, shaking away loose water. He tugged the rope to a similar stout pine growing in the rocks, circled the trunk, pulled the line tight, and tied off the end. A taut line stretched over the water, suspended two feet above the rocks and the rapid current.

Siriman signaled Lionel, who waved to the subadar. Gurkhas descended, gripped the rope, and in single-file, four hundred soldiers inched through the current and over the slippery rocks. Once the last soldier crossed without mishap, eleven British officers and dignitaries mounted and followed, crossing the shallow water without difficulty.

"Leave the rope secured," Skene said to Lionel while shooting a glance at Lieutenant Lugard.

Lionel nodded.

Lugard will need the rope for his detachment's mysterious rapid return.

Lionel picked up Siriman's pack and rifle, mounted, and followed the last of the column across and up the narrow path to the southern bank. There, the men of the expedition gathered.

Where are the Manipuris?

The princes and the two regiments of Manipuri irregulars had departed.

"They left in a hurry," Skene said. "They call that a welcome?"

"So much for our escort," Quinton said. "I wonder why they thought they needed to get so far out ahead of the parade."

The Gurkhas stomped the hard ground, shaking wet trousers, and then removed and dumped the water from their sloshing boots. As the column reformed, Lionel strolled among the ranks, looking for Siriman.

"Nice work, Naik," he said.

Siriman sat donning his boots. He saluted, smiled back, and then stood and hoisted his backpack.

"I am glad we did not lose you downstream," Lionel added. "The rocks were tricky."

"Yes, sahib," Siriman said. "Very tricky rocks—once or twice."

Lionel brushed singed fibers on the shoulder of Siriman's uniform and said, "The flames scorched your shirt."

Siriman craned his neck, trying to look over his shoulder. "Not to worry, sahib," he replied grinning. "Dragon fire is much hotter."

Lionel laughed as he mounted and rejoined the officers at the front.

"That little escapade has put us an hour behind schedule," Skene said.

"We must arrive in time for the durbar," Quinton said.

"Let us do one better," Skene replied. "I would prefer to arrive in time for breakfast."

Skene addressed the subadar. "Up for a quick march?"

"Yes, sahib!" the Gurkha shouted. "We will see if these Manipuris can keep ahead."

The column reformed, four-abreast. Skene waved, and the expedition moved forward. Emerging from the river forest, the road stretched southeast following the line of the telegraph poles for the final six miles to Kangla. The quick marching Gurkhas soon caught up to the two regiments of Manipuri sepoys, forcing the irregulars to trot to stay ahead.

An hour later, the walls of Kangla appeared. Lionel looked through his field glasses. Thousands of Manipuri citizens lined the battlements and both sides of the road ahead. A man on horseback galloped toward them.

It is Frank Grimwood, riding out to meet the column.

Lionel waved, hoping to catch Frank's eye, but when Frank arrived, he focused attention on Quinton, leaning over and whispering in his ear.

Lionel raised his field glasses again, studying the approaching fort. High on the battlement, he spied a banner waving in the hot breeze—a coiled golden dragon on a green field. Below the banner, figures gathered around an all-too-familiar object.

One of Tikendra Jeet's cannon!

"Sir!" Lionel shouted to Colonel Skene. He offered the field glasses. "I believe they are aiming a seven pounder in our direction!"

"What on earth!" Skene said, taking the glasses. "What are these fools doing now?"

With a mighty boom, the cannon fired.

Chapter 44. The Reunion

10:00 a.m. that morning...

Karna

An explosion echoed from the walls of Kangla. A wispy smoke trail rose above the battlements and drifted past the green dragon banner. Karna Sunwar raised his field glasses toward the smoke and the sound of the gun.

The expedition is late. Cannon fire from the fort! Is this an attack?

Karna scanned the Residency grounds. White tents dotted the field of the expanded bivouac area, and more dodged trees, stretching from the lake to the perimeter wall. A crop of shelters, planted ahead of the column's arrival. Tents emptied and Gurkhas bearing rifles ran to the gate from every direction. Lieutenant Simpson arrived on horseback, galloping up the carriage lane from the house.

"Sahib!" Karna shouted. "Gun fire from Kangla."

"Not to worry!" Simpson said. "It is a salute. More will follow. The expedition arrives—better late than never."

Simpson directed the Gurkhas to assume honor guard positions, and one hundred soldiers assembled astride the carriage lane, fifty to a side. With rifles shouldered and standing at attention, they formed a welcoming corridor.

As Simpson predicted, the cannon fired a second time. Manipuris gathered along both sides of the road. After the third explosion, the nearby bustees and villages on the south and west sides of Kangla emptied. Shop owners and patrons spilled from the women's bazaar. The groundswell surrounded the Western Gate and spread south to the walls of the Residency.

"Open the gate!" Simpson directed.

Karna grabbed the left handle, a comrade the right, and the barricade between flanking stone buildings swung open. The mob of Manipuris surged toward the opening—men wearing white turbans; women in colorful phanek saris and headscarves; Naga and Kuki men and women in straw skirts and feathered headdresses; and swarms of screaming children.

"Keep them back!" Simpson shouted. "Clear the road!"

Gurkhas advanced, using rifles to stiff-arm the crowd aside. Simpson urged his horse forward and barked in Manipuri, driving the mob back further.

Karna counted the shots of the cannon salute. After the twelfth and final explosion, the crowd parted, drawing back to avoid the hoofs of a dozen horses striding at the head of a long column of marching men. Cheers erupted from all sides as three men rode through the gate. One was a late-middle-aged man wearing a brown tweed suit, one a middle-aged man in a British army uniform, and the third man wore a gray suit. Karna recognized the face.

Sahib Grimwood!

Frank Grimwood stood in the stirrups, waving to the cheering crowd, and then sat with eyes straight ahead, wearing a grim expression as if in haste to get home. Nine men on horseback—the remaining British officers and officials—followed, riding single-file through the gate. Then came the stream of Gurkhas clad in khaki uniforms with white caps held by tight chinstraps. With rifles shouldered and packs on backs, they marched in a crisp line, four abreast, arms swinging, eyes straight ahead.

The column is long—it goes forever!

Karna scanned each face as it passed, hoping to see friends or acquaintances. The first few rows marched past without a familiar face. Then, a bolt of joy shot head to toe.

Siriman! He is here!

Karna could not believe his luck. He had not seen Siriman in months. He had not expected to see his cousin march through the gate as a member of Quinton's Expedition.

I thought he was in Wuntho!

Karna had heard Siriman was in Burma, stationed with the Wuntho Field Force. The sight of Siriman in Manipur brought sheer joy. Karna remained at attention, but he trembled with excitement, suppressing the urge to attract Siriman's attention.

There will be time for that soon.

As the last Gurkha marched past the gate, Simpson urged his mount forward, warning the crowd back. Karna closed and secured the barrier, grinning at the chattering faces pressing against the bars.

"More sentries to the gate!" Simpson ordered.

The column disbursed into the bivouac area to make camp, and the sahibs rode to the house. With the gate secure, Simpson turned his mount, preparing to follow the British officers and dignitaries.

I have an idea!

"Sahib Lieutenant!" Karna said, mustering the courage to get the officer's attention.

Simpson pulled back on the reins and faced the Gurkha.

"Sahib, my cousin arrived from Kohima. Could someone relieve me at the gate?"

Simpson smiled and nodded. "Stay close, Sunwar. The royal party from the palace arrives at noon for a durbar. Meet me back here at the gate in two hours. I have a special assignment for you."

"Yes, sahib!" Karna saluted, grinning.

Simpson tugged the reins, wheeled, and galloped away up the lane. Karna slung the strap of his Martini-Henry over his shoulder and ran toward the white tents. At the bivouac area, Karna hurried from tent to tent, group to group, looking at each face. He asked for Siriman and called his name.

"Sunwar, 44th GR!" he cried. "Sunwar!"

Karna approached a cluster of soldiers and called. One Gurkha—a bugler—looked up, pointed at Karna, and called to another. "Look, dragon slayer! Someone is calling you."

A young man in khaki turned and Karna at last faced his cousin. The men rushed forward, met, and embraced.

"Look at you," Karna said. "You are a naik while I am still a sepoy."

Siriman shrugged. Karna pulled away to study Siriman—he pinched his cheeks, turned his face side to side, and shook his shoulders. He looked him up and down as if to convince himself it was his cousin.

"I thought you went to Burma!"

"No, I did not go." Siriman wiped a joyful tear. "The Madras Infantry has Wuntho handled."

"How did you come to be here? I thought the column was all from 42nd GR."

"The sahibs doubled the column size," Siriman said. "They needed two hundred more rifles. They picked from the 44th GR, so here I am." He leaned closer and whispered. "How have you been? Has the murmur returned?"

"Once," Karna said. He told Siriman of his adventures, including the dragon's murmur; his punishment spent guarding the memsahib; encountering the prince at the tower; the jade dragon idol; and goat's death at the hand of the old woman he called a witch.

Siriman laughed. "Always the women with you! You became involved with a memsahib—I am not surprised."

"Stop!" Karna glanced around to make sure no one was listening. "It is not as it sounds. I am serious. This prince is bad—untrustworthy. The old witch—something evil is happening. I sense danger here. I hope you have not joined me in a trap."

"Trap?" Siriman said. "What have you heard?"

Karna eyed a group of chatting Gurkhas wandering closer. "Never mind—save it for later. What of you? How have you been? Why did that bugler call you dragon slayer?"

Siriman told Karna of the campfire—how he became emboldened and spoke of dragons.

Karna shook his head. "What possessed you? Dangerous to speak of such things."

"I do not know why I talked, but I caught myself before I said too much. I stopped, went to my tent, fell asleep, and had a strange dream."

Siriman recounted the dream—how he had relived meeting the dragon; the trip to the temple to speak with Ramnath; the long hike across Nepal; and meeting the gallawalla in Bhaktapur.

Karna looked down, murmuring, "Poor Ramnath. Sometimes I miss him. It was hard to leave him the way we did."

"Yes," Siriman said, "it was difficult saying goodbye. I hope the old priest made it to Kathmandu. Sometimes I feel guilty for abandoning him, but I have no regrets for joining the army, despite lying about my age. We did the right thing."

"Remember the trials?" Karna asked.

"They were hard, but we made it."

"Remember how soft those other recruits were—the ones from the towns and valley farms?"

The cousins continued chatting until the bugler came by to warn they would miss the midday ration of rice and beans. They hurried, grabbed tins, and got in line. They sat together, apart from the others, and ate as they reminisced further. Karna laughed until his sides hurt. He could not recall such happiness. When they caught up to present day, Karna became serious.

"Has anyone written you—with news?" He looked down and mumbled. "From back home."

"Yes, mother and father," Siriman said.

"I mean, from Akuti."

"Why would she write me?" Siriman leaned close and studied Karna's face. "Have you heard nothing?"

"I thought..." Karna paused. His face reddened, and he cleared his throat. "Never mind. It has been five years—she would have married someone by now."

A shout interrupted the tender reunion. "Naik!"

A Gurkha motioned at Siriman. He jumped up, and after hurried whispers, the soldier left. Siriman returned and reached for his rifle.

"Who was that?" Karna asked.

"The havildar—we will have to continue later. I have a guard duty assignment at the house."

"What are you guarding?"

"He did not specify," Siriman said.

"Oh!" Karna jumped. "I remembered—the gate! I must get back! Sahib Simpson said he needed me."

The cousins parted and hurried in opposite directions. Karna arrived at the treasury as Simpson reappeared on horseback. The lieutenant dismounted and approached Karna.

"There you are Sunwar. I trust you found your cousin."

"Yes, sahib!"

"Ready for your mission?"

Karna nodded, beaming.

"You remember the Yuvraj, correct?"

Karna scratched his head and shrugged.

"Tikendra Jeet—the one you called the bad prince."

"Oh, yes, sahib!" Karna nodded. "Sunwar remembers!"

"You would recognize him if you saw him?"

"Yes, sahib."

"Even at a distance?"

"No question, sahib! Sunwar never forgets that man's face."

"Good," Simpson said. "There will be a durbar soon. A royal party will arrive from the palace. It will be a large party, with royalty and an entourage with many soldiers and dignitaries. Do you understand?"

This assignment is unusual.

"Yes, sahib." Karna frowned and said, "The bad prince and many Manipuris are coming here. What do I do?"

"Stand outside the gate," Simpson said, pointing. "Watch for the Yuvraj—the bad prince—to arrive. Make sure he is there—if needed, use your field glasses. As soon as you see he is among the arriving visitors, signal."

"How do I signal?"

Simpson handed Karna a piece of red ribbon. "Tie this to the end of your rifle. When you are certain he has arrived, move back inside the gate. I will be further up the lane with the British welcoming party. Raise your rifle high and wave the ribbon as if waving a flag. Make sure you see me. Keep waving until you are sure I saw the signal. I will wave back when I see your sign. Understood?"

"Yes, sahib!" Karna nodded. He examined the ribbon—two feet long.

Simpson continued, "After signaling, keep both eyes on the prince. Watch him—every move. If he turns back and does not enter the Residency..."

"Sunwar will stop him!"

"No!" Simpson shouted. "Do not go near him! If he leaves, find me straight away. Reenter the gate and come straight to find me. No scenes—just get my attention, take me aside, and tell me. I will handle things from that point—understood?"

"Yes, sahib," Karna said. "Sunwar understands. You can count on Sunwar."

Simpson remounted and rode back up the lane. Karna stuffed the ribbon into a pocket and wandered toward the entrance. The gate stood open again and a detachment of Gurkha sepoys formed a line across the opening. One motioned to the curious crowd to clear the road and stay back from the entrance.

Karna straightened his cap, brushed off his uniform, and stepped through the line and outside the gate. As he left the shade of the treasury, he noticed the midday sun.

The heat and glare are oppressive!

Karna wiped his brow, wishing for a shelter from the hot rays. He swallowed hard and his brow furrowed with worry.

Must not give in to heat. The dragon's murmur must not return.

Hooves pounded and two horses galloped hard up the lane. Each horse had a Gurkha rider and a red-coated Manipuri sat behind one. Karna stepped aside as the riders exited the gate.

Where are they hurrying? Is that a chuprassy with them?

Karna fidgeted in the heat, wiping his brow several times. Fifteen minutes passed, and then the horses galloped back from one of the southern bustees and sped through the gate. A red-coated chuprassy rode behind each rider.

One chuprassy rode out, but two returned. Was the second the head chuprassy?

The noon hour approached. More Gurkhas arrived from bivouac and assembled near the gate. Lieutenant Simpson returned and directed the soldiers into formation on either side of the lane. British officers gathered in a welcoming party at the end of the ceremonial line. Karna waved to Simpson. The officer saw Karna, nodded, and waved back. Karna shuffled back into position, standing nonchalant with the crowd outside the gate.

Minutes passed. The crowd continued to grow, hemming Karna in, pressed from all sides. The heat increased, and he mopped his brow. Then, without warning, guards shut and locked the gate. Karna stared open-mouthed. He was the lone soldier outside the wall, stuck mingling in the masses of Manipuris.

Why did they secure the barricade? What of the visitors coming?

At high noon, a gong rang from somewhere inside the fort. Then an eerie howl erupted from Kangla as first one, and then an entire chorus of conch shells bellowed. A commotion ensued—the crowd surged into the road and cheered. Unseen and beyond the mob, a brass band struck up a stirring march, creating a chaotic cacophony of clashing sounds. Then came the royal parade. In the lead were three palanquins, each carried by four strong sepoys.

The first palanquin shimmered like burnished gold. Carved dragons adorned both sides, each looping and devouring its tail. Plush, green velvet upholstery decked the interior, and a canopy rose partway overhead. A pompous chap with a white silk uniform and red turban sat in the chair and gave limp waves to the cheering crowd.

He must be the maharaja.

The second palanquin was less ostentatious than the first, shaped more like an ornate box. An occupant sat huddled back in his chair, sheltered from the bright sun, his face hidden in shadow.

The third palanquin was the least elegant of the three. It was a simpler frame with a green silk canopy. Karna saw a young man with a full mouth, chomping.

Behind the three litters, a long line of uniformed men on ponies followed three abreast. Next came the brass band, belting out a rousing march. A large company of armed sepoys brought up the rear. The parade halted a few feet shy of the locked gate. The band played to the end of the song, and then silence followed—the gate remained shut.

Gurkhas stood at attention behind the bars but made no move to open the barrier. The silence lasted a long two minutes. A hubbub began in the crowd. Whispers became chatters. The man in the lead palanquin leaned and spoke to a servant who trotted back to the band director. Seconds later, the band struck up another snappy marching tune. Karna became nervous.

Why is the gate not opening?

He glanced at the gate and considered asking why it remained closed, but then he looked at the palanquins. The bearers set down the litters as the blasting music quieted the crowd.

Remember your mission. You must find the prince first.

Karna knew the first and third palanquins did not contain the one he sought. The middle must hold the bad prince—the one Simpson called the Yuvraj.

If he is in the parade.

Karna lacked a clear view of the middle palanquin. He had to be certain, so he straightened the rifle strap on his shoulder, melted back into the crowd, and inched toward his target. He did his best to avoid contact but bumped into a short Manipuri woman. She poked his stomach, jabbering, and pointing at the gate and the hot sun. Karna did not know the woman's language but her message was clear. He smiled, shrugged, and sidestepped. He continued to weave through the mob until he stood beside the middle palanquin. The man inside spoke to another man—gray-haired, dressed in a green uniform and orchid-colored turban. Karna observed the lead pony had no rider and assumed the man had dismounted. The turbaned man stepped aside, revealing the face in the palanquin, and in that instant, Karna knew...

It is he! The bad prince! Must signal the sahib!

Karna melted back into the crowd and weaved his way to the gate.

The heat is oppressive!

Sweat escaped Karna's cap and streaks marked his face. The band finished its song and another awkward silence followed, but then murmurs from the restless citizens grew to angry shouts and shaking fists. Karna elbowed his way to the bars and faced a fellow sepoy.

"Why is the gate still closed?" Karna asked.

The sepoy shrugged. "Sahibs say they are not ready. Sahibs say Manipuris must wait outside until they give the order."

Karna shook his head in disbelief. "Well, I have to give a signal to Sahib Simpson."

"So?"

"So step out of the way!"

Karna tied the ribbon to the end of his barrel, raised his rifle high, and waved the ribbon like a flag. Through the shimmering air, he found Simpson. The officer sat at the end of the long line of the honor guard with a party of mounted officers, but was not looking Karna's way. The Gurkha waved the ribbon again, and that time, Simpson looked up, raised his sword, and waved back a similar piece of red ribbon, signaling he received the message.

Karna shouldered his rifle and moved back into the crowd, intending to return to his surveillance point near the prince. He turned and smacked into the sturdy chest of the gray-mustachioed man in the green uniform. The elderly man's deep-set eyes glowered at Karna.

"You, Gurkha." The man spoke stern, halting English. "You with British?"

Karna nodded.

"Why make royal princes wait in hot sun?" he grumbled. "Why keep gate closed? Heat is unbearable. This is insulting and rude!"

"I—I am uncertain," Karna stammered. "Sahibs say, not ready yet. That is all I know."

"Most inappropriate!" the old soldier continued.

Karna nodded and sidestepped the officer. As he reentered the crowd, he glanced back at the old man arguing through the bars with the Gurkha at the gate. The band played a third march, brighter and catchier than the earlier tunes. Karna weaved back toward the middle palanquin and then halted. His jaw dropped, his pulse pounded, and his temples burned. He clenched his fists. The hunched figure of an old woman stood next to the palanquin, speaking to the prince.

It is the old witch!

Karna wanted to rush and tackle the crone but remembered his orders. He restrained himself and peered at the woman as she offered the prince a bouquet. He accepted the gift, reached among the flowers, and drew out a little object—the color of green jade flashed in the sun.

It is the memsahib's dragon idol!

An itch flared in his palm. He remembered the pleasant, tingling sensation he felt holding the smooth figurine.

To touch it again—just once!

Karna remembered his reluctance before giving back the idol.

You should have kept it.

No, it belongs to the memsahib.

Karna struggled to breathe. His temples pounded, salty sweat stung his eyes, and his vision blurred. Voices spoke from deep inside his head. Darkness came, but he remained conscious and touched his eyelids.

Lids open—but I am blind! No! I will not surrender! I will keep control!

The darkness passed and his vision returned. The pounding quieted but his ears rang with a high hiss. When he looked for the prince, his heart sank. The lead palanquin remained in its place, but wide empty spaces followed—the second and third palanquins had vanished.

The bad prince—gone!

Part VI. The Fit of Absence of Mind

"There is something very characteristic in the indifference which we show towards this mighty phenomenon of the diffusion of our race and the expansion of our state. We seem, as it were, to have conquered and peopled half the world in a fit of absence of mind."

From *The Expansion of England* (1883)
By Sir John Robert Seeley

Dramatis personæ

In order of appearance (*denotes a fictional character)

1891 Manipur

Frank Saint Clair Grimwood	British political agent to Manipur, 37
Ethel Saint Clair Grimwood	Frank's wife, 24
Lieutenant Walter Simpson	Bengal infantry, 43rd Gurkha Rifles, 31
Prince Tikendra Jeet Singh	Yuvraj (crown prince), former Senapati, 35
James Wallace Quinton	Chief Commissioner, Assam, 57
Lieutenant Lionel Brackenbury	44th Gurkha Rifles, banjo player, 23
Colonel Charles M. Skene	Expedition commander, 42nd GR, 47
Rassik Lal Kundu	Head chuprassy (messenger), 40
Regent Kula Chandra Singh	Maharaja-in-waiting, former Yuvraj, 37
Prince Lekharjit "Zillah" Singh	Youngest prince of Manipur, 21
Tongol General	Senior military leader, king's protector, 74
Captain Thomas S. Boileau	Senior officer, 44th Gurkha Rifles, 40
Lunatic	Mentally-challenged hunchback, 30
Blind woman*	Aged-looking apparition, oracle,??
Bandmaster	Naga, royal bandleader, formerly 44th GR, 40
The Naga	Naga soldier, native militia, 30
The Kuki	Kuki soldier, native militia, 30
Pukhramba "Kajao" Phingang	Jamadar (lieutenant) Manipuri regulars, 36
Niranjan Subadar	Half-caste Gurkha, formerly 34th Infantry, 39
Siriman Sunwar*	Naik (corporal), 44th Gurkha Rifles, 20
Heema Chund	Subadar (major), 44th Gurkha Rifles, 50
Karna Sunwar*	Sepoy (private), 43rd GR, Siriman's cousin, 22
Captain G.H. Butcher	Senior officer, 42nd Gurkha Rifles, 41
Lieutenant Edward J. Lugard	D.S.O. (1890), 42nd Gurkha Rifles, 26
Moonia	Ethel's former ayah (personal maid), 60
William Henry Cossins	Assistant to Chief Commissioner, 27

Chapter 45. The Long Wait in the Hot Sun

Before sunrise that same Sunday morning...

Frank

Frank Grimwood woke with a start, shocked at finding Ethel snuggling at his side. He smiled and relaxed, basking in a satisfied glow.

I love her so much, but I do not deserve her.

He remembered his predicament, the glow faded, and concern grew.

I love having her by my side, but I hate myself for exposing her to such a danger. Quinton is playing with fire. I must convince him.

Frank stood and rummaged in the dark for clothing. Nervous excitement tied his stomach in knots.

I dread facing my obligations.

As he finished dressing, Ethel stirred and rubbed her eyes. "You are up so early. Today is a Sunday—not yet dawn."

"Today is the day," Frank whispered. "Remember?"

"What day?"

"Quinton arrives this morning. Fifteen for breakfast. Recall now?"

"Oh!" Ethel moaned. She pulled the sheet over her head, pouting. "Must I?"

"We could manage without you."

"Oh, bother!" she said.

Ethel tossed the sheet, stood, and reached for her robe. She embraced Frank, pressing her cheek against his chest. "Why you? Is there no one else to do this—terrible deed?"

"No point in belaboring matters," Frank said. "Things will work out— you will see."

Frank left Ethel to finish dressing. He wandered down the hall, stepped outside onto the verandah, and plopped into a high-back wicker chair. The bright moon cast shadows, and the night sounds filled the still air with somber melodies. The khidmutgar appeared, carrying a lamp and a tray.

How did he know I was awake? The bearer told him, I suppose—the bearer always knows.

The khidmutgar set the tray next to Frank, poured a cup of hot tea, hung the lamp, and departed. Boots crunched gravel, signaling the approach of a shadowy figure in the moonlit darkness. A moment later, Walter Simpson stepped into the pale lamp light.

"Hullo, Walter," said Frank. "You are up early, too. Take a seat and have tea."

Walter did so.

"So tell me," Frank continued, "how did *you* know I was awake?"

Walter took a sip and cleared his throat. "I saw your lamp while out by the gate. I thought I would join whoever was on the verandah and wait for the sun to rise."

"Why were you by the gate?"

"Learning things," Walter said. "Ever since old Moonia vanished, I have had active eyes and ears out in the bustees, picking up intelligence."

"By any chance," Frank said, "would these eyes and ears belong to a certain slender young dark-haired lady friend?"

Walter nodded. "Good guess."

"Is she working for both sides now?"

"When it suits her."

"Can you trust her information?" Frank asked.

"We will find out soon."

"Did she have anything interesting to report?"

"Yes, very interesting," Walter said. "Two regiments marched out of Kangla, heading north, up the Kohima Road."

"That is interesting. Irregulars, I assume."

"Yes, but led by Tikendra Jeet, Angao, and the general."

"Hum," Frank said. "That is a big welcoming party. What is their real mission?"

"Two thousand armed men? My guess is they do not trust your word. Someone believes Sura Chandra is coming back, or at least, is not taking chances. That army left to arrest the former maharaja."

"Blast!" Frank exclaimed. "You are no doubt right. I hope the trigger-happy fools do not blow off their fool heads." He set down his cup. "I suppose I should ride up there and make certain."

"Watch no one blows off your fool head."

Frank smiled and nodded. "Right!"

The men spent long minutes in quiet thought until the first hints of red appeared in the eastern sky. Walter broke the silence. "Something has upset you. Am I correct?"

Frank fidgeted but kept still.

"If about the kiss last night," Walter added, "I can explain that."

"No, not that," Frank said, chuckling. "In fact, I have a favor to ask."

"Another favor?" Walter said, holding up his hands. "I hope you do not want me take another wild woman off your hands."

Frank grinned. "How did you guess?"

"No!"

"Well, something of that sort."

"Who?"

"Look, Walter," Frank began, "things may get very dangerous—soon, maybe today. I must—well, something could happen. Please promise to look after Ethel."

Walter's jaw dropped.

"With my full blessing," Frank added with a quick nod.

"Oh, come now!" Walter scoffed. "Things cannot be that bad. This drama, this sudden nervous atmosphere—this concerns Tikendra Jeet. Am I right?"

Frank nodded.

"This is why Quinton came," Walter added. "Right?"

Frank folded his arms and sat back. "I am not at liberty to discuss. Since you mentioned Tikendra Jeet, you reminded me. I need a more immediate favor from you."

"Ask."

"The durbar today at noon…"

"Yes, yes. Dress uniform, etcetera," Walter said. "What favor?"

"When the Manipuri royal party arrives, could you keep an eye out for Tikendra Jeet? It is essential he shows up, and if not, I must know straight away."

"I see," Walter said. He scowled and bit his lip. "Say no more. I will handle it. What time does Quinton arrive?"

"He said to expect him at eight o'clock for breakfast."

"We better get ready. The sun will be up soon."

They parted to go about their duties. Time sped and eight o'clock arrived with no sign of Quinton. Frank dressed for riding and ordered his horse brought from the stable. Walter and Ethel watched from as he mounted.

"No doubt everything is fine," Frank said, "but I should go. I would have more words with Quinton. Not to worry, I will fetch them home soon."

Frank galloped up the lane and past the guards at the open barricade. Outside the Western Gate, he found Manipuri servants preparing for Quinton's arrival. They erected a colorful shamiana tent, rolled out red carpets, and adorned tables with fresh flowers. A steady trickle of Manipuris gathered.

Numbers could soon swell into the thousands. Well, that is a good sign. Why would they bother if they planned an attack?

Frank sped on, rounded Kangla, and turned north onto the Kohima road. After a mile, he encountered pony riders headed his way. He recognized three in the lead—Tikendra Jeet, Angao Sena, and the Tongol General. Tikendra Jeet raised a hand, and the riders halted.

"Good morning!" Frank called. "Nice day for a ride. Did you run into Chief Commissioner Quinton and his party?"

"We did, Mister Grimwood," Tikendra Jeet answered. "You will find them further up the road. We gave them a warm welcome at the bridge. Now, if you will excuse us, we must get back to Kangla and make further preparations."

Frank tugged at his reins.

"Oh," Tikendra Jeet added, "please forgive the congestion. You will run into the rest of our party ahead, crowding the road."

Frank nodded, waved, and rode on laughing. A mile ahead, as Tikendra Jeet had warned, he found the road clogged with two regiments of irregulars.

Looks as if Walter received good intelligence.

The Manipuris trotted, panting, and Frank soon realized why. The irregulars were hard-pressed to stay ahead of the closing column. British officers and dignitaries led the way on horseback and four hundred quick marching Gurkha riflemen kept pace. Frank brought his mount alongside Quinton and the men exchanged quick greetings. Quinton gave Frank an update on the morning march and the meeting at the burning bridge.

"Ah!" Frank said. "That is what he meant by a warm welcome."

"The scoundrel has a gift for understatement," Quinton said.

I must change topics.

Frank looked around, leaned toward Quinton, and whispered, "Were you able to reach Lansdowne with a final appeal?"

Quinton nodded, frowning. "Yes, but his answer was not what we hoped. It is full steam ahead as planned." He patted his coat's breast. "In this pocket is the decoded reply. The message was direct—you and I need rehabilitating and today we take the first step."

Frank frowned. "You confuse me."

"The Raj sees this mess your and my doing, dating back to the coup and abdication. In fact, earlier than that."

"Earlier? How?"

"He said your familiarity with the royal family clouded your thinking. You took sides and were too quick to push Sura Chandra to abdicate."

"Preposterous!" Frank exclaimed. "He ran away to become a fakir—after being attacked by his brothers. He had to choose—fight back or surrender. Since his choice was to run away, abdication was the decent thing to do. All I did was help him write the letter. No idea why he changed his mind and went to Calcutta."

"That aside," Quinton continued, "you are now an easy scapegoat. They hold me responsible, too, because I supported your actions—and I still do. Now you will make amends by arresting Tikendra Jeet. I will salvage the rest of my career by ensuring the rascal goes into exile for a few years where he will lead a very comfortable life. Then he returns home as if this never happened."

Frank muttered a curse under his breath.

This makes it easier to ask for a transfer once this ends. In fact, if they think so little of me, I may have to resign.

"What is wrong with people in Calcutta?" Frank grumbled. "Are they dim-witted or self-destructive?"

Quinton sighed and shook his head. "John Seeley wrote that England seemed to have conquered half the world in a fit of absence of mind."

"Is that what we face?"

"Yes—a fit of absence of mind."

"So they still insist the coup was the fault of Tikendra Jeet?"

"They do," Quinton said. "Tikendra Jeet is the smartest of the brothers and thinks he should rule. Left to his own devices, he will get there, step by step. They expect, after a few years or perhaps sooner, he will force Kula Chandra to abdicate and crown himself maharaja."

"They are speculating," Frank said. "So what if he does? Is that England's business?"

"Forces at work here see the entire world as England's business."

An officer on horseback trotted up beside Colonel Skene. "Excuse me, sir! I believe the barrel of a seven pounder is being aimed in our direction!"

Lionel!

Frank had been so absorbed speaking to Quinton that he realized for the first time Lionel Brackenbury was riding nearby. Frank spoke scant words to Brackenbury the prior day.

I was in a hurry to get home before dark.

"What on earth!" Skene said, holding field glasses. "What are these fools doing now?"

The gun erupted and Frank cringed, waiting for the telltale scream of the falling shell. No scream came. Kangla drew nearer and the crowd awaiting their arrival had grown large. A second shot fired. No shell fell.

"Well!" Skene said, chuckling. "We are receiving a welcoming salute. A lot of powder making a lot of noise. First, they try to burn us, then drown us, and now frighten us to death. We appear to be in a friendly country."

The column reached the north side of Kangla and turned west, then south, and arrived at the Western Gate. There, between gun salutes, the party paused and Quinton, Skene, and Frank dismounted. The regent Kula Chandra waited in the shade by the red carpet under the shamiana tent. Manipuri princesses carried flowers and servants brought bananas and sugarcane to the officers and dignitaries.

Lionel Brackenbury translated for Quinton as the regent spoke words of greeting and friendship. Quinton thanked the regent, returned words of friendship, and stated he looked forward to the durbar with the regent and *all* of his brothers at the Residency at high noon.

"Emphasize the word *all*," Quinton told Lionel.

The regent assured Quinton he and his brothers would arrive on time for the durbar with all the pomp and ceremony befitting the auspicious occasion.

The column proceeded south to the Residency and a twelfth and final salute sounded as they passed the gate. Frank waved to the cheering crowd but his thoughts centered on his unpleasant duty. He clenched his teeth and rode ahead.

I am more worried now than ever.

Ethel and Melville waited on the verandah as the riders reached the house. Walter Simpson galloped up last, joining after the last of the Gurkhas had passed the gate. Frank dismounted and began the introductions. He introduced Chief Commissioner Quinton and Colonel Skene; followed by Captains Butcher and Boileau; Doctor Calvert the company surgeon; Quinton's assistants Cossins, Gurdon, and Woods; and then junior officers Chatterton and Lugard.

Ethel greeted each with warmth and grace. Frank noticed the bright faces of the officers, smiling as if captivated...

By the most beautiful woman in India!

"Last," Frank said, "one you know well."

"Lionel!" Ethel said, beaming. "What a wonderful surprise!"

She stepped forward and hugged Lieutenant Brackenbury. She took hold of his hands and met the eyes of the young officer.

"So good to see you! It has been too long. We must find time to chat. So much catching up to do."

Brackenbury blushed and looked at his boots. "Yes," he mumbled. "I hope so. That would be capital."

Frank scanned the faces of the officers. Many were open-mouthed, stunned to see his wife making over their youngest comrade. Frank cleared his throat and asked, "Is breakfast ready?"

"Oh, yes," Ethel replied. "This way, gentlemen. You must be famished."

As Ethel and the officers stepped onto the verandah, a Manipuri messenger approached in the company of a Gurkha sentry. The messenger handed Frank a note, and Quinton and Skene drew close, waiting as Frank huddled with a chuprassy.

"It is from the regent," Frank announced. "He requests we postpone the durbar. He claims, today is a Manipuri holy day, requiring fasting and rest."

"Nonsense!" Quinton replied. "We spoke to the man moments ago. Brackenbury—you interpreted—did he mention anything of the kind?"

"No sir," Lionel said.

"They gave me bananas and sugar cane, for God's sake," Quinton added. "How is that fasting?" He turned back to Frank and nodded at the messenger. "Tell him I said no. They know we are having the durbar. I will expect them on time as he agreed earlier."

Frank gave the reply to the messenger, and then he, Quinton, and Skene joined the rest of the party inside for breakfast for fifteen.

The hearty meal was a welcome treat for the hungry British newcomers, but Frank lost his appetite and ate little as his thoughts drifted far from the table conversation. The party broke as the officers left to don dress uniforms and Frank likewise went to his parlor to change. As he slipped on a clean necktie, Ethel stepped in close.

"You picked at your food," she said. "You should be famished, having missed dinner last night."

"Jitters I imagine," he muttered.

"Anything new from Quinton?"

Ethel never gives up hope!

"No. Sorry," Frank said, shaking his head. "The die is cast."

"It is still a secret. Several officers have asked questions. They dance around the topic as if to discover what I know of the mission."

"Testing you perhaps."

"I believe they are in the dark," she said. "Still—a military man should handle dangerous police work."

"A military man like Walter you mean?" Frank chuckled.

Her shocked look is so amusing!

Frank frowned, adding, "One thing is ironic. On one hand, they blame me for being too friendly with Tikendra Jeet but, on the other, because he trusts me, I am the natural choice to arrest him."

Ethel straightened a kink in Frank's tie. "If you must, at least you will look very handsome while performing the duty."

"Me? Handsome performing? Are you perhaps remembering my performance last night?"

Ethel laughed with a mischievous twinkle in her eye. "I might be."

"Ah!" Frank said, raising a finger. "Perhaps you are thinking of your handsome friend Lionel."

"Oh, stop!" Ethel said. "Do not be such a cynic. He is handsome, true, but he is a boy." She gave the tie a finishing twist. "*You* are a distinguished gentleman."

"Ha!" Frank scoffed and then blushed. "By distinguished you mean I am too old for you."

Frank and Ethel left Frank's dressing room and strolled toward the durbar hall, hand in hand, as if they were walking to a wake. On the way, as they passed a window, Ethel observed bustling activity—British officers had directed Gurkhas into positions at the foot of the verandah steps.

"I want to see," she said.

They stepped outside and meandered the entire perimeter, finding sentries placed every few feet.

"It does not look like an honor guard," Frank said.

"Anyone can see we set a trap," Ethel replied. "The officers must suspect by now."

When they reached the front, they reentered the house to find guards positioned at each exit. Someone had locked all the doors to the durbar hall save for the main entrance where, just inside, Quinton stood.

"There you are, Grimwood," Quinton said. "Ah." He cleared his throat and nodded to Ethel. "Missus Grimwood."

"Ethel knows," Frank said.

"Hum," Quinton mumbled. "Right! No matter. I—ah—Grimwood! We have a problem."

Quinton elaborated—protocol required Frank serve a written arrest order to Tikendra Jeet and present a copy to the regent. Protocol also mandated documents written in the recipient's native language.

"Why did you not translate them earlier?" Frank asked.

"Secrecy," Quinton said. "I saved it for last out of necessity. In addition, I did not have access to a Manipuri translator. You must translate."

Quinton handed Frank the papers. Frank thumbed through the pages and shook his head. "I cannot do this."

"Why not?" Quinton said. "You speak Manipuri."

"I do, but Manipuri script is complex. I do not read or write the language well. This is lengthy and time is short."

"Missus?" Quinton said, looking to Ethel.

"Oh, no!" She held up her hands. "I do not read or write Manipuri at all."

"What of Simpson then?" Quinton asked. "Or Brackenbury?"

"Neither does," Ethel answered, then turned to Frank. "What of the chuprassies?"

"They would learn the secret."

"Would they abide by sworn oaths?" Quinton asked.

"Yes, but I would not trust them longer than an hour."

"That should be enough," Quinton said. "If all goes well, that is. There is no other choice. Send for one at once. Better, send for all at once. No time—must divide the work."

Frank sent a servant running for the chuprassies. Ten minutes later the poor fellow returned with one red-coated chuprassy and a Burmese translator. Frank chattered at them and threw up his hands.

"Damned worthless chuprassies!" Frank shouted. "Neither man can write a word of Manipuri."

"Where is the head chuprassy?" Ethel asked.

"Right!" Frank tugged the messenger's red sleeve. "Where is Rassik?"

"Sahib, head chuprassy not here."

"I see that!" Frank said. "Where is he?"

"Holy day, sahib."

"The durbar is a higher priority," Frank said. "He must come to work."

"Something else, sahib. Unfortunate incident. Head chuprassy wife found dead this morning."

"What? How?"

"Someone slit her throat slit in the night."

Ethel shrieked and covered her face. "Moonia!" she gasped.

Quinton looked at Ethel, shook his head, and then shouted at Frank in exasperation. "Sad, but I have no time—bring the chap in this instant. Offer him my condolences and an extra month's pay to soften the blow."

The chuprassy said Rassik lived in a village by the southern walls of Kangla. Frank led the man outside and ordered two steeds and riders brought from the stable. Soon the party galloped toward the gate with the chuprassy behind one rider.

"Every minute counts," Quinton said. "We will not have much time!"

Fifteen minutes later the riders returned with the head chuprassy. Rassik was willing and able to translate the document. Quinton first swore the man to secrecy and Frank assigned sentries to watch the men until the durbar was over and the prince in custody. It soon became plain the translation effort would take too long—Rassik kept stopping to ask definitions of terms used in the document.

Quinton pulled Frank aside and whispered, "Your translator requires constant hand-holding."

Frank whispered in return. "It is almost noon. The Manipuris will arrive soon—the translation is not ready."

"Tell the guard to lock the gate," Quinton said. "We cannot have Tikendra Jeet walk in with the work ongoing."

Frank relayed the order. The gate closed and moments later the noon hour struck. A bellowing chorus of conch shells began, followed by the sounds of a brass band.

Ethel returned from the verandah holding field glasses—Quinton was busy explaining a phrase to Rassik. "They are coming," she said. "Large party—palanquins, ponies, a band, and at least a half-regiment of sepoys."

Quinton nodded. "More the merrier, if Tikendra Jeet is in the party."

The work continued as painful minutes dragged. The band began a second march. An officer hurried up and spoke to Frank who nodded and returned to the hall.

"The heat is oppressive," Frank said. "The party at the gate is restless—asking questions."

"More time!" Quinton said, pleading. "Almost there. A few more minutes."

The minutes ticked past and when Frank looked at the clock, it read twenty minutes past the hour.

"Finished!" Quinton exclaimed. "Open the gate!"

Frank passed the order to a signaler who relayed the message to the honor guard. The barricade opened. Gurkhas stepped forward, pressing back the crowd. A single palanquin, followed by a dozen men on ponies, entered and proceeded down the lane. Next, a company of one hundred Manipuri sepoys streamed past the guards, hurrying around the ponies and the royal litter to surround the house. The armed men fanned out on all sides, studying the sentries and the security perimeter.

"We have kicked a hornet nest," Ethel murmured to Frank. "They are certain to suspect a trap."

"Did you notice the number of armed men?" Frank asked.

"They outmatch the sentries surrounding the house," she answered.

The procession continued down the lane. The band finished its rousing tune as the golden palanquin reached the verandah. Pony riders drew close and halted as sepoys lowered the palanquin to the ground.

Walter Simpson galloped up, dismounted, and hurried up the steps. He found Frank and took him aside. Darkness clouded the lieutenant's face.

"Why is there only one palanquin?" Frank asked.

"We have a problem!"

Frank sighed. "Now what?"

"No Tikendra Jeet!"

Chapter 46. The Durbar Debacle

Continued...

Ethel

Frank's face reddened. He quivered with clenched fists and then exploded in disbelief. "Bloody hell!"

Ethel flinched—only tremendous stress could unleash her even-tempered husband in such dramatic fashion.

Never-ending bad news has pushed him over the edge.

Walter shrugged and said, "He *was* in the party." Then he added, as if elaborating would soften the blow, "I stationed a trusted man outside the gate who identified Tikendra Jeet first hand. At an undetermined point during the long wait, he and Angao Sena left the parade."

Frank fumed. "Both returned to Kangla?"

"We must assume so."

"Assume?"

"I could not get a definitive answer."

Frank set his jaw and remained speechless for painful seconds. Then, with a shake of his head, he moved toward the steps.

Ethel stopped Frank. "What of Quinton? He is still in the house."

"Protocol—Quinton will not meet without Tikendra Jeet."

Walter shot a glance at Ethel and then hurried after Frank. The two joined the welcoming party of Colonel Skene, Captains Butcher and Boileau, and Quinton's assistant William Cossins.

The Tongol General and Prince Zillah dismounted and met Kula Chandra climbing out of his palanquin. The three Manipuris approached the British officials as Ethel eavesdropped from the verandah.

After opening pleasantries, Frank apologized for the long wait, blamed it on a clerical matter required for the durbar, and then addressed the regent. "Why are your brothers Tikendra Jeet and Angao Sena not in the procession?"

Kula Chandra shrugged. "They were, but left. They tried to attend, but have been in poor health. The long wait in the hot sun sapped everyone's strength. They fell ill, and not knowing how long of a wait they faced, returned to the palace. It was for the best, considering their condition."

Tikendra Jeet showed signs of illness in recent days, but not Angao Sena.

"In fact," the regent added, nodding toward the Tongol, "the General is also not well."

The old man nodded, coughing into his fist.

"I see." Frank's face remained blank.

Frank suspects he is lying!

"I must inform the chief commissioner. Your brothers' absence could force a delay. As Mister Quinton stressed earlier, all the princes must attend."

Frank returned to the house—once more leaving the royal party waiting in the hot sun. Minutes dragged, and after five minutes, Walter whispered to Skene and left the others. He rejoined Ethel in the shade of the verandah, removed his cap, and wiped his brow.

"Hot out there?" Ethel asked.

"Like an oven."

"Skene let you escape?"

"I told him I need to tell you something important."

"I see," Ethel said. "So tell me—what happened to Tikendra Jeet?"

"He was there—Sunwar saw him."

Walter told Ethel about the sudden disappearance of the palanquins, including Moonia's arrival with the bouquet and the jade dragon.

"No!" Ethel's face burned. "He gave it—it was mine!"

"So he has it back." Walter cocked his head. "Is it that consequential?"

"It was a precious gift."

"I know that, and you told me the real reason he gave it to you."

"Moonia was my servant—he may assume I sent her with the idol to rebuff his marriage proposal. He may be angry and never return."

Walter raised a finger and said, "Perhaps he believes you meant to warn him. What if he thought you sent Moonia to signal it was not safe and he should stay away?"

"Even worse!" Ethel gasped and shook her head. "How could anyone believe such a thing?"

"Many would recognize Moonia as your servant."

"Horrifying!"

"Either way," Walter said, "the question is what next?"

Ethel bit her lip.

Does he know what is happening? Should I risk telling him?

"How much do you know?" she asked. "Of—all this…" Ethel nodded toward the officers and princes mingling on the drive.

"I pieced enough of the puzzle together. My question is, how long before the Manipuris figure out Quinton is here to arrest Tikendra Jeet?"

The door burst open and Frank returned, looking as grim as ever.

Not good news!

Walter followed as Frank strode straight to Kula Chandra and spoke. "I am sorry, but the chief commissioner was adamant—we cannot hold the durbar without *all* of your brothers present."

The Manipuris stepped away and huddled. The general's face darkened, and he coughed. Young Prince Zillah showed his hot temper, shouting and waving arms in protest. The regent calmed his brother and then turned to Frank.

"I will send a messenger and direct my brothers to come without delay."

The proposal pleased Frank, and the regent summoned a sepoy who soon trotted away on a borrowed pony, note in hand.

"While we wait," Kula Chandra said, with a hand to brow, "may we seek shelter from the heat inside the Residency?"

"I will ask." Frank left Boileau in charge and returned inside with Skene and Butcher. A moment later, Frank emerged and motioned. Boileau escorted the regent, his brother, the general, and three ministers to the durbar hall. Ethel and Walter remained on the verandah where Frank soon joined.

"Now what?" Ethel asked Frank.

"Quinton and the others are in my study," Frank said. "I will have to join them—Quinton insists he will not meet the regent face-to-face until Tikendra Jeet arrives."

"What do *we* do meanwhile?"

"I need you two to help Boileau keep them entertained."

"How?" Ethel asked.

"Be yourselves, be pleasant, converse, show them my photos—do anything coming to mind—but do not allow them to leave the room."

They entered the house and Walter and Ethel proceeded to the durbar hall where Ethel did as asked and passed time in light conversation with Walter, Boileau and the regent. The ministers fidgeted, as if growing bored, and drifted away from the conversation, wandering near a rear window.

Where are they looking? Oh no! They are noticing the sentries.

One minister grew animated and called to Kula Chandra who joined them at the window. A moment later, the regent stamped his heel on the wooden floor, calling his brother and the general. The three then retreated to a corner, whispering and casting sidelong glances at Ethel.

Ethel and Walter exchanged worried looks. Ethel whispered, "How long do they expect to keep this secret?"

Walter shrugged and whispered back, "Here they come."

Kula Chandra and Zillah returned, but the general stayed in the corner. He leaned back, and…

"General!" Ethel cried.

The old soldier inched down the wall, legs splaying, and his boots skidded on the hardwood. He hit the floor with a thud and flopped to the side. Ethel rushed over and searched for a pulse, but his eyelids fluttered and snapped shut—he lay silent.

"General!" Her voice trembled.

I think he expired.

"Please, General—oh!"

Ethel shrieked and jumped as the old man's bushy gray eyebrows sprang up and his eyelids popped wide open.

Thank goodness!

Ethel tugged at his arm. "Please stand!"

She pulled harder and shot a pleading look at Walter. Simpson took hold and together they stood up the old man. The regent and his party watched the drama with mild interest before returning to their private conversation.

"Set him on the couch!" Walter said.

They helped the general to the sofa, his old joints creaking as he shuffled. There he plopped, and before Ethel could find a pillow, he tipped to one side and fell asleep, snoring. Ethel wedged a pillow under his head, stood, and sighed in relief, hand to forehead.

I have entertained for an hour and I have had my fill!

Ethel excused herself and walked straight to Frank's study. She knocked and Frank opened the door a crack.

"I need to see you," she said.

Frank stood aside, and she entered, facing Quinton, seated at Frank's desk, as Skene, Butcher, and Cossins stood to one side.

"Sorry to interrupt, gentlemen, but…," she fought back tears, and then cried, "A debacle!" She unleashed a vivid description of the events—the probable discovery of the trap and the general's antics.

"All right, dear," Frank said, taking hold of her arms. "I better come have a look at this—debacle."

When Frank and Ethel reached the durbar hall, a new arrival was speaking to the regent who stood, reading a note.

"Messenger from Kangla," Walter whispered.

The general groaned and with a slow, creaking effort, stood up and joined Zillah and the ministers next to Kula Chandra. The regent looked up from the dispatch, cleared his throat, and pursed his lips.

"My brothers have replied," he said. "They are still too ill to attend today. They hope the meeting will carry on without them."

Frank's face froze, and he excused himself. "I will relay the news to the chief commissioner." He returned minutes later to announce, "The chief commissioner cannot hold the durbar without all the princes present."

"In that case," Kula Chandra said, "we will return to the palace, see to my brothers' health, and weigh our options."

"I understand," Frank said. "If acceptable, I want to come along and discuss the options."

"If you wish," the regent replied. He turned to leave, then stopped, and raised a hand. "Oh—I understand my band was to play music here this evening. If you wish, they may stay for your evening entertainment."

"Most generous," Frank said with a slight bow.

Frank followed the Manipuris outside and called for his horse. Kula Chandra reentered his palanquin, and the sepoys regrouped. The parade reformed—minus the band. Without fanfare, the party marched up the gravel lane with Frank following on horseback.

Ethel smiled and waved until the gate closed, then her smile vanished and she turned to Walter.

"Now—I want to learn the details myself!"

Walter sent for Karna Sunwar, and when the Gurkha arrived, he and Ethel probed and prodded for information on his sighting of Tikendra Jeet. Ethel satisfied herself that the soldier had seen Moonia give the dragon figurine to the prince. She stared at the lake, arms folded and fuming, as

Walter pressed Karna further. At last he gave up, frustrated that the Gurkha could not explain how two palanquins vanished.

"I am sorry, sahib," Karna said. "It was the heat."

"Dismissed."

Once Karna left her sight, Ethel turned, shaking, and said, "That is twice the heat got to him! Something not right with that little chap!"

Walter frowned but made no reply. They returned inside and gathered to wait in the parlor with the officers. An hour passed before Frank galloped back through the gate. He dismounted and headed straight for his study to deliver his report to Quinton. A few minutes later, Quinton and Frank appeared on the verandah and called the officers to assemble.

"Agent Grimwood has good news," Quinton announced. "The regent has agreed to reschedule the durbar for 8 o'clock tomorrow morning. He promised, this time all of his brothers will attend. So rise early, prepared to carry out your assignments as planned."

Frank stepped forward and spoke, "I must caution everyone—stay alert. We have lost the element of surprise. The Manipuris may suspect treachery. Let us all pray the durbar happens as planned tomorrow morning."

"Hear! Hear!" Quinton said.

"Dinner is at seven o'clock," Colonel Skene said. "Our hosts, Mister and Missus Grimwood, have arranged for a band concert for our after-dinner entertainment." The officers murmured their thanks and offered a few claps in appreciation as Skene continued. "Inform the men—until dinner time, those not on-duty may relax or explore the immediate vicinity. Stay in groups, close to the Residency, and keep an ear out. Be ready to respond to a bugle call. Company dismissed."

Ethel rushed to Frank's side, smiling. "Nice work, rescheduling the durbar and all."

When Frank did not reply, she studied his demeanor—ramrod straight, but tight jaw and a slight trembling of hands.

So pale! He is under such stress!

She placed a hand on Frank's forehead.

No fever.

"Are you feeling all right?"

Frank nodded. "Long day—I have a headache."

"Not surprising—after no sleep or food. You have been under stress for days. Perhaps after a nap your appetite will recover."

Frank nodded, squeezed her hand, and entered the house.

With Frank napping, how best to spend the afternoon?

Ethel had noticed furtive glances from Lionel during the announcements.

Should I catch up with Lionel now?

Brackenbury had surprised her by showing up with Quinton's expedition.

I hope he is not here because of my letter!

She remembered the letter's personal tone and the scent she applied.

Was I too forward? Perhaps I should not have sent it, but Frank and Walter upset me so.

She resolved to save catching up for later.

I will talk to Lionel tonight—a drink may put me in a proper mood.

Chapter 47. The Last Dinner Party

Continued...

Ethel

Chief Commissioner Quinton strolled off and stood alone in the shade of a tall oak, staring at ducks on the lake. To that point, Ethel had not given Quinton much thought. From his unkempt, thick gray hair and bushy gray eyebrows and mustache, she guessed he was approaching sixty.

He seems deep in thought. Maybe I should try to get closer. Frank had no luck, but maybe I can persuade him to abandon this insane plan.

Ethel took a deep breath, mustered her courage, and strode toward the tree. Quinton looked up and smiled as she approached. They exchanged greetings and then Ethel struck up a conversation.

"Is it your first time in Manipur?"

"Yes," Quinton said. "It has been two years since the Raj assigned me to Assam and until now I never got closer to Manipur than Kohima."

"How long have you served?"

"Most of my adult life."

"Oh, my...," Ethel stopped herself before declaring that was a long time. She cleared her throat and started again. "Where were you assigned?"

"I spent the most time in Northwest India."

"An awful place—they say."

"It can be insufferable—hot and dusty."

"And dangerous, I suppose—the Khyber Pass and all that."

"True," Quinton said, smiling.

He is warming!

"I hoped Assam would be a welcome change—somewhere quiet, where I could finish my career, be at ease, spend time, and enjoy social comforts with my wife and daughter."

Ethel nodded. "I can appreciate that wish!"

"Then, along came this regrettable Manipur business. I hope we can get this matter over with tomorrow."

Ethel bit her lip and cracked a mischievous smile. "I have a thought! Take your mind off for a while. I could show you sights."

Quinton cracked a wide smile. "Wonderful—what is there to see?"

Ethel suggested a tour of the Khwairamband women's bazaar. The large open-air market stood close by, astride the Cachar Road, and opposite the Western Gate of Kangla. It had remained unchanged for centuries and, by tradition, women owned and operated the shops.

Quinton accepted and had the stable hands bring their horses. Captain Boileau happened by, on his way out for a ride.

"Mind if I tag along," he asked.

Ethel agreed, and the three left on horseback, rode the short distance to the bazaar, and tethered horses outside the entrance. Women ran the shops and stands, but customers of all ages, genders, tribes, and social classes mingled, examining the wares. Here and there, groups of Gurkhas from Quinton's expedition wandered through the aisles and between the tents. Ethel escorted her guests past a myriad of open-air fruit, vegetable, and fish stands. Quinton stopped to inspect the apricots.

"So many choices," Boileau said. "Fresh, too!"

"Too bad," Quinton said, shaking his head, "we must leave Manipur soon."

Ethel tugged Quinton's arm. "Come! See the other side first. It has clothing, jewelry, and utensils. My ayah ran off yesterday after stealing my precious figurine. I would love to find one to replace it, but I suppose that is too much to hope."

They crossed the road, and the men followed as Ethel meandered from stand to stand, browsing rings, bracelets, and carvings. A small dragon carved from sandstone caught her eye, and while examining, she said, "How much...," as the shopkeeper stiffened and turned away. "What...?" Ethel said, and women merchants behind nearby tables backed away, eyes darting.

What is happening? They fear something!

Ethel set down the carving and as she turned to leave, a grotesque, bug-eyed hunchback leapt toward her with arms flailing. She shrieked and shrank back, wide-eyed as he howled and growled gibberish from the twisted mouth in his horrid, distorted face. The hunchback grabbed for Ethel's arm and she tripped, fell backward screaming, toppling a table.

Quinton sprang forward brandishing his riding crop and gave the man a sound whack across the back, knocking him to the dirt. The chief commissioner then placed a firm boot on the man's back and raised his hand, threatening a second blow.

"No!" Ethel cried. "Please, do not hurt him! He is harmless!"

Quinton lowered his crop and pointed it in the hunchback's face. "You know this lunatic?"

"No—I mean, yes!" Boileau helped Ethel stand. She brushed and straightened her dress as the captain righted the table. "I suppose I know him after a fashion. He is insane, but a simple fellow. I had not seen him in many months and was not expecting him, so he startled me."

"He accosted you more than once?"

"Oh, yes—many times," she said. "Tikendra Jeet ordered him locked up in the afternoons and early evenings. Those are the times I visit the bazaar and he did not want the poor chap frightening me anymore."

"Well," Quinton said, "the poor chap, as you call him, is out now. Did Tikendra Jeet release him, knowing you would be here?"

"Oh, no," Ethel said. "He would never..."

Quinton turned to the wretch and shook the crop. "Be off with you then!"

The hunchback grasped Quinton's intent and crawled, slinking out of reach of the crop.

"Damnedest bloody country!" Quinton kept an eye on the lunatic until he was out of sight behind a shop tent.

Ethel said, "I want to thank...!" She halted and stared, open-mouthed. A stooped figure appeared nearby, and from behind, Ethel thought she recognized...

Is that...? Can it be...?

"Moonia!" Ethel rushed and grabbed the woman's shoulder. The aged figure spun and Ethel gasped.

It is not Moonia!

Ethel faced a shriveled woman of size and appearance like her former servant, but the drawn face had deep wrinkles and pale cataracts dulled shrunken eyes. Ethel released her grasp and, as she drew back, bony fingers shot forth and gripped her arm.

"You seek the dragon!" The woman's voice hissed and dark eyes stared into space. "You want to touch it—to hold it one more time—but the dragon seeks you!"

Ethel twisted, trying to pull free, but the claw-like grip was too tight. "What do you mean?" Her voice trembled.

"Beware!" the woman said. "Prepare to flee—go west! Time is short—the end is near!"

Ethel struggled, pulling back harder. "Please—you are hurting me!"

A voice behind her spoke. "Missus Grimwood?"

As Ethel at last pulled loose, she glanced over her shoulder at Quinton and Boileau. She turned back—the woman vanished.

"Where did she go?" Ethel asked.

"Who?" Quinton replied, squinting, head cocked.

"The old woman…," Ethel said, tears welling. "She was—she hurt my arm!" Ethel held up her arm to show a black and blue bruise.

"Old woman?" Boileau said. "There was no one—you were alone."

"Are you all right?" Quinton asked. His hard face softened, and he took her hand to study the bruise.

He has a genuine concern.

Then a deep, eerie sound erupted from somewhere east of the market. Quinton dropped Ethel's hand and his eyes opened wide.

"Conch shells!" Ethel said.

A chorus of the horns bellowed, like those in the morning parade. Women screamed—customers and shopkeepers alike.

"The Yuvraj!" a woman shrieked. "Prince Tikendra Jeet is coming!" Manipuri shoppers and merchants rushed at once toward the market entrance.

Then, from south of the market, a bugle sounded. "Assembly!" Boileau said, pointing. "Skene is ordering everyone return to the Residency."

Groups of Gurkha soldiers strolling through the bazaar broke for the entrance, shouting, and bedlam ensued. The soldiers dodged screaming Manipuri women, upsetting tables and spilling merchandise.

"Make for the horses!" Quinton shouted, taking Ethel's trembling hand.

Ethel followed in stunned silence and the three weaved through the panicked crowd, exiting the bazaar near the tethered horses. The conch shells bellowed again, and a parade spilled onto the road from the Western Gate. A priest in a white robe led a procession of worshipers blowing shells, ringing bells, and beating gongs and drums.

Young Maiba!

"Turns out—we have a holy day," Quinton said. "Just as the regent warned. Well, I have had my fill of the bazaar. Would you agree, Missus Grimwood?"

Ethel sniffled, blinked back tears, and nodded. The three mounted and rode toward the Residency, passing crowds of native villagers and straggling Gurkhas along the way.

"I hope you are all right, Missus," Quinton said.

"Better, thank you."

"Good! We shall see you at dinner then."

"Oh—you reminded me," Ethel said, smiling. "I had such a special dinner planned for this evening."

"Had?" Boileau said.

"I purchased and fattened a wonderful goat—but sad to say, it was not to be."

"What happened?" Quinton asked.

Ethel explained how she bought and fattened a goat and then told of its poisoning. When she came to the part where the groom tried to save the poor creature, pouring brandy, Yu wine, and beer down its gullet, the men burst out in laughter. Ethel blushed—she had thought the story upsetting, not funny, but soon she laughed, too.

"I am certain whatever we have to eat will be perfect," Quinton said, still chuckling. "You and your husband have done a wonderful job, preparing for our visit. I am certain all will appreciate the band this evening."

"Oh, we worked for weeks," she said. "We have an entire programme planned—a polo match one day, a Naga dance one night, and a nautch on another…"

"Nautch?" Quinton said. "What is a nautch?"

"Oh, you must see one," Ethel said. "Manipur is famous for its nautches—elaborate stories told in music and costumed dance. All the young girls dance in Manipur, and they are all so beautiful."

"You have convinced me!" Quinton laughed. "I hope we can do everything. After the debacle of today—I wonder."

"I wonder, too." Ethel rode in silence. She shuddered, sighed, and then broke into a smile. "I will need a drink soon."

"I will drink to that!" Boileau said.

The three riders arrived to find the bandstand brought from cellar storage and assembled near the house. Servants were setting up chairs and standing on ladders, stringing paper lanterns. Ethel thanked the gentlemen and said she would see them soon at dinner. She then left to inspect the preparations for the party.

At seven o'clock, fresh and changed, Ethel greeted her guests. The dining room filled with British officers and dignitaries, young and old. Frank sat next to Ethel and appeared refreshed.

Fifteen at one time! The Residency never saw so many guests.

To Ethel's mind, the dinner of fish and fowl was ordinary.

A sad substitute for the feast I planned.

The officers found the meal fabulous. Wine flowed, with many toasts complementing the hosts. Ethel hoisted her glass each time, motioning to servants for refills. As the servant filled her glass, she caught Frank looking at her. Frank opened his mouth to make a comment when another spoke.

"Feeling better, I hope," Captain Boileau said.

"Why?" Frank peered at Ethel. "Is something wrong?"

Boileau told the story of the afternoon trip to the bazaar. The captain turned an afternoon that Ethel thought terrifying into a funny story. Ethel found herself the center of attention, one woman surrounded by fourteen laughing men. The joke was on her, but soon she surprised herself by laughing, too. She drained her flask and raised a finger for yet another refill.

"Whatever were you doing?" Frank asked. He had smiled during the story but his tone signaled concern. "Why did you stand in the bazaar alone talking to yourself?"

"Oh, who knows?" Ethel cooed, making a silly face. "Hallucinating, I suppose!"

When laughter burst out, Walter Simpson frowned and stood.

"A toast," the lieutenant said. "William Melville is leaving us early tomorrow morning. I offer a toast to our friend. Safe travels!"

"Hear! Hear!" the group shouted, raising flasks.

Ethel took another gulp before raising hers. "Oh, now, William, William!" she moaned. "Please—do not leave us so soon."

Melville reddened and rose, wincing in pain from his bum leg. He raised his flask to Ethel. "I am so sorry, Missus, but I must get on about the Empire's business."

"Whatever would we do without the wonderful telegraph machine?" Ethel laughed and almost tipped her glass. "All those complicated wires, needles, and codes—who but a wizard could make sense of it all?"

Mumbles of agreement went around the table.

"That calls for a toast," Melville said. "To Misters Cooke and Wheatstone, inventors of the British telegraph!"

Everyone including Ethel drank again. "Please, William," Ethel said, leaning forward and batting her eyelashes. "Do not leave so early—stay the morning. We can see you off that afternoon. Please?"

Melville turned beet-red, downed his drink, banged the glass on the table, and bowed. "As you wish, Missus!"

Laughter and cheers erupted. Ethel clapped, then raised and downed her flask, which sparked more cheering. She stopped laughing, raised a hand, and cocked an ear.

"Listen!"

The men quieted. Music filtered in from outside the house. The band had set up during dinner and had struck up a brass rendition of Strauss's "Blue Danube."

Ethel stood and said, "I love this waltz! I must go have a listen."

The men rose and the dinner party dispersed outside into a clear evening lit by bright moonlight and strands of paper lanterns with burning candles. The glowing shells hung above, strung from tree to tree, creating a magical atmosphere.

In her rush down the verandah steps, Ethel stumbled, caught by a steady hand. She looked up and beheld the beaming face of Lieutenant Lionel Brackenbury.

"Oh, Lionel," Ethel purred, gripping his arm. "You are a gentleman, and so handsome in uniform. Such a good friend—I missed you so. You received my letter, I hope."

Lionel grinned and gave a quick nod.

"I am so glad you came," she said, still holding tight. "We must catch up on old times."

Brackenbury blushed and pointed toward a tree. "How about those two chairs?"

"Luffely!" Ethel said, slurring the word. "And so romantic!"

Ethel and Lionel strolled and took the two seats facing the band just as the waltz ended.

"The Nagas are in exceptional form," Lionel said.

"They are such wonderful musicians, and—oh, look—the bandmaster saw us. Here he comes!"

A little man leapt from the bandstand and rushed to greet Ethel. His uniform was outlandish—a fashion nightmare of mismatched colors and styles. The bandmaster tipped his ancient top hat to Ethel.

The Naga conductor had learned music in Kohima from the bandmaster of the 44th Gurkha Rifles and so he greeted Lionel with bow and said, "My regimental brother!" Then he grinned and added, "Does the dear memsahib have any requests?"

"Hum," Ethel said, tipping her head back in thought. "I have always been partial to your version of 'the William Tell Overture,' but I have a special enthusiasm for your English dance favorites. Perhaps Lionel will ask me to dance." She stuck out her tongue at the lieutenant and laughed.

Lionel turned red as a rhododendron as the bandmaster cracked a wide smile. "It shall be as you wish!" He hurried back, leapt onto the bandstand, and raised his baton.

As the song began, Ethel craned her neck.

"Something wrong?" Lionel asked.

"Excuse me," Ethel said. "I will see about drinks."

As she neared the verandah steps Walter Simpson blocked her path. "You are making a scene," he said in a terse whisper. "You are drunk."

Ethel held up a hand in protest. "Please! Walter! I am not a child! I have had a trying day."

"We all have—and we face another trying day tomorrow. I would hate to carry you to your bed."

"Would you hate that so much?"

"Behave yourself!" he said. "You are hanging on that poor young fellow."

"Why, Walter," she hissed, "Are you jealous?"

"No! You should not lead on the lad."

"He is my friend! The only one in the entire lot of new arrivals."

"Well, everyone is staring at you two. I am advising you as a friend."

"Everyone?" Ethel craned her neck. "Where is Frank?"

"Where else?" Walter said. "Talking to Quinton."

"Well, he had a nap so I suppose now he will be up half the night, busy talking strategy, and intrigue."

Ethel then glared at Walter until he shook his head and stepped aside. Once inside, Ethel encountered the bearer who, to no surprise, expected her arrival. He apologized for the delay and assured her drinks were on the way. Ethel nodded and took a step toward the door, but stopped. She changed direction, went to her study, and pulled a note card from a drawer in her writing desk. She dipped a pen in ink, scribbled a note, folded the card, and walked back to the music. As she passed Walter, she slipped the card into his hand and kept walking. She retook her seat next to Lionel and glanced in Walter's direction.

Good! He is reading my note.

Ethel sat and listened, but in a more subdued fashion—made self-conscious by Walter's comments. She conversed with Lionel, catching up and reliving old times, but her hands stayed in her lap. When a servant brought drinks by, she declined.

"Are you feeling all right?" Brackenbury asked.

"I have had a long day. We all face an early start tomorrow. Perhaps I should retire. Please convey my compliments to the bandmaster and my regrets for turning in so early."

Lionel stood as Ethel departed. She passed by the other guests and said goodnight. The men stood and issued a chorus of protests. Ethel smiled and blushed. She gave Frank a light kiss on the cheek, and then took Quinton's hand, thanking him for his noble concern earlier at the bazaar.

Walter Simpson stood by a nearby tree, arms folded, staring. She smiled, waved, and walked on to the house. As she reached her bedchamber, she had a thought.

For once, I do not miss Moonia.

Ethel undressed and reached for her nightgown. She changed her mind and instead turned down the lamp to a mere glimmer and drew a silken sheet around her slender figure. She waited, sitting on the bench at the foot of her bed. The band droned on, with the thump, thump, thump of the tuba, bass, and drum. One unrecognizable song followed another like a hazy, endless dream. Then the music stopped and the faint hubbub of male voices signaled the evening's end.

Minutes later a knock came. Ethel stood, and the sheet fell open in front. She remained silent as the knob turned. The door creaked open revealing a man's shadowy figure.

"I am over here," she whispered.

Walter Simpson came to her. His warm hands circled her naked waist.

"Are you certain about this?" He kissed her ear as his hands moved higher and the sheet fell away.

"Yes." Her breathing was heavy. "Time is short—the end is near."

Chapter 48. The Hornet Nest

Before dawn, Monday morning, 23 March 1891...

Frank

Frank had another restless night, but nervous energy won out over the dread of the task ahead. He woke before dawn and, being careful not to wake Ethel, slipped out of bed and pulled on his clothes.

Ethel sleeps like a top after her evening of music, laughter, and too much wine.

Ethel stirred anyway, draping an arm over her face, moaning, "Walter?" Her other hand patted the empty spot on the bed. "You best leave. Frank will come soon."

"It is me—Frank," he whispered. "It is dawn. Walter left before I came to bed."

Ethel yanked away her arm and raised her head, staring wild-eyed as if Frank's dark figure was a ghost. The disheveled head of hair plopped back onto the pillow as she shut her eyes and sighed, muttering, "Oh, bloody hell!"

"Take your time," Frank said. "The durbar is at eight—I will handle the preparations. You need do nothing. I will send in tea and breakfast later."

Frank grabbed a bite, reviewed the ceremonial preparations, and ordered a breakfast plate sent to Ethel. Outside, Gurkha sentries took positions around the perimeter. Inside, officers locked doors and placed guards at each exit. Frank joined Quinton on the verandah to watch and wait.

"I try to stay hopeful," Quinton said, "but expect bad news."

The hazy sky turned grayer, foreboding lackluster sunshine—a welcome change after the intense rays of the earlier day.

At eight o'clock, a solitary turbaned pony rider ambled down the lane. Frank and Quinton exchanged frowns.

"From his slow pace," Frank said, "I wager he is not delivering good news."

Rassik, the head chuprassy, read and translated for Frank and Quinton. "Note says, Yuvraj still ill, unable to attend, so maharaja sees no reason to come."

"Nice touch," Quinton said. "Calls himself maharaja, knowing full well Britain still regards him as a regent."

"Sad," Frank said, "but not a surprise."

Quinton and Frank discussed their next move. Unable to think of an alternative, they decided upon one last try to entice the princes to a meeting. Frank dictated a response to the messenger, requesting the regent reschedule the durbar for noon.

A dour mood settled over the Residency and the four hours dragged. Telegraph superintendent William Melville prepared to leave for Sengmai as servants gathered his baggage and saddled his horse.

"Stay another day, why don't you?" Frank said. "Those clouds look ugly."

"I already delayed my original plan for a morning departure. I will leave no later than one o'clock."

"But—a storm could break," Ethel said.

"All the more reason to start—I face a twelve-mile ride."

"You cannot be blind to all that is happening!"

"Missus Grimwood," Melville said, smiling, "your concern is much appreciated. Do not fear for me—I am not worth capturing. I shall get along fine."

At twelve o'clock, the messenger returned bearing a message.

"Like the other?" Quinton asked.

"Just so," Frank said. "No Yuvraj—no durbar!" He asked the messenger and Rassik to wait for a reply as he took Quinton aside on the verandah.

"Now what?"

Quinton shrugged. "I am out of ideas, and patience is thin. I will author an ultimatum."

"Ultimatum? You cannot send a message like that via a messenger!"

"Do you propose to deliver it in person?"

"If I must," Frank said.

They went back inside to Frank's study where Quinton sat at Frank's writing desk and secured paper, pen, and ink.

"Sir…," Frank said.

"James," Quinton corrected.

"James—perhaps we should think again. Is it worth all this drama? It seems such a minor matter in the scheme of things. Why not admit defeat, pack up, and return to Kohima? What difference will it make in five years or ten?"

Quinton sighed and reached into his coat's breast pocket. "Yesterday," he said, "I told you of the coded telegram I received. I alluded to its contents, but I did not tell the whole story. Here." He handed Frank the folded paper.

Frank opened the message, read, and turned pale. "So!" he spat. "They are dead serious. Either Tikendra Jeet leaves Manipur and goes into exile or—they sack us—cashiered, our careers destroyed. Is that it?"

"That is how I read it," Quinton said. "I am sorry. The allegation of moral impropriety was a low blow. My career has few years left but my wife and I will need the pension to live. You are younger and, if you can get past this obstacle, could yet have a bright future. We must do what needs doing." He returned to writing his ultimatum.

"I will tell the messenger," Frank said. "Shall I say the regent should expect me at—four o'clock?"

"Fine," Quinton replied, still writing.

At one o'clock, after a bite of lunch, Melville left for Sengmai. Ethel waved goodbye from the verandah as Frank and Walter watched.

"I worry for him," Ethel said.

"I worry even more for us," Walter replied.

Ethel shot an ugly look at the lieutenant and left the verandah.

"I stepped in it," Walter said.

Frank shrugged. "Everyone is on edge now."

"So, I hear you are going to the palace."

"Right—at four o'clock. I will meet with the regent, explain in person the government's orders, and demand the peaceful surrender of Tikendra Jeet."

"You are taking an escort I assume."

"No—I am going alone."

"No you are not," Walter said, standing tall and straightening his shoulders. "I at least am going with you, and I will not hear otherwise."

"Yesterday I asked a favor—to care for Ethel should anything happen…"

"Look, Frank," Walter interrupted. "I have feelings for Ethel—I cannot hide the fact. She deserves the best and you are the best man I know. You are my friend and I want to be part of your lives—both of you. I cannot stand by while you sacrifice yourself. If my going along ensures your safe return then I am going, for both you and Ethel. There is no more to say."

Frank stood and stared at his friend—wide-eyed, open-mouthed, and red-faced. "Right!" Frank choked back emotion, able only to shake Walter's hand.

Two hours later Frank and Lieutenant Simpson prepared to leave.

"Three are going?" Walter pointed to three saddled horses.

"Yes," Frank said. "Last minute change. Rassik Lal Kundu is coming—I may need more writing translated."

The head chuprassy appeared and mounted the third horse. The translator looked shaky, thinner, and gaunter than usual, almost swimming in his ornate red coat.

Quinton came down the steps and presented papers to Frank. "The translated orders from yesterday and..." Quinton looked around and then whispered, "My new letter—you know."

Frank scanned the ultimatum letter and nodded to Quinton. He waved goodbye to Ethel and three riders set out for Kangla.

Outside the gate, Walter said, "What does Quinton's letter say?"

Frank rubbed his neck and said to his translator, "Rassik, please ride on ahead!" He waited until the chuprassy was out of earshot, and then said, "Quinton demands the regent surrender Tikendra Jeet forthwith or the Yuvraj will suffer forceful arrest."

Walter gulped. "He cannot mean that. He threatens an act of war."

"I cannot in good conscience deliver such a message!"

"What *will* you do?"

"I am not sure. Negotiate, or—I do not know. I must think of something."

They continued in silence on the deserted road and neared the Western Gate. The sky darkened further as ominous clouds gathered.

Walter broke the silence. "Frank, I must confess something..."

"If about last night, never mind."

Walter turned red. "Ethel told you?"

"Not in so many words, but—damn, Walter, you two are so indiscrete, you make poor fodder for a decent scandal."

"The others? They—they know?"

Frank laughed. "I cannot say on that score. The way Ethel downed Yu I suspect their imaginations ran wild, fantasizing every manner of shenanigan. If not by you, then poor Brackenbury."

"Blast—I am such a cad."

"Nonsense," Frank said. "If you want to hear a confession, here is one—I thought she wanted it and so I wanted it for her. What does that make me?"

They spurred their horses, caught up with the chuprassy, and together entered the Western Gate. The atmosphere changed—Kangla crackled with tension. A threatening crowd of armed sepoys approached and surrounded their mounts.

"We are going to palace," Frank said. "You know this already—let us pass."

The soldiers backed away, and a path opened as they rode forward under the ever-darkening sky. Manipuri citizens kept their distance, glaring in silence.

Walter craned his neck, studied the ramparts, and said, "Rifle barrels sprouting like weeds!"

The walls and roofs of buildings crawled with riflemen, most only watching, but a few made as if they were training their weapons.

"Yesterday, Ethel said we kicked a hornet nest. Today, we strolled into the nest."

They passed the Kangla-sha and arrived at the Uttra (coronation hall). The three dismounted and, surrounded by escorts, climbed the palace steps. Guards led them down a torch lit hall to the council chamber where the regent sat on his dead father's throne. The Tongol General, princes Angao and Zillah, and six ministers stood to his side.

After greetings, Frank said, "We saw many irregulars brandishing firearms."

"Yes," the regent said. "You may recall your wife's entertainment schedule calls for Chief Commissioner Quinton to review Manipur's troops—following the durbar. Our standing army is small, but many loyal citizens answered the Lallup call for that ceremony."

"We came without weapons and pose no threat, yet we felt threatened and unwelcome inside your gates."

"Please accept my apologies," the regent said, bowing his head.

Frank looked around the room. "Your other brother—Prince Tikendra Jeet—is not here. Is he better?"

"I am uncertain," the regent said.

"It could help matters if we confirmed first hand his poor condition. Then we could report our findings to the chief commissioner."

Kula Chandra nodded to the Tongol General who left to seek the prince somewhere within the palace.

Walter whispered, "I thought he lived in his own compound. Outside the inner fort."

Frank nodded and shrugged.

Minutes later, the general returned followed by four sepoys carrying a litter bearing a robed figure covered by a blanket. The bearers set the cot on the floor. As Frank took a step toward the litter, Rassik Lal Kundu, the translator, grabbed his arm.

"Sahib," Rassik said, "let me examine the Yuvraj. His illness could be catching. Not good for you."

Frank nodded, and the chuprassy knelt by the cot and lifted the blanket.

Tikendra Jeet!

The crown prince's face was sallow. He shivered, clenching the blanket, despite the warm atmosphere in the room. Rassik laid his hand across the prince's forehead. Rassik drew back. "Hot!" he said. "The prince's head is like fire."

Rassik returned and told Frank and Walter his findings—the prince was feverish and appeared to have not bathed in days.

Frank called to Tikendra Jeet. "My poor friend! I pray you do not have the Russian flu. It is wreaking havoc in Europe. It can be deadly."

The prince answered in a weak voice. "Sometimes I felt death could be a blessing."

"I am very sorry for your condition," Frank said. "Thank you for permitting confirmation of your illness. Perhaps it would be best if you returned to your chamber and rested."

"Take me from this place," the prince commanded his bearers. "I should be in my home and not risk infecting the healthy. Take me to my compound now." With that, Tikendra Jeet fainted. The four sepoys lifted the litter, carried the sick man toward the palace entrance, and disappeared.

Frank turned back to the regent. "May Lieutenant Simpson and I speak with you in private?"

Kula Chandra nodded. The room emptied of everyone including Rassik, and the door closed, leaving Frank and Walter alone with the regent.

"I have always been honest with you and your family," Frank said. "I hope it will always be thus between us."

Kula Chandra nodded. "You are honest," he said. "You have been trustworthy and a good friend to Manipur."

"I now confide something I should not say—I pray I can trust you to keep the information secret and not allow it outside this room."

I cannot give him the ultimatum—I must try a conciliatory approach first.

Frank explained that his closeness, honesty, and trustworthiness backfired. Sura Chandra, the regent's older brother and former maharaja, blamed Frank for his abdication. The former monarch protested to the highest levels of the Raj. Quinton's mission was, in part, to mete justice upon Frank. As Kula Chandra listened, his face grew pale and body limp.

"Your news is very unsettling."

"Sura Chandra demanded reinstatement as the maharaja," Frank continued, "but the Sirkar rejected his demands. Britain wants to recognize you as the new maharaja."

Kula Chandra's eyebrows raised and his eyes lit. He leaned forward, smiling, and said, "Now tell me the condition—the price I must pay."

Frank nodded. "The chief commissioner and I will suffer career setbacks because of my familiarity—but that is our concern, not yours. The price, you may have guessed, concerns your brother, the Yuvraj. Your coronation depends upon the surrender of Prince Tikendra Jeet."

Frank handed the regent the translated government orders. Kula Chandra's hand trembled as he read the pages in silence. He looked up, his face darkened.

Frank stayed steady but firm. "I am asking as a friend of Manipur—end this drama in peace. Persuade your brother to surrender. The terms of exile are generous—he will want for nothing and will receive respect befitting his rank. In time, depending on good behavior, he may appeal, and have the banishment ended. If you wish, he may keep the title of Yuvraj and even succeed you in event you were to suffer an unfortunate death."

At those last words, the regent trembled. "Unfortunate—death…"

No—damn it! I said too much!

Chapter 49. The Storm of Desperation

Continued...

Frank

Kula Chandra clapped his hands, the doors opened, and guards and minsters reentered.

"I cannot decide a matter of such gravity on the spot," the regent announced. "Please return to your home now and I will send my final answer by seven o'clock this evening."

Frank and Walter gathered Rassik and trudged in silence out of the palace and to their horses. They mounted in threatening darkness and headed back the way they had come.

Walter Simpson broke the silence. "Rassik, are you are positive the Yuvraj was ill?"

"Oh, yes, sahib," the chuprassy said. "A sick, bedridden man."

"At least now we know," Walter said. "That is something."

Frank nodded. "Yes, poor chap. I felt sorry for him. Thank you, Rassik. Please ride ahead." With the translator out of earshot, Frank said, "Well, I mucked things up even worse."

"How so?"

"Kula Chandra now fears Tikendra Jeet more than he fears the British Empire. That is the last thing I wanted. I uncovered distrust and jealousy between the brothers. The future maharaja now fears his brother Tikendra Jeet would return from exile, exact revenge for his surrender, and seize the throne."

"You sensed all that?"

Frank nodded. "I could smell the fear on him."

"What about the rest you told him? Was all that true—about you and Quinton—your careers?"

"Every word." Frank clenched his teeth. "If I were Quinton, I would say, damn the career and do the proper thing. I would tear up the orders and march straight out of here."

Walter opened his mouth to reply then stopped and rode a silent minute before stirring. "I had a thought. Neither of us examined Tikendra Jeet."

"No," Frank said, "but Rassik did."

"Right. That is what I mean. Was Rassik not on our list of potential spies?"

Frank considered. "Yes, he was—before Moonia showed herself."

"Ah," Walter said. "Can we be certain she was the only one?"

Frank had no answer. They galloped ahead, caught up to Rassik, and the three reached the house at six o'clock. Frank and Walter handed over the reins to the stable hands and stepped up to meet a concerned Ethel waiting on the verandah.

"I am relieved to see you both return," she said, "but from your faces I fear the news is not good."

"It is not yet hopeless," Frank replied. "Not very promising, but we shall know for certain within an hour."

"This early darkness has brought an evil atmosphere," Ethel said. "The bazaar closed early—that is unusual, despite the bad weather approaching. The main roads have emptied. Worse news—our servants are abandoning us, slipping off one-by-one, like rats leaving a sinking ship. There is a palpable fear growing."

Frank left Ethel with Walter and stepped inside to deliver the news to Quinton, omitting mention of his failure to deliver the ultimatum.

"It is time," Quinton declared. "I will give matters over to the military."

"I would counsel against such action—even at the ruin of my career and reputation. Military action risks unnecessary deaths, including our own. We do what we must, but I have concern for my wife's safety."

"Understood." Quinton's face darkened. "I will take your recommendation under advisement. Leave me now—I need time to consider next steps."

Frank left his study and found Walter waiting with Skene and Boileau. "You had best hurry," Walter said. "You need to hear this for yourself."

They proceeded to the durbar hall. Gurkhas stood beside two native men—one a Naga and the other a Kuki.

"These men," Boileau explained, "arrived at the gate minutes ago asking to meet with the sahib—you, that is. They claim to have vital secrets worthy of a great reward."

"Speak, then!" Frank commanded.

The men claimed an armed force had gathered and would soon launch an attack against the Residency. It would swarm the gate, scale the walls, and overrun the house.

"When?"

"Tomorrow evening," the Kuki said. "At midnight."

"Who will commit this crime? Manipuri regulars, irregulars, or both?"

"Not Meiteis," the Naga answered. "Only Naga and Kuki warriors will attack. Meitei soldiers will not attack."

"Why not the Meitei?"

"Meitei rule Manipur," the Kuki replied. "British sahibs see the Kuki and Naga as wild tribes, out of control. No blame given to the Meitei."

Frank sneered. "Why tell me this? Are you mercenaries? Do you have no loyalty to your rulers?"

"Nagas and Kukis do not want war," the Kuki said. "Sahibs will kill many Nagas and Kukis. Meitei force dirty work on Naga and Kuki people. Meitei will not suffer, will make peace with British, and sahibs will punish Nagas and Kukis."

"Badmash (cad)!" Frank shouted. "You are filthy liars! These lies are not worth a single rupee! Be off with you before I have you beaten!"

The Naga fell to his knees. "No, sahib!" he pleaded. "We speak truth! There is more to tell!"

"Be quick about it then!"

"Orders specify—no unnecessary killing, except one Britisher only."

"Who?" Frank said, and then he straightened and shuddered.

Quinton! They intend to kill Quinton!

The native men said nothing.

"Who?" Frank repeated, raising his hand to slap the kneeling man.

"You, sahib!" The Naga cried.

"Yes, sahib, you!" the Kuki said, holding up his hands and nodding. "They will assassinate you!"

Frank gasped and stepped back, eyes open wide.

"More to tell!" the Kuki cried. "They are to capture the memsahib alive and take her to Kangla."

"Why?" Frank cried. "As a hostage?

"No, sahib," the Kuki answered, "to become a wife to Tikendra Jeet! Prince says the memsahib wishes this—to be queen of Manipur—but sahib must die first. British will not make war on Manipur with the memsahib as queen. Sahib is unfaithful to the memsahib. British blame sahib for all Manipuri problems and will not shed tears."

Frank swung his fist, striking the Kuki full in the face. The man fell flat and Frank moved toward the Naga.

"Stop, Frank!" Walter grabbed Frank's waist and yanked him back.

"I will kill both lying, bloody sons of bitches," Frank shouted, temper lost, out of control, face blood red.

Walter turned to Skene and Boileau. "Sirs, please lock up these two men in the guard house. Then, with all due respect, please leave me alone with Political Agent Grimwood."

The Gurkhas dragged the Naga and Kuki from the room. Skene led and Boileau followed, closing the door.

"Release me!" Frank cried. "I have to kill the dirty bastards!"

Walter gripped tighter. "Frank, listen—their words have truth."

Frank stopped struggling and relaxed. "What truth? How can there be any truth?"

"Sit first." Frank sat as Walter poured. "Here—drink this brandy."

Frank sipped and took a deep breath. "Now tell me," he murmured. "What truth is there?"

Walter told Frank the details Ethel shared—her dinner with the Yuvraj; their conversation atop the tower of Vrindavan Chandra; Tikendra Jeet's marriage proposal; and how Ethel delayed her answer until after Quinton's visit.

Frank buried his face in his hands. "Why did she not tell me?"

"She could not bear to," Walter said. "She only told me as a confession to a friend, to purge her soul of guilt."

"Why did she not reject the lout on the spot?"

"She thought she was helping us, Frank. I was trying to get access to the arsenal—remember?"

Frank wiped his eyes on his coat sleeve and stood. Seven o'clock struck and, right on schedule, the messenger from Manipur returned. Frank and Walter went outside to receive the message. Frank glanced at the evil sky and suggested the rider try to outrun the storm and not wait for a reply.

"What would be the point?" Frank asked. "We know what it says."

No sooner had the rider cleared the gate than lightning flashed and the black sky opened with a tremendous boom. Frank and Walter stood sheltered under the verandah roof as Frank opened the note.

"What does it say?"

"I cannot read it—looks like Bengali. I need Rassik."

Frank called for the chuprassy and Rassik translated.

> **Maharaja welcomes British recognition but Top Guard has ruled Yuvraj innocent, undeserving arrest and exile, and cannot surrender Yuvraj Bir Tikendrajit.**

"That is the end then," Walter said.

Frank sighed in resignation, stared at the downpour a full minute, and then turned back to Walter. "How could those natives have known the Raj blamed me for this mess?"

"You told the regent," Walter said. "I suppose he let it out."

"Not enough time—we rode straight here. Skene and Boileau had the natives in custody. The plans must be many hours old."

"Then someone else knew."

Frank frowned. "How could anyone else have known? I myself learned—what is today? I have lost track."

"Monday," Walter said.

"Right—Monday—Quinton told me on Saturday, in Sengmai. I rode straight home and told Ethel—and only Ethel—that evening. She said nothing to you?"

"Not a word."

"I was taking precautions," Frank said, "even listening to the walls with Calvert's Stethoscope, but Ethel told me Moonia fled the compound. We concluded she was the spy…"

Frank stopped and stared at Walter wide-eyed. "You were right," Frank said. "A spy is still in our midst."

Lightning flashed again, revealing Skene and Boileau behind, returned from jailing the Naga and Kuki. Frank asked Walter and Boileau to wait and invited Skene to go with him.

"We will see Quinton," Frank said, "but first, I must find Ethel." Frank found her at her writing desk in her study next door to his. "I need your help," he said. "That map of Kangla you showed me—the one you drew after your dinner with the Yuvraj—bring it."

Ethel raised her eyebrows and blushed as she fumbled with papers on her desk. She held up the map and followed the men next door to Frank's study. Frank knocked.

"Enter," Quinton said.

"Sir, we have received final word," Frank began. He cleared his throat and continued. "The regent will not surrender the Yuvraj."

"I see," Quinton replied, staring down at the desk.

"I have reconsidered," Frank said. "After receiving new information, I have had a change of heart."

Frank told Quinton of the Naga and Kuki and the threat to overrun the Residency, but said nothing of the threat to capture Ethel or his own assassination. Skene, who attended the natives' interrogation, stared ahead and made no additions or corrections.

"I now believe we have no choice," Frank said. "We must arrest the Yuvraj—at whatever cost—as soon as we can, before they attack us."

Frank looked at Ethel. She was wide-eyed and pale but made no comment. He pointed to Ethel's map and said, "Tell him."

Ethel cocked her head and frowned.

"Tell him; tell all of us! Show us where we can find Tikendra Jeet."

Ethel cleared her throat, managed a weak smile, and laid her detailed ink-on-parchment map on the desk. "Gentlemen," she said, "if I may direct your attention." She pointed. "There—where I wrote Yuvraj—Tikendra Jeet lives there. It is a walled compound between the inner and outer walls. The gate to his home is here, but you must first get past the Northern Gate—here. The weakest point—is here." Her index finger circled the northwest corner of the outer wall. "Cannon fire breached the wall here and is still in disrepair—almost wide open. The ditch on the north side here—dry, and the opening offers the easiest access. I saw all from the tower—here." She pointed at the square marking the temple. "The breech is the best attack point."

Quinton studied the drawing, looked at Ethel with wide eyes and parted lips, and then returned his eyes to map. "How can we be certain Tikendra Jeet will be there?"

"We cannot know with total certainty," Frank said. "But Simpson and I heard him direct his bearers. They bore him in that direction. It is his home, and the best, most fortuitous place for us if he is there."

Quinton looked to Skene.

"Right!" Skene answered. "My officers and I will draw up the attack plan. We will move in and, if all goes well, arrest the wretch before dawn."

Chapter 50. The Last Moonlight Stroll

Later that evening...

Ethel

The savage storm ended and the coal-black sky cleared. An evening sun emerged and its orange warmth challenged the chill air. The roads remained desolate, the citizenry out of sight. Most of the servants sensed the danger and fled, melting away in dribbles, vanishing into the local population. The Residency grew quiet—almost eerie. A gloomy cloud descended upon Ethel as she realized the impact of having no servants.

Tomorrow the military will take over and do its job. Death and destruction is a serious possibility. Here I am without servants. How will I manage?

Ethel grew up eldest daughter of a British judge—not upper crust, but well to do. She never lost her way about the kitchen, but she became accustomed to having servants and to servants serving.

At least the bearer, the khidmutgar, and a few others are standing firm—and to my surprise, so is the head chuprassy.

After Rassik translated the arrest orders, Frank ordered the chuprassies put under guard. Once the secret of the impending arrest was out of the bag, Frank released the poor chaps. The pompous, red-coated messengers, translators, and office clerks all fled—save the head chuprassy, Rassik Lal Kundu, who had the greatest justification to flee. Ethel shuddered, thinking of the horrible death of Rassik's wife on Sunday.

Imagine waking to find one's spouse dead, throat cut.

An unsolved mystery connected Moonia, Ethel's former servant, with Rassik's wife.

That vicious fight between Moonia and Rassik's wife!

Ethel spoke to Rassik. She showed compassion, trying to comfort him, but asked questions, hoping to learn details of his wife's death. Rassik knew little and said even less.

"Rassik knows nothing!" he said, staring at the ground.

"Why do you stay, while other chuprassies run?"

"Rassik has nowhere to go." He brightened. "I can help sahib with the telegraph!"

Ethel summoned her husband.

"Have you any experience?" Frank asked.

"Oh, yes, sahib! Rassik was once a babu—much skill with telegraph devices."

"Jolly good, then!" Frank said, patting Rassik's shoulder. "As the only remaining babu, the treasury is yours. Chief Commissioner Quinton will appreciate your help tomorrow."

As the redcoat hurried to his new station, Ethel said, "I wish I better understood the animosity between Moonia and Rassik's wife. A wicked hatred existed between those two. I hope Moonia had nothing to do with the murder. We may never learn the answer."

"Moonia called Rassik a spy—remember?"

"Yes, but, do you think he is?"

"I hope not," Frank said. "We need his help. When this ends, we should track Moonia down and make her talk."

"Do you think we shall?"

"I wonder."

"It occurs to me," Ethel said, "Moonia also clashed with the bearer—each detested the other. He was the first to call Moonia a witch."

"Did you ever ask him why?"

"I did," Ethel said. "He only said—something wrong with Moonia."

Frank looked at the red-coated man trotting up the lane toward the stone building. "Perhaps I should follow Rassik and see how he handles himself."

"Meanwhile, I will see about dinner."

Ethel went to the kitchen. With staff gone, Ethel took command. She recruited the bearer and the khidmutgar and together concocted a dinner. Soon fowl simmered in the pan and two tall pots of soup boiled.

Misters Quinton, Cossins, Gurdon, and Woods sat at the dining room table, engaged in a competitive game of whist. When the aroma wafted from the kitchen, Quinton called, "Something smells delicious! You are working miracles in there, Missus!"

Ethel poked her head, smiling in appreciation, but scolded the men, "After dinner, maybe one of you will help. When you finish that hand, please clear the table."

"Set table for fifteen again, memsahib?" the khidmutgar asked.

"Fourteen only—Mister Melville left for Sengmai this afternoon."

Splendid chap—safe in Sengmai, I hope!

The bearer announced dinner and the other officers and gentlemen trickled into the dining room. Ethel found the dinner more somber than expected.

I can recall happier wakes.

The younger officers spoke of the day ahead.

"I hope the Manipuris put up a good fight," Lieutenant Chatterton said.

Skene frowned but made no comment.

Perhaps he remembers his own foolish, youthful passion.

Ethel ate in silence, growing weary of being one woman among thirteen Englishmen. She imbibed no wine or brandy after her earlier excesses. When dinner at last ended, Ethel, the bearer, and the khidmutgar tidied up, with welcome voluntary help from lieutenants Gurdon and Woods.

"As a reminder to all," Colonel Skene said, "we must rise early. I suggest calling it a night."

Howls erupted along with calls for Lionel Brackenbury to fetch his banjo. The young officer soon took a seat in the parlor, strumming and singing an assortment of comical songs.

Ever bashful and quiet, yet eager to be the center of attention.

Ethel sat by Frank and listened, smiling, hands folded in her lap.

I should recognize these songs but cannot recall having heard a single one.

Walter Simpson joined Lionel and belted out the funniest lines of the choruses.

"Frank is too tight to requisition a piano," Walter joked between songs. "He spent all his money on photographic equipment."

Frank nodded, smiling and clapping. Ethel chuckled, but her mind drifted to happier days.

I miss Shillong—Walter pounding the keys—I should have stayed.

Her smile faded as the weight of the coming events hit home.

Frank leaned and whispered, "Let us slip out and walk in the moonlight."

Ethel lit up at the offer. They sneaked out of the room while the younger officers belted bawdy lines from a chorus. Outside, the cooler air was fragrant, scented by garden flowers and, from near the lake, hints of apricot and plum trees in bloom. As they turned up the carriage drive, Ethel spoke of the beauty of her home and the many good times in Manipur.

"Will you miss it?" Frank asked.

"Perhaps, but then I remember—oh, to see England again."

She spoke of places; friends and family back home; and how long it had been since she spent time with her loved ones.

"Except for Alan," Frank said, chuckling. "Your brother—if one can call him that."

Ethel smiled, but remained serious. "When *will* we see England? I want to go home."

"Soon, I hope." Frank frowned. "I blame myself for allowing you to stay when you could have been steaming homeward by now."

"Do not blame yourself. I wanted to stay—to be with you—and Walter."

They kept further thoughts to themselves as they strolled up the lane. As they neared the wall, a call came from a sentry. A Manipuri entourage was at the gate. Frank approached the bars and spoke to the man in charge.

"Ethel, dear!" Frank turned and called. "Is there a nautch this evening?"

"Oh, goodness!" Ethel said with hands to face.

A company of young dancers and musicians were at the gate—with a crowd of parents and relatives—arriving to dance and play for Quinton and his men.

"Oh, look at all the pretty girls!" Ethel said. "I had forgotten, what with the terrible rain and all, and now—I fear now is too late to start the dance. Everyone will turn in for the evening soon."

The man pleaded, but Ethel laughed and joked that they already had entertainment underway. She promised the Manipuri his pay, but he argued money was not the issue and even offered the girls to dance free. After further back and forth, Frank spoke.

"Good night," he said. "Sorry we could not accommodate. Thank you for coming. Have a safe journey home."

Frank and Ethel turned away and strolled back toward the house.

"I scheduled the nautch weeks ago, when we were so optimistic it would be a wonderful time. I cannot imagine holding a dance now—so late and with matters as they stand."

"Do not worry about it," Frank said.

"I feel horrible sending them away. They seemed so eager to please. You must pay them regardless!"

"You know I will pay them, but I do not feel sorry. That chap at the gate had a soldier's air—an officer even. I sensed he wanted in to spy on us."

Ethel laughed. "That would be silly! What could they find different from yesterday? A few guards redeployed at the wall. You always suspect everyone!"

Ethel and Frank reentered the house and found Brackenbury and Simpson still at it and taking requests for more. Frank suggested to Ethel that they sit a few minutes longer and Ethel agreed. She tried to enjoy herself. The khidmutgar offered flasks of Yu, but she declined. Lionel finished his song. After applauding, Ethel rose to excuse herself and Frank did the same. In their bedchamber, Frank turned down the lamp, and they crawled into bed.

"Everything will turn out fine tomorrow," Frank murmured. "You will see."

"I know, dear—I have confidence in you." She gave Frank a light kiss, and they hugged. Frank was soon snoring, wearing a warm smile.

At least he seems happy in his dream.

"Good night, Frank," she whispered. "I love you so."

Chapter 51. The Ras Lila Nautch

Earlier that evening...

Kajao

Lord Indra, king of the Devas, came down from Mount Meru, riding Airavata, his white elephant. He tore the sky apart with Vajra, his magnificent thunderbolt. Vayu, lord of the winds, howled his displeasure, and the broken heavens poured forth a dark torrent of desolation and despair. Then Surya the sun god came, driving a chariot pulled by seven mares. The rain stopped, the clouds parted, and the evening sun shone once more. Vayu blew a final blast and a bitter chill descended upon the bosom of the Land of Jewels. In his watery abode, the sleeping god Pakhangba opened one eye and smiled.

At eight o'clock, a knock came at the portal of the mud cottage. Kajao cracked the door and spied a short turbaned man. He opened wider, leaned out, and looked around for others, but the man was alone.

"The rain stopped I see," Kajao said, looking at the sky, "but the air has a chill. What brings you, Niranjan Subadar?"

"May I come in, Jamadar?" the shorter man asked. "Or must I stand in this mud puddle?"

"You may enter," Kajao said. "Are you not my commanding officer?"

Kajao invited the subadar with a nod and the man stepped through the doorway.

The subadar dispensed with small talk. "I understand that your daughters are to dance for the sahibs tonight in the Ras Lila nautch."

"Yes, they *were*," Kajao replied, "all three of them—but I assumed the sahibs cancelled the nautch because of the storm, and because..."

He glanced behind to see if anyone else listened, finishing in a terse whisper, "You know why."

"Collect your daughters and their costumes," the subadar said. "Take your wife—the more the better. Round up the musicians and the other girls of the nautch and their families and lead the entire group to the sahibs' compound. Tell the musicians and girls to prepare to play and dance."

"But—the storm—late now." Kajao fumbled for the right words. "It is cold and will be too dark soon."

"No matter—the Tongol General sent me—orders from the Yuvraj himself."

"But my girls have another—a pre-dawn moonlight performance early tomorrow at the Rasmandala. The Dol Jatra festival is upon us—the full-moon day of March has come. They are young girls—just teenagers—they need rest."

The subadar answered with a smug smile. "Practice makes perfect. Consider it a dress rehearsal."

Kajao stared at his superior.

I dislike him—he is not Manipuri.

Niranjan Subadar was half Gurkha, half Hindustani. He had been in the Indian Infantry until he met a beautiful Manipuri woman. Niranjan fell in love and deserted, fleeing to Manipur to escape punishment. To the surprise and displeasure of many, Niranjan shot up in the ranks, becoming the feared right hand of the Tongol General.

Kajao sighed, resigned to his task. "What do I tell the sahibs?"

"Go to the gate—ask permission to dance, as they requested. Once inside—watch, listen, and reconnoiter. Learn as much as you can of their defenses—prepare to report anything useful for when—you know."

This is not a good idea. I must push back.

"What if they tell us go away?"

"Then ask to reschedule to tomorrow morning—as early as they will agree, say, after the sun has risen. Dance later at the Rasmandala. I am sure the cast can manage two performances in one morning."

Kajao did not argue further and did as commanded. Within the hour, the performers gathered, and he led the crowd of musicians, pretty girls, and proud parents across the road to the British compound. The young girls chattered with excitement. They gripped their costumes high in their arms as they took careful steps, avoiding mud puddles left by the hard rain. The musicians followed, quiet but for the jingling and jangling of their instruments. Kajao strode to the gate, rattled the bars with a stick, and called for the guard.

A Gurkha sentry stepped up and spoke a terse command. "State your business. It is late!"

"We came for the nautch," Kajao said. "The memsahib scheduled it for tonight. May I speak to the sahibs?"

The Gurkha turned to another, and they chattered in high-pitched voices.

Now they will say go away.

Kajao's eyes widened as two figures appeared in the moonlight. They drew closer on the gravel lane, walking hand-in-hand.

A British man and woman!

They came closer still. The British sahib wore a dark gray suit.

I recognize him! Grimwood—the one the Nagas and Kukis will assassinate.

"You are in luck," the Gurkha said. "By coincidence, the sahib and memsahib are close by—out for a moonlight stroll. Wait here."

Grimwood approached the gate and stood before Kajao, separated by the wide iron bars.

I could save everyone time and trouble—stab him now, right through the bars!

Kajao could not kill the sahib—his wife would lose a husband and his daughters would lose a father.

My wife and daughters are everything.

Grimwood spoke in Manipuri. "So—what is all this?" He looked past Kajao at the eager faces of the musicians, young girls and their parents.

The sahib seems pleasant.

Kajao bowed to the British gentleman. "Sahib, we are here for the nautch—to play and dance for the sahibs! The memsahib scheduled a nautch for tonight. It is the most fine of all nautches, sahib—the Ras Lila—the most famous nautch of Manipur."

"Ethel, dear!" the sahib said. "Is there a nautch this evening?"

"Oh, goodness!" The woman's hands covered her face.

A chill traveled Kajao's spine as the memsahib came to the bars.

She is the one—soon the Yuvraj's new wife. So beautiful.

"Oh, look at all the pretty girls!" the memsahib cooed. The dancers giggled and blushed. "I had forgotten, what with the terrible rain and all, and now, I fear now is too late to start the dance. Everyone will turn in for the evening soon."

"But—memsahib…," Kajao pleaded. "Girls are excellent dancers—can make a fine entertainment for British guests."

The British woman laughed. "We have entertainment. An officer is trying his best at least. He is inside playing his banjo and singing silly songs."

"Banjo—memsahib?"

She laughed. "Oh, never mind! So sorry—now is just too late. I will see to your pay—all we promised."

"Pay not the issue, memsahib!" Kajao insisted. "Girls will dance for no rupees—girls dance for pride and pleasure of performing—to make memsahib and sahibs happy!"

The memsahib's face grew sad. "I am so sorry, but it now is too late. Perhaps another time."

"When, memsahib? When another time? Tomorrow, memsahib?"

"Well—maybe..." The woman the sahib called Ethel fumbled for words. "So much to do tomorrow—we have a busy day planned—I am so sorry."

"Good night," the sahib said. "Sorry we could not accommodate. Thank you for coming. Have a safe journey home."

They turned away and strolled back down the lane toward the house.

Kajao led the dejected dance troop back to the bustees and villages huddled along the south wall of Kangla. The musicians grumbled, girls cried, and angry parents chittered.

"I am sorry I had to drag you all there!" Kajao apologized with heartfelt sincerity. "Orders were orders. See you all again before dawn at Rasmandala for the moonlight performance."

Niranjan will castigate me for failing, but I do not care.

Kajao's girls needed to get home and into their beds.

The scouting report was unnecessary.

Once home, the girls went to bed and soon slept. Kajao gazed with pride and hugged his wife, who laid her head against his shoulder and wept.

I love my three girls so much. They are my life, not that half-cast Gurkha!

The night passed and the next day, in the cold pre-dawn, the troop of musicians, dancers, and parents reassembled and trudged once more through the darkness. They entered the Southern Gate and soon reached the Temple of Shri Govindajee where bright moonlight gleamed off the golden domes. Nearby, southwest of the temple, lay the Rasmandala. The secluded copse resembled the sacred moonlit forest grove where the young Lord

Krishna played his flute and danced a Night of Brahma with the Gopis, the milkmaids of Vrindavan.

The girls donned their elaborate and colorful woven costumes and placed veils over their faces. Proud parents gathered in the grove, securing the closest points of observation. Faithful Manipuris swelled the crowd—they came to watch, worship, and thrill at the joyous revelation of divine love.

The gathering crowd waited as the maiba came from the temple to give a rousing introduction.

"Ras Lila dance is an honored tradition, telling a story from Hindu scriptures. The Gopis, milkmaids of Vrindavan, hear Lord Krishna's flute and sneak away to a forest to dance all night. Lord Krishna stretches the night to last billions of years—one Night of Brahma. Watch and listen with faith to find Lord Krishna's pure love and devotion."

The musicians played and the singing and dancing began. Kajao clasped hands with Pankheibi, his wife. They thrilled at the sight of their beautiful daughters—Kairembi, Kangjaibi, and Kebisana. Kebisana, the youngest, played the part of the young Lord Krishna, dancing and playing the flute.

Manipuri girls rank among the most beautiful. Teenagers hold on to their childlike innocence—happy brown eyes fill with dancing, sparkling lights, like tiny twinkling sprites performing their own joyful nautch. Their fair faces shine, framed by black hair, cut straight in front, and left long on the sides. All the girls of Manipur are bright—educated, like the boys.

Kajao taught his daughters bravery, to think for themselves, and never be a slave to any man. His oldest daughter was sixteen. She could marry, but she declared she was not ready. She was willful and her pride in herself made Kajao happy.

So happy!

The musicians played, and the dancers sang as the first streaks of daylight challenged the full moon. Tears of happiness filled Kajao's eyes as he watched with pride. He was so intent on listening to the sweet sound of their singing he missed the first crack of the rifle.

His young daughter dropped her flute and Kajao gasped.

She only stumbled!

Then Kajao watched in horror as blood spread across the breast of his daughter's tunic and she fell to the ground.

Nor did Kajao hear the second shot or the third as two more children fell, struck dead by invisible bullets from nowhere. The music crashed to a discordant end, replaced by screaming, as children and grownups ran in every direction, tripping and colliding in their panic.

The screams could not mask the cracks of the next several shots. Kajao dropped to the ground and yelled for his wife but could not stop her—she ran toward her daughters and then toppled backwards as if yanked by a rope. More shots, more screaming, and more blood.

Then the shooting stopped. No more cracks—only the sounds of agony and terror—crying, sobbing, and screaming. Bodies lay scattered, and splattered blood covered the grass amongst the trees of the sacred grove— young bodies, but adults, too.

Kajao looked at the figures lying on the ground, noted the direction they fell, and his military training told him the source of the firing. The shots traveled far—from the tower.

The Temple of Vrindavan Chandra!

Kajao crawled to his wife and daughters—his legs were too weak to carry him. He sobbed and wailed as he pulled the four lifeless bodies to him and their blood stained his uniform. He looked up at the distant tower through blinking eyes too wet to see and shook his fist.

"I swear by all the gods!" he cried. "I swear—I will give death to the sahibs! Death!"

Chapter 52. The Dry Ditch

3:30 a.m., Tuesday morning, 24 March 1891...

Siriman

That morning no bugle sounded—no reveille call, neither long nor short. Gurkhas woke and rose in the dark and bitter cold, either on their own or with a gentle shake of a shoulder by a comrade. Siriman required no shake. He slept in his uniform and finished dressing, adding boots, cap, kukri, Snider-Enfield rifle, bayonet, ammunition belt, and a coil of rope. Little else needed—no great distance to march, no provisions needed, and no heavy pack to carry.

This morning I go to battle—speed and silence are the day's order.

Siriman joined his company—thirty Gurkhas of the 44th, each hand-chosen by Lieutenant Brackenbury. The company led the other detachments out the gate. They assembled in a field north of the Residency perimeter serving as a temporary campground and staging area. The Gurkhas in Brackenbury's company formed three lines and stood in silence as Subadar Heema Chund checked his list, counting. Once satisfied, the subadar gathered the twenty-nine men into a semi-circle, and speaking in a low voice, bade them kneel.

"The sahibs honor us today—first wave. We leave soon—before first light. We will move fast and in silence—we avoid encounters. Keep off the road when possible. We will swing wide, first west of the fort and then back east to the north side. We must cover more than a mile without discovery. When we reach the Northern Gate, we will take cover, stay unseen, and guard the Kohima Road. No Manipuris will pass our line. No firing until the Sahib Lieutenant orders. The mission today is to capture a rebel prince and return, not to kill enemies, or hold territory. Protect yourself, but avoid unnecessary killing. Remember—speed and silence, speed and silence. Use the bayonet when possible—if you must shoot, take clear shots—save your bullets as we have few and none to spare."

Twenty-nine heads nodded and eager smiles filled faces.

"Questions?" the subadar asked.

"What of our dead or wounded?" one young soldier whispered.

"Speed, silence, but everyone comes back—alive, wounded, or dead."

"What if we run out of ammunition?"

The old soldier grinned. "Do not run out of ammunition." He waited, but no questions followed. "Assemble for departure in one half-hour. Sahib Brackenbury chose each of you for your experience and dependability. He is counting on you, and so am I. Now, go—get something into your stomachs—fast and in silence. Dismissed!"

An overpowering urge hit Siriman.

I must share final words with Karna!

A larger party, more than twice the size of his company, was meeting a few yards away. In the darkness, he recognized Karna among the soldiers kneeling and receiving hushed orders. Their meeting ended and, following dismissal, Siriman approached from behind and tapped Karna's shoulder.

"What are you doing?" Siriman whispered.

Karna turned, and the cousins embraced, arms wrapped in a bear hug.

"Where is your Martini?" Siriman asked.

Karna held up a Snider-Enfield rifle. "Second wave—Captain Butcher's company. We cross the dry ditch, climb the broken wall, rush the compound, and capture the bad prince."

"You are 43rd Regiment," Siriman said. "Butcher and these others are 42nd. Why are you going with them?"

"Sahib Simpson requested me." Karna thrust out his chest and held his chin high. "He is coming as a guide and I am the spotter. I am the one Gurkha who knows the bad prince by sight. Only I have been in his house."

Siriman wagged his head and patted Karna on the back.

Karna's eyes glinted as he flashed a twisted half-smile. "If I see the stolen dragon idol, I will take it and return it to the memsahib..." Then a more sinister look crossed his face. "And I will kill anyone that tries to stop me. If I see the old witch..."

Siriman's eyes widened, and he shook his head. "Take care! Do not get into misadventures. No time—stay focused, follow orders. Speed, silence—come back in one piece."

"Eat now!" Karna's smile broke the tension but left the matter unresolved.

They lined up for rations, devoured flat bread, beans, and boiled eggs, washing it down with weak green tea. They embraced a final time.

"Subhakamana (good luck)!" Karna said.

"You as well!"

At a quarter of five, under a clear sky and cover of darkness, Siriman's company went into action. Brackenbury led his thirty men north at a fast trot along the planned route. The bright moonlight shone upon an empty road where cold puddles glimmered to mark cart ruts and potholes. Wary citizenry deserted the lane before the storm struck and all remained silent.

They trotted in silence, passed the Western Gate without incident, and sped further on to the northwest corner of Kangla. The road turned east, parallel to the dry ditch on their right, and a darkened village on their left. After traveling over a mile, they reached the Kohima road and spread out on either side. The Gurkhas disappeared into the brush north of the dry ditch and crouched near the gate. A few positioned further east within sight of the river. There they hid, watching and waiting. The doors of the arched gate stood open and unguarded. No sentries were visible atop the high brick wall. Jungle night sounds on the far side of the river filled the air.

Siriman looked to his far right. The northwest corner was the point where Karna's party would scale the broken wall and raid the prince's compound. Siriman would have a clear view of Karna's arrival. Brackenbury and his company made good time but no sign yet of the second wave.

It should have followed within fifteen minutes.

The company waited five minutes, then five minutes more. The first glimmer of gray light appeared in the east beyond the jungle mist. Siriman saw no sign of activity at the northwest corner. Lieutenant Brackenbury crouched low and crept to the center of the road. There he called to Siriman in a whisper.

"Dragon slayer!" Brackenbury motioned to Siriman, who left his spot behind a bush, scurried, and crouched at his officer's side.

"Something delayed Butcher." Brackenbury cracked a wide grin. "Are you game for a little exploring?"

Siriman nodded, grinning back.

"Right! Follow me."

Brackenbury drew his pistol, hunched low, and hurried toward the gate. Siriman followed in like fashion, gripping his rifle in one hand. They reached the arch and took cover in shadows beside thick, wide-open wooden doors.

Brackenbury inched forward with Siriman following and they passed into the open area inside the outermost perimeter. The river stood close, having looped inward around the long outer wall, and a grassy field on their left led down to water. Straight ahead, lay the wet moat before the high barrier of the inner citadel and, to their right, stretched a long, six-foot-tall mud wall. Two arched gates broke the long stretch—twin entrances to the Yuvraj's compound. The wicker gate at the first arch stood open.

The men pressed their backs against the mud wall and inched sideways, avoiding the moon and keeping in shadows. They inched toward the open arch ahead and when they stood aside the opening, Brackenbury raised his left hand. He showed Siriman three fingers and counted down, three, two— and at the count of one, the lieutenant spun around the corner to enter the gate. Brackenbury halted, standing face-to-face with a Manipuri sepoy.

"Ah, hullo there!" The lieutenant said in a bright, cheery tone.

"What is sahib doing here?" the turbaned man shouted.

"Out for a moonlight stroll," Brackenbury answered, grinning. "But, I say, old chap, may I have a word with the Yuvraj? Is he at home?"

The sepoy shouted an alarm in Manipuri, raised his rifle, and fired, missing both men.

"Run!" Brackenbury shouted, and he shot the sepoy down with his pistol.

Siriman turned and sprinted hard for the outer gate. Harsh voices answered in Manipuri and the outer battlement came alive with shouting men brandishing rifles. Shots cracked and projectiles struck the road at Siriman's feet. Reaching the safety of the outer arch, Siriman stopped and waited for his lieutenant. Shots came from two directions—the battlement and the mud wall. The bullets chased Brackenbury away from the outer gate and toward the river on their left flank. The officer dodged left and right as bullets hit the earth all around and then Brackenbury dropped, as if struck, and his figure disappeared in darkness near the bank.

"Sahib!" Siriman shouted. He kept flat against the wall under the arch, staying out of the line of fire from the mud wall. "Sahib Brackenbury!" Shots fired from the battlement hit close to his feet, kicking dust.

A faint voice came from the riverbank. "Dragon slayer! I am hit!"

"Where hit, sahib?"

"My ankle—maybe," the reply came. "Not sure I can stand, but I will try to run for the gate. Can you squeeze off a few rounds at the mud wall? I am giving it a go."

Siriman raised his rifle, searched for a target. A shadowy shape like a turbaned head poked above the mud wall. He aimed, fired, and the shape disappeared. As he reloaded, voices shouted and withering fire returned his way from the mud wall. Siriman pressed his back flat against the bricks and held his breath as bullets struck near his head and close to his boots. A dark figure rose from the bank and hobbled toward Siriman at the arched gate. The Gurkha turned, picked another dark target above the mud wall, fired, and dropped another sepoy. As he reloaded, more cracks, but that time the shots sought Brackenbury. The lieutenant fell and crawled toward the river beneath a torrent of bullets. As the officer crept, Siriman saw the body take another hit. Then Brackenbury vanished behind the crest of the bank.

A shout came from outside and Siriman looked to the ditch. A figure bearing a rifle rose from the brush near the road and broke for the river.

"No, Subadar!" he shouted, but too late.

A barrage of shots erupted from the battlement and chased the native officer. The dark figure dropped and toppled over the riverbank north of the wall. Answering shots erupted from the brush as angry Gurkhas returned fire at the sepoys on the battlement. Two Manipuris screamed and fell over the parapet. More shots cracked from atop the wall and a furious firefight ensued. Siriman knew his comrades outside could not fire back for long.

They will use up their ammunition!

"Sahib!" Siriman shouted toward the river. "They shot the subadar!"

"Go find Butcher!" Brackenbury shouted back. "Tell him we have wounded. Tell him the Manipuris have the company pinned. Perhaps he can spare reinforcements and get us out of this mess."

"How, sahib?" Siriman shouted. "Where is Butcher from here?"

"Use the ditch!" a weak voice answered. "Godspeed, dragon slayer!"

Siriman inched from under the arch and peered to his left, inspecting the outer face of the wall and the dry ditch. He measured the distance to the broken corner and shouted to his comrades.

"It is Sunwar! Sahib ordered me to get help. Do not shoot me—shoot the sepoys atop the wall!"

Siriman took a deep breath and exited the gate. He spun left and ran down into the dry ditch beside the high brick wall. He ran hard, carrying his rifle in both hands, and covered over two hundred feet before voices shouted from atop the wall and fired. Lead streaked, hissing past his ear, striking the dirt behind and on either side. A Gurkha volley answered from the brush. Manipuri rifles fell silent as bodies dropped behind the parapet. Heart pounding, Siriman ran another one hundred yards before hearing more rounds fired. The shooters were too far away and harried by the covering fire—he was clear. He drew near the corner of the ditch where tumbled bricks marked the broken wall. Twenty Gurkhas appeared ahead, holding rifles with mounted bayonets. Several turned, lowering points to thrust position, and others took aim.

"Do not shoot!" Siriman shouted. "Sunwar, 44 GR, with Sahib Brackenbury's unit!"

"What are you doing here?" a Gurkha shouted.

Siriman drew close and stopped to catch his breath. "Officers—wounded," he managed. "Men pinned—much fire—need reinforcements. Where is Sahib Butcher?"

"Inside the wall," the Gurkha answered. "With fifty men. He goes to arrest the prince. We are the rear guard. We go in now. Lugard's detachment arrives soon. You can wait or come with us—maybe you will find Butcher. Affix your bayonet first—Captain's orders."

As Siriman drew and attached the long blade, the Gurkhas swarmed up and scrambled over the broken bricks. The last soldier disappeared through the gash by the time Siriman climbed over dirt and bricks. As he reached the top, a pile of bricks shifted beneath his boot and he lost balance. He reached to steady himself, grabbing a pier cap atop a baluster, but the cap shifted and gave way. Siriman tumbled backward into the ditch and landed on his back with his head pointing downward. He slid and came to a rest wedged between two jagged-edged sections of the smashed wall. His consciousness dimmed, but he held on and cleared his head. He tested his limbs and flexed his back.

Nothing broken! Lucky fool! You could have cracked your head wide open!

As Siriman sat up, he discovered a rectangular object lying flat across his stomach. He brushed the object aside and scrambled to his feet. As he leaned over and retrieved his hat, he snatched and inspected the rectangle. It had an envelope shape and appeared made of paper, coated with smooth, hardened wax. He glanced up at the brick pier and down at the fallen end cap.

I must have dislodged it from under the end cap and it landed on me as I fell.

As Siriman examined the object, thoughts echoed—a strange voice from another time and a distant place.

Remember the shape. Someday you will find something similar. When you do, save it, and give it to the angel.

Siriman shook his head, clearing the distracting thoughts.

No time now! Save for the sahibs to inspect later!

He unbuttoned his shirt, stuffed the object inside, re-buttoned, and returned to his mission. He climbed, crossing the bricks with greater care, and in moments stepped down into a courtyard within a lush garden behind the house of the Yuvraj.

Now which way?

Shots cracked.

Always move toward the shooting!

Siriman stepped over bodies on the ground—Manipuri sepoys, young and old—dispatched by bayonets. Another turbaned sepoy sat, back against a wall, face frozen in a blank stare—a round bullet hole between his eyes.

He rounded the main house and faced sudden chaos. Burning thatched roofs cast shadows. The outnumbered Gurkhas swarmed the grounds and chased Manipuris between the outbuildings. The Manipuris fired wild shots and had no time to reload. They dropped their single-shot smoothbore muzzle-loaders and died in their tracks, bayonetted by the efficient Gurkhas.

Siriman saw a Gurkha pulling his bayonet from his kill and he called to the soldier, "Where is Sahib Butcher?"

The Gurkha pointed toward a brick tower and ran. Siriman made sure the path was clear and sprinted toward the building. The tower featured entrances on each side and he made for the closest tall portal. He stepped through and beheld a high, torch-lit chamber. A line of wounded Gurkhas spread across the brick floor and Captain Butcher knelt beside one, tending his wounds.

Siriman approached and stood close. "Sahib Captain?"

"One moment—I am trying to save this man's life!"

Siriman waited and watched the captain tighten a bandage around a bloody wound. Butcher made the final wrap and glanced. "Who are you?"

"Sunwar, 44 GR," Siriman said. "Brackenbury's detachment…"

"Far from your position—what is the report?"

"Heavy fire, sahib! Officers wounded and men pinned."

"Brackenbury?"

"Hit, sahib, but alive, stranded by the river. He sent me to find you."

"The river!" the captain exclaimed. "What the bloody hell is he doing by the river? Are you certain?"

"Yes, sahib. I was there."

"Well, if he wants reinforcements, we have our bloody hands full here. We have stumbled into a nest of five hundred regulars and no sign of the Yuvraj. Once we secure the compound I can spare a few men—did you say you are a Sunwar?"

"Yes, sahib."

He will give me bad news about Karna.

"There is a Sunwar up those stairs." Butcher nodded at a brick staircase. Flights rose, circling the inner sanctum.

"My cousin, sahib."

"He went up to scout—said he once encountered the Yuvraj in the upper chambers. I decided it was worth him having a look. He has been up there a while. Perhaps you should check on your cousin."

Siriman saluted and headed for the stairs. He climbed four flights and reached a wide chamber where open arches led to balconies on four sides.

A garbha griha!

It was a sanctum, a sacred place of worship—but there were signs of struggle and death. Two slender bodies, one headless, lay across puddles of blood. Red smears profaned the floors and walls. Smashed idols littered the bricks and, sitting on the altar, ghoulish eyes stared from a severed, turbaned head.

A rifle shot cracked and Siriman started. The second shot confirmed the source of the shooting was higher, somewhere above his head. A door led to a central stairwell. He checked his rifle.

Loaded!

More shots. He climbed three short flights. Shots continued at regular intervals, each loud crack echoing in the well. When he reached the top, a door opened onto a flat rooftop surrounded by an iron railing set between brick balusters. The light remained dim but a cold dawn was breaking over the misty jungle.

Siriman rounded a corner as another rifle shot cracked. The shooter stood before him at the edge of the rail. Siriman's eyes opened wide at the sight, his jaw dropped open, and he cried out in terror.

"Karna!"

Chapter 53. The Tower of Vrindavan Chandra

Two hours earlier, at 4:00 a.m....

Karna

Karna Sunwar woke and dressed in the chill and darkness. He exited his tent and raced in silence to join his detachment—seventy rifles of the 42nd Regiment, commanded by Captain Butcher. The Gurkhas assembled in the field outside the wall, north of the Residency. Jamadar Gurung counted and checked each name, ending with only Karna unaccounted.

"Who are you? You are not on my list!"

"Sunwar, 43rd GR," Karna said, grinning. "Sahib Simpson sent me—I am the spotter!"

The jamadar nodded and whispered to a sepoy. The man sprinted off and returned bearing a Snider-Enfield rifle and an ammunition pouch.

"No Martinis!" The jamadar handed Karna the rifle. "Sniders only. Here..." He handed Karna the pouch. "Forty rounds—use with care—and make sure bayonet is sharp."

Karna set aside his Martini-Henry and his pouch of rounds.

Martini rounds do not fit the bore of a Snider.

The native officer bade the kneeling group to draw closer as he spoke in hushed whispers, outlining the mission.

"We are second wave—we leave fifteen minutes after the first. We move fast and in silence to the northwest corner. There we cross the dry ditch and enter through a break in the wall. Once inside, we secure the compound and then locate and capture the Yuvraj. Sahib Lugard's third wave of forty rifles follows fifteen minutes later to reinforce our position."

The jamadar looks like he sucked on a lemon!

"We go in waves, because of the noises you clumsy oafs make. You *will* be quiet, and you *will not* alert the Manipuris, or I will slit your throat myself. Understood?"

Smiles vanished as sixty-nine heads nodded and a few gulped, gripping their throats.

"We go to *arrest* the prince, not to kill him." He turned to Karna. "You know him by sight?"

Karna nodded.

"Good! When we secure entry to the palace, Sunwar will lead the way as we search room by room."

Karna nodded again and looked around, beaming, noting the jealous glances of the others.

Granting such trust in a sepoy is a great honor!

The jamadar added further instructions—to work fast and in silence; to use bayonets first before firing; to fire only if ordered; and, above all, to preserve scarce ammunition.

"Meet in a half-hour," the jamadar finished. "Now, go eat!"

As Karna stood, someone tapped his shoulder. Turning, he found his cousin Siriman standing behind, and the two leapt with joy, meeting in a mutual bear hug. After breakfast and a brief conversation, Siriman rejoined his detachment. At 4:45 sharp, Karna watched as Siriman and the thirty men of the first wave, led by Lieutenant Brackenbury, headed north along the muddy road.

Fifteen slow minutes passed. Karna thumbed the point and edge of his bayonet and found it sharp. Captain Butcher and Lieutenant Simpson joined the detachment. Simpson nodded to Karna, smiling. Karna smiled back and returned the nod, excited.

The sahib lieutenant still trusts me! I will not fail him this time!

At five o'clock, Butcher signaled and the detachment of seventy-two men padded toward Kangla, passing the women's bazaar on the left, opposite the Western Gate. One hundred yards further on, Butcher raised a hand, and the company halted while Butcher and Simpson huddled.

The lieutenant and captain disagree!

Simpson shook his head but at last shrugged and motioned to the jamadar. The native officer drew the sixty-nine Gurkhas aside and delivered hushed orders.

"New plan!" he said, frowning. "We will station a rear guard here, out of sight. I need twenty men—count off—you there, over to you!"

It took another minute to achieve the proper count and two more to find a suitable hiding place for twenty men under cover of brush.

"Guard the gate," the jamadar said to the twenty. "Watch the bazaar and the Cachar Road. When you sight Sahib Lugard's reinforcements on the move, head to the northwest corner, find the entrance point, and rejoin us inside the wall."

The rear guard scattered to their hiding places. Karna followed Simpson as the fifty-two remaining soldiers regained the road and proceeded north. After another one hundred yards, Butcher halted again.

Why stop? We are too far south of the northwest corner!

Karna stayed close and overheard Butcher and Simpson whispering.

They are arguing again!

"There!" Butcher said, pointing. "A broken wall—and the ditch is bone dry, too. We will enter here."

"This is the wrong place," Simpson said. "This is not where Ethel—where Missus Grimwood—said we should enter. Her map showed a spot farther ahead, around the corner, on the north face."

"Is she your commander? This spot is much closer with a broken wall and a dry ditch. We can make up time we lost splitting out the rear guard."

"Why did we lose time," Simpson said. "A rear guard was not part of the original order."

"It was in *my* orders!" Butcher looked at the jamadar. "Why was the company not told?"

The native officer stood stoic and looked away.

"What of Brackenbury?" Simpson said.

"What of him?"

"His party will not see us arrive and enter. They will think we are late and fear something is amiss."

"Nonsense!" Butcher hissed. "They have their own area to defend and have no business worrying about us. Now, come!" The captain waved his arm and led the way off the road.

Simpson grabbed Karna's arm and whispered in his ear, "Stay at my side—no matter what happens."

Fifty men followed Butcher and Simpson into the dry ditch, scrambled up the broken rampart across scattered bricks, and dropped from the banquette. Karna followed and his boots hit the ground in time to hear Simpson's terse whisper.

"Bloody hell!"

Where are we? This is not the Yuvraj's compound!

They gathered in an open area between the inner and outer battlements. Many yards stretched ahead to the mud wall surrounding their destination. To their right stood a ramshackle bustee—a jumbled collection of darkened mud-and-thatch huts.

The men continued toward the wall in silence save the slight rustle of leather on khaki. To their right lay the wet moat and tall brick wall of the northwest corner of the inner citadel.

No sentries visible!

They neared the southwest corner of the compound and discovered a pond to their left where an old Manipuri man drew water. A boot snapped a dry stick. The man looked up, dropped his bucket, and shouted an alarm. Turbaned heads rose from the citadel wall. Rifle barrels lowered over the parapet and took aim. Answering shouts broke the quiet and a first shot cracked.

"Run!" Butcher shouted.

The captain waved the men to follow. Karna kept at Simpson's heels. The company flowed behind, sprinting into the ditch along the south face of the long mud wall encircling the Yuvraj's compound.

Bullets flew, striking the mud wall above their heads and the dirt path beside the ditch. Darkness and surprise hampered the accuracy of the Manipuri muskets. A Gurkha ahead of Karna took a grazing shot in the leg. Karna grabbed an arm and helped his comrade limp and keep up with the others.

Simpson shouted at Butcher, "Now where?"

"Follow the wall to the southeast corner! When we round the corner, the gate should be ahead to our left."

As they neared the halfway point, shouting sepoys boiled from the bustee behind and gave chase. One hundred yards ahead, more shouts came followed by shots, and then explosive clamor and shooting erupted.

We are running toward a firefight!

Simpson grabbed Butcher's arm. "Stop! We cannot go this way. All hell has broken loose ahead!"

Butcher examined the mud wall. "Here then—forget the gate. The wall is at its shortest point right here. We can scale and escape the snipers. Once inside, we move to outflank the fight ahead."

"Right," Simpson said. "Go—I will cover you."

Simpson pulled aside Karna and a dozen men. The soldiers knelt and fired, leveling enfilading fire at the bustee and picking off snipers atop the inner fortress wall. Butcher and the rest of the company paired up, linked hands, and boosted comrades up, over, and into the compound. Simpson, Karna, and the last dozen climbed as helping hands reached and pulled. Karna landed inside, right after Simpson. The rest of the men dropped and as the final soldier prepared to jump, he took a bullet in the shoulder. Karna caught the man as he fell, cradled in waiting arms.

The fifty reformed and Butcher assigned two soldiers to tend the wounded.

"Also, watch for any comrades following," he said.

"Who?" Simpson said. "The rear guard is unaware we took a shortcut. They will stick to plan and head for the northwest corner."

Butcher said nothing and waved the company forward, heading for the sound of the fighting.

Inside is more alive than outside the wall!

The narrow streets and outbuildings swarmed with hundreds of Manipuri sepoys.

"They must outnumber us ten to one!" Butcher said.

"Is that all?" Simpson laughed. "They will soon realize they are under attack from a superior force!"

The Gurkhas set to their grim work. Manipuris fired wild shots and, before they could reload, bayonets flashed. Karna killed three himself. The scattered bodies of turbaned sepoys soon lay bleeding wherever he looked.

Butcher lifted a torch from the wall. "Let us have a little more light!" He tossed it high onto the thatched roof of an outbuilding and flames erupted. Other soldiers followed his example and soon the entire compound was aflame.

It was a butcher's work and Butcher led his company, rushing forward and scattering the defenders. Soon they reached their destination—the northeast corner of the compound. As they neared the palace of the Yuvraj, a Gurkha ran up, and Butcher paused for news.

"Lugard is arriving soon," Butcher said. "We wait a moment."

"With all due respect, Captain," Simpson said, "We should go after the Yuvraj."

At that moment, Lieutenant Lugard arrived with forty reinforcements and the Gurkhas left behind at the wall.

"You followed our route?" Simpson said.

"We heard the shooting," Lugard said, "and took the shortest path to the fighting. Why did you come that way? That was not the plan."

"No time to explain now," Butcher said. "Simpson, take our company to the palace and search for the Yuvraj. Lugard, take your men and clean the west half of the compound. I will take the wounded and setup a command post and hospital in that temple."

"Come on, Sunwar!" Simpson said. "This is your moment."

Karna led the company to the wooden door of the palace, rattled the knob, and shouted, "Locked, sahib!"

Simpson stood back and pointed at the lock. "Shoot it!"

Three Gurkha rifles fired at close range and the wood exploded, scattering splinters. Simpson kicked, the door flew open, and Karna led the Gurkhas into the foyer.

"Which way?" Simpson said.

"Courtyard in middle, sahib," Karna said. "Rooms go both ways, around the courtyard."

Simpson pointed left. "Take half that way—move through the rooms clockwise. I will take the rest and work counter-clockwise. When we meet, take care. Do not shoot each other!"

Karna took the lead, trying to show confidence.

I never saw this wing!

He had only seen the kitchen and dining area.

On the other side.

Karna moved forward, room by room, knocking down doors, searching closets and under beds. The Gurkhas found huddled servants hiding in behind doors, in corners of pantries, and under beds.

No sign yet of the bad prince!

They moved on, encountering a swarm of guards, but the Manipuris fell to the well-trained Nepalis. The Gurkhas took prisoners, but killed many, including servants.

Too many killed!

A few Manipuris died from rifle shots, or beheaded by kukri knives, but the points of Gurkha bayonets did most of the work. They soon reached the central courtyard and met Simpson's company.

"House is clear, sahib," Karna said.

"Any sign of the Yuvraj?"

Karna shook his head. "No sign of the bad prince."

"Same here," Simpson said. "The clever tiger smelled a rat. He is somewhere safe behind high walls by now."

Simpson stationed sentries at the entrances and the rest of the company, including wounded and prisoners, headed back to the chaos of battle. They worked back the way they had come, moving south along a narrow alley parallel to the eastern mud wall. They secured the east gates of the compound and shot at pesky snipers atop the outer battlement near the Northern Gate.

"Too much firing!" Simpson called. "We soon will be out of ammunition at this rate."

The company rounded a corner between two burning storehouses and met Lieutenant Lugard at the head of three dozen Gurkhas.

"Where is Butcher?" Simpson asked.

"He secured the temple." Lugard turned and pointed toward the medieval-looking brick tower. "He set up a makeshift medical station for the wounded and a stockade for prisoners."

"Is all clear?"

"A lot of work remains to call this compound clear."

"We will join you, then." Simpson turned to Karna. "Pick six able-bodied soldiers—take the wounded and prisoners to the temple. Offer help to the captain."

"What of the prince, sahib?"

Simpson shook his head. "We will not find him here."

Karna led the small company between the burning buildings to the temple. Once inside the torch-lit chamber, he herded the prisoners to a corner under guard, and then helped wounded hobble to the captain who was kneeling, busy treating wounds.

"Where is the stockade, sahib?"

Butcher pointed toward the open door to the inner sanctum. Karna peered past a dead Manipuri sitting slumped in the doorway. Bullets had despoiled the chamber—dead bodies, broken statues, and pieces of smashed idols lay strewn. A dark trail marked the path of a dead body dragged aside.

Defiling Lord Krishna's temple!

Karna jabbed at the prisoners, forcing them into the room, and stationed two guards at the door. He scanned the rest of the temple chamber.

The staircase! I remember!

Four flights of brick steps wrapped the inner sanctum.

The upper chamber! Altars and idols! Memsahib's dragon could be in its original place!

"Did Simpson send you, Sepoy?" Butcher asked.

"Yes, sahib."

"Any sign of Tikendra Jeet?"

"No, sahib. Not yet."

Karna stared again at the stairway and Butcher glanced that way.

"Something interesting over there?"

"Has anyone checked upstairs, sahib?"

"We gave it a quick look—it was clear."

"Sahib, may I look?" Karna bit his lower lip, trembling with anticipation.

Must not seem over anxious!

"Once I was there with—the Yuvraj. There is a shrine—very cluttered. There may be places to hide."

Butcher nodded, pressing a bandage against the bloody arm of a wounded Gurkha. "Right—but be quick and watch yourself."

Karna saluted and sped to the stair. He gripped his rifle two-handed, bayonet-forward, and raced up the four flights, reaching the torch-lit upper shrine to the old gods of Manipur. Karna approached the altar and there, among a crowd of statues, he found the object he sought.

Memsahib's idol!

The jade-green dragon figurine was back in its original spot and light from the torches sparkled across its delicate wings.

Karna stood his rifle against the altar and took the little statue in hand. His palm tingled, and as he stared at the dragon, a familiar rumbling rose in the back of his mind.

Not the murmur! Not now!

He shook his head. "No!"

The rumbling stopped and Karna returned to his senses.

Footsteps! The captain is coming!

Karna slid the idol into a breast pocket and turned, expecting to see Butcher, but his eyes opened wide, shocked by an unexpected sight.

The old witch!

Moonia, who two days before he had seen hand the dragon to the bad prince, stood before him, closer than ever. A Manipuri guard stood on each side. The two soldiers were handsome lads in black turbans, skinny and smooth-faced. They were young, too young, more boys than men. Each youth held a wicked-looking dao knife in a trembling hand.

They are too young! I do not want to kill boys!

Karna noticed the open door to the stairwell leading to the top of the temple.

They hid on the roof.

"So now it begins!" Moonia cackled. "I warned him! I told him someone would come for the idol, but he would not listen. All he would spare for guards are these two boys." She smirked and wagged her head. "So here they are—sworn to defend the shrine against the likes of you, a lone, filthy Gurkha."

She studied the altar and frowned. Her eyes narrowed and rose to the bulge in Karna's shirt pocket. She cracked a wry smile and chuckled.

"You want it for yourself. I see that now. You care nothing for your lovely memsahib."

"No!" Karna said. "Prince gave dragon to memsahib. It belongs to her now. You stole it! Now I will take it to her. I will give dragon back to memsahib."

"Hah!" the old woman scoffed. "It was not his to give. No one *owns* the dragon; no one *gives* the dragon away. The dragon finds its own keeper in its own time. The prince ignored this, so it became his undoing."

"Where is the bad prince?" Karna said, voice trembling.

Moonia laughed. "Such fools you are. You will not find him here. You will never catch him. He is too smart for you. You British are so predictable, so easy to manipulate. British sahibs think they are so smart, so powerful, and so superior. Sahibs so uncivilized—barbarians, so disrespectful of Vedic ways—ready to kill and eat unsanctified meat and blaspheme the gods. You British deal out death to the innocent and seal your dooms."

"I am Gurkha! Not British!"

She laughed louder. "Oh, I see! Mighty Gurkhas! No one conquers the Gurkhas—not the British or anyone. So different are you? So free?" She emitted a long cackling laugh. "How can you be free when you have such fierce love for the Queen Empress? Like little dogs for your British master. A dog cannot have the dragon. The dragon eats little dogs like you. So try to give it to your memsahib—if you can. At least she has potential she has not yet realized. Perhaps she can learn to control her power in time."

Karna placed a hand over his breast pocket.

"Oh, but perhaps the dragon wants you to have it—for now—to use you for a purpose. You think you have won, but you lost—it has you. You had no choice—you became weak—an agent. The dragon uses you to change the world—a war, to resurrect a dead empire."

"Old witch! You lie! You are—a Rakshasa!"

"Rakshasa?" Moonia doubled with laughter. "At least use the right name—Manushya Rakshasi!" (Shape-shifting female demon in human form.)

Moonia straightened and grew taller, transforming before Karna's eyes. Taller and taller she grew until she looked down, a rail-thin figure standing three feet taller than Karna. Reptilian eyes flickered in the torchlight and scales shone on her temples beneath bedraggled white hair.

"So!" she shouted. "Do you believe your eyes now, or is this a witch's trick?"

The young guards shrank, trembling in terror at the sight of the giantess. She stretched a bony finger toward Karna.

"Kill him!"

They looked at each other, raised their blades, and sprang toward Karna, wild-eyed and screaming. The closest swung his blade. The Gurkha ducked, and the blade struck a shelf of idols. Statues flew, crashing to the bricks. From his crouching position, Karna reached for his rifle, gripped the barrel, and lunged upward. The long bayonet blade impaled the youth's neck and the point shot through the top of his skull. Karna yanked with both hands. The rifle pulled downward, and the blade sliced the slender throat lengthwise. The youth fell gurgling as blood sprayed across the bricks.

"Good!" Moonia shouted. "Blaspheme the shrine, British lap dog! Profane the temple and earn the wrath of the gods. Give yourself to the dragon if that is your decision. Suffer the fate!"

The second young guard leapt toward Karna, swung the blade backhanded, and it sank into Karna's left side. The force knocked Karna backward, and he fell across the altar. More idols scattered, crashing into pieces on the floor. Karna stood and swung his right fist. He connected and sent the young guard flying across the altar, smashing more figurines. Karna yanked the blade from his side and placed his hand over the wound. Blood oozed between fingers. He lowered his blood-soaked hand, drew his kukri, and turned to speak to the witch.

Where is she?

Moonia had vanished. Karna stepped forward, looking in each direction, and then stopped. There was no sign of the giantess. Karna cocked an ear—idol fragments clattered and scraped as the young sentry struggled to his feet. Karna noted the crunch of clumsy footsteps, turned, and swept his kukri upward. One powerful stroke sent the young guard's head flying onto the altar, and the headless corpse crashed to the brick floor, spewing a dark puddle.

Karna dropped his kukri and doubled over, grabbing his side. He straightened, swooning, and scanned the room. Everywhere lay smashed idols, dead bodies, and blood—dark, broad strokes painted everywhere. Karna patted his breast pocket.

The dragon idol safe!

Karna found his rifle and looked at the stairway leading to the roof. He staggered toward the door, blood dripping, and left a dark trail across the bricks as he climbed the three short flights to the roof. He walked to the railing and looked out at the fire, burning roofs, and fleeing Manipuris chased by Gurkhas. Manipuri riflemen fired at the compound from the citadel across the moat. He lifted his rifle and took aim, intending to return the fire and pick off a few of the turbaned sepoys.

No, not them!

Who then?

Look at my temple. Do you see the gold domes?

Yes, still dark, but I see.

Now look right—the nearby grove. They defile my temple. Stop them!

Between the distant trees, tiny figures—musicians and dancers—filled the grove. What were they thinking? Did they think they were revealing the glory of divine love? Did they not realize how they had upset his master— that the old religion wanted revenge? Karna raised his rifle and took careful aim. They were far away and at that distance, he had to aim higher.

They are within my range.

Karna squeezed the trigger, fired, and a tiny figure fell. He reached into his ammunition pouch, reloaded, and fired again. Another body dropped. Reload, fire, another hit. He fired, again and again, like an automaton—a mindless killing machine.

Why am I killing innocents?

You only do that which your master demands.

Yes. I have no choice.

"Karna!" a voice cried.

The speaker sounded far away. The word was strange. It was a name. His name.

That name means nothing now.

A force crashed against his side. Someone had tackled him—someone he once knew. He fell to the rooftop deck. A Gurkha sat on top, holding him down, stopping him from his duty.

The figure knelt over him. "Oh, Karna, what have you done?"

Karna studied the other Gurkha's face.

There was something—what was it? Unfinished business!

"I told you once before," Karna said. "I said I would kill you, Siriman Sunwar. Now you will die!"

Karna grabbed Siriman by the throat and squeezed. Siriman knocked Karna's hands away and scrambled for his rifle. As Karna rose and lunged, Siriman turned, raised his bayonet point, and Karna fell on top. The long blade impaled Karna's chest near his heart.

"No!" Siriman cried. "Karna! What have I done? I am so sorry. I have killed you!"

Karna? Yes, Karna was my name.

"No," Karna said, gurgling blood. "Siri—man. You—saved me—at last."

Take the dragon from my breast pocket.

Karna thought the words and his jaw moved, but he only coughed, gurgled, and sputtered from his blood-filled mouth.

"Dragon…," Karna said. "Pocket…"

Siriman fumbled with Karna's shirt pocket and pulled out the little dragon figurine. It glittered in the dim light, still intact.

He must not keep it. He must not give it to the memsahib. It is evil. He must destroy it!

Karna tried to warn Siriman, but through the coughing and gurgling all Karna could manage was…

"Memsahib…"

"Yes, Karna," Siriman cried, holding up the idol. "I understand—I must see the memsahib gets her dragon back. I will tell her how you rescued it for her!"

No!

The word failed, drowned in the blood in Karna's throat. Darkness came and then light. Karna rose, amazed. A body—a bloody mess, a dead Gurkha—lay next to Siriman. A light appeared, whiter and brighter than any light in his memory, and a voice spoke.

"Come." The calm voice was familiar somehow—smooth and soft. "It is time."

"No," Karna answered. "Not yet—but soon. Siriman still needs my help."

He drew back from the light. Darkness grew, but he found a place in between, a gray line of twilight. There he lingered—safe, peaceful—and he waited.

Chapter 54. The Bloody White Linen

A few minutes earlier…

Walter

Simpson and Lugard brought fire and death wherever they trod. They flushed Manipuris from behind barriers and hiding places and the sepoys fled the Yuvraj's compound in a stampede. Many ran through narrow alleys and out the gates. A few scrambled over the mud wall. Others trapped themselves, running into dead ends where they dropped to their knees and begged for mercy. Most of the time, the Gurkhas showed quarter and took prisoners, but too often the little soldiers acted like the well-trained, efficient killing machines they were. As if unleashed in a blood lust, the Gurkhas thrust and stabbed, either unwilling to listen, or incapable of comprehending the pleas of surrender.

Walter Simpson walked among the dead and dying, inspecting the carnage, and shaking his head. Here and there, amid the lifeless bodies of Manipuri soldiers, were women and young boys, youths far too young to have been fighters, but many showed bravery—or foolishness. Most looked to be servants whose misfortune placed them in the way when the wave of death broke over the compound. Soldiers know they face death in their trade and accept their fate, but—so many civilian lives cut short.

Did I know any when alive?

He could have seen them in passing as he strolled through the market, spoken to or transacted business with a few. Perhaps at one time, he knew a few of their names. He might have tossed back an errant ball, receiving thanks from the handsome youth lying dead at his feet—a tangle of arms, legs, and bloody white linen.

"Five hundred," Walter said, removing his hat and wiping his face with his sleeve.

Lugard frowned. "Sorry?"

"There must have been at least five hundred regulars here when we first arrived. I joked to Butcher about the odds being in our favor—but did not realize. There are too many dead Manipuri civilians in the mix. Far too many. No matter how this ends, today is an evil day. England and Manipur can never recover after today."

"It is their fault," Lugard said. "This was a trap. They knew we were coming. Someone warned them."

"It does not change things."

"Listen, Simpson," Lugard answered. "Indian dust soaked up a lot of blood over the years. Remember Cawnpore!"

Walter scoffed. "Cawnpore? 1857? Sorry—before my time—and yours, too. Manipur stayed out of the Great Rebellion. In fact, they sided with Britain. Blood leads to more blood."

Lugard referenced an event thirty-four years earlier when rebels cornered European civilians in the town of Cawnpore. The civilians surrendered and at first, the Indians accepted their surrender, but then anger and blood lust won out. The rebels slaughtered hundreds of innocent women and children and tossed dismembered bodies down a well. It was the rebellion's blackest day. The impact upon British sensibilities was so great it produced a rallying cry of "Remember Cawnpore!" along with acts of revenge just as despicable. Evil slaughter on both sides left a wound still not healed.

"Look, Simpson," Lugard said. "Perhaps you have been living amongst these people too long. The compound is secure. Maybe you should take a breather. Round up these prisoners and take them to Butcher. I will station sharpshooters at the wall to stop the sniper fire from the citadel."

Walter opened his mouth to argue and then remembered.

Sunwar. I sent him to the temple—I will retrieve him and we can make a final pass to search for Tikendra Jeet.

"A breather!" Walter snarled. "I *will* take the prisoners and wounded to the temple and check on Butcher. Then I will conduct a second sweep and rejoin you at the wall. Tell the shooters to mind the ammunition. I hate to think how few rounds are in their pouches."

Walter soon arrived at the temple with the prisoners. He provided Butcher an update on their success in clearing the compound and failure in finding the Yuvraj. Walter finished by expressing concern for the number civilian deaths.

"A shame, I agree." Butcher shook his head. "What to do? War *is* a dirty business."

"Are we at war?" Walter said. "I thought we came to arrest one rebellious prince."

Butcher's face reddened and veins raised. He opened his mouth to speak and then clenched his teeth. Darkness faded and became a frown and he returned to dressing a wound.

He is ignoring my comment. Discussion ended. I must get a grip.

Walter looked around the chamber for Karna. "Have you seen Sunwar?"

"Which one?" Butcher replied. "There are two."

"My Sunwar. The spotter—sepoy with the 43rd."

Butcher scratched his head. "Now I recall—it does not matter which you want because they are together." He nodded toward the stairway. "Both are somewhere up those stairs. Your sepoy wanted to search for Tikendra Jeet. He left a while ago so I sent the other up to check on him." He glanced at his pocket watch. "Blast it! What is going on up there?"

Walter signaled to three Gurkhas to follow and padded up the stairs. He reached the sanctum and halted—stunned by the scene of carnage and destruction.

"What the bloody hell?" he whispered.

He pointed, and the Gurkhas fanned out, checking each corner of the chamber and each of the four balconies. Walter strode over a pool of blood, idol fragments crunching under his heels, and studied the two young corpses.

"More boys!" He noticed the decapitated body. "Where is your head, I wonder?" He looked around and grimaced at the sight of wide eyes staring back from atop an altar. "Sweet Jesus!"

The three Gurkhas returned, heads shaking.

No sign of anyone else on this level.

Walter nodded toward a door. "I suspect that leads to the roof."

Heavy boots echoed in the stairwell and Walter exchanged glances with the Gurkhas. The soldiers gripped their rifles, bayonets raised and ready, as the iron-trimmed door screeched and swung open. Out stepped Naik Siriman Sunwar of the 44th Regiment, soaked in blood, rifle strap slung over his shoulder, and a limp body in his arms.

The three Gurkhas glanced at Simpson—he nodded, and the Gurkhas sidestepped Siriman and sprinted up the stairs to the roof. Siriman laid the body on the bricks.

Walter knelt and turned the head. He saw the face and swallowed hard. He touched the neck, checking for a pulse. "Dead." Walter looked up at Siriman. "He was—a relative—correct?"

"Yes, sahib," Siriman said. "My cousin, but more like my brother."

"I am sorry." Walter nodded toward the nearby carnage. "What happened here?"

"Not sure, sahib." The Gurkha's shoulders slumped. He fidgeted and avoided Walter's eyes.

"What *do* you know?"

"I came too late, sahib." Siriman nodded at the two corpses. "Manipuri guards must have attacked Karna. He fought and killed both, but he suffered wounds in the fight and then he died."

Walter inspected the slash wound in Karna's side. A wicked dao knife lying in the nearby pool of blood would account for it. Next, he examined the chest wound.

"Strange," Walter said. "To my eye, this looks to be a bayonet wound." Walter noticed blood on Siriman's bayonet...

A bloody bayonet—like every other damn bloody bayonet.

Walter stood and took a deep breath.

Why do I feel attached?

The young Gurkha had become someone Walter depended on, despite his episodes of erratic behavior.

He could not mask his frustration. "What the hell..." Walter choked. "What was he doing on the roof? How did he manage with those vicious wounds? This chest wound was fatal."

Siriman blinked back tears. His mouth opened, but he shrugged and looked away. A tear ran down Walter's cheek. He wiped his face with a coat sleeve, shook his head, and stood.

"Was he dead when you found him?"

"Almost, sahib," Siriman said. "I have something else to show you." Siriman reached into his shirt pocket. He fished and pulled out the dragon figurine. "Before dying, Karna gave me this." He held up the idol. "He found it—said it belongs to the memsahib. He wanted her to have it."

Walter's eyes widened. He shivered, feeling an electric surge up his spine and a trembling weakness in his knees.

This will make Ethel ecstatic when I give it to her.

"Let me see that." The lieutenant reached, but the Gurkha looked aghast and drew back.

"For the memsahib!" Siriman said.

"Hand it over!" Walter insisted. "That is an order. I am familiar with Missus Grimwood's little statue. I must make certain that one is the right one."

Siriman hesitated and then handed over the idol. Walter studied it, holding it up and turned it back and forth. The red jewel sparkled in the torch light.

"Yes!" Walter said. "That is the same one!"

The officer slipped the object into his breast pocket and Siriman's mouth opened and eyes widened in a look of horror. Walter cracked a wry smile.

"Not to worry," he said, chuckling. "I will see she receives it."

One of the Gurkhas from the roof reappeared in the stairwell. "Sahib!" he shouted. "Roof clear of Manipuris but many spent cartridges."

Walter sprinted for the stairwell followed by Siriman. Up on the roof the officer knelt and examined the empty casings scattered near the railing.

"Snider shells!" Walter lifted the Snider-Enfield rifle and examined the bloody bayonet. He looked across the expanse, past the moat, to the tall battlement of the inner citadel. The turbaned heads of snipers were visible.

"Good man," Walter muttered. He stood and addressed Siriman. "Your cousin must have spent his last ounces of strength shooting at snipers. He tried to take down a few for us before he gave up the ghost." The lieutenant turned to his escorts. "You three go find Lieutenant Lugard. Tell him—get rifles up here now! This is an excellent spot for firing at the citadel."

"Yes, sahib!" The three Gurkhas ran for the steps.

Walter turned back to Siriman. "Your cousin was a good soldier. You should carry his body down and place him with our dead."

Siriman took a step to leave and then stopped. "Sahib?"

"Yes?"

"I spoke to Captain Butcher..."

"What is it?"

Siriman explained to Walter the reason he was at the tower. He had come seeking relief for Brackenbury's detachment. He told of the firefight at the Northern Gate and the predicament his comrades faced.

"What on earth was Brackenbury thinking?" Walter exclaimed. "What possessed him—going to the gate and asking for Tikendra Jeet?"

"Sahib Brackenbury worried something delayed Sahib Butcher."

"Ha!" Walter shook a clenched fist. "I knew there would be consequences. We came in the wrong entrance and had to scale a mud wall. That explains the gunshots we heard up ahead."

The door burst open and a dozen soldiers appeared. They took positions along the railing and fired at the Manipuris on the walls of the inner citadel. A few minutes later Lugard followed with a dozen more men. It did not take long for sniper fire to wreck devastation on the enemy across the moat.

"Look, Lugard!" Walter pointed at a stream of sepoys racing east through the open Eastern Gate, heading for the river.

"Hurrah!" Lugard cheered. "Watch the beggars run! They are trying to escape!"

"I am not so certain," Walter pulled a set of field glasses from a case on his belt. "That gate never opens. I suspect they have something else in mind."

From his vantage, and with the field glasses, he saw the Manipuris splashing across the rocks of the shallow river and reassembling in the jungle on the far side.

Musket barrels raising!

Walter saw a puff of smoke and shouted, "Duck!"

The officers and Gurkhas ducked just as a bullet whistled over Walter's head and struck the brick wall.

"They found a safer place," Walter said.

The Manipuris fired from new positions, hidden behind rock walls and low, brush-covered mounds across the river. The distance was greater, affecting accuracy, but the native soldiers had shelter from attacks from the tower.

"Sahib!" Siriman shouted. "They now endanger Brackenbury, the subadar, and the detachment watching the Northern Gate!"

"What is he saying?" Lugard asked.

Walter explained the dire situation with Lionel Brackenbury.

Lugard nodded. "We must do something."

Walter turned to Siriman. "Come with me. I will speak with Captain Butcher."

Walter raced down the stairs and found Butcher still with the wounded. Walter gave an update from the roof and then requested fifty men to search for Brackenbury. "We need to attack the river encampment."

Butcher would not hear of it. "Fifty men!" he shouted. "That is half my force! I have my orders. Colonel Skene was specific—search for the Yuvraj, secure the compound, and await further orders."

"Then I will see Skene!" Walter said.

"Fine," Butcher said. "Take a shortcut through the Western Gate. While you were upstairs Chatterton pulled off a neat bit of work."

Butcher explained how Lieutenant Chatterton had led a company across the wall at the point selected by Butcher. They started as if to reinforce Butcher at the compound, but then turned south and surprised the guard at the gate. After a short firefight, the British had captured the gate and held the entire outer ring of Kangla.

Siriman arrived carrying Karna. He laid the body in the line of dead soldiers, stood and stared in silence. Walter touched Siriman's shoulder. "Come—we will see Skene."

It was eight o'clock by the time Walter and Siriman reached the staging field and found Colonel Skene and Frank Grimwood with the reserves. Skene listened and approved Walter's plan. He ordered Havildar Dhap Chund to assemble fifty fresh men with an extravagant allotment of sixty rounds per man. As the force gathered, Walter patted his shirt. The comforting hard lump meant the dragon figurine was still there, safe in his pocket.

It feels so warm. Is it my imagination or is it tingling?

He looked toward the Residency.

Should I take time, return the idol to Ethel?

He took a step toward the gate but stopped, reaching to touch the comforting tingle.

It can wait. Brackenbury first. Ethel will have it soon—if I can stay alive, that is.

Chapter 55. The Last Line of Defense

Earlier that morning...

Ethel

Ethel closed her eyes, but could not sleep, so she did something she had not done for longer than she could remember—she prayed. When it seemed as if she had prayed the entire night, she woke with a start.

I have been dreaming! It is three o'clock!

She gave Frank a gentle shake and so began the day of destiny.

Ethel dressed, shivering in the dark and bitter cold, pulling on tighter-fitting winter wear. She hurried to the kitchen to find the bearer and khidmutgar up and waiting. The three renewed their assault on the stoves, pans, and larder. They brewed tea, set out loaves of near-stale bread, and boiled four dozen eggs. At half past three, officers trickled in from bivouac.

Ethel pointed to the counter. "There are eggs and bread, Gentlemen—tea is here. We all must fend for ourselves today."

A few officers sat at the table, others stood while eating, and the rest stuffed pockets and proceeded to the campground. Ethel heard Frank's voice and turned.

"Where are you going?" she said, voice cracking with dismay

Frank stood in the doorway, a holster strapped to his waist, a pistol on his hip.

"I thought you would stay with me," she implored, "a safe distance from camp."

"Not this day," he said. "After a quick bite, I must join Skene with the reserves."

Frank gobbled his food, kissed Ethel and left. By four o'clock, all the officers had reached the bivouac area. Ethel peered from the verandah—movement was visible in the moonlight, but all was silent, save the occasional creak of leather or crunch of gravel beneath a boot.

The mission should start any moment. So many active men—quiet as mice!

The detachments left the compound, collecting in a staging field north of the mud wall for final instructions. The soldiers would attack on foot, so the few remaining stable hands kept the officers' horses stabled and quiet.

A familiar voice said, "Missus Grimwood, would you care to join Mister Cossins and me at the telegraph office? The action is about to begin."

"Oh, yes!" Ethel said without hesitation.

She followed Quinton and Cossins to join Rassik, their acting babu, at the end of the lane where twin two-story structures framed the gateway to the compound.

Sturdy stonewalls should keep us safe!

Quinton and Cossins collaborated on a dispatch detailing events leading to the decision to attack, and the babu transmitted the message to the Raj. Amid the clicking sounds from the telegraph, the unmistakable crack, crack, crack of gunfire came from Kangla's direction.

Ethel's ears perked. "What is happening?"

Quinton glanced at the window and muttered, "It begins." He showed scant interest and turned back to watch the babu work the needles and dials of the telegraph device.

"It is first light!" Ethel said, running to the window. "Daybreak is almost upon us. At least it looks to be a fine, clear day for our men."

Quinton kept his eyes on the telegraph. "My dear woman, I would stand back from that window if I were you."

Ethel turned away and an instant later, the window shattered. At the opposite wall, plaster fragments exploded and a tiny dust cloud settled to the floor. Ethel shrieked, hands covering face, and dropped to the floor. She crawled and huddled beneath a desk, stammering, "Should—we—flee? To—somewhere safer?"

Quinton continued his work with the babu, seeming unconcerned. "Not—quite—yet. We are half way through the transmission. It is quite a missive."

Ethel trembled and said, "I never imagined!"

"Imagined what?"

"They shot at us—here! The Yuvraj's palace is so far away."

Quinton chuckled. "It was not personal, Missus—it was just a stray—could even be one of ours. Best to avoid windows facing the fort. Perhaps below you would feel safer."

Ethel crawled from beneath the desk and scurried to the stairway. She crouched and scooted down the steps to the dank basement and hid behind stacks of wooden crates. She sat on a box, shivering in the cold, and kept an ear cocked. Muffled voices filtered down the stairs.

Quinton is talking to Cossins.

The door banged shut and thirty minutes later, Cossins returned. Ethel mustered courage and poked her head up from the stairwell to listen closer.

"I made out nothing!" Cossins said.

Ethel listened further to piece together the story.

Cossins ran to my house!

Quinton's assistant had risked the bullets by running back to her house, climbing onto the roof, and trying to catch action from that vantage. Ethel had thought the slight man bookish—like a schoolteacher or librarian—someone best suited to push paper or run Quinton's errands. Her opinion of the man moved up several notches.

I could never manage that! The man is braver and more resourceful than I imagined!

The next several hours were torturous. After an hour alone in the basement, Ethel mustered the courage to rejoin the men upstairs where Rassik had just finished sending the long missive.

"Message sent?" she asked.

Quinton nodded.

"What happens now?"

"We wait for a reply."

Ethel grew braver and crawled back to the window to peep through the broken glass. A barrage of bullets passed high above the roof and Ethel watched Gurkha sentries rush out the gate.

Poor things—they are such fighters they cannot help themselves. So eager to wade into the fray.

Quinton rummaged drawers as if hunting something. "Ah! Here!" He handed Ethel a pair of field glasses. "Those may help."

Ethel raised the glasses and peered. Seconds later she said, "Something is on fire!"

Smoke rose from the far side of Kangla near the Yuvraj's compound. Officers came and went at the staging field and another wave of soldiers ran up the road to join the action. The clock on the wall struck eight o'clock.

"I see Lieutenant Simpson returning from the front!" she said.

I hope he visits!

Instead, Simpson soon returned to the fort with a troop of fresh soldiers and orderlies carrying doolies.

"Doctor Calvert is going back with him!"

Calvert, orderlies, and doolies! Doolies—litters to carry the wounded. Wounded!

A vision unfolded, and she blanched, struck by the implications. Gunfire meant bullets; bullets meant wounded; wounded meant blood; and blood meant loss of life or limb.

It is real—war is happening!

Embarrassment swept over Ethel like a battering wave. She swallowed hard and despaired, thinking of her place in the vast scheme. Men were fighting and dying while she crouched and hid. She resolved to help—not to keep safe, stay out of the way, and avoid being a bother.

I swear, when the time comes, I will pitch in and help the doctor in any way I can.

Nine o'clock came and Ethel squinted through the glasses, recognizing two officers arriving at the staging camp.

"Lugard and Woods are reporting to Skene. I hope they bring good news!"

A boom erupted, and the glass rattled.

"Bloody hell!" Quinton cursed. "Now what?"

"I know that sound," Ethel said. "Prince Tikendra Jeet just fired a seven-pounder."

"You can tell?"

"Oh, yes," Ethel said, nodding. "I watched him many times at his favorite hobby. He is outstanding at gunnery."

"Well, confound it!" Quinton said. "If true, that means the scoundrel is free. I wager he was not at home when our boys raided his compound. Ha! Too ill to attend a durbar, but not too ill to fire artillery. A miraculous cure!"

Ten o'clock came and minutes later, when Frank appeared at the door, Ethel's heart leapt.

I hope he brings good news and will stay.

"In a rush!" Frank said. "Must tap my ammunition store—the troops need my cache of Snider-Enfield rounds."

Ethel's eyes widened with hope, and she clasped her hands. "Then—will you stay?"

"No time—must rejoin Skene!"

Her face fell. "What news from the battle?"

Frank shook his head and sighed. "Good news—and not so good. The Yuvraj's compound, temple, and the Northern Gate are secure. Chatterton now holds the Western Gate."

"Wonderful," Ethel said. "What is the bad news?"

"Tikendra Jeet was not home when they called and now he is firing at the tower. Skene has the bit between his teeth and wants to storm the inner citadel. We will take scaling ladders to the front."

"Ladders?" Ethel said. "Where did you find those?"

"Bamboo—Gurkhas rigged them overnight—Skene's idea."

"Are the officers all right?"

Frank bit his lip and shook his head. "Brackenbury is missing."

Ethel gasped, and a hand covered her mouth.

"What do you mean missing?" Quinton said.

"No one knows what happened—stories conflict. Lionel took wounds—that is certain—and now he is missing."

Ethel's chin quivered and her eyes filled with tears. "Is anyone searching?"

"Try not to worry," Frank said. "He will turn up soon. I must go."

Frank stomped down two flights to the cellar and returned to ground level carrying a wooden box. As he turned, writing on the box's side read:

```
BOXER AMMUNITION
FOR '577 BORE
SNIDER RIFLES
CARTRIDGES 500
```

I hid behind boxes of ammunition!

Four kahars waited outside with two doolies. Frank loaded the box on one litter and led the kahars back down for more. They carried up five more boxes and loaded three crates on each doolie. With that, the party trotted back through the gate to rejoin Skene at the staging field.

Quinton checked with Rassik at the telegraph. "Any reply?"

"No, sahib," the babu said. "Nothing."

Minutes crawled by but still no reply was forthcoming. "Try sending again," Quinton said.

Rassik fiddled with the dials. "Telegraph not working, sahib. Maybe wires cut!"

"Blast!" Quinton shouted. "Let me have a look!" Quinton tried, but neither man could make the needles move.

"Did the Manipuris cut the wires?" Ethel asked.

"We can count on it."

"Where? Can anyone repair it?"

"No way to tell. There are twelve miles of wire from here to Sengmai. The cut could be anywhere."

Sengmai! William Melville is at Sengmai!

The noon hour approached, and the telegraph was still not working.

"We should return to the house," Ethel said. "Have lunch."

"I am not sure…," Quinton began.

"We have tea, and leftover fowl. We can make sandwiches for ourselves and the officers."

"Well…," Quinton rubbed his neck. "All right, but first…"

He jotted a short message and ordered Rassik to keep trying—in case the telegraph returned. Then Ethel, Quinton, and Cossins scurried back to the house. Quinton entered with Ethel but Cossins made another ascent to the roof, hoping for better luck spying with the field glasses.

Ethel went to her dressing chamber first and doffed her winter gown. She chose a looser fitting, blue serge skirt with deep pockets, and then added a white silk blouse and patent leather slippers.

The morning chill passed but, if required to work chores of a servant, I will do so in a more comfortable costume—better suited to household work.

Quinton made no comment about her change of dress and, a short while thereafter, while cutting sandwiches, Ethel heard a tinkle and sensed—something.

Is Quinton staring at me?

She turned, smiling, but Quinton was in the durbar hall, gazing out a window toward the action.

I wonder if the officers are coming. I must see.

Ethel approached the window and felt a crunch under her shoe.

Broken glass!

She studied the wall opposite the window and found two bullet holes in the plaster.

"My house!" she cried. "They shot my house! Bullets came all this way!"

"Afraid so, Missus," Quinton said. "The action grows hotter out there."

Ethel hurried to the dining room, looking for more damage, and halted, exclaiming, "Whatever are you doing?"

In a corner, the two remaining maidservants sat on the floor before three statues. A woman hid face behind clasped hands. "Praying, Memsahib—to Ganesha, the goddess, and Lord Krishna!"

Ethel reddened and her cheeks grew hot.

Praying. Worshiping—my decorations.

Statues—things Ethel regarded as quaint works of native art livening her home—were sacred objects, the focus of worship by frightened servants.

"Please," Ethel said, choking back tears, "pray for us all!"

While returning to the kitchen, Ethel passed a bookcase. A book's spline caught her eye, and she snatched it from the shelf, smiling.

The Princess and the Goblin. I received this as a child.

Ethel had carted the book everywhere.

Ages since I thought of it. Reading may help pass the time until I can help the doctor.

At half-past-twelve, Ethel and the bearer set out fresh sandwiches and flasks of tea, hoping officers would return for a meal. She then followed Quinton and Cossins back to the telegraph office.

"No luck, sahib," Rassik reported.

While Quinton joined and fiddled with the device, Ethel sat in a corner to read. She thumbed through the book, stopping here and there, looking at the illustrations, and smiling at certain passages.

Nanny read this aloud—so many years ago!

She stopped at a well-worn, dog-eared page—eye captured by an underlincd passage.

It is when people do wrong things willfully that
they are the more likely to do them again.

Male voices interrupted her contemplation. The door opened and in walked Frank, Skene, Boileau, Lugard, and Woods. They looked tired, dirty, and somber. A war conference commenced, with scant good news reported. Simpson, Gurdon, and Calvert still looked for Brackenbury. Butcher held the Yuvraj's compound and Chatterton held the Western Gate, but they faced a stalemate. The day was passing fast, ammunition was running low, and the chances of capturing Tikendra Jeet were dwindling.

"If the battle lasts much longer," Boileau said, "the tide will turn. The Manipuris will gain the upper hand."

Ethel took Frank aside, asking, "What news of Lionel?"

Frank shook his head and frowned. "No word on Brackenbury—Walter is in the thick, searching. He is clearing the jungle past the river."

The officers look so tired and famished.

"You should eat," Ethel said. "Convince the others. There is food back at the house."

Frank agreed, spoke to the officers, and Ethel led the men to the house to serve lunch. As he ate, Frank suggested, "A servant could wrap lunches for me to take to Butcher and Chatterton."

"You mean me?" Ethel said. "No help remains so I will see to it."

She stepped into the anti-room to make the sandwiches. As she sliced the bread, a window near her head shattered and a hail of bullets hit the opposite wall. She screamed and dropped to the floor. Men shouted and dishes crashed. Boots stomped, chairs tumbled, and a door banged.

Heart pounding, Ethel crawled to the kitchen.

Empty! Where are the men?

The backdoor banged again—unlatched and swinging free.

Manipuris are attacking! They have us surrounded and will kill us all!

Ethel panted and whimpered as she crawled to the dining room. She reached a rear window and lifted her nose above the sill.

I am not far off the mark.

Manipuri sepoys climbed the ditch and mud wall behind her house to assail the Residency grounds from the west. A large force used the jungle and nearby Naga village as cover, flanked their position, and crossed the thick brush and a bordering stream. There, the Manipuris struggled, fighting to enter the backyard, hampered by a thorny hedge.

My last line of defense!

Ethel had the hedge planted two years earlier to keep cows away from her garden. She joked to Frank at the time that the hedge was her last line of defense from attack.

No longer a joke! This is life or death!

Gurkhas abandoned the front of the house and eastern wall and raced to defend the rear. Ethel watched in horror as a bloody battle raged. Officers fired pistols, dropping Manipuris raising muskets. Gurkhas used bayonets to impale, and their wicked, curved knives to hack the enemy to pieces. The Gurkhas drove back the Manipuris and recaptured the wall. Bloody bodies and dismembered parts lay tangled in her thorny hedge of last defense. Ethel's ears rang with the screams of dying men.

Please make the screaming stop!

She crouched beneath the window—back to the wall, hugging her knees—then buried her face and sobbed.

"I cannot do it! I cannot keep my promise to help the doctor. So much blood—I cannot bear the sight of death!"

Chapter 56. The Retribution

Continued...

Ethel

Gunfire ceased, screams faded, and then a door creaked.

The kitchen door! Oh, God, please—no!

Footsteps—like heavy boots on hardwood.

Men in the kitchen!

An incomprehensible muddle of deep voices...

British men's voices! Has the worst passed?

One voice rose above the others, saying, "I demand retribution!"

Skene—the colonel is furious!

"Boileau, take all the men you need. Save ammunition—use bayonets, swords, knives, and torches. Burn the bloody village down—burn it all to the ground! Bushes, trees, huts, livestock—anything in your way! I want a clear field of vision so the bloody beggars think twice before attacking our rear!"

"Yes, sir!" Boileau said.

The backdoor slammed. Ethel's head swam and her heart pounded.

Where is Boileau going? Attacking the village!

More muffled sounds from the kitchen—Frank, Skene, and other officers conversing. Ethel tried to move, but her arms and legs froze, and she remained a crouching ball hidden in a corner.

What is Frank saying? Words run together. I must stand!

She strained, trembling—too weak, drowsy, and confused to move.

"Ethel!"

Frank—at the dining room door!

"Frank!" she answered in a hoarse croak.

"There you are!"

Boots clacked, clothing rustled, and Frank knelt at her side.

"Are you hurt?"

Ethel shook her head; face still buried in her knees.

"What is wrong?"

Ethel sobbed, "So much blood—the screams…"

"I am so sorry," Frank said. "They attacked, everyone ran off, and I gave no thought to your safety."

Ethel's eyes lifted, and she gaped at Frank's holstered pistol. Words stuck in her open mouth. Frank took her hand, eased her to her feet, and led her to a seat in the durbar hall. When Ethel's focus drifted to the floor, Frank placed a palm on her forehead.

"Ethel—dear—are you in shock?"

Ethel gazed through Frank as if he was invisible and murmured, "My things."

"Sorry?" Frank shifted, studying the path of her gaze.

Ethel stared at—things, her things—decorative household possessions. Beautiful things lying broken, smashed, and scattered—casualties of bullets shot through windows during the attack.

"Our paintings—that beautiful vase—it was a wedding gift, a favorite of mine, now broken…"

"Never mind."

"Your photographs…"

"Ethel! Stop!"

She looked up startled, eyelids fluttering, and shook her head. "I am sorry—they are—things. Our safety is paramount, but then…"

Ethel stood, drifted to a wall, lifted a painting, and stood it against the wall on the floor. She did likewise with a photograph and knickknacks on shelves, arranging them on the floor as if preparing to pack.

"I should move them somewhere safer—is there a place?" She set a statue near the stack and then reached for another. "I fear nowhere safe exists anymore."

"Dear…" Frank took her hand. "Forget these things. Perhaps you should retreat to the cellar. You would be safer there."

Ethel shook her head. "I cannot keep hiding in cellars."

"I could make a snug nest in a corner." He winked, cocked his head, and grinned. "Stone walls all around—very secure—no bullets to dodge."

"No. I promised myself I would help the doctor." She bit her lip and nodded. "I will keep that promise—when he returns."

"Are you in any condition…?"

"I will be fine." She put hands to cheeks and sighed. "I need a minute."

"We can move the hospital to the cellar."

Ethel cracked a wide smile. "Then we each could have our way."

Frank laughed. "Now you are feeling better!"

With Frank's help, Ethel scoured nearby rooms for valuable items to move, finding every window had taken a bullet.

It will only worsen.

Ethel held up a vase and shook her head. "I packed these things two weeks ago."

"We should have sent the crates ahead, instead of unpacking," Frank said.

"Then Tikendra Jeet would not believe I was staying."

"I wonder—would that matter now?"

"Frank," Ethel asked, "tell the truth—have we hope? Can we win?"

"Win?" Frank answered, "Hum—difficult question. Boileau clears the Naga village while Walter searches for Lionel. Butcher holds the Yuvraj's compound, including the tower, and Chatterton holds the Western Gate. We control the outer ring of Kangla, but cannot attack the inner citadel."

"Why not?"

"Skene decided after assessing matters from atop the tower. Manipuris raised the drawbridge and shut the inner citadel gate. The inner moat is wet, too deep to cross without swimming."

"What of the scaling ladders?"

"Skene had the Gurkhas erect a bamboo bridge over the moat, but that effort failed. He considered storming the walls, but it would be suicidal— the Manipuris are poor shots, but any fool with a musket becomes a marksman at point-blank range. They outnumber us—we cannot afford serious casualties."

"Mister Quinton and I heard cannon fire. I said it sounded like Tikendra Jeet."

"You were right," Frank said. "He fired at the tower after we put snipers on the roof."

"What? No! His family's temple—priceless artifacts."

My dragon figurine may be back in place!

"The building is brick—thick and solid—the seven pounder did little damage. In summary, to answer your question—no, we cannot win. We have a stalemate, but ammunition dwindles. They outnumber us and soon will out-gun us, too."

Ethel set the vase down and folded her hands. "So, what to do?"

"I wish I had the answer. This was an ill-considered venture. I regret speaking in favor of attacking."

"You were dead set against the arrest, but favored action after returning from the palace. What changed?"

Frank paced, fists clenched. "My temper clouded my judgment."

"What do you mean?"

"I wish you had told me."

"Told you what?"

"About Tikendra Jeet and his marriage scheme."

Ethel gasped, wide-eyed and hands flew to cheeks. "How did..." She stopped and smirked. "Walter!"

"He had to tell me—Nagas and Kukis would assassinate me and carry you off to wed Tikendra Jeet." Frank gave Ethel details of the confession by the natives.

Ethel held her forehead, heart racing.

Why did I say I would answer later? I should have slapped him and left, or let Sunwar shoot him!

"I see...," she muttered. "You wanted revenge because of my weakness."

"No!" Frank shook his head. "For what Tikendra Jeet did to you. We had to act—it was him or us."

"Then why have regrets?"

Frank tossed his hands. "I fell for his trap—Tikendra Jeet fooled us— he was never ill, and I guessed wrong where he would be. It was too risky— we were fools chancing it. We should have packed up and left. Instead, we picked a fight we cannot finish—too few men, too little ammunition—a disaster."

Ethel fell into Frank's arms. "What happens now? Can we get out of this alive?"

Frank shrugged. "Ammunition supply exhausts soon. We must seek a truce, or surrender—just a matter of time."

"No!"

"If we surrender, Tikendra Jeet will not harm you."

"You would not give me over to him!"

"Not while I live," Frank said. "I must corner Quinton and Skene— time we chatted."

Frank left to find Quinton, and Ethel sat alone, sobbing.

I thought meeting Tikendra Jeet would help! Instead, my actions brought disaster!

Ethel slumped, stunned by distant sounds of Boileau's counterattack—cracks of gunfire, cries, shouts, wails of animals, and bitter shrieks of dying men. A half hour passed in a wink and Frank returned.

He looks somber—the news is not good.

"What did they say?"

"We wait."

"Wait for what?"

Frank sat next to Ethel and took her hands. "Quinton sent word of the sneak attack to Butcher. We have done all we can inside Kangla, and Tikendra Jeet remains free as ever. Quinton will order forces fall back and defend the Residency."

"Then what? Can we hold out here?"

"Perhaps," Frank said. "Skene and I have similar thoughts. We spoke moments ago—he let slip critical pieces of information. He agrees we must admit defeat and retreat, but he has a trick up his sleeve."

"Tell me!"

"Skene sensed something rotten from the start. The Raj used weak pretenses to justify arresting Tikendra Jeet; the threat to cashier Quinton for failure was criminal. A force of five hundred Gurkhas seemed designed to stoke Manipuri fears. With no field guns, limiting ammunition made it certain the expedition could not defend itself. It reeked of sabotage or total incompetence."

"You describe an evil conspiracy," Ethel said.

"Politics most evil is at play. Someone wants Skene's men defeated so England will declare war and seek revenge. Someone wants to add Manipur to the empire, but first needs a good excuse."

"Who could be so diabolical?"

"Whoever they are, they did not take Skene into account. Orders limited ammunition to forty rounds per man but said nothing of the rifle model. When Walter sent word of my cache of Snider-Enfield cartridges, Skene switched from Martini-Henry rifles to Sniders, doubling the available rounds."

"No one was the wiser?"

"No, but it gets better. Orders mandated four hundred Gurkhas march from Kohima, but said nothing of reinforcements. In secret, Skene ordered a relief column from Cachar—a standard procedure within his discretion, requiring no permission."

"What are you saying?" Ethel asked, eyebrows raising. "A rescue force is on the way?"

"Correct!" Frank said. "Even as we speak, two hundred Gurkhas from the 43rd Regiment, led by Captain Cowley, are marching from Cachar! With plenty of ammunition for both Snider-Enfield and Martini-Henry rifles—and they have field guns!"

Ethel clapped and her face lit. "Wonderful! When do they arrive?"

Frank grinned. "With luck—in two days."

"Two days?" Ethel gasped. "Can they not hurry?"

"They know nothing of our predicament."

"Can we not send word?"

"The telegraph is out," Frank said, "but regardless, no stations along their route. I suppose we could send messengers on horseback and hope one makes it."

"Can we hold out two days?"

"Uncertain, but I have doubts. This is why Skene and I argued for retreat. There is a hill two miles west, halfway between the Cachar and Kohima roads—you know the one."

Where Walter and I had our picnic.

"If we reach the top," Frank continued, "we can defend it for days, and Cowley's arrival will shock the hell out of the Manipuris."

"Wonderful!" Ethel laughed and clapped. "I am ready. When do we leave?"

Frank shook his head and frowned. "Quinton would not hear of it."

"Why not?"

"More politics!" Frank spat the word as if he tasted sour milk. "Quinton believes abandoning the Residency would admit defeat and show failure on his part. He still hopes for a diplomatic solution."

"He sounds more worried for his career than our lives."

Frank shook his head. "I allege nothing like that, but he was firm. For now, to survive, we have to marshal our forces, conserve our remaining ammunition, hunker, and hope for the best."

The clock struck three, and a commotion erupted at the rear of the house. Frank left to investigate, and Ethel crept behind to eavesdrop from the dining room. Boileau had returned unharmed from his mission of retribution against the Naga village.

He looks dejected.

"The good news is," Boileau reported, "my men drove off the attack party—five hundred Manipuris. We destroyed the village, burned huts and brush far past the stream. We will have a clear field of vision to our rear. Further sneak attacks from that direction will be difficult."

"What is the bad news?" Skene asked.

"I did not manage things well," Boileau said, looking at his boots. "I lost control of the Gurkhas. After a stray shot hit one, the rest fired without discriminating. There were civilian casualties—too many, I fear."

Ethel returned to the durbar hall, stomach churning, tears filling her eyes.

Retribution! So horrible!

Frank arrived moments later, despondent and cursing. "Another bloody disaster!"

"How can England and Manipur sort out this mess? How can they have relations again?"

A bugle call sounded.

"What is that?" Ethel asked.

"Quinton's orders—the bugler blows recall."

Part VII. The Prophecy

"It was about two in the morning that we left the Residency, and we marched steadily on until daybreak. We had not gone four miles away from the station, when I turned to look back, and found the whole sky for miles round lit with a red glow…"

From *My Three Years in Manipur and Escape from the Recent Mutiny*
(1891)
By Ethel St. Clair Grimwood

Dramatis personæ

In order of appearance, (*denotes a fictional character)

1891 Manipur

Lieutenant Walter Simpson	Bengal infantry, 43rd Gurkha Rifles, 31
Siriman Sunwar*	Naik (corporal), 44th Gurkha Rifles, 20
Doctor J.T. Calvert	Medical officer and surgeon, 42nd GR, 27
Lieutenant Edward J. Lugard	D.S.O. (1890), 42nd Gurkha Rifles, 26
Dhap Chund	Havildar (sergeant), 44th Gurkha Rifles, 35
Singhia Lama	Naik (corporal), 42nd Gurkha Rifles, 28
Jaimani Thapa	Sepoy (private), 42nd Gurkha Rifles, 22
Frank Saint Clair Grimwood	British political agent to Manipur, 37
Ethel Saint Clair Grimwood	Frank's wife, 24
Captain G.H. Butcher	Senior officer, 42nd Gurkha Rifles, 41
Lt. Lionel Brackenbury	44th Gurkha Rifles, banjo player, 23
Haribans Tiwari	Calvert's medical assistant, 42nd GR
Colonel Charles M. Skene	Expedition commander, 42nd GR, 47
James Wallace Quinton	Chief Commissioner, Assam, 57
Rassik Lal Kundu	Head chuprassy (messenger), 40
William Henry Cossins	Assistant to Chief Commissioner, 27
Bearer	Major-domo at British Residency, 50
Captain Thomas S. Boileau	Senior officer, 44th Gurkha Rifles, 40
Gunna Ram	Bugler, 44th Gurkha Rifles, 23
Tongol General	Senior military leader, king's protector, 74
Yenkhoiba Major Rudra Singh	Lalupchingba, officer over the irregulars, 35
Pukhramba "Kajao" Phingang	Jamadar (lieutenant) Manipuri regulars, 36
Leishna (name fictionalized)	Tongol's daughter, Walter's consort, 19
Young Maiba*	Vaishnavist priest, Sanamahist shaman, 49
Angom Ningthou Girid Singh	Chieftain of the Angom tribe, 40
Mongjam	Tongol General's valet, 20
Moonia	Ethel's former ayah (personal maid), 60

1891 Peru

Siriman Sunwar*	Brevet Havildar (sergeant), 44th GR, 20
Zoluti	Angelic blonde woman in white, 25
Bahadur Thapa*	Naik, 44th Gurkha Rifles, 22

Chapter 57. The Rescue

Earlier that morning, 8:00 a.m., Tuesday, 24 March 1891...

Walter

Skene sent Lieutenant Lugard and Doctor Calvert, the company surgeon, with Walter's rescue party. Calvert brought four kahars with two doolies—for Lieutenant Lionel Brackenbury and Subadar Heema Chund. The detachment left camp and, with the convenient shortcut of the captured Western Gate, soon reached the temple. Calvert stopped to administer opium to the worst of the wounded and, having done all he could, rejoined Walter. The soldiers moved forward through the arched gates on the east side of the Yuvraj's compound.

Siriman pointed. "Ahead, sahib—over there! By the bank!"

"You are certain?" Walter asked.

"Yes, sahib! That is where Sahib Brackenbury fell."

The party crept forward with heads low, mindful of shots from across the river, and reached the crest of the bank. Walter and Siriman dropped, inched forward, and peered through the low brush.

Walter studied the lay left, right, and to the river. "So, where is he?"

"This is the place, sahib. He must be here somewhere."

Shots cracked, bullets struck the bank a few yards in front, and Walter pulled back.

Siriman held his ground and continued inspecting the location. "Sahib! I see a trail through the foliage. Sahib Brackenbury dragged himself south to escape."

"Is he lost?" Walter said, shaking his head. "Why go south?"

"North, south—danger everywhere, sahib. Residency closer going south."

Walter inched forward to inspect the trail, but shots hit the bank, and both men pulled back. Walter crawled to Lugard to discuss the situation.

"We cannot conduct a proper rescue with Manipuris firing at us," Walter said. "Take Calvert and twelve men north—find the subadar. The rest of us will cross the river and clean the bloody jungle."

Siriman spoke, "Sahib! May I go south to search for Sahib Brackenbury?"

Walter considered, smiled, and nodded. "Do it! Wait until we cross the river, then stay low—do not be a target." He patted Siriman's arm. "Good luck."

Walter waved the company forward, drew his pistol, and led the charge, splashing across the rocky ford. He chanced a glance to see Lugard and company moving north under heavy fire. Seconds later Walter reached the far bank, stormed a mound, and shot two Manipuris. The Nepali soldiers screamed a battle cry and ran headlong into the enemy fire.

"Ayo Gorkhali! (The Gurkhas are upon you!)"

Nervous Manipuris fired wild shots, and before they reloaded, bayonets and kukris struck. The natives scattered into the jungle, leaving behind dead and wounded. Brave souls stood and fought hand-to-hand, wielding dao knives. They paid with their lives, but bought their comrades precious seconds to stop and reload. A salvo of musket fire killed a Gurkha and wounded three.

Now is the time!

"Fire at will!" Walter shouted.

He unleashed his company of killing machines, and a half-hour-long firefight ensued. Gurkhas shattered the Manipuri formation and the remaining natives fled deeper into the jungle—dead and dying lay scattered amongst the thick brush.

"Drive them south!" Walter ordered.

Half his force chased the Manipuris as he led the rest to gather dead and wounded comrades, re-cross the ford, and rendezvous with Lugard. Walter found the lieutenant and Doctor Calvert on the west bank kneeling beside two unconscious bodies—Gurkhas from Brackenbury's detachment—a havildar and the old subadar, Heema Chund.

Thank God! They found the old soldier!

Calvert finished dressing a wound. "I have done all I can. Amazing—the old subadar took four bullets, but is still alive."

Kahars lifted the wounded onto doolies and hurried for the temple.

"There go brave men!" Lugard said, pointing at the sprinting kahars. "I have never seen such fearlessness. They carry those litters through musket fire as if bullets were raindrops."

"Where are the rest?" Walter said. "Brackenbury's detachment had thirty guarding the north gate."

"We found a few dead," Lugard replied. "The balance is missing. The brush provided no cover once the sun rose. Without ammunition, it was impossible to hold this position. Pray they make it back to camp."

"I am giving you more men," Walter said.

"Why?"

"Take care of the dead and wounded, then take Calvert and locate survivors."

"What of you?"

Walter looked at the jungle—gunfire echoed. "More cleanup work here—most will cross and clean the east bank. I will comb the west bank for Brackenbury—follow the trail south."

Lugard smiled. "Do not die a hero. And do *not* make us send a detachment for *you*."

Walter laughed. "Do not do that! Not under any circumstances."

Lugard and Calvert led their party west toward Butcher's temple infirmary. Walter selected three trusted Gurkhas—Sepoy Thapa, Naik Lama, and Havildar Chund—and sent the others across the ford to rejoin the jungle fight. He gave instructions to drive the Manipuris into the jungle and then rendezvous along the river further south.

Walter and his three Gurkhas followed the west bank under heavy musket fire from the eastern wall of the citadel. As they took cover beneath the scrawny brush of the riverbank, there came a distant boom.

Cannon fire! A seven-pounder—at the fort.

Walter counted, listening for the telltale whine of a falling missile.

Not shooting at us!

The cannon continued its steady firing but at a safe distance from the rescue party.

Tikendra Jeet is firing his guns—but at what target?

Walter found more signs—a second trail of scuffs and bruised vegetation. "Sunwar followed Brackenbury's trail."

Minutes dragged as sporadic rifle fire from the battlement on their right flank limited forward progress to brief intervals. Walter wiped sweat, grew frustrated, and cursed, "It will take us bloody hours at this rate!"

We will find Brackenbury, but too late!

Slow progress continued along the bank, and then the havildar pointed. Forty yards ahead, under cover of a thicket, a lone Gurkha crouched beside a man in British uniform.

Pinned down, but—good man, Sunwar—you found Brackenbury!

Walter checked the sun.

The afternoon is slipping away.

Sunlight flashed from the twin domes of the Shri Govindajee Temple inside the fortress wall.

We followed the trail the entire river loop.

The rescue party had made a clockwise circuit along the river, past the royal palace, almost to the southern side of the citadel.

How did Brackenbury ever crawl so far?

Ahead lay forty yards of open space, then another exposed forty yards to the road between the southern walls. The bank spread wide and flat down to a shallow river ford. The brush had thinned—sparse except for a thicket in the middle. Lionel and Siriman occupied the single point of cover in eighty yards. Erratic musket fire struck sand and gravel near their position.

So close—but how do we reach them?

Then—musket fire cracked—and more bullets struck close. Across the river, Manipuris emerged from the jungle to attack their rear.

Siriman shouted over the musket fire. "Sahib Simpson! I made a litter from bamboo—for Sahib Brackenbury!"

"Brilliant," Walter shouted in answer, "but we are easy targets and would not get far."

A long moment later, Siriman answered. "Have you any rope?"

Walter looked at the havildar. The Gurkhas slipped off packs and rummaged, each producing a coil.

Walter shouted back. "Fifty yards total—what do we do?"

"Sahib," Naik Lama said, "Thapa and I can do this."

Lama knotted the coils into a single line, and then he and Thapa rose, scurried forward ten yards, and dropped, lying prone as shots struck the ground. They rose, scrambled another ten yards, and dropped again. In this manner, they covered the forty yards to Siriman and Lionel unharmed.

Siriman tied the rope to Brackenbury's litter. Lama and Thapa took the other end and ran, repeating the evasive maneuver. They dodged bullets and advanced in stages until they reached the shelter of brush and boulders near the road. The Gurkhas waited out the salvo, and then reeled in the line, pulling together, dragging Brackenbury's litter across sand and gravel. Erratic musket fire chased the litter the entire distance.

Walter's cheer froze in his throat as loud cries turned his head. Manipuris surged into the river, firing as they crossed.

This is the end!

Walter checked his revolver—the cylinder chambers were full. He planted his back against the bank and took aim. The havildar raised his rifle and Walter signaled to wait.

At least we will take a few Manipuris with us.

Walter watched the eyes of the lead soldier, struggling through the rushing water, leveled the barrel, and, as he prepared to squeeze the trigger, a shot rang. The sepoy dropped into the foam and surfaced downstream, face down, carried over the rocks by the rushing current. The other attackers paused.

"Ayo Gorkhali!"

Gurkhas burst from the jungle and attacked the Manipuris from the rear.

My company—rendezvousing as ordered!

Walter's smile vanished when half of the Manipuris returned fire at the Gurkhas and the rest charged forward across the river. He settled back, raised his pistol again, picked a new target, and prepared to squeeze.

"Hold on, Simpson!" a voice shouted. "We are coming!"

Shots cracked and the lead Manipuris staggered and dropped into the waves. Walter lowered his pistol and looked toward the road.

Lugard and Calvert!

The British officers hurried up the road leading a host of riflemen. Gurkhas knelt, aimed, and opened fire, attacking from two sides. The withering fire caught the Manipuris mid-river. The survivors swam to deeper water and escaped downstream, carried by the rapids.

"Now—run!" Walter shouted, and he and the havildar sprinted for the road, collecting Siriman on the way.

An abandoned bustee stretched from the road to the citadel wall and the joint company found shelter behind mud huts. Gurkhas took Brackenbury's litter and scurried away, bearing the wounded officer to the temple infirmary.

Walter inspected Lugard's company. "Where did you find these reinforcements?"

"They arrived from Sengmai. I left twenty men there, and Melville sent them ahead when the Manipuris cut the telegraph wires."

Walter shook Siriman's hand. "You showed bravery back there—rescuing the lieutenant. You can follow Lugard back to the tower—or you can stay with me."

Siriman grinned. "Stay with you, sahib."

"Why? Safer at the temple."

Siriman eyed the bulge in Walter's shirt pocket. Walter reached and patted the object. "Do not trust me to stay alive?"

"Sunwar trusts, sahib, but does not take chances."

Walter smiled and said, "Come on then—make sure the memsahib gets her precious figurine."

Lugard took six Gurkhas and returned to the temple, leaving the twenty from Sengmai with Walter and Calvert. The officers assembled a company of forty rifles and organized forays searching for the missing men from Brackenbury's detachment. They searched the jungle, locating a dozen men alive and many bodies. After two hours of searching, a bugle call issued from the Residency.

"Is that recall?" Calvert asked.

"Yes," Walter said. "We have to fall back!"

Fifty exhausted soldiers trudged out of the jungle bearing dead and wounded. They crossed the river, dodged sporadic shots from the battlements, and followed the road to the Southern Gate.

"Which route is safest?" Calvert asked.

Walter nodded south. "Ahead to the Southern Gate, then we turn west and follow the road straight to the Residency."

Walter patted his breast pocket.

The little dragon survived the day's action.

The company proceeded toward the gate. Ahead, abutting the wall to the right of the road stood a ramshackle bustee. A crowd gathered, blocking their way—unarmed Manipuris and a smattering of Naga and Kuki tribespeople. Old men glared. Women stood holding babies, children at their side.

"They do not look happy," Calvert said.

"Small wonder after today."

Walter addressed the crowd in Meitei. "Stand back—let us pass and we harm no one."

The mob remained silent, and no one moved. Flies buzzed, and a baby cried.

"What do they want?"

"I hope they will clear out and let us pass," Walter said. "Gurkhas have been high strung all day. Anything could set them on fire."

A shot rang out, appearing to come from the crowd. Before Walter could utter a command, the Gurkhas sprang upon the villagers, firing, stabbing, and hacking. The crowd screamed and panicked, trampling children and elderly in the confusion.

"Stop!" Walter screamed. "Cease firing! Stand down, damn you!" He waded forward, trying to pull his men back. He lost his temper and struck a soldier in the face, knocking the man to the ground. "Stop! Stop!" Walter pleaded to no avail. He sank to his knees and sobbed, "Why do you not stop?"

The bloody and battered bodies of men, women, and children lay before him, scattered across the ground and through the tall grass. Walter broke down and wept, devastated by a day of senseless killing he had been powerless to prevent.

Walter's chest burned—as if his shirt's breast pocket was on fire. He opened the flap and dug for the dragon figurine. He winced and yanked his fingers away.

It burns—too hot to touch!

Walter reached again and gripped, flinging the tiny statue aside. He raised scorched fingertips to his mouth. The idol landed in the dirt before Siriman's boots and the Gurkha reached to pick up the object.

"Do not touch it!" Walter cried. "It will burn you!"

Siriman paused, fingers inches away, and stared wide-eyed at Walter. He waited, hand trembling, and then, as Walter gasped, Siriman snatched the idol and stood.

"It is fine, sahib," Siriman said. "Not hot at all—cool."

"Take it then!" Walter shouted as tears streaked his cheeks and he nursed his burned hand. "I do not want it near me! It is evil—evil, I say. It was an evil day when I first set foot in Manipur. I pray to God that I can live with myself after this day. I pray he has mercy on us all."

Chapter 58. The Untenable Position

4:00 p.m., Tuesday, 24 March 1891…

Ethel

Ethel drew the curtain and Frank peered at Butcher's company returning from the tower. Kahars bore wounded on doolies and makeshift bamboo stretchers.

"Heading for the infirmary," Frank said. "Too small to serve as a proper field hospital—it will overflow."

I must keep my promise.

Ethel looked over Frank's shoulder. "We should go—help the wounded."

"Too dangerous—that building is nothing but mud, thatch, plaster, and wattle. The walls will not withstand rifle fire, let alone artillery."

"I must take the chance—I promised myself I would help the doctor. Silly knickknacks should be the last of my worries."

They rushed to the white building near the bivouac area, mindful of random shooting from Kangla. As Ethel entered, her eyes widened at the sight of bandaged and bloodied men.

So many!

"Where is Doctor Calvert?" Ethel asked Butcher.

"With Simpson—searching for survivors. I hope they heard recall."

Ethel inched past stretchers—blood-soaked bandages covered faces, chests, and limbs; groans filled her ears.

Such agony!

She reached the far side and, lying packed alongside a dozen wounded soldiers, found Lieutenant Brackenbury.

"Lionel!" Ethel exclaimed, rushing to her friend's side.

Bandaged head to foot!

"Lucky to be alive," Butcher said. "Six bullets! Simpson found him by the river near the palace—he must have crawled a half-mile."

"Oh, Lionel!" Ethel sobbed. "Look at you—so brave—I am so sorry. Have they given you something for the pain?"

Brackenbury winced and nodded.

"Calvert administered opium," Butcher said, then motioned Ethel and Frank from the infirmary.

"What happened to Lionel?" Ethel asked.

Butcher told an implausible story of Lionel sauntering up to a door, knocking, and asking for Tikendra Jeet.

Frank shook his head. "A brave act, or very foolish."

"We are all in that basket," Ethel added.

A commotion rose from the gate—Chatterton arriving with twenty men.

"There is a strategic mistake," Butcher said.

"Why?" Ethel asked. "Where were they?"

"They guarded the West Gate and kept Tikendra Jeet bottled inside the inner citadel. We abandoned the outer ring—Manipuris will reoccupy the battlements and shoot from closer range."

"What choices have we?" Frank said. "They cannot hold without ammunition."

"We will never know," Butcher replied.

At half past four, Simpson's company reached the gate. Walter and Doctor Calvert returned with fifty Gurkhas bearing bamboo stretchers. The company carried the wounded straight to the infirmary where Ethel and Frank greeted their friend.

"Your party is last to answer recall," Frank said, shaking Walter's hand.

Ethel gave Walter a quick hug. "So relieved to see you!"

Walter wiped his brow. "This is an evil day." He described the dead civilians at the compound that morning and the recent deaths at the bustee as they returned.

Frank told of the attack from the Naga village and Boileau's counterattack.

"Manipur will never forget," Ethel said.

"We will pay a price." Walter motioned a nearby litter bearer forward. "The day is not a total loss. This weary soldier has a surprise for Ethel."

Ethel studied the Gurkha, frowning. "Who is this?"

"Sunwar," Walter said.

I do not recognize him.

"Not the Sunwar you knew," Walter explained. "His cousin."

Ethel smiled. "How nice—where is your cousin?"

"Among our dead," Walter answered.

Ethel gasped, placing hand over heart.

"Before dying," Walter said, "he recovered something and gave it to his cousin to give to you—if you still want it."

Siriman took an object from a breast pocket and extended a palm. There sat the jade-green dragon figurine—wings and emerald eyes glittering, red jewel sparkling. Ethel's eyes lit, and she broke a broad smile.

Against all hope!

She reached for the object and paused. "You said—if I still want it? Why should I not?"

"At risk of sounding unhinged," Walter said, "something is—strange. I carried this—object—all day, but I will not touch it again. The thing has a—strange power. You care for it, I understand, but toss it in the lake while you can."

Have grievous civilian deaths affected his mind?

Ethel studied Walter—set jaw and tight lips. She looked at the smiling Gurkha presenting the idol. She snatched the figurine and thrust it into a dress pocket.

Never out of my possession again! Not even for a moment!

Siriman bowed and backed away.

"Not yet, Sunwar," Walter said. "I am taking you to Colonel Skene. When he hears of your bravery today at the ditch and by the river—well, I am recommending you for immediate promotion. We lost a good havildar today. I trust he will agree you fit the bill."

Walter and Siriman left to find Skene. Frank went to the treasury for more boxes of ammunition. Ethel approached Doctor Calvert and volunteered her help. Calvert accepted and suggested getting straight to work.

Calvert stood Ethel beside Haribans Tiwari, his medical assistant, to watch and, when asked, fetch instruments and supplies. After a few minutes, Calvert let Ethel dress wounds herself. He inspected her efforts, answered questions, and offered encouragement.

Lionel and Subadar Chund had the most bullet wounds but other soldiers had more severe injuries. Ethel trembled, shocked and saddened by the horrific wounds. She mustered strength to withstand the sight of blood and the sounds of the dying.

I am facing my fears!

A wounded Gurkha issued a low groan.

A hoarse voice whispered, "Subadar? Someone—help him!"

"Shush!" Ethel said. "Keep quiet, Lionel!"

Ethel rushed to tend the dying man, but Calvert edged her aside. She stood back, gripping the idol in her pocket, watching in horror as Calvert and Tiwari worked to save the subadar's life. A few minutes later, Calvert pronounced the old soldier dead. Ethel took Lionel's hand and the young officer gripped with surprising strength.

"The subadar," Lionel whispered. "Is he gone?"

Ethel bit her lower lip and blinked back tears. She nodded—but did not cry.

Something is happening—I have grown numb to the sight of blood and death.

"Yes," she murmured. "He was a brave soldier."

"Best soldier I...," Lionel said, coughing. "Best I—will ever know."

"Shush—rest!"

Time passed—twenty minutes, then thirty—as Ethel worked nonstop treating the wounded without further loss of life.

I made myself useful!

Her spirits lifted as if her efforts atoned for her mistake leading on Tikendra Jeet. She found a rhythm to her work, did everything the doctor asked, learned the tools and supplies, and then...

A boom—a sound she knew so well—announced the start of the barrage.

The first blast came a few minutes past five o'clock. An ear-splitting whine followed, and then a shell exploded in treetops near the lake. Ethel reached for the comforting tingle of the smooth jade dragon nestled in her dress pocket.

As Butcher warned, the Manipuris reoccupied the outer ring of Kangla and moved rifles and field artillery to closer battlements. First, the seven-pounders fired, and then a musket battery opened fire from atop the western walls.

Ethel poked her head outside to see puffs of gun smoke at the high walls, followed by a hail of bullets striking her house, riddling the verandah steps. A second volley landed higher, hitting windows and shattering the last of the unbroken glass. Bullets next penetrated the infirmary's mud walls, sending plaster fragments flying across the room. Calvert and Tiwari cleared supply tables and tipped them on end against the wall. The wood splintered but stopped the bullets.

Cannon fire came nonstop, raining shells upon the Residency grounds. A bomb exploded midair above the infirmary and the roof caught fire. A missile fragment whizzed through the thatch, and hot metal grazed Ethel's arm, leaving a long, red streak. She clutched the wound, gritted her teeth, and stifled a scream by stamping her foot and leveling evil looks at the thatch ceiling.

You can endure this pain! You have lived such a charmed life. It hurt far worse when your bear clawed your shoulder!

Calvert and Tiwari had hands full and gave scant notice. Ethel fought back tears and dressed her shrapnel wound. More bullets struck and splinters flew from the makeshift shield of tables.

"We cannot work under these conditions!" Calvert shouted. "We must move the hospital."

"The cellar beneath my house!" Ethel said. "Enough room, and safer!"

Frank was right.

"Let me go," Ethel volunteered. "I can run to the house and make preparations."

"Uncertain that is a wise idea," Calvert said. "The danger…"

More bullets struck the mud wall and another cloud of splinters sprayed from the wooden tables.

"All right," he said, studying the rickety barrier, held together by shards. "You might be safer outside than inside the infirmary."

Ethel prayed as she sprinted for her house. Bullets whistled as she weaved between trees, making a harder target. She stopped and hid behind a tree to catch her breath, and her hand stole to her dress pocket, gripped the little idol, and found comfort in its tingle.

For good luck!

Perhaps her prayers worked, or the dragon's luck was with her, but Ethel reached the backdoor—winded but unscathed—and hurried into the kitchen.

"Help!" she shouted. "We must move the infirmary to the cellar!"

Lieutenant Lugard ran off to organize a company of Gurkhas to carry supplies and help Calvert and Tiwari move the wounded. Next Ethel enlisted help from the bearer and khidmutgar in clearing the stairs, making a safer path to the cellar. They lit lamps and lanterns, and then lifted and stacked boxes, making as much room as possible. Ethel strained, dragging and shifting crates to one side, creating a long, flat table space.

Doctor Calvert soon arrived, with a limping Lugard following, leading a column of soldiers carrying doolies loaded with wounded soldiers and boxes of medical supplies. The company parked the litters and took shelter in the rear of the house. Calvert and Tiwari carried supplies to the cellar and set up the hospital. One by one, the kahars brought down the worst of the wounded. The sole casualty of the move was Lugard who had taken a stray bullet in the leg.

"What irony!" the lieutenant said, laughing off pain as Calvert examined the wound. "Shot at all day at close range—but struck only by chance—a long-distance shot."

Frank returned from the treasury and joined Ethel in a sweep through the upstairs gathering sheets, blankets, and pillows. Ethel set up a stove in the cellar and put water on to boil for sterilizing bandages.

The house shook from a close concussion as a shell exploded above the house. A fiery fragment set the thatch roof aflame and Gurkhas and officers scrambled for buckets, making a line, fetching water from the lake, and dousing the flames. Quinton, Cossins, and Gurdon moved to the basement for safety and soon Frank and Skene followed.

At six o'clock, another close shell rocked the house. Calvert tossed aside a stack of blood-soaked bandages and confronted Quinton.

"Our position is untenable!" the doctor shouted. "We must evacuate!"

"Doctor!" Ethel said. "Shush—think of the wounded."

Calvert glanced at the stretchers and whispered, "Serious wounds need amputation or men die. What is your plan?"

Quinton looked at the row of cots, listened to the groaning wounded, and shook his head. "No decision reached yet," he said. "I will inform you if things change."

At that moment, twin explosions shook the house.

Closer that time!

Men shouted and terrified horses neighed.

"Oh, dear God, no!" Ethel cried. "The stables!"

Frank joined officers sprinting up the stairs and sounds of horror, anguish, and gunfire filtered down to the cellar. Ethel winced, but clenched her teeth.

Focus on your work!

An hour passed with no word and, at last, at seven o'clock, Ethel could stand it no longer. She climbed the stairs to see what she could. Black smoke rose, but from her vantage, she could not see the stables. Outside the backdoor, Frank stood, speaking with Quinton and Skene.

I hope Quinton will now decide.

Ethel returned to the cellar and a few minutes later, looked up to see a grim-faced Frank trudging downstairs.

He is so wan—I fear the worst.

"Gone!" Frank shook his head. "All gone!"

"Not the horses!" Ethel shrieked.

Frank nodded. "Direct hit—most died in the explosion. The fire killed many, and we had to shoot the rest—too burned, legs broken from collapsing walls. Stable hands dead, too—boys—the groom. All destroyed—burned to the ground—a horrible loss."

Ethel burst into tears.

My horse! The young groom!

"When will it end!" she cried.

"Soon—Quinton tossed up the sponge and Skene sent for the bugler. Quinton is calling a truce to discuss surrender."

Chapter 59. The Truce

Minutes earlier, 7:00 p.m., Tuesday, 24 March 1891 ...

Frank

Frank aimed and squeezed the trigger twice, silencing the last two horses. Crippled and maimed animals—his and Ethel's—once beautiful, now dead, killed out of mercy.

They served us well during our time here.

Frank blinked tears, turned his back to the burning ruin of a stable, and joined the party trudging back to the house. The slump-shouldered Englishmen payed scant attention to indiscriminate shots, as if no hope remained.

"Waste of good horses…," Quinton muttered.

"Waste of ammunition," Skene added.

Frank, Quinton, and Skene reached the house and waited until the other officers passed. Frank looked at the rising moon in the red sky. "Beautiful evening—another bright full moon tonight." He spoke without emotion—as if the stable still stood and nothing threatened their lives; as if they could sit at leisure on the verandah, smoke cigars, drink brandy, and engage in idle chitchat.

Ethel stood at the backdoor, bright eyed, biting her lip, as if hoping for good news, but expecting the worst. Frank looked at his boots to hide his face, and when he glanced up, Ethel had vanished. Bombs exploded near the lake, bullets whizzed over the roof, and a full minute passed before anyone spoke.

"Look, Quinton!" Skene spat. "We are in a bloody bad spot! Manipuris surround us—outnumbered ten-to-one. We are out of ammunition while their supply appears limitless. Cowley will be too late—we cannot survive two days under bombardment. I belabor the bloody point, but what more to say?"

"I repeat what I said three hours ago," Frank added. "Retreat west to a tall hill and wait for Cowley. I can lead us to the spot."

Quinton stared at the ground, hands behind his back, as Frank argued points Quinton rejected earlier.

Is he listening?

Quinton shook his head and smacked a fist on palm for emphasis. "We must seek negotiations!" He turned to Skene. "I want a truce—negotiate terms for retreat. How do we signal we wish to parlay?"

"Blow cease-fire," Skene replied. "Manipur holds the upper hand and may ignore us, but unless we try..."

Skene called for the bugler and Quinton sent for Rassik, the head chuprassy, to compose a message. Frank gave Ethel the news and returned upstairs as Quinton emerged with the letter.

Frank glanced at the page and shrugged. "I cannot read Bengali."

"Manipuris do, I assume," Quinton answered. "Rassik does not trust his Manipuri skills for something so critical."

"Yes," Frank said. "Their last messages were in Bengali. What does yours say?"

"I wrote, 'On what condition will you cease firing on us, and give us time to repair the telegraph and communicate with the Viceroy?' Short and to the point."

Frank opened his mouth to speak and shut it.

He was to ask for safe passage out of the country. He refuses to admit defeat.

Frank nodded, took the message, and proceeded with Skene and the bugler to the gate. At half past seven o'clock, bugler Gunna Ram first blew the call.

Da-da-da-daaaa. Da-da-da-daaaa.

Bugle echoes faded, but firing continued unabated. Skene ordered the call repeated once, and then three more times. After cannon fired another volley, the reverberations faded. Seconds passed without following shots.

A voice broke the silence, shouting in in Manipuri, "*You* came, and *you* attacked us! How can *you* ask *us* to stop fighting? Are you men or women?"

Cannon and muskets opened fire again. The bugler continued blowing cease-fire, and at last, at eight o'clock, firing ceased, and an eerie silence fell over the battle scene. Then came the ominous, deep *bong, bong* of a great gong inside Kangla. Skene eyed Frank, head cocked.

"There it is," Frank said. "Manipur agreed to cease firing."

Frank chanced stepping out the gate into clear sight.

I make an easy target in this moonlight.

He cupped hands to mouth and shouted in Manipuri. "We have a message for Regent Kula Chandra and Yuvraj Tikendra Jeet! Come down to receive the letter!"

Minutes passed and Frank and Skene exchanged glances. Frank sighed, shook his head, and said, "What can be...," when the Western Gate creaked and a Manipuri sepoy appeared.

Skene handed the letter to Gunna Ram. The Gurkha bugler trotted out, met the Manipuri half way, and handed over the paper. The Manipuri retreated, and the gate slammed.

"Now we wait," Skene said.

Frank and Skene returned to the house and Frank found Ethel waiting on the verandah steps.

"Doctor Calvert is putting the cease-fire to good use," she said. "Kahars are replacing expired soldiers with new wounded from stations about the grounds.

Frank only nodded.

"What happens now?" Ethel said.

"We wait. How are you managing?"

"I am well, but grieving for these poor men—wounds so horrible I cannot believe the little chaps are still alive. Lionel is one of the worst off—such pain."

At nine o'clock, the Manipuri messenger delivered a reply to the Residency gate and Gunna Ram ran the message to the house.

"They responded in Bengali," Frank said, handing the paper to Rassik to translate.

Rassik studied the note, cocked his head, and grimaced. "Message says, 'Jadi astra shastra pheliya deba.'"

"Which means?" Quinton said.

The translator did not answer, but continued staring at the page.

"Well?" Quinton said, frowning and raising his voice.

"Message says 'throw down your weapons,' or perhaps 'lower your arms,' or it might mean 'surrender your arms.'"

"Well, man, which? Those are different matters."

"Astra is clear—refers to firearms, weapons of distance—rifles, pistols, and such. Shastra means close fighting weapons such as swords or spears."

"Fine, but we are to do *what* with our weapons?"

"In Bengali," Rassik said, "the word *pheliya* as used here has two or three meanings. To throw, or lower—in one context, to surrender. The intended meaning is uncertain."

"Well, blast it!" Quinton shouted. "Yes—we will lower our weapons and cease firing, but we are not dropping or throwing or surrendering any of our weapons—that much I can say."

"Perhaps we should ask for a parlay," Frank said. "Seek clarification from the Yuvraj."

"Fine," Quinton agreed, "I will parlay, but first—seek assurances of safe passage."

Frank walked to the gate and spoke to the messenger.

"We wish to parlay," Frank said. "We need clarification—to understand the message's intent—and wish to speak to the Regent and Yuvraj."

The messenger bowed. "I shall deliver sahib's message."

"Another thing," Frank said. "If Chief Commissioner Quinton attends the parlay in person, can Manipur guarantee safe passage?"

"Yes, sahib!" The man cracked a sly grin. "Why should *we* harm *you*? Are you British not superior—godlike compared to us?"

The messenger left, returning at half past nine o'clock with a verbal reply.

"Manipur," he announced, "will allow a few unarmed sahibs to approach under truce and parlay at the Western Gate at ten o'clock."

Frank nodded and returned to the house.

"I am attending," Quinton declared. "Skene, as the highest-ranking British officer—you should come, too. Grimwood should come to translate, and his close relationship with the princes might smooth matters."

Frank considered and felt a twinge in his stomach.

Something is wrong.

"Is that an order?" Frank asked.

"No, damn it!" Quinton said, fuming. "I am asking—you in or not?"

"Let me go!" Walter Simpson interjected. "I know the princes, speak the language, and understand the people and their customs."

"No," Frank said. "I will go—I insist."

"Right," Quinton said, nodding. "Grimwood goes—sorry, Simpson."

"The higher ranking Manipuris will have seconds," Walter insisted. "I ask permission to be Frank's second."

Frank raised a hand to object when Quinton nodded, saying, "Agreed!"

Cossins spoke up, saying, "In that case, Mister Quinton—I want to be your second. I have contributed little to this point."

"All right, William," Quinton said, nodding, "if you insist, but I disagree you have not contributed. Done! Let us five prepare ourselves and wait for the hour."

Frank descended to the cellar and motioned Ethel aside for words in private. Ethel followed to the corner by the little cooking stove. As Frank explained the plan, Ethel's face paled, and her hand slipped into her dress pocket.

She is a bundle of nerves—always fondling that blasted figurine!

"Oh, Frank!" Ethel exclaimed. "I must come, too!"

"I cannot allow that—too dangerous. Much safer in the cellar."

"But, if I was by your side it would show Tikendra Jeet he has no hope of—you know."

"He might think I brought you as a shield, or see it as a sign you were on his side. He could take you hostage on the spot—we cannot chance that."

"Frank, I must tell you," Ethel said, biting her lower lip. "The day Quinton arrived, when the durbar debacle happened, I went to the bazaar."

"I remember—Quinton and Boileau saw you talking to yourself. You said you hallucinated."

"It was more like a vision. A woman—old, blind, like a seer, or oracle—told me the end was near, go west while I could."

Frank chuckled. "Whoever she was, she offered sound advice."

"Please, Frank!" Ethel pleaded. "Please do not go! Let us use the cease-fire—escape and take anyone who wants to come."

Frank frowned. "Too late for me—duty calls. I must go, but you raise a good point. If anything happens, captured or worse, go west."

"Without you?"

"Yes, you must chance it and not wait."

"How will I know?"

"If we do not return and Manipur opens fire—something has gone wrong, and it will be time to escape—it could be your last chance."

Ethel's eyes opened wide and her mouth quivered.

"You know the way to Cachar? Right?" Frank continued. "You have traveled each way several times."

"Yes, I could find my way blindfolded. Make for the Peak of Leimatak."

"Then be ready—do not think twice."

"Frank—I cannot leave here without you!"

"Do not worry over me. English forces will straighten this out, but you are a prize. Tikendra Jeet will not let you go without a fight. You must escape—you will know when."

Frank embraced Ethel—she pressed her face against his chest and clung with an iron grip.

"Oh, wait!" Frank pulled free. "I have a gift." He unbuckled a wide belt around his waist and handed Ethel his holstered revolver and ammunition pouch.

"What—why?"

"We must go to the parlay unarmed," Frank said. "If anything happens—wear it." He had given Ethel many lessons in target shooting during their months in Manipur. "You remember how to use it?"

Ethel nodded. "But—you should not go unarmed."

"Do not worry," a voice said. "I will look out for him."

Frank and Ethel turned to find Walter watching, arms folded, chuckling, and Ethel ran to Walter's open arms.

"Trusty old Enfield pistol, eh?" Walter said. "At least a Mark II. Have my Webley—newer, smaller, and easier to handle. Oh, you can have my sabre, too."

Frank laughed and Ethel blinked away tears.

"I feel so hopeless," Ethel said. "The two men I care for are leaving, going unarmed into danger. What if something happens?"

"I promise I will look after Walter," Frank replied, smiling.

Why does seeing my wife embrace my best friend make me happy?

"Twice now I tried telling Walter he could not come, but I keep losing the argument. Not to worry—all will be splendid! We will return soon."

Chapter 60. The Last Bowls of Soup

Continued...

Ethel

Frank and Walter climbed the cellar steps. Halfway up Ethel's heart leapt as Frank stopped and turned, pausing as if preparing to speak.

He changed his mind!

Her heart sank again as Frank delivered a final admonishment.

"Remember, if we have not returned and Manipur opens fire..."

"I know!" Ethel hung her head and sighed. "Time to flee!"

She looked up as Frank winked and smiled. She wiped her eyes on her sleeve and turned to smile back but Frank had disappeared. Ethel flopped into a nearby chair, covered her face, and cried. For the first time in her life, she experienced every sense of alone—solitary, cut off, left behind, abandoned, and rejected. Her heart was breaking.

I wanted to go, too! I should have insisted—argued harder. Something bad will happen. I know I can help with Tikendra Jeet. I may not have another chance.

Ethel stood and took a step toward the stairway.

Go after them! Do not let them leave!

She set foot on the first step and halted.

I cannot face another rejection, and I would only embarrass Frank.

Nor could she bear watching her husband and best friend trudge off to face uncertain fates at the gates of Kangla.

Our safety is in their hands. If they negotiate our retreat—or even a delay, buy us time for Captain Cowley to arrive with reinforcements. The next hour will decide our future.

Ethel's hand slipped into her pocket, without conscious thought she sought the dragon figurine and the comfort of its strange tingle. She closed her eyes and sighed.

So weary.

Something nudged Ethel, and she straightened, wide-eyed. Doctor Calvert loomed before her. She yanked her hand from her pocket and wiped her eyes. The doctor smiled and took hold of her hands.

He seems to have aged ten years in a single day.

"Sorry to wake you," the surgeon murmured.

"Was I sleeping?" Ethel said. "I did not mean to doze. How long was I sitting here?"

"Not so long," he said. "A few minutes."

"Goodness." Ethel shook her head and shuddered. "I am so sorry." She sniffed and straightened her dress. "I will return to work straight away."

"The men are quiet now. We should keep using the truce to our advantage. We have more deceased to remove."

"How can I help?" Ethel asked, trying to sound bright, energetic, and eager for anything.

"Perhaps you could go upstairs," he said, smiling. "Forage dinner."

"But—but I...," she said.

Ethel swore to help tend the wounded—and even the dead, if she found strength. She would stand no one thinking her in the way—shuffle her aside, send her to the kitchen—when serious duties arose.

"It is all right," the doctor said. "You have been a wonder. Expect more deaths as the night wears. In the meanwhile, save your strength and help the living. The wounded must eat, and so must the sound and healthy among us."

She stared back but did not move. The doctor cleared his throat.

"In plain English, my dear—I am hungry!"

Ethel blushed and nodded. She rose and rushed upstairs to the kitchen. From habit, she opened her mouth to call for servants, and then stopped herself. She shook her head and stamped her foot.

Foolish girl—on your own now—almost. Yes, I remember. I will manage.

She searched the larder and found it all but empty, save for a large pot of leftover soup from last evening; a few unopened jars of stewed vegetables; bread, almost but not yet stale; and several tins of condensed milk. She collected anything else of use and made ready to haul it all to the cellar when the bearer appeared.

"Kahars finished with dead, memsahib. Now moving wounded."

I will test his loyalty.

She put the bearer to work lugging pots, jars, and cans down to the little kitchen in a corner of the cellar. Then Captain Boileau appeared.

"May I help, Missus?"

"Wonderful!"

Ethel sent the captain rummaging for empty bottles. He found a half dozen, filled each with water, and Ethel mixed in the condensed milk. Then Ethel and the captain, arms full, descended the narrow wooden stairs. The welcoming aroma of steaming hot vegetable soup met their noses. A crowd of British officers caught whiffs and surrounded the stove, blocking her path.

"Gentlemen, please!" she complained, pushing through the crowd. "Allow me to serve the wounded, the poor doctor, and his assistant. After that, you may all help yourselves to whatever remains."

Ethel ladled cups and bowls for the patients. Those with minor wounds sat up and fed themselves while those with serious injuries accepted sips from cups or spoons. Others were unconscious or too wounded and unable to eat. Most expressed gratitude for her efforts and it warmed her heart. Once she had made the rounds, she returned to Lionel's side. She took over spoon feeding duties from Tiwari and sat by her wounded friend. Lionel tried to sit up, but winced and laid back. He managed a faint smile.

"What time is it?" he whispered.

"Half past ten," Ethel replied, "but never you mind what the time is. Eat your soup."

Lionel cracked a half-smile and accepted another sip.

"I am so thirsty..."

"Drink all you can," she coaxed. "Good for you."

He managed a few words between sips and coughs. "I am sorry—if I appear—a mess."

He is a mess—all four limbs broken and bound. So gaunt and gray.

Clammy perspiration glittered on the brow of his boyish face.

Heavy bleeding at his ankle—seeping through fresh bandages.

"You *should* be sorry!" she said, feigning scorn. She mopped his brow, softened, and smiled. "You look fine. Very handsome, considering the number of bullets you collected. Whatever were you thinking, wandering into such danger?"

"Thinking...?" He chuckled and coughed. "I am—not much good—at thinking. I am just a banjo player—in a uniform. What happened to my instrument? Will you fetch it for me?"

"Oh, to be sure!" Ethel laughed. "Perhaps after dinner!" She grew serious and changed topics. "Lionel—what happened to you? I heard the strangest story. Can it be true—did you walk up and knock on the Yuvraj's front door?"

"True somewhat...," he replied, wincing. "A—slight—exaggeration."

"What possessed you?"

"Butcher—delayed." He sputtered and coughed. "I decided—to take initiative..." He broke into a long, wheezing cough. Ethel set the bowl aside and wiped his mouth.

"Poor Lionel!" she said. "I wish you *could* play for us. It makes me so happy when you play and sing your silly songs." She paused and bit her lip, debating what to say next. "I missed you so much—during your time away from Manipur."

"I missed—you, too," he said, managing the slightest smile. "Do you know—why I came back?"

"Back to Manipur? With Quinton, do you mean? I assume your regiment had orders..."

"I volunteered..."

"But—why?" Ethel feared she knew the answer.

Oh God! No.

"Your letter..."

"Oh, Lionel—it was my fault—I am so sorry. What have I done?"

"You—made me happy," he said, choking. "I wish—to read it one more time. If I—I wish—I want to hear you read it. I misplaced my coat somewhere—it was in the pocket..."

Ethel blushed and her eyes grew moist.

"Such—a joy...," he managed and then closed his eyes.

Ethel leaned close and listened for signs of breathing.

Thank God—he fell asleep.

She stroked his hair, bent, kissed his cheek, and whispered, "Rest now, dearest Lionel. Stay strong. We will get out of this together."

Ethel stood and inspected the rows of cots. Wheezes and heavy breathing. The wounded slept or rested. Calvert dimmed the lanterns and ate with Tiwari. A few officers dozed or rested. Ethel approached the doctor and asked what she could do next.

"Go back upstairs," he said. "Find someplace quiet—take a rest."

"What if you need help?"

"I will send for you if need arises."

"Promise?" she said.

He promised and Ethel climbed the steps, convinced she was not abandoning her duties. Once upstairs, she stepped onto the verandah and took a deep breath. The strong fragrance of her flower garden was like a welcome balm, diminishing the smoldering stench of the burned village. She listened to the croaks and chirps from the peaceful jungle. There was no other sign of activity.

I will first check for news from Kangla.

Ethel wandered up the carriage drive and found Captain Boileau staring at the bright moon.

"Such a singular evening," she said.

"Yes, Missus," he said, continuing to look skyward. "Never a brighter moon—almost like day."

"Odd how one's priorities change," she said. "Seems so long ago now, but it was only yesterday evening, after the storm. Frank and I strolled by the gate and a dance company arrived—young girls, just children—begging me to let them inside to dance. We sent them away, and they were so disappointed. I felt so sad—worried I hurt their feelings, so I insisted to Frank—he must pay them, regardless. I made him promise me. Something so vital then seems trivial now."

"Your husband is a good man." Boileau turned from the moon studied Ethel with sympathetic eyes.

Ethel smiled.

My husband is a good man. Please, God, keep him safe.

She sniffed, wiped a tear, and looked toward Kangla. "Any word?"

"None yet—all quiet."

"Where are our men?" she asked. "Are they in sight?"

"It appears the party passed the gates."

"Inside?" Ethel exclaimed. "I thought they were to parlay outside, somewhere in between, or before the gates."

"They were," the captain said. "Something changed. Quinton must have felt safe if he agreed to an inside meeting."

"I wish we had news."

"Perhaps I will stroll out to the mud wall," he replied. "Get closer, maybe see something."

"Thank you, Captain!" she called. "I will rest for a while. Wake me if any news."

Boileau waved, turned, and walked away up the gravel path.

Chapter 61. The Final Durbar

Minutes before 10:00 p.m....

Frank

As ten o'clock approached, Quinton, Skene, Frank, Simpson, and Cossins gathered outside the gate and then left the road for the field, taking a position beside a broad oak. There they waited until ten o'clock when Quinton nodded, and the five walked forward, reaching another oak halfway to the gate. There, they waited several minutes.

No sign of activity at Kangla.

"Keeping us here cooling our heels," Quinton complained, checking his pocket watch. "I suppose those with the upper hand have that privilege."

"Blast!" Skene said. "I asked Chatterton to have five chairs brought to this spot."

"Sahib!" a voice called.

A moonlit figure trotted toward them from the Residency—a Gurkha hurrying across the field bearing a large bundle. Gunna Ram, the bugler, arrived, dropped his heavy load, and set to work assembling five canvas campaign chairs.

"So sorry, sahib!" the bugler said to Skene. "Ram is late with chairs!"

"Thank you, bugler," Skene said as the Gurkha assembled the last chair. "Best to hurry back while you can."

Gunna Ram eyed the five Englishmen selecting chairs. "But—Sahib Colonel has no second! Please allow Ram to stay as Sahib Colonel's second."

The Englishmen eyed one another, and Frank suppressed a grin.

"All right, bugler," Skene said, chuckling. "Stay and be my second."

"Thank you, sahib!" The excited soldier took his place behind Skene and stood ramrod at attention.

"That makes six," Walter said. "Even numbers are luckier!"

"Lucky!" Quinton scoffed. "So lucky are we—six unarmed gentlemen of the British Empire, out on a moonlight stroll on such a glorious Manipuri evening."

The men sat, waited, and conversed for ten more minutes, appreciating the night air as the bright moon rose higher and cast shadows.

"Frank," Simpson whispered, "I thought of something—did you mention to Ethel we suspect a spy is still at the Residency?"

"Huh, no," Frank groaned. "I did not—such a long day. I will when we return."

At that moment, the gong inside Kangla rang and the Western Gate creaked open. The Englishmen stood as a turbaned dignitary in a white uniform approached.

"Prime minister," Frank whispered.

The minister bowed and Frank translated as he spoke. "My name is Haobam Dewan, sahibs. I will escort you to the entryway."

Quinton nodded and Dewan led the six to the crossroad where a man in military uniform waited.

"Commander of the palace guard," Frank murmured to Quinton.

"They sure make a grand showing."

The commander introduced himself. "I am Nilmani Singh, sahibs. I will escort you past the moat."

The party stepped forward—dry ditch at their left, wet ditch on their right—and entered the shadow of the arched gate where three more uniformed men waited. Two of the men had familiar faces—young Prince Angao Sena and the venerable Tongol General. The third bowed and introduced himself.

"I am Yenkhoiba Major."

A close military advisor to Tikendra Jeet.

"Where are the Regent and the Yuvraj?" Frank said.

"Inside," the major said. "Waiting for sahibs."

"We were to meet them here," Quinton said, after Frank translated.

"Durbar inside now," the major insisted.

"Too late at night for a durbar!" The general spoke to Frank with a gruff tone. "Not a good idea."

"Why?" Frank asked.

"Not safe!" The general muttered, shaking his head. "Angry crowd outside the palace. Crowd has blood lust to make revenge on sahibs."

"So what should we do?"

"Go back—hold durbar tomorrow. Perhaps crowd will calm."

"Not possible!" Yenkhoiba Major shouted. "Yuvraj insisted officers must come inside fort for durbar. Must come now—truce requires durbar now."

"Sir," Frank said to Quinton, "they changed plans—now want to meet in the fort. The general recommends we leave and try again tomorrow, but the major implies the truce will end. They could bomb us again."

"They guarantee us safe passage?"

The major nodded and smiled but the general frowned.

"Then...," Quinton said, "*now* it shall be. No point delaying matters further."

As they started through the gate, the general blocked Gunna Ram, growling, "No children!"

Skene put a hand on Ram's shoulder, saying, "He is with me!" and pushed past the glowering old soldier.

They marched on and followed the main causeway toward the palace. Armed soldiers lined the high walls and angry citizens holding torches lined both sides of the street. As they passed the Laktong Gate, the crowd drew in and followed until they reached the Kangla-sha before the durbar hall where great torches burned and flames leapt high.

The tall dragon statues stood as they had for centuries, frozen with mouths open, as if laughing at the full moon. Before the durbar hall stood Prince Tikendra Jeet and four more dignitaries. Two rows of chairs sat outside—empty and waiting—facing each other at the foot of the stairs.

The crowd grew and pressed close around the meeting site. A pretty face caught Frank's eye in the long line of angry faces. She smiled and waved.

Leishna—one friendly face at least!

Walter nudged Frank. "It is Leishna," the lieutenant said.

Frank nodded. The general shot a dirty look at his daughter and the girl shrank into the shadows.

I wish I had not slept with her while Ethel was away. Someday there will be an accounting for my indiscretions. God, how I miss Ethel. I must end this and get home soon.

The crowd noise grew. Manipuri guards held rifles and spears, shoving the mob farther away. One guard with a spear glared at Frank.

Where have I seen his face?

The two parties met by the chairs. During introductions, Tikendra Jeet named the four dignitaries.

"Ningthou (chief) of the Angom yek (tribe); Lokendra Singh; Wangkheirakpa (chief judiciary official); and two military officers, Major Mia Singh and Colonel Samu Singh."

All venerable, well-respected Manipuri figures.

Frank studied Tikendra Jeet. "You are looking better—healthy even. You looked to be at death's door yesterday. A miracle perhaps?"

"Not a miracle." The prince glared and leveled stern words. "When enemies attack one's home, one finds inner strength."

"It would appear so." Frank looked at the other faces. "Where is the regent? We expected him for the parlay."

"When you British attacked, he left Kangla for his safety. Manipur's defense is in the hands of military commanders."

Quinton nudged Frank. "Ask him why we are meeting here. The crowd is too close—angry and threatening. Would we not be safer in the durbar hall?"

Frank translated Tikendra Jeet's reply. "The people are angry because of your ruthless attacks. They have suffered grievous losses."

"I assure you," Frank said, "civilian casualties were unintentional. Hostilities have consequences—we intended no harm to civilians."

"I wish I could believe you," Tikendra Jeet said, "but you cannot explain many deaths." He turned and pointed past the golden-domed temple toward a grassy meadow circled by trees. "This is a holy time. Yonder is the sacred grove of Rasmandala. Young dancers performed the Ras Lila nautch there early this morning with proud parents watching. Many killed—children, women—slaughtered like animals. Assassinated in cold blood by British rifles fired at a great distance from the roof of my family's temple. That is no accident and unforgiveable."

Frank translated and noticed Walter's face was red.

What is wrong with Walter? The prince's remarks shocked him.

Frank finished translating.

"Preposterous!" Skene shouted. "I was at that temple—so were you, Grimwood. You, too, Simpson. We all stood on the roof and the balconies. No such shooting took place. Our Gurkhas would never commit such a terrible crime. We had our hands full with attacks from the citadel walls."

Tikendra Jeet glowered. "Yet innocent children lie dead, awaiting funerals as we speak."

Quinton grew impatient. "That aside, what good comes of the crowd breathing down our necks?"

The prince answered through Frank. "Intended or not, a great evil happened. The people know their leaders trusted Britain—now the people do not trust their leaders. We cannot pacify the citizens of Manipur meeting behind closed doors. The people must see their leaders meet with the attackers in good faith, and the British cannot buy their way out this time with guns or gold."

"Are we to stand here all night?" Quinton said. "Let us get down to business."

Tikendra Jeet motioned, and the parties sat. Ten Manipuris faced the Kangla-sha, and five British men faced the durbar hall. Gunna Ram, the bugler, stood at ease, behind Skene.

"We read your reply to our message," Frank began, "but the Bengali interpretation was not clear as to what you intended about our firearms."

"You British and your Gurkha mercenaries must surrender all arms—pistols, rifles, and swords," Tikendra Jeet replied. "You must turn over all weapons and remaining ammunition to the Manipuri army."

"And in exchange?"

"The cease fire will continue. You may stay, under watchful guard, and wait inside the mud walls of your Residency. Manipuris are not barbarians—we do not slaughter unarmed innocents as you made Manipur bleed."

Frank translated and Quinton's face darkened. "We cannot surrender our weapons! They are not ours to give. They belong to the Queen and Indian Government. We must first repair the telegraph and inform the Viceroy in Calcutta who may have to petition the Queen. Will the prince allow us time and safe passage to repair our telegraph lines and communicate these terms?"

Tikendra Jeet laughed and shook his head. "More messages? Messages about bagging a great tiger in Manipur? Oh yes, I heard of that message. No, chief commissioner. The telegraph must stay disconnected—no further messages."

The debate continued, back and forth, without progress, until the eleven o'clock hour approached. As the crowd grew more restless, the din made hearing difficult.

"The Tongol General proposed rescheduling the durbar," Quinton shouted. "He suggested tomorrow."

As Frank translated, Tikendra Jeet's eyes widened. The prince eyed the general who shrugged as if saying, "what if I did?"

"His suggestion makes sense," Quinton continued, "given the crowd noise. We will retreat to the Residency and ponder your demands. I propose reconvening at eight o'clock tomorrow morning. Let us meet somewhere else—not in the middle of the crowd—outside the gate, perhaps."

Without waiting for agreement, Quinton rose to leave and his comrades followed, stepping away from their chairs. Tikendra Jeet rose but did not move. Sensing something had happened, angry voices grew louder, and the crowd erupted in a terse, repetitive chant.

"What are they saying?" Quinton asked Frank.

"They want us dead," Frank answered.

"They are chanting 'kill, kill,'" Walter added.

Frank led the British party back toward the Laktong Gate. As they passed the Kangla-sha, Frank met the guards holding back the crowd.

"Let us pass," Frank said.

The gate swung shut, and a guard gripping a spear blocked Frank's path. Frank studied the guard's dark eyes and shrank back, shocked by a sudden recognition.

"Now I recognize you!" Frank said. "Last night at my gate. You brought dancers for a nautch."

The man stood firm, with clenched jaw and burning eyes. Frank turned to look for Tikendra Jeet. A Manipuri man wielding a polo mallet tore loose from a guard's grip and lunged at Walter Simpson. The mallet rose and fell, striking the lieutenant a vicious blow across the temple. Walter staggered and fell. As the mallet raised a second time, a woman screamed.

Leishna!

"Walter! No!" Leishna shrieked as she ripped free, ran past the guards, and fell upon Simpson, shielding his head with her body.

More men broke through the ring of guards and pressed forward. The surging mob separated Frank from his comrades and he lost sight of Walter and Leishna.

"Simpson!" Frank searched for Tikendra Jeet but the angry mob surrounded and pressed close. Frank shoved a man aside and, as he grabbed another to clear a path to his friend, he stiffened and gasped.

Pain seared, greater than Frank imagined possible. He looked down, shocked to see the point and shaft of a spear protruding below his sternum.

The crowd screamed and fell back, opening a space before the feet of the Kangla-sha.

Blood filled Frank's mouth. He coughed and spat as he sank to his knees, feeble fingers grasping at the shaft, slippery with his warm blood.

As Frank's vision blurred, the dim figure of a man appeared, standing at the feet of the Kangla-sha—someone he recognized. Someone from a dream many months before, whose shade had appeared uninvited and spoiled his photo. Someone who once took Frank's job and learned the dark danger of Manipur the hard way.

Heath! Damn you, I told you to stay the hell out of my dreams!

"You did, Frank," he answered. "Sad to say, not a dream." He extended a hand. "It is not as bad as you suppose. Come—I will show you."

Frank closed his eyes, surrendered, and accepted his fall into a place somewhere between light and darkness.

Chapter 62. The Prophecy Unveiled

Seconds earlier…

Tikendra Jeet

Tikendra Jeet froze as a guard—a man with clenched teeth and a scowl of darkest hate—raised his spear.

"No!" the prince shouted. "Stop!"

His voice faltered—too late, too far away, drowned by chanting. He reached in futile, grasping thin air, and then…

The guard thrust the point through the sahib's back. The impaled Englishman dropped to his knees coughing blood, clutching the shaft with feeble fingers, and toppled face-forward onto the brick pavers. Frank Grimwood—who the prince once regarded as a friend—passed beyond that chasm separating the living from the dead.

Tikendra Jeet drew his sword—torchlight glittered off cold steel—and sprang into the fray. Durbar comrades swarmed after, following him into the surging mob. He pointed at the guard beside Grimwood, shouting, "Seize him!"

The turbaned man gripped the spear shaft and grimaced as he continued thrusting, pinning the white man's torso to the brick courtyard. Looks of anger and hatred turned to surprise and frustration as sentries grappled the guard and pulled him to the ground.

"No!" voices screamed from the crowd. "Release him!"

"He is a hero!" others cried.

"Get back!" the prince bellowed. "I am Yuvraj, and I say, stand back!"

Darkened faces paused, glaring—with clenched jaws, or with flaring nostrils and bared teeth—all with the bitter look of desperate souls ready to die to right an injustice.

They will tear the sahibs to pieces, and me along with them!

Sentries rallied to the prince's side, waving swords, forcing back the angry crowd.

What of the other sahibs?

Wangkheirakpa and Angom Ningthou faced the mob with drawn swords, shielding the British dignitaries. The Tongol General waved a bloody polo mallet—the weapon that struck Walter Simpson—forced from an attacker's hand. The old soldier loomed above his daughter, mallet raised, ready to strike anyone within reach. Leishna sat at his feet, sobbing and cradling the bleeding head of the unconscious Simpson. Tweed-suited civil servants Quinton and Cossins crouched behind the uniformed figures of Colonel Skene and Gurkha bugler Gunna Ram standing, fists clenched, ready to strike.

Quinton looks bewildered.

Tikendra Jeet ordered, "Lift Simpson—take the sahibs to the durbar hall!"

The Tongol General's lip curled and deep-set eyes burned. "To do what with them?"

"Guard them!" the prince replied, glaring back at the old soldier. "Keep them safe from the crowd!"

"For now, perhaps." The gray-haired soldier reached under his daughter's arm and pulled. "Stand!"

Sentries lifted Simpson, and the general and Prince Angao Sena led the way. Sentries shielded the captives as they climbed the steps. The general unlocked the door and sentries prodded the captives inside the durbar hall.

Angom Ningthou nodded at the crowd where sentries held the struggling guard. "What of the murderer?"

"Who is this assassin?" Tikendra Jeet said. "He looks familiar."

"Kajao—a jamadar. He rebelled against your older brother, and after Sura Chandra abdicated, you released him from prison and made him an officer."

The prince nodded. "I remember. Why did he attack Grimwood?"

"His wife and daughters—killed in the Ras Lila slaughter. He is a hero—a symbol of the mob's anger. The people will not stand seeing him punished."

Tikendra Jeet looked up at the bright moon and shook his head.

I might have done the same.

"Lock him up," Tikendra Jeet said at last. "Keep him well-guarded until his trial."

The Angom Ningthou nodded toward Grimwood's corpse. "And the dead sahib?"

Tikendra Jeet looked at the lifeless body.

A day ago, I ordered his assassination, and now—I have regrets?

An authoritative voice rang out, demanding, "Do not touch the body!"

Tikendra Jeet spun and faced a late-middle-aged man in a thin white robe. His wide eyes shone red in the torchlight.

Young Maiba! He missed the durbar.

"Listen to the priest!" Tikendra Jeet leveled a stern stare at the angry faces in the crowd.

"The Thawai fled!" the holy man continued. "Sahib's Hakchang is unclean! We must treat the corpse according to our customs."

An angry woman screamed, "Murderers deserve no ceremony!"

"Feed them all to the pariah dogs!" another shouted.

Tikendra Jeet's sword raised higher, and the mob shrank back. "The priest has spoken! No one touch the body—the dead sahib stays where he lies."

Tikendra Jeet placed sentries guarding the corpse. Young Maiba drew close to his ear and whispered, "Come to the temple—we must speak of vital matters in private."

The prince nodded and motioned to Subadar Jatra Singh. The officer approached and Tikendra Jeet said, "I am going to the temple. Go to the durbar hall—see no one harms the sahibs. If anyone threatens their safety, tell me at once." The officer nodded and moved toward the stairs. "Wait!" the prince shouted, motioned the officer back, drew close, and whispered, "Watch the general in particular."

The subadar stiffened, raised an eyebrow, and then nodded and sprang away up the steps.

Tikendra Jeet followed the priest past the durbar hall and polo grounds toward the temple of Shri Govindajee. The moonlit Rasmandala grove caught his eye, and he studied the path northwest toward the tower with a tarnished green roof. He squinted, measuring the angle and distance.

How could a bullet travel so far with such deadly effect? That is no accident.

"You are thinking of the slaughter," Young Maiba said. "I, too, wonder how an act so vile could happen. Perhaps answers are in the temple."

They climbed the brick steps, entered the darkened outer hall, and navigated the torch lit ambulatory pathway. Tikendra Jeet's long shadow fell across the first of the surungs where, legends claimed, the dragon-god

Pakhangba still roamed. He looked into the deeper darkness as the priest watched.

"Your breathing is heavy," Young Maiba said. "Do you sense anything?"

Tikendra Jeet sighed and said, "No—I tried before but feel nothing. Sometimes I question belief in the old gods."

"Your face is flush. I see your weariness—this was an evil day."

"For many."

"You should take a rest."

Tikendra Jeet shook his head and straightened. "I cannot—if I lay down, I may not wake for hours. My duty is in battle."

"Come then." Young Maiba led the prince to the inner sanctum. "What I will say cannot wait."

They approached an ornate hardwood table stacked with books. The priest reached for an open leather-bound volume and said, "I fear the day has come."

Tikendra Jeet frowned. "What day?"

"A day foretold in prophecy two centuries ago. My master, the Old Maiba, knew it would not come in his lifetime, or your father's. He expected it to happen in my time and yours. I told your brother Sura Chandra of the prophecy years ago, knowing his reign would end before the fateful day."

The maiba presented the open volume with reverence.

"What book is that?" Tikendra Jeet asked.

"The Ningthoural Singkak—the great book of prophecy written in King Khagemba's time—over two hundred years ago."

"I thought the Puya Meithaba burned all copies."

"As you see." Young Maiba held up the heavy volume. "A copy survived—kept secret in this temple, guarded, and passed down from maiba to maiba. Your brother Sura Chandra learned his fate from these pages. Now you must learn the prophecy. Unlike him, you might avoid your fate."

"What are you implying?" Tikendra Jeet said. "That book predicted my brother's overthrow?"

"Yes."

"Predicted it two hundred years ago?"

"Yes." The priest nodded. "Sura Chandra knew his fate—we pondered the meaning together. He respected supernatural forces, but hoped to fight the tide and change history. Your brother Kula Chandra should learn this, but he fled and left you to manage the crisis. The matter is too vital, so my duty requires me to make sure *you* learn the warning and act in his place while still time."

"What warning? Time for what?"

"Listen and it will become clear."

The priest read aloud the centuries-old parchment, beginning with innocent passages establishing the timeline, and ending with an ominous phrase.

"The next raja will rule for one year. In his reign, five white heads shall fall at the feet of the Kangla-sha." Young Maiba paused, as if waiting for reaction.

"I heard this prophecy," Tikendra Jeet said. "I cannot remember where or when—maybe as a child, whispered rumors told to frighten—but tonight was the first time I heard the actual words. Many say we live in a Time of Prophecy, but I pay scant attention to stories. Do *you* believe the time is upon us?"

"Consider the timeline—it aligns to your father's era. The next passages describe the reigns of your older brothers Sura Chandra and Kula Chandra. In addition, you hold five white men in custody…"

"Only one is dead!" Tikendra Jeet said.

"Yes, only one. Four live—for the time being."

"Their heads stay attached—no plan to remove them. Why is this the time of prophecy?"

"We must, at least, remove the dead sahib's head—our customs demand this."

Tikendra Jeet looked down and muttered, "Mleccha."

"Yes, sahibs are Mleccha—foreigners, outsiders, unbelievers—not of our faith. The dead body is unclean—it cannot defile holy places. We can only bury his head."

I dislike it, but these are our ways. I cannot violate this law.

"This is no dream," Young Maiba continued. "We act out perilous moments in Manipur's history. The time of prophecy is upon us—that is clear—but we may yet escape doom."

"Doom?" Tikendra Jeet scoffed. "I thought the prophecy foretells a golden age for Manipur."

"Only in children's tales." The priest shook his head. "I have a story—you will see what I mean. My story begins thirty-four years ago—before your birth. I was a teenager, the Old Maiba's chela, on the eve of the Great

Rebellion. A European sorceress stopped in Manipur on her way to Burma. She came to this temple, stood where you stand now, and sought wisdom in the old books. The Old Maiba showed her this book!"

Young Maiba held the book higher and continued.

"He read the prophecy, but not all—I told her the last part. 'The west gate shall close and the east gate shall open; and when the white heads fall before the dragons, three rajas shall come by three roads, each with an army, and the kingdom shall fall.' She humbled my master with stern warnings of the fall of Manipur."

"So what?" Tikendra Jeet said. "Why should I care what a European sorceress said?"

"There is more," the priest said. "That night, in the durbar hall, she impressed your father with more prophecies. Powerful spirits surrounded her—the room shook, dishes and table cutlery rattled."

Tikendra Jeet laughed. "Parlor tricks! An earthquake. I do not believe in sorcery. I am certain she did not impress my father as you claim."

"Let me finish," Young Maiba pleaded. "The spirits stopped at her command. She predicted the Great Rebellion; told your father to ally with the British; and warned his cousin princes were threats he should remove. She even predicted the rise of the Tongol."

Tikendra Jeet shook his head. "The British, the Rebellion, the Tongol, my cousins—you claim these relate to the prophecy?"

"No claim—truth. Your father betrayed his cousins and India but he saved Manipur. His reward was a knighthood."

"My father and the old Tongol allied with the British, betrayed my cousin princes, and helped quash the Great Rebellion?"

"Yes."

"What is the purpose of this story?" Tikendra Jeet asked.

"Your father made hard choices, but acted as a leader—a great king. When the time came, he kept his wits and listened to inner voices, to the supernatural, and what he did saved his country. Learn from your father— do not ignore the supernatural elements."

"What would you have me do?"

"A struggle begins soon, perhaps tonight," the priest said. "A battle for Manipur's future. Tradition holds, the five heads mark the dawn of a golden age, but the prophecy says the sahibs will die and Manipur will fall. The sahibs are in danger—you must keep them safe."

"I gave orders—armed guards keep the sahibs safe."

"I believe you want no harm to befall the sahibs, but rebellious voices call for vengeance. Be careful whom you trust—show vigilance."

A voice spoke. "Forgive me, Yuvraj." Subadar Jatra Singh and a young sentry stood in the sanctum doorway. "You asked we inform you—you must come to the durbar hall."

"What happened?"

"The general," the officer said in a grave tone. "After you left, he gathered the Top Guard. He is demanding the sahibs' execution. He said if they stand together and insist then you will give the order."

Tikendra Jeet bolted past the priest and exited the inner sanctum.

Chapter 63. The Dragon Wakes

Continued...

Tikendra Jeet

Tikendra Jeet rushed from the temple and raced for the durbar hall. Subadar Jatra Singh and the young sentry Usurba kept pace.

"Tell me his exact words!" the prince shouted.

"Prince Tikendra Jeet!"

Tikendra Jeet slowed and looked back. "Someone called my name. It sounded like a woman."

"I heard nothing, Yuvraj, except you, asking what the general said."

"Yes, tell me."

"The general said, 'we must shut the mouths of the sahib captives—shut them forever.' He fears the surviving sahibs will testify if released. They will declare Grimwood a martyr and rally against us."

"Has he a plan for hiding the deaths?"

"He says blame the Kukis and Nagas—it was your original plan—claim they took revenge for burning their village."

"The British will not believe it," Tikendra Jeet said, shaking his head.

They reached the torch-lit courtyard near the Kangla-sha where the angry crowd milled, still hovering near the guarded corpse. Tikendra Jeet shoved past the mob and sprang up the steps to the durbar hall. He waved aside the gauntlet of armed guards and burst through the door.

Five men huddled in a corner surrounded by armed wardens and bound at the ankle with iron fetters. The Tongol General's daughter sat holding Simpson's head in her lap, bathing his bloody wound. Quinton, Skene, and Cossins conversed as the Gurkha bugler watched.

The general stood in the middle of the room addressing the Top Guard—a council of Manipuri officers, tribal leaders, and dignitaries. He shot a dark glare at the prince as he strode into the mix.

"Ipu (great old man)! You foment rebellion behind my back! Did you propose executing the sahibs? My orders were clear—keep the sahibs safe!"

"How long can you keep them here?" the general spat.

"As long as necessary."

"To what end?"

"To make peace with Britain."

"Fool!" the general shouted. "We cannot make peace now!"

"We have no choice!"

"Why fear these sahibs?" The general pointed to the huddled group. "See how they cower—weak, defeated." The general motioned toward the door. "See the people's anger and passion. This is our moment! The British committed outrages and our fervor will drive the sahibs from Manipur. Others will join our fight—Burma and others will follow. India will unite in a second great rebellion. We will defeat the British—drive the sahibs from India."

"Now who talks like a fool?"

"You sound like a frightened boy!"

"Be careful how you speak to your commander."

"My commander?" the general scoffed. "What battles have you fought? I served your father two decades before your birth. I fought the Burmese..."

"Yes!" Tikendra Jeet shouted. "You served my father! We both know you and he colluded with Britain during the Great Rebellion. You betrayed the Rebellion and led the sons of Nara Singh into a trap! Why would India back Manipur when Manipur sided with Britain?"

The general's nostrils flared as his face turned purple. The room quieted, and the stunned Top Guard stood speechless. Tikendra Jeet glowered and then softened his tone. "You did the needful—you and my father—you both swallowed pride to save our country. I ask you to trust me as you trusted my father. Help me keep the sahibs safe."

"I will not!" the old man exploded. "Grimwood died because of you, not me! I argued for postponing the durbar, but you ignored me. I warned the sahibs the crowd was too big, too angry—told them, come back tomorrow. They might have listened, but you sent Yenkhoiba Major to overrule me."

"Yes, I erred," Tikendra Jeet said, "but did not want Grimwood killed."

"No? Yesterday you plotted his murder. Everyone knows! You paid the Nagas and Kukis to kill him. The sahibs discovered your plan and struck first. We know what *you* want–the pretty memsahib—another wife for your harem. Another skin for the tiger hunter's wall!"

Tikendra Jeet searched the faces of the Top Guard for support, but few eyes met his.

They agree with him! I am losing control!

He tempered his anger with a slow, even tone. "You look tired—go home, take a rest. I cannot trust you so stay away. Do not return unless I summon you."

The general uttered a curse and hobbled to his daughter. "Give up the charade!" he barked. "Stop prostituting yourself—no secrets to learn from this dog."

Tears streaked Leishna's soft cheeks. "I cannot leave—I love him!"

"Fool! Simpson used you, as you used him—he knew you spied, so did Grimwood."

Leishna shook her dark-hair and shielded the lieutenant's bloodied head with her body.

"The mob will tear you both to pieces," the general continued. "Is that your wish?"

Slender shoulders trembled as she sobbed. The general shook his gray head and glared again at Tikendra Jeet.

So ancient and frail looking.

Blood drained from the general's face and he sank to his knees. His young valet ran to his side, took an arm, and helped the old man back to his feet.

"Come, Mongjam," the general murmured. "Nothing for a patriot here. Take me home."

The valet draped the general's arm over his shoulder and helped him stagger to the door. After they left, Tikendra Jeet faced the Top Guard. Tikendra Jeet cracked a grim smile when only one counselor met his gaze.

"Angom Ningthou, my friend—will you guard the sahibs?"

The chieftain drew his sword. "Yes, Yuvraj. I will do this."

"Good!" Tikendra Jeet clasped his friend's shoulder. "I charge you with the sahibs' safety. No harm must come to them." Tikendra Jeet searched the faces of the Top Guard for signs of disagreement. "This discussion ends now."

Angom Ningthou studied the huddled prisoners. "Did they understand?"

Tikendra Jeet shook his head. "Simpson speaks our language, but is unconscious. Leishna knows too little English to translate. Look at their faces—helpless—they understand nothing."

"Will you now take a rest?"

"Soon, but not yet. First, I return to the southwest rampart and resume firing. We must force a surrender."

Sentries brought a pony to the foot of the stairs. Tikendra Jeet mounted and urged his mount through the parting crowd. In the distance, the Tongol General staggered homeward, assisted by young Mongjam. Tikendra Jeet rode on toward the Laktong Gate where the moon reflected on the quiet waters of the Nungjeng Pukhri. As he neared the portal, the weight of the long day struck. He left the road, ambled to the sacred pond, and dismounted under circling trees.

Resting place of Pakhangba, legends say.

He knelt at the silvery shore, splashed water over head and neck, and blinked back weariness. Then he sat and studied the moon's reflection, whispering, "Has the moon ever been so bright? Almost like daylight—as if Lord Chandra studies us." He chuckled, waved, and shouted, "Are you enjoying the show? Are we entertaining?"

Ha! What am I saying? Speaking as if I believed in the moon god.

Soft grass invited him—lay back, rest your heavy eyelids.

No! I must stay awake!

He splashed more water, and asked, "Can I escape this predicament?"

Grimwood's death has consequences.

"I jailed the assassin, and will deliver him to the British for trial."

That will not save you. The British came to arrest you—now you lead a rebellion. The Sirkar will hold you responsible.

"A trial will prove I did not order Grimwood's assassination, and I prevented further murders."

One murder, or six—does it matter?

"Yes, it matters. I must keep the mob—and the general—far from the captives."

The British entered Kangla under a truce. Grimwood's murder violated the truce—a vile act in the eyes of civilized countries, including Indian tradition.

"I did not order the killing! A father took revenge for his family's murder. His trial will prove this."

What will the Nagas and Kukis say?

"They are tribespeople, not civilized, not believable."

What of the sahibs at the Residency? You cannot pretend the truce stands.

"I will end the truce and force their surrender."

Who but a fool would trust you a second time?

"They have no choice. The memsahib will plead my case to the Sirkar."

You have a high opinion of yourself. Why would she take your side? Her husband is dead—killed by an officer under your command.

"She does not know he is dead. When she learns, I will remind her of his philandering, and my spy says she is having an affair with Simpson. With Grimwood dead she will do anything to keep Simpson alive."

Anything?

"She—at least will want Simpson kept alive…"

Tikendra Jeet ended his internal debate. He remounted his pony and took a final look at the moon on the smooth water.

"Lord Chandra, protect her from the hellfire I must unleash."

Why pray to Chandra? Why not Krishna? Better—why not Pakhangba?

"The old gods?"

You fly the dragon banner. Pakhangba has been Manipur's symbol for thousands of years. Your father kept the old gods alive. The family duty now becomes yours.

"Yes, my father kept the old traditions, but I wonder if he believed."

Tikendra Jeet dug into his tunic, pulled a chain necklace over his head, and studied the medallion—the image of a looped dragon devouring its tail.

"The old gods!" he laughed. "Dragons, myths, and vague prophecies I first must understand and then fight to prevent. Why waste time on nonsense?"

He flung the chain and medallion far out into the still water. The necklace vanished with a faint plop and moonlight glimmered on widening ripples. Bubbles rose and burst.

No time for moonlit bubbles.

"Midnight—the time to send a message to the Residency."

Tikendra Jeet arrived at the southwest rampart to find the artillery officer waiting with seven-pounder field guns and ordinance at the ready.

"Common shells?"

The officer presented a nearby row of pointed missiles, ready to arm and load. Common shells held low-grade explosives. Fuses ignite the gunpowder and the shells burst mid-air, showering incendiary fragments across a wide target area.

Tikendra Jeet grinned. "Trim fuses longer—this time, set fire to the house."

He raised his hand and, at the stroke of midnight, gave the signal. With two mighty booms, the twin RLM seven-pounder Mk IV field guns erupted in unison. The explosive shells fell and burst amongst the Residency treetops. Distant figures of Gurkhas scurried as branches crashed earthward.

Tikendra Jeet shouted over the wall. "Thanks to Queen Victoria for the fine weaponry!"

He ran giggling along the rampart toward the Western Gate and found the officer on watch. "Signs of forward observers?"

The turbaned officer pointed. "There—in the brush. Gurkhas hide, but we see them."

Tikendra Jeet patted the officer's shoulder and smiled. He turned toward the brush, cupped his hands, and shouted in Manipuri. "The sahibs will not return!" He chuckled and turned to the officer. "I think they got the message. Watch and see."

The brush stirred, and a solitary figure broke for the Residency gate. A rifleman raised his musket but Tikendra Jeet shook his head, watching the soldier scramble. "Let him scurry—I want the message delivered. They must know why the cannon fired and despair. If they surrender fast, we may escape this mess alive."

Tikendra Jeet beheld the carnage and turned to the artillery officer. "Before I collapse—I will take a rest. Keep firing until I give the order."

He retreated to a guardhouse and fell face first onto a cot. Exhaustion took its toll, and he slipped into a deep sleep. Darkness parted, and he stood once more in the silver moonlight at the bank of the Nungjeng Pukhri.

You lost something.

Tikendra Jeet looked for the speaker, but saw no one. On the moonlit bank, at his feet, a chain necklace and medal glittered. He lifted and studied the symbol—a looped dragon devouring its tail.

"My medallion," he said. "I tossed this into the lake. How did it get here?"

Safer where it belongs—back around your neck.

He placed the chain over his head and, as he slipped the medallion into his tunic, dark figures approached. A young man bore a frail-looking man draped over his back. The older man released his grip by the bank and sat.

He wore a green uniform and a lilac turban. Moisture glistened in deep-set eyes and tears ran over his bushy white mustache.

"Ipu! General!" Tikendra Jeet called, but the men did not respond.

The general knelt at the water's edge, splashed his face and neck, and then dunked his head. He slipped, almost toppling in, but the valet caught his tunic. The old man raised his head, drops dripping from his shaggy mane, and wailed as if with a broken spirit.

"Please help me." He extended open hands over the waters. "Lord Pakhangba, tell me what I should do."

You know what to do.

Tikendra Jeet jerked, startled by the voice in his head.

"Tell me!" the general pleaded.

Fulfill the prophecy.

"General!" Tikendra Jeet shouted. "No!"

That time the general tensed. He turned and stared through the prince.

He heard me, but he cannot see me!

A female voice said, "Who are you?"

Tikendra Jeet spun to see who spoke.

No one there again!

A man spoke. "Yuvraj!"

Tikendra Jeet stirred but did not wake, too weary to climb to consciousness.

My neck itches!

He reached to scratch and discovered his lost necklace—back around his neck where it belonged.

I dreamed I tossed it in the lake.

He smiled and snuggled deep into the pillow, drifting back toward the darkness.

"Yuvraj!"

Tikendra Jeet jerked and woke—still lying on a cot in the guardhouse. "What time is it?"

"After two," the officer replied. "Your order is underway."

"What order?"

"The sahibs."

"Where are they?"

"With the executioner."

Chapter 64. The Evacuation

An hour earlier, approaching the 11 o'clock hour…

Ethel

Ethel returned to the house and wandered the halls in dismay. Sight of the havoc wrought by bullets—her precious belongings destroyed—twisted her stomach.

Nothing can be as it was!

She blinked back tears and took a deep breath.

Think of survival. You can replace objects!

Ethel reached her bedchamber, collapsed onto her bed crying, and discovered her little dragon tingling her hand.

I do not remember taking it from my pocket.

Green jewel eyes twinkled as moonlight poured through the window, and heavy eyelids embraced blackness.

Black curtains parted, and she emerged from a gray mist, standing in a moonlit grove. Naked toes wriggled beneath a flowing white gown, caressing cool grass. Long dark hair flowed over her shoulders.

The way Moonia always brushed it!

Ahead in the clearing, a circle of silent figures—young girls in pastel dresses—performed a slow, moonlight dance. Amongst the trees, handsome women with proud smiles watched the graceful dancers.

"I recognize you," Ethel whispered. "The dance company—at my gate last night."

The girls linked hands, formed a semi-circle, and gazed at the moon. Ethel stepped closer, smiling, marveling at the pale glow of translucent bodies.

Like phantoms!

"Are you—dead?" Ethel asked.

Heads lowered and shimmering eyes met hers. Dark stains covered fronts of dresses and ghastly wounds disfigured young faces.

"What happened?"

The youngest turned and pointed toward a temple. Ethel glanced and nodded in recognition. "Shri Govindajee," she whispered. "Should I go there?"

One by one, the ghostly figures looked skyward and vanished. A silvery path appeared, leading to the temple. Bare feet glided, and as she reached the verandah, three men emerged, flew down the brick stairs, and sped toward the Kangla-sha. A slender man wearing a white turban and tunic led the sprint.

"Tell me his exact words!" he shouted, turning his head.

Ethel recognized the face and called, "Prince Tikendra Jeet!"

The man stopped, looked, spoke with the others, and then ran on, paying Ethel no heed. They disappeared from sight near the Kangla-sha.

He heard me! Why did he not see me? Why is he not with Frank?

Ethel started after, but stopped.

The girls want me at the temple.

She climbed the short flight, bare feet scuffing over rough bricks, and took cautious steps into the ambulatory passage. She edged forward, holding her breath, with outstretched hands touching total darkness.

What is that? A tiny point of light!

The point moved toward her, grew to a flicker, and disturbed the black, showing a male figure carrying a burning torch. He wore a gown—thin, white, and feminine—not a priest's robe. The torch lit a familiar face.

"Young Maiba!" Ethel exclaimed. "Your face—painted—like a woman! Why?"

Ethel's presence went unnoticed—unseen, unheard. The priest raised the torch and approached a chasm in the hall floor.

"This is the end," he said, standing at the edge. "I stayed true—did all I could. The prince must stop the prophecy now. If I understood your will—I could..."

The torch lifted higher and then dropped. Fire blazed as the brand fell—light dwindled and vanished. Silence followed, and then sounds—metallic scrapes, like steel blades on hard stone, heavy breathing—and stale air rose from the black opening.

Ethel edged away, terrified of gaping holes in total darkness, turned, and wandered forward, hands outstretched. A blind, cautious effort to retrace her steps brought panic as the passage stretched forever and she lost track of time and direction.

Wrong way—lost!

Then, at last, a faint glimmer appeared, and she emerged into moonlight. She ran for the steps and paused, sighting a man in a white gown walking toward the Kangla-sha.

Young Maiba—going to the dragons? Is Frank there? I must find Frank and Walter.

She hurried down, intending to follow, but halted.

What stopped you?

Fear.

What frightens you?

The statues—I fear what lies at their feet—something from a dream. I must face my fear and follow.

"No!" a cracking voice said. "Do not!"

Ethel spun and there—hid by moon shadows of brick columns—stood a hunched woman.

"Moonia?"

"Now is time to leave." The old woman's voice grated Ethel's spine. "I told you—go west—do not delay."

"Not time yet!" Ethel argued. "Frank said I would know when—if Manipur attacked. All is quiet and calm."

"Go now!"

Twin explosions erupted and Ethel woke to a telltale whine. A shell detonated, the house shook, and a mighty crash followed.

"Frank!" she cried. "Oh my God! Manipur is attacking. Where is Frank?"

She sniffed.

Smoke—the house is on fire!

Then voices—high-pitched chattering—followed by banging and sound of activity.

Outside—the Gurkhas!

She cocked her head, listening, trying to glean meaning from the strange mix of English, Hindi, and Nepali.

Another bucket brigade—bringing more lake water!

Ethel stowed the dragon idol in her dress pocket, leapt to her feet, and rushed for the bedchamber door. She grabbed, tugged, and rattled the knob.

Unlocked, but stuck!

Smoke drifted through the crack under the door and wafted past her shoes. Ethel braced one foot against the frame and grabbed the knob with both hands. She pulled with all her might—with a screech, the door opened an inch and stopped. Through the narrow opening, she saw glimmering flames, and terror struck.

The shell collapsed the roof over this wing! The other door!

Ethel ran to the far side of the bedchamber—the door to her study opened with ease.

Thank God!

She sidestepped her writing desk and reached the door to Frank's study. The knob turned—she yanked, but the ceiling groaned and the header beam creaked, compressing the doorframe.

It will not budge! Trapped!

With a loud crash, the bedchamber ceiling collapsed, and her bed disappeared under a pile of timber, plaster, and thatch. A cloud of dust and smoke billowed through the open door.

Ethel coughed and yelled, "Help! Someone—please—help me!"

"Missus Grimwood!" a man's voice answered.

"Yes!" she shouted. "Captain Boileau? I am in here. Go in through Frank's study."

"I see the door! Stand back!"

With a heavy thud, his shoulder struck the door. The wood shuddered, but the frame held. The captain flung his weight again, and that time the portal burst open. Boileau entered, grabbed Ethel's hand, and pulled her to safety.

"Thank you!" Ethel said, panting. "You saved my life—how—how were you so close?"

"I was looking for you," he answered. "You asked me to come wake you if there was news."

"News!" Ethel exclaimed. "Are they back—Frank and the others?"

The captain set his jaw and shook his head. "The guns...," he began and then stopped.

Ethel *had* received news. The guns fired—Manipur *had* attacked—truce at an end. The parlay failed with the negotiators still inside—as prisoners—or worse. Tears welled and her hand stifled a cry. Blood drained, and the room darkened. She wobbled, weak-kneed, and Boileau caught her arm. He kept her steady and led her back to the kitchen. At the door to the cellar stairs, color returned to Ethel's face, her vision cleared, and she remembered Frank's instructions.

"We *must* evacuate!" she announced.

"The Gurkhas have the fire under control. The cellar stairs are clear. Only one wing is in ruin."

"I mean—we must abandon the entire compound. Everyone—now!"

"But—but...," the officer stammered. "I must discuss this with Captain Butcher."

"Consult as you wish," she replied. "I am leaving, along with any wanting to come."

Ethel left the open-mouthed officer and clattered down the wooden steps to find Doctor Calvert. The surgeon required no convincing.

"I argued for retreat hours ago!" the surgeon exclaimed. He and his assistant packed medical supplies and prepared to move the wounded.

Ethel located the sword, pistols, and holsters Frank and Walter had trusted to her care and carried them upstairs.

Must pack—first find a travel bag for essentials.

Ethel started for her bedchamber, stopped, and sighed.

Off limits—roof collapsed—stuck with what clothing I wear.

She located a suitable carpetbag on a pantry shelf and tossed in the sabre and revolvers. She rummaged shelves and drawers in the dining room for anything useful and voices came from a conference in the durbar hall. Captain Boileau waved through the open door, motioning her to join.

"Come in, Missus—this concerns you, too."

Two Gurkha soldiers were delivering a report. She recognized one as Sunwar, the man who rescued Lionel and saved her figurine. As she entered, the captain bade the other continue his report.

"The voice spoke in Manipuri..." He stopped and looked at Ethel.

"Please go on," Ethel said. "I know my husband is in danger. Tell us what you heard."

"A man on the wall said...," He paused, swallowed, and blurted, "'the sahibs will not return!'"

"You are certain?" Boileau said.

"Yes, sahib!"

"You understand the Manipuri tongue?"

"Yes, sahib! At least—I understood that much."

There is no doubt now.

Butcher and Boileau whispered, and then Butcher nodded to the Gurkhas. "That will be all."

The Gurkhas saluted, turned to leave, and as Sunwar passed, he gave a huge grin. Ethel smiled back.

I can never repay him!

"Missus Grimwood," Captain Butcher said after the two men left, "Captain Boileau tells me you want to evacuate, and we discussed your suggestion…"

Ethel shot the men a stern look. "It is *not* a suggestion."

Butcher ignored her comment. "We cannot let you to leave on your own. We cannot spare the men and ammunition."

"I promised my husband," Ethel answered. "He was firm—resuming hostilities means the truce failed—time to flee. I am sure Colonel Skene gave similar orders."

The officers exchanged glances. Boileau cleared his throat. "Yes," he said, "the colonel did, but—it may be too soon. We do not know the status of our party. We cannot abandon brave men to an uncertain fate."

"Do something!" Ethel shouted. "We must evacuate! You had your chance! I am finished with the indecisiveness of military officers and career politicians. I will honor my husband's final instructions. The doctor is coming, too—we are bringing the wounded and any natives in camp wishing to follow."

Gurkha sentries gathered outside the window, rifles ready, chattering, eying the house as gunshots cracked, and explosions rattled broken glass.

Men are listening—they know we argue. Not good—I must end this discussion.

"But—where will you go?" Butcher implored.

"West—to Cachar—to find Cowley's reinforcements."

"You do not know the road," Boileau protested.

"I do."

"Even in the dark?"

"With my eyes closed!"

"With native warriors behind every tree?"

"We have no choice!" she said. "Do something, or stay here and die if you see fit, but I am leaving with the wounded and non-combatants. This conversation is at an end."

Ethel left without further words. She found the bearer, set him to spreading the word, and exited the house through the front door, barking orders. Back inside, as she reached the cellar stairs, kahars emerged, removing the first of the wounded.

Lionel!

The lieutenant cried in pain as the orderlies set the litter down behind the house. Sunwar was at his side. Doctor Calvert edged away the Gurkha and Ethel kneeled beside her friend.

"Do not move me!" Lionel cried. "I hurt too much!"

"We must," Ethel said. "We are evacuating and cannot leave you."

"Yes, leave me! I will slow you. I cannot make it—too much pain!"

Ethel looked at Calvert, eyes begging the surgeon for a sign of hope. He tightened his jaw and shook his head.

He can do nothing—out of morphine!

"I have something to say," Lionel whispered. "Before I die..."

"Shush!" she answered. "You are not dying. Keep quiet—save your strength."

"No—before I go—I must speak..."

"All right, Lionel," Ethel said, tears welling. "What is it?"

"I—I love you..." He coughed blood. "I always have—I—hoped..."

"Oh, dear Lionel!" she cried, tears streaking. "Listen—Listen! Shush! You must not die—do you hear me? Stay strong—you are all I have left. I cannot lose you, too. You can make it. You must!"

"I—love...," he whispered, closed his eyes, and issued a long sigh.

Calvert felt for a pulse and shook his head.

Ethel gripped Lionel's shirt and buried her face, sobbing. Calvert touched her shoulder and then peeled away her clinging fingers.

"We cannot—leave him—here," she sobbed. "I know their evil ways—they behead enemies—even dead ones. They will defile his body—I cannot abandon him to such a fate."

"We cannot take him," Calvert replied. "No time for burial."

"Hide him in the cellar then," Ethel said. "Use the bandstand lumber. If the house burns, it will be his pyre. Flames will guard his remains."

The kahars lifted the doolie, carried the dead officer to the cellar, and laid the body on a sheet. Ethel knelt at Lionel's side, closed his eyes, and prayed for him and for herself.

Please forgive me. My vanity lured this young man to his death.

She sobbed, and when Calvert placed a hand on her trembling shoulder, she shrank and said, "He deserves a proper eulogy!"

The doctor cleared his throat. "Here lies Lieutenant Brackenbury of the 44th Gurkha Rifles—a good officer, cut down before his time. Rest in peace, Lionel." He took Ethel's arm. "Come now—we must go!"

Ethel pulled the sheet over Lionel's face and stood back, fighting tears and mustering strength, as Gurkhas piled planks atop the body.

I am finished crying. I am now numbed, immune to the sight of death.

She drifted outside and turned attention to the evacuation. Lieutenant Lugard hobbled forward leading a company of fifty Gurkhas.

"Butcher and Boileau reconsidered," he said. "Will you take help from a lame escort?"

Ethel accepted without hesitation and put the Gurkhas to work rigging more litters.

The bearer collected the remaining servants and chaos erupted as a jabbering swarm of bunnias (merchants), coolies, and camp followers crowded the assembly, pushing, shoving, and jostling others aside. They chattered with clasped hands, pleading fear of abandonment, begging the bearer to include them in the company.

Ethel's westward escape route faced an obstacle—the thorny cattle barrier—her last line of defense.

"I will come for you after we cut a path," Lugard said. "Wait by that tree—do not move from that spot."

"I promise," Ethel said.

As Lugard set Gurkhas hacking at the hedge with kukris, shells exploded near Ethel's tree and limbs crashed earthward. Ethel flinched, cringing, eyes darting each way. She reached into her dress pocket to made sure she had her cherished possession—the dragon figurine. She glanced at her footwear—the patent leather shoes she donned at lunchtime.

Comfortable inside, but not for hiking one hundred miles!

She considered sneaking inside and finding another way into her bedchamber.

No, the shell destroyed any possibility—but other useful items might still be reachable. Should I make one final sortie?

She remembered her promise to Lugard to stay put until summoned.

Should I risk them leaving me behind, like one bunnia too many?

The temptation was too great. Ethel stepped toward the house, but stopped as a telltale shriek filled her ears. A massive explosion followed, and her world went dark.

Chapter 65. The Wages of Sin

An hour earlier...

Walter

Walter Simpson ground out a painful slog to consciousness, as if climbing a dark well, dragging himself brick by brick by his fingernails, only to slide back and start again.

Voices!

Distant at first, then closer and louder—men murmuring, then shouting, speaking in Meiteilon, the language of the Meitei of Manipur—followed by banging and more voices.

Arguing—Tikendra Jeet and the Tongol General. Sounds as if the general wants us dead!

Walter slid back down, drifted, and lost sense of time. When cannon boomed, he stirred and faced reality.

The truce is over—the attack resumed!

His forehead and eyes ached as someone wiped his tender brow.

Something cool, refreshing—a damp cloth!

Eyelids fluttered, and he moaned, "Oh, my head hurts. Light is too bright—hurts my eyes."

"Shush!" a young woman's voice answered. "It is only torchlight—outside is even brighter. The moon shines like nothing ever seen. Chandra is watching."

"I know that sweet voice," Walter mumbled. Through a blurry haze, a familiar profile emerged.

Leishna—so pretty!

Delicate hands of his friend and mistress wrung the cloth into a bowl and placed cool comfort across his wounded forehead. Walter lifted his feet a few inches and something clattered when his heels hit the stone floor.

"My legs are so heavy."

"You wear iron fetters."

Walter shook his feet—chain jangled and iron clanked. "It appears so—why?"

"So you will not run away, silly."

"Oh." He tried to swallow but his mouth was dry. "Good plan—otherwise I am certain to flee."

"Do not talk so much."

Walter licked his lips and blinked as the room came into focus. "So—what hit me?"

"A polo mallet." Leishna dabbed the cloth and moistened his lips. "It may have cracked your skull. It could have killed you if it had struck a little higher."

"Polo is such a brutal sport," Walter mumbled. "Always figured it would be the death of me."

"You should not make jokes!"

Ah, such sweet scolding!

He winced. "You saved me, I suppose."

She smiled. "Maybe I did something."

Such a heavenly smile!

"My father helped, too."

"Your father—the venerable Tongol General? I do not believe it."

"He did," she said. "He disarmed the man before he could strike me…"

"Oh, I see," he said. "Perhaps he saved you, not me. Well, thank you, and thanks to him, too, for the protective gesture."

Walter stroked her smooth cheek and smiled. "Sweet child. I woke to such a pretty face—the sight alone almost makes the pain vanish. I do not deserve a good friend like you."

"You are right!"

"Ah, and who is making light now?"

The smooth cheeks flushed as she bit her lower lip and changed topics. "Do you remember anything?"

"Hm. I remember—the crowd. They chanted, kill… kill. Then they attacked. Did we all survive?"

Leishna frowned, shook her head, and looked away. She turned back with moist eyes. "Sahib Frank," she whispered.

"Dead? How?"

"Stabbed, run through with a spear."

Walter shook his head as tears welled and flowed. He tried to speak but coughed and winced, bit his lip, and forced words to come. "I promised

Ethel I would protect him—not much of a protector, was I? We became best friends and I loved him as a brother."

"I loved him, too," Leishna murmured, tears streaking.

"Are the others safe?"

"Yes." She looked to his left. "Safe and right here beside us."

Walter raised his head, but the agony was too great. He turned back to Leishna. "Who killed Frank?"

"An officer of the guard—his wife and children died in the massacre at Rasmandala."

"Oh," Walter said, sighing. "I cannot blame the poor chap. I might have done the same."

Seconds passed and then Leishna shed her dour demeanor, straightened, and brightened. "The Yuvraj ordered the guards to arrest the murderer!"

"Oh, fabulous," Walter replied. "That is a relief—one less worry."

The girls face fell and Walter turned inward.

Frank, I am sorry I failed you, my friend.

Walter looked back at the young woman, brushed a strand from her eyes, and smiled. "So now, here we all are—in one fine mess."

She pouted. "You are alive, at least. You are with me and I will not leave you."

"What will your father say? I dreamed he wanted us dead—that he argued with Tikendra Jeet in favor of killing us."

"That was no dream!" she whispered. "It was a big argument—much tension. My father wants to start another Great Rebellion. The Yuvraj is wiser—he protects you—for now, at least."

"Where are we? What is this place?"

"The durbar hall."

"Ah, makes sense. Close by, up the steps. Very convenient."

Leishna turned back to the bowl of water and rinsed the cloth. Water dribbled as she squeezed the excess and placed the damp towel back on his brow. "Too much talk. Rest now."

A man's gruff voice erupted from Walter's left. "I say, Simpson," Chief Commissioner Quinton said. "What is all that jabbering? Can you two not speak English?"

"Sorry, sir."

"Are you back among the living?"

"It appears so, sir. To a point, at least."

Another voice spoke, this time Colonel Skene. "Simpson, were you awake to hear any of the shouting a short while ago? Tikendra Jeet and the Tongol General were going at it."

"Yes, sir," Walter answered. "They were arguing over us. The mob wanted us dead—now the general does, too. Leishna says the Yuvraj is keeping us alive for the moment. I cannot say for how long."

"We should get word to the Residency," Quinton said. "Tell them we are alive—most of us. Your—woman friend—could she do this for us?"

Walter asked Leishna in a hushed voice. She looked at the guards and dignitaries and whispered back. "I am no prisoner—I can leave any time. My father even wanted me to leave—but if I tried to make it to the Residency, I fear one side or the other would shoot me. What good would it do? The sahibs will assume you are prisoners, but the firing has them pinned down—they cannot rescue you."

Walter relayed her answer.

"Hum," Quinton said. "This entire situation is my fault. I want that made clear—I accept full responsibility."

"You were following orders," Skene replied. "The same way any of us must."

"Blast them and their orders!" Quinton shouted. "Despicable politicians and snobby elites—criminals all! I am a free agent. I should have thought of our lives and not my career."

"Such conversation is not useful," the colonel countered. "I directed my officers to draw up the battle plan. Grimwood, after a while, argued for attacking the fort. Enough blame—nothing gained from recrimination."

"Humph!" Quinton replied.

Skene turned back to Walter. "I assume they have the outside well-guarded. Ask her."

Walter asked.

"Sentries all around," she answered. "To keep the mob out. You are unarmed, and with your fetters, you would not get far. It is best to trust Prince Tikendra Jeet. He will keep you safe."

Walter relayed her answer. Quiet followed, punctuated by the sound of vicious firing outside in the distance.

"Poor devils," Skene muttered. "At the Residency, I mean. The bombardment sounds merciless."

"Well," Walter said, "if Ethel—Missus Grimwood that is—respects her husband's orders, by now she should be on her way to Cachar."

"What do you mean by that, Simpson?" Quinton asked.

Walter explained that Frank had given Ethel a directive to flee west. "He was emphatic—I was there—she promised."

"Is she capable of such a feat?" Skene said. "In the dark—under attack?"

"Well capable," Walter insisted. "Resourceful when she puts her mind to it. I would wager she could find her way to Cachar blindfolded."

"Jolly good!" Cossins said. Skene and Quinton stared at the bookish man and he added, "Well, nothing wrong with hoping she escapes."

"If we can hold out here...," Quinton added, "and, if they can reach Captain Cowley's column..."

"Butcher and Boileau would have to keep the bulk of the forces in place," Skene interjected, "so the Manipuris do not suspect. I wonder if they have the good sense."

Walter struggled to a sitting position and shook his head. "I suspect if Ethel goes, then they will all go. Any staying to face that fierce bombardment would sacrifice themselves."

"You reminded me, Simpson," Quinton said. "A while back, during the durbar, all that nonsense about slaughtering innocent women and children—you looked as if you knew something."

Skene studied Walter's face. "*Do* you?"

"It is possible," Walter said.

He told the story of his sepoy named Sunwar and another Sunwar carrying his dead cousin down the steps at the tower; the suspicious-looking bayonet wound; and finding empty cartridges on the roof. He described the jade-green dragon figurine, his fears, and reluctance to return it to Ethel.

"Poppycock!" Quinton shouted. "Stuff and nonsense! That polo mallet did something more than bash your skull—it scrambled your brain. Next, you will tell us you believe in ghosts."

"Well, funny you should mention that..." Stern looks from Quinton and Skene cut him short.

The room remained silent for several minutes. Walter turned back to Leishna, speaking in her language. "Did you spy on me?"

"Oh, yes."

"You spied on Frank, too, I suppose."

"Yes, I did. Like you, I must follow orders."

"I suppose so," Walter said. "There are other spies, too—right?

"Yes."

"Moonia?

Leishna laughed. "That old witch! No—not a spy! She loves and protected the memsahib."

"She poisoned the goat!"

Leishna chuckled. "Goat would have died—eaten by heathen sahibs. The old witch tried to save the memsahib from the anger of Agni the fire god. Bad to eat a goat without proper Vedic ceremony."

"So I hear," Walter muttered. "Still—she stole Ethel's little jade-green dragon figurine and ran away. She gave it back to Tikendra Jeet."

"Idol does not belong to the memsahib. The idol came from the dragon king himself. It belonged in the temple. It is very dangerous for any ordinary person to keep. Moonia was trying to save the memsahib from the danger."

"I can vouch for the danger!" He inspected his burned fingertips. "Well, the old witch had everyone fooled. I gave the idol back to Ethel. It was foolish, but did it anyway. I wonder why."

"Maybe the idol uses memsahib for its own purpose."

"Are you sure the mallet did not hit you, too?" Her ugly scowl wiped the smile from his face. "Sorry—if not Moonia, who spied?"

Leishna shrugged. "There are free agents, too, with their own designs and purposes. Not everyone works for Prince Tikendra Jeet. Who can say who is a spy? I do not know everything."

Walter leaned back on one elbow and studied Leishna's eyes. "You know an awful lot for such a delicate young lady. You are a much better spy than I imagined. Why did you save me? Why are you helping me now?"

Leishna blushed and shrugged.

"I remembered something," Walter said. "I may have dreamed it, but I thought I heard you tell your father you loved me."

Leishna turned redder. "Not a dream," she said. "I said that, but you do not love me—you love the memsahib."

"How would you know?"

She shrugged. "Everyone knows. Now that Sahib Frank is dead, you and she can be together at all times."

"Can we? I wonder. I must first escape this mess."

The door opened, and a man entered and spoke with Angom Ningthou. Other Manipuris gathered and a hurried discussion ensued. Walter tensed, sat up straighter, and caught several dignitaries looking at the prisoners.

"Who is that?" Walter whispered.

"Rudra Singh—Yenkhoiba Major—Lalupchingba, leader of Manipur's irregulars. He is a cousin and trusted advisor of the Yuvraj."

"What are they discussing? I understood only a word or two."

"It is hard to say." Leishna listened. "I dislike their tone." She became agitated. "Something has changed."

"What do you mean?"

"Hush!" she said. "I fear…"

The guards gathered and Yenkhoiba Major approached with Angom Ningthou. The major kicked Leishna's foot. "Stand!"

"Why?" she demanded. "What is happening?"

"New orders."

Leishna squared her shoulders and crossed her arms as if challenging the major's authority. "Where is the Yuvraj?" Her eyes narrowed. "Where is Prince Tikendra Jeet?"

"Simpson!" Quinton said. "What is happening?"

"Uncertain, sir. Something ominous, I fear."

The major met Leishna's stare, wavered, and signaled for the guards. The men seized Leishna's arms and pulled her standing.

She faced the major with burning eyes. "No!" she shrieked, straining at their grip. "You cannot do this! Where is the prince?" She thrust her face toward Angom Ningthou. "You swore to protect the sahibs!" Her voice cracked with icy scorn. "He called you his friend!"

Leishna struggled and bit restraining hands. The major grabbed hair, twisted, and she screamed. The guards won the test of strength and dragged the young woman from the room.

Yenkhoiba Major turned to Walter. "Stand! All of you—come with us."

Walter pointed at his feet. "As you can see, you fettered us." He shook his legs, and the chains clanged.

The major nodded to the guards. Two men grabbed Walter by the arms and yanked him to his feet. The major grew close, locked eyes, and hissed through gritted teeth, "Shuffle!"

Guards lined the four Englishmen and with Gunna Ram leading the way, the five shuffled toward the door. Walter followed the bugler, with Skene, Cossins, and Quinton next in line. Walter blinked as he stepped into the moonlight.

Leishna was right! I have never seen a moon this bright!

The parade waddled down the stairs to face a mob of several thousand crowding every corner of the courtyard, save a broad opening near the Kangla-sha. The guards led the prisoners past sputtering torches to the clearing before the dragon statues. A middle-aged man in a thin white gown stood waiting, face down, hands folded. His head rose, and the torchlight flickered over a grim, painted face.

"Who is that?" Cossins asked.

"The Manipuris call him Young Maiba," Walter answered. "He is a priest, or a shaman—Krishna worship, dragon worship. No idea why he is here. It is not like him to leave the temple and get involved in such matters." Walter scanned the line of faces in the crowd and muttered, "Where is Tikendra Jeet? I do not see the Tongol General either. Who is in charge, I wonder?"

The guards forced the five into a straight line, north-to-south, at the feet of the Kangla-sha. Gunna Ram stood at the northernmost position and Quinton was southernmost. A gruff guard moved up and down the line, barking at the men, grabbing, squaring shoulders to the line, backs perpendicular to the statues.

"What is he saying?" Skene asked Walter.

"He wants us facing due west."

The priest in the white gown, the man Walter called Young Maiba, raised thin arms and bony elbows above the sleeveless gown. A hush fell as the maiba addressed the crowd.

"Now is the time!" he said. "The time foretold in the great prophecy is upon us. The dragon god has risen and retaken his rightful place. He has spoken and his wishes are clear. We welcomed the sahibs in peace, but they attacked us, burned our villages, and slaughtered our livestock. They destroyed sacred relics in our temple and desecrated our altars and sanctums with the blood of patriots. They killed women, children, and elderly, profaning our sacred grove with the blood of innocents—mothers with young daughters—celebrating a holy day. Must the sahibs now pay for their crimes?"

The crowd erupted. "Yes! Make them pay! Death to the sahibs!"

"Send forth the public executioner," Young Maiba commanded.

A tall man emerged from the crowd bearing a ceremonial dao blade. He hefted his large sword and took practice swings.

"What is happening, Simpson?" Quinton said.

"Something bad, I fear, Chief Commissioner. I recognize the pattern of that blade. The Manipuris call it Tendol Thang—wicked sharp. If you have anything to get straight with your Lord and Savior, I suggest you get to it. It appears we are to give the last full measure of devotion to the Queen."

"So they propose to execute us then," Skene said. "We came here under truce. This is their sense of justice. Where is the Yuvraj? Can he not face us while they commit this crime?"

"Execute us!" Cossins exclaimed. "This—is—preposterous," he sputtered. "Nothing we can do? Say something, Simpson. You speak their language."

"I will try," Walter said and cleared his throat. "You!" He shouted at the priest. "Young Maiba! What do you mean by this?"

The man in the white gown strode forward nose-to-nose with Simpson who smirked, studying the priest's garb. "What are you made up to be?" The maiba snarled, and Walter added, "Where is Tikendra Jeet? We demand to see the Yuvraj."

"The prince signed your death order by inviting you to enter our gates. You must pay now for your crimes."

Walter lunged, fetters clanking. The maiba shrank back and guards sprang, raising spears to Walter's neck.

"Will you face your deaths as men," the maiba said, "or must we bind you like sheep to sacrifice?"

Walter shuffled back a step and translated for the others.

"Right," Quinton said. "So that is it? Well, I need no bonds. I will show them how an Englishman dies."

"Is this it then, sir?" Cossins asked, voice trembling.

"Sorry, William," Quinton murmured. "Sorry I dragged you into this—sorry for everything."

"I would not have missed it, sir."

The executioner stepped to the end of the line, faced north, and hefted his sword. Young Maiba raised and dropped his hand. Walter closed his eyes as the swordsman swung the blade with a great swish. A hollow thud followed as Chief Commissioner Quinton fell dead. The executioner stepped over the body and faced Cossins. The blade swung again and the little man in the tweed suite fell beside his superior.

Skene grinned at Walter and the bugler. "I will greet you both in Hell!"

Walter nodded and gave a quick salute. "Jolly good, sir! I will be along soon."

The blade swung and Skene fell. Walter squeezed Gunna Ram's arm.

"Have courage, soldier."

"Better dead than a coward! You know this, sahib!"

Walter nodded and managed a final smile as the blade swung.

Something happened to the moon!

One moment so bright and then—darkness—everywhere black. Then, from somewhere—a light.

From above or below—I cannot tell.

Yet, Walter Simpson knew...

Everything will be all right.

Chapter 66. The Red Glow

Seconds before...

Tikendra Jeet

Tikendra Jeet's pony galloped hard through the Laktong Gate to the royal courtyard where a massive crowd blocked his path. From mounted vantage before the Kangla-sha, he observed the swift swing of the executioner's blade that dropped Lieutenant Simpson.

Too late!

Four headless bodies sprawled at the feet of the massive dragon statues—splattered blood darkened the paws and thick legs. Only the Gurkha bugler remained standing, feet shackled by iron fetters. The executioner lifted his sword, awaiting the final signal, and a man in a white gown raised a hand.

Young Maiba! Is he responsible?

"Wait!" a voice cried.

The maiba spun to face the crowd, hand still high. The mob quieted, all eyes on the speaker, as a black-turbaned Manipuri soldier stepped forward.

"Who speaks?" the priest shouted.

"Niranjan Subadar speaks! Kajao, an officer under my command, slew the Britisher Grimwood. Hear what I say before executing the Gurkha!"

The maiba motioned, and the executioner lowered his blade. The emotionless Gurkha bugler stood, facing west, staring straight ahead.

"Speak then, Subadar, but be quick."

Niranjan faced the crowd. "This man is no Britisher—no sahib! He is a servant—a British slave! He is as I once was. Let us offer him redemption." Niranjan faced the Gurkha and spoke in Gorkhali. "Join us, bugler! I was once like you. I may be half-Gurkha, but I, too, once fought for the British lion. Do you see the error of your ways? Will you, here and now, before the aggrieved people of Manipur, before the temple of Lord Krishna and the mighty symbols of Lord Pakhangba...?" he pointed at the stark moon.

"Before the watchful eye of Lord Chandra, renounce the sahibs! Save yourself! Join us, bugler, and I will fight any man trying to harm you!"

The words echoed in the night and an eerie silence followed. The crowd inched closer as torches flickered, and flames leapt higher.

Gunna Ram, Nepali Gurkha, bugler with the 44th Gurkha Rifles of the Bengal Infantry, durbar second to Colonel Skene, spoke in a clear voice. "Kafar hone bhanda morne ramro (Better to die than to be a coward)." Ram then spoke in Hindi. "Turncoat!" He spat at Niranjan. "Half-cast!" He sneered at the mob with burning, torch-lit eyes, and the front line shrank back. "Death, I say, to you all! You have sealed your fate! The sahibs will paint your green country red with blood, raze statues, burn temples, and cast down brick walls. You will beg for mercy but receive none. God save Queen Victoria, Empress of India!"

Young Maiba gave the sign; the executioner hoisted his blade, reared, and swung. Steel flashed and the final body fell.

Tikendra Jeet dropped from his pony, sank to his knees, and wept, face buried in hands.

I failed—no longer in command—lost my country!

Silence deepened—as if the finality of death stunned the mob. The moment passed, and the crowd erupted—cheers, then drums. A slow beat at first—thump, thump, thump. The pattering tempo rose to a fever pitch, like the roar of a dragon. Men and women of every age and caste embraced. Clenched fists rose high. Many clasped hands and danced.

A voice cracked behind the prince. "You appear upset."

Tikendra Jeet raised his head, prepared to turn, but stopped.

The old witch!

He was in no mood.

"She has it, you know," Moonia said. "Your precious memsahib has the dragon idol. I told you—I said, keep it from her—but you assigned two worthless boy guards. Now they are dead, and she has the jewel."

"I had a battle to fight," the prince grumbled, glancing over his shoulder. "I could not waste soldiers guarding an idol. What does it matter? The figurine may be priceless, but locked away in a tower—worthless."

"Priceless—worthless—hah!" She chuckled. "Much more than that, you fool. The dragon holds the Mani—the magic gem of Ananta, King of the Dragons, from the treasure of Babhruvahana. It is the namesake of Manipur, a five-thousand-year-old link to the *Mahabharata*. What possessed you to give it to her?"

"She desired it—I wanted her to have it. I thought it would attract her, and I still think someday it will."

"So now she has it, and soon she will discover the power to wield it."

"Wield it?" He stood and faced the old woman. "Nonsense! Valuable, yes, but carved jade and jewels. Myths and legends—a trinket—nothing more."

"Wrong! You released a power into the world. The consequences will be on your head."

"Go, old witch!" He waved her away. "I do not believe in magic or your supernatural nonsense."

"No? You still doubt after what happened. You could not stop the prophecy."

"I tried—it was not my fault. The priest—I—I fail to understand why…"

She laughed and wagged her head as if sizing up the prince. "Too little! Too late! Legend will link you to the prophecy and deaths. You have no choice but to fight a war you will lose. You cannot win without the jewel. Manipur will burn."

"I will get the idol back."

"How?" she scoffed.

"I will storm the walls—capture the Residency."

"Too late," she said.

"Why?"

"You will not find her."

"We shall see," he said. "The dragon will not leave Manipur. I will get it back."

"No harm must come to her!" She shook a crooked finger in his face. "I have warned you!"

"No one shall harm a hair," he mumbled.

"Your spies are still at her side," Moonia said. "That may be your one hope—for a spy to seize the idol—but powerful forces want the dragon loose in the world." She sighed. "Sometimes I weary of the Great Game."

"Look!" a Manipuri man shouted. "The Yuvraj!"

"Prince Tikendra Jeet!" a woman shrieked.

Revelers broke from the mob, surrounded the prince, and lifted him high onto strong shoulders. Swept away into the dancing crowd, Tikendra Jeet looked for Moonia, but she had vanished. The bearers wove through the crowd and delivered the prince to the feet of the statues, set down before the maiba. Tikendra Jeet studied the five headless bodies and leveled a contemptuous glare at the priest.

"You arrived in time!" the maiba exclaimed. "Now we complete the prophecy—must have five heads—one more required."

"You have five!"

"The bugler is of no consequence—the prophecy demands five *white* heads."

Tikendra Jeet shook his head and spread his hands. "After all your talk—all of your warnings of the prophecy, and how I must stop it—and then, *you* had them killed. Why did you do this?"

"I saw him!"

"Saw whom?"

"The dragon!"

Tikendra Jeet squinted in the bright moonlight. "What dragon?"

Young Maiba's eyes glowed red in the torchlight. "All my life I waited—studying, learning from Old Maiba, praying the dragon would choose me. I swore to do anything asked." He looked down at his white gown and pinched the thin cloth. "I even humiliated myself, dressing as a woman."

"You are mad!" Tikendra Jeet spat.

"No! He is beautiful—all I hoped for and more—so intelligent. He spoke—said it was my time—showed me what to do. He chose me—me!"

Tikendra Jeet grabbed the maiba's arms and shook. "Who gave the order?"

"You did—do you not remember?"

"Nonsense!" the prince cried. "I did nothing of the kind—even gave explicit orders to the contrary. I was at the wall—I fired guns at the British and then slept."

The maiba threw up his hands. "Why does it matter? A new day dawns for Manipur. We must complete the prophecy." He shouted to a nearby sentry. "Summon the executioner!"

The tall man reappeared, elbowing his way through the dancers, still carrying his long blade.

"There is more to do!" The maiba pointed at the five bodies. "Separate the fetters from the unclean corpses."

The executioner nodded and swung his blade, severing the feet of the first corpse. The iron fetters clanged as he kicked them aside. He moved body to body freeing all fetters, and then faced the maiba, blood dripping from the blade.

The maiba turned to the crowd, shouting, "Clear a path! We must attend the final sahib!"

Dancers stopped and backed away, opening a passage to Frank Grimwood's body lying face down, still untouched. The executioner strode forward, lay his blade across the neck, and chopped. More cheers erupted as dancers leapt and thrust fists in the air.

"The feet are unfettered!" the priest shouted. "Leave the body untouched—retrieve only the head."

The executioner reached, grabbed hair, and returned through the crowd carrying the severed head. Tikendra Jeet blanched and looked away, unable to face the shocked stare of his former friend.

"Gather the other four white heads," the maiba called.

Guards did as ordered and kicked poor Gunna Ram's head aside.

"Show the white heads to all!"

Five guards held five British heads high—dangling by their hair, open-mouthed, wide ghoulish eyes staring back at the cheering mob.

"Behold!" the maiba said. "The prophecy fulfilled!"

Howling cheers echoed and pounding drums shook the walls.

"We must dispose of the Hakchangs!" the maiba cried. "What shall we do with the unclean bodies?"

"Feed them to pariah dogs!" a woman screamed.

"Drag them outside the Western Gate," one shouted.

"No!" another cried. "The gate is sacred. Drag them over the walls!"

Men brought ropes and grappling hooks, tossed from a safe distance, and snagged uniforms and suits of the headless corpses. The excited crowd cheered and surged west, pulling the ropes, dragging six bouncing corpses. Headless torsos flew, sliding back and forth, towed with reckless abandon through brush and dirt, kicking up dust, skidding and scraping over brick and stone.

Tikendra Jeet winced, but swallowed his sorrow and joined the maiba and stragglers. They followed the narrow causeway past the inner gates to the outer wall near the Western Gate. The leaders hauled the ropes up steps to the top of the battlements. Others raced out the gate and waited below in the ditch.

"Drop the ropes!"

The ropes fell to waiting hands in the crowd. Strong arms pulled cords, hand over hand, dragging the bodies up, painting ghoulish smears across the brick wall. When the six corpses reached the banquette, more joined below and pulled harder. The bodies strained, hung up on the battlement, and then broke free. The corpses hopped, flew over the wall, and landed in the mud with dull thuds. Pariah dogs rushed forward, snarling, fighting over the corpses.

Tikendra Jeet stood inside, far from the echoing snarls beyond the walls, when a new sound—a deep rumble—blanketed the howls, and cries. The prince faced the Residency where the southern moonlit sky above the high wall glowed an eerie red.

"What is happening?" a woman screamed.

"Red sky!" another shouted. "Blood on the moon."

The crowd surged—out the gate and up the stairs—seeking better views.

Tikendra Jeet turned to Young Maiba and sneered. "Is this part of the prophecy?"

The priest scratched his head. "I do not know what this means. An explosion perhaps? The Residency may be on fire."

The red glow dimmed, and as the rumble faded, a group of officers approached. "Strange lights and sounds at the Residency!" one said. "The sahibs are up to something!"

"Muster the soldiers!" Tikendra Jeet said. "Regulars, irregulars, anyone bearing arms—rifles, pistols, or dao knives. Send half to the Western Gate and the rest to the Southern Gate. Find ladders—as many as you can. We attack from the north and the east—cross ditches, scale walls, swarm the gate. This battle ends now!"

"What of prisoners?" an officer asked.

"Take prisoner any who drop weapons and surrender. Any that fire at you, or refuse to disarm—kill them. One exception! Pay close attention!" He scanned the crowd, seeking attentive eyes. "No one harms the memsahib, no matter what. Do you all understand? Find her and deliver her untouched and unharmed. I want that message understood and relayed to all troops before the attack begins. Am I clear?" Heads nodded. "Wait for my signal. No war cries—we attack in silence. I will lead the charge from the Western Gate. Where is the Senapati—my brother Angao Sena? I want him leading the eastern charge."

The officers scattered to muster armed forces at the two gates, as an old figure, held upright by his valet, limped toward the prince.

Tongol General! Did he have a role in this?

Tikendra Jeet met the general with gritted teeth and a penetrating gaze. "Ipu, did you order the execution?"

The general shook his head. "The mob is saying *you* did. I slept— dreamt I washed and prayed at the Nungjeng Pukhri, but woke with boundless joy on hearing the news. A great moment for Manipur!"

Tikendra Jeet turned in disgust.

No time! Must focus on the matter at hand. We can wait no longer!

Tikendra Jeet signaled the advance. His forces streamed south from the Western Gate, and to his left, his brother's column swarmed from the Southern Gate.

As they ran, the rumble returned and the red glow brightened. Many stopped and covered eyes and ears. Then the light and sound faded, as if a fiery god had risen, disappearing into the heavens.

Tikendra Jeet staggered, blinking, rubbing his eyes, dazzled by the red glow. Soldiers on each side stumbled and dropped to their knees, rubbing eyes, trying to regain vision.

Angom Ningthou appeared beside the prince and asked, "What has happened?"

Tikendra Jeet shrugged. "An unknown phenomenon—perhaps ball lightning—a vestige of yesterday's storm."

The forces reached the perimeter and threw ladders over the ditch and atop the wall. They scrambled by the hundreds into the interior, rifles, pistols, and swords ready, but encountered no resistance—the British had deserted the compound.

Manipuris raced up the carriage lane and reached the damaged remains of the house. One wing had collapsed, fire smoldered in places, and flames still flickered in others. Sepoys fanned out and scoured the building and vicinity. They searched the cellar, shacks, outbuildings, tents, and sifted through stones at the damaged Treasury astride the main gate. After a half-hour of fruitless searching, officers gathered before the verandah, and the prince studied the line of tired, confused faces.

"Gone, Yuvraj!" one said. "No one remains in the British camp."

"I found a dead body," another said, pointing toward the lane. "Over there! A Gurkha—shot mid-stride, perhaps while fleeing."

Tikendra Jeet rushed to the side of the dead Gurkha, knelt, and examined the body. "He was not fleeing," he announced. "He was running away from the house and toward the gate—perhaps to announce the retreat to men at the perimeter."

"We have searched the entire compound," an officer said. "They buried their dead in shallow graves. This man died last—never buried."

A soldier ran from behind the house waving a little black object. "Yuvraj!" he shouted. "The sahibs hacked a hole in the hedge. They crossed the river—heading west toward Cachar."

Tikendra Jeet regarded the man's hand. "What did you find?"

The soldier presented the object and Tikendra Jeet held it close to one eye. "This," he said as he tossed and caught the object, "is the heel from an Englishwoman's shoe."

She escaped, but could not have traveled far!

"Summon all officers!" When they arrived, he addressed the group in somber tones, saying, "The tired must rest or collapse. Those with strength remaining must catch the sahibs and their Gurkhas. Send a company north on the Kohima Road to Sengmai and stop any going that way. Others go east on the Burma Road—capture the cantonment at Langthabal and prevent escape at the border. Send the rest west along the Cachar Road. Kill any Britisher or Gurkha you find, but do not harm the memsahib. A thousand rupee reward to the man who captures Grimwood's wife and delivers her alive and unharmed."

The officers disbanded as a lone pony rider cantered down the lane. "I could not charge on foot," the general said, dismounting. "Too exhausted!"

"Well, old man," Tikendra Jeet said, "you have your wish—I hope you will have strength for your war with Great Britain."

"Strong enough—when the time comes."

Prince Tikendra Jeet looked at the moon, brighter than ever. "We are all puppets. We believe we are free, in charge of our lives, but we dance on strings for the amusement of others."

"Who pulls the strings?" the general asked.

"The wealthy and powerful, the gods, supernatural forces—I wonder which this time."

Chapter 67. The Avenging Angel

The early hours of Wednesday, 25 March 1891...

Siriman

Zoluti's terse whisper breathed the word Siriman feared most.

"Dragons!"

The simple utterance cracked his head like a polo mallet. Eyelids fluttered and cheeks grew hot. A sharp hiss stabbed his ears and the top of his head crackled like a lightning-sparked wildfire. The golden-haired woman's face dwindled to a pinpoint.

Must not pass out—focus! This cannot be happening.

It is happening.

Karna?

You predicted what she would say. Come back—now!

Soft hands gripped Siriman's arms. The pinpoint became a hazy circle, and the room swam into sight. Everything looked the same except the walls and deck, once sharp and bright white, appeared blurry, dingy—as if a flood drained, leaving a yellow-gray film.

The worst has passed.

Blue eyes studied his. "Are you back to reality?"

Ears burned, but he gulped and nodded.

Zoluti smiled and kept the Gurkha upright. "For a moment I feared we lost you. You should sit."

Siriman nodded, looked for a spot, and she eased him to the deck. Fellow Gurkhas gathered—tight jaws belying concern. Thapa knelt at Siriman's side and touched his comrade's forehead.

"You sensed what I was about to say," Zoluti said, "but I did not expect the word to affect you—like that."

Thapa's grin widened. "No fear, memsahib—we call Sunwar the dragon slayer."

"Dragon slayer, you say!" She rose, hands on hips. "I *have* found the right people."

Siriman shook his head as the other Gurkhas laughed. He cracked a bashful grin and mumbled, "Thapa gave Zoluti Memsahib the wrong impression. I did not slay a dragon. I met a dragon once, back in Nepal, five years ago, but did not kill it—I only wounded it."

Her eyes peered deeper. "How?"

Siriman cocked his head.

"How did you wound it?"

"I—threw my kukri—struck its shoulder."

"Dragons have shoulders?"

Siriman nodded and Zoluti threw back her head and laughed. "Knowing a detail like that makes you an expert on dragons. Did it bleed?"

Siriman nodded again.

"Good," she said. "What of creatures that bleed?"

"If it bleeds…" He paused and gulped. "We can kill it."

"Correct!" She exclaimed, clapping hands.

Siriman signaled to Thapa for help to regain his feet. Zoluti stepped back, and the Gurkhas crowded closer.

"Tell us more of your battle," she said.

"Yes, tell us," Thapa echoed.

The Gurkhas murmured agreement, fidgeting in anticipation, and then quieted. Two nights earlier at the campfire at Sengmai, Siriman left them dangling when he declined to tell his tale and retired to his tent.

They will hound me until I tell it.

Siriman shrugged in surrender and began his story, telling how he and his cousin Karna met a dragon in a bone-dry ravine in the mountains of Eastern Nepal. He spoke of the cart toppling in the rocky bed of the once raging rivulet; beloved ox Saktisali's death; the dragon's hypnotic stare; his cousin's poisoned mind; and their narrow escape from ravenous flames. He told how the rivulet raged the following day and ended his narrative with a brief mention of the pilgrimage to Kathmandu with the priest Ramnath; his dream of the Smoking Woman; and meeting the gallawalla in Bhaktapur.

"Was that when you became soldiers?" Zoluti asked.

Siriman nodded. "The British assigned us to different regiments, but we kept in touch. We were both at Kangla. Karna's company arrived first, before the main column."

"Where is your cousin now?" Zoluti whispered, and her frown signaled suspicion.

"Dead—killed—atop the temple tower." It was all Siriman could manage before choking back tears. He wanted to tell everything, but the voice stopped him.

Say nothing for now of the slaughter or Memsahib Grimwood's dragon idol.

Zoluti took Siriman's hands. "The story is painful to recollect. Did the dragon ever release its grip on your cousin's mind?"

"The dragon's murmur killed Karna at the end; he broke free moments before he died."

A long silence followed. "I see," she said at last.

What does she see? How can she understand anything?

Zoluti released Siriman's hands, bit her lower lip, and then lit up as if an idea had come to her.

"So—this matter of fighting dragons—is it personal for you now?"

A tear worked a slow path across one cheek. "Zoluti Memsahib, what does it all mean? The dragon, the Smoking Woman, the disease in Karna's mind, his death in Manipur, the letter I found and gave you, the insane attack on Kangla—nothing makes sense. I lived it and almost do not believe. Why me? Why us? Who or what are these dragons? What do they want?"

"They want the world. It was theirs once, and they bided their time— hidden, underground. Little stands in their way because those few who believe they exist lack the power to stop them. The Scientists need your help."

Siriman took a deep breath. "Then I, at least, will fight the dragons, not for the Queen, or for you—or for the Scientists, whoever they are—but to avenge my cousin. Whatever plans the dragons have are a mystery, but my destiny is to stop them…"

"And?"

"But dragons are dangerous—it will be a suicide mission. I was lucky to survive one meeting and will not be as lucky the second time. I cannot ask anyone to join me. You must release the others so they can return to duty."

A few Gurkhas protested, but many muttered in agreement.

"Is return possible?" Siriman continued. "Thank you for the rescue, but will the Scientists allow the men to go free?"

"I can arrange that," she said.

"Are you certain? They will set them down somewhere safe and release them? Are they not afraid they will tell stories of you and this flying craft?"

Zoluti laughed. "Who would believe such a tale? Did anyone believe you about the dragon?"

Siriman thought, shook his head, and then perked. "The Smoking Woman believed!"

"Ah, yes, her—she would."

"How do you know her, memsahib?"

"She and my mother were friends—a long time ago. I am here now, doing what I am doing for—for both, I suppose."

Zoluti turned away, hiding moist, red eyes. Siriman waited, counting the seconds, until the young woman cleared her throat, turned back, and continued. "No one returning will remember anything—the Scientists will make certain."

"Havildar…," Thapa said, "I, at least, wish to help fight dragons."

Each decision I make affects lives.

"We arrive in Peru soon," Zoluti said. "I suggest we finish the trip, set down in Peru, rest a while, and discuss it further. Those willing to fight will stay, and the Scientists will accommodate those wishing to return home."

Siriman brightened, but then frowned. "How can you be certain?"

"Because I will go home, too, after our stop in Peru."

Siriman scratched his head and wrinkled his nose. "You, going home? Why are we going to Peru? What do you expect to find there?"

"I expect to find my replacement. In fact, I am counting on it. At least, that is what the letter you gave me implied."

Siriman gulped at her words. "Replacement?"

"Yes. Someone who can translate, speak for the scientists. I agreed to this mission as a favor but I have a husband and a three-year-old son and I must return home."

"You will not be there when we—when I—fight dragons?"

"I hope not!"

Siriman's smile vanished.

That changes things!

His brave fantasy—standing firm, rifle in hand, bayonet fixed, jaw set, ready for anything; an avenging angel in white by his side, golden hair streaming in the wind, fiery sword raised high—disappeared, burned away like a morning mist. A nightmare replaced the fantasy—he cowered alone, crouching, cringing as flames erupted all around, unable to communicate with unseen masters, expected to do something, but unsure what.

"After you—go home—will you remember any of this?"

Zoluti grinned and said, "They may find me a tough nut to crack."

I cannot do this alone. How can I back out now? Wait!

He remembered something significant. "Ammunition!" he shouted. "We have none. We cannot fight without rifle shells."

"How many rounds have you?"

Siriman and Thapa conversed and removed their caps. They dug into pockets and dropped the discovered shells, clinking, into the hats. Between the two, they located five cartridges. They chattered at the nearby soldiers and passed the caps. More furious fumbling and digging resulted in infrequent clinks as precious few rounds dropped as the hats made the circuit and returned. Neither cap was full when presented to Zoluti.

"Too few rounds," Siriman said. "Less than two hundred is my guess— from one hundred and six men. Very hard to fight dragons without ammunition."

"Hum!" Zoluti stared at the clinking shells, dug fingers into a hat, and pulled out a handful of the gray-tipped 577 brass cartridges. She closed one eye and studied the metal canisters in an open palm, then gave a twisted smile and clenched her fist. "I will ask the Scientists!"

Off she sped up the ramp to the unseen upper decks. The Gurkhas drifted apart, chattering in small groups, and Siriman stared at darkness through the porthole. The dead black of night hid passing landscape.

We could be over plains, mountains, or open sea—impossible to tell.

Thapa joined Siriman staring in silence for uncounted minutes. "Where is the sun?" Thapa asked. "We flew many hours. It should be morning."

"We outrun the sun."

Siriman and Thapa turned to find Zoluti standing close.

Hands empty!

"The earth turns on its axis," she continued. "The sun chases us, racing east to west, a thousand miles per hour at the equator, but we fly faster. When we arrive in Peru, it will still be dark, still March 25, and earlier in the morning than when we departed. The sun will rise upon the eastern side of the Andes—the great mountain range of South America."

A half-hour later the saucer landed. Once more, there was no discernable sense of motion other than a slight bump when the struts touched the earth. The ramp lowered and Zoluti urged the Gurkhas to gather their rifles and packs and descend. Siriman and Thapa kept a tight grip on their caps as each hat held half of the precious few remaining Snider-Enfield rifle cartridges. Zoluti followed, last down the ramp.

As she predicted, they arrived under darkness. Between the scattered clouds, against a jet-black dome, a myriad of stars pierced the thin air. Siriman was at home at the high altitude, but observed Zoluti breathing with difficulty. She looked up, noticing his concern.

"I will be all right." She gave a quick wave. "This thin air requires effort."

"We Gurkhas love this air, memsahib. It is almost like Nepal."

"I can imagine."

Siriman wrinkled his forehead and turned a complete circle studying the sky.

Zoluti smiled. "Now *you* appear perplexed."

"Where is the moon? So many stars, bright as diamonds, but no moon. Manipur's moon was so bright."

"We reached the world's far side."

"Oh!" He shrugged. "Seems impossible, but must be so."

A soft hiss came from the saucer. Almost invisible in the starlight, round hatches opened and telescoping tubes extended from the bottom hull to the ground. Chest-high panels opened, revealing tube interiors stacked high with packages, large and small.

"Supplies," Zoluti said, pointing, before Siriman could ask. "Please have your men move the packages a safe distance from the saucer."

The Gurkhas crowded about the tubes and carried, or dragged, the bundles three hundred feet away. Once emptied, the panels snapped shut, and the tubes raised, disappearing into the hull bottom. Zoluti motioned everyone to back away. With a red glow and a rumbling locomotive sound, the ship rose and, in seconds, dwindled to a point and vanished.

Siriman stared skyward. "Where are they going?"

Zoluti pointed an index finger. "Up—that way! To solve your ammunition problem. The saucer is just an excursion craft."

"Excursion craft?"

"A larger ship is far above—somewhere. Think of the saucer we traveled in as a ship's boat."

Siriman shrugged. "What is that?"

"Imagine a smaller boat hoisted and carried by a great, ocean-going steamship—the boat makes short excursions to shore with passengers or crew. It is the same principle."

This is all too much for me!

Siriman shook his head. "I have never seen a steam ship." He walked to the pile of packages delivered via the tubes. "What is in these bags? This outer covering is a strange material."

"We will open the packs when the sun comes up," she said. "It should not be long."

Chapter 68. The Brown Wide-Brim Felt Hat

Continued...

Siriman

Dawn broke an hour later, revealing a stark landscape.

"We landed on the Collao Plateau," Zoluti explained.

A mountain rose in the west and the sun glinted off too many rivulets to count. Raging white foam tumbled over cliffs, raced east downhill through deep ravines toward pockets of green forests and bright sunshine reflecting off the surface of a distant great lake.

Zoluti pointed west. "Over that mountain is Arequipa, and there," she turned east, "is Lake Titicaca—the highest navigable lake…"

She stopped and smiled at Siriman shaking his head and shrugging.

"Sorry, memsahib," he said, "I know nothing of this…"

"Geography?"

"Yes—that! Where did you learn so much?"

"I taught school and became headmaster. Then I got married and—I had to quit." It was her turn to shrug. "It was for the best I suppose."

"Oh, I see." He frowned then brightened. "I went to Hindu school in Nepal—and, I can read a little English—I taught myself."

"Very creditable—good I mean—excellent." She took a deep breath of thin air and exhaled. "Let us deal with the supplies now. We should unpack and make camp. The Scientists could be away a while."

The transparent packaging material was strong and smooth, but the Gurkhas discovered they could yank little handles and rip the packs open. Larger packages contained rolls of strange cloth—thin as gossamer and shimmering with the colors of the rainbow. Boxes and cylinders of color-coded provisions tumbled to the dirt from the smaller bags. The Gurkhas sifted through the piles—jostling, arguing, and bartering.

"Why are they fighting?" Zoluti asked.

"They tire of the provisions."

"After only a few hours?"

Siriman shrugged. "They learned the better-tasting food and drink by color. Gurkhas prefer real food. Does your—geography knowledge—tell if we can forage edible wild vegetables here?"

"Yes, you are in luck—Peruvian ground apples!"

Zoluti described a perennial daisy with tasty roots, found growing wild on the eastern slopes of the Andes, with visible shoots and tubers easy to unearth.

"Wait until we assemble the tents," she said. "Then they may forage all they want."

"Tents?"

Zoluti found circular sheets of shiny paper decorated with colorful pictures. "Instructions," she said, "for assembling tents. These rolls of gossamer are tents." She studied the figures and then handed a sheet to Siriman. "Study the pictures and follow the steps. It should not be hard."

Siriman studied, turning the circle, then looked up and shrugged.

She is right—easy!

The Gurkhas first cleared rocks making a flat surface. Then, following steps shown in the pictures, stretched shiny fabric over level ground and secured the circumference with sharp, U-shaped stakes. Siriman snapped a white cube into a square in one corner and the fabric popped into a dome-shaped tent.

In similar fashion, the Gurkhas soon had a dozen such tents erected. As soldiers entered and exited tents, Siriman scratched his head.

Peculiar—the tents are invisible!

The fabric blended with the landscape so well it took close examination by Siriman to find shimmers outlining each tent.

"Magic tents!" he exclaimed.

Zoluti laughed. "There is no such thing as magic." She ran her fingers across the surface of a tent. "Look closer."

Siriman studied the material. "Tiny mirrors—reflecting the surroundings."

"Ingenious, are they not?" she said.

"How long will we stay here?"

"I guess a night or two." She looked at the cloudless heavens above the mountains. "Your men should forage while the sky is clear. This is the rainy, growing season. Expect unexpected storms and watch for sudden flooding in the ravines."

Siriman organized food foraging teams—six parties, two armed men each—a dozen riflemen sent to search for the six-foot-tall stalks.

"Look for little yellow flowers," Zoluti said. "They mark the hiding places of the sweet tubers."

Siriman doled out precious cartridges—six rounds per man—and gave instructions to fire only in an extreme emergency.

"Use kukris or bayonets first."

Zoluti addressed the foragers before they departed. "This county has a sparse but friendly population," she said. "You should have no problems, save perhaps…"

"Dragons?" Siriman said, grinning.

She laughed. "Maybe—who can tell? Let us hope not. You could meet jaguars or bears but you are more likely to frighten them. Be cautious and do not linger. Stay within two or three miles."

The tuber foragers fanned out along six routes, heading toward the mountain slopes to the west, toting empty transparent supply bags for lugging back roots. Siriman next organized similar teams to trek toward the forests near the lake to seek dead wood for campfires. Fresh water was plentiful in the many nearby streams and rivulets. A quick search of the Gurkha backpacks yielded a dozen cooking pots for tubers. Anticipation grew for a tasty evening meal.

Siriman then organized the campground—situating campfires, establishing a perimeter, and assigning sentries for night watch. At noon, foragers filtered in with firewood and ground apples and by one o'clock Siriman accounted for all save two. Sepoys Rai and Lama were the only party still at the mountain slopes.

We wait another hour before worrying.

The hour passed with no sign of the Gurkhas and he confessed his worry to Zoluti. "I have a bad feeling, memsahib."

"Let me try something," she said. "Our need outweighs any consequences."

Zoluti strolled a short distance away and sat on a flat boulder. Siriman followed and watched as she dug into the neckline of her dress and removed a fine gold chain from which a gold object dangled.

A Christian cross!

Zoluti kissed the crucifix and released it. Then she reached again and pulled out a second necklace—a silvery chain looped through a pewter-gray ring—the face sported a looped dragon devouring its tail. Siriman stared open-mouthed as Zoluti gripped the ring and closed her eyes.

"Memsahib," he ventured, voice trembling. "You have a Manipuri ring—with dragon…"

"Yes, I know."

"Is it—safe?"

"Safe for me. A gift from my mother long ago—before I realized she was my mother."

"You did not know your mother?"

Zoluti opened her eyes. "Long story for another time. Please—allow me to concentrate!"

Siriman kept quiet as Zoluti closed her eyes and her face went blank. A sudden gust of the eastern breeze tossed her hair. A cool raindrop hit Siriman's face, and he frowned, glancing up at the graying sky. After a minute, Zoluti sighed and opened her eyes.

"What happened?" he asked.

"Nothing—but I fear we have a problem."

"What must we do?"

"Find insects."

"Insects?"

"Bugs—anything creepy-crawly, or winged, six-legged creatures—as many as you can catch alive."

Siriman's face slackened. He opened his mouth to ask why she needed insects.

It must be necessary! Best to not waste time!

He ran shouting for help, and soon Gurkhas scrambled everywhere, lifting rocks, digging in the damp soil, catching flying insects in cupped hands. Minutes later Siriman and Thapa returned running, each holding a transparent provision bag filled with crawling beetles, wriggling grubs, and buzzing winged insects. Zoluti backed away from the flat boulder.

"Place them on the rock," she said and Siriman and Thapa did as she bade. "Now move back, far back." She scanned the sky. "Not too late, I hope."

Siriman followed her gaze and looked skyward.

What does she seek?

A bird appeared. "There!" Zoluti said, pointing. "A snowy plover!"

The tan-and-white plover circled, swooped, and landed atop the rock. It hopped once and pecked its curved beak at the insects.

"No one disturb me!" Zoluti said. "No matter what happens, do not touch me or try to talk until I am finished."

What is she finishing?

Zoluti kept her distance, staring at the winged creature, and soon the bird trained one eye sideways, staring back. Then the plover leapt and flew away west, but Zoluti remained standing—motionless, frozen like a marble sculpture. Thapa inched closer and opened his mouth to speak but Siriman grabbed his arm.

"Quiet!" Siriman whispered, finger to lips. "Wait!"

They waited in silence. Siriman counted to sixty fifteen times before Zoluti stirred, shook her head, and cleared her throat.

"Pick good men," she said. "Bring rifles and as much ammunition as you have. We have a rapid march ahead and must leave straightaway."

Siriman did not ask questions. He picked Thapa and ten other men. The Gurkhas armed themselves and followed the hurrying Zoluti, already a hundred yards ahead. Siriman ran, waving on the men, and all sprinted to catch their angel in white. Siriman caught up, matching her strides.

"Your ring…," he said between breaths, "the dragon ring—is it magic?"

"I told you before," she answered, staring straight ahead, "no such thing as magic, and no time to waste. Your missing men are in danger. Another man is there, too."

"Who?"

"Uncertain, but I suspect he is my replacement. We must hurry."

They covered two miles in thirty minutes. The terrain became more rugged, and they entered a ravine—a winding gash in the mountainside. Rocky cliffs sprouted scrawny bushes and crooked trees and a trickle of water rippled over sharp rocks.

"This rivulet should rage like the others," Zoluti said. "This is the rainy season—these streams should be strong and turbulent."

"Why this place?" Siriman asked. "How can you be certain?"

"I saw."

"You saw? How could you?"

"From the air."

"How…," Siriman stammered, "how could you—see from the air?"

Zoluti glanced Siriman's way but said nothing. She pressed forward, climbing rocks, and splashing through the shallow stream.

"Was it the bird?" Siriman pressed. "It must be—you saw through the bird's eyes! How is that possible?"

"This way," Zoluti answered, waving on the soldiers, ignoring his question.

"You said—no such thing as magic."

"We are almost there," Zoluti said.

The party rounded a curve in the winding ravine and stopped. Before them, on the rocky bed of the dribbling stream, was a hat—a brown, wide-brim felt hat. Beyond it lay a body, face down in a pool of blood—a dead Gurkha soldier. Thapa knelt and turned the dead man. Something razor sharp had gutted the Gurkha, slashing him from groin to chin.

Thapa examined the frozen face. "Lama!" he said, turning to Siriman.

"His rifle?"

Thapa lifted the weapon and examined the breach. "Empty—but fired."

"Where is Rai...?" Siriman scanned the ravine.

"And the other," Zoluti added. "The one who dropped this." She reached and picked up the brown hat.

Siriman gritted his teeth. "Who is the owner of the hat?"

Zoluti shrugged. "How should I know? If the letter you gave me is right, he is American—so a cowboy, perhaps. He and Rai could be up ahead. We must press on and hope we are not too late. Ready yourselves for battle."

"Two must carry Lama back to camp," Siriman said. "Warn the others."

Zoluti nodded. "First, cut off his uniform—his shirt at least."

"Why?"

"We may need material to make torches," she said.

Siriman motioned and two Gurkhas knelt and cut away poor Lama's shirt, tossed it to Thapa.

"Check for ammunition, too," Siriman said.

They searched the dead man's belt and pockets, yielding three rounds.

"He had six so he must have managed three shots," Thapa said. He picked up the rifle and bayonet and stood. Two Gurkhas lifted the body and headed back toward camp.

"Affix the bayonet," Siriman said. "Hand Lama's rifle and ammunition to the memsahib."

Zoluti blushed as Thapa thrust the rifle into her hands. She fumbled with the weapon and the brown hat.

"I—I have not fired a rifle," she said. "How do I use this?"

"Learn!" Siriman regretted his terse tone and softened. "Hold it, memsahib, and thrust. Stab at something—like so." He thrust his rifle and bayonet forward, impaling thin air.

Zoluti hefted the rifle, took a practice jab, and nodded.

"Memsahib," Siriman said, "I know where this ravine leads. You saw something from above, but I lived this exact moment. What are you not telling us? What else did you see?"

"Dragons," Zoluti said.

"How many?"

"Two, three, perhaps more," she sputtered. "With men—or something like tall men…"

"Dragons, tall men, and you did not tell us? Why, memsahib?"

"I do not know," she said, tears welling. "I am sorry but we waste time. We can discuss all that later after we save those men."

Zoluti, Siriman, and nine remaining Gurkhas pressed forward. They hurried around the next bend of the ravine and reached the end where massive boulders rose ten feet. Above yawned the open mouth of a cave as tall as a standing man, with a trickle of water splashing across rocks. Zoluti headed for one side, gripped the smaller, tumbled boulders, and climbed.

"Memsahib," Siriman shouted, "where are you going?"

She scaled the first sharp stone and turned. "After them! They have to be in the cave. Are you coming or not?"

"Hold up—the cave is a dragon lair. I told you I faced one—it was very dangerous. You must come down from there."

"Stop wasting time!" she cried. "Make yourself useful! Cut those bushes and tree limbs. Take strips from Lama's shirt and rig torches. It will be dark inside the tunnel."

The Gurkhas did as she bade and, minutes later, the woman and ten soldiers stood at the cave mouth. Three raised lit torches and Zoluti and the others held rifles.

"Everyone ready?" Zoluti asked.

Siriman looked around, checking his comrades' faces. "No matter what happens—avoid the dragon's eyes!"

The Gurkhas grunted and mumbled their understanding. Siriman turned back to Zoluti and nodded.

"Then follow me," she said, stepping into the dark tunnel.

Epilogue. The Tea-Space-Time Continuum

Fifty-six years later, Thursday, 8 May 1947

Mary

The late afternoon sun shone through the parlor window. Outside, the warblers twittered from oak branches. Tiny heads tipped sideways and peered at the clinker-brick cottage, studying Mary and her visitors.

Mary entered sporting a bright smile. The helpful Gurkha trailed, crossing the creaky wooden floor bearing a tray laden with a teapot, a sugar bowl, biscuits, and four sets of rattling cups, saucers, and teaspoons.

"Nectar and ambrosia," she announced, "for the long-lost travelers!"

Siriman set the tray on the tea table between the couch and the chairs. Mary distributed the cups and saucers, glancing at James and Donald huddled in a corner in quiet conversation.

What are they debating?

"Mary, who is this?" James pointed to a framed black-and-white photograph hanging on the wall.

Heat rose in Mary's checks. "Oh, him?" She forced a chuckle. "That is Douglas Fairbanks Junior." The three visitors stared, eyebrows raised.

The name means nothing to them.

"He is a famous cinema star. This year he was in *Sinbad the Sailor*, but it was not his best performance. Now—*Gunga Din*—that is my favorite. It was so exciting. It reminded me of our adventures." More blank stares. Mary pointed at the bottom of the photograph. "He signed it—you see there?" James leaned and inspected the signature. Mary turned to the other two. "He wrote, 'To Mary, my best. Douglas.' I wrote to him and told him how much I enjoy his acting and he sent me this autographed photo. Oh— that reminds me—the other day I read of Mister Sam Jaffe who played Gunga Din in the film and try to guess the year of his birth." Shrugs and polite smiles came from the three visitors. "1891! Is that not interesting?"

James frowned. "These chaps—Fairbanks and Jaffe—are they stage actors?"

"Yes—no!" Mary tossed her hands. "Too hard to explain moving pictures. We must go to the cinema sometime—then you will understand."

"You must admit, James!" Donald leaned closer to the photo. "You and Fairbanks could be twins."

The three visitors exchanged mischievous smiles. James turned his head to one side and studied the photo. "Do you think so? I had not noticed."

"Oh, yes, a strong resemblance."

James straightened "You wound me! I am better looking than this chap."

Mary shook a finger at Donald. "Do not be a tease!" Her voice quivered more than it scolded. She cleared her throat and forced a smile. "Any slight resemblance between James and Mister Fairbanks is coincidental."

"Yes, for sure," Donald said. "A total coincidence."

Siriman clapped hands, grinning. "The first coincidence in history, memsahib!"

Mary glared at Siriman and cleared her throat. "Sorry to intrude, Gentlemen. Tea, anyone?"

James and Donald settled and Siriman, ever the gentleman, waited for Mary to sit. She lowered her eyes in silent prayer. The men reached for cups and china clinked. Mary filled James's cup. He sipped, closed his eyes, and sighed. "My goodness! Excellent, Mary. Assam tea?"

Mary finished her sip and placed her cup on the table. "Always! None better." She put on her glasses and pulled the paper from her apron pocket. "Let us see what the letter says." She flipped the page, examining front and back, and smiled. "That settles it—Madame Blavatsky wrote this."

"Where do we go next? Does she say?" Donald said.

"She does! Back to the American West!"

Siriman's eyes lit. "Texas again, memsahib?"

"Not Texas. Farther west—New Mexico—near a town called Roswell, by early next month. There is more—she rambles, as usual."

"The American West!" Donald patted the top of his head. "I wish I still had my old hat."

"Ah," Mary said, "that brown, wide-brimmed felt hat. I had forgotten it. Whatever happened to it?"

"It fell off—midair—high over Dublin, Texas. We were rescuing you." Donald looked at James. "Was that the second or third time someone rescued her?" Mary studied her teacup, tears welling. "Oh no!" Donald exclaimed. "I am so sorry! I meant nothing! In fact, now I remember, you rescued me first!"

"No," Mary said. "You are right. I was always in the way. I am more trouble than I am worth. You risked your lives for me too many times. I best leave you three to it this time and stay home."

James stood. "Nonsense! You must come with us. We are counting on it. We cannot leave you for the government to—do whatever they plan to do."

"I am too old now. Kind of you not to mention how decrepit I have become during your absence. I am sorry if I have disappointed you."

"You could never disappoint us," Donald said. "None of us can help what has happened to any of us. The world survived because of you."

"You are still our angel!" Siriman said.

Mary sniffed and straightened "I will not get emotional! Stiff upper lip, and all that! As for going with you—blast! What is that infernal tapping?"

Siriman walked to the window. "Memsahib, you have another visitor. There is a bird on your sill, tapping at the glass."

"Ignore it. It will go away in time."

"What does it want?"

Mary shrugged. "I have not the foggiest. Maybe they think I am a bird."

Siriman tapped back, and the bird flew away. He returned and knelt before Mary. "The birds love you—how could they not?"

She smiled, reached, and smoothed a wild spot of Siriman's dark hair. "Dragon slayer!"

Siriman blinked glistening eyes, grinned, and said, "Zoluti Memsahib!"

The End

Thank You!

Thank you for reading *Seven Breaths of the Dragon*—my first novel. I hope you enjoyed it! You may wonder if there will be a follow-up. Rest assured the story is not over. You can help make sequels happen by supporting my work. Please tell your friends, family, and acquaintances about *Seven Breaths of the Dragon*, and the overarching series, *The Secret History of the Gurkha-Dragon War*.

Online reviews matter, too. Reviews inform readers and constructive comments help writers improve. Thank you in advance for taking time to post honest, thoughtful reviews. I welcome your feedback.

If you want to learn more about the universe of the Gurkha-Dragon War, please visit my Web site, **RobertStMichael.com**. There you will find background information and you can register for access to news and early drafts of new content.

If you want to reach me with questions or comments, you can email me at *gurkha.dragon.saga@gmail.com*. I look forward to hearing from you.

Thank you once again for reading my book and I hope you will enjoy my future work.

Warm regards and happy reading!

Robert St Michael

Acknowledgments

Thanks to Krista, the love of my life and my biggest fan. She reads and critiques every word, always telling me when I go off the rails, but her relentless encouragement, insisting I am doing something worthwhile, keeps me going. Krista is also a talented poet and artist and she created the cover to *Seven Breaths of the Dragon*.

Many thanks as well to Trevor, Janel, Barbara, and Georgia for reading early drafts and offering encouraging feedback, and to Sharath for support, insights on Hindu culture, and for naming the oxen.

I spent years researching the characters, settings, and scenes depicted in *Seven Breaths of the Dragon*. Over time, I will post a complete list of references on my Web site, but I wish to acknowledge here several important works and sources of information about the Manipur Disaster of 1891.

Ethel St. Clair Grimwood's definitive, autobiographical account: *My Three Years in Manipur and Escape from the Recent Mutiny*, Richard Bentley and Son publishing, 1891.

Lady Belinda Morse's fine biography of Ethel Grimwood: *Calamity & Courage, A Heroine of the Raj*, Book Guild Publishing, 2014.

Caroline Keen's detailed historical account: *An Imperial Crisis in British India, The Manipur Uprising of 1891*, I.B. Tauris publishing, 2015.

Col Ved Prakash's insightful account: *Queen Empress Vs Tikendrajit, Prince of Manipur* from *Encyclopaedia of North-east India, Volume 3*, Atlantic Publishers, 2007.

I also acknowledge and express gratitude to **E-Pao.net**, the excellent Web site and source for learning the news, geography, history, religion, and culture of Manipur.

About the Author

Robert St Michael worked in computer software development before becoming a full-time fiction writer. His jobs ranged from engineer to consultant to technology officer of a public company. He made several trips to India while writing *Seven Breaths of the Dragon.*

Robert married his high school sweetheart after graduating from college. After moving around, they settled in Georgia near Atlanta, where their three grown children and spouses live close. He enjoys seeing his grandchildren as often as possible and is partial to black-and-white English Springer Spaniels.